Praise for

THE TOSS OF A LEMON

"[*The Toss of a Lemon*] pads in on little cat feet and rips you along. You don't realize you're on an epic journey in the midst of a generational saga until you're well along and it's far, far too late to turn back. Not that you'd want to. Not that you even could . . . [A]stonishing. Brilliant. Beautiful."

—*January Magazine*

"[H]aunts us well after closing the back cover."

—*Minneapolis Star Tribune*

"Full of vivid detail, strengthened by Viswanathan's meticulous research, this book is both a fascinating human story and an impressive social history."—*Hartford Courant*

"A brilliant tour de force."—*India Today*

"Lovers of Rohinton Mistry and Vikram Seth will want to get hold of this Brahmin family saga."—*Vancouver Sun*

"*The Toss of a Lemon* records a passionate love affair with the English language. Many of the maximalist sentences are satisfyingly lush and rendered with a light touch."

—*The Tennessean*

"[Viswanathan] makes a vanished world feel completely authentic. Superbly done." —*Booklist*

"Of a piece with the recent works of Vikram Seth, and reminiscent at times of García Márquez—altogether a pleasure." —*Kirkus Reviews*, starred review

"This is a rich, sensual book that uses life itself as its plot... reading it is an experience of immersion . . . There is a whole world here between two covers." —*National Post*

"[A] captivating novel, one I wanted to continue long beyond its 600-plus pages. I recommend it most highly."

—*Historical Novels Review*

"The story is heartbreaking and exhilarating, exotic yet utterly recognizable in evoking the tensions that change brings to every family." —*Asian Star*

"[A] stunning first novel . . . The brilliance of *The Toss of a Lemon* rests not so much in its intricate plotting as in the compressed, poetic precision with which Viswanathan depicts a lost world." —*Walrus*

"This soaring new novel, inspired by the Edmonton author's family history, will draw comparisons to *The God of Small Things*, but Viswanathan has a voice and a vision all her own." —*Chatelaine*

"In *The Toss of a Lemon* we see exactly how magnetic, how sinkingly seductive that life was, and how difficult it must have been when the habits and customs of millennia were overturned by the shock of the new . . . Leaving the book feels like getting out of a warm bath on a cold day."

— *Globe and Mail*

"With its rich and complex background and often sharp insights, *The Toss of a Lemon* is a valuable and evocative work." — *Montreal Gazette*

"The portrait [Viswanathan] paints is dazzling . . . [A]n important work of historical fiction."

— *Library Journal*, starred review

"Viswanathan's absorbing first novel, based on her grandmother's life, goes deep into the world of southern India village life." — *Publishers Weekly*

"[This] fine and ambitious debut novel . . . beautifully (and effortlessly) opens a window on the life of a Brahmin widow."

— *Uptown*

"Viswanathan performs a wondrous balancing act of words. Rich with sensual detail, *The Toss of a Lemon* is the story of a community centred on tradition during an era of upheaval and change. Above all, it is a moving and deftly-drawn portrait of a family."   —ALISSA YORK, author of *Effigy*

THE TOSS OF A LEMON

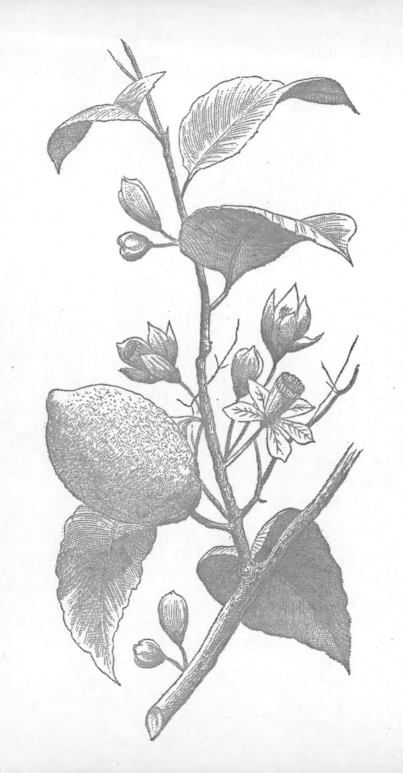

TOSS

of a

LEMON

PADMA VISWANATHAN

MARINER BOOKS
HOUGHTON MIFFLIN HARCOURT
BOSTON NEW YORK

First Mariner Books edition 2009
Copyright © 2008 Padma Viswanathan

For information about permission to reproduce selections from this book,
write to Permissions, Houghton Mifflin Harcourt Publishing Company,
215 Park Avenue South, New York, New York 10003.

www.hmhbooks.com

Published in Canada by Random House Canada.

Library of Congress Cataloging-in-Publication Data
Viswanathan, Padma, 1968–
The toss of a lemon/Padma Viswanathan.—1st U.S. ed.
p. cm.
1. Women—India—Fiction. 2. Family—India—Fiction.
3. India—Social life and customs—Fiction. 4. India—Social conditions—
20th century—Fiction. 5. Domestic fiction. I. Title.
PR9199.4.V57T67 2008
813'.6—dc22 2008013369
ISBN 978-0-15-101533-7
ISBN 978-0-547-24787-8 (pbk.)

Designed by Kelly Hill

Printed in the United States of America
DOM 10 9 8 7 6 5 4 3 2 1

for

Bhuvana and S. P. Viswanathan

...and for

Dhanam Kochoi

Most of what matters in our lives takes place in our absence: but I seem to have found from somewhere the trick of filling in the gaps in my knowledge . . .

Salman Rushdie, *Midnight's Children*

MAIN FAMILY TREE

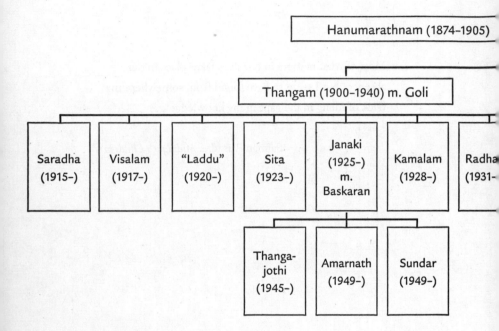

Hanumarathnam (1874–1905)

Thangam (1900–1940) m. Goli

Saradha (1915–)
Visalam (1917–)
"Laddu" (1920–)
Sita (1923–)
Janaki (1925–) m. Baskaran
Kamalam (1928–)
Radha (1931–

Thanga-jothi (1945–)
Amarnath (1949–)
Sundar (1949–)

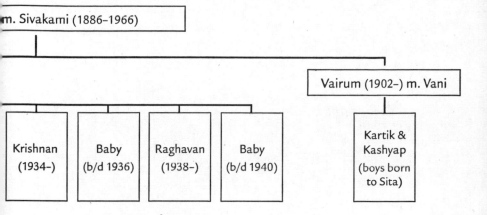

m. Sivakami (1886–1966)

Vairum (1902–) m. Vani

Krishnan (1934–)

Baby (b/d 1936)

Raghavan (1938–)

Baby (b/d 1940)

Kartik & Kashyap (boys born to Sita)

OTHER CHARACTERS

Sivakami's servant: Muchami (m. Mari)

Sivakami's next-door neighbors: Annam (widow), her son Murthy and his wife Rukmini

Sivakami's friends up the road: Chinnarathnam, his wife, their son "Minister" and his wife Gayatri

Sivakami's brothers: Sambu (m. Kamu), Venketu (m. Meenu), Subbu (m. Ecchu)

Janaki's school chum: Bharati

Baskaran's family. Dhoraisamy and his wife "Senior Mami," three unnamed daughters and three sons, Madhavan (m. Vasantha), Easwaran (m. Swarna), and Baskaran (m. Janaki)

I.
Thangam
1896

THE YEAR OF THE MARRIAGE PROPOSAL, Sivakami is ten. She is neither tall nor short for her age, but she will not grow much more. Her shoulders are narrow but appear solid, as though the blades are fused to protect her heart from the back. She carries herself with an attractive stiffness: her shoulders straight and always aligned. She looks capable of bearing great burdens, not as though born to a yoke but perhaps as though born with a yoke within her.

She and her family live in Samanthibakkam, some hours away by bullock cart from Cholapatti, which had been her mother's place before marriage. Every year, they return to Cholapatti for a pilgrimage. They fill a pot at the Kaveri River and trudge it up to the hilltop temple to offer for the *abhishekham*. These are pleasant, responsible, God-fearing folk who seek the blessings of their gods on any undertaking and any lack thereof. They maintain awe toward those potentially wiser or richer than they—like the young man of Cholapatti, who is blessed with the ability to heal.

No one in their family is sick, but still they go to the healer. They may be less than totally healthy and simply not know. One can always use a preventative, and it never hurts to receive the blessings of a blessed person. This has always been the stated purpose of the trip, and Sivakami has no reason to think this one is any different.

Hanumarathnam, the healer, puts his palms together in a friendly *namaskaram,* asks how they have been and whether they need anything specific. They shyly shake their heads, and he queries, with a penetrating squint, "Nothing?" Sivakami is embarrassed by her parents, who are acting like impoverished peasants. They owe this man their respect, but they are Brahmins too, and literate, like him. They can hold up their heads. She's smiling to herself at his strange name: a hybrid of "Hanuman," the monkey god, and *rathnam,* gem. The suffix she understands; it's attached to the name of every man in the region. *But no one is named for the monkey!*

Her mother and father cast glances at each other; then her father clears his throat. "Ah, our daughter here has just entered *gurubalam.* We are about to start searching for a groom."

"Oh, well," Hanumarathnam responds with a wink, "I deal in medicine, not charms."

Sivakami's parents giggle immoderately. Their daughter stares at the packed dust of the Brahmin-quarter street. Her three older brothers fidget.

"But you have my blessings," Hanumarathnam continues, making a small package of some powder. "And this, dissolved in milk and drunk each day, this will give you strength. Just generally. It will help."

Then he looks at Sivakami. She doesn't look up. When he asks her parents, "Have you done the star chart yet?" his voice sounds different. They haven't. "Come at dusk. I'll do it for you."

What could be better? The humble folk trip back to their relatives', four doors down the street, for snacks and happy anticipation of their consultation with the auspicious young man, who also has some fame as an astrologer.

At that strange hour that gives the impression of light even though each figure is masked by darkness, Sivakami's father, with two of the male relatives, finds Hanumarathnam on his veranda. He cannot make out the young man's features, but the slant of his chest and head suggests wisdom and peace. So young and a widower, by a freak accident: his wife drowned in the Kaveri River before she ever came to live with him. His parents were already dead. He lives with relatives while his own house—his parents' home, the second to last on the Brahmin-quarter—stays locked, dark and still.

Hanumarathnam stands to greet them; they take their seats; they make brief small talk as his aunt brings tumblers of yogourt churned with lemon water and salt.

He examines the chart by a kerosene lamp while the men finger their shoulder towels. He makes some calculations. He purses his lips and takes in a sharp breath before speaking. "I, well, I must say it. I have just entered gurubalam myself."

Sivakami's father hesitates. "Oh?"

"I will make more detailed calculations, but this is my reasoned guess . . . Your daughter's horoscope is compatible with mine."

The young man licks his lips, no longer the astrological authority but instead the nervous suitor. He speaks too quickly. "I am obliged to mention, of course, or perhaps you have already heard: the weakest quadrant of my horoscope has a small shadow . . . It . . . it faintly suggests I will die in my ninth year of marriage. But, as that prediction is contained in the weakest quadrant, it holds no weight, as you know, though ignorant people let it scare them."

The men do not know but are not ignorant enough to say so, and anyway, Hanumarathnam has not paused in his speech.

"And most often, the birth of a son changes the configuration, as you know. I understand it must be difficult for you to consider giving your daughter as a second wife. My first wife, she drowned to death in her tenth year. Only three years after our marriage, you see, and it was not I who died, you see? It was her. Quite contrary to the negative quadrant of the horoscope. An, an unfortunate, accident. So I have no children, and I am still young. I have money and manage well. I am speaking on my own behalf only because I have no father and I know the horoscopes better than anyone."

He blinks rapidly, the lamplight making him look younger than his twenty-one years. He takes a breath and looks at Sivakami's father.

"I have never looked at, nor ever proposed to any girl before now. Please . . . consider me."

That night, Sivakami's father relates his impressions to her mother. They are positively disposed toward the young man and feel they trust his astrology and his good intentions. They ask their relatives in the morning: have they heard anything against Hanumarathnam or his kin?

The relatives assure them that they have heard only good things: fine, upstanding Brahmins all. The young man not only has special talents but has just come into his inheritance, some very good parcels of land. They think it could be a good match, more: a shame to waste the opportunity.

In the morning, Sivakami's father bathes and prays. Then he picks up quill and ink and writes a gracious note, pretending they, the girl's family, are taking the initiative, as is right and conventional, and inviting Hanumarathnam for a girl-seeing as if his already having seen the girl had nothing to do with any of this.

> *Most Esteemed Sir, Village Healer and Knowing One,*
>
> *The humble man who Writes this Missive to your
> Gracious Self invokes the Blessings of the Gods and
> Stars on his intentions. The writer would be Honoured
> above Reasonable Expectation, if he were to have the
> Pleasure of Welcoming Your Good Self to the
> Samanthibakkam home of his family, where his Revered
> Ancestors have Bestowed their Blessings Through the
> Ages. With the Wisdom and Learning You have
> acquired through Great Sacrifice and Effort, please
> Choose an Auspicious Time, and send word that Your
> good Relatives will Accompany you to Grace the
> Threshold of our Poor but Pious Dwelling. We will be
> Eagerly awaiting your Word. And the Opportunity to
> shower our Hospitality on Your Presence.*
>
> *I remain, Yours humbly,*

The note is in Tamil, a script without capital letters, but this is the idea—inconsistently the most flowery and archaic Sivakami's father can muster.

The note is delivered by Sivakami's brothers after they also have bathed and prayed. With a great sense of accomplishment puffing his modest chest and head, Sivakami's father leads his wife and children on the trek back home.

Word from Hanumarathnam follows. He comes to Samanthibakkam accompanied by a distant uncle and a male cousin. Sivakami's family offers the stiffest, most formal reception they are able to raise above the brim of their excitement and happiness. Sivakami is ushered in. She keeps her head bowed and her eyes down, since, by unspoken convention, this is behaviour appropriate to prospective brides. She serves sweets she has made herself, the solidity of her upper back giving her movements a linear grace. Asked to sing a couple of devotional songs, she does so with gusto, closing her eyes.

By the time he leaves, the observant young man is even more smitten than that day, short weeks before, when he had seen the pride flash in Sivakami's eyes.

They are married, like everyone else, at an auspicious time on an auspicious day in an auspicious month. After her marriage, she continues to live with her parents, like everyone else who has parents, though she is escorted to her husband's village several times a year for festivals, at which times she is feted, and brings gifts for her new relatives. In Cholapatti, she stays with her parents, at their relatives' house up the street from where her husband lives with his relatives. They are present at the same functions, where she participates in the ceremonies, but her husband remains for her a person known only in public and in glimpses.

After three years, she comes of age, like everyone else lucky enough to survive childhood, and finally the great change is upon them. Her family readies her to join her husband for good.

When Hanumarathnam, now twenty-four, learns he will receive his thirteen-year-old bride, he unlocks his parents' house. The aunt and uncle who raised him (double relatives: his mother's sister married his father's brother) make a ceremonial fuss at his declaration of departure; their house is just next door, after all, and their son Murthy's bride may also arrive soon.

Hanumarathnam's own house has not been opened for a full generation. Generations are short in this time when girls marry as children and have children as soon as they are able, but still, the house has not been opened for a while. Hanumarathnam has brought the servants with him who will make the house ready to receive a new bride. These are servants his inheritance has supported in rice and lentils, year in, year out. Generations of their families have served generations of his. While his parents were alive, these people had worked around the house. Hanumarathnam's mother died before his second birthday, his father less than a year later, and since then, whenever the servants have met him on the street, they have wept noisily for his dead parents. Eventually, they also wept for his dead little wife. When they learn that they will once more have domestic employment, they express great joy. One then becomes untraceable for some weeks. He will later be rounded up sternly by Hanumarathnam, with his uncle, who will come along to lend authority. But the others come immediately, and these two are with Hanumarathnam as he gently tries to open the great, rusty padlock.

The key turns suddenly, and he's afraid that it has broken along its collar of rust. But the lock is opening and the thick door of grey-weathered wooden boards is swinging to. They are in the vestibule, a narrow passageway with a high ledge on either side—too high to be a seat, too low for storage. The next lock has not been so exposed and opens more easily. A buttery smell of bats wings over them while the creatures themselves flutter farther back into the dark. Hanumarathnam already has the next key ready—for the tall, narrow double doors into the garden that runs the length of the house. There are two such door-ways, about five paces apart, in the wall of the main hall.

The servants with Hanumarathnam are old enough to remember his first steps in that garden. They shuffle, atypically quiet, in the silent dust of the house. Maybe they are letting him alone in case he is mourning those early years, just a few months, really, possibly before memory, when he was not an orphan. Maybe they are mourning their own lost time. Or maybe they are just thinking of all the work to be done, and the happy times to come for Hanumarathnam, as a family man and householder at last.

Hanumarathnam opens the doors from the main hall to the pantry, from the pantry to the kitchen, from the kitchen to the back courtyard, where an extended family of monkeys screeches and leaps at his appearance. Hanumarathnam screeches and leaps back into the house. The monkeys have been eating from the fruit trees in the garden: the courtyard stinks of rotting fruit, including half-eaten mangoes and overripe bananas evidently used as missiles in monkey food fights. Several bananas are still stuck on the walls where they were smashed. The monkeys must have been attracted to the courtyard by the shade afforded under the partial roof.

Hanumarathnam, like his servants, who are tucked safely behind him, stands with the tail of his jasmine-white *dhoti* held over his nose and mouth against the rancid smell and his horror at the colonizers' aggression. The courtyard is crawling with their clan. Fifteen, perhaps twenty, mothers, babies, adolescents. There are two dominant bull monkeys. One is a patriarch with a silvery thatch of hair, his muscles a bit stringy. His manner, as he bares his teeth and boxes a yearling's ears to show off, is defensive. The up-and-comer, who has probably defeated every bull but the old one, is sleek and barrel-chested. He squats, shaking his head and puffing his cheeks, inches behind the old fellow.

Now, all the monkeys are looking their way, except one, about two years old, who has caught a little bird and is absorbed in plucking it. The bird squawks ambivalently. The monkey rubs the bird's head on the courtyard bricks, then inspects it as though this might reveal the source of the protest. Hanumarathnam, to the relief of his employees, gently shuts the courtyard door and bolts it.

Seconds later, there is a pounding against the wood, a single fist, then a multitude, then the monkeys start to squabble and scrabble among themselves and forget the interlopers. The door from the courtyard to the garden is still locked; the monkeys have been going over the wall to get the fruit. Hanumarathnam, back in the main hall, shuts the garden doors and sends the servants to their homes. The house cannot be cleaned without water, and the well is at the centre of the jealously guarded courtyard. The water at least is probably safe: the well has no bucket right now and, unlike the big agricultural wells, no ladder.

Three hours before dawn, Hanumarathnam returns. He opens a garden door, straining his senses to perceive life or movement.

Detecting nothing, he slowly swings a kerosene lamp out in front of him. Still nothing. With increasing boldness, he creeps, then stalks through the garden. There are no monkeys sleeping here.

He returns to the main hall, closes the door and proceeds to the back of the house, which splits into the pantry and kitchen to the right and a small room, beneath the stairs, adjoining another small back room, on the left. He takes the left passage this time and tries the bolt. It is a little sticky. He rotates it up, down, up, down, pulling steadily on the handle. It opens with a bang. He pulls it shut again just as quickly and sets his ear against the door, his heart pounding. He can almost feel the old monkey's overdeveloped canines penetrating his soft, scholarly flesh. When Hanumarathnam was a child, one of the Brahmin-quarter children died of a monkey bite. She had been a beautiful girl; the enraged monkey tore off half her face.

There is no sound from the courtyard: as he suspected, his house is just one stop on the monkeys' circuit. They don't sleep here, cramped quarters, but rather in some forest glade, on grooved branches above leaf-padded floors.

Monkeys, like cows, cobras, peacocks and mice, are sacred— their mythological associations give them immunity from harm. So Hanumarathnam, as a good Brahmin, must find some means of reclaiming his house without violence toward the invaders. At three the next morning, he and three of his servants return. Illuminating the garden section by section with the gaseous glare of kerosene, they strip every tree of its ripe fruit. It is not a large garden, but severely overgrown, and it takes them until six before all the fruit is stacked neatly in the pantry.

As Hanumarathnam locks the garden doors, a female servant prepares several platters: two of fruit and a third heaped with cooked rice mixed with fatty yogourt, mustard seeds, curry leaves. Hanumarathnam carries the rice, two others the fruits. They place these ceremoniously at the bottom of the steps into the wasteland behind the house, just outside the courtyard door.

That day, Hanumarathnam opens the front doors of the house so neighbours from up and down the street can come and help themselves to fruits. He monitors the sounds of the monkeys over the course of the day and hears them discover the plates. They feast, and waste food, and waste time and then come over the walls into the courtyard and garden. Their chattering grows progressively more outraged as they discover nothing but hard green fruits. These function well as weapons, or toys, and they batter the walls and doors for a time. But they are still hungry and soon scuffle off to other locales.

Hanumarathnam has reserved a portion of the ripe fruit. This, with a plate of yogourt rice, becomes the next morning's offering, half as large as the day previous, but still generous. It is placed four paces away from the back wall, four times farther than the day before. The next day he halves the offering again, and doubles the distance. By the end of the week, the monkeys lackadaisically lap up the token offering left by the side of the canal a furlong from the courtyard door. They have stopped coming to Hanumarathnam's garden.

On a day deemed favourable by the religious almanacs, all the doors are flung open, and the cleaning is done in earnest. Hanumarathnam, with the servants, works to clear the garden, uprooting dead trees and installing seedlings. Two female servants use a new bucket to haul up well water, which they sluice top to bottom and side to side, from the very front of the house to the back. They scrub the courtyard thoroughly with coconut coir to remove all stains and traces of the monkey invasion, then scour it with cow dung. Hanumarathnam himself perfumes the corners with sandal paste and incense.

Hanumarathnam hires a Brahmin lady to do a final cleaning, to bring the house up to caste standards so his wife will have to do only a few small things for ceremony's sake, such as hanging bundles of mango leaves and spiny cactus above the door, against the evil eye. Their first act, on her arrival, will be a *puja* for the black stone Ramar installed in the main hall, the Ramar that was the object of his mother's devotion and that has stood neglected, though still noble, since her death.

Three weeks after she comes of age, Sivakami is escorted to her husband's home. Before she mounts the bullock cart, she falls at her elders' feet. All of their blessings are the same: Bear your husband many children. May your first child be male. Always be modest. A family's honour is a woman's responsibility. The blessings cut through the wonder and fear of departure: she is confident these accomplishments can and will be hers.

She alights in Cholapatti, feeling elegant in a silk sari of red and yellow checks, ornamented with less gold than on her wedding day but still quite brilliant in thick gold bangles and dangling *jimiki* earrings. A gold chain threads the sides of her sternum; her wedding pendants fit snugly between her small breasts, hidden beneath sari and blouse from any jealous glance. Hanumarathnam greets her in front of their home, together with his aunt, his uncle and his cousin Murthy. This is the only time when it is proper for a groom's family to show hospitality to a bride's. Sivakami's parents and uncles will be put up next door.

The party goes there first, to socialize until the sunset, when the young couple are seated side by side and served a meal with much banter. Tonight, they say, is the night of "Rudra Shanti Muhurtam," the pacification of the bride's passions. Sivakami is not sure yet what her passions are, but supposes it is good they will be calmed. After they drink cups of sweetened saffron milk, the couple are escorted to the chamber on the second floor of Hanumarathnam's house, where the bed has been made with the new quilts Sivakami has brought, and strewn with flowers. The couple are seated there, blushing so that sweat beads attractively on their foreheads and upper lips. After singing to them, the party closes the door, going to make merry and leaving the newlyweds to do the same.

~⌒⌐

SIVAKAMI'S TERRORS AND SORROWS in the early months of her marriage are much the same as any new bride's. It hardly seems worth troubling the imagination to find pity for her, so common are her woes. At first, she tries constantly to please her husband, but he is easily pleased. Sivakami has no mother-in-law, so her own mother comes twice in six months to ensure standards of household management and nutrition are not being thrown to the four winds. Hanumarathnam's aunt, Annam, who raised him and lives next door, might have done the honours, but her own new daughter-in-law, Rukmini, is using up all her attention.

Essentially, Sivakami is alone with her husband. She appreciates this but will appreciate it even more in retrospect. Each morning, she bathes at the Kaveri River and does the *kolam,* the design a girl or woman of a house draws daily in rice flour on a freshly swept threshold. Then she does a puja for the Ramar. Before sunrise, she lays out fruit and rice beside the canal for the monkeys. She cooks. Each afternoon, while her husband naps, she cries a little in a corner of the pantry. She cooks. Each evening at sunset, she watches the parrots swooping low over the roof. At night, she and her husband have sex. They talk, mostly about the village and religion and the daily matters of their shared life. She likes her husband and comes quickly to rely on him.

She comes also to know the Brahmin quarter and her neighbours. Hanumarathnam's aunt Annam, who apparently looks and sounds just like her late sister, Hanumarathnam's mother, and her husband, Vicchu, are kind and helpful, even while they are preoccupied with training their daughter-in-law. Rukmini arrived six months before Sivakami, and Sivakami alternates between feeling sorry for her, having to accommodate her parents-in-laws in exactly the way Sivakami herself has been spared, and feeling envious of the extended family and parental surrogates she has been denied. Rukmini and Sivakami see each other daily to exchange cooking or gossip, and so Sivakami hears the older girl's mild complaints about her mother-in-law, which are never venomous or even very specific. Rukmini's complexion is uneven, marked by evidence of some childhood malady, measles or chicken pox, but she is tall, with broad shoulders, and an exceptionally good cook, which her in-laws appreciate, though they're more likely to tell others this than tell her. She has frizzy hair that won't grow past the shoulders, and irritates Sivakami with excessive attention to her glossy, waist-long tresses—*What does it matter, really?* she thinks, though she knows she is proud of her hair.

Murthy is slightly shorter than his wife and has a high-pitched voice. He chiefly endears himself to Sivakami with his pride in Hanumarathnam's abilities. Since a mother's sister is considered a second mother, and a father's brother another father, Murthy considers Hanumarathnam to be his own brother and takes personal credit for his accomplishments. He himself barely made it through eighth standard before stopping. He nominally assists in looking after the family lands, which have been split now that Hanumarathnam has received his share, but mostly spends his days snoozing on the veranda and occasionally holding forth on some article he has read, say on recent advances in science and technology. Hanumarathnam commented once to Sivakami that Murthy always mangles the details of these reports, and she has never since been able to respect Murthy, though she is fond of him nonetheless.

They live in the house to the left. Sivakami never meets the people to the right. She hears their story from Hanumarathnam's aunt, though when she repeats it, wide-eyed, to her husband, he tells her not to take all the details so literally. No one ever sees the wife of that household, because she is ashamed, knowing everyone on the Brahmin quarter fears her. Her mother-in-law was a witch, and bribed the young woman to become one too. She accepted a necklace of gold coins, along with her mother-in-law's hellish, itchy craving to periodically cast a spell. When, every so often, some old, weak or retarded person snaps and becomes crazy, the village understands the young witch has satisfied her demonic urge upon this victim. The craving tormented the elder woman; she died soon after passing it on and now rests, supposedly in peace, not knowing the real tragedy of her family: one of the young witch's early spells was misdirected at her husband's sister, a beautiful, bitter woman, who now crouches and gibbers, incontinent, in a corner of their house. Sivakami hears the sister-in-law sometimes—howling for food, chuckling eerily or delivering obscene diatribes—and shudders.

Cholapatti's Brahmin quarter is a single street of some fourteen houses, ending in a Krishna temple. At the other end, closest to where Sivakami lives, the road curves out past a small Shiva temple and joins the main road into the nearest town, Kulithalai, the Taluk seat, where there is a sizable market, a courthouse, a club, even a small train station. Although Samanthibakkam, the village where she grew up, is larger than Cholapatti, it is much farther from any town of size, and she enjoys the sense of proximity to bustle and importance, even if she rarely sees it herself. Cholapatti's Brahmin quarter is surrounded by fields, but there are small settlements of other castes, agricultural workers mostly, tenant farmers on the properties owned either by Cholapatti Brahmins or by the better-off residents of Kulithalai.

Once in the early months of her marriage, she goes to a wedding in Kulithalai: the Brahmin quarter there consists of two streets whose mix of prosperity and humility is similar to that on the street where she now lives. It is bordered on one side by a large quarter of Chettiars, whose opulent homes rise above their shops: jewellery, fabric, pawn and moneylending. When Sivakami goes shopping with Murthy and Rukmini, she sees there is variation in the Chettiars' prosperity, but this doesn't alter her perception of that caste as uniformly money-grubbing and flashy. Streets of other castes: Reddiars—she's not sure what they do, business of some kind; a few families of Marwaris, with their fair, sharp features and gold hoop earrings, competing with the Chettiars for moneylending business; others she cannot name, including members of the agricultural classes wealthy enough, by wile or inheritance, to live in town; these streets bow out to enclose the circular stone bench at the market square, petering out beyond the train station, or at the river, which runs alongside the main road from Cholapatti. The untouchables' neighbourhoods are in the hinterlands, though she has never seen them, nor even thought of them: the barbers, the funeral workers and so on, who all have their own traditions and hierarchies.

Once Sivakami saw a white man alighting from a horse cart in front of the train station. She asked Murthy if white people lived in Kulithalai, and he laughed, "No, no!" Hanumarathnam told her that might have been a circuit-court magistrate, paying a bi-monthly call, or a revenue supervisor visiting from Thiruchinapalli, the city, some hours away by train. He has promised her they will visit someday.

As to the rest of the Cholapatti Brahmins, Sivakami made their acquaintance when she and Hanumarathnam paid their post-wedding calls. There are three grand households. Hanumarathnam is great friends with the husband of one, at the far end. The other is a duplex, five doors down, brothers who built across from their father's more modest house. And there are three very poor households, including that of the woman Hanumarathnam hired to clean his house. Her husband is a cook-for-hire, the lowest profession available to Brahmins. At their house, Hanumarathnam and Sivakami did not take a meal but, with cordial remove, accepted tumblers of churned yogourt and stale snacks that Sivakami supposed the husband brought home from weddings where he worked.

In other words, for all that this life is so new to her, she has a profound sense of order: everyone in their places, easily found when needed, otherwise comfortably unseen.

Then this.

It is strange. Even if all of Cholapatti insists it is normal, she will refuse to believe it. But what if it is normal? Will she live with this for the rest of her life?

She sits on her haunches and rocks back and forth while she adds up, in two separate mental columns, the factors that make her marriage normal and the factors that make it strange. Before now, reflections on her marriage were either smug or self-righteous, depending on how she felt toward her husband in the moment. At present, alone—she has never been alone before, she's barely got used to being alone in a room once in a while, and now the whole house balloons empty around her—she is terrified.

The long list of normal factors gives her some satisfaction, and thus a little calm. She wants to demonstrate to herself that, on balance, her marriage is not materially different from any other Brahmin union. Next, she tackles the strange.

1. She is the second wife of a widower. Widowers with children marry their deceased wives' sisters, if they can, because such women have maternal feelings toward their nieces and nephews. Widowers without children marry girls no one else will have. Neither condition applied to Sivakami, a fair-skinned, able-bodied, obviously intelligent girl of good family. But her parents offered her no explanation and she had come to see it as of little significance: he never even met his first wife, after the wedding. That long-ago girl must seem as unreal to him as she does to Sivakami. Sivakami edges this factor, in her mind, toward the normal column—Hanumarathnam, so young, barely qualified as a widower.

2. It is a little unusual that he is a healer, but there are others who divine people's ills and offer remedies of holy ashes, each-each unique but looking each-each the same. Also, he doesn't consult any priest for astrological advice but goes straight to the stars and makes the calculations himself. Though unusual, these are at least activities appropriate to Brahmins with a *paadasaalai* education—natural extensions of his training.

Sivakami takes a breath.

3. Her husband has just wandered off into the forest with a small band of itinerant ascetics, *siddhas,* naked but for their hair and some holy ash, or maybe dirt, smeared in patterns on their blue-black or mud-brown skin, stretched taut on bony bodies . . .

She shudders. Her husband, a young, healthy, even slightly flabby Brahmin man, has walked off in a jolly manner with three siddhas, men who know no caste boundaries, whose origins are obscured by their membership in this mystic cult, who have no right, as far as she is concerned, to come in contact with respectable caste householders.

The fiends had come to the front door. She had heard Hanumarathnam's brisk step behind her and stepped back, gaping at their audacity, to allow him to chastise them. He passed through the door, said, "I'm going out," and then she was watching him disappear. She had looked around, hoping, at least, that the neighbours hadn't seen, but they all had. She had closed the door, something never done in daylight, too shocked to resume what the siddhas had interrupted: her afternoon cry.

She enjoys this cry, as she enjoys the parrots at sunset, and sex, and being mistress of her own home. She is only thirteen years old and misses her mother's hands in her hair each morning, and the little puppy her brothers had found a few weeks before she left, and so she weeps a little each day. A little less each day, but still she weeps because she is on her own with her husband—even though he is handsome and gentle and is teaching her the ways of love.

Sometimes, during the day, she thinks about what happened the night before, in the dark of the closed house. He's always giving her some instruction or another, which often makes her giggle. When she finally manages to do what he is telling her, however, he is usually correct about the result. (You may imagine him as a young scientist in his first laboratory—many theories and, finally, the opportunity to try them.) Last night's was challenging, but she is slim and supple . . .

Sivakami snaps herself from her reverie. He is gone! He has disappeared into the forest and here she sits idly beneath a window with a stupid smile on her face. She walks briskly to the well in the back, draws a bucket of water, cool even now in the hot season, and roughly washes her face. Stalking back into the main hall, she falls on her knees in front of the large black stone Ramar that dominates the room.

That morning, she ground fresh sandalwood pulp to anoint it, the figures of noble Rama, who stands in the centre, chest out, holding his signature bow; chaste Sita, to his left, her palms together, head modestly inclined; warriorlike Lakshmana, to his brother's right; and faithful Hanuman, the monkey god and Rama's deputy in the war on Lanka, who kneels before them. Every day Sivakami decorates them with sandalwood and vermilion, ornaments them with blossoms of marigold and jasmine and then proves the gods' beauty by burnishing their features with chips of lighted camphor, held aloft. Her mother-in-law's devotion to this statue had been legendary. She called her son after Hanuman, the monkey, Rama's most ardent devotee, and appended it with "rathnam," a common suffix for boys' names in this region, in honour of the hill temple in whose shadow they live, the founding myth of which concerned a gem lost then found.

Hanumarathnam's name is a constant reminder to Sivakami (whenever she hears it; she herself would never say her husband's name) of the legacy she has inherited. The statue is the household embodied.

She prays, but on this dark afternoon when their home has been seemingly sundered by prehistoric wraith-men, she feels she must do more. She plucks flowers from her garden, weaves fragrant garlands, drapes them on her gods and falls again before them in supplication.

It's still not enough. She needs not cold stone but warm eyes. The neighbours have all seen anyway. She goes out her back courtyard and next door, to see her husband's aunt, Annam. Sitting on the step behind her kitchen, she pours out her heart.

Annam laughs, then stops at Sivakami's expression and pats her knee. "He has always done that, ever since he was a small boy. They come and look for him, he spends a few days with them. He used to ask me to prepare a packet of food to give them when they returned. That will be your job now. No one knows what they do, what they tell. One very naughty boy, you know, Jagganathan, he tried to spy on Hanumarathnam once, some fifteen or twenty years back."

"Mute Jagganathan, up the road?" Sivakami frowns.

Rukmini comes into the kitchen from their main hall, rubbing her eyes, her sari dishevelled as she wakes from her afternoon rest.

"The last time he spoke was to boast that he was going to find out the secrets of the siddhas, whatever they share with your husband. 'Why not me?' he said. 'I'm as good as him.' Stupid boy. We never found out what he saw. Swagger on his face, he opened his mouth to tell us what he had learned. No sound came out."

"Can't he write things on a slate?" Sivakami lets herself be drawn into the story.

"He has never written what he saw. Your husband was only a boy. He went and spoke to Jagganathan's mother, tried giving cures, but nothing worked. I think he was not the one who did it. I suspect he could cure Jagganathan now, if he wanted. But maybe he thinks . . ."

She pauses until Sivakami prompts her. "Thinks . . . ?"

"Maybe he thinks it is better if Jagganathan has no chance to speak."

Sivakami looks away, pouting, and wonders if she has betrayed him by coming here.

"Go home. Have your supper, lock the door, go to sleep. Hanumarathnam will wake you if he comes in the night. If he doesn't, he will come soon."

"Is he safe?" Sivakami asks finally, betraying a little anger that this was not her first concern.

"Was he safe all those times before you were his wife?" Annam snorts and gets up. "How many people have what he has? It is a gift and you are very lucky. I'll send my servant's daughter to sleep in your house tonight so you won't be afraid."

As soon as it is cool enough, Sivakami goes up on the roof to scan the countryside. Dusk finds her numbly watching the parrots as they take their low sunset swoops. Shortly after dark, the servant girl arrives and silently sleeps in the main hall as Sivakami lies awake.

Nearly two days pass in long hours. The elderly servants come at their usual times, to sweep, bring vegetables and kerosene from the market, sort the rice for stones, shape cow dung into patties and slap them onto the courtyard walls to dry into fuel chips. They give no indication that they think anything is wrong, as Sivakami sits half willing them to notice her fuming in a corner of the main hall.

She is the cherished only daughter of a not unknown family. She was not raised to be left alone. She didn't marry to be left alone. She reviews again the details of her marriage, which echo in her mind like her footfalls in the empty house.

When Hanumarathnam returns, Sivakami is haggard. Though thinner, he seems renewed, vigorous, faintly glowing even. He asks her if she has cooked. She has, as she has three times every day of his absence, anticipating his return.

"Pack four meals, my dear. Large meals," he says, his eyes dancing with hidden thoughts, new knowledge, non-Brahmin fascinations of which she is no part.

He knows things he has no right to know.

But he is her husband and he has asked for food, so she packages rice with sambar and vegetables into plantain leaves and binds them neatly with long fibres pulled from palm leaf stems. The yogourt rice course she wraps separately with tidy daubs of pickles. She is numb. She is packing food for her husband's abductors, his friends, his mentors, who are just the sort of people she has been taught are dirty— which anyone can verify by looking at them. By smelling them.

They are not only smelly, they are sarcastic. Sarcastic to the point of blasphemy: as they saunter along the Brahmin quarter in the direction of the Krishna temple, no doubt savouring the pollution their naked, non-Brahmin forms are bestowing on the sanctified land, they cry, "Here is a body, feed it!"

It is the cry that distinguishes mendicants from beggars. In the old days, before Brahmins secured land and, thus, income, when they were strictly priests and scholars, living in righteous poverty, they would gather their daily sustenance by walking the street, carrying nothing but a brass jug and a walking stick. Hearing their cry, "Here is a body, feed it!" villagers would run after them and press upon them paddy and lentils. Now this drama is being re-enacted before Sivakami's own house, except that those offering are Brahmins and the criers are non-Brahmins and Sivakami's husband, a Brahmin, is the non-Brahmins' great friend.

So now that he's back, she asks herself, Who is he, her husband? Is marriage not a known quantity, a thousand and one inconsequential variations on fixed roles and results?

Sivakami becomes pregnant the night her husband returns.

Which is to say that things go a little differently from usual. After it happens, her husband explains that this is the required conclusion if they are to create children, but that it has not happened before because the philosophy in which he is receiving instruction teaches that men must learn to conserve their life force, to keep it within them and not jet it from their bodies at the first hint of pleasure. This night, though, for him, it was not possible. Perhaps he was weak from three days without food, perhaps exhilarated by his learning, perhaps just a little too glad at holding her again. Sivakami was at first frightened by seeing his eyes roll, his body tense and spasm. She had thought for a moment that he was having a seizure—could this be one more thing about him she hadn't been told? Following his explanation, she is relieved, and testifies also to her happiness at his return, though she is a little disappointed by the brevity of their fun.

Now that they are together again, in the pre-dawn, post-coital calm and commonality, she is emboldened to ask about these siddhas, suddenly so central to her marriage. Her husband replies, "They are men. Men concerned with perfection."

"What perfection?" She tries not to scoff.

"Lower metals can be made into gold," he says, and his tone makes her wonder for a moment if he means this literally. "Have you heard of that? The siddhas are teaching me how. And, by an analogous process, the body can attain spiritual freedom. Perfection, like gold, but while still in life, not after, you see?"

He is not really asking and so she just allows him to continue.

"But it is a very, very long process. These men, the siddhas, how old do you think they are?"

"I don't know." She doesn't want to show too much interest.

"Guess." He smiles.

She sits up, her arms wrapped around her knees. "I can't see them very well, their hair snakes to their knees, they're all dusty, and I didn't look, sort of, directly."

"Hm?"

"They wear no clothes, am I supposed to inspect them?" Hanumarathnam begins laughing and her irritation increases as she continues. "Go up and stare at these naked men up and down to determine the depth of wrinkles beneath their coat of mud and ash?" She stops and waits, sulking, until he answers his own question.

"They are some hundreds of years old."

"Hah!"

Hanumarathnam looks a little taken aback at her vehemence, and she is both scared and glad.

"Truly I am saying," he continues a bit cautiously, "they extend their lives. It takes so much time to transform the soul, and since the body is the soul's vessel, its life, too, must be extended. And their practices increase vigour and so naturally extend the life. They must live long, else how to learn and practise sufficiently? How to find time?"

"Is that what you are doing?"

"I am not a siddha." He stretches and yawns.

"I thought they hated Brahmins."

"They do," he says lightly. "They mock Brahmins."

"Then how have they come to call on you?"

"Brahmins have knowledge too."

"They want to learn . . . what? Astrology? Healing arts?" This, at least, is something in which she can take satisfaction: they are interested in his scholarship.

"We sometimes debate."

This is less welcome: a debate implies he treats them as his equals. "And you are learning their . . . to . . . extend your life? You are going to live for hundreds of years?"

"I said, I am not a siddha."

"But you are doing their practice, philosophy, whatever you call it." What, exactly, is his relationship with them?

Hanumarathnam sighs. "I am living here with you in the Brahmin quarter," he says, his mouth a bit tight as he speaks in the minor-key singsong reserved for unnecessary explanations. "Once or twice in a year I go with them, then I come back to my nice house and I try some experiments. There are forces at work in my life which do not enter into theirs."

"Is it true that they write obscene poetry?" Surely this, she thinks, should cap her case.

"It has other meanings also . . ."

"Anti-Brahmin messages and so on."

"Yes, yes. Anti-Brahmin messages. Is this what the neighbours have been telling you while I was away?" He doesn't wait for a reply. "The poetry is satirical. It is critical of the idea of caste."

"I should hope you debate this, at the least."

"Yes . . . but the poetry is more. It is also about spiritual life. Transformation. The perfection of base matter . . ."

"Like base metals into gold."

"Quite." He pats her knee. "They have means."

Sivakami maintains what she thinks is a look of resolute skepticism, though she feels a little reluctant excitement at the idea that her husband may be learning a means of prolonging his life.

_____ᘒ

HANUMARATHNAM IS HAPPY about the pregnancy, though worried because his wife is so small. Sivakami's confidence and self-assurance grow with the itty-bitty body within her own, and she reassures him. They have created a child, they are carrying on an important work, one he cannot undertake without her, and one for which she is fully equipped. The unmarried Sivakami was passionate but reserved; the newly married Sivakami was determined yet unsure; the pregnant Sivakami sits on a solid sense of her worth in the material and spiritual universe.

By the third month, though she is not getting large at all, she is getting a little uncomfortable. Her belly is becoming heavy. Not swollen, not churning—this is not a fictional sensation nor is it gas. She is bearing a significant wombal weight. She continues to be active and cheerful, but as the fourth and fifth months pass, the slight roundness grows and distends downward, slung in her pliant skin. By the end of the sixth

month, though no one would even know to look at her that she is pregnant, she can barely stand. When she does, she must lift her middle
against her interlaced fingers. She finds ways to manage.

Her nervous husband makes sure she is never without household
help, instructing the two old woman-servants never to go home. They
have five betel-stained teeth between them and have suffered a significant loss of memory with age, especially memory for all difficult tasks.
But they enjoy the status conferred by age, and most days, Sivakami
finds one of their nieces or granddaughters washing the pots and clothes,
pounding the paddy and sorting for stones. The wise old women wisely
confine themselves to the sedentary tasks of stripping leaves for thatch
and cracking jokes, chewing betel in the courtyard or on the step out
back. Newsmongers stop by to ply them with frequent gossip.

Hanumarathnam also arranges for a penurious Brahmin lady to
come in to cook. She slips quietly in and slips out, so as not to have to
acknowledge the humiliation of labour. Sivakami, who is a snob but
not cruel, tactfully ignores her. It's easy because most of her concentration is taken up with sitting, walking or lying down. She cannot turn
over once she lies down but has to grasp her middle, sit up and steadily
descend onto the other side.

As the nine-month mark nears, Hanumarathnam and one of the old
women-servants escort her to her mother's home, as is customary and
expected. They leave her there to be doted on for a few weeks before
the birth. She is fed sweets; her nieces sing to her; her sisters-in-law
loop strings of fragrant jasmine into her hair. Though she never complains, her brothers' wives watch her heaving her wee belly around and
dryly wonder what she will do when she has a pregnancy of substance.

One day, with the unexpected prescience of some fathers-to-be,
Hanumarathnam departs in a rush for his wife's village. He arrives to
find Sivakami in the concluding hard stages of labour. A barber's
scrubbed wife has been working with Sivakami for some eight hours.
Sivakami's mother can't stand the sight of blood and is dithering around
the well in the back. Hanumarathnam's father-in-law is pacing the street
and veranda, a wreck, trying to think nice things to block out his
daughter's groans and cries. He attempts to smile at the arrival of his
son-in-law, but there is an undercurrent of blame. He blames

Hanumarathnam, who is directly responsible for Sivakami's present trials, but he also blames himself, because he would have ensured that Sivakami be put in this position eventually, if not with Hanumarathnam, then with someone else. (He wants but cannot quite bring himself to blame society, which insists it must always be so: women marrying men, bearing their children. If they are at all able, it must always be so.)

Hanumarathnam can see how he feels. He feels rather the same. He touches his father-in-law's feet. This makes the older man feel worse, even as he twinges with pride, a vestige of the wedding. Hanumarathnam proceeds into the house and finds himself ushered straight out the other end. He walks into the garden and along the side of the house, until he finds a window in the vicinity of the birthing room. He calls out, "Ayah! Ho, ayah!"

The exasperated barber's wife finally appears at the window and asks, "What do you want?"

"How is she?"

"You have ears."

"Here." He holds out a lemon.

She stares at it and grunts distractedly, "Huh."

"You must throw it out the window the second the child's head appears."

"Okay."

"The exact moment, you . . ."

She has caught the lemon and vanished back into the birthing room. He imagines her tucking it into one of the hundreds of secret pockets created by the random wrapping of the saris their class wears and finding it three days later. He gives himself over to fate. He sits and paces and prays for his little wife and baby.

But she is good, the barber's wife, a very cool head, and the second the golden orb makes an appearance, she extracts the lemon with a flick of her hand in the region of her waist and tosses it to a niece who is seated on the threshold of the birthing room, a little girl whose curiosity far outweighs the smack and reiterated forbiddance whenever someone notices that she is still there. There is one in every household. "Run, run. Throw this out the window to that ayya. I have seen his baby's head."

The ecstatic child (who loves work as only children can) runs and hurls the lemon as hard as she can out the window, which is far above her height. So intent is Hanumarathnam on watching his hourglass and repeating a mantra that he doesn't see the fruit's flight, and only looks up when he hears a slap. He sees the lemon rolling toward him from the roots of the coconut tree it hit. Fortunately, he noted the time, the moment he heard the sound. He has a figure he can use to make his calculations.

Sivakami is up on her elbows, panting and sweating. The barber's wife, though intent on her task, wordlessly conveys her boredom at this act that never was and never will be new.

Finally, it's a push and a rush, a new mother nearly lifting off the cot with relief, and a baby girl sliding into the midwife's hands, nearly pulling her to the floor because this is one heavy baby. Small to average size, but heavier than an iron skillet. As they gently wipe her with a warm, damp cloth, like a cow's tongue on its calf, they notice this child is exceptionally beautiful.

"Jaundice," says the barber's wife at the child's colour. But Sivakami, who doesn't have the age or experience to question the ayah aloud, knows she is wrong. Though the baby will formally be given her paternal grandmother's name, she will be called Thangam—gold.

Six weeks later, the small family returns home. Sivakami is relieved to see how her husband dotes on the little girl. Everyone prefers a boy, but this is just the first child. You can still hope.

Sivakami cannot lift the baby. Her middle is still a little weak and the baby heavy as a sack of bricks. Hanumarathnam lifts Thangam to the breast or lays her in her little cloth hammock so Sivakami can rock her. He even regularly puts his daughter in the crossed legs of his own lap to dandle her, something Sivakami has rarely seen fathers do. But Thangam is unusually good and calm. Everyone says so. Everyone loves to hold her. They need to hold her, even if their arms fall asleep and they stagger and sway and give themselves backaches. The baby doesn't cry or even coo. Sometimes she smiles a faraway smile, and all around her are transported, stroking her golden skin, looking into her golden eyes.

2.
Vairum
1902

THANGAM GROWS INTO A SOLEMN, obedient child. Even if she were not so heavy, one would have to say gravity is her chief characteristic. Sivakami recalls the feisty, fightingish child she was herself, battling three elder brothers and winning. It was hard for her as a girl: she was required to grow out of this and even now she is not sure she succeeded in leaving this part of herself behind. She is glad to see her daughter is not like her.

Sivakami is pregnant, again, four months along. But this new life is not heavy, neither is it soft. When Sivakami, curious, palpates her tummy, she feels a hard centre, like a coin, or a marble, or a gem.

One morning finds her in the kitchen, as usual, grinding rice and lentils into *idli* batter. Her left hand rotates the huge black obelisk of the pestle into the pit of the black stone mortar, polishing the pestle with her palm. As each rotation swings away, her right hand guides escaping batter back into the black stone pit. Thangam watches. Sivakami herself finds the motion mesmerizing and enjoys even more seeing her child engrossed.

Suddenly Thangam looks to the front of the house, where her father is holding his healer's court on the veranda. She pushes herself to her feet and toddles forward with intent. Her weight grounds her. It enabled her to balance early, so walking soon followed. Sivakami calls her name, but Thangam doesn't stop. Sivakami quickly wipes her

hands and follows, but she is fearful of running, and so doesn't catch
Thangam before the little girl exits the front hall to the vestibule. She
is confident, though, that her watchful father will keep her from leaving the veranda. When Sivakami arrives at the doorway, she sees
Thangam framed in sunlight and, beyond her, three siddhas. The men
return Thangam's gaze, neither stare the more innocent or knowing,
each curious and mildly calculating.

The trio is led by a tall man whose grey hair, yellowing at the temples, winds into smoothly matted locks that hit the backs of his knees.
He has sharp, sculpted features and an imperious bearing. The others
are younger and shorter. One appears to be in his forties, his wide face
filled with sunny-looking, upturned features. The third, in his early
twenties, has a surly, rebellious manner. He projects active defiance,
while the others give off an air of amused inevitability about their
Brahmin-quarter invasion.

Sivakami tries to lift Thangam into her arms, but of course the little girl is too heavy. She does succeed in turning her damply glowing
child around and hustling her into the house, where she kneels and
clutches her to her breast. She is furious: Hanumarathnam is telling the
crowd of supplicants to come back another time, which means that,
once more, with no notice, no thought for her feelings or preferences,
he is off. He looks around the door at her and—without even a note of
apology in his voice!—says he will not be away long.

The next day, they are to attend a wedding in Kulithalai, twenty minutes
from Cholapatti by bullock cart. All Cholapatti Brahmins of stature are
invited; the groom is one of their own. When Hanumarathnam's aunt,
Annam, calls from the road that they are ready to depart, Sivakami bustles out sullenly and pretends she will be able to lift Thangam onto the
bullock cart alone, until Murthy is signalled by his mother to help.
Rukmini, innocent and unobservant, asks after Hanumarathnam.
Sivakami responds with a shrug, then feels shame at her own rudeness,
which in turn prods her to cheer up and pretend to enjoy the day.

At the bride's house, a sea of primped matrons seethe round and
among the festivities, cords of jasmine and roses tucked in their hair.
Their husbands hover or sit, contented or nervous; their children race

around. Girls twirl and squat, so their stiff silk *paavaadais* pouf out in bells that they pop like inflated cheeks; the boys twist and tweak the girls' plaits and upper arms. In one corner is a sacred fire and around it are gathered the parties required to be relatively attentive—bride and groom, parents, bride's brother, groom's sister, priest. To satisfy a need for spectacle, puffed rice and ghee are sacrificed to the fire; any kind of animal sacrifice would admittedly command more attention, but at some point, for some reason, this came to be shunned in favour of things that don't squeal or bleed. Once in a while, the priest intones the Sanskritic phrase that signals those gathered in witness to hurl rice or flowers to bless the union, which they do while hardly pausing for breath from their chattling-prattling.

The groom is from the last house on Sivakami's street in Cholapatti, one of the grandest families on the Brahmin quarter. His father, Chinnarathnam, comes almost daily to exchange the news of the world with Hanumarathnam. The son, at thirteen, has already earned an English nickname, "Minister," owing to his anglophilia and oft-declared political ambitions. Sivakami has met the boy often, since Minister accompanies his father whenever possible, interrupting pompously with opinions his father affectionately challenges him to refine. Sivakami has the impression that Chinnarathnam is more intelligent than his son, but skeptical in his essence and so unmotivated to join public life. Hanumarathnam also prefers the father but doesn't hesitate to say it is Minister who will be remembered.

The bride is seven. Sivakami's first glimpse of her is in the bride-and-groom games, keepaway coconut, which she wins, and the one in which the couple are put on a swing and sung songs with teasing, sometimes even lewd, lyrics. The little girl shouts to her mother from the swing, a question about a word she doesn't understand. She elbows her groom until he looks cowed, half hanging off the end of the swing. Sivakami recalls her own marriage, so long ago already. She defensively feigned uninterest in Hanumarathnam—at least, she thinks she was pretending. She had enjoyed the games and new clothes, but when, on the second day, she told her mother she had had enough and tried to ignore the priest's instructions, she was reprimanded sharply by a half a dozen people she didn't know.

Chinnarathnam greets Sivakami, one eye straying to look for Hanumarathnam. Unlike the many other people who have asked after him, Chinnarathnam is tactful enough not to confirm what he knows. Sivakami cannot guess whether he is offended by Hanumarathnam's absence, though she feels it must be a serious gaffe.

This, the second day of the celebration, is the most important. The couple will be made to walk seven steps together in imitation of their future life, with the fire as witness. They will swear eternal fidelity on the unwavering pole star. They will exchange garlands like exiled royalty in myths, those who have no family but the forest to help bind their fates. The bride will be collared with the saffron-threaded *thirumangalyam*, the emblem of her new state: two graven gold pendants that tell the world, in symbols neither she nor anyone else can decipher, whose family she has married. Vermilion is rubbed into the parting of her hair and the gold medals hung at her throat, so she becomes warm colour and wealth—everything good to look on.

Any of these ceremonies is individually sufficient to declare a man and woman one. But then the whole thing would be over so quickly, and how to choose among them? Bride and groom are jostled upon the shoulders of maternal uncles for the exchange of garlands; they feed each other bananas in sweetened milk; they pray, together and individually.

Three times a day, roughly corresponding to the ending of each ceremony, the gathering is fed. This does not include the many— early, late or simply hungry—who are fed in between. But three times daily, talk goes up a decibel as the gathering seats itself at rows of banana leaves laid out on the floor of the dining hall with the narrow end to the left. Each diner sprinkles the leaf with water, wipes it off with a hand, waits. The servers—hired help mixed with relatives— begin with a dollop of a gooey sweet onto the lower right corner of the leaf. The eaters lick this up: the first flavour to touch celebrants' tongues must be sweet. Then along the half of the leaf above the bisecting vein, in order from left to right, are dished vegetables in dry and wet curries, *pacchadis* of yogourt and cucumber, of sun-cured mango with palm sugar or, in more fashionable homes, of shredded beet flavoured with essence of rose. The arrangement ends with *vadai,* deep-fried patties of lentil and chili, and a spicy pickle, say of lemon or baby mango, in the top right corner. Some sweet in the form of a square or ball goes on the lower left side of the leaf, along with *pappadum* to offset the mushy main item: rice, lower centre, without which this is not a real meal.

The first course is rice mixed with *sambar*, a thick lentil sauce; the second is rice with *rasam*, and thin lentil broth, which the diner must chase continually until it is eaten to keep it from running off the leaf. Next, another helping of the first sweet, warm and runny or sticky. Last, more rice, with home-brewed yogourt: "Scrubs the teeth and tongue!" Sivakami always overhears some pompous uncle saying to an uninterested youngster. "And aids the stomach in digestion!"

Flavours and textures and the order of a meal are arranged according to the *Shastras* that proclaim that if a meal is taken as prescribed, it will settle happily. Those who violate the prescriptions take their stomachs into their own hands.

In the afternoons, the corners of the hall, the small rooms adjacent to it, even the veranda, are heaped with sated, sleeping guests.

For days, it will continue: a ceremony peaking every few hours, every chant and gesture worn smooth as pebbles on the Kaveri riverbed by repeated practice since the Aryans first entered the south, bringing with them new gods and myths, pushing into the forests the fierce deities they found the darker natives worshipping; bringing with them a system for dividing people according to function, which the Portuguese, thousands of years later, would call caste. In halls such as these, they gather, the Brahmins, hardly newcomers now, yet slightly apart from this place where they have lived for millennia. The marriage fire forges another link in the chainmail of caste; every sound, sight and smell is a celebration of the clan.

When Sivakami and the others return from the wedding, Hanumarathnam still is not back. The next night, she lies awake, angry, though unsure whether she will say so. She has already wrapped packets of food to send the siddhas on their way, the third night she has done this, just in case they return. She doesn't like their audacity and she doesn't like their taking her husband, but she is never sure how to put that, or to whom. She hears him at the front, hurries to unlock the doors and fetches the food.

He has followed her, takes up the packets and goes back outside. Sivakami hears a musical voice mutter, "Where is the golden child? The transformation of your seed, your soul-breath?"

Hanumarathnam laughs a little and answers ruefully, "Yes, the only alchemy I have ever effected."

"No less miraculous, brother. And she will grow, flesh upon bone, to face the trials of this well-worn cycle."

"You are kind."

"Blessings on her, and the next, and on your home," replies the voice.

Her husband enters their house once more and locks the locks against the night and the moon's glow, and all is as it should be. From deep down the Brahmin-quarter path, the cry floats back at them, "Here is a body, feed it!"

Hanumarathnam chuckles.

Sivakami's objections are at a standstill. From anyone else, she would have had suspicions of *dhrishti,* evil eye, from such a compliment. Still, she goes and waves a fistful of salt over her daughter; it doesn't hurt to take precautions. Siddhas don't want family or home, so why would he put the evil eye on them? It's not logical, not likely. She doesn't let Hanumarathnam see her with the salt—he has no patience with superstition. She flushes the salt along the drain out the back of the courtyard and feels cleaner than she has for days.

Sivakami is much more mobile than she was with her first pregnancy, and keeps a closer eye on the hired help. The servants are a little resentful but do not take her too seriously.

Every pregnancy has its peculiar discomforts, though. This time, Sivakami finds it hardest when the baby kicks or she squats. His swimming within her is like being prodded with an *iddikki,* an iron pot-tongs, all angles and edges.

She says "him" because she knows—and her knowledge is bordered with single-minded wishing—that this baby will be a boy. If you have a girl and a boy, it doesn't so much matter what the others are after that. Everyone says you raise a girl for someone else—you pay for her wedding and then the fruits of your investment are enjoyed by others. She is the wealth that leaves your family. A boy is the wealth that stays. Still, you must have a girl *and* a boy, a girl, then a boy, or a boy and then a girl, but she already has a girl . . . Everything is going so well, it would be very hard to have a disappointment now.

She has seen couples who seem very happy for the early years of their marriages. Then, if they have no children, they enter a state of suspension. If they have girl after girl, they enter a state of constant worry. The ones with boy after boy, though, say, "Oh, yes, shame, isn't it, seven sons, we would have liked a girl, but at least we will have grandchildren and our boys to live with in our old age!"

And the parents of five girls say nothing but wonder if one of their daughters will be tending these idiots in their dotage, and make a mental note not to let it happen.

Disappointment and lack of change wear down the life of a couple, she concludes. It should not happen. In her last trimester, she takes some quasi-medical advice from old ladies to ensure it does not: rubbing holy ash on her belly and using compresses of fresh herbs they gather for her at specific times of day.

Finally, she is off to her mother's house for the delivery. Her husband comes just before the birth. He hands the lemon to the barber's wife and reminds her, "As soon as you see the top of the baby's head."

She nods, she nods, she waves him away. He says over his shoulder, finger wagging in the air as he is shunted out the door, "It's very important!"

May as well be shouting to the trees. The trees, in fact, nod at him condescendingly as he enters the garden, and then they, too, ignore him. No choice but to take up his position, to pace and fret.

No one pays him much mind because he is behaving like any expectant father. He wishes his concerns were those of any expectant father. He wishes he were just concerned for the health of his wife and baby. Instead, he is concerned for himself—a concern that has pursued him ever since he first pursued Sivakami.

A man must marry. A man must have children. But what if a man's horoscope—the weakest quadrant, but nonetheless—says he will die in the ninth year of his marriage? Because of its placement, this really is not likely to happen, but it is difficult not to feel qualms. But say a son is born at an auspicious moment: the conflagration of father's and son's stars, the conflation of their horoscopes, could change destiny. A son has the ability, with his birth, to assure his father's longevity. Some people think of children as a means to immortality; Hanumarathnam doesn't want to live forever but wouldn't mind just a few more years. Then, the boy's birth might make no difference at all, in which case he will live with the same uncertainty as everyone else.

With Thangam, he had no such worry, because he had a strong feeling the first would be a daughter. He was not ready for a boy, then. He was not ready to know. This time he does not know even if this child is a boy. He might be pacing and fretting for another girl.

Nothing to do but wait.

Hanumarathnam stomps the garden to a pulp while, within, Sivakami concentrates on the hardest thing she's ever done.

"Oh," says the barber's wife. "Hmm ... well ... don't worry," she mutters, as though encouraging herself.

"What?" Sivakami pants.

"Bum first. No matter." She nods at Sivakami. "We're going to have to do this fast, all right? It's your second time at this, you know what you're doing ..."

Sivakami feels another contraction coming on and the barber's wife commands, "Get it out!"

A few moments later, Hanumarathnam hears a squalling. He throws his arms up in frustration, notes the time, goes to the window and yells, "Lemon!"

It is hurled out the window at him, but he pays no attention. "Girl or boy?" he shouts.

"Boy!"

A boy. The barber's wife finishes wiping the child and hands him to Sivakami with the suppressed satisfaction of one who has accomplished a feat much more difficult than those around her appreciate. Sivakami doesn't even look at her as she receives her son. He's a little skinny, and darker than his parents, though she doesn't notice either of these qualities until her sisters-in-law point them out. The baby calms as she rocks him and starts to sing a nursery rhyme that was one of her own favourites as a child. He opens his eyes to gaze at her, his irises nearly black yet strangely brilliant, diamond sharp.

3.
Only one, as an eye
1902

"Onnay onnu, Kannay kannu."
"Only one, one, as an eye, an eye."
When there is only one, how precious is that son.

SIVAKAMI IS AT ONCE PROUD AND COMPLACENT—complacent because she knew she would deliver a boy, and proud that she took every available measure to ensure it. When she emerges from her dive into her new baby's eyes, she asks about Thangam. Since no good wife can say her husband's name, everyone understands she's asking after her husband. She expects to hear his voice responding. Instead, her youngest sister-in-law walks Thangam to the door of the birth room and tells Sivakami, obviously curious to see her reaction, "He's gone already."

Sivakami feels an unjustifiable pang.

At Thangam's birth, Hanumarathnam had called to his wife, "I hear she's a beauty—won't tell a soul. I'll return. Send word if you want anything."

His presence at his children's births was highly unconventional, after all. He attended only because he trusted no one else to record their birth times and make the consequent calculations.

Sivakami tells herself if he hadn't said those few words to her after Thangam's birth she wouldn't be feeling this disappointment; she tells herself it is far more proper for him to leave, saying nothing, and return for the eleventh-day ceremonies as though he'd never come before; she tells herself he was too excited the first time and couldn't restrain himself, but now he's more mature. She tells herself he's overwhelmed with emotion because she delivered a boy. She doesn't tell herself that none of these excuses suffices.

Hanumarathnam is fleeing. He speeds, to the degree that he can in a bullock cart, toward his home and his instruments: his home, where he can think straight, and his instruments, which will tell him, finally, his fate.

He reaches Cholapatti as the sun is setting, at that time of day when what is known appears unknown. A sickened feeling in the pit of his stomach has nothing to do with village roads and the swaying cart. He says nothing about it to himself because that would be fatalism: a person irresponsibly deciding, on some caprice, that a terrible fate awaits him. Such a man will be continually preoccupied with his doom until something, anything, happens so he can say, "Aha! You see! I am doomed, it was not my imagination!"

Hanumarathnam has no patience with such whimsy. Destiny can be read precisely, scientifically, and this is precisely, scientifically, what he intends to do. Only after that, if necessary, will he fall into despair. Or sink into relief: he keeps himself optimistic.

On the Cholapatti rooftop, he works through the night. He notes his son's birth time and birth location in tables, then creates other tables to repeat the calculations from different angles and starting points, checking them one against another, consulting charts and books. Every equation takes him back in time, so changed is the sky already from the moment whose influences he is enumerating as the night moves past the moon.

Every so often, he peers through his telescope, scavenged by a distant relative from the house of a dying British surveyor and bon vivant, and brought to Hanumarathnam in recognition of his talents. Where his ancestors relied on handed-down documents, he, always interested in other traditions' teachings, supplements his Vedic calculations with measurements he has learned to make using telescopic observations.

He brings the stars close, through the lenses; he looks in their eyes. To those who merely admire the heavens, as they admire a new building in the city or another man's wife, alterations in the sky are mere degrees of difference. They are interesting to observe, chart, identify. They are fine to forget. But, as all experiences, however fleeting or superficial, leave residues, so the moment-by-moment turning of heavenly bodies has momentous repercussions.

Hanumarathnam, all too fully aware of the ability of the heavens to sustain life, bring death and cause all the ups and downs in between, cannot simply stare in dumbfounded awe for a couple of seconds at the beauty of the skies and then go down to supper and sleep. What he sees writ is destinies untold.

Dawn breaks upon him. He has been sitting still a long time. Dew trickles down his neck, as if the morning sees he's not sweating and thinks he should.

He has read that he will die.

Sooner, that is, rather than later. His weak quadrant has an astrological alignment with his son's birth time, and this has darkened the shadow of death. The discus of the little boy's stars will cut Hanumarathnam's lifeline within three years.

At the eleventh-day naming ceremonies, Hanumarathnam goes through the motions. It's not conspicuous: everyone is just going through the motions, as people do at these things. But Sivakami notices and is concerned: Hanumarathnam has not tried to get close to his son. With his daughter, he is still all fond smiles and lifting and swinging, though Sivakami perceives a sadness there too.

Why not the boy? Why not the boy? Sivakami wonders as she waits out the remainder of the thirty-one days' seclusion. After a girl baby, seclusion lasts forty-one days, so Sivakami has another reason to be grateful for a boy: she couldn't have borne this strange worry as long as that. Finally, Hanumarathnam comes to escort her home.

He makes his wife comfortable with the baby, who is a bit of a fusser, in the back of the bullock cart. Maybe that's it, she thinks, the whimpering and whinging. It doesn't bother her, but maybe that's why his father keeps his distance. Or the baby's looks: they don't make her feel strange, but maybe they do his father? Sivakami is feeling sensitive: her eldest and youngest sisters-in-law had made a few remarks—the sort that sound kind-hearted but sting. "He's obviously so alert, must be very intelligent, and what do good looks really matter for anyway?" and, with a little shudder, "Oh! Those eyes just look right through a person, don't they?"

Hanumarathnam sits up front with his lovely daughter, showing her the sights, until her eyes are heavy. Then she leaves him to come and lie in back with her mother, where she insists on keeping one hand on the baby, as though the cart were a big cradle for both of them. Thangam has said nothing about her new little brother, but it is clear that she doesn't share the world's repulsion. Daily, since his birth, she has brought him gifts, sweets Sivakami pretends to feed him, for Thangam's sake, and pretty leaves he crushes in a fist. She would squat on small haunches watching him almost without blinking, for half an hour at a time, until an aunt startled her by calling her name. If anyone asked her about him, though, she gave no answer but her vague, incurious gaze, and since the questions rarely needed answers—"You must be so proud, a big sister, eh, Thangam?"—the asker just pinched her cheek and turned away.

When Hanumarathnam brings Thangam to the back, he looks at the baby without speaking, and then returns to the front to sit with the servant who has come along as driver. Sivakami's mind keeps running on in speculation: maybe he thinks the boy doesn't look like him? But who can tell with a mashed-up barely one-month-old? She is feeling ill now, much as Hanumarathnam did on this journey just after his son's birth. It is a variety of motion sickness, caused not by the rock-bump-sway of the animals and cart, but by the ringing and ricocheting of her thoughts as they tumble along and drag her behind.

They reach home by nightfall. That night, he sleeps, she doesn't.

In the morning, they go through more motions. Sivakami watches Hanumarathnam: his movements look stiff, his face unnatural. She can feel the pressure of whatever he is thinking on her temples, on her chest, but she cannot guess at it and finally cannot bear it any longer. When he comes into the main hall for his mid-morning meal, the baby is napping and Thangam has gone next door to play with the still-childless Rukmini. Sivakami crumples to the floor and cracks out a plea through clenched teeth and tears, "Oh, my lord, my lord. What is happening? What is wrong?"

He immediately drops to his own knees, lifting Sivakami's face to his and thinking how he loves her.

"Little one . . . I . . ." Where should he begin? With which small fact or hope? "I'm sorry, I . . ."

Sivakami is watching his face, her lips parted, trying to read what he is not telling her. He turns away so as to be able to tell her himself.

"I told your father when I proposed that . . ." He glances back and away again. "Let me explain. You know that if something is written in the weakest quadrant of one's horoscope, it is extremely unlikely, yes?"

"Okay . . ." She has never heard this before, but the interpretation of horoscopes was never of particular interest to her.

"Your father and uncles knew that, and for the sake of honesty, I told them that my death in the ninth year of my marriage was written in that very weakest quadrant."

Sivakami sits back on her haunches, no longer weeping, looking resolute and skeptical. "But . . ."

He will not be hurried. "Often, the birth of a son changes the relation of the stars, can even erase the shadow of death from the father's horoscope."

"Our son cannot have done that," she says, sad and matter-of-fact.

"My calculations following our son's birth show that Yama's water buffalo has advanced from the weakest quadrant to the strongest," he quietly agrees. "The god of death will surely come to take my soul in the third year of the boy's life."

"Ayoh!" Sivakami cries now. "Ayoh, Rama!"

"It is not the child's fault . . ." Hanumaratham says as though it could be. "But he has killed me."

She is now leaning on a pillar, he kneeling in front of the Ramar triptych, the glare of the street just out of sight through the front doors, reflecting into the hall along with the distant sound of daily life, but they don't stay like that for long.

Sivakami soon pulls herself to her feet, and her feet carry her mechanically to the well. She washes her face, the face she has had and known for more than sixteen years—a long time, by some standards. She feels hard new lines drawn there by her husband and son. What will be written on those lines? Maybe they can read what she can't, these men who know so much. She returns to the hall and asks, "And so. What now?"

Her husband sees what she has felt on her face. He thinks, *Look, two children, and no trace, now, of the girl. She has become a woman. How wonderful, how miraculous, that we go through these stages, walking the path of our lives one foot in front of the other, one in front of the other, this is how we live, this is how to live.* He comforts himself with circular, cloudy thinking, the sort that makes respectable conversation in the face of grief. As if he's rehearsing to attend his own funeral.

For now, though, he is still living, and so is Sivakami, and so are their two children, whose needs must be met, so the requirements of life put their feet one in front of the other. They eat and sleep and conduct business even though their life has been poured into a rice-sorting basket and tossed two foot, four foot, six foot in the air.

———

HANUMARATHNAM TELLS SIVAKAMI that he is going to teach her about household finances, administration of agricultural income, market relations and management of personnel, and that he has hired a new servant, a young boy, who will learn to assist her. If he works out well, and Hanumarathnam has good reason to believe he will, then he will be retained. If not, they will dismiss him and try quickly to find someone else. They cannot be dilly-dallying with this servant as they normally would. It is not enough that he is related to one of their old servants, not enough that he needs a favour, not even enough if he is entertaining or pitiable. He must be efficient, confident and worthy of trust. Hanumarathnam doesn't need to say the reason: that Sivakami and the servant will be managing the lands on their own in a little more than two years and both must prove themselves capable.

A few days later, the new servant starts. Sivakami is giving the children their baths when she hears the boy call out from behind the door at the rear of their property. How can she help but hear his as one of the voices of death? Yet she herself opens the door. She forces herself, because the few times she has acted maudlin, it only made Hanumarathnam impatient.

The servant, a thirteen-year-old by the name of Muchami, accepts a cup of sugared milk and then leaves to accompany Hanumarathnam on his daily round of some portion of the properties. He walks behind Hanumarathnam out to the fields, then along the narrow hump separating paddy fields one from another and from the plots of other crops. Social imperative dictates that they cannot walk abreast on the street, agricultural imperative that they walk single file between the fields: the dividers between plots are less than a foot wide in places.

Muchami notes his new employer's sure-footedness. It separates those who walk among the fields from those who don't. Most landowners sit in their big fine houses and wonder lazily when to expect the rent, not giving it any more thought than that until some crisis passes the point of resolution. Hanumarathnam is obviously a landlord who likes to know what's transpiring out among the folk, to sort out tangles while they are still small, even to anticipate them. Muchami is of the same mind. He marches proudly in step with his new employer. He decides he likes Hanumarathnam's looks and tries to match his step to the seigneur's.

They pause to clear fallen leaves from irrigation canals. They come slowly up beside the white herons that stand in the six inches of paddy water every morning. Only a few move away. Muchami listens patiently as Hanumarathnam tells him things he already knows, such as who the tenant is on each piece of land, his rent, his character and temperament. Muchami has always made it his business to know things. He finds knowledge more interesting than ignorance. So he doesn't listen too closely but dreamily soaks in the sound of Hanumarathnam's voice, which he might have likened to chocolate had he ever known chocolate. (He never comes closer to chocolate than the sound of that voice.)

When they return, he waits while his employer completes bath, prayers and meal. Hanumarathnam takes his rice meal at ten; Muchami receives the same. He ate already that morning but eats again because he is an accommodating sort of boy and, at thirteen, especially accommodating toward extra meals. Hanumarathnam sits in the main hall, Muchami in the courtyard.

As they eat, Hanumarathnam quizzes Muchami through the open doors of the pantry and kitchen.

"Shanmugham's sesame field—what's the northern border?" he calls.

Without missing a mouthful, Muchami calls back, "The teak stand that's the southern border of Kantha's turmeric field, Ayya."

"Shanmugam's paddy yield last year?"

"What he really got, Ayya, or what he told you?"

"Either one."

"He paid you seventeen per cent of twenty-two bushels."

"Other particulars?"

"Particulars you told me or *other* particulars?"

"Hm . . ." Hanumarathnam purses his lips. "The latter."

"His brother's wife has a cousin who went to work on a rubber plantation in Malaysia and never returned. News came on the wind that he married a beautiful village girl, but she is only a girl during the blue nights. By day, she becomes a monkey, called 'orange-utange,' or something."

Hanumarathnam already has a strong feeling that he and Muchami share a point of view on relations with tenants and have a mutual appreciation of the importance of obscure if irrelevant information to everyday business. For instance, Hanumarathnam is certain that, in the past, tenants were tempted to cheat him. He thinks that he has succeeded in dissuading them by strategically mentioning "other particulars" about the party in question—giving the impression that he knew much more than he said. He's sure Muchami also knows how to deploy such details to effect.

Next, Sivakami gives Thangam to Muchami to entertain while she begins her portion of the training.

Sivakami must also walk the fields, though she cannot actually walk the fields: were she truly to walk in public view, she would be risking their social position in an attempt to maintain their economic grip. Any respectable Brahmin matron keeps largely out of sight if her family can afford that modesty; a widow must be kept entirely hidden, so as not to expose her shame at her condition.

So Hanumarathnam has laboured to create a middle ground: a detailed map of the holdings for Sivakami to walk through with her eyes and mind. Hanumarathnam has accurately portrayed those properties: real and perceived distances, sizes, and productive capacity of each plot. It is not simply a matter of drawing a map to scale; one must choose what sort of scale: physical? psychological? This map has to show how a property relates to its owners, to itself, to tenants, to the community. This is business—not geography, not math.

Each holding is labelled with the tenant, fee and probable current and projected output. Each of these wants discussing: the age and character of the tenant, the age and character of a particular plot of soil, the problems and promise and possibilities of each. Some tenants have special agreements. They grow plantains for themselves among the coconut trees, for instance, until the coconut trees grow large and require that space. Hanumarathnam gets a slightly larger share of paddy for this, since he and Sivakami have plantains in plenty from their own garden. And what of the paddy to be sold? Selling at the market is an art and the middlemen are crafty. Sivakami and Muchami must be equipped to play this game; they must operate as a team.

Muchami is out back playing horsie, letting wee Thangam ride around on his back while Sivakami peers at the map, rotating it, biting her lip. Muchami is slight but must have considerable strength to give a horsie-ride to the world's heaviest child, Hanumarathnam notes with satisfaction, just as the boy collapses in a pile of giggles. He had wanted a young man, someone who would be Sivakami's legs and back, eyes and hands, throughout her life. But there are dangers, for a . . . a . . . (he does not let himself think *widow*). He had to find someone he could trust with his wife, who would be no more than eighteen and left alone in the world.

In the weeks between his son's birth and his wife's return, Hanumarathnam had found reasons to casually observe the young people of the servant class at play. The rough and tumble of pubescent boys, their teasing and taunting of the girls, the girls' half-hearted escape attempts ... and he noticed a young man who didn't participate in the taunting of the girls. He observed this young man more keenly and saw the youth was not gentle or shy. In Hanumarathnam's opinion, this boy didn't refrain from teasing out of an inordinate respect for females. He refrained because girls did not interest him. Hanumarathnam saw Muchami's eyes gleam when the boys alone ran off to play kabbadi in the dust. He saw him tackling the tallest and best-looking boys and sitting on them a little longer than necessary; when he saw this, he guessed that this boy would not outgrow his boredom with girls.

Discreet inquiries revealed the boy to be called Muchami, to be the only son in a family of three children and to have a widowed mother. By way of one of the couples who work for him, Hanumarathnam summoned the widow to his house and explained his interest in employing her son. He met with the boy, who impressed him as sharp. The pact was secured, conditional on performance, the widow was eternally grateful and Muchami was instructed to show up a week or so after Hanumarathnam brought his wife from Samanthibakkam.

After the morning meal, the whole household naps, Hanumarathnam a little apart from Sivakami and the children in the main hall, Muchami on the narrow, sheltered platform that extends from the back of the house into the courtyard.

Around tiffin time, an agent comes to the house to purchase paddy. Muchami asks permission to handle the transaction on his own. Hanumarathnam complies, then watches with increasing admiration as Muchami bullies and shames and achieves a much better price for the paddy than Hanumarathnam ever has.

After the muttering and defeated middleman leaves, Muchami asks Hanumarathnam, "Ayya, why do you deal with that particular agent with your paddy?"

"I ... because I have always dealt with him."

"He's been cheating you."

"I know ..."

"But less than the others would have."

"I know." Hanumarathnam wonders why he sounds defensive, given that he feels amused. "That's why I always go to him."

"Well, you can see he will cheat far less now. Today I did not permit any cheating at all, though I will, with your permission, Ayya, allow him to cheat now and again, just to keep him interested." Hanumarathnam nods as Muchami continues, "The balance will still be more profitable for you than it has been."

After this it's market hour. Muchami will assume this not from Hanumarathnam, but from one of the other servants, a diligent man, but one for whom age is becoming an obstacle. Hanumarathnam takes Muchami to the market himself, to spare the old man the journey and to evaluate Muchami's bargaining ability.

With the sellers of dry goods, vegetables, fruits and kerosene, Muchami uses much the same bullying and shaming techniques that were so effective with the rice agent. Hanumarathnam observes at a distance, thinking it would have made good business sense to hire such a savvy assistant much earlier. Muchami will pay for himself in no time.

Hanumarathnam has only occasionally gone to market—when he was young, and a servant was sick or perhaps away at a wedding. Every time, he wanted to bully exactly the way Muchami is doing now, especially when dealing with those merchants known to be particularly bad cheats. His caste consciousness would not permit him: such behaviour seems ungracious from Brahmins. It provokes jokes about mercenary priests, and Hanumarathnam is particularly sensitive owing to his role as village healer. If he were perceived as grasping, the villagers would still come to him for medicine, but his relationship to them would be altered by a lessening of confidence in the purity of his goodwill.

So he never tried, though sometimes he intervened on someone else's behalf, because merchants cheat poor people even more than they cheat the rich and Brahmins. Hanumarathnam reflects momentarily that a poor person working for a middle-class household has the greatest bargaining advantages—the power to purchase in quantity and the knowledge and status of the street.

When they return from the market, Hanumarathnam comes in by the back courtyard, washes his feet, then proceeds to the veranda to sit on a jute-strung daybed and contemplate the *Hindu* newspaper.

Muchami enters the courtyard behind him and empties the bag of vegetables on the platform behind the kitchen. Sivakami squats to do the sorting. This was a ritual, enacted by her mother and various servants, that she had observed daily as a girl and looked forward to assuming: the mistress criticizes the servant's choices, goes into shock at the expense, has all the fun of market banter without leaving the house.

But when, in her first week as mistress of her own house, Sivakami launched some imaginative criticisms of the produce, the old servant barely glanced at her. He just put the change down on a corner of the platform and wandered away, leaving her mumbling to fade into silence. The day following she asked him to stay while she inspected the goods, and he complied but shrugged at bruises and rot, claimed not to remember prices and was altogether no fun.

Now, unexpectedly, Muchami addresses her. "Beans are better than most. It's not been a good season for beans. Don't know how he gets such good beans, considering he's such a coward."

Sivakami is too surprised to respond. She has been silent with him till now, resenting him, hating what he represents. Now, she's uncomfortably aware of her reluctance to risk a remark that might cause him to stop talking. He doesn't seem to mind her silence and continues, "His wife and son are always ganging up with her sister and the sister's husband. They ridicule him until he cries and runs away to sleep. They all live with him—he's too scared to stop them. Must spend all his time finding these great beans."

Sivakami, though still trying to be unfriendly, can't help asking, "Why is he so scared?"

"Because he's a coward, like I said. Look at these eggplants. I know they're not gorgeous, but they were a free gift owing to my acquaintance with the seller. He used to beat up on me because I was a friend of his younger brother. Now he won't try it because I'm working for you, Amma. Just cut off the bad parts, there'll still be lots. Where do you want the lentils?"

He bounces the sack of lentils off one knee and then the other while waiting for her answer. She hurries to fetch the canister, and he puts away the other dry goods and the kerosene.

That night, Hanumarathnam talks to her about their newest employee. He is satisfied that he has chosen well this caretaker for his wife and children but is also aware that he may be giving this boy some power. He likes the idea that he has the power to give it and thinks Muchami will still know his place.

In those early weeks, Hanumarathnam continues the work of checking on crop yields and collecting the rent while Muchami tags along. The servant has adopted Hanumarathnam's posture and stance, the slight stoop, the outward turn of the knees. He has found himself a walking stick, which he uses to dredge plantain leaves from irrigation tracts. He leans on it as he watches Hanumarathnam leaning on his own stick and talking to the peasant cultivators. Muchami's dhotis become whiter, his hair smoother, and he adopts Brahmin turns of phrase and pronunciations, adding curlicues to a manner of speech that had already sounded a bit forced among his social equivalents.

Many of the tenants, along with Muchami's uncles and mother, find his affectations silly, but the few who are impressed give him more than enough reason to continue. He begins monitoring and collecting on his own. Though he is tougher than Hanumarathnam, he never bullies the tenants. In the market, people expect to be bullied, but bullying peasant farmers in front of their homes is gauche. His family and close friends call him the landlord's *goonda*, but they are only teasing. Muchami knows this and doesn't get defensive; instead he swaggers around and pretends to be a real goonda. He knows he is successful.

Sivakami, too, senses that Muchami hopes to be something more than most among his class, and wonders if they might be of help along that path. She also finds herself, daily, looking more and more forward to his reports from his rounds, less and less inclined to hide her amusement. She has a few friends, Brahmin matrons like herself, who drop by from time to time, but they seem to tell the same few stories, about saris, deaths and slights ad nauseam. These things do interest her, in the candyfloss way of pulp novels. It is wholesome gossip, because everyone does it, and because it comes with judgments: proper versus improper, decent versus indecent. In contrast, Muchami's tales are meaty and illicit. He tells her everything about people she knows and those she will never meet. He is more respectful when speaking about Brahmins but makes no attempt to censor himself—in fact, he is encouraged by Sivakami's attention into increasingly outrageous mimicry.

One day a few weeks after he starts work for them, Muchami is sorting through the produce in the back courtyard by the well, entertaining Sivakami, who sits on the platform behind the kitchen with the baby in her lap, by commenting on the vegetables in the voice of their preferred kerosene merchant. The kerosene seller has a strange condition: his voice, every few phrases, shoots up briefly and involuntarily into a falsetto. Muchami maintains a deadpan monologue on the vegetables, not breaking rhythm at all for the falsetto interludes. "Okra aren't bad, though he kept slipping these *little-little rotten ones* in among the good. I called him on it, picked them out and said, 'Who're you trying to fool?'"

Sivakami, after a brief attempt to restrain her giggles, breaks down. Muchami starts adding effeminate prancing to the high-pitched bits, still with no break in work or words, until Sivakami is nearly collapsing with laughter.

Glancing up, she sees Hanumarathnam has come to the pantry entrance, attracted by her laughter. He looks amused and curious, but Muchami stops when he notices his employer and stands with his head bowed. Sivakami, too, stops laughing, and Hanumarathnam says, "What? Why so solemn as soon as I show up?" They smile at him shyly and he withdraws with affectionate exasperation, but Sivakami feels sick with anger now, at herself, and even more, at Hanumarathnam. Muchami tries to resume clowning a little but quickly sees that she is no longer in the mood.

How dare my husband trick me into accepting this? Sivakami stomps inside and puts the baby in the cloth hammock where he sleeps, rocking it silently and a little too hard, until the baby's wails jolt her into slowing down and beginning a lullaby. She takes a deep breath. *Here I am, acting normal, after my husband has said he is going to die.*

꩜

WEEKS ACCELERATE INTO MONTHS. Sivakami and Hanumarathnam's son has come to be called Vairum, "diamond," in contrast to Thangam's gold. One of Hanumarathnam's sisters created the nickname, when, holding the baby, she said with a little shiver, "Ooh—look at how his eyes glitter—so cold!" She stopped, suddenly aware of how Sivakami might take this. An elder sister-in-law didn't really need to be concerned with Sivakami's feelings, but she didn't want to offend her little brother. "Your little diamond!" she added in a shrill disclaimer, and Sivakami accepted the suggestion, choosing to pretend the entire comment had been in goodwill and good taste. (The sister-in-law had not yet discovered ice, or Vairum might have been named for that chill substance.)

Vairum is a very different child from his elder sister. Unlike Thangam, he craves attention. He complains loudly until he is picked up and comforted. Fortunately, also unlike Thangam, he is the normal weight of a skinny Indian baby, and so not a great burden to his tiny mother. While Vairum's stare contains unmistakable longing, no one but Sivakami and Thangam is tempted to carry and cuddle the boy with the pinched features and cold, dark eyes. Tempted least of all is his father. Hanumarathnam keeps very occupied with healing and agriculture, his studies, his training of Sivakami and Muchami. He always has a small joke and a cuddle for his daughter, but nothing for his son. Sivakami holds Vairum tight whenever she can, covering him with kisses and words of adoration. Where Thangam, at six months, nursed six times daily with perfect regularity, Vairum demands the breast capriciously like the little king he is and should be. Sivakami nearly always complies, stopping what she is doing to take him into the room under the stairs, holding him in her lap as he idly sucks and fiddles with her thirumangalyam, the wedding pendants that otherwise are dropped out of sight in her blouse.

On one afternoon, after Vairum finishes nursing, Sivakami is playing with him, lifting him horizontally to blow against his tummy, luxuriating in his baby skin and the rich sound of his giggles. She looks up to see Hanumarathnam, watching through the doorway as though it's a portal between this life and the next. She holds the baby out to him, exasperated: no matter what is coming, nothing in life is denied to him now. But he takes a step back and she clasps Vairum again to her breast.

She wishes she could talk to Hanumarathnam about the despair and estrangement she sees on his face, but when she tries, she finds she pities him too much. She is grateful she doesn't have to live with such feelings toward her children; she doesn't know how she could talk Hanumarathnam into feeling any different. She persuades him a couple of times to hold the child, thinking he can't help but fall in love if he does so, but Hanumarathnam looks so stiff and helpless that she takes Vairum back. And the little boy's eyes, so often trained on his father, are full of unreciprocated desire.

Perhaps through some ineffectual cosmic attempt to remedy this injustice, Thangam is as infatuated with her little brother as the rest of the world is with her. She insists on helping her mother bathe the baby; she rocks him, pats him, sings to him, seems oblivious to any child's existence save his, even while children on the veranda call for her daily.

When Vairum is nearly eleven months old, they shave his hair—it takes three of them, Sivakami, Murthy and Rukmini, to hold him still—and make a pilgrimage to Palani Mountain, where they offer it to the deity. On his first birthday, he is held on Sivakami's eldest brother's knee and his ears are pierced. He screams and thrashes so violently that Sivakami wonders if one of the demons who should be placated by these rituals has got the wrong message. Thangam stands close by—she who whimpered as her head was shaved and burbled with silent tears at her own piercing—trying to soothe the baby.

Hanumarathnam, on these days, says nothing. He always turns so as not to have to see the little boy, who watches his father as Thangam watches the baby, and Sivakami watches them all, knowing nothing can compensate for Vairum's deprivation. None but a father can give a father's love.

～ℰ

MONTHS SPEED PAST. Hanumarathnam and Sivakami have been married now for almost eight years.

She has been enjoying her new responsibilities. She has known many women who do their families' accounting and make their financial and strategic decisions. Many wives do these jobs because their husbands are less than competent. The wives' work is accepted but never acknowledged. She is the first she has known whose husband has trained her at these tasks, shown faith in and approval of her abilities. And with Muchami's presence already so strong in the fields, her husband's absence will hardly be noticed out there.

She realizes that she has begun to accept the way he has tricked her into being practical, into living with his death. She hardly recalls the resentment she first had toward Muchami.

And in the night, every night, Hanumarathnam turns to her. They might go through the movements for procreation or pleasure, but on these nights, the fire is fed on fear of death. Sometimes, as Sivakami marches tenderly through the requirements of his siddhic practices, she wonders with each movement, is this the one that will give him long life? She is a Brahmin, she cannot make him into a siddha. She supposes he could become one, if he chose. But then, that would mean renouncing caste, and if he were not a Brahmin, she could not be married to him, so what purpose would that serve?

She often rises after Hanumarathnam's rough breathing has deepened into post-coital rest. Her sleep now is rare and slight, between her worries and Vairum's nocturnal wakings. She lights a kerosene lamp and does beadwork by the bad light. Night after sleepless night, contrary to all her mother's severe warnings, Sivakami finds her sight improves from the exercises. The tiny glass beads dance with the flame, sometimes they seem to her almost to sing, as she sits before the Ramar, working and praying and wondering about the future.

She wonders, if they have more children, another son, maybe things, astrological things, would shift again. But she somehow knows there will be no more children.

She recalls Savitri, that most devoted wife and daughter, whose story is told in the Mahabharata. Savitri had insisted on marrying Satyavan, in spite of all her elders' objections that he was cursed to die within a year of their marriage. She would not be put off, and when Yama, god of death, came riding his water buffalo to claim Satyavan's soul, Savitri went after him and, with clever arguments and bulldoggish perseverance, got her husband back.

Sivakami wonders what choice she herself would have made, given these conditions. She admits to herself in the small, bleak hours before morning that, given the choice, despite all she feels for her husband, she would not have chosen to be a widow.

But she was not given the choice. And when the time comes, will she follow Yama's water buffalo into the netherworld, over rocks and by harsh seas, to reclaim her husband's soul for his body? She sensibly concludes that all she can do is prepare. Her husband, bless his cursed soul, is doing everything in his power to help her do that. She falls asleep praying for strength.

4.
Fever
1904

The years hurtle past them, like rain and parrots,
like rice and rose petals.

VAIRUM, NOW TWO AND A HALF, is outside playing under Muchami's watchful eye. He has grown from a complaining baby into a child who plays alone. He plays energetically and needs many people to populate his games, but since he lacks friends, he uses Muchami for every role. Vairum is fractious, bossy and tiring, but the patient servant generally does whatever the child commands, pretending perfect comprehension of Vairum's cryptic and sometimes semi-intelligible orders. Muchami is an energetic young man, but Vairum taxes him completely.

Vairum is spoiled. Not just because he's an only son, though this might have been enough, but because Sivakami pities him. She coddles and cuddles and feeds him extra sweets. He laps it up, going to her many times each day to bury his face in the folds of her sari and thighs.

He has begun to exhaust even Thangam, who continues to love him for reasons of her own. Vairum responds by pinching his sister, pushing her away when she tries to help with his games and then screaming and clinging when she leaves him, once kissing her so violently his tooth breaks her skin. He doesn't seek her out, though, as if to prove he doesn't need her the way everyone else does.

In his favour, Vairum is generous to a fault. He never eats treats without first offering others a share, even giving up his own portion if some urchin looks at it with big eyes. He can't stand for anyone to go without. Even Thangam is never excluded, though she will never take from him. Sometimes, he approaches his father with an offering. Always, his father declines.

It is hard to say whether Vairum is doing this to win friends. If he is, it's not working: smaller, more timid children are scared of him; larger, bolder children tease him mercilessly; small and large run at him to take whatever delicacy he has on offer, then run away. Vairum cries in a far corner of the house, goes on feeding the opportunistic children and plays with Muchami.

Thangam spends most of her time sitting in the hall or on the veranda. She doesn't chatter, she doesn't do handicrafts, she just sits. She is willing and prompt in completing her few chores, and Sivakami is satisfied she will make a good homemaker. If she needs no entertainment, this is an asset.

The little girl has always been quiet, but, since Vairum was born, she has become increasingly so. This could, Sivakami thinks, be owing to Vairum's demanding nature: Sivakami knows she pays more attention to the boy, but everyone else pays so much attention to Thangam. Neither has Thangam ever shown her parents the passionate affection that Sivakami receives from her son. Once or twice, however, Sivakami thought she saw, mixed in Thangam's adoring glances at Vairum, some shame, as she herself received from Hanumarathnam the easy fondness he has never been able to bestow on his son.

Most of the neighbourhood considers Thangam's beauty itself to be a community service. Burnished hair, molten eyes—for Thangam's sake, many children come to their house. They ask her to come away, to play with them. They touch her golden skin. She smiles a fleeting smile, rebuking, mischievous, skeptical and warm. The children never give up asking and Thangam never goes with them.

The world loves Thangam and does not love Vairum, because Thangam is easy to love and Vairum is not, and people, given the choice, do what is easy.

IT IS THE HOT SEASON. The children of Cholapatti lie moaning, felled by a fever and pox, in rooms all up and down the Brahmin quarter, in huts in the village and fields beyond. Sivakami prays daily to the stone Ramar, guardian of their home, for her children's safety. She ties extra charms around the children's necks and wrists. She prays to the goddess Mariamman, who visits houses in the guise of such sickness, by muttering welcomes, because she mustn't make the goddess angry, and by appeasements, because this goddess is always angry. Despite her precautions, both Thangam and Vairum contract the illness, which has already taken three children in a month.

The children lie in the front room for five days with sweats and chills. Each awakens with nightmares. Thangam will be sleeping and flip suddenly onto her back. Her eyelids will shoot open and she will stare at the ceiling as though facing down her fears, lips troubled but silent. Vairum thrashes and lashes out in his sleep, hits himself and howls. He weeps from bad dreams and must be consoled.

Sivakami wipes their small bodies with warm water. When they are chilly, she covers them. When they sweat, she fans them with sprays of neem branches, kept always near sick babies, because neem gives the goddess Mariamman pleasure and so satisfies her that she feels she may depart. Muchami quietly does what Sivakami does, attending to one child when she tends the other.

Hanumarathnam is behaving very strangely. The village families have come to him for remedies, but he has told them he can do nothing for this sickness. He has never said such a thing before. He even gives his own children a wide berth, though he watches them from a distance. When Sivakami asks him if he is concerned for them, he says no.

One night, as she lies awake listening to their laboured breathing, Sivakami becomes aware that Hanumarathnam, whom she had thought asleep for some time already, is saying something. She quietly asks him to repeat himself, but he continues mumbling. She leans in close, but the phrases are nonsensical to her. She watches him with her dark-sharpened eyes for a while: he is asleep. She rises to take up her beading. She is working six scenes from the child Krishna's life and is midway through the third.

In the morning, she asks Hanumarathnam if he recalls his dreams of the night before.

"I never dream," he replies without looking up from his newspaper.

"You were talking in your sleep last night," she says.

"Why didn't you wake me?" He is already impatient with the conversation, and she reciprocates, "Why should I?"

He sighs. "Did it frighten you?"

"No." The subject is dropped, and Sivakami goes about the morning's chores, mystified and suspicious.

That afternoon, she is attending to the children, praying under her breath continuously. Like all the women in the village whose children are sick, Sivakami has offered a deal to Mariamman, that her children will participate in the village goddess's annual festival if only she will remove the scourge. It has been five days, without sign of recovery, but Sivakami has faith yet.

Hanumarathnam is napping on the other side of the main hall. Sivakami starts as his lips begin moving and realizes she has been staring at him for a long time. She rises to move closer and in doing so happens to catches a glimpse beyond the open front door.

The siddhas have come.

The eldest nods as she catches his eye. She is, as always, unhappy to see them. She crosses to her husband, who is muttering softly, intense emotion working his brow, his breath fighting in his nostrils. She takes his shoulder and he startles, panting, sweating, looking around wildly.

"What, dear, what is it?" Sivakami asks. She feels she knows; she feels she is about to cry; she feels a little feverish herself, hot and cold at once.

"I dreamt . . ." Hanumarathnam is calming. "I dreamt . . . that you and the children will lead long, healthy lives." He backs away from her to lean against the wall. "And that I will not recover from this fever."

Sivakami stares at him. "You are not even afflicted with the fever."

"I will not recover from it."

"You are not stricken." She is aware of her damp palms, twisting the folds of her sari at her waist. "It doesn't affect adults." In fact, two adults have contracted the pox and have suffered even more than the children did.

Hanumarathnam rises and joins the shadows blocking the light from the door. Sivakami sinks to the floor, still protesting. "You are hale and strong. You never dream. Why should I wake you just because you talk in your sleep?"

He has gone.

In the evening, Muchami comes in through the back. Seeing the main hall empty, he retreats through the rooms to the courtyard. He addresses Sivakami from outside the kitchen door.

"Where is he?"

"Out," she says without looking up, slicing vegetables with alarming speed. The children are asleep in the pantry, where she can watch them.

"Out?" Muchami asks.

"He's out." She sounds as angry as she feels and feels no need to hide this from Muchami. "I don't know when he'll be back."

"Oh . . ." Muchami nods. "Oh. The siddhas?"

"What else?" She leans out the door to toss some peels into the courtyard. Her face is puffy.

Muchami's eyes narrow. "You aren't crying over this?"

In some other servant, some other household, Muchami's manner might be considered audacious, even insolent, but his are the liberties of those lifelong servants who become closer than family, and more trusted.

"Stupid." Sivakami sniffs wetly, wipes her face on the end of her cotton sari and starts to sob. "I just can't stop. I'm making onion sambar, that's why. When we stop eating onions, I'll stop crying."

"Onions never make you cry," Muchami reminds her gently.

"So I'm crying because it's about time he gave them up!" She rises, slams the blade down into the block and dumps the vegetables into the blackened iron pot on the fire. "After all, he says he's going to die anytime, he should start getting ready for it . . ."

"You angry?"

"Of course not, don't be ridiculous." She pokes another dung chip into the fire and fans it. "Can't he do as he likes?"

"Sure, he's the husband." Muchami wags his head. "But he shouldn't be taking off and leaving us alone like this."

Sivakami cries harder.

When Hanumarathnam returns, two mornings later, he faces identical resentful glares from both of these souls who adore him.

That night, Hanumarathnam drops a pinch of *veeboothi* on the small gold tongue of his daughter and the small pale tongue of his son. He places his hand on the head of each. His touch on Thangam is lingering. His touch on Vairum is brief, but the little boy glows rapturous under his hand, and Hanumarathnam's eyes become tender for a second. Then that is over.

Before going to bed, Hanumarathnam gives Sivakami a large packet of veeboothi and instructs her to distribute it among the parents of the village, for all of their children, sick and healthy.

"That should do it," he says. She accepts the packet silently and he lies down to sleep. *Siddha medicine,* she thinks, and shudders, but still, she hopes it works.

That night, when he begins mumbling, she puts her hand on his arm to wake him. The arm is very warm, and she feels his forehead and stomach. A fever has taken hold of him, and there are pustules forming on his neck and arms.

5.
Buried Treasure
1904

A WEEK PASSES, during which Hanumarathnam never once completely awakens. Word spreads. People drop in constantly, whispering words of pity that wear on Sivakami. Each of the visitors brings some remedy, Ayurvedic compounds from famous practitioners or family recipes, steeped green leaves or pounded buds, bitter barks or shaven twigs, the resulting broths sweetened with sugar or softened with butter. Sivakami dutifully pours them all down Hanumarathnam's throat. The guests quarrel over their remedies, disagreeing on which is best. Each argues that the other remedies are interfering with the effectiveness of her own. They make a lot of noise and bustle in the house, whose occupants are unaccustomed to such cacophony. Sivakami summons silent endurance. Muchami enjoys the spectacle, until he recalls its cause.

Murthy is particularly aggressive with some veeboothi from the Palani temple; Sivakami lets him administer it to Hanumarathnam himself, in light of their relationship. Hanumarathnam's sisters arrive with accusing eyes and suggestions that Sivakami try all the remedies she has already tried. She does her best not to disagree and to avoid them. She has to believe she has tried everything. She had retained a small amount of the veeboothi Hanumarathnam brought back with him from the forest and administers that too.

It certainly has been effective on the children. Thangam and Vairum are no longer ill. They have returned to their old activities:

Thangam sitting out front and being fawned over, Vairum giving orders to Muchami, but they are unsettled by the crowds.

Vairum has a set of rocks he has named for their family: Appa, father, a long thin grey rock; Amma, mother, a slim oval of smooth black rock; Akka, big sister, soft, golden sandstone; Vairum, a small slab of unpolished quartz (it glints in places); Muchami, a great chunk of unfired brick. The rock family spends all its time exploring, usually places a little boy is too small to be permitted or too big to fit. They crouch in the fire under the bathwater. They take daily flights through the air to roll off the roof. Vairum, the smallest family member, once navigated a cow's entire digestive tract. Today, they will explore a small soft spot in the foundation of the house, on the side of the garden.

"Dig," he says to Muchami, handing him a stick. The overworked servant looks at him blankly, pretending, this time, not to understand. Comprehension is a subjective and fleeting art.

Vairum points and stamps his foot, repeating, "Dig! Dig."

Muchami examines the stick and starts using it to pick his toenail. Vairum cuffs Muchami's shin and grabs the stick. Muchami wrests it back. Vairum whines a little, then settles down to watching his good pal Muchami create a little tunnel home, a homey little cave, under the house.

Inside the house, Vairum's aunts are alternately relaxing and rearranging everything. They are fifteen and thirteen years older than Hanumarathnam, and lived with him only a few years before going to their husbands' houses, which perhaps is why they didn't fight harder to take their little brother in when their parents died. Later, they were able to justify it, saying that he received an excellent education and upbringing with their aunt and uncle, who *genuinely wanted him,* as they would say to one another, and to Hanumarathnam, and to others who hadn't even asked. *And of course we soon had small children of our own to care for,* the eldest would assert, with the younger parroting her, and *How would we have asked our in-laws for such a favour,* and *Murthy got to keep his brother!* It had worked out so well for all concerned. Annam and Vicchu, his aunt and uncle, had sent him to spend holidays with them from time to time. Since Hanumarathnam's marriage, his sisters had come to visit several times, a thing they had rarely done before. It was as though they needed to assert their presence in his life a little more, now that they were in danger of displacement.

Visitors continue to arrive, even from neighbouring villages and towns, people whom Hanumarathnam has healed. Not one child in his village is now sick with the fever. Each family will carry out its pledge, to carry fire or milk to Mariamman's temple during her annual festival, yet each grieves the imminent passing of the man who came as close to science as any they have known. Sivakami hears their remarks, floating in from the main hall to the kitchen with the tch-tch of clucking tongues.

"Such a shame . . ."

"Such a young man . . ."

"Oh, what will we do!"

"You know, his first concern was always for us . . ."

She stays in the kitchen, churning out delicacies to keep their mouths busy so they'll talk less, to keep her hands busy so her heart will forget to break.

Vairum charges in from the garden, looking for his mother, wanting her to come and see how cozy the stone family is, stowed in their cave against the elements. He gallops through the main hall toward the kitchen, but his father's eldest sister grabs his arm. It's nearly yanked out of its socket, so intent is he on the kitchen and so abrupt is the detention.

The aunt pulls Vairum toward her large face and booms, "Hallo, my boy, taking care of your father?" and then speaks to the others over Vairum's head. "This is the ugly one. His sister's out on the veranda."

Vairum wrenches away from her and barrels once more for the kitchen. Now he is intercepted by a neighbour, who wants him to eat a snack from a large tray she carries. He doesn't want any, but her grip on his arm is tight. When he tugs the captive limb free, it flings upward, slamming into the tray and sending its contents airward. Consistent with his generous nature, Vairum has distributed the snacks equally among all persons in the room.

Silence falls with a thud and awakens Hanumarathnam, who sits bolt upright from a mumbling sleep. With calm resolve, he seeks out Sivakami's eyes where she stands in the kitchen doorway. Across the multitude that separates them, he summons her with a slight movement of his head.

Now: no middle-class Brahmin wife with any kind of breeding walks through the main hall and talks to her husband in front of guests, and today these guests include her sisters-in-law, who would subject her to no end of criticism, both to her face and behind her back, alone and in mixed company. Though Sivakami is spirited, brave and has had reason to feel encouraged in her life, she cannot obey her husband this time.

Instead, she silently iterates the names of the gods, her children's need for a father, Hanumarathnam's relative youth. She cannot completely banish, though, the feeling that if his time has come, she is powerless. How can she stop the progress of Yama's water buffalo?

Hanumarathnam looks at her a long moment, and her eyes are held in his. His sisters will later liken her to a frightened young goat, unable to move though a tiger walks toward it. A little part of them wants to hear her bawl like a captured kid, but this doesn't happen. They never see Sivakami cry. She doesn't permit it.

When Vairum ran into the house, Muchami had left on rounds of some landholdings. He has tried not to let the worries at the house keep him from his tasks. He goes along the canal that runs behind the houses, since he will not walk on the Brahmin street except in the company of a Brahmin, and at the end pauses a moment to spit a red stream of betel juice into the long, green grasses. As he straightens, his eyes grow wide. The largest water buffalo he has ever seen, its coat a lustrous pewter, its massive horns curving out at their tips, is strolling along the Brahmin quarter, unaccompanied by cart or driver. Muchami moves to behind the temple and, mesmerized by the water buffalo's swaying hump, watches it until it is in front of Hanumarathnam's house. Then the servant pivots and darts back along the narrow path behind the Brahmin-quarter houses.

Inside the house, Hanumarathnam's head falls back, exhaling a word that sounds, to at least half the people in the room, like "podhail."

His sisters, standing closest to him, hear the word and their eyes meet. Podhail: buried treasure. The possibilities of that word occupy the sisters' thoughts as their younger, only, brother dies.

In that moment, Vairum, having run out to the garden in a tantrum, has kicked all the carefully cleared earth back into the hole under their house. He wets the earth with tears and stamps it and pounds it, his mouth pulled down in an ugly shape, until the place is packed flat. The child of the black-diamond eyes, his golden, oblivious sister, his tiny mother, his slim, dead father, their Muchami—buried forever. Podhail.

They will find Vairum here later, asleep with his head on the ground. They will awaken him, wipe his earth-streaked face and explain that now he is the man of the house. He will learn he has work to do.

6.
Siddha Song
1904–1905

IT IS INCREDIBLE TO SIVAKAMI that Hanumarathnam spent years preparing her for his passing. She is shocked by the heat of bereavement: a pyretic pain behind her eyelids and in the unseen caverns of her body. She doesn't cry and is aware that observers, such as her husband's sisters, remark this. She feels she contains floods of tears, but they are boiled dry before they can spill.

And the house, too, is alight with funereal activity, the throngs of well-wishers turned chorus, ushering Hanumarathnam's spirit forward. Sivakami is bidden to wear her best clothes, her finest jewels, during the ten days it will take for that to happen.

His body is dressed in new, unsoiled clothes such as are worn only by the dead and taken to the cremation ground. Little Vairum will light his father's pyre. This is one reason everyone needs a son.

At the cremation ground, Sivakami does not tell her children that their father is within the blaze. This seems unnecessary. When Vairum runs ahead and picks something off the ground, Muchami slaps it from his hand. It is a bone, but no one explains this. As he throws a burning faggot on his father's pyre, Vairum is crying because Muchami wouldn't let him have that white stone.

A little shrine is built beside the Ramar, to house Hanumarathnam's soul. Thangam, her hair loose, like Sivakami's, to show their grief, learns to make rice balls, which are offered daily at the tiny shrine.

This is one reason everyone needs a daughter.

Sivakami tells her children that their father has gone away, and that the little shrine is like a playhouse where his soul lives, and the rice balls are like pretend food for him. Thangam seems to like this idea. Over the thirteen days of mourning, brushing her long, unbound hair out of her face, she brings extra decorations for the shrine, some tiny play dishes and her own picture of baby Krishna. Vairum takes little interest.

Now that her husband is truly gone, Sivakami feels an odd eagerness for the ceremonies that will brand her a widow. A woman whose husband dies before her is, in some cosmic, karmic way, responsible for his death, and must be contained. The best way to do this is to make her unattractive: no vermilion dot to draw attention to the eyes, no turmeric to rub on the skin for brightness, no incense to suffuse the hair, no jasmine bunches to ornament it. No hair to suffuse, but that comes later.

Still wearing the bright colours she now loathes, she is paraded down the main street to the Kaveri, escorted by her father, her eldest brother and Vairum. On the riverbank, in a ceremony as old as men and women, her brother tears Sivakami's blouse at the back, and she is made to remove it. She unties the saffron thread of the thirumangalyam and drops it into the pot of milk her son holds for her. She feels her bile rise and viscerally understands why her wedding pendants' hot anger might need to be cooled.

She will never see those gold medals of wifehood again. All her bright silk saris are packed with neem and other bitter leaves against moths. Thangam will receive them someday, and the wedding gold melted down and transformed. No one wants to waste gold.

Sivakami accepts the two white cotton saris that will be her only garments and her badge.

She watches Vairum as she goes through each stage of her transformation: *see, I am to blame, it is my fault—everyone thinks so*. She offers her yoked shoulders for this burden: *see, my son, it wasn't you.*

On an appointed night, Sivakami waits in the courtyard while the rest of the house falls asleep. She sits and looks into the dark, the cotton of the new sari still stiff. It chafes against her bare and tender breasts but will soften with many washings. She combs out her hair with her fingers. Curly and unruly, it tumbles past her waist. Not as long as some women's, but quite long, considering how wilful it is. She wishes her hands felt like her husband's, stroking her hair, but one's own touch can never have that delicious strangeness.

She has a feeling suddenly of being very, very large, twenty times larger than the average woman. Her hands, when she holds them up, look small and far away. The night is cool on her face and she feels both drowsy and unpleasantly alert.

The courtyard door opens. She jumps up and takes the kerosene lamp from the blackened wall niche. She holds it out to see: the one she waits for has come.

She motions to another doorway; beyond it is the garden. The barber follows her there.

He has brought a small wooden stool. She seats herself. The moon is scant days from its darkest phase so he needs the lamp with its flame leaping large and greasy.

He is experienced and efficient and has kept dozens of such appointments, and before he begins, he says, "Amma. I'm sorry."

As he lifts the first hank from her neck, Sivakami's deprived body thrills to the sensation, and the shame of this thrill makes her glad that he is cutting it off. Then he begins shearing her head, leaving only a quarter-inch pelt to protect her delicate scalp.

It is complete. She has finished the crossing from *sumangali*, married woman, to *aamangali*, widow.

The barber cleans up and departs with the dignity of those who do the work the world despises. The locks he gathered will be sold as hairpieces. Sivakami bolts the courtyard and garden doors, then douses herself with buckets of cold water. Barbers are untouchables and she has been temporarily reduced to his status. The water makes her an untouchable of another kind. From now on, she will be *madi*, maintain a state of preternatural purity from dark to dark, so that no one may touch her after her pre-sunrise bath until the sun sets. And she will be as invisible as any untouchable in the Brahmin quarter, going to her river bath in pre-dawn dark, returning before light so as to spare her neighbours the sight of a widow. Such a bad omen.

She drops the bucket over and over into the blue-black iris of the well, still feeling the barber's fingers in her phantom hair. Her eyes are terribly dry.

As she finishes, she hears a sound from the sheltered corner of the courtyard where Muchami sleeps when he stays the night. She holds the lamp up. Muchami is turned to the wall, weeping. This is not the first time she has seen him thus since Hanumarathnam died. A twinge of affection shakes her head. She almost reaches out to touch him: her head has been touched by a non-Brahmin man, why should she not touch the head of one? Is there a separation any longer between Muchami and her?

Yes, there is. Muchami still has his middle-caste status, while she, now, is so pure as to be an outcaste. They never touch, not even accidentally, for the duration of their separate and inseparable lives. The barber is, she thinks with revulsion, the only man permitted now to touch her regularly: he will return, every few months, to ensure her continued ugliness.

She goes to lie beside her children. Vairum stirs and reaches for her thirumangalyam. He only occasionally still nurses, but playing with her pendants is a remnant of babyhood, and he reaches for them whenever he feels insecure. Frustrated at not finding them, he bats at her neck. Sivakami shushes him and presses him close, easing him back into sleep.

She keeps her breathing shallow so as not to disturb him, her chin lightly touching the top of his silky head, as the night slides and blurs against tears that will not free themselves.

The crowds eventually drizzle away. Sivakami's brothers depart, after receiving Sivakami's pledge that she will move back to their village, Samanthibakkam, to their father's house, where they can help her manage her affairs. A woman alone is a target, they say, and she agrees. The shrine is dismantled and Sivakami tells her children that their father has sent a telegram saying that he has reached the stars and must continue travelling. He is studying the heavens and doesn't know when his researches will be completed, when he'll be allowed to return home. Even if the gods let him go, she tells them, we won't recognize him because he no longer has his body. The children appear doubtful but ask no questions. They look hurt, and Sivakami tells them Hanumarathnam didn't undertake this journey by choice, but she doesn't sound convinced.

Sivakami's brothers return for her three days later, weeks sooner than they had agreed. Their mother has been ruined by Sivakami's widow-making, and is on her deathbed. At the time of the marriage, her husband had told her what Hanumarathnam had said and implied that worrying about his horoscope would be an indication of her ignorance. She felt that if Sivakami had better timed her son's birth, none of this would have come to pass. As Sivakami's mother, she, too, was to blame. Who knew what karmic drama was being replayed thus to punish them? For clearly they were being punished.

In her lucid periods, she tells her sons not to permit Sivakami to visit. She doesn't want to see her daughter in white, she says, with shaven scalp, no ornament or decoration save for a streak of holy ash on her forehead. But in her sleep she cries out over and over for Sivakami, her youngest, her only girl.

Sivakami craves her mother, but she is ashamed to be seen in widow's whites; she feels guilty for the tension in her brothers' faces. She has failed; her family did not thrive. But she wants to kneel and put her head in her mother's lap, just as her own little boy does in hers, to feel her mother's hand stroking her head. She is only eighteen years old.

Thangam and Vairum go next door to stay with Annam and Vicchu, and Sivakami's brothers escort her to Samanthibakkam for a visit.

When Sivakami arrives, her mother is awake. Shrunken and wasted, she lies on a cot while her eldest daughter-in-law, Kamu, reads to her and the youngest, Ecchu, presses her feet. At Sivakami's appearance, her mother shuts her eyes and rolls onto her side, clutching her knees to her stomach and moaning, "Oh my daughter, oh my youngest, oh my dearest, youngest child, my golden girl."

Behind her, Sivakami's brothers whisper, "You see, that's what she does. Come, bathe and eat." Sivakami obeys, but she knows her mother is watching her. Sivakami's father stands in the puja room. He counts off mantras on his beads, and every five rounds, he makes a mark in a book. Sivakami sees him on her left, then sees herself in the cracked shaving glass outside the kitchen on her right. She inherited the stiffness of her shoulders from him.

In the next few days, Sivakami and her mother have two or three private audiences. During one, her mother extracts a promise, then falls asleep. Sivakami slips her moist hand into her mother's dry one, though she should be observing madi, and somehow falls asleep herself, her shaven head half-resting on her mother's hip, the crumpled white cotton of her sari shrouding the rich maroon of her mother's. Her face, at rest, is as pouty, self-absorbed and carefree as that of the adolescent she might, in another life, have still been. The next day, her mother dies.

The same funeral procedures that they so recently observed for her husband now follow for the mother: new clothes, a pyre, a little shrine like a dollhouse. Sivakami makes the rice balls and recalls her daughter's small hands and the care Thangam applied to this task. She works to apply herself as her little girl did. And now, Sivakami cries. She weeps at the shrine and at night and alone in corners, expecting and receiving little comfort from her brothers and their wives, who are sensitive enough to leave her alone, nor from her father, who has his own burdens. She cries for her mother in this house where she is a child.

After nearly three weeks at her father's house, though, she must return to Cholapatti and her children, to pack up their lives.

Back in Cholapatti, she and Muchami decide that, after she and the children have moved, he will periodically collect the paddy percentages from the tenants. He will take his own share and those of the two remaining old servant couples. He will then sell the balance, tie the cash in a cloth and toss it through one of the high windows into the front room. The house, thoroughly padlocked, will function as a giant safe, and every few months, Sivakami will return to count the income and put it in the real safe, which sits in the northwest corner of the main hall.

Annam, Hanumarathnam's aunt, will set out the daily offering for the monkeys, which tradition Sivakami believes she inherited from her late mother-in-law, yet another expression of reverence for Hanuman, Rama's monkey devotee. Since the house will be locked, that daily offering will have to replace Sivakami's daily pujas for the Ramar.

Murthy is still grieving, so dramatically that Sivakami would resent it if he weren't so sincere. "He was my brother," she hears him sighing whenever she goes to talk to Annam or Rukmini. "Ah"—she sees him pinch the bridge of his nose and sniff loudly—"but not even he could dispute what was in the stars." Annam and Rukmini smile consolingly at Sivakami, almost as if in apology, but she is mute.

Muchami is bearing up bravely. He avoids meeting Sivakami's eyes because he thinks she looks like tragedy. He has had his own head shaved to a half-inch too. He has worn only white since coming into their service, so he cannot adopt white garments in mourning, but he robes himself in a look of bereavement.

Vairum now is insatiable in his need for attention. At night, Sivakami holds him. He has stopped looking for her thirumangalyam but instead plays with her index and middle finger, obsessively and rhythmically twirling them through his own until he falls asleep. During the day, though, from sunrise to sunset, he is not supposed to touch her. These are the new rules. When Vairum comes to her for the comfort of her lap, she must back away from him, offering explanations he doesn't accept. Finally, he gets angry and slaps out at her knee or her hand, and once, her head. This is not mere violence, it is sabotage: she must bathe again and wash her sari. From time to time, she gives in and permits him the lap, since she will have to bathe anyhow. This sometimes happens twice in a day, so that her saris haven't time to dry. Vairum gets damp, sitting in her lap and holding onto her; they both catch cold.

The day before their departure from Cholapatti, Sivakami has just finished her penultimate puja for the Ramar, asking the stalwart gods to guard their home in her absence. Her needs at her brothers' house will be few, and she intends to return to Cholapatti every four or six months to look after the business. She is taking only a single trunk— no pots, no furniture, no jewels. She has only the two white saris, one of which she will wear, and the children's clothes hardly fill one-third of the trunk; they have many clothes, but they are small children. She is also taking a book, the Kamba-Ramayanam, the Tamil telling of that epic story, the only book she reads.

She fetches the keys to the safe. This gesture, too, is enveloped in nostalgia. As she lifts the loose brick between the doors to the garden, revealing the keys beneath, she permits herself to wallow in memory, as in sun-warmed mud: her first week as a bride, newly come of age, learning to be mistress of her own house; her husband's delight at showing her the Dindigul safe. Dindigul: a brand to rely on.

There are four iron keys, only two of which are key-shaped. Another is a rounded stick, like a hairpin, and the fourth is flat, a lever. Hanumarathnam had deposited the bundle of keys in her palm and pointed to the safe without a word, challenging her to figure it out. She had poked and tickled and pounded the safe, neither wholly haphazard nor exactly methodical, but determined. Finally, Hanumarathnam had wrested the keys back from her, near helpless with laughter, and shown her the way:

1. Use the flat stick to remove the screw from the trim on the top right-hand side of the door.
2. Poke the rounded stick into the hole and the "L" in the safe's nameplate will pop loose, revealing a keyhole.
3. Insert the key with the clover-shaped end and turn it once counterclockwise. Pull open the front of the safe. Within you'll find a second, smaller door with a keyhole in the conventional place, halfway up on the left side.
4. Turn the second key a half turn clockwise in this hole, just until you feel a soft click.
5. Slide the flat stick between the door and the wrought iron trim on its left edge. The lever will catch and the inner door pop open.

It sounds like her heart popping open. She feels her shoulder blades locking across her back. From the safe's inner sanctum drifts the scent of sandalwood.

She takes out the bundles of ancient palm leaves on which were recorded mysteries of the universe: her husband's treasures. She pushes their clothes aside and puts the palm-leaf bundles in the bottom of the trunk even though he didn't give her the keys to unlock these mysteries. Now she takes out a slim sandalwood box. It contains the leaves on which the children's astral portraits are scratched. She doesn't open the box, just lifts it quickly from the safe and drops it in the trunk, among the children's clothes. She shuts up the safe and the memories and the scent. She shuts the trunk lid on the little clothes, and her spare sari, and the scent. She lifts her hand to her nose. The smell of the soft, golden wood is upon her fingers.

The children play in the sun on the veranda. A familiar shadow darkens the light from the front door. Her hand falls from her face and resentment and fear rise in her throat: it is them again, the siddhas. She wonders if they know that her husband is dead. She has not allowed herself to be seen.

Before she decides whether to move to the door, the siddhas begin to sing, accompanied by a little *dholak* drum, finger cymbals and a rough lute. Their voices are more strident than melodic, yet everyone on the Brahmin quarter will hum this tune, without admitting it, for weeks.

> *Where there is onion, pepper and dry ginger*
> *What is the use of other remedies?*
>
> *Pus and filth, thick red blood and fat*
> *Together make an ugly smelling pitcher.*
>
> *A few morsels for the cremation fire am I*
>
> *Like a bubble that arises on the surface of water and perishes,*
> *So indeed perishes this unstable body.*
>
> *Salt will dissolve in water*
> *Be one with the incomparable.*

The wish to master science does not halt
I wish to master powers undissolved
To transform all the three worlds into shining gold.
Use as your riding beast the horse of reason
Use as your bridle, knowledge and prudence
Mount firmly your saddle of anger and ride in bright
      serenity.

When there is no solace in the world
There is still solace
In the holy names of the lord who rides the bull . . .

The song's undertow pulls Sivakami to the open door, but the siddhas have already begun to move off. They travel the length of the Brahmin quarter, singing.

At the end of the street, they keep walking, but one of them—which?—calls out mockingly, "Here is a body, feed it!"

PART TWO

7.
Her Father's House
1905

AT HER FATHER'S HOUSE in Samanthibakkam, where her brothers live with their families, Sivakami takes on the lion's share of household work. The cotton of her saris grows thick and soft with washing. She draws the end over her head, sheltering her scalp from the sun or stray looks: white reflects all sunlight, any incidental looks glance off her. Bad omen. Her narrow shoulder blades protect her heart from the back and her sari now protects it from the front.

Others might have dwelled or moped or made life difficult for themselves and others, but Sivakami has tucked her grief away. No one expects her to chit-chat. As part of her extra-pure madi state, she has also resolved never to eat food cooked by any other person, so she volunteers to cook for all of them. Since she cooks very well, her sisters-in-law are only too happy to give the kitchen responsibilities to her.

Kamu, her eldest brother's wife, had childhood polio that left her with one foot shrivelled and bent so that she walks, rolling, on its callused "top." She is a bit loud and demonstrative for Sivakami's taste, but also very kind. Sivakami likes her a lot, and wonders if it is, in part, their temperamental differences that make Kamu so appealing. Sivakami also admires Meenu, married to her second brother, who is brisk and busy, as industrious as her husband, at least in non-domestic matters. Their considerable energy is focused at present on their burgeoning traffic in Ayurvedic remedies for new mothers. They are packaging a gripe water brewed with fennel seeds, and "Cure-All Concentrate," garlic and sweet herbs reduced in ghee to a medicinal paste, said to shrink the womb and enhance milk production.

Sivakami is as fond of Kamu and Meenu as she is suspicious of Ecchu, Subbu's wife. Her youngest brother is also the sweetest, a gentle and incorruptible soul who always gives in to the children's clamouring for candy or soda pop. Ecchu is stingy, but too insecure to tell Subbu to cease his indulgences. Instead, she mutters reprimands she refuses to clarify or repeat. For Kamu, housework is strenuous; for Meenu and Ecchu, it is an inconvenient distraction. Sivakami is given full rein.

Sivakami's concerns for her children in the aftermath of their father's death are soon allayed. Vairum's cousins accept and include him as the Cholapatti children never did. Vairum is thrilled and opens himself entirely to the clique. He is out of the house every day, running and playing, coming in for lunch and a nap, too hungry and tired to think of anything else, and then only returning after sunset, so he and Sivakami no longer clash over her madi state. By the time she calls him home, she is able and glad to enfold him in her embrace. Thangam seems little affected by her surroundings and indeed keeps much the same routine as she did in Cholapatti, sitting on the veranda with admirers clustered round.

One of the children's favourite pastimes is trade. Cowries are coveted items, and the rarity of a glass soda bottle stopper with the wax rubbed off makes it valuable, though a marble is more easily utilized. Girls tend to go for long and colourful feathers, boys for unidentified metal objects. Once in a long while, the skull of a bird or mouse makes the rounds, and bidding is fierce. Vairum lets his small treasures go at bargain prices, gaining the reputation of a sucker . . . but everyone likes a sucker.

Most coveted of all is money, because it is the only item of currency with equal value in a child's and an adult's realm. Money breaks barriers, and Vairum puts this principle into effect as soon as he figures it out. When he is the one his uncle Subbu favours with a coin, Vairum runs immediately to his companions and asks how they would like him to spend it. Suggestions usually centre on a round of candy.

Vairum has also discovered a talent: he has an instinct for elementary arithmetic. He amuses himself and the other children by doing long calculations and reciting litanies of large numbers. Unlike in Cholapatti, here he is appreciated for who he is, so as he discovers his gifts, they blossom. He is becoming, in small increments, who he was born to be.

8.
The House Safe
1906

WHILE SIVAKAMI IS SETTLING HER CHILDREN at her father's house, Muchami, in Cholapatti, tends to business alone. This is the role for which he was intended—Sivakami's right-hand man.

Every few days, he collects the rent of some tenant or other. Someone is always late, or needing to make a partial payment; schedules are flexible. He makes rounds every day and has no difficulty keeping track. The tenants pay in paddy, when they harvest paddy, and silver the rest of the time. If Muchami receives paddy, he converts it to silver, as agreed. Hanumarathnam required all his tenants to plant a variety of crops, so they would have steady incomes and continually rich soil. Some landlords encourage the planting of entire fields with single crops they consider up-and-comers, convincing tenants with promises of jackpots. Always, the tenant goes into debt within five years, and the landlord ends up profiting from a protracted legal battle. When Muchami had asked Hanumarathnam if he was interested in this, he was relieved to hear that his employer disapproved.

As he and Sivakami agreed, he bundles the collected coins in paper and tosses the packet through one of the high windows of the main hall, which are barred and shuttered, except for one. Sometimes it lands with a thud and sometimes with a ring and spinny clatter, depending on how well he has folded the packet and how strong the scrap of paper he used. Either way, all the silver morsels are safe inside the stronghold.

He makes a deposit whenever the pile of collected coins becomes too great for him to carry in the waist-roll of his dhoti, about twice a week. Before doing so, he goes to the courthouse veranda to locate the scribe Hanumarathnam retained before his death. There are men on the Brahmin quarter whom Hanumarathnam could have recruited as volunteers, friends who would have been happy to help Sivakami with business matters, but he had thought it best not to give them responsibility or information.

Though Muchami cannot read, he's no slouch in the math department, at least for the purposes of business. Still, he has the squatting-squinting scribe double-check his tally sheet and record it in longhand, next to the place where he himself recorded it in numerals. When the sheet starts to get worn and torn, Muchami has the scribe write at the bottom, "All fine. R. Muthuswami," and address an envelope. Muchami inks his thumbprint above his name, the paper practically refolds itself and Sivakami receives it regular as trains out of Madras station.

In the fourth week after Sivakami leaves, Muchami is rising from doing his business with the scribe and notices the customer behind him giving him an odd smile. He nods; Gopalan is from his own caste community, and they meet most evenings in the market, along with everyone else interested in the news of the day.

"Rent, is it?" Gopalan remarks casually.

Muchami gives him a vague and uncomprehending smile. After Muchami leaves, Gopalan confirms with the scribe, whose code of professional ethics includes nothing about confidentiality, that he had been writing the names of Sivakami's tenants next to numbers that could plausibly be plot rents.

That evening, Muchami and Gopalan are both among the men clustered around the circular stone bench in the centre of the Kulithalai market.

Gopalan asks loudly, "What do you do with the silver, Muchami?"

Muchami waves at him in friendly acknowledgement and continues paying careful attention to a vendetta story being related by a man beside him.

"Hoy, Muchami! Muchami-o!" Gopalan is not to be put off, and his cronies are also intrigued, since he has, of course, told them as much as he knows, on which information they have speculated as extensively as they are able. They move over to engulf Muchami. "Where do you keep the coins? Are you putting them in one of your mother's pots?"

It would be no good to have word get around that he is storing Sivakami's silver in his mother's house. It doesn't occur to Muchami to suggest he is depositing the money with a bank or moneylender. He must decide rapidly, and so, since he thinks their system is a good one, he opts against his better instincts to tell the curious men the truth.

"No, all the money goes back in the house. It couldn't be more secure, no one in the village has keys to the padlocks, and you know there are several doors on each side. It's as good as a safe. Anyway, Sivakami Amma will come back from time to time and put it all in the real safe inside. A Dindigul safe. The whole thing is impenetrable."

The men are nodding evaluatively.

"But how do you put the money in the house?"

"Oh, there is a way." Muchami makes as if to go.

"Where there's a way in, there's a way out." Gopalan prods.

"No, no, this is a way only to put the money in," Muchami says, trying to turn away. "It can't be taken out the same way, no."

"A hole in the wall?"

"A chute?"

The men sound as though they are trying to offer suggestions.

"No, please, nothing so complicated. But tell me"—Muchami turns to the man whose tale of a sordid family feud had been interrupted—"how the sisters of the dead boy took revenge."

"An open window." It's Gopalan who hits on this. "There are bars—you throw the bundle in, yes, Muchami? You never said you didn't have keys to the courtyard, right, and from there you go to the garden . . ."

The men need no further contribution from Muchami; they can continue debating the merits and drawbacks of the house safe system on their own.

In this discussion, one of their number thinks he recognizes an opportunity.

Cunjusamy's father had been a ruthless usurer and had accumulated a substantial fortune. Cunjusamy inherited his father's values but none of his skill. His debtors take advantage: they don't pay interest; they claim early to have paid off their pawns; they carry home collateral that is not their own. His once-considerable inheritance is dwindling.

He waits a month, long after everyone in the marketplace has ceased even to think about the house safe. Then he waits for a night when the moon is half full—half light so he can see, half dark so he cannot be easily seen—and walks along the canal behind the Brahmin quarter until he reaches Sivakami's house.

Cunjusamy tried and failed to be subtle in his inquiries regarding Muchami's methods, and so Muchami had, for some time, been watching Cunjusamy's house. When he sees the moneylender leave his house in the dead of night, waving an iron spike, Muchami goes to the houses of several men, including one in Cunjusamy's close circle, he has enlisted for this purpose, wakes them and goes to Sivakami's house, expecting to find Cunjusamy there.

He finds Cunjusamy heading out of the courtyard.

Muchami inquires solicitously, "Going somewhere?"

"Yes. Home," Cunjusamy replies officiously and tries to push past, but the labourers are much more solid than the doors were, and he is prevented.

Muchami takes a step toward him and asks, "Find anything interesting?"

"Sure, your four policemen," Cunjusamy retorts and turns on his supposed friend accusingly. "So no one's guarding the house at night, is it? Muchami's just tossing the money in and letting the locked house keep it safe, is it? Huh?"

The friend looks at him like he's crazy. "All anyone said was what they knew. Anyway, were we talking so you could come here and steal? From a widow?"

"Oh, she's just hoarding."

Muchami draws himself up to his full five feet three inches and spits back, "She needs every paisa."

"Oh, is that how it is? Then how can she afford four policemen every night? Do policemen work for free now?"

"What are you talking about?"

"The policemen looking after Sivakami Amma's money."

Muchami stares at him for a moment, then looks at the other men and shrugs. Cunjusamy thrusts out his iron spike and parts the human doors. "Lock up, will you?"

There doesn't seem to be much reason to stay. Muchami does a quick inspection of the courtyard and notices a hole in the weather-smoothed planks of the kitchen door. He points to it and barks, "Are you responsible for this?"

"So small, and you are worried about it? You can hardly see it. I put a hole in each door so I could see if anyone was inside, keeping watch. Good thing I did, or I would have played right into the policemen's hands."

Muchami has finally had enough. "What are you talking about? She couldn't afford policemen, to pay them and bribe them and all other costs."

Cunjusamy, who had been lingering, reluctant to step back out into the dark alone, becomes self-righteous. "Are you calling me a liar?"

"What should I call you? A thief?"

"Did I take one paisa?" Cunjusamy steps back into the centre of the courtyard, jabbing his finger at Muchami. "Not one!"

Muchami matches him, jab for jab. "You would have, except the policemen stopped you."

"You just said there were no policemen!"

"There aren't any policemen! Yes, I am calling you a liar! And a thief! Liar! Thief!"

Muchami had mentioned his suspicions to Murthy, asking him, also, to keep an eye out for nocturnal activity. Now that neighbour comes over, attracted by the noise, and starts shouting at Cunjusamy to cover his own negligence, alerting still other neighbours who had heard rumours of Cunjusamy's interest through one source or another. Only the witch's husband, who has problems of his own and therefore pays little attention to gossip, is surprised to look down from his roof into Sivakami's courtyard and see a bulky rich fellow and a servant shouting at each other.

Finally Muchami humbly offers a decision.

"No action can really be taken, because no robbery occurred. I don't think there are policemen guarding the house, because I would have known, and because someone would have seen them coming and going. Besides, where are they now? No one but Sivakami Amma has a key to the house. So, I don't know what happened, but I will inform her and find out what she wants to do."

They all file off into the night, still berating Cunjusamy, who refuses to look at anyone and instead scans the sky for owls and waves his iron spike at darting shadows.

The next morning, Muchami goes to the courthouse veranda and has the scribe write a letter to Sivakami. Murthy had offered to write it, but Muchami insisted he would get it done He need not explain much since everyone knows the story, which has circulated the village several times already, gathering momentum, dust, branches and extra leaves at every turn. If anything, he finds he has to limit the scribe to the details he himself knows. "I was there!" he yells at the man, who says he's only trying to help. "I'm the one in charge," Muchami replies loudly. He is worthy of this responsibility, he tells himself. He is sick over how close his mistress came to losing what was in his charge to protect.

Even as the letter is posted, Sivakami is already on her way to Cholapatti. Early that morning, during her brief sleep, she dreamt of the black stone Ramar that dominated her main hall at home. In the dream, she was doing puja for the gods. But when she anointed each of their foreheads with sandalwood paste, as she had every morning of her life in that house, each turned to sandalwood. Then she garlanded each with roses and each turned to silver. And when she held the oil lamp aloft to reveal their features more brightly, each turned to gold. But when she finished, she began to pack her trunk, to leave for her father's house, and the Ramar turned to khaki cloth and she picked each one up, shook it out and folded it and packed it away in her trunk.

She woke, awash in guilt and homesickness. She must return and do a puja for that Ramar, she thought, she has been neglecting it, the Ramar that had been her responsibility as wife and mistress. She departed for Cholapatti the same morning, with an adolescent nephew for an escort.

It is early evening when they arrive, expecting no one since no one is expecting them. They walk in the failing light from the train station at Kulithalai, Sivakami as excited as her nephew is bored. When they pass the market stalls that proceed from the roundabout, someone calls out and runs toward them: Annam's servant girl. She is round-eyed and panting. "Oh, Amma, Amma, you have come so quickly. You got Muchami's letter, already?"

Sivakami bypasses puzzlement and goes straight for concern. "What's happened?"

At this sign of trouble, her nephew looks a little more interested. The girl stretches out the drama. "Didn't Muchami tell you?"

A few more people gather, the men hanging back a little and not acknowledging Sivakami out of respect, making Sivakami even more aware of her discomfort at being in public. She has to know what happened, though, and tries to hear the men's loudly muttered contributions from four feet away. The servant girl holds her ground, not to be robbed of this juicy revelation. "Well . . ."

But then, a shout: Muchami is coming. Everyone bursts into babble and the servant girl is drowned out. She pulls back to pout silently as the crowd parts to admit Muchami to the inner circle. "Amma, you didn't get my letter already, Amma?"

"What letter? You often send me letters. What's going on?"

"Nothing really bad happened, Amma, it would have, but it didn't . . ." Muchami would prefer she had read it. He doesn't want to see her disappointed with him. "And what it was, was—you know Cunjusamy, the *gundu*, whose father was Kandan?"

"Yes, yes."

"He . . . tried to get at the money, your money, that's in the hall."

Everyone around them begins to break in and augment. "He made holes around each window, pulled out all the windows and climbed in . . ."

"Muchami brought the police in through the front door, while Cunjusamy was coming in through the back."

"Muchami and the labourers had dressed up like policemen . . ."

"He used witchcraft to go in through itty-bitty holes in the doors, without opening the locks . . ."

Muchami shushes the thousand and one well-meaning informants and asks if Sivakami wants to wait for him to get the bullock cart. When she insists on walking, he follows at a discreet distance. They encounter several Brahmin men on the cart path, but they pretend not to see her, exposed as she is by the necessities of modern travel.

At home, Muchami explains what he knows, showing her the holes by the light of kerosene lanterns. He doesn't know how the invented story about the policemen served Cunjusamy's motives. Maybe he heard Muchami coming and decided to make a dash but didn't want to admit it.

Sivakami asks Muchami how Cunjusamy knew about how the money was kept. He explains fully, undefensively, the scene and what he understands, his voice wobbly with shame: Cunjusamy bored a hole in each door from the courtyard to the main hall, not knowing if Muchami or someone else might be sleeping there. Finding no one, he broke through, but stopped before he entered the main hall and effected the robbery, because, he said, Sivakami had four policemen guarding the riches. She asks how he happened to catch Cunjusamy in the act. In telling her, he regains a little pride.

The next morning at four, he is waiting, as he did before, behind Murthy and Rukmini's house, where she and her nephew are staying, to escort her to the Kaveri River for her bath. She goes, fighting waves of nostalgia, forcing herself not to pretend she has just awoken from her late husband's arms. On her way back to her house, she stops in at the roadside temple, as used to be her habit.

Back at the house, she does a long, sincere puja to the Ramar. At about eight o'clock, she asks Muchami to tell her once more what happened, so she can examine the house by the light of day. She finds it essentially in order. Then she and Muchami count the money, using his letters, which she has brought. All accumulated wealth is present and accounted for, not a paisa short. Muchami isn't looking for compliments and Sivakami doesn't pay any, but they are in the air: Muchami can both count and be counted on. After counting out Muchami's salary, plus a little bonus, miscellaneous retaining fees—for the scribe, for example, and the two old couples she supports—they roll the coins in rags torn from Hanumarathnam's old dhotis and Sivakami deposits the rolls tidily in the Dindigul safe.

Just as she finishes, Chinnarathnam, Hanumarathnam's old friend from up the road, stops in to inquire whether she needs any assistance in dealing with this intrusion. She asks Muchami—whose proximity to Sivakami is never questioned by anyone, including her—to give Chinnarathnam a storytelling tour of the house while she sequesters herself in the room under the stairs. Even were Sivakami still married, she would not talk to him directly, but now that she is widowed, her orthodoxy dictates that she not even permit this male non-relative to see her. When they have finished and gone back out to the vestibule, she emerges to stand half behind the door to the main hall, and talks to the concerned neighbour through Muchami.

Since no money was taken, Sivakami is inclined to do nothing, but Chinnarathnam advises that it would not be a bad thing to engineer a little something to discourage Cunjusamy, or others like him, from trying such a stunt again. Chinnarathnam is friends with the police commissioner at Kulithalai, and could request that someone from the police interview Cunjusamy. He doesn't have to be charged with anything, even though what he has done can't be particularly legal.

Sivakami accepts the advice, asking that Chinnarathnam invite Murthy to come along. Hanumarathnam's cousin has looked in several times with stalwart offers of help, making Sivakami feel there was nothing in particular he felt he could do. Her nephew also perks up at the suggestion of police involvement and, late that afternoon, Muchami, Murthy and the nephew call on Chinnarathnam and they, under escort of a keen-looking young officer, proceed to Cunjusamy's house. As per Chinnarathnam's suggestion, they make themselves seen. Everyone they pass gawks and squawks. No one asks where they're going.

The mission finds Cunjusamy on his veranda, popping peanut sweets in his mouth and staring into space. Muchami later imitates him when he re-enacts the story for Sivakami's benefit: Cunjusamy's eyes look nearly as empty as the sockets of the enormous deer skull on the wall above him; in fact, the long-dead deer looks more perceptive. The party is almost at his step before he jumps up and chokes. He spits the offending morsel past them onto the road and recovers a little of his dignity, the sort that owes less to character than to bulk. He hesitates a moment, before deciding on belligerence as the only available avenue. "What do you want?" he shouts.

They feel his hot, peanutty breath whoosh past them, and the nephew edges behind Muchami. Chinnarathnam replies, "The facts. Just the facts."

The policeman steps forward and explains, "We just want to get to the bottom of this. Won't you come along, sir?"

"I didn't take anything!" Cunjusamy's chins wag indignantly.

Murthy steps forward with a finger raised, saying, "Aha!" while Chinnarathnam muses, "That's what's so curious."

The policeman gracefully gestures Cunjusamy to precede them into the street, also glancing pointedly at his billy stick. Cunjusamy marches out, still spluttering. All of the village is quiet before them, and noisy in their wake.

At Sivakami's house, they come into the main hall, where Cunjusamy is waved to a bench. Sivakami positions herself in the pantry to witness. The policeman pulls a notepad from his breast pocket and paces to and fro, then stops and stoops in a single action, his nose level with Cunjusamy's, his eyebrows beetled penetratingly. He booms, "Where were you on the night of _____?"

Cunjusamy's voice is a full octave higher than normal. "Home! Asleep!"

"All night?"

"I can't remember!"

The policeman, who is young and smartly turned out, wheels away. He walks along the bench to the end of the hall. Facing the door, he pulls out his billy stick and whacks the bench on the far end of which Cunjusamy is quivering. It cracks down the entire length of its grain. The policeman sighs, regains his composure, turns around and flips to the next page of his pad. "Can you remember yet?"

Cunjusamy starts to blubber. "I told them, I told them everything, I am not a wealthy man. I know I have a big house, but I have a big family, and so many people are not paying me, and . . ."

Chinnarathnam leans forward. "You made a hole in each door."

Cunjusamy answers through boo-hoos, "Yes."

"You picked the lock. With a pin?" the policeman asks.

"Yes."

"You went through three doors, then made a hole in the door to the main hall, then you didn't go in and didn't steal the money."

"Yes. No! I mean, no. I mean . . ."

"What I said was right?" the officer says.

"Yes."

"Why didn't you steal the money?"

"I told them, it was the policemen. Four policemen, posed, like a picture, three standing, one kneeling, like, like . . ." Cunjusamy casts around. "Like that!" He points to the Ramar.

Muchami has backed up against the eastern wall of the house so that he alone can see both Sivakami and the interrogation. He looks at her; she wags her head: the house will be safe, not because of policemen or neighbours, but because her gods are protecting her.

Muchami clears his throat. "Sir, thank you, sir. Amma is satisfied that he won't do it again."

The police officer frowns. "Are you sure? This blackguard . . ."

Muchami looks to Sivakami again, and she wags her head more definitively.

"Sir, yes, that's enough, sir." Muchami, too, is wagging his head vigorously. "Please, sir, keep the notes, yes, everything, but that is enough, sir. The house will be safe."

Murthy, too, wags his head as though satisfied. Chinnarathnam, too, concedes. It seems a bit abrupt, but he can't dispute her judgment. He glances quizzically at the Ramar and, on their way back along the Brahmin quarter, asks Muchami what he thinks happened. The servant echoes Sivakami's thought: the policemen's appearance is a miracle.

The nephew, who had to suppress a cheer when the billy stick broke the bench, is disappointed that the interview is so brief. He points at Cunjusamy: "And don't you forget it, fatso."

Cunjusamy sneers and pulls back his hand as if to strike. The nephew insolently turns and saunters after the policeman. By the time they reach the main road into Kulithalai, he has asked three times to carry the billy stick.

9.
High Time
1907

WHEN THANGAM COMPLETES HER FIRST SEVEN YEARS,
Sivakami's family starts making noises on the subject of the girl's marriage. Sivakami's father begins and Kamu, her eldest sister-in-law,
nods her lip-pursed agreement. Their strong opinion (stronger for
being not at all original) is that it is high time. Kamu's husband,
Sambu, a roomy, sedentary man, is less enthusiastic than he should
be—arranging a wedding is a lot of work and all that work is the
brothers'. Their father, since his wife's death, has largely withdrawn
from family life and obligations. The middle son, Venketu, who is
unnaturally energetic, annoys his elder brother with ambitious proclamations about the match they will make their niece.

With respectful comments on their brother-in-law's renown as an
astrologer, they request Thangam's horoscope. Sivakami goes to her
trunk, which now contains only the palm-leaf bundles and the carved
sandalwood box. She had aired the clothes out on arrival, set them on
their allotted shelf with her Ramayana and not opened the trunk
since. Now she lifts out the long, slim box and sets it on the floor in
front of her.

She bends to breathe the ancient scent—rich, antiseptic, vaguely
obscene—of the sandal tree's protected parts, the heartwood and
roots. She is trembling a little with an old, familiar flush of resentment
at her responsibilities: she has never opened the box, inside which are

the leaves whose graven words have caused her loneliness. In the scent is every morning, when her husband ground a block of sandal against a dampened black stone to make a paste, to anoint the foreheads of their gods and each other and their children. It is the scent of her husband's forehead when she bent over him as he slept.

Sivakami exhales and straightens, and as she does so, her shoulder blades, which had spread slightly, lock back into place. The breath of good memory has steadied her to open the box. As she lifts the lid, she feels an icy breeze escape and curl around the back of her neck. Thangam's horoscope is on top. Sivakami lifts it out and shuts the box without looking farther. She doesn't think until later that Vairum's would have logically been in that place, since he was born after Thangam. Hanumarathnam must have put Vairum's beneath their daughter's. He would have known that Thangam's marriage would come before their son's, and he must have realized that if Sivakami, not he, was opening the box, she would have reason not to want to see Vairum's horoscope.

The brothers take the palm leaves to the corner astrologer. He quacks over them briefly, threads a silver stylus through the hole in his index fingernail and doodles out his pronouncements on a supplementary leaf. He slips this appendix onto a couple of pegs and stacks the original four leaves on top of it. The holes line up, but he seems to cut his leaves slightly larger than the standard two-by-eight-inches, or Hanumarathnam cut his smaller: the edge of the update leaf protrudes as though the little-known local garnished and trimmed Hanumarathnam's predictions, readied them to be served.

The brothers return with long faces. Sivakami, scooping rice onto a plate in the kitchen, hears her eldest brother, Sambu, telling his wife, "She's got a tough one."

The wives are not ill-intentioned, but the eagerness of their concern is evident as they ask, "What—what does it say?"

Sivakami pauses to listen to Sambu's reply.

"It says . . . whoever she marries, he's going to die young."

"Ayoh!" The exclamation comes from Kamu, Sambu's wife.

Meenu, the second, echoes her, muttering, "Ayoh, ayoh." She shakes her head and whispers, "Young widow."

Sivakami comes out to serve lunch and they fall quiet. Ecchu raises her hands to her lips, seemingly to hide a nervous grimace. Sivakami goes back into the kitchen to fetch other items and thinks, *This is also the fate that awaits my daughter?*

While the men have their afternoon rest, the women discuss marriage even more than usual—and this is a much-discussed subject. With the subversiveness that compensates for but never threatens the domestic hierarchy, Sivakami's sisters-in-law talk to her of the inaccuracy of horoscopes.

Ecchu overcomes her customary remove to tell of a boy in her family who wanted to marry his cousin. "She was a nice girl, beautiful girl, suited to him in every way except that her horoscope said her husband's brother would die. So the boy's elder brother's wife objected, 'No. If this marriage is conducted, I will be a widow!' But the boy insisted, 'If I do not marry this girl, I will not marry. At all.' What could the family do? They could not leave their son unmarried. The older brother had already had children. So the cousins married, and guess what? No one died, not the brother, nobody. Thirty happy years later, the boy himself, the groom, died. Just last year. The older brother still lives, even today."

The sisters-in-law nod and pat their babies. Meenu chips in spunkily with another story. "Yes, my sister, she had a horoscope that said her mother-in-law would die. My brothers showed it around, but no one would accept. Then they heard of a widow lady and thought she might consent, but when she saw the horoscope, she chased them out of the house with a big stick!"

The women laugh hard, startling toddlers silent and babies awake. A smile even breaks through the anxiety cobwebbing Sivakami's face. Meenu laughs hardest of all. "They had to run pretty fast, or they would have got a nice whack. They came home crying and yelling, 'What's her problem? She's a widow anyway, what does she care if she lives or dies? We're not going to arrange this marriage any more!'"

"What happened?"

"Another widow. She had been a second wife, she didn't mind. The marriage was for her youngest son, the last of her responsibilities. The marriage took place, oh, twenty, twenty-five years ago, and the old lady is still going strong. Sweet, mild-mannered lady, but strong as a plow-ox."

The women wipe the laughing tears from the corners of their eyes—imagine their husbands being chased by widows with big sticks! They go back to absentmindedly joggling babies and mending clothes. "Marriages are made in heaven, that's what. No one can say how one will turn out."

Their chatter is cut off by the tiffin hour. Sivakami's father wanders past in a cloud of his musings, moving toward the dining area. Sivakami and Ecchu rise to serve him his meal.

The stories of wrong horoscopes serve as distraction but certainly not as consolation. Her husband's own horoscope was accurate, and he did Thangam's horoscope himself. Sivakami feels sick but all too confident that he got it right.

The brothers return from a day of searching with an unexpected proposition.

They have called on three families—enough, in their opinion, to take a decision. This is the report, which Sambu, the eldest brother, delivers in a slow, sonorous monologue, regularly interrupted by the impatient Venketu. Subbu, the youngest, doesn't try to contribute but smiles comfortingly at his little sister. She smiles warily back.

"The first family asked us if we were kidding," Sambu relates. "They have only one son, they have waited so long to marry him, until their duty was done by all his sisters. Will they marry him to a woman who is just going to kill him off? No. The second family: they hesitated because they have been searching for a long time for a bride. Their son is an ascetic, a renunciant. He has been so since a very early age and has said he can only marry a woman who accepts this lifestyle. Since he wants nothing so much as to be taken to the next world, his family thought he might take our option, but after some discussion, they finally said no, they could not be party to this union. Although any wife of his would have a more austere life during marriage than during widowhood, they need to find a girl who is already inclined to a spiritual life. We said Thangam is a very undemanding girl, but they were not sure. So we went to a third house. They were recommended to us as a great landowning family, but it was clear when we arrived that they are very much in debt. I'm sure that's why they are having trouble finding a match for their son. We saw him—extraordinarily handsome, talkative, smiling face."

Here Sambu pauses for even longer than usual. He normally speaks so slowly as to make it seem he is choosing each sentence from a dwindling supply. Sivakami's face, which had been frowning in concentration, now smoothes into wariness. She looks around at her sisters-in-law, who look back inquiringly to their husbands. Their husbands look down at their food, and Sambu continues. "This is the best option. There is a catch, but this is still the best option."

They each eat a mouthful.

"The catch is," Sambu drones, "that the son has something in his horoscope that suggests . . ."

Venketu breaks in, "Well, suggests strongly . . ."

"Yes," Sambu reasserts. "Strongly suggests his wife will . . . die married." Here he takes one of his customary pauses, permitting Sivakami's shock to jell. "Far preferable to being a widow, certainly."

"Of course," Venketu yelps, "it suggests this will happen after many, many years."

"Yes, many years," Sambu eventually adds.

"Yes, many," Subbu chimes in at the last.

Sivakami waits a long time, but Sambu has nothing else to say. They resume eating, nervously.

This is a choice between frying pan and fire—and the women know, as men do not, the consequences of such choices. Sivakami's mouth is dry and she feels a bit dizzy with tension but decides to plunge forward.

"How old a married woman?" she asks her eldest brother. "How many years will she have?"

"Many years, many years," Sambu replies without looking up.

"How many?" Sivakami insists, feeling close to tears while knowing she will not cry.

"Well, let's see . . ." Sambu frowns.

Venketu helps him. "She's seven now, so that would make thirty-three more years. Practically a lifetime."

"And 'strongly suggests,'" Sivakami presses them, surprised that her voice is not shaking. "What does that mean? How 'strongly' does it 'suggest' his wife will die married?" She can't bring herself to use "Thangam" and "die" in the same sentences.

"Hm. Well," Sambu begins, and Venketu finishes, "More strongly than Thangam's suggests its opposite."

Sambu glares.

There is silence as each woman in the room compares her own lifespan with the one Thangam's uncles want her to accept. It is a little less than twice Sivakami's current age. More time than she wants but not nearly enough for her daughter. Venketu offers Sivakami the courtesy of a little consolation, and she sees that, despite his early proclamations, he has put all the effort he intends to into this match. "Anyway, when she has children, remember, chances are very good that their horoscopes will change all this. Children give all women a new lease on life, isn't that right, ladies?"

The ladies pretend they haven't heard. Sivakami does not let herself reflect on whether children are a reliable method of altering one's destiny. She thinks instead that her brothers will not be so hasty in selecting mates for their own children: good children, but ordinary. Plain, some of them very plain, and not exactly brilliant either. Her brothers will have to work double-time to pair them off and they will too. Without looking up from his slurping-burping, Sambu concludes, "They want a girl-seeing next week."

Sivakami retreats to the kitchen in disgust. It will be concluded at the girl-seeing. No one has ever laid eyes on Thangam without tumbling headfirst into the well of love where she dwells, a little golden frog. She is a delicacy not to be resisted, the sweetest of sweets laid over with pure, pounded gold. Thangam melts on the tongue.

She hears her father calling from the far end of the house for his bedroll. He has concerned himself with nothing about the marriage since making the demand that his sons do their duty by their niece. That was his duty, to make the demand.

If only horoscopes were less impartial, Sivakami thinks, feeling sorry for herself, since to feel sorry for her daughter, already, would break her heart. The stars strike without pity. And they collude through generations. She, her husband and Vairum were all victimized by Hanumarathnam's and Vairum's star charts, and now, because of Hanumarathnam's death, Thangam's stars have shredded her life in advance. The stars' effects can be altered in combination—look, Thangam's destiny was reversed by this match. Surely her father, had he lived, would have found a way to turn hers to advantage.

Had he lived. Her brothers had asked her to come here so they could look after her: a woman alone is vulnerable, they said. They are right. Clearly, no one will protect her and her children now that her husband is gone.

As Sivakami predicted (see: she, too, has such powers), the boy's family comes, sees, consents. The groom, called Goli, is eighteen, handsome, with the sort of creamy complexion customarily called red. (A tinge of aristocracy? Romance and good fortune?) He's all charm and dash, glib compliments and a restless eye. Sivakami's sisters-in-law are a-titter.

Sivakami can't deny that Goli is good-looking, but his behaviour is suspicious. Has he affected this manner or is it natural? He acts like he cannot stay still. He has no obligation to find Thangam's family interesting, nor even to act as though he does. But is something wrong with him?

Vairum began pouting even before the interloper arrived. He has been scrubbed and oiled and made to sit still, withheld from his cousins and the grubby roaming day that calls to him in sun and dust. He sits obediently in the main hall, a sad, bored expression on his face, determinedly reciting numbers, his lips barely moving.

Thangam serves sweets to her prospective groom. Sivakami observes the pair keenly. She believes she sees the light of attraction between them, like something seen close by the window of a moving train—Goli looks at the girl as she serves; Thangam looks at him as he looks away. Sivakami knows this may be merely wishful: Thangam is only seven, after all, and not a child whose feelings are easy to read. Next Thangam turns to serve Goli's mother and father, and when they ask the little girl to sing, she treats them to a gentle, indulgent smile and sits to one side, silent and absent-looking. Her aunts hurriedly bring out the little girl's needlepoint, evidence of her industry and intelligence. She may not speak much, but she is clearly no dolt. The embroidery is primitive; she is still small. Anyway, the handiwork's beauty cannot compare to the girl's, and all is forgiven with laughter in the warmth of Thangam's glow. The families feel themselves on the brink of an agreement, and this makes the gathering even more agreeable.

A little apart, Vairum sits as dourly as only a precocious five-year-old can, keeping one cautious eye cocked on Goli, who continues to bounce about the salon, admiring trinkets and babies and pictures of gods, peering out at the street, tossing out non-witty non sequiturs that set the aunts adrift in gales of giggles nonetheless. No matter how he moves, his clothes hang perfectly on his body. Now he stops in front of Vairum, saying jovially, "Hey, mite!" He ruffles Vairum's hair, bats his shoulders and generally takes liberties.

"Not the prettiest kid, eh?" Goli addresses the group.

Thangam leaps up, looking alarmed and hurt, as the rest of the gathering burbles and hiccups. Vairum glitters cold scorn. Sivakami bristles, but no one notices her, or Thangam, who eventually sits without speaking but also, now, without smiling.

Throughout this sparkling exchange, Vairum has continued to recite under his breath, "Four hundred and eighty-three times four hundred and eighty-three is twenty-three lakh, three thousand, two hundred eighty-nine. Four hundred and eighty-three times four hundred and eighty-four is twenty-three lakh, three thousand, seven hundred seventy-two. Four hundred and eighty-three times four hundred and eighty-five is twenty-three lakh, four thousand, two hundred fifty-five."

Now his sister's intended—for that is what he clearly is, though no one has bothered to explain anything to Vairum—peers at the younger boy's lips, which immediately still. Goli asks, "What are you saying?"

Vairum turns away, repulsed by Goli's scent of new rice and lemons—he is nauseated by everything about Goli, by all that everyone else clearly admires. The aunts explain: "Arithmetic. He is doing arithmetic."

They turn to Goli's parents, still as brick compared with their son, and elaborate, "He picked it up somewhere; he does it all the time. The children ask him to name two big numbers and add them divide them we don't know what all, but they seem to find it amusing."

The fiancé likes this. He crows, "O-ho! A smarty-pants we have here, have we? So do some. Go ahead, let's hear your arithmetic."

Vairum is lost in his own thoughts, and startles when Goli repeats his request: "Come on, smarty-pants. Show us your tricks. I'll get you started. What's seven plus five?"

Vairum fixes a squint on him and says, in order to end the conversation, "Eleven."

Goli leaps away shuddering and addresses the crowd. "Ugh, those eyes give me the creeps. Don't they give you all the creeps?" He starts examining the beamwork of the house and asks, "So what's this wood holding up your house?"

Vairum's had enough. He rises and heads for the door. His aunts admonish him sharply to stay, but he keeps moving. Goli leaps in his way, the chivalrous knight, barely glancing at his quarry. "Stop right there, little man."

Vairum ducks past him into the vestibule. Goli grabs his arm and yanks him back over the threshold. "I said stop."

Vairum tries without success to wrest away. "I don't have to listen to you."

His elder uncles slide fast from sycophancy to sharp authority: "You do have to listen. He is going to be your brother-in-law." They slide back to ask the parents with jollity, "We are assuming?"

The in-laws-to-be give hurried assurance, lest anyone change minds. "No, yes, yes, you are quite right, quite right. All very satisfactory. Must get on to details immediately!"

Vairum, under cover of everyone's etiquette, escapes Goli's hold and bounds outside. From there he yells, so the whole street can hear, "Don't tell me what to do!"

Goli poses briefly as though to give chase, but Vairum is gone and the older boy really hasn't a spark of interest in a sweat-drenched trot through the sun-drenched village. He saunters back into the salon, but there is an unhappy tilt to his mouth. Sivakami sees it as a flag. Might these boys grow to understand each other as men or has she just seen an enmity enter her family?

Her father now rises from his corner. Everyone is mildly surprised, having forgotten he was present. He shuffles out to the veranda, where he will await the next meal to punctuate his existence.

Wedding plans are amicably contracted between the responsible parties. Thangam's uncles ask for her feelings with questions that cannot be answered, such as "All seems very suitable, doesn't it, Thangam dear?" and "Weren't in a mood to sing, were you? Well, it doesn't seem to have hurt anything." There is no way to respond, and so Thangam doesn't. All has gone as God intended and the day waves sunnily ahead.

To his immense credit—though he might have been goaded either by his conscience or by his wife—Sambu negotiates for a dowry to be given in land instead of cash and jewels. He has concerns about Thangam's future family's debt status and tries for one more condition: he would like to continue to manage the land and thereby improve it for the couple. To their surprise, the in-laws agree.

Sivakami is somewhat cheered by this small proof of her brother's concern for Thangam. She feels doubly secure because, of course, he will not manage the land—she will. She trusts her own ability and industry above his.

Despite this discussion, Thangam will still come with a large trousseau. Her sisters-in-law do the shopping. The jewels from the Cholapatti safe will be displayed on the child at the wedding and go with her to her new home. Sivakami hears, even through the cacophony of her feelings about this marriage, the voice in her head making practical arrangements. She doesn't trust Goli and doesn't exactly know why, other than that he acts so strangely. But she also feels some relief at having the marriage contracted: Thangam had to marry someone and, who knows, maybe another union would be worse. Maybe this one will turn out all right. Still, she wonders as she bends sleepless over her beading that night, *What is on this Goli's mind? What is Thangam in for?*

10.

A Woman Alone

1908

NINE MONTHS AFTER THE BETROTHAL, the days of the wedding
arrive. Everyone has a role to play, in giving and receiving the gifts of
silks and lands and bride. The drama begins with the procession of the
bridegroom in the streets, dressed up in parasol and eyeliner and a stiff
swirl of silk dhoti. As is customary, he pretends he is off to Benares to
complete the Sanskritic studies with which so few modern Brahmin
boys bother. Goli's primary education was interrupted prematurely by
his sense of fun. His nickname, which means "marble," was bestowed
by a tutor who left, as all Goli's tutors did, within a year, after observing that he couldn't teach a child who spent every session ricocheting
off the walls and furniture. Goli liked the moniker and it became one of
the few things he retained from his education.

Customarily, when the parade passes the bride's house, her father
intervenes in the chaste young scholar's journey and persuades him to
marry his daughter. This is a Brahmin boy's big break from the
cocoon of youth and scholarship, his chance to transform into a
householder who is qualified, and indeed, obliged, to own property
and produce a family.

This happy moment of intervention and invitation should have been
Hanumarathnam's. Today, his cousin Murthy, here from Cholapatti
along with half a dozen of their other neighbours, fulfills the role,
solemnly and with evident excitement, as the closest equivalent of a

paternal uncle. Muchami has also come, at Sivakami's request, ostensibly to help, though everyone knows it is a treat and he is given no real work.

Vairum has been instructed as to each of his obligations and is too bored, by now, even to resist. He sullenly repeats, with flat affect and eyes out to space, each scripted word fed him by the priest, flaring up the sacred fire with ghee. In the process, he accidentally sets Goli's puffily starched silk dhoti on fire.

Goli streaks straight out back to the courtyard to plunge his leg into a brass basin as Vairum and Thangam make unexpected eye contact, a quavering beam of horror that turns instantly into suppressed laughter. Sivakami, whose widowhood confines her to the courtyard because the wedding is everywhere else, scampers through a gate in the wall, just ahead of the crowd that soon surrounds the smoking groom. In a forgotten garden, behind a scrubby old margosa, Sivakami, too, has a good laugh, and then a good cry, though she cries only from her left eye. Her right stays dry.

If she were not a widow, she and her husband would have escorted Thangam to and from her in-laws' house for festivals in the years between the wedding and her coming-of-age, at which time she will join her husband for good. She and Hanumarathnam would have got to know Goli and his family at home—though, of course, it would not have been Goli, she reminds herself with shame, since now it is done, and to think of Thangam with anyone else is tantamount to sin. Now her brothers will escort Thangam, and she will have to glean what knowledge she can from their careless, partial reports. Oh, for a spy, someone on her side! A Muchami of the marriage, that's what she needs, she thinks, as she watches her servant watching the now-resumed festivities. Who will tell her what she needs to know?

Her sisters-in-law approach her, interrupting her thoughts. She has not seen them since Hanumarathnam died, though she dutifully sent them letters, to which they didn't respond, after settling at her brother's place.

"Oh, how thrilling to have such a wonderful excuse to come and see you and the children," the elder sister effervesces. Her jowls, which started forming in her early forties, have a strange rigidity to them now, giving her a formidable look despite her gay tone.

Sivakami is cowed.

"Your brothers have done a fine job," sniffs the second sister primly. "You must count yourself as lucky."

"Yes, I suppose so," Sivakami replies.

"Now you must let us help you," trills the elder, and Sivakami is alarmed, since they have never offered any help she wanted before. She has been grateful for their lack of communication since Hanumarathnam died. "Your house is standing empty and you must let us look in on it from time to time. Give us the key, there's a good girl. We'll wait here. You don't seem too busy right now."

Sivakami looks at her, trying to think quickly. Samanthibakkam is a little closer to Cholapatti than their husbands' places, and they have never seemed inclined to inconvenience themselves for her before. "I . . . thank you. I do manage to go back every three or four months, and . . ."

"But, my dear, you really shouldn't, and don't need to!" says the elder sister, cocking her head impatiently. "We will look after it. Go on, fetch the key and no more objections. You shouldn't be worrying about this, with everything else on your mind!"

Sivakami looks at the younger sister, who has been silent through the elder's speeches. She looks nervous and guilty. Sivakami says nothing more but goes to the shelf where she and the children keep their few possessions. Beside her second sari, the children's clothes and her Kamba-Ramayanam is a small pile of possessions Vairum has accumulated here, things he likes to look at, things he has acquired in trade or intends to give away. Among them is an old key for the Cholapatti house, which she saved for Vairum after the attempted robbery, when she had the locks changed. She'll have to compensate him, she thinks, as she brings it back to her sisters-in-law.

"For the courtyard door padlock. It's a little stiff, but if you work it . . ." she is telling them, but they are already rising to go.

"Don't worry, Sivakami! You worry too much!" says the elder, tucking the key in her bosom. Her younger sister smiles stiffly in Sivakami's direction but cannot hold her gaze.

Sivakami knows she has just postponed giving them whatever it is they want but knows that Muchami will tell her what happens when the sisters come to Cholapatti and that this will be enough to help her decide her next move. A woman alone is a target, she nods grimly to herself as she prepares the next meal.

11.
This Is for You
1908

THE NEXT ORDER OF BUSINESS will be Vairum's education. Several of his cousins, slightly younger, are ready to undertake the *poonal* ceremony—the conferring of the holy thread, which ceremony and emblem signify that a Brahmin boy is ready to begin learning. Vairum might have passed through this gate a year earlier, but Sivakami's brothers suggested she wait until these cousins could join him, and given the confusion of resettlement, she thought it might not be a bad idea for him to wait to start school.

The family's Brahminism is a great point of pride for Venketu, Sivakami's second brother, and so he takes the lead on having his son and nephews initiated into the caste. He drums up a few more participants from the Brahmin quarter: the more boys the priest can do at once, the more everyone will save on fees and feast, so it's not hard to convince a few cash-strapped parents that their four-year-olds are old enough to understand what it means to be sworn into the caste, to commit to a life of study and prayer with no remuneration. All of these parents want their caste status confirmed, and all will be disappointed if their sons actually honour the letter of this commitment. The sons will be married to Brahmin girls, live in Brahmin quarters, eat only with Brahmins—they will behave like Brahmins socially, but, the parents hope, not economically. Parents with means send their sons to secular schools. Their fond hope is that they are cultivating lawyers or

administrators or earners of some white-collar sort. Only families too
poor to afford a non-Brahmin education will send their child to a
paadasaalai, a Vedic school, to be educated as a priest and remain both
Brahminically pure and Brahminically poor.

On an auspicious day, at an auspicious hour, seven little boys
gather shivering before dawn, oiled and clean, in new silk dhotis and
shoulder cloths. Vairum, a few months short of his sixth birthday, is
proudest of all, buddying about with his cousins, giving useless instructions to the confused younger boys. They are all told, by the wise and
kindly priest heading the morning's events, that this is the day of their
birth. Anyone can be born from a mother, he tells them, but what sets
us apart as Brahmins is this second birth into caste, into knowledge.
Each boy huddles beneath a cloth with his parents, who reveal to him
the prayer with which, each daybreak, he will petition the sun for
illumination. He is given the three intertwined poonal threads that will
signal to the world his special status: his right and obligation to knowledge, his right and obligation to poverty (except, not really).

Sivakami is as proud and happy as Vairum is. How nice for him to
have a second birth, she thinks, given the circumstances of the first.
His birth into learning will be his real birth into life. Vairum turns
from the fire and flashes his crooked little smile, his narrow, uneven
eyes crinkling. She smiles back shyly, proudly, from behind the kitchen
door, and watches as he leans and whispers something to the cousin
beside him, who smirks and passes it on, and then all seven are in an
uncontrollable fit of giggles and the uncles and fathers get angry with
them, but they can't stop, the ceremony is so solemn and they so gay.

A couple of months later, the school year approaches and the household begins to prepare. There are things to be bought, uniforms,
books, tiffin containers, forms to complete and documents to secure.
Vairum is of an age to begin first standard and clearly ready in other
ways, given his math skills. He has even received his poonal, and so is,
in every way, it seems, sanctioned to commence.

Before Sivakami has a chance to ask about how to go about regis-
tering him for school, Sambu harrumphs one morning at breakfast,
"Vairum is more than ready to begin his education."

"Yes," she rejoins. "I was going to say the same."

"He is a bright child," Sambu drawls. He takes longer than anyone else to eat his meals. "The math tricks, they prove his intelligence. Did you know the Vedas are highly mathematical? Not that we would know about that, but that aspect will probably hold all kinds of interest for him."

"Yes," Sivakami answers, more hesitant now. Do they teach Vedic mathematics in the schools? Maybe it's an option. "We'd better find out what he needs, especially since he doesn't have a father to testify for him on those forms."

Sambu frowns indulgently. "Paadasaalais don't require forms or fathers. Not much to worry about at all."

"A paadasaalai?" she repeats. "But he's not going to a paadasaalai."

"It's all fixed, Sivakami," Venketu breaks in. He is a natural-born salesman and takes every conversation as a challenge to his powers of persuasion. "Don't argue. He is a very intelligent boy, and if he goes to a secular school, he'll leave you. Your only son—you don't want that, surely? A boy educated to some English profession will need to follow his work to cities, but a priest won't have fancy opportunities to give him ideas. Solid Sanskritic education, because you need him. Anyway, it's good to have a priest in the family. Father says so. Someone has to respect tradition, with all these boys going the way of the big, bad modern world!"

Venketu shakes with false jollity while she stares at him. Subbu takes his brothers' side, wheedling, "Who better than the son of Hanumarathnam, who was a one-man repository of tradition, so scholarly, mystical, so famous? Your son will carry on his father's life work."

Sivakami is silenced. She has carried with her, her whole life, a faint guilt with regard to her brothers. One of her earliest memories: she was four and Subbu saved her life. She had been about to jump into the family well—out of curiosity and defiance, not despair. She struggled violently against him and when he set her down in front of her mother, she turned and broke his nose. She always felt herself to be stronger than them; she has never, she thinks, fully given any of them the respect and obedience elder brothers deserve to command.

Even now, she thinks with resignation, that hasn't changed. She had no choice in the matter of Thangam's marriage: a widow has no power to dispute such matters. But she need not let go of her son's shoulders at this fork in his path. She's not about to let go unless she absolutely has to.

As it happens, there is a paadasaalai conveniently up the street. It doesn't have any sort of reputation, but her brothers would consider one paadasaalai much like another, using the same methods and the same curriculum with the same results since the beginning of time. This one is run by charity, so there is no cost. No cost for supplies, no cost for exams, no cost for extra tutoring, no cost for college afterward because Vairum won't be going to college, that's for sure. Any costs would have been paid from her money, of course, given to her brothers to manage while she was living in their house. A paadasaalai education would mean no work for them.

And why should they trouble themselves over her son? Any wealth he accumulates is nothing to their family. Even the dowry he will someday attract—certainly more substantial for an engineer than a priest—would only be his, or, at best, Sivakami's. What use has she or Vairum for wealth? Sivakami wonders if they admit, in the privacy of their own minds, that they are a little jealous of Vairum, of his brains, of the possibility that he might outshine their boys.

She wouldn't be able to endure seeing her son educated in Sanskrit to waste himself performing occasional ceremonies for the rich, demanding their gifts and gossiping and never leaving the veranda to check on the world without. Priesting is a profession for the poor, the choiceless; Sivakami is not rich, but she is too rich for her son to become a priest. She is a snob, but this is not snobbery. This is cold reason. Firstly, she fears that, because her son has an inheritance, he would grow lazy and corrupt. And then, say he wastes his inheritance and does want for money, the rewards for chanting over fires are no longer sufficient to support a family. The world has changed and shirtless priests, walking the street with nothing but a brass jar, haven't the opportunities they once had.

Vairum is diamond needle sharp. She fears that if he is not challenged, his intelligence will turn inward and damage him. He must be educated in English to take his place in the new world. Even if he leaves her to fend for herself while he makes his way, even if she will know nothing of his values or career, she must give him this chance. Even if she will lose him by doing so. She didn't take any such stand on behalf of her daughter because her daughter was not hers to lose. Daughters are born to be the fortunes of other families, but her son's fortune is hers to find, for him. While she lives with her brothers, however, she cannot take any initiative that is not theirs.

Standing silent on the veranda with her brothers now imitating (badly) their father's detached and philosophical gaze, Sivakami decides that it is not, in fact, right for her to live with them. She married into another house, and to there she will now repair.

After she serves the night meal, she announces, sounding quieter than she feels, "I'm . . . I have decided to move the children back to Cholapatti."

Her brothers cease wiping their mouths, and Sivakami sees Sambu decide he must not have heard her correctly.

She repeats, too loudly this time, "We are very grateful for having had this time here. We are returning to my husband's—to my house."

"My dear sister," her eldest brother says, "that is out of the question."

She looks up from the floor and nervously at her sisters-in-law. She feels rising in her the stubbornness of the child she was, when she went and played at the river alone every day, despite slaps and warnings, or when she built nests for abandoned baby birds who then filled their courtyard with squawks and offal. When confronted, she sometimes was not able to think of a reason or response, but even when she knew exactly why she was doing what she was doing, she explained nothing.

"Talk to her!" Sambu commands the women, who commence wailing as their husbands retreat to confer. At a look from Sivakami, though, Kamu and Meenu's weeping stops, while fragile Ecchu's turns genuine.

Sivakami is as surprised as anyone else to find herself, a twenty-two-year-old matron, behaving just as she did when she was five. She had convinced herself that she had grown to be pliable-reliable and demure. But the next day, she sends her brothers to buy her railway tickets for early the following week, and they obey. When Venketu asks sarcastically how she will pay for her son's education, the steadiness of her own voice surprises and reassures her, "My husband trained me to manage the lands. The income will be sufficient, and I know how to administer it."

She has carefully considered all obstacles. In five days, she will march her children out the door and back to the household where she alone is head. It is only after she has overcome her brothers' objections and made all arrangements that she permits herself to acknowledge— to herself, never to them—that she really would rather have stayed. Her visits back to Cholapatti have been brief, but each time, she has been overwhelmed by the loneliness of the house and glad to return to the affectionate company of her family in Samanthibakkam. Now she has closed that door, and the future sidles from sight.

On the eve of their departure, she wants the children in bed early so she can rouse them early for the train. Thangam is sitting on the veranda as always and comes in as soon as she is called. Vairum is running up and down the street with his gang, pretending to do battle on the plains of Kurukshetra. He gallops past his mother three times, once as horse, once as cart, once as charioteer, until Sivakami gets the attention of one of his elder cousins and commissions a capture. Vairum nobly resists arrest. Then he resists bedtime. They go finally to sleep, Thangam swiftly and sweetly, Vairum with much violent affection, hugging and kissing his tiny mother who is touched but not quite so athletic as to cope with his caresses.

At night's darkest hour, Sivakami does an oblation for the gods of her father's house as all its inhabitants sleep, save her. By tradition and by her heart, she no longer belongs here, but she is grateful to have had it as a stopping-place between grief and the rest of her life. She turns to leave the peace of the altar where she worshipped with her mother so many fond years ago and is startled by a listing white figure.

It is her father, roused from sleep, his gossamer hair leaping into the air above him as he moves. He pauses a moment to register her presence, then continues out back for his night business. Sivakami leans against the door of the puja room, thinking how he has aged—so quickly!—from the trim and prideful little man she knew. Her widowhood, and then his own, within weeks of one another: each death sparked in him a minor stroke, so now his left foot appears to be slightly more burden than support, and the left side of his jaw is slung low in the loosening skin of his face.

She hears the shufflestep of his return. He passes her and then stops and, without turning, says gruffly, "I still cannot decide if we were cheated on your behalf. I simply cannot decide."

She says only, "He left me well provided for, in every way."

Her father remains motionless; his hair rises and sways in unseen breezes. Their silence admits all the noises of the night beyond and the bricks cooling underfoot. He is the one who speaks: "You know a paadasaalai would be best—ah, for your son, for you. But the world is changing. Maybe the boy should be prepared to meet it when it comes to his door."

He lurches into motion. He takes his place alone on his bamboo mat; he lays his head on the wooden pillow. The world turns beneath him, and sometimes, he thinks, he feels it move.

In the grey morning, the family bids them farewell at the veranda. Subbu will see them to the station. Sambu has wafted, for several days, an air of puzzlement, as though more concerned for Sivakami than for his own pride, though the opposite is transparently the case.

"I wish you success, little sister." His gaze rests on her heavily, like the burden he thinks she is shouldering. "I hope, should you need help, that you will come to your brothers."

Sivakami can see he is sincere, regardless of how slow he will be to act on any such request. And she is touched by his sincerity. She takes leave of her elders by performing oblations for them and making her children do the same, requesting and receiving blessings on this departure. Then children and baggage are bundled sleepily onto the bullock cart, she mounts beside them and they are trundled toward the train.

Mistress of my own house. On the train, her mind ticks with business. She will have to get caught up on all the tenants. Muchami had included a note in his last letter to say one of them was resisting payment and another had fallen ill. Muchami's mother had also written her—that was a surprise—saying Muchami was acting oddly and refusing to attend his own marriage. She beseeched Sivakami, as his employer, to make him comply. She has already rehearsed what she will say to him. She feels charged with responsibility, as though it's some species of lightning. She turns and hugs her children close as the train pulls out of the station. She cannot be madi on a train.

If Thangam is excited about a return to Cholapatti, Sivakami can't tell. Vairum has no use for the place of his infancy, little as he remembers it. He complains but assumes they are going for a visit, as Sivakami has, every four or five months since they moved. Sivakami has not had the heart tell him he is to live out the rest of their days there, in the place where he was friendless and sad and where his father died. Children this young, she thinks, recover quickly from moves. He'll cry for a few days, then he'll forget he ever left.

She is saying this to herself as she watches him awaken on the train. He raises his gaze to hers, eyes like leaded-glass windows behind which his trust shines softly. She strokes his head. He takes advantage, cuddles up. She strokes his head, thinking, *This is for you, this is for you,* to the train's rhythm, *this is for you.* She feels steel spark against steel, wheels on rails. There is no other way, she winces. Stroking his dear, quiet head, bracing herself for his misery. *This is for you, this is for you.*

PART THREE

12.
Muchami Gets Married
1908

ANGAMMA, MUCHAMI'S MOTHER, stands in front of the little roadside temple, her fingers clamped around his wrist, waiting for a lizard to chirp. It has to come first from the left, next the right—the other way around would be a bad omen and would put her to a great deal of trouble, coming up with good omens to counter the bad until she felt satisfied the wedding could proceed.

Men of Muchami's caste generally marry in late adolescence, but there has been in his case a delay. The elder of his two younger sisters took overlong to marry, owing, so people said, to her buckteeth and pointed tongue. His plump, malleable younger sister was snapped up in no time at all, liberating Muchami of his obligation to wait, but then she divorced and all was thrown into confusion. Fortunately, she remarried with equal haste and now Angamma is hustling to get him settled before anything else changes.

At least there was, in his case, almost no question of whom he would marry: the second of his mother's five brothers has a girl of thirteen. Muchami probably would have married the girl cousin just elder to him, had his sisters not taken so long (his caste permits boys to marry older girls, though he would have had to do something to compensate, like swallowing a coin or gifting a coconut for each year of the age difference); he might have married the girl just elder to his now-intended, but she was bundled off with someone else in that brief period of uncertainty and lowered family reputation when his younger sister returned home.

Even this alliance is not without matters to be resolved, though. The birth order is not ideal, for example: both Muchami and this girl, Mari, are the eldest children in their families and Muchami's mother forebodingly quoted the proverb that says, "The contact of two heads of family is like the clashing together of two hills."

Mari's father, Rasu, claimed that this was just another minor and obscure objection Angamma thought she could use as a bargaining chip. He actually accused her of inventing superstitions and conditions, which was silly because she clearly was not capable. Everyone, including him, knew Rasu would be crazy not to take Muchami as a groom—a sister's son, employed, of sound mind and body, and appropriate height and colour. The only real question was when.

And, of course, the verdict of the omenistic lizards. "At least everyone knows we have to do this," Angamma huffs as they wait. The lizard chirps. Muchami looks to the right of the little shrine, but his mother looks left. They look back at each other. "So far, so good," Angamma says, and Muchami shakes his head and looks as though he's about to say something, but his mother raises a hand to stop him.

"Chirp."

Angamma looks to the right though he looks left. "That's settled then!" she says and raises his hand in triumph as though this was his prize fight. He resists ineffectually. "We can choose a date. Now we just have to get that cheapskate bustard to settle on the terms." Angamma never swears but often says things that sound close.

Mari, Muchami's bride, is an irritating girl in many ways. Everyone agrees that her pretensions make her a perfect match for Muchami, as do her looks, which are similar to his, perhaps owing to the fact that they are cousins. She is skinnier than is considered attractive, with a wilful set to her protruding lower jaw. Her eyes, though, are quick and dark, and she cuts an energetic figure. Muchami's mother finds Mari unbearable, but, in the lead-up to the wedding, feels more kindly toward the girl than she ever does again.

Muchami's caste, almost without exception, pays bride-prices. Angamma had been forced to return most of what she received for her younger daughter's first marriage because her daughter was at fault and she couldn't pretend otherwise, though she indignantly did not pay the interest the other side implied was due.

But Mari's fondest aspiration is to practise Brahminhood even though she can never belong to any caste other than the one into which she was born. Individuals can be robbed of caste—temporarily, by means of such brief pollutions as haircuts or funerals, or permanently, by transgressions. Or they can be exalted within their caste—as much as Mari can hope for. She is laughingly referred to as "more Brahmin than the Brahmins," and most of her affectations involve imitating the higher caste.

Owing to her convictions, she forbids her father to accept a bride-price for her—she tells him he has to pay a dowry. There is no reason he should listen to her, and his brothers say he's setting a bad precedent when he gives in. But there is a growing fashion these days for claiming that one's caste is higher in the hierarchy than others think, and one way of substantiating such claims is by adopting higher caste practices. His wife is also in favour: she thinks they would gain more status from paying a token dowry than from receiving a fat fee.

Brother and sister still jockey for form's sake. (Until movies arrive, there's little in any village or small town that's as much fun as fighting.) They settle on a dowry of three chickens and a sixteenth-harvest each of millet, rice and peanuts—a list more typical of a bride-price than a Brahmin dowry, but why would they give things they don't have and don't want? This is theatre—they get the gesture right, and the negotiations conclude to everyone's secret satisfaction.

On the eve of his marriage, Muchami does his rounds of the fields in the morning and comes back to Angamma's hut to eat. Late in the after-noon he goes out again. His mother calls after him, "Home early—got that? None of this gadding-about-late-night-seeing-your-friends. You have to wake up in the very early morning. All the women will be arriving to help by three o'clock and you must get dressed up . . ."

Her voice fades behind him as he walks away, waving his hand in what could be farewell but looks more like he wants to be left alone.

Angamma lies down at eight-thirty. She lies on her side on the mud floor, her arm tucked under her head, muttering her to-do list, along with increasingly strong, partially accurate, imprecations at her son. She gets up, lies down, gets up, rearranges clothes, jewels, betel-nut coconuts, switching them from one tray to another.

She has never asked her son where he goes when he goes out at night. She thinks it's risky, but Muchami knows the fields better than anyone and she finds it difficult to restrain him. Too, there are in her vocabulary rude words, sexual insults, that she fears may apply to her son. No one has ever said anything like this to her, and this is one of the reasons she has never asked about his friends. But this night, of all nights, she would have thought he'd have the respect to stay home.

Eventually, she dozes, but even in sleep she mutters and twitches, and when the Kanyakumari train runs along the nearby tracks, her eyelids flip open. She leaps to the doorway and checks the time by the position of the moon. Midnight.

She fumes curses against her son. She starts to cry a little, with hurt and helplessness. Promptly at three, five women arrive to help. Angamma normally would bluff, but she feels weak. She knows a couple of these women are jealous of her: Muchami gives his mother most of his salary. He doesn't drink. Really, he has been the ideal son before this, the women remind her, affectionately or with gloating tones. He will come soon, they say, he will come.

She accepts their reassurances, though they do nothing to assuage her nervousness. Dark drains into a hostile-looking day, and the hour arrives when she must step across to her brother's. Angamma looks even worse than usual. She has fair skin, in contrast with her brothers, and though she is not heavy, her face is always puffy, with purple half-moons under the eyes, as though she were once prey to some terrible vice, which she never was. Today, her eyes are swollen with crying and sleep loss; her hair and clothing stick out in odd directions.

Under the canopy, the witnesses are assembled and in full gossip. The bride is bedecked and bejewelled. All wait expectantly. Finally, Angamma has no choice but to tell them that the groom has gone missing.

She so wants everyone present to think some huge and possibly violent misfortune has overtaken him. Her defiant eyes beg them to be alarmed. A tactful few react this way, even going so far as mildly to suggest a search party. To them she is forever grateful. Most, however, develop knowing expressions and ready themselves—not to depart but to witness whatever comes next. They hope it's a fight.

Rasu demands of his sister, "Where is your son?"

Angamma is forced to reply with humility, "I . . . don't . . . know."

What can Rasu say? He is not going to insult his sister or call his beloved nephew bad names. The things he said before were a matter of form. He marches out to the toddy shop, shaking his head.

He has to admit he had a small worry all along. There are others like his nephew. But they all marry, have children. It is not a question of whether women interest a fellow, in general or in particular. It's a question of what is done.

He arrives at his regular clearing and purchases a cup of cloudy amber drink from the slatternly woman who minds the brew. She pokes an escapee tuft into her matted coif and grins at him lewdly. Her husband is passed out not a quarter furlong away. Rasu doesn't notice the woman, so taken up is he with the thoughts shadowing the backs of his eyes. She curses him; he makes a cursory reply. It's the kind of ritual observed between men and strumpets the world over, almost obligatory, somewhat comforting. He sits by himself.

He's not wholly unsympathetic to Muchami: he himself had to marry his uncle's daughter. Not the prettiest nor the liveliest girl in town, but Rasu had an obligation and he fulfilled it. One gets married.

He drains his cup and gets another. The vendress of drinks is rolling in some shrubbery with one of the guests from the aborted wedding. Four or five others squat around the vat, retelling the morning's events. They would have enjoyed a longer confrontation, and now embellish the story, for fun and to make it more plausible. Rasu ignores them all.

There is no question of calling the marriage off—he won't leave his own sister in the lurch. Muchami must be made to face his obligations just like anyone else. Soon his brothers join him. They are slight but muscular, labourers all, dark and glossy. Squatting together, they look like a society of ravens.

The eldest says, "We will fix another date."

They all wag their heads in assent.

The third says, "We will keep an eye on him, before the ceremony."

They all wag. They drink.

The fourth says, "He won't try this again."

They drink. The youngest says, "We won't let him."

They all wag. They drink deeply. Rasu, the second eldest, says nothing. His lips, plum-coloured and full in the manner of that country, are pressed into a rigid frown. But he is reassured.

They had planned this as a day of relaxation and overconsumption. They decide they may as well stick to that plan. Together they drink, and when sufficiently past satiation, sleep off the day in the shade of the toddy palms. The youngest gets fresh with the bar matron. She rebuffs him good-naturedly with a lot of crude language and he passes out, smiling. The others accuse her of cutting slits in the leaves used to make the cups, to force them to drink her swill too quickly. She calls them a bunch of fucking fabulists. They show her the leaks. She punches two or three in the face, tells them to suck the outside of the cups and that's the end of the matter.

MUCHAMI SLOUGHED OFF HIS MARITAL OBLIGATIONS, but he would never be so cavalier with his job. He doesn't come home but still makes his daily rounds and so is easily traced. His uncles come after him one day and forcibly remove him home, soiling his blindingly white dhoti in the operation and causing him to lose his favourite walking stick. Angamma boxes his ears, which does nothing to improve his frame of mind.

A new date for the wedding is established. In the days leading up to it, one of Muchami's five uncles accompanies him at all times. They think of their security detail as assisting their nephew to live up to his commitments. It's the sort of thing family does. Uncles and nephew have always enjoyed one another's company and these days in fact pass pleasantly for all of them.

The evening before the marriage, Muchami invites his uncles to the toddy palms. He never touches the stuff himself, but he knows how they enjoy it. The uncles appreciate his thoughtfulness and get drunk. They accompany Muchami back to their sister's house. She's disgusted with them. They tease her and prepare to share the final vigil. The youngest will watch for the first two hours while the others sleep. He will then wake the third, who will watch for two hours before passing the responsibility to the next eldest and so on. The father of the bride is exempt this evening. The three settle down to sleep and the youngest to watch. Muchami lies on his back beside this uncle and chats with him. The other three uncles approvingly fall into a peaceful sleep. After they do so, Muchami pretends to fall asleep. Soon, he hears his youngest uncle's resistance begin to falter. Tiny snores are interrupted by snuffles and the sound of him rising and pacing in an effort to stay awake. This carries on for a mere ten minutes before he succumbs. Sometime between then and daybreak, Muchami departs.

The feast is wasted again. The uncles are angry at one another and themselves and their sister, and she is angry with them. They are all furious at Muchami. The uncles find him again and, near brutal in their embarrassment, drag him home.

Muchami's mother decides she can't trust her brothers any more than she can trust her son. If the only obligation he feels deeply is to his employer, then the order to marry must come from her. She marches with a couple of her brothers down to the sub-judicial court veranda, where the scribes lounge in wait, and has a letter written and posted to Sivakami.

Sivakami had just determined on her return to Cholapatti, and sent a letter informing Muchami of that, which included an assurance for Angamma that, in accordance with her dharma as his employer and patron, she will do her utmost to ensure that Muchami treads the correct path.

She arrives and Muchami meets her at the train. Though there is gladness in his aspect, there is also something fugitive.

Sivakami has no idea why Muchami is behaving in this bizarre manner, but she assumes it is some sort of fear. She herself was afraid of marriage. Who isn't? She will just appeal to his sense of duty; wasn't that the reason her husband hired him, after all?

Because he is the most trustworthy, hardworking, intelligent boy of his class in the district?

The day they arrive, she and the children take rest. The next day is spent in reviewing with Muchami the accounts and the state of the property. Sivakami is pleased and tells him so. He accepts this as his due. They intend to finish up the next morning, but on that day, Muchami is accompanied by Angamma and a couple of uncles, so other business must be delayed.

Sivakami holds court in the courtyard at the rear of the house. The uncles stand at a respectful but firm distance while Angamma screams and wails, tears her hair and pleads. She invokes the spirits of their dead husbands—with marginal propriety, in Sivakami's opinion. It's all very well to invoke one's own dead husband, but invoking another's seems a bit bold.

These people have a different manner from ours, Sivakami thinks, as she listens patiently. They are prone to displays of emotion, which Brahmins eschew. One must accept their theatrics, of equally alarming proportions in positive and negative circumstances, without giving them undue weight. Of course she will put her foot down, she reassures them, and receives Angamma's histrionic gratitude in response.

Sivakami would have preferred to give Muchami the dignity of a private conference, but this is not a private matter. Mother and uncles keep their eyes stonily upon the recalcitrant Muchami as Sivakami raises her eyebrows at him. He stands, hands clasped respectfully before him, looking very tired of the whole business. Sivakami instructs, "You must obey your mother and marry your uncle's daughter."

Muchami looks at the ground.

Sivakami continues, "Your mother and uncle are going to fix another date and then there will be no more of this nonsense. How can I have a man working for me who is not married? It is my duty, as much as a parent's, to make sure you live in a correct way. I forbid you to persist in this behaviour. And I give my whole and hearty blessings on your marriage."

Angamma flings herself into blessings for Sivakami and her children and her children's children. She and the uncles and a subdued Muchami depart.

After his rounds, Muchami returns to finish going over the accounts. He gives no sign of resenting the admonishment.

Angamma brooks no more delay. Within a week, the marriage is done. Sivakami is not invited to attend the marriage—as a Brahmin, she cannot attend lower-caste weddings (and as a widow, she cannot attend Brahmin weddings)—but she hears that all has proceeded in a satisfactory way.

Now all that remains is for the bride to come of age so the happy couple can be united physically, as they already have been spiritually.

13.
A Hidden Coin
1908

IT'S BEEN TEN DAYS SINCE THEIR RETURN, and Vairum is sitting in the front hall, waiting to go back to the place where he was a happy child.

He had had fun on the first day, helping to gather coins from all over the main hall. They had even let him keep one that he inched out from a crack in the base of the Ramar statue. He tied it in the waist of his dhoti and is fingering it now.

The second day, he had gone out with Thangam. She took her old place on the veranda, while he circled the gathering children from behind. Half the crowd drew near her, half approached him. He could hear them, gently asking his sister questions to which she softly replied. The children around her got quieter and gentler. When they realized they would never coax her from the veranda, they settled around her, one girl holding her hand, another patting her hair, several others calmly sunning themselves in her presence.

The children who encircled Vairum were those who could not get near Thangam, and yet they seemed a different breed entirely.

"Hey, ratface!" one boy taunted in a low voice, poking Vairum in the side experimentally.

Vairum recoiled, shaken, but then thought to distract these potential playmates by asking the question that had started so many enjoyable hours in Samanthibakkam: "What have you got to trade?"

It was a simple question, but these children seemed not to understand. Vairum tried another. "Want me to add or subtract anything?"

They had grown silent but were still peering at him, moving closer and closer, until, of a moment, one's hand reached out to tug his hair and another cried, "Boo!"

Vairum leaped from the veranda and broke into a run.

The children gave chase, straight down the length of the Brahmin quarter and past the temple onto one of the small paths leading into the farmlands. Vairum streaked ahead of them, wondering why he was running and where he was going and how he would find his way back afterward when his ankle caught on a root and he sailed into the road with such force that he slid a couple of feet.

He rolled onto his back and propped himself by inches until he was sitting, knees bent, bum dirty, wiping dust from his lips and teeth. The children were panting and laughing. One of his knees and the opposite elbow were badly scraped. A little girl with square, tough-looking features cuffed him, hard but not unaffectionately, on the head.

He shouted at them, "Two thousand, eight hundred and thirty-five times sixty-nine is one lakh, ninety-five thousand six hundred and fifteen!" and defiantly waited for them to be impressed.

They looked at one another, trying, apparently, to see how they should react. The boy who poked him first made a "cuckoo" sign, twirling his finger against his temple; another, hiking up his dust-stained dhoti, asked Vairum, "Yeah, so?"

But they didn't stop him from trudging home. He wiped his nose so roughly on his dhoti that his eyes stung. He felt for the silver coin knocking warm and heavy against his hip, took it out and thought about how the children back in Samanthibakkam would appreciate it, what fun it would buy them on his return.

A blur of children were clustered at the front of his house. As he passed them to enter, a few wrinkled their noses and whispered, "Ratface!" A couple laughed. Thangam softly said, "Stop that," and the children immediately around her froze in apology, but Vairum didn't hear her and mounted their front steps without looking at his sister. He continued whispering a multiplication table: three thousand six hundred and fifty-four times two, times three, times two thousand nine hundred and eighty-five. He turned the silver coin over in his hand. He went inside and didn't come out.

————— ॐ

MANY NEIGHBOURS CAME TO CALL on Sivakami in those first days, curious and condoling. With some, the most pressing business was to find out why Sivakami had returned. Others came to shed tears, the weight of which they had borne since her departure, wishing her there to cry with them.

Questions and tears were equally intolerable for Sivakami. She tried her best to respond, though everything in her resisted. She could see that her neighbours were leaving unsatisfied, thinking she was aloof. The days left her drained, with very little energy for her son, who seemed content at first, keeping his solitary counsel in the hall, or pantry, or courtyard, doing arithmetic under his breath, sometimes playing marbles or *dayakkattam* or tic-tac-toe against himself, chalking all the necessary grids onto the courtyard bricks, like arcane, alchemical formulas. Muchami was too preoccupied to attend to the little boy at first, busy as he was settling Sivakami's accounts and then settling his own accounts with his uncles regarding his marriage, but after a couple of days he began to join Vairum in the occasional game.

By the sixth of these long, confined days, the courtyard bricks were covered in chalk markings, and Vairum was bored and restless. When Sivakami suggested he might go see what the neighbourhood children were up to, his response was to run from her, to the front end of the main hall and back to the courtyard, and back and back, twelve or fifteen times, until his shoulders slumped and his breath rasped. Then he walked slowly past her, dragging his hand across the back of her thighs. She didn't have the heart to reprimand him. She went to take a second bath, after which Vairum strolled past and slapped her knee. She bathed again. An hour before sunset, he rubbed her head.

He ignored Muchami's invitation to go on rounds with him; he kept out of sight of the children gathered round his sister on the veranda; he thrashed and screamed when Muchami and Sivakami said it was time they registered him for school. He played less; he whined more. On the tenth day, the whining, too, ceased.

When Sivakami asks him why he is sitting near the front door—still out of sight of passersby—he tells her he is waiting.

"Waiting for what, my dear one?"

"Waiting to go home to my Samanthibakkam," he answers, impatient and helpless.

She cannot touch him and cannot help him, and so she turns away.

The next morning, as Vairum is mumbling his prayers in front of the Ramar, Sivakami notices a speckling of white from his armpit to his shoulder blade. He is shirtless following his bath, as prescribed, and wearing a fresh dhoti. She comes closer, thinking he must have spilt some holy ash, though it seems a strange place to manage to spill it. There is none on his neck or shoulder. She comes close, squints and reaches out her hand. She doesn't care if she has to take another bath; she catches her son with her left hand and rubs the spray of white freckles, hard, with the other. They don't come off.

Vairum, shocked at her touch, shrugs her now-trembling hand away and then tries to see what she is looking at.

"What is it, Amma?" he asks, annoyed.

"Nothing," she murmurs with a stiff smile, though she is already muttering horrified prayers against leprosy, *sotto voce*. "It's nothing. Finish your prayers."

Some hours later, she hears a female voice, and Vairum's in response. It couldn't be Thangam, because Thangam hardly talks, and it couldn't be a neighbour, because Vairum doesn't talk to the neighbours. Sivakami moves to the pantry and looks before she is seen. A young girl, probably fifteen years old, is laughing, addressing her son. Though Vairum looks bashful, he doesn't seem to resent her. The girl tosses her head and then notices Sivakami, who moves out toward her.

"I'm Gayatri. I'm married, up the street, you know. The big house." She smiles, forthright, friendly, and hands over the fruit she has brought.

Ah, Minister's bride. She had not yet come to join her husband when Sivakami left Cholapatti. A Kulithalai girl, she didn't have far to come. "You're married to Chinnarathnam's son?" Sivakami eyes Gayatri's strong shoulders and good height. Her sari is of an excellent silk.

"I used to come for holidays when you lived here—before, I mean—but I was just a kid, so you probably don't remember me. But now I'm a proper lady of the house and all."

"I came to your wedding," Sivakami tells her, feeling drawn to Gayatri's liveliness. "Do you know how indebted I am to your father-in-law, how much he helped me, when we were away, and our house was vulnerable to thieves?" She is glad for a chance to revisit this debt. "My husband had great respect for him."

"Oh, so do I. He's eased my homesickness so much. He's such fun, a real father to me." Gayatri casts around for a place to sit.

Vairum is once more gazing gloomily at the door.

"Hey, bright eyes," Gayatri addresses him as she claims a spot against a post, waving away Sivakami's offer of a mat. "Why don't you get us a tumbler of water?"

Sivakami clucks and hurries to do this herself but notices that Vairum, without changing his expression, was rising to obey the newcomer.

Sivakami returns with snacks and water, for Gayatri and Vairum. She takes another plateful out to Thangam and the crowd of children that play quietly around her as though Thangam's gravity weighs down their wildness. She returns to her guest with a bit of the usual apprehension. This girl didn't know Hanumarathnam and so won't try to ferret out and share Sivakami's grief. Sivakami calculates that she'll be one of the curious ones, and summons those of her stock responses most successful in forestalling questions.

But Gayatri doesn't dig for the reasons Sivakami has returned to Cholapatti. She talks about her own family and married life, what she enjoys, what bothers her. Polite and interested, she asks Sivakami questions about herself for an hour or so before announcing regretfully that she must return to home and chores.

"I'll come again tomorrow. Do you need anything?" she asks. "Anything your servant can't get you?"

Sivakami can't think of anything. She hasn't had a conversation as such since she left Samanthibakkam. Her loneliness is more acute for having been briefly relieved; the sick feeling of worry over that archipelago sparkling on Vairum's back also reintensifies.

Gayatri asks Vairum, "Do you play *palanguzhi*, loudmouth? Something about you makes me think you'll be good at it. You can count, can you? Add, multiply?"

Vairum takes a second, then assents.

"I'll bring my board tomorrow when I come," she says. "You better be here, got that? No gallivanting with those roughnecks outside, no school, no going back wherever you were before. We have an appointment, you and me. Okay, sport?

"Bye, Akka," she says to Sivakami, using "big sister" as an honorific, as opposed to "aunt." Gayatri apparently has decided Sivakami is more friend than elder. "Send your man if there's anything you need from me."

After she leaves, Sivakami and Vairum raise their eyebrows at each other. He continues to dream by the door, and Sivakami feels a bit lighter as she goes about her chores. She determines that she will ask Gayatri's father-in-law, Chinnarathnam, what to do about Vairum's condition.

It is in those days that the letter from Hanumarathnam's sisters arrives. The sisters had sent it first to Sivakami at her father's house, and Sivakami's brothers had sent it on.

Safe.

(One always puts this assurance of well-being at the top of a letter, to avoid causing undue alarm.)

Dear Sivakami,

Hope this finds you and the children and your father and brothers and all their family members well!

You must have been quite overwhelmed at Thangam Kutti's wedding to give us the wrong house key! Silly-billy! Did you forget you had had the locks changed?

Muchami told us about the nasty robbery attempt! You
should have told us! How were we to know?!
  As we explained, matters must be seen to! An empty
house is a target!
  Send to us the right key, and we'll make sure that
everything with the house is grand!

                        Your loving Akkas . . .

Sivakami folds the letter and goes out back to the courtyard where Muchami sits on the stones, taking his mid-morning meal. He is still on the first course, rice with okra sambar, and a fried plantain curry.

"More sambar?" she asks. "Curry?" She prefers to serve him, unusual as that is for a Brahmin mistress, though she keeps a decorous distance even while she does.

"Sambar," he nods.

She fetches and serves it from a small blackened iron jar that she holds with tongs. "So tell me what happened when my sisters-in-law came to see about the house."

"Ayoh, Rama, that's right, we were interrupted when I started telling you about it before." He signals that he has enough by holding his hand above his rice. "Why did you give them the old key?"

"I didn't know why they wanted to get into the house." She puts the sambar back in the kitchen and returns with more rice on a plate.

"Podhail."

Sivakami straightens. "What?"

"Buried treasure. I'm sure of it." He's ready for more rice, which she pushes onto the now-cleared space on his banana leaf. "Remember—" He pauses, unwilling to upset her, but continues softly, "Ayya's last word?"

Hanumarathnam's head falls back, exhaling a word . . . Sivakami has thought back on that moment dozens of times in the years since it happened. If it had been night, and they had been alone, she would have been at his side. She doesn't think he could have said anything important: he spent so long in preparation for his death and was so methodical.

"It might have been anything," she mumbles, swiping at her left eye, which had started to tear, and going back into the kitchen with a sniff.

"A lot of people thought he said 'podhail,'" he explains.

"Including my sisters-in-law, you think?" she asks from the kitchen.

He has carved a well in the mound of rice for ghee and rasam, and Sivakami fetches these and pours them in.

He scoops and presses his rice to mix in the lemony broth. "I'm sure of it. They tried first on their own, then sent for me when they discovered they had the wrong key. When they learned I didn't have any key at all, they had their manservants climb into the garden. With spades. I felt really torn, because this is not their house, and I'm supposed to be keeping it from harm. So I asked, Have you come to do some gardening? 'Yes,' they said. 'Gardening.'"

Sivakami squats on her haunches in the kitchen door as he continues.

"I think they must have been planning to inspect the floor of the house to see if there was any seam, you know, some place that had been dug and then bricked over. But they had only the garden. The servants were lazy buggers, pardon me, so at first they said there was nowhere to dig. But the ladies and gentlemen were so anxious, they called the servants back and *had themselves helped over the wall.* Can you picture it? Your sisters-in-law, with their great big—" he indicates with his hands the width of the sisters' widest parts—"in their nine-yard saris, and, ayoh, Rama. Not to be disrespectful. Curry?"

Sivakami brings it, on a plate. "Then?"

"I went over with them, what else could one do? The garden was a mess, of course, with fallen fruit and rotting coconuts. I said it was very nice of them to take care of it. I was thinking that if you weren't coming back, what was the point? Let it grow over, like it did after their parents died. When little Vairum returns to take his house, then is the time to clear the garden."

"They wouldn't have accepted such advice from you."

"That's why I didn't say anything. I helped them to clear the garden."

"Oh, I thought you had done all that in anticipation of my return," Sivakami responds, bringing more rice and then yogourt.

"Well, I would have, when you told me you were coming back, but no, in fact, all this happened a month before. It's when they ordered the manservants to dig that I remembered your husband's final word. *Thokku?*"

Sivakami goes to fetch a dollop of the condiment and deposits it on one side of his banana leaf. She trusts Muchami absolutely, so she has no worry about discussing the possibility of buried treasure with him.

"If my husband thought there was treasure here, he would never have waited to tell us from his deathbed."

"You're right, I say." Muchami takes a mouthful of food. "They would have dug up the whole garden, but I pleaded for the trees. They said what's the point, it would be fifteen years before Vairum returned, but I begged, I'm telling you, and so they just dug around the roots and after each one I would pack the soil back in. I didn't ask any more questions. Anyway, all the weeds got cleared."

"Yes, it looks very tidy," Sivakami says wryly.

"So, at the end of the day, the sisters and husbands are barking at one another, the servants are dirty and sweaty, none of them have eaten since morning, and they're no richer. We all go back over the wall. They go to Murthy's house to bathe and eat, and I'm sure they must have told Murthy's mother the real reason, or she guessed. So then, my sources tell me, they hit on the idea that they should go talk to Jagganathan. About what he saw."

This was the boy who once followed Hanumarathnam to spy on him with the siddhas, and lost his voice in the adventure.

"Did I tell you that, since your husband died, he's got his voice back?" Muchami folds the bottom half of his now-empty banana leaf over the top, picks it up, stands and belches and goes to throw the leaf out the back door of the courtyard.

Sivakami squats against the house, under the eave. "Mm-hm, you told me. He didn't discover it for some months, until he stubbed his toe and yelled."

"After so many years without use, it was more of a croak. He still doesn't talk much—he's out of the habit. But that mother of Murthy's was inspired to ask him. Now that your husband is gone, maybe, she thought, he wouldn't be afraid to talk about what he saw."

"They thought he would say he saw my husband turning lumps of clay into bricks of gold, and so our house and garden have golden bedrock?"

Muchami rinses his mouth with well water and pours a half-bucket over the spot where he just ate, a Brahmin habit he has picked up in this house, cleansing the spot not only of a little spilled rice, but of the largely theoretical contaminations of cooked food, a horror to Brahmins for obscure reasons.

"Jagganathan probably knew what they wanted, but he wasn't talking. If he couldn't have such a reward, he who had suffered so much, why should they? I saw them after, glum faces . . ."

"Don't be gleeful," Sivakami tut-tuts. "It's not classy."

He smirks. "Then they went home."

Sivakami rests a cheek on her knee, frowning in thought. "The soil is all turned, it's a good time to put in some new plants . . ."

He's a little puzzled at the switch in topic but goes along with his mistress. "When?"

Three days later, a jack tree, two papaya trees, a banana tree and a rose bush are delivered to Sivakami's house. Muchami had told the tree vendor that the lady of the house wanted them to come to the front, strange as that may seem. When he arrives, the whole street sees Sivakami telling the shrubbery parade that no, they are mistaken, come around the house to the back, oh, okay, come into the garden through the front hall, then. Muchami does the planting and she supervises.

That evening she calls a scribe to pen a letter to her sisters-in-law:

Safe.

My dearest Akkas,

Hope this finds you and my brothers-in-law and nieces and nephews and your in-laws in the pink of health.
  Oh, I am so sorry and embarrassed to have given you the old key! Where was my head? It's not every day

one's daughter gets married, so I guess that's my excuse! Now, as you may have heard, I have returned to live in this home, my son's home, where I belong. I am his humble custodian, and so of course, you must come again, and see to matters which must be seen to, as such.

Thank you so much for making the effort to tidy the garden for me. I so appreciated it! Just today, I planted jack, papaya, banana and roses in the newly turned soil. But guess what? When we made the holes, we dug up more than worms: a little metal box, no lock, just a latch. Inside was a tiny kumkumum box and a note, in my late husband's hand. The note said, "My only success at transformation, save for my two children." With the date and his mark. He would have buried it just months before he got the final fever. In the kumkumum box: you could barely see it, a sifting of gold dust, so fine and scarce we would have missed it inside, but outside in the Cholapatti sun, it shone.

What do you make of that? Pretty unexpected, isn't it? He never said anything to me.

Although this has reminded me of something I had nearly forgotten. I'm sure you may not remember for grief, but the moment he passed on, he said something. I myself thought he said "poonal," but I was all the way across the room. Some others heard "padigal" but I couldn't think of what he might have wanted to tell me about the stairs, inside or out. I heard from others, though—who thought I should dig up the floor of the house—imagine!—that they heard "podhail."

I'm still not really convinced: it would have been a lot of work searching for that box, for not much return. Perhaps he wanted me to find the proof that he really did some transformations; perhaps he was too shy to tell me earlier. And I did find it! I'm sure he would have wanted you to know also.

Sivakami finishes the letter with chat, verbose as she's never been with those two.

The scribe is suitably impressed with the information he has just learned, and Sivakami knows it will be all over the marketplace by sundown. Muchami has already been instructed to confirm and clarify rumours. Sivakami sits up with her beading long into that night, thinking how nice it would have been to find a note from her husband testifying that his son was one of his successes, how nice it would have been to show Vairum something like that.

WHILE SIVAKAMI IS WORKING UP THE NERVE to talk to Chinnarathnam about Vairum's condition, she has been taking measures of her own. Each night before Vairum goes to sleep, she has rubbed veeboothi on the patch of white, which has become increasingly solid in only a few days. Vairum asks what she is doing, but she refuses to tell him and perhaps he senses how serious she is because this is one of the few instances in which he obeys her and submits, both to the topical application of the ash and to a pinch Sivakami makes him ingest, which she administers with more mutterings.

It is the third morning after she noticed the freckles, and Gayatri comes, as she has made a practice of doing daily, to drink a cup of coffee and play a game of palanguzhi with Vairum. The coffee-drinking is proof of her modernity; Sivakami never touches the stuff. When they sit down, Gayatri says to the little boy, "Go wipe your mouth, squirt. You left some yogourt in the corner from breakfast. I'll set up." She starts counting cowries into the small bowls carved into each side of the board. "Is the game of fours all right, or do you want the twelves again?"

"Twelves," Vairum replies. He likes this game best: twelve cowries in each of the three bowls to either side of the centre bowl, which is empty at the start but accumulates cowries, round after round, like a bank. Either player—if he or she counts right—can claim either bank, even both. Vairum feels intoxicated by the sight of the cowries piling up and even overflowing a central bowl as the game progresses.

He returns and Gayatri says, "You go first." She looks at him closely. "You missed it again. Don't you know how to wipe your face?"

"I did it." He swipes at his mouth with the back of his hand.

Gayatri frowns and, grasping his chin, tilts his face up. "Sivakamikka," she calls, letting go and rubbing her hand on her sari. "Have a look at this."

Sivakami comes from the pantry, already knowing what Gayatri is going to tell her.

Gayatri fetches her father-in-law at Sivakami's request. He comes and has a look at the new white patch, which has appeared like the beginnings of a clown's mouth around Vairum's frown, as the little boy huddles defiantly in a corner of the main hall, playing palanguzhi solitaire, barely looking up when he is asked.

"I'm sure it is not what you think it is," Chinnarathnam calls to Sivakami, who is staying decorously out of sight in the pantry. "My advice is that you have a licensed medical practitioner come and see the child."

"What is it, Amma?" Vairum says, rising.

"It's nothing, child," says Chinnarathnam. "We will have it looked after. I know an LMP," he says to Sivakami, using the English acronym. "He comes through Kulithalai once weekly. I will call for him."

Chinnarathnam and his son (Gayatri's husband—the man who has been called Minister since he was small, though he holds no official post yet) arrive with the LMP a few days later. Chinnarathnam will mediate because Sivakami will not come out in front of the LMP, nor speak to him directly.

The LMP examines the child. Palpating the patches, he asks, "Can you feel this? Is it numb?" Vairum looks at him with a catlike expression of defiant incomprehension until Chinnarathnam gently asks him, "Vairum. Tell him, little one—does it hurt?"

"No," Vairum grunts, but the LMP sighs sharply and repeats, "No—*numb*. Can he feel anything at all?"

"Ah, yes," Chinnarathnam clucks with mock humility, the sound conveying the superiority landed gentry feel toward the working man. "My apologies. Child, can you feel this man's fingers on your face?"

"Of course," Vairum snorts.

Chinnarathnam smiles at the LMP, who is officiously not making eye contact with anyone as he continues pressing Vairum in other places and firing off further questions, interrupting their replies.

"It's called vitiligo," he finally grunts, repacking his black bag. "A condition of the skin: not painful, not contagious, as far as we know, and incurable. Do you understand?"

Chinnarathnam smiles. "So it is not"—he drops to a whisper— "leprosy? This is what the child's mother fears."

"No, no, no. Damned village superstition." The LMP leans in to Chinnarathnam, who leans away from his overfamiliarity and smell of sweat. "My mother thinks the same way. We must impress upon these people that it is quite different."

Chinnarathnam sees the doctor to the door and instructs Minister to walk him to the end of the Brahmin quarter and bid him farewell.

He then comes back to the rear of the main hall and asks, "Sivakami? What do you think?"

Muchami is waiting in the garden to relay her response to Chinnarathnam. Sivakami is aware of the unusual importance of re-enlisting the servant in her son's care—she has always felt that when Muchami looks after Vairum, he is overcoming some native distaste. Now she has to persuade him that Vairum's condition won't affect him—before trying to persuade the entire Brahmin quarter of the same.

"I am quite satisfied," she says, with forced authority.

Muchami conveys this to Chinnarathnam with a passable imitation of her quavery confidence.

"What do you think?"

"Yes, it confirms what I thought," Chinnarathnam says, polite but genuinely relieved. "There is no way that a child being raised in such hygienic and sheltered surroundings could have contracted . . . the l-word."

Muchami relates this to Sivakami verbatim, again bringing his skills in mimicry to bear.

"But now you must do something for the boy's condition."

"Mm, yes," Sivakami hurries to agree. "I want to pledge a golden armour for the Rathnagirishwarar Lingam. Vairum can carry it up the hill to give."

"A very good idea for skin maladies. Shall I order that for you? There is one Kulithalai goldsmith I trust to do a very good job."

Sivakami consents.

"May I also suggest a puja to ward off possible ill effects of the planets?" Chinnarathnam continues. "One relative of mine, he had exactly the same condition, and an astrologer advised the family that it was a time of bad planetary alignments for the man. I can't remember which . . . Saturn? Venus? Something not good. I can call an astrologer for you, also. There is one man here your late husband respected."

Sivakami thinks this a very good idea.

When Chinnarathnam goes, Vairum, who, despite his theatrical displays of uninterest, has been paying close attention to these exchanges, runs straight to Muchami, who shrinks from him.

"What's wrong with me?" the little boy demands.

"Nothing, sir." Muchami shakes his head insistently. "Don't you worry yourself about this. Come on, I have time for a round of dayakkattam. Come chalk the board on the courtyard. Come."

This is a house without mirrors, and so until Vairum leaves it to go out into the world, he will have to take Muchami at his word.

⁂

THE OLD MEN AND WOMEN who had been in Hanumarathnam's employ have, after years of pretending they were too old to work, finally grown into their pretense. Sivakami asks Muchami if his wife would like a job.

He doesn't see why she wouldn't. So Mari begins, only an hour or two daily at first, then staying to serve Muchami his mid-morning meal, and then staying to help with the late-afternoon cleaning. She is appropriately shy and deferential with her husband and his employer, but her strength of personality is evident. Like Gayatri, Mari is a confident young woman who did not know Hanumarathnam and who therefore comes unaccompanied by residual sadness. Unlike Gayatri, however, Mari is very strict in religious observance. One of the reasons she wants to spend time with Sivakami is to learn the practices of the caste she considers closest to God.

Mari appears determined to make herself a Brahmin woman in every way she can—which is to say, every way except birth, marriage and where she makes her home. Since everyone in Cholapatti considers Sivakami a paragon of Brahmin widowhood, Mari replicates all her habits, which are, apart from her shaven head and white sari, simply orthodox practices that any person with deep concern for his or her spiritual well-being might adopt. Most often, Brahmin men and women take on these renunciations late in life, when their children are gone and their material obligations with them. But Mari is impatient to improve her spiritual welfare and starts immediately. She maintains madi from sun-up to sundown. She takes food prepared only by her own hand, or Sivakami's. She refuses foods such as *pazhiah sadam, dosai* and *idli,* which involve fermentation; at home, she will eat only food cooked the same day, and if it's not available, she eats raw fruit. It's a sacrifice but she relishes it. Visibly.

Almost all the Brahmins on Sivakami's street who learn of Mari's imitations are flattered; she basks in their approval. She knows many in her own community are contemptuous; she takes their contempt as proof of her success. But Gayatri, who comes over daily to keep Sivakami up to the minute on gossip and opinions, new purchases and the news of the day, is openly amused by Mari's pretensions. She unapologetically drinks her daily cup of coffee at Sivakami's, teasing Mari about it, pressing her to imbibe. Worse, Gayatri never once says she wishes she could be so strict with herself. It is of Gayatri alone that Mari might be jealous—not because she wants to be like Gayatri, but because Gayatri doesn't want to be like her.

And now Vairum, in Sivakami's opinion, is refusing to become what he already is, what he was meant to be. After all her efforts in bringing him back here, he will not attend school.

Thangam, despite being the elder, spends all her days on the veranda. She has small chores to do, a few minutes of helping her mother with food preparation, a few minutes of embroidery, which she does without resistance or engagement. Always the children await her outside, from first light to dusk. She is not likely to attend school, but Sivakami registers her, hoping this might goad Vairum into it too. When Sivakami reminds him of the ceremony of rebirth he so proudly undertook in Samanthibakkam, saying that his education commenced with that moment, he replies, "So take me back there so I can start school. I told you, that's what I'm waiting for."

She jabs her hand in the general direction of her brothers' house. "If you go back to Samanthibakkam, the school you will go to will make of you nothing more than a Brahmin."

"I am a Brahmin," says her son.

"Yes," she cries, "you are already a Brahmin, and I think you can become something more, if you go to a proper school."

"Well, I don't want to and I won't!" He stomps upstairs, to the attic room he has begun to adopt as his refuge.

Gayatri, who arrived early in this conversation, signals to Sivakami that she will go after him. She mounts the stairs and persuades him to come down for their twice-weekly palanguzhi match, and, as usual, he does multiplication tables under his breath between turns at the cowries. Today, she casually inquires, "Do you have any idea how much more maths you will learn, how much more math there is to learn, by going to school? You can't imagine." For her trouble, she receives a scowl.

Muchami also makes his contributions to the campaign. Sivakami overhears him at the close of a game of courtyard tic-tac-toe, saying, "Look, I beat you. Me, your family servant. Go to school, little boy, or that is going to happen more and more."

It is Minister, Gayatri's husband, who makes the obvious suggestion. "Bribe the boy!" he proposes in his marvellously English-accented Tamil. Only a would-be politician would think of this, but Gayatri agrees it is a simple and brilliant solution.

She immediately conveys the suggestion to Sivakami in whispers by the well, just in case Vairum should find their conversation interesting. But with what should they bribe him?

They offer:

1. **New clothes.** Wouldn't he like a bright shiny shirt and dhoti to

wear to school? But Vairum, though he sits out of view of the street, can see the street quite well. He can see that every child wears a bright shiny shirt and dhoti to school. He rejects the deal.

2. **Money.** Wouldn't he like a few more coins to jingle against the one at his waist, maybe to buy candy on his way to and from school? But Vairum already knows that money has no value in this place. The only way he will accept cash is if he's going back to Samanthibakkam, where he has friends on whom to spend it. No deal.

3. **Toys.** Wouldn't he like a new palanguzhi set or a top he can show off on the street? But Vairum likes palanguzhi with Gayatri just fine on the set they have—and he's not showing anything off on the street. Forget it.

Gayatri had witnessed Vairum's first encounters with the village children as they ran past her own veranda and can imagine that his condition would now make him even more self-conscious. Her father-in-law has gone to considerable trouble to smooth Vairum's path into the local school, meeting with the headmaster and teachers. He succeeded in overcoming their objections to the child's presence, though he could not persuade them against prejudices. Gayatri thinks she understands Vairum's reactions to the bribes but cannot come up with anything better. During their afternoon rest, she asks her husband if he has any other ideas.

"No, no, you must offer him something special, something different . . . something more . . . English," Minister muses. "Shoes. Offer him a shiny pair of brown leather shoes, foreign-made. I will take him to Trichy"—it's one of Minister's idiosyncrasies that he thinks the English name for the city of Thiruchinapalli, "Trichinopoly," more attractive than the Tamil—"and buy them for him. Get him off on the right foot, so to speak." He chortles at this last expression. It's rendered in English, so Gayatri doesn't understand it, but she understood what he had said before and so chortles along and pecks him impulsively on the cheek, which leads, one thing to another, on to something else. It's early evening by the time she makes the trip to Sivakami's house.

Wholly convinced this suggestion will work, Gayatri beckons Sivakami in from the kitchen with a call—"Hoi, Sivakamikka!"—and squats before the glum little boy whose education is their collective mission. Vairum regards her with wary curiosity.

"Okay, mister, what about this? My husband has offered to take you into Thiruchi with him tomorrow and, if you are the good little boy he thinks you are, the little boy who is going to start school and be brilliant and become rich, he wants to buy you a pair of English shoes. No one can expect to be successful and work in an office without shoes. And think about it, you will be the only child from Cholapatti who walks to school in glossy, brown, leather . . ." Her descriptive powers fail her for a second, and Sivakami breaks into the pause indignantly.

"Hooves! They will be like bullock hooves. What Brahmin wears the skins of killed animals? No, I'm sorry. Vairum will not be clip-clopping to and from the school smelling like a tannery worker no casted person would go near."

Vairum pays a good deal more attention upon hearing his mother's objections. The idea of shoes does appeal to him. He's seen them on tax collectors and on Minister. If his mother had been enthusiastic about the idea, he might have had to reject it. Now, seeing her willingness to relinquish his education over caste objections, he stamps his foot and insists, "Yes, yes, I want English shoes to wear to school. I must have English shoes to go to school."

Sivakami gapes at him in astonishment. "But you told me you only wanted to go to the school that would make you into a Brahmin. Now you will only go to school if you do something Brahmins do not do?"

"Oh, pish," Gayatri interrupts with one of her husband's favourite ejaculations. "In cities, offices are full of Brahmins, all of them wearing both sacred thread and leather shoes. Times are different. If you want your son to go to a paadasaalai, he can go barefoot. If he is going to step into the new world, he has to do it shod."

Vairum is agreeing vigorously, and Sivakami concedes defeat with the flicker of a feeling that she has brought this upon herself—and Vairum. If she had stayed in Samanthibakkam and sent him to a paadasaalai, he wouldn't be getting shoes, that's for sure. What kind of Brahmin will he become, walking the path along which she has aimed him? Maybe he needs the shoes.

No more than two days later, Vairum steps proudly up the Brahmin quarter and to his front door. Sivakami hears him coming. It can't be, not in the soft dust of the road, but she is sure she hears the soft thuds of Minister's tread, and the smaller clip-clop of her own son's new feet. Born into caste to begin school and now uncasted for the same reason.

She meets him at the door and sees his expression of cautious pride when confronted with all the veranda-gathered children become defiance when he sees her. She silently indicates where he is to leave his shoes, in the vestibule between the doors. He shucks them with his toes and lines them up carefully in a corner.

The next day, as per the bargain, Muchami drives Vairum, kudumi slicked and shoes buffed, in the bullock cart, to the Tamil medium school at Kulithalai, some twenty minutes away. He is wearing a new dhoti and shirt, each with a bit of vermilion kumkumum rubbed into an unseen corner, to soil it appropriately.

She watches them from the door, listens to the rustle, snap and clip-clop of her little boy's outfitting, watches him clinging tightly, more tightly than he would ever admit, to Muchami's hand as he mounts the bullock cart. He rides in front with Muchami since the two of them are alone. She turns away only after they turn the corner. Vairum never glances back.

In the schoolyard, though, holding Muchami's hand again, he walks more and more slowly as they pass the other children, some recognizable from the Brahmin quarter, some from the merchants' colony, some from Muchami's own quarter. There are more high-caste than low-caste kids, and more Brahmins than anyone else, and none wearing shoes. Muchami feels a little uncomfortable about the freakish child hanging from his hand: there is something slightly awkward about his gait; his clothes look boxy, his eyes too intense. The effect is heightened by the spreading patch of white on his face, as well as another sprinkling on his knee beneath his dhoti and on the hand clasping Muchami's. The servant would have felt this way even before Vairum's condition arose, and only convinced himself to touch the child in the course of convincing his own mother that he could not catch Vairum's malady. He gives a menacing glance toward the first giggle, and all the children along that flank fall silent. Vairum's hand is slippery against the servant's and the child squeezes harder to hold on.

MID-MORNING, Sivakami steps out to the front to call Thangam in. She sees one of their neighbours withdrawing a hand he seems to have placed on the child's head in an attitude of blessing. He continues along the Brahmin quarter, not having seen Sivakami, and the blanket of children around Thangam reseals in the wake of his departure. Looking down the quarter after him, Sivakami sees Gayatri leave her own house and come toward Sivakami's, along with another neighbour on her way back from the temple. Not in a mood to speak, she withdraws slightly. This woman, also, stops to place a hand briefly on Thangam's bowed head. She, too, continues home. The children register no surprise. Gayatri arrives, and Sivakami speaks: "Thangam, it's time for your food." Sivakami backs away a little more to avoid their touch as they pass, and asks Gayatri, "Have you eaten?"

She knows that Gayatri has—it's a formality to ask—and so gets her a cup of coffee, seats Thangam and serves her first helpings before asking Gayatri, "Is everyone on the Brahmin quarter coming daily to bless my daughter?"

Gayatri tilts her head back and raises her eyebrows. "Everyone is *receiving* her blessing . . ."

"You too?" Sivakami asks.

"Of course. Every time. She's done wonders for the children, as you can see. There are no children yet in our house," she says smugly, five months pregnant and finally showing, "but all the parents are saying their children have become quiet and manageable, and everyone . . ."

Here Gayatri pauses.

"What?"

"Well, I don't know about your husband, except what people have said. Is it true, he had friends among the siddhas? My husband said they used to come and your husband would go off with them, that he had great healing powers, and that they, the siddhas, haven't come since he died."

"Yes, my husband could heal."

"Your daughter can too." Gayatri blurts and then shuts her lips quickly as though unsure of whether she should have said this.

Sivakami is more surprised than skeptical.

"People think," Gayatri tentatively explains, "she inherited his abilities."

"But they haven't been around, have they?" Sivakami asks warily. "The siddhas—since we left?"

"Not since I got here," Gayatri shrugs.

"I don't want them to come." Sivakami shakes her head, but she is recalling the words of the siddha that day when he saw her baby daughter: Brahmin flesh becoming siddhic gold. It's impossible, preposterous anyway, that he would have given something to the child. But Hanumarathnam had gifts, to transform sickness into health, translate mystery into reality. It's not strange that his efforts and gifts are manifest in his daughter; it would be stranger if they were not. It remains to be seen whether the father's disciplines or lack of discipline will dominate in his son, whether Vairum will be the product more of experiments in transformation or of the blood and conditioning of caste.

Muchami escorts Vairum to and from school every day for a week or two and gradually identifies which children of his own caste community attend regularly. He visits the homes of these boys and instructs them to keep an eye out for Vairum. Any child who tries to harass him should be reminded that Muchami will hear about it. Muchami inspires awe across caste.

When Vairum realizes that these boys have begun to follow him, he makes some cautious attempts at friendship. He does some math equations, and they are very impressed, though they don't seem inspired to familiarity. He gives them every interesting item in his tiffin case and they accept, but they still pass the lunch recess at a slight distance. He invites them to the sweet stand to buy them some treats, but Muchami stops them before they get there.

The boys confess to Muchami that they are a little afraid of Vairum's speckles, as well as of the other Brahmin kids, who seem to want to pick on him, but he tells them they are doing a good job and keep it up.

As the weeks roll forward, Vairum trudges resignedly to and from the schoolhouse and ceases to talk of Samanthibakkam.

Sivakami thinks he has forgotten the wandering-pondering fun of his gang and his pre-school years. She doesn't see the silver coin always in his pocket, polishing itself against his school clothes, and if she did, she would not know he set it aside to trade with those left-behind cousins. She would only think, *What a good and thrifty boy not to have spent that coin.*

14.
Festival Days
1908

SIVAKAMI RETURNS FROM HER BATH at the river and is horrified to learn that Thangam has, alone and unsupervised, drawn water at the well and taken her bath. At least she took her bath water cold; she's not yet been taught to light the bathroom stove. It is early September, the eve of Navaratri, nine nights of feasting to celebrate goddesses and girls. The first three nights are dedicated to the goddess Durga the perfector, the next three to Lakshmi, the bringer of wealth, and the last three to Saraswati, who governs education and music. It must be that Thangam is excited.

Sivakami is not sure how to take the little girl's enthusiasm: she has never seen Thangam show excitement about anything before, apart from her passion for her little brother, the expression of which has been muted since he grew out of infancy.

This is the first of the major festivals they have celebrated at home since Hanumarathnam's death and their return. Sivakami is re-establishing their family in the Brahmin quarter as modest and conventional beyond reproach. Their *golu* will be simple, no more and no less than three shelves, displaying a good selection of dolls in conservative, indigenous attire. Thangam unpacked all the dolls the night previous, inspected them for breaks and tears and mended as required. Today, she will repaint faces. One or two dolls may get a change of costume, but the sari must still be wrapped in an orthodox manner, and jewellery and hairstyles remain consistent. Thangam takes the single liberty of grouping a few around her little flute-playing Krishna, to admire his musicianship and pectoral muscles.

Fortunately, Gayatri, who has none of Sivakami's concerns, has invited Thangam to help her and her mother-in-law set up their golu, which will require much more time and creativity. This is Gayatri's first Navaratri in her husband's village, where she has no sisters, nor sisters-in-law, and so she has invited Thangam to come and help with this, the most pleasant of feminine chores, always more pleasant in a crowd. Gayatri does, at least, have an ad hoc ally in her mother-in-law, an avid and competitive collector who has decreed that their golu should be the grandest on the street. Her daughter-in-law is, for once, wholly complicit in her wishes. Sivakami is amazed as she watches Thangam gallop down the Brahmin quarter to Gayatri's house.

She arrives as Gayatri and her mother-in-law are unpacking their collection. They greet her as servants shuffle away the boxes. Thangam stands silent until she's impatiently beckoned.

Some of the dolls are exotic, such as a little boy figure in green felt short-pants held up by two straps. He has a mate in a green felt skirt. "Both are albino," the mother-in-law points out. They were a gift from a man who photographed her wedding for display abroad, from "Soovisterlund," a place the mother-in-law says, authoritatively, is "between Iroppia and Aappirikka." Gayatri exclaims that another doll, with reddish-brown skin, looks like pictures she has seen of north Indian indigenes: tall and severe, clothed in stiff skins, beads, feathers and face paint. The mother-in-law explains condescendingly that the doll is, in fact, from "Ikanahda," gifted to her by a British engineer.

None of the other dolls are as exotic, but they are exciting. Three are dressed like dancing girls, in cheap jewellery and cunningly wrapped costumes. One even has a torso that wobbles in its blouson and hinged legs that spread the pleats of her costume into a stiff fan. Another wears a sequined, Persianesque veil.

Thangam is most taken with four tiny, exquisite, carved figures, each all-of-a-piece: a woman bending over a grinder, a man putting his shoulder to a plow, another woman inspecting her loom, and a man cutting coconuts from the top of a tree. The mother-in-law's face softens with pleasure at Thangam's choice.

"These, child . . . the most precious. They are the only dolls I brought out from my father's house. They were carved by our old servant. He took me everywhere. On his hip—he never let my feet touch the ground. He's been dead now . . . thirty-five years? More."

She quickly becomes all business. "So, Gayatri, what? What are we doing?"

Gayatri shrugs.

There is one thing that Thangam has not yet examined, and she goes to it now: a three-storey dollhouse, sitting on a green-painted wooden plinth. It's taller than her waist and has a veranda spanning its front, while the back is painted in red bricks, with window frames filigreed in green and violet.

Gayatri comes over to where Thangam is conducting her inspection and explains, proud and a little possessive, "My father bought this for me in Thiruchi when I was nine, just after my first Pongal in my husband's house. Guess you'll have yours in a couple of months, right? I begged and begged for it, but he said no, and I cried so hard that night. I wasn't spoiled," she says as if warning Thangam. "My whole life, I never asked for anything but this. The next day, he came home with it." Two little bound-straw dolls huddle over clay pots and an even smaller pair nap on tiny mats. "My sisters said I must bring it with me when I came to live here. Aren't the dolls sweet?" She rearranges them around minuscule tin plates, but the realism is spoiled because they are too stiff to sit. "Let's try and make some more things for them."

(Is Thangam remembering that other wee house, long dismantled, where she served her father's soul his last meals? She says nothing about that, but brings her own tin play dishes to Gayatri the next day and insists on an extra place setting at each meal.)

Gayatri's mother-in-law breaks in. "How many shelves for the golu? I say eleven."

Thangam gapes.

"Eleven, yes, and an extra platform to run the perimeter of the pool. Panju! Panjunathan!"

Their servant comes hurrying to remove the two-foot-square wooden cover that sits year-round like a trap door in the main hall, flush with the floor. It conceals the hollow whose sole purpose is to become a pond every year at this time, a fixture in homes of status. The servant clatters off the board and squats to examine the state of the square basin, much like a temple tank in miniature, its surface slippery and green from eleven months under cover. This will give the "lake" an authentic cast once the basin is filled with water and baby lotus plants, but Panjunathan's job is to find cracks, dry them and plug them with mortar. He picks diagnostically at fissures with a long, reddish fingernail.

They work on the golu until the wee hours of the morning. It is magnificent. At eleven shelves, it is taller than anyone who will come to see it. The top shelf is crowned with pictures of gods, heavily garlanded by Gayatri, who balances precariously on a bench dragged into the main hall for this purpose. The servant guards her, no doubt praying he will not have to touch her, since to do so is forbidden in several ways: first, a male servant can't touch a young mistress, and second, she is Brahmin and his touch would be polluting. Her pregnancy adds an extra frisson of fear and his jaw is clenched as he stands by.

Reams of new silk cascade down the shelves in bands of peacock and aubergine, so much fabric, of such good quality, that its weight holds it in place without tacks. On each shelf, a scene plays out. Thangam and Gayatri will change the dolls around each morning of the festival, so that the small figures meet one another in a variety of social settings: a concert, a party, a school, a wedding, a Dravidian religious festival, a trial, a pilgrimage, a diplomatic incident (suggested by Minister), a bridge inauguration and an exorcism. Two bars, normally used for hanging saris on, extend from the sides of the ninth shelf, and three marionettes hang from each bar.

For nine nights running, Thangam and all the other village girls run house to house after dark, admiring the golu, singing a song and accepting a treat: sweet crunchy balls of black sesame, teardrop bubbles of fried batter tossed with nuts, sugar crystals ground with toasted lentils and compressed into balls. On the ninth night, the lady of each house makes an offering to a young girl, invited for this purpose. A beautiful virgin from a good family embodies the goddess, perfect in everything—no girl is feted who is deformed or sickly, blind or bad-smelling. Not surprisingly, Sivakami has received many requests for Thangam, though she has made her available only to houses without virgins of their own.

Thangam's enthusiasm has got Sivakami curious, and on the first night of the festival, when she's putting Thangam to bed, she asks her about it.

"I had no idea you loved Navaratri so much, *kunju*. You never showed such excitement, even last year in Samanthibakkam, when your cousins and aunts got up a display."

The girl is quiet a moment. "They had all the dolls."

"They didn't have that many dolls."

"No."

"Not like Gayatri."

"The big aunty already had so many, Amma—remember when we went, when I was small?"

This is Gayatri's mother-in-law. Sivakami knows she and Thangam would have paid a call there together before, before everything changed, but she has no recollection of it. Clearly, it made a much greater impression on Thangam than she had realized.

"And Gayatri Mami told me she has just as many, Amma, and she does and she specially asked me to help arrange them!" Thangam's eyes shine in the dark.

Sivakami strokes her head. What else has Thangam seen, been changed by, fallen in love with without her mother noticing? "Maybe next year you can get a couple more for our golu."

"Puppets." Thangam has clearly thought this through. "Not the big ones, the small ones."

In contrast with his sister, Vairum's joys and sorrows are all too evident: she sometimes wishes she could notice his unhappiness less, along with the way he blames her, for his exclusion, for his nostalgia, for noticing his skin problems. She knows she is to blame. She didn't bring him back here so that he could be happy; she brought him so that he would be fulfilled. She just wishes she weren't reminded of this every time she looks at him.

Now it is early November and time for the next festival: Deepavali, the festival of lights, when oil lamps are lit and fireworks shot off, perhaps to celebrate Rama's triumphant return from defeating the demon king of Lanka, perhaps to celebrate one of Krishna's many victories, perhaps to celebrate a victory of the god Vishnu, of whom both Rama and Krishna are earthly incarnations. Regardless, it's a chance to celebrate, and why should any god or incarnation be excluded?

This Deepavali is the first of Thangam's life as a wife, Sivakami's first great act as a mother-in-law. Custom dictates it should be half as grand as the wedding, but many make it grander than that, hoping attendees will double it in their heads and be even more impressed with the wedding in retrospect.

Sivakami's preparations are anxious and exacting. In-laws have been known to make demands on the spot—for extra dowry items, saris or jewellery. Thangam's in-laws don't seem the type, but maybe she should hold something in reserve, just in case? Like what? No, she will give what is appropriate; she has never done less, nor more. If they make demands, she will meet them.

Murthy travels to the in-laws' village to extend the invitation, thrilled to be the family envoy. He thinks of himself as fastidious and preaches this almost as a kind of morality, but he always overlooks some detail of his grooming. The day he embarks, for instance, bright with the honour of his mission, Sivakami notices a line of red betel-stained spittle marking a trail down his chin. She works hard to over-look his flaws, which are almost endearing: he is quite genuine in his affection for her family, as he was in his fondness for Hanumarathnam, and he sincerely desires to help.

Murthy returns home three days before the Deepavali celebration, gushing over Thangam's husband's beauty, of which he had, sadly, only a glimpse toward the end of his trip. It's a shame, Goli's parents had said, he must have mistaken the time. They sent someone to fetch him, but he'd been unavoidably detained. Guess Murthy would have to greet him at Deepavali in Cholapatti, with the rest of the Brahmin quarter. When Murthy was being taken to the station, the driver pointed to a tall boy crossing the street, and Murthy recognized him from the wedding—high colour, immaculate clothes. But Goli disappeared before they could catch him. "As with our Thangam," Murthy says, "just a sight of him is enough to fill a heart with peace and gladness. What a couple they will make!"

Sivakami thinks, *But that's inexcusable!* and wonders if Murthy is being honest or trying to make her feel better about her son-in-law's rudeness. Surely guileless Murthy is not capable of dissembling?

The day before the festival, Muchami takes Vairum, Murthy and a cotillion of garland-bearers to greet the in-laws. Sivakami is so hoping that this meeting between the brothers-in-law might go better than the last. It would be so nice for Vairum to have a friend in the family. Thirty minutes later, Vairum tears into their vestibule, kicks off his shoes so hard they hit the ceiling, ducks out of the way of their descent and shoots into the farthest corner of the cowshed. Sivakami guesses he still has no such friend.

The rest of the party is half an hour behind him, slowed by the many who come out to greet them. Goli's parents look wan and wary, but Goli is fresher, shinier and handsomer even than before. Sivakami wonders again why she cannot see his charms and resolves to try harder, if only for Thangam's sake.

The next day, the house is crowded with feasters and gawkers who come to see the new son-in-law. Hanumarathnam's sisters come. They ask nothing about matters related to the house. Sivakami's brothers come. They ask nothing about matters related to the children. Sivakami greets them with affection and respect, enhanced by the feeling that she is, truly, mistress of this home.

Happily, Thangam's in-laws make no extra demands. They meekly, mutely receive their gifts and, in turn, present Thangam with a sari. Various matrons rub it between their fingers and pronounce it, among themselves, not gorgeous, but respectable. Goli is as pleased as a child with the diamond ring he receives from Sivakami, the ring her father had presented to his own son-in-law. As Goli leaps about the room displaying it, Sivakami squints to blur the crowd and see, for a moment, only the light of the jewel, as though it were still winking from her husband's hand.

Then Sivakami instructs Thangam to lay banana leaves for the feast. But in the brief interval between diamond and dinner, Goli vanishes. His wife and parents dine without him. Everyone is uneasy, but they proceed. He is not back for the second seating. Several packs of youngsters and a posse of men volunteer to look for him. He remains unlocated. His parents remain mum. Sivakami begs everyone to sit for the third seating, but no one will. She walks to the back of the kitchen and leans in the doorway facing the courtyard, where Mari and Muchami are nervously conferring, and Vairum, who insisted on taking his supper out back and alone, is playing palanguzhi against himself. Sivakami beckons Muchami, and after hearing what she has to say, he goes, quick and solemn, through the cowshed to the northernmost garden door.

Sivakami comes to the door of the main hall with an optimistic look at Gayatri and says, so that she can be overheard, "Please, Gayatri, make them sit. The poor boy has just gone to the *chattram* to lie down. Some stomach problem, it seems. Not my cooking—at least I know that! Your husband sent Muchami to tell us." Sivakami emits a brittle laugh. Minister's schedule is strict, including tea and a constitutional in late afternoon, and a snifter of brandy before bed, and he had departed following the first seating.

Several men look confused and protest hesitantly, "But we asked at the chattram."

Muchami now offers the definitive version from the garden entrance. "Bah! They didn't know anything. We asked, too, and they told us he had not returned, but luckily Minister Sahr bade them move aside so he could have a look in the room." They can almost hear Minister's commanding tone as Muchami continues. "He even insisted that I come too."

This is pushing credulity, but all are too interested in the story's outcome to challenge the servant on whether he would have been invited into this Brahmin bastion. Muchami waves his arms. "There he was, curled up in a ball, holding his . . . his stomach?"

Sivakami blinks confirmation, and Muchami goes on. "Holding his stomach. Don't know how he got in without them noticing."

"Just the way he left here without anyone noticing, I guess," Gayatri offers, and she and Muchami look just as mystified and impressed as the gathering. Gayatri continues, encouraged, "Strange that such an eye-catching young man . . ." She fades out at Sivakami's disapproving look—Gayatri is too young to be commenting on the attractiveness of others' husbands—but the party, bewildered at its own blindness, is meekly seating itself for food.

Muchami takes two steps back into the garden where Vairum has just completed a celebratory dance, kicking his heels out and punching his fists in the air. With a fiercely cheerful grin for Muchami, he goes in search of flowers to offer Lord Krishna, child hero and perpetrator of mischief, to whom he has been praying all day for the disappearance of his brother-in-law.

Goli's parents return at two in the morning, the prescribed hour, when Thangam's mother-in-law is to pour oil on the bride's and groom's heads before they take their baths. But Goli is not with his parents. Sivakami does not ask after him. Muchami and Mari do not ask after him. Thangam bows her head for the oil. She goes to her bath, while her mother- and father-in-law stand, their heads bowed, unmoving. Gayatri runs in, breathless and excited. She's hastily taken her own oil bath and wants to be the first to offer congratulations to the couple. Not seeing them, she waits. Thangam emerges from the bath. Gayatri's body settles, particle by particle, in understanding, and it is she who addresses Goli's parents in their attitudes of shame.

"Oh. I'm sorry that it seems your son's stomach is still troubling him." Her voice sounds as though cooled over blocks of ice, the kind one sees now in Thiruchi, glowing mysteriously beneath layers of sawdust and straw.

But what's that sound? The ice cart, drawn by a pony? No, it's little Vairum. He had gone to sleep content—thrilled, in fact—at his brother-in-law's absence. Now he trots in, making pony-hoof clicking noises with his tongue, and pulls up short at the sight of Thangam's mother-in-law and father-in-law. A quick glance around assures him that Goli has not come, and he restarts his pony with a whoop and trots into the bathroom, wide awake and wriggling with excitement at the thought of his fireworks. Two days ago, he laid them out on the roof to dry. Today, on Vairum's command, Muchami

will light them in the street. Vairum has invited his schoolyard bodyguards to come and watch from just beyond the Brahmin quarter.

Thangam sits with her back to Rukmini, Murthy's wife, to have
her hair plaited. Rukmini and Murthy have not yet had children of
their own, but Rukmini, a good-natured innocent, is full of affection
and care for Sivakami's kids and Thangam goes to her daily for this
small, intimate chore, which Sivakami can no longer do because she is
madi.

Rukmini's own hair is, by general agreement, the worst kind: so
kinky it never grows past her shoulders. Puffs of it gather in front of
each ear; a halo of frizz rises from her rectangular forehead. Her memories of daily tears, owing to her mother's vigorous efforts to tame her
curls, make her gentle with Thangam.

Sivakami remembers that Vairum should have put some oil in his
hair, also. She takes the bottle of oil to the bathroom and persuades him
to wrap his six-year-old modesty in a towel. Finally, he opens the door
and she dribbles oil into his hair. He massages his scalp distractedly
with one hand, the other clutching his towel. He closes the door and
begins again to splash.

Rukmini holds Thangam's hair in her left hand while she strokes
the comb through with her right, careful to scratch the scalp healthily
with each pull. Reflexively, she tilts Thangam's head to inspect for lice;
Thangam spends her days surrounded by children with their heads
inclined toward her. Sivakami leans forward for a look.

They see no bugs, though there is dandruff nestling in the little
girl's part. Not much, but Thangam is a bit young for this problem.
Probably Rukmini has not been scraping the scalp properly each day.
Sivakami chastises herself for not monitoring Thangam's toilet more
carefully. Perhaps it's the change in seasons. At Thangam's next oil
bath, she will have Rukmini rub extra coconut oil into her knees and
elbows, with vigour for heat, and give her scalp a healthy massage. She
now notices a sparkle of dust inching along the drain from the bathroom with the water from Thangam's bath, as Vairum splashes within.

Rukmini tilts Thangam's head toward the lamp, and the flakes
glint as she extends the part down the back of Thangam's head and
makes three smooth ropes on each side. Thangam's plaits are looped

back up on themselves in the fashion of little girls from then to now, and tied behind each ear with a purple ribbon, just as the Deepavali dawn bends through a sulphur haze kicked up by the fireworks circling, shooting and trailing through the early light.

After the formalities of the bath are concluded, Thangam sits to witness the festival fun from her usual spot on the veranda, but without her crowd, because all the children who dare are busy running from their own verandas into the centre of the street with exploding devices to scatter and impress the others. Vairum makes a satisfying morning of it, watching his stash go up in smoke. Not permitted to handle fireworks himself, he stands with his group, just outside the Brahmin quarter, while Muchami juggles the sparkling, flaming or smoking cylinders and cubes.

Only one small mishap mars the morning—it wouldn't be Deepavali without some trifling injury. Some naughty boys tie a string of crackers to a sow's tail, intending to watch the fun from the fence post, but panic pushes the big pig over the bar and out of her pen. She tramples two of the pranksters before escaping through a paddy field and extinguishing hopes of further entertainment.

Sadly, Goli misses all the fun. No one fails to inquire after him, and each is told his stomach is keeping him indoors. All day, his parents mope from chattram to house and back again, no son and no explanation. Sivakami is not clear on how long they intend to stay, and cannot ask.

The day after Deepavali, Thangam wears royal-blue ribbons to match the borders of her silk paavaadai, which is, in the main, a salmon pink worked in gold thread with a tasteful density of flowers. Sivakami instructs Rukmini to comb Thangam's scalp harder. The tender-hearted woman reluctantly complies, but when Thangam winces and blinks back tears, Rukmini starts crying herself. The flaking is getting worse, and not only from Thangam's head. As the child rises, her hair pulled into braids so tight her eyebrows have lengthened, sprinkles fall from her elbows, sliding down the slippery silk paavaadai to shine in a half-sun against the courtyard bricks. She pads out to the veranda, leaving a faintly glistening trail of footprints.

Mari arrives to sweep and swab the floor, as she does daily. When she pours out the wash water, Sivakami can't help but check the courtyard drain. This has been the worst Deepavali she has ever experienced, waiting for this boy who doesn't seem to think any of the rules of propriety apply to him. It probably bears no relation, but, appearing when it has, she can't help feeling as if this dust is evidence of Thangam's humiliation. She hauls and pour bucket after bucket of water along the gutter, but the golden specks must be heavier than dirt, than skin, than flesh and blood, because they settle again to taunt her from the trough.

Goli's parents linger for two nights after Deepavali and then take their leave. When Muchami returns from seeing them off at the train station, he reports the puzzled inquiries of a dozen townsfolk, wondering why Goli wasn't there with them.

"I told them he had gone already and asked them, Didn't they see him go? I said he had said goodbye to as many people as he could, and that I didn't know how they had managed to miss him. They asked if he was recovered and I said, Well, no, but . . . and then I waited, but his parents didn't say a thing, not a thing, just stood there, the mother looking at the ground and father looking at the sky. So I said he was called away on family business, that he had to go and look after some things, things to do with their land. Okay?"

"Yes, yes. What else could you say?"

Muchami responds, even more indignant than when he had started, "Right, what else could I say? Certainly not the truth."

He is deeply alarmed and insulted by Goli's behavior, though he chose not to share this with Sivakami until now. He made his own inquiries—he needed to know what they were in for, and planned to decide later how much Sivakami had to be told. He had found and followed Goli, who patronized several local haunts, including the relatively respectable Kulithalai Club, where, after dark, men played cards, as well as establishments of lesser repute, including one "house of gaiety" in the street of prostitutes. Muchami had ferreted out one man who appeared slightly less infatuated with Goli than others in his crowd (for Goli already had a small gang of "friends," most of whom he met only in the course of this short festival), and learned that this man was a relative of Goli's and that they grew up on the same Brahmin quarter in a village two hours away.

Yes, Goli is a careless person, the man said, when Muchami skilfully isolated him at the edge of the village square one morning. He is egotistical and spoiled. This Muchami could tell—but what of his parents? His parents, said the man, are melancholy, deeply melancholy; they had enough money so Goli had whatever he wanted, but they never disciplined their son and never paid him much attention. Then, in his youth, Goli fell in with a gang of petty criminals. The relative hastened to say that he didn't think Goli had ever committed a crime, but he liked being liked by those small toughies, and they liked him for his money.

"He's a dreamer, though," said the man, in a tone that sounded appreciative. "Goli always has a scheme up his sleeve. One day, one of them has to come to something. I think he'll do well." Muchami hoped he was right. He told Sivakami none of what he had learned.

Sivakami narrows her eyes, raises her brows and replies, "That is the truth. He is a little better, though still in some pain. Where is he? He is off on family affairs."

They fall silent for a moment as Thangam walks through the hall from the front to the back, on her way to the washroom, or to get a drink of water, or some other ordinary task for an eight-year-old who perhaps shouldn't be worrying about the whereabouts of her vagabond husband. She passes through a shaft of sunlight and puffs of gold dust dance off her shoulders and toes.

Sivakami whispers to Muchami, "That is the truth. The end."

They look toward the door. From without, there is a sound of celebration, some kind of parade. Goli is entering the Brahmin quarter with a small and cheerful collection of villagers in a hip-hip-hooray mood of celebration. He gives a jaunty salute, less to his mother-in-law than to the neighbourhood, calling out, "Namaskarams! My train leaves in ninety minutes." There's no train in the direction of his home village until dusk: apparently, he's going somewhere else.

"You must not go without eating something," Sivakami says from the kitchen, disconcerted at his band of friends, half a dozen Brahmin men, some of whom she knows from the Brahmin quarter, some of whom must be from Kulithalai. Clearly others had been able to find him. "You've eaten nothing in our house since your arrival. Come in, please, come in."

156 ~ PADMA VISWANATHAN

Goli puts his arms round his new friends and extends invitations. "Come in! Have a small bite of something, but you'd better get me to the station before the nine-thirty!"

Sivakami runs to the kitchen and assembles small silver plates with a sweet and a savoury snack on each as Goli and company enter the main hall. Vairum pushes past them to the door. He needs to put on his shoes and go to school. Goli smiles hugely at his little brother-in-law, and extends a hand to ruffle his hair. Vairum ducks and scowls, which makes Goli laugh and shrug. As Vairum passes, Goli slaps the back of his head.

Thangam carries out a silver tray with seven tumblers of water while Sivakami makes polite, formal inquiries. "I trust your health has improved? And your business has gone on well?" Goli doesn't answer, busy as he is, working the room, making sure everyone's looked after. He receives a plate and pays attention just long enough to lift the sweet toward his mouth. A moment before it goes in, though, he exclaims, "The train! The train!" He drops his plate and dashes for the door.

Muchami has hitched the bullock cart and driven it around to the front of the house. Goli tosses his valise in the back, climbs up after it, reaches over and whacks the bullock's buttock. It starts to trot. Muchami gives an exasperated look back at Sivakami as Goli bids his cronies farewell.

"So long! Don't forget what we discussed—I'll be in touch. This idea is really going to take off. Don't tell anyone else. Just between us!" he shouts, as the cart rounds the corner to exit the Brahmin quarter.

This episode is the end of the all-important first Deepavali. Thangam spends the rest of the day on the veranda, refusing lunch, rising only at Sivakami's insistence, around half past four. When she rises, gold falls from her paavaadai as though all its forget-me-nots were shedding their petals.

A few minutes after Thangam vacates the veranda, Vairum arrives home from school, removing his shoes before dragging his satchel over the threshold. It gathers a thin gold line of dust along the broad bricks. Muchami departs for his late-afternoon tour of the fields; Mari sorts rice; Sivakami organizes snacks for her children.

Thus, she does not see a neighbour's disappointment at just missing a chance for Thangam's blessing, she doesn't see him pass close by their veranda on his way home and be arrested in his passage by the thin dusting of gold on the spot Thangam just vacated. She doesn't see him take a pinch and stroke it across his forehead, the way he did with a pinch of ash given him once or twice a week by Sivakami's late husband when he held his healing court on the very spot where Thangam sits daily.

Sivakami doesn't see one or two neighbours note the glisten across this man's forehead as he proceeds home, she doesn't hear his wife exclaim over it, she doesn't even hear the crackling up and down the lines of gossip as the news spreads like fires in the dry season. What she does hear is the sound of squabbling, maybe an hour after the original incident. What she sees, when she goes to investigate, is three of her neighbours trying to scrape their own small mounds of Thangam into small paper cones, while a crowd of ten or twelve others try to get a glimpse of the substance, on the veranda, or the road, or the steps, before it is all gone.

In the days following, whenever Thangam is out on the veranda, adults come one by one to receive her blessing. As before, she does nothing to offer it. Those who need must simply take. They lean across the veranda and pinch a pinch of dust from the sprinkling around her or from the small drift against the wall where she sometimes leans. Small babies have the dust rubbed on their tummies for their perpetual ailments. Some is given, folded in a bit of paper, to a servant whom caste does not permit to walk on the Brahmin quarter. Old people receive a pinch on the tongue, just as they take a daily dose of holy ash brought home from favourite temples to ease their undiagnosable internal malfunctions. The villagers remind one another that once upon a time it was said a morsel of pounded gold taken internally had great medicinal value. It was the vitamin pill of nobility. All in the village swear that they feel its invigorating effects. Their good health gains renown, and people come from elsewhere, too, just as they did for Hanumarathnam, to pay respects and receive some holy ash toward prevention or cure, just as Sivakami's parents did all those years ago.

At first, Sivakami feels a vague indignation at her neighbours' greed and opportunism. She can't bring herself to think of Thangam's dust as a gift; to her it feels like a symptom of some malady, the root of which she tells herself she cannot yet fathom.

She eschews the auric dust. The village presumes this is because of her widowhood: widows do not wear gold—her forehead should be marked by nothing but ash, the leavings after a flame goes cold. But this does not explain why neither Muchami nor Mari applies Thangam's dust to their furrowed brows or tired limbs. Gayatri queries them. Muchami doesn't say that he, too, is widowed, though this is how he has felt since Hanumarathnam's death. He replies as he and Sivakami determined together in advance. He tells their young neighbour, "All who are frequently in Thangam's presence are coated with her blessed presence at all times." He holds out his hands for inspection; the glints beneath his purplish fingernails and in the creases of his velvet-dark knuckles prove his claim.

Vairum has overheard, though, and pipes boldly his own explanation, "I'll never take gold from my sister. I'll only give her gold, I will never, never take it."

Gayatri feels inexplicably shamed by their answers and determines from that moment not to take the dust by pinches, but to feel content with whatever traces drift upon her by accident during her daily visits.

A week after Deepavali, however, it is clear that the quantity of gold Thangam is shedding is somewhat reduced. Within a month production has ceased. Thangam has returned to her previous magnetic, but not magical, self. The village resigns itself to taking her blessing as before, with a hand on her head. Straggling pilgrims who come seeking the girl who makes gold must content themselves with a sight of her. As the locals point out, and the religious travellers must agree, that sight is reasonably miraculous in and of itself. The pilgrims depart protesting their perfect contentment. And when, inevitably, a few visitors come with glints in their eyes more entrepreneurial than spiritual, all rumours are hotly denied, and the would-be capitalists turn away shrugging.

―☙

SOME MONTHS LATER, the seasons turn, and crops mature. It is Pongal time. This harvest, the big harvest, is the busiest time in Muchami's work year. Accounting suddenly becomes more compli- cated. There are three growing seasons, not to mention year-round income sources such as coconuts or bananas, but in this time when every possible crop can be reaped, bushels can be lost or disguised. This year, Muchami's sixth in this household's employ, will be excep- tionally stressful for him because he, together with Gayatri, Murthy, and Rukmini, will escort Thangam to her in-laws' house for the holi- day. There, Thangam will initiate the festival by placing the pongal pot on her in-laws' stove to symbolize the bounty she brings them as a bride. Her escorts know that, given her in-laws' straits, their charge is a fortune both literal and figurative.

Muchami has become silent and tense. This is not due to the stress of his work. Normally, he thrives under this kind of strain, becoming more authoritative and authoritarian with each additional demand. He is proud to be taking Thangam, and will be fiercely watchful.

It's just that he wishes he could take her by bullock cart: he is scared of the train. He doesn't find it difficult to meet trains at the sta- tion. He displays a good deal of confidence when putting people on and taking them off, certain that the train is stationary while he does so. None of this leaping on and off while it is in motion, no sir. To ride on one himself? It seems an unnecessary risk.

Mari and Sivakami reassure him that frail women and little chil- dren ride them all the time. Yes, he agrees, but those passengers are lit- erate, high caste. He is the toughest guy around when it comes to market and merchant. He can hold his own in the rowdiest toddy shop in the deepest forest. But this great big roar of metal and smoke . . . He hopes he can keep his dhoti clean, within and without.

Mari accompanies them to the station, counting baggage, ensur- ing the gifts are always in her husband's hands. Even if he's gripping them numbly with fear, at least he's got them. A clutch of dishevelled children, including a couple of Vairum's bodyguards, stand with her on the platform. They run around, chattering, helping her settle

Thangam, Murthy, Rukmini and Gayatri. Finally, a couple of minutes before the 3 p.m. departure, Muchami must mount, ashen beneath his mahogany complexion. The children imitate his knees shaking and laugh until they choke. He stands to yell at them, but the train gives a preliminary lurch and his voice fails him. He sits down and feels the floor shudder up to speed.

Two hours later, it is a suave and cosmopolitan gent who swaggers from the train with his party. They have befriended a number of fellow travellers, exchanged news and opinions, and addresses. There had been, in their own compartment, a range of caste such as you would never run across in such close proximity anywhere else. Muchami is not really sure this part is such a good thing. He has heard of agitations to promote such mixing. One of the men in their compartment seemed to lean that way. Muchami is not persuaded, not at all. He knows his place and so should everyone. Else how would anyone know anything? What would be one's occupation, one's realm of expertise? But the conversation was lively and two hours couldn't really harm anything. Best of all, he no longer fears the iron horse, and his compartment companions concur: it is initially harrowing, but ultimately a very agreeable and efficient way to travel.

The in-laws' servant brings them by bullock cart to the chattram where they will be accommodated. Muchami will sleep in the courtyard out back, since the building is Brahmin-only. They tidy themselves, organize the gifts and go to take their evening meal at the in-laws' home. Murthy, in a kurta neatly pressed except for one wrinkled sleeve, is being insufferably knowledgeable, having travelled here once before. Gayatri is so curious that she can't get too irritated with him; Rukmini, also curious, is naturally deferential to her husband; Thangam shows no curiosity. Just before they enter the house, Gayatri inspects the girl, and absentmindedly, with her thumb, wipes a little sparkle of sweat off the child's upper lip. But the lip is not moist, and now Gayatri's thumb shines with a faint gold, the sort that Cholapatti has not seen in months.

No time to wonder, though, because here are Goli and his parents, and neighbours who have come to greet them, and Thangam's maternal uncles who have come also, and there are gifts to be distributed and inquiries to be made and the evening meal to be taken, and . . . Goli is gone again. His parents appear utterly unsurprised and offer no explanation. Half the guests want to take the same approach, the other half are more inclined to wild speculation, until Gayatri pipes up, "Why is everyone so mystified? He had to go look after business. He's a very responsible boy. Too responsible," she gently chastises his parents. "He should learn to take it easy sometimes. He would be forgiven on a night like this."

Muchami overhears her and is so grateful, because from his place in a foreign courtyard, in a foreign land, he can do nothing.

Anyway, Goli returns at noon the next day, plainly exhausted, for a meal and a nap. He is gone again by late afternoon. Thangam pathetically, exquisitely, performs her functions, stirring the pongal pot on the first day of the festival; on the second, she makes rows of seven balls each of sugared rice, yellow rice, red rice and yogourt rice. These are left as an offering for the crows, who are models for familial behaviour since the common wisdom is that they never eat without calling their fellow crows to eat with them. This is also the day women pray for the welfare of their brothers; when brothers give gifts to their sisters. Thangam is given a cash token by proxy, from Vairum, and Sivakami's brothers give her a few rupees to take home to her mother.

Rukmini and Murthy eat and talk heartily and Muchami and Gayatri silently collude in their relief: if Rukmini and Murthy don't find Goli's absence suspicious, neither will anyone else. Besides, the village is distracted by a miracle: Thangam is shedding again.

When the party returns to Cholapatti after an absence of almost seventy-two hours, they are all coated in a dusting of gold. It is in the corners of their eyes and in their hair, it speckles Murthy's shiny bald forehead so he resembles a new species of egg. As they disembark the train, all their compartment companions compete for a fingerful to smear on the foreheads of near and dear.

Rukmini and Murthy are flushed with celebrity as they arrive back on the Brahmin quarter. They excitedly relate the events of Pongal to Sivakami while Gayatri listens in uncharacteristic silence. The in-laws' village had been so impressed to see Thangam in the full bloom of her powers. She just started a little the night before Pongal, but by the following evening, there were puffs of gold jetting from her heels with every step. The house streamed with people all wanting a bit, and Thangam satisfied them all. Oh, how Sivakami's brothers had been amazed!

That evening and the day following, chattering hordes mill about Sivakami's veranda, replenishing their supplies. "Thangam does look happy to be home," Sivakami says to Muchami, who agrees. He has told her that, in those seventy-two hours, they saw Goli for perhaps two, one and a half of which he spent asleep.

Sivakami shakes her head. She is about to ask, rhetorically, "Where does he go?" but then it occurs to her that Muchami might know, and she is not ready to be told. Men disappear from time to time, and women must cope. Knowing where they go and why sometimes just makes that harder.

Three days later, the village is restive. Thangam's glut of gold is receding once more. Where does the miracle come from? Where does it go? How to make it stay? Murthy, who likes to spend his days pacing and pondering questions of import, hits upon a theory: marriage completes a woman, does it not? It was only when Thangam found her other half that she became fully what she was meant to be, is it not so? Naturally, her capacity for magic waxes when she is near her husband, and wanes when he is far away.

The explanation is readily received by the village. But what to do? The child cannot live close to her husband until she comes of age. They would not want to lose her any sooner than necessary. When she goes, oh, that will be a sad day! Murthy's scientific and deductive clarity has helped the townsfolk to understand what they can expect. They resolve to be satisfied with what they receive.

Sivakami hears snatches of the debates skirling in the wind down the street. She doesn't participate. She has a strong feeling that the gold dust is a product of the marriage, and her orthodoxy compels her to believe that marriage completes the girl, but every fibre of her understanding strains against the idea that Thangam is becoming more what she was meant to be. As the gold drains from her child, Sivakami despairs that Thangam is becoming not more, but less and less and less.

15.

A Coming of Age

1914

AT FOURTEEN, THANGAM SHEDS FIRST BLOOD. "Ah," the village sighs, "how sweet that she's survived to come of age, and how bitter, that she will now leave us!"

In the style of her mother, the celebration will be thorough but not grandiose. Sivakami believes feasts should please the tongues of the gods, not the gossips.

Thangam, dressed in red, sits in the back room, on a mat laid over grains of raw rice. Brahmin-quarter girls, those who used to cluster at the veranda, now cluster at the doors so that she won't feel alone in her isolation. When the villagers come, they greet Sivakami, "Congratulations on your grandson!"—anticipating the required fruit of of the union to come. The married women sing songs about the games of love to make Thangam blush and the girlfriends giggle. All the women dance *kummi*, circling and clapping hands before the Ramar statue, and sing a song congratulating curvaceous Sita on her noble, attentive husband. Every marriage starts out as perfect as Rama and Sita's, the matrons imply. Every marriage, like theirs, faces trials. But today we'll sing not of battles or hardships but of rose petal beds and curtains of jasmine and milky moonlight veils concealing nothing.

For three days, Thangam languishes in peaceful isolation and the village dances around her. For the fourth-day ceremonies, Rukmini will perform the part Sivakami would have had were it not for her widowhood. On that morning, Thangam's in-laws appear before dawn, while she is out back, bathing for the first time since her first menses began. They stand in the hall beside an immense kolam while Rukmini, blushing with the pleasure of her office, gives Thangam a *dhavni,* and maternal instructions for womanly comportment. Under silver vessels at strategic points on the kolam are hidden a small conch dripping milk, some cowries, a little doll and some seeds. These are whisked into Thangam's dhavni and tied at her waist, and then she is seated at the kolam's centre.

The matrons try to place the ritual silver pieces on Thangam's head, shoulders, palms and feet, but the coins slip and fall. Is she trembling? Why would she be? The ladies laugh at this difficulty which in any other girl would seem ill-omened in the extreme. "Why even try? Who piles silver upon gold?" They dance more kummi and sing more songs and feast, and when the gaiety is finished and the celebrants depart, nothing is left but the wait until Thangam, too, must go.

Where will she go? Sivakami wonders. To her in-laws', at the start, but after that? Goli, now twenty-five, has charmed his way into a revenue inspectorship and will be required to change districts every two years for the rest of his career, lest he become attached to locals and tempted into lenience and corruption. Thangam will leave a trail like a small golden snail criss-crossing the presidency. None of them, not Sivakami, not Muchami, none will be able to follow.

A few months later, when Thangam's new family is due to come again to take her home, Sivakami takes it upon herself to explain to Thangam whatever she can imagine of what her life might be like.

"Do you know, Thangam, that your husband has secured a job?" she asks as she serves both children their supper.

Vairum breaks in. "He's a revenue inspector."

Thangam looks at him.

"Big deal," he says, bent over his meal. Thangam quickly turns her head back to her own food.

"It's a very good job," Sivakami says, feeling obliged to sound positive, for Thangam's sake, even while she abhors the sound of her brothers' voices in her own, instructing Vairum on how to feel. Neither child looks up. "It will place very interesting demands on you,

Thangam, as his wife. You will move to a new district every two years!" Her voice sounds brittle to her. Thangam is looking at her now, clearly alarmed. "Won't that be interesting?"

"It will be terrible, Amma!" shouts Vairum, and Sivakami jumps. "Will her in-laws travel with her, at least? Is she going to be all alone, in a new place, every two years?"

"Well, she will be with her husband," she says defensively.

"You can't count on him! When he comes here, he's never here. When Thangam Akka goes to his home, he's never home!"

"Vairum, we need to help your sister prepare, to feel confident and ready." She watches as he folds his banana leaf and storms to the back of the house. She looks back at Thangam, who has stopped eating and started to cry. "Oh, no, *kuttima*. Please, dear, everything will be fine." It is after dark, so she reaches to stroke Thangam's hair. She looks up to see Vairum has returned and is standing over them.

"Thangam Akka, you have to write to us and tell us if you need anything. Okay? I will come and see you." He squats beside her. "I will make sure everything is all right." She nods a little.

Sivakami looks at Vairum to express her gratitude, but he rises without acknowledging his mother's presence and goes upstairs to his attic room.

The next day, Sivakami can't help confessing her fears to Gayatri, who now takes her daily coffee accompanied by her three sons, the baby a little less than six months old.

"Oh, I know," says Gayatri, nose to nose with her youngest, his black eyes flashing toothless delight. "When I have girls, I'll just worry about them all the time, like my mother does about me, like your mother did about you. Won't I worry about your sisters, little baby? Won't I?"

Sivakami feels irritated at Gayatri's response—what does she know of it? But later that day, as she readies her daughter's trousseau, she reconsiders and decides Gayatri is right. What is she feeling that every mother has not undergone? She is accustomed to reading her own emotions in Muchami's face and his dour farawayness shows her how much she has come to look like her own mother, powerless over her daughter's fate.

Thangam's in-laws come to fetch her. This is a strange departure from tradition, but they had written to say they wanted to spare her the bother of asking her relatives to escort the girl—since Thangam has no father, either Murthy or Sivakami's brothers would have gone. Sivakami understands that Thangam's in-laws cannot afford the expense of hosting the relatives properly, and she accepts their offer with outward grace and inward resignation.

They have grown thinner in the years since the marriage. Though they have the fair skin and drooping eyelids of the highly bred, their clothes are almost threadbare. This is an occasion calling for grandeur, but Thangam's mother-in-law wears, apart from her wedding pendant, only two measly strands of gold about her neck. Her bangles, earrings and nose rings are perfunctory. Sivakami knows of their financial struggles. Every time she sees her brothers, they ask after Thangam's in-laws, shaking their heads but heartily insisting, "Good people," before going on to gloat—good-naturedly, publicly—over the in-laws' financial incompetence. She hears from them that this once-wealthy family is auctioning off its real estate, taking prices far below the land's worth. "Creditors," the brothers speculate in self-righteous tones as they buy parcels of the in-laws' land on Sivakami's behalf, using the money she had set aside for Thangam's dowry.

The departure blessings, as needed, are done. The cart arrives and is packed.

"Coffee?" Sivakami asks the in-laws, and Thangam catches her eye.

Gayatri laughs and winks at Mari. "Our girl's become corrupt!" She means it as a joke, light-hearted.

Sivakami can't rebuke her daughter in front of her in-laws; it would be a rebuke to them as well. But Thangam has never before drunk coffee. Mari whispers to Sivakami that she should not give her daughter any of the polluting drink, but Sivakami ignores her, thinking, *I don't have a daughter.* Thangam is now someone else's child.

Sivakami brings the coffee in flat-bottomed silver bowls and tumblers, with a half-inch lip around the top. Thangam accepts her coffee from her mother and begins pouring it, tumbler to bowl and bowl to tumbler, mixing from ever greater heights so that it curls and foams:

caustic liquid gentled with sugar and milk, like a truth made palatable. Thangam relishes each tongueful as Sivakami watches her, imagining her in faraway places Sivakami will never see. Is Thangam drinking the coffee to postpone the moment of departure? Is she experimenting with this foreigners' drink because she, too, is about to become a voyager?

When she is through, she and her in-laws take their leave. Thangam performs an obeisance for her mother, one her husband should have been there to do with her. Vairum stands to one side, watching woodenly. When Thangam rises, her eyes fill and she steps, almost jumps, suddenly toward her brother, putting her palm on his cheek. Vairum jerks his head as though to clamp her hand there, and then shakes her off. Thangam backs toward the cart, which her in-laws have already mounted. Once more, Sivakami has to shake off some petulance—so uncharitable!—at the sense that her children have an understanding that excludes her.

Muchami hovers until Thangam, too, is seated on a bench in back, then leaps up into the driver's seat and flicks his switch. Little puffs of gold jolt from the side of the cart with each pothole and fall twirling in the sun to the thick dust of the road.

Sivakami turns to her son. "Our family grows smaller to grow bigger."

He gazes at her skeptically. "I don't see how you could have let her go with them."

"You're not talking sense," she says, sounding sharp and liking it. "I didn't 'let' her do anything. Her destiny is written by God and I am nothing but an executor." She catches her breath against tears.

"If you're not worried, you're stupid. If you are worried, you should do something about it!" Vairum storms past her.

"What can I do about it, son? I am a widow." She is shaking: how dare he speak so rudely to her?

"None of this would have happened if our father hadn't died." He stands at the bottom of the stairs and starts hitting his forehead with the heels of his hands. "My fault. It's all my fault."

Sivakami gapes. "Where on earth did you hear that?"

He stops and looks at her. "You think it too." Then he runs up the stairs.

"I do not!" she says after him, and again, "I do not," weakly. She can't bring herself to follow. What can she say?

When he comes down, hours later, for his meal, she still has not thought of a way to broach the subject. She has been able to think of nothing but their exchange, but can't think beyond what he said. She serves him silently. While he is eating, she says gently, "It's no one's fault, Kanna. Or, that is, it's my fault, of course, I'm the wife, and if I . . ."

She is foundering, but Vairum excuses her. "Don't talk about it, Amma. Forget it."

She obeys, with uneasy relief, and they go about the routines of their days until they establish, in Thangam's wake, new rhythms not unlike the old.

16.
Another Coming of Age
1914

WHILE MARI HAS BEEN WORKING at Sivakami's house and still living at her mother's, she has passed her fourteenth, then fifteenth, then sixteenth birthday, but she has not yet gotten her period. It does happen, sometimes, everyone knows of such cases. It doesn't mean there is anything wrong with her, but Muchami's mother has spent these years glaring at her brother and sister-in-law and making comments: She should have had several grandsons from her son by now. Maybe there's something really wrong with the girl. Maybe her brother has known all along. She might be within her rights to demand another dowry.

But neither Mari nor Muchami has shown any impatience or desire for the situation to alter. Mari works right alongside her husband at times, serves his meals, hears his problems and goes home each evening to her own mother's house.

"How can Mari not be frustrated?" Angamma frequently demands of him. He shrugs and sucks his teeth; she jabs her hand at him. "How can you not be frustrated?"

Finally, when Mari is well past her seventeenth birthday, the miracle occurs. All are surprised, though her parents would never admit that. She's been obediently taking herbal doses and douches for years. They throw a big celebration. Mari herself insists on staying away not only from the temple, but, Brahminically, from all of the guests. Her family finds these pretensions insufferable. But that's Angamma's problem now!

No one has worries like Muchami, though. For most young men, a bride's coming of age announces imminent delights. For Muchami, it represents terror sheer as a veil or a cliff. Most young men would be thrilled to receive a wife after so long, even a thin one like Mari. Muchami gets tenser and tenser.

On the day of Mari's procession from the house of her childhood to the new phase of her life, Muchami disappears again. No one is alarmed, really. All understand this cannot be easy for him, so let him live out his fears alone for a day. Though it would be nice for him to welcome his bride, he has to come home at some point and needn't be present for the ceremonies.

Just as the procession is concluding in a great swirling of vermilion water and tossing of flowers, a naked panic of five young boys come running from the eucalyptus woods, shouting and crying, "Muchami! Muchami!" Out of deference to Muchami's mother and his uncles, no one answers them. They yank the adults' arms, wailing, "Muchami! Muchami!" and are ignored, until one child's mother notices her son's hair is wet. She clamps his shoulder, shakes him and yells, "You've been swimming, haven't you? Huh?" He puts his thumb in his mouth and refuses to look at her, but the other boys are still weeping and shouting. Muchami's youngest uncle has a dreadful premonition. He tears away from the crowd and runs toward the river. One by one, the uncles are swept by dread and peel from the crowd, running.

Angamma stops swirling the *arathi* and watches them go. The lip of the brass plate droops until she looks down and sees the vermilion water has all spilled and is running along the ground toward the river. She cries out and drops to her knees, but the water has soaked into the earth. She wipes her hands across the red-veined dust and whimpers. She hurries after her brothers.

The youngest uncle wades out into the Kaveri. Muchami, whose body moves like a river weed in the current, is anchored by an arm stuck in a crevice of rock creeping out from the opposite bank. Red radiates from his head in a pump and slap that could be caused by the water or his heart. His eyelids are purple and swollen shut.

The uncle is up to his shoulders in the deadly water, unconscious of risk, when an undertow sweeps him down and away. He fights, as he did as a boy, when the river was forbidden to him as it is to his sons now. He wrestles the river and finds the opposite bank. His brothers, one by one, do the same, except the eldest, who runs puffing to the bridge and crosses there. He arrives as his brothers are climbing out upon the stones, their hearts in their mouths. They free their nephew from the clutch of rocks, lift him from his pale ruby halo, press him to their chests and lay him on the riverbank.

But he is breathing. He coughs and some water runs from his nose and mouth. They start to laugh, in small, tense bursts, like eager dogs, barking and panting. How can this be? Muchami is unconscious, bruised and badly cut, but he is alive. The five little boys had swum the river and now climb the bank to stand beside the uncles. The eldest asks them, "What did you see?"

"He came around the bend—"

"He wasn't moving. His face was in the water."

"Suddenly there was a big swell—"

"Like a big wave—"

"It pushed him at the rocks—"

"It hit his head and flipped him over—"

"And then we saw his face!"

"It was Muchami Ayya!"

"And then we came running—"

"We ran! We were scared!"

The uncles, too, are still scared, since Muchami, though he is breathing, has not yet opened his eyes.

Angamma arrives, out of breath, and wails, "Does he live?" She is so relieved at the answer that she attacks him and must be pulled off, berating her unconscious son for all his rebellion, all his life. "When you were small, I forbade you to go to the river, but you defied me, you went, and went, until you became an expert swimmer, don't deny it, I know, the proof was when you rescued Gopi Ayya's daughter. So what's the meaning of this? You went to take your bath this morning and forgot to stand up?"

The uncles carry Muchami to his mother's hut, as she trots along-side, still lecturing him. They lay him down in his mother's hut, and as Angamma argues with her brothers about whom to call to treat her son, Muchami's eyes open to bright slits. His bride catches his glance, but he closes his eyes again. She thinks no one else has noticed, and this is proven correct when one self-appointed healer pushes through the crowd, flips Muchami over and begins pounding on his back. Muchami recovers quickly enough to escape much bruising.

Only a few days behind schedule, Muchami and Mari are installed in their hut, adjacent to his mother's. They make their first physical acquaintance as patient and nurse.

One afternoon, while Angamma naps in her own hut, Mari speaks up. "Do you know I don't care if I have children? Of the womb, I mean. I want you to know. Your sisters are having plenty, we can adopt one of theirs."

Muchami laces his arms into a pillow and regards her calmly. He hasn't gone to the fields in days; Sivakami forbade it. Nothing is expected of him as long as he is infirm. He has never taken his ease like this. Mari has just made it easier.

Beyond their thick mud walls, a chanted chorus arises, an obscene ditty with the names "Muchami" and "Mari" filling in the blanks, childish voices that then disperse in foot patter and laughter amazed at its own audacity.

"How can you not want children?" Muchami inquires wryly and Mari laughs, covering her mouth.

"I want respect. I want my husband to be clean and not shame me and not drink. My father is a good man, but I could not cope with the drinking."

"I don't drink."

"I know."

Another burst of children's laughter comes through the window on a heat wave, from far away. Muchami knows he should be silent and grateful and never mention the subject again, but something in Mari's manner makes him persist.

"Doesn't everyone want children?"

"I am a religious person, I don't fight fate. God has reasons. If I am meant not to bear children, I can be content with this."

For the first time since his mishap, Muchami attempts to rise, but the room tilts and he wobbles down onto his knees before his wife. He casts his eyes down. "I am thankful."

She nods.

17.
Vairum Steps Up
1914

AT TWELVE YEARS OLD, Vairum thinks little of the past, much of the future. He is religious, and disdains superstition and folkways. His academic performance is exceptional. His loss of colour, too, appears to have slowed or halted: although a fresh snowy patch appears at the start of each academic year, and with each anniversary of his father's death, and although there is still some chittering gossip about those that show on his neck and arms, most of the Brahmin quarter has accepted the truth of Chinnarathnam's aggressive proclamations on the condition. And since Vairum has never had friends, he hasn't lost any. He causes his mother little trouble, so she chooses not to worry about him.

For a time, she worries about Muchami instead—cautious, conscientious Muchami nearly drowned in the Kaveri on the very day he was to bring home his bride. Why is it, Sivakami wondered—and then wondered if in wondering she was tempting fate—that terrible accidents so often happen on the happiest of days? It's obviously the evil eye, cast by some poor soul festering with loneliness, but there is also a susceptibility that comes on such days—giddy joy that renders one unable to negotiate the rivers, kitchens and roads one has managed every day of one's life.

Sivakami forbids Muchami to work for some months, until Mari and his mother judge him recovered. Muchami will not disobey but sends a return message: who will walk the fields? He names the tenants whose rent is due, along with three separate cases of complications and exceptions. The messenger, who was, until recently, Vairum's schoolmate, stammers the details of the cases earnestly and with thorough incomprehension. Sivakami, who still walks the fields in her imagination, with the map her husband left, and so knows enough to know what makes sense, recognizes that the ex-schoolboy's report is garbled and illogical.

However inauspicious the precipitating event, this does seem the opportunity for young Vairum to learn the landscape and methods that support his household. They sit down with the map his father constructed ten years earlier, and she goes over the basics. A few borders have changed, families grown, crops shifted, but Hanumarathnam made the chart flexible enough in its conception to admit evolution. It is soft and creased, like Sivakami's two white saris, but it is still the best guide an heir could have.

"I know it's a lot to absorb," she smiles at him, "but if I can do it . . ."

"No, I get it, Amma," he says, without looking up. He's on his hands and knees and his shadow falls across the topography of their lands like a bird's.

"You'll have to take it to Muchami, because of course he is the one who goes out and talks to the tenants, as you will be doing. He keeps track of the day-to-day details. I only need summaries."

"Mm-hm. Got it."

"I'm proud of you."

He looks up, a little shy.

"And your father would be proud of you, on this day."

Vairum scowls. "If he were around, I wouldn't even be doing this."

"Of course you would: he would have given the map straight to you. I wouldn't have even been in the picture." He's listening. "All this was meant to be yours, to manage as well as he did. Very hands-on, your appa. Knew everything that was happening. Make it your business to know."

Clutching the map to his breast, Vairum marches over to Muchami's hut to collect the correct information. On the community's outskirts, he pauses at the sight of a small crew of his classfellows, Muchami's castemates. They are horsing around in a game of keep-away; Vairum recognizes the disputed object as one boy's prized cap. He slows to a halt and watches them, these boys who are not his friends. Once or twice a year, some boys (always Brahmins) start jeering at or teasing Vairum. Though these boys of Muchami's caste readily do the same or worse to one of their own, they come instantly to Vairum's defence.

They notice him and the game stops as they wait for him to approach them. His attention shifts to what he will say and how he should conduct himself, and so he is distracted from thinking that he wouldn't mind being teased as mercilessly as the boy with the cap, if it meant he belonged.

"Muchami?" says Vairum, and they point to Muchami's hut. It's the longest conversation he's had with them since his earliest overtures with trades and math. In the hut, Muchami tells Vairum it's these talents he must summon, to determine if he is cheating his tenant, if his tenant is cheating him, if a merchant is cheating him or anyone else. The acceptability of the cheating involves other sorts of skills, he explains to the solemn boy, other varieties of calculations.

"Don't mistake me," Muchami says. "Your father managed his lands by the code of your caste. You can see that your mother, too, is as strict as strict can be with herself. A person must have a code. Then, if any man says, 'You have done a wrong thing,' you will be able to stand up and say, 'According to my principles, it was right. And I can live by the principles of no other man.' Understand?"

Vairum had grasped all the methods of calculation using weight, cost, quality and season on first explanation, but now wags his head with deep and evident uncertainty. Calculating on the principle of caste? What kind of maths is this?

"You see, Vairum, your father was a real Brahmin. He was a scholar and a healer. He could not be taken for a fool, nor could he appear greedy. How could he one day chastise a poor man for keeping back some few extra grains, and the next, give to the same man holy ash to quell his child's diarrhea? He couldn't. Yet he also couldn't make of himself a laughingstock when every Mussulman market-man is giving him half-half his lentils' worth. So, first thing first: I do most of the negotiating. These peasants are my castefellows. I know all of what they know, and more, and I know how to make them believe I know even more than that. Until I'm better, don't bother doing any negotiating. You are just keeping an eye on things. Secondly, I will tell you all I know—and they know this. Good?"

Vairum nods with somewhat more confidence or, at least, relief: it's evident that until Muchami returns to work, he'll be able to stick to familiar territory.

That evening and the next, Vairum works diligently to make his own copy of his mother's map. On parchment the exact size of the original, he measures, draws and annotates, first in lead and then, meticulously, in ink. He returns his mother's copy to her and tells her, "Ask me any question, any property. Go on."

"You don't want to be looking at your copy?"

"No need. Ask. Come on."

"Veerappan."

"What do you want to know?"

"Crops and yields, nine months ago."

"... Mm. No, not like that." He waves his hand impatiently. "Ask me about now, not ancient history."

"Oh, yes. Well, tell me who-all owns the pond and the well on Achchappan's plot."

He is silent for a second, then bursts out impatiently, "Why do you keep asking me things that are not even on the map? How am I supposed to know all that? I'm in school, not out gossiping with the tenants."

"I'm sorry, dear one. I ... thought all that was on the map." She believes this because, if it weren't, how would she know the answers?

"Well if it were, I would know it."

"Of course, my dear," she says, eager to keep their feeling of complicity.

"I know everything I need to know," he reminds her. "I got all the calculations right, first time."

"Of course." She knows how smart he is.

He neglects to mention that this applied only to the mathematical calculations. Calculations that factor caste by profession to the power of social status, divided by wealth—these, he will have to grow into. His mother guesses at this and is pleased anyway that he has learned enough to become interested, and is interested enough to learn more.

Each day of Muchami's absence, Vairum rises an hour earlier than usual and walks the fields before school. In the late afternoon, he walks the lands for another hour or two, beginning and ending this walk with a visit to Muchami, to discuss his findings. Several people cheat Vairum; several people who always try to cheat Muchami don't try to cheat Vairum, perhaps out of sympathy for the fatherless child. Vairum prefers being cheated: he wants to be treated like a man.

In the first weeks of Muchami's recovery, Vairum shares every detail of his discoveries with his mother. His evening meal sits untouched as he relates litanies of rules and exceptions in ownership, announces projections of profits and shortfalls, and even starts making tentative pronouncements on various feuds. His mother reminds him repeatedly to eat, but each time, he takes a mere mouthful and starts talking again.

Sivakami already knows much of what he tells her but enjoys his enthusiasm hugely. She delights in watching her son learn, and learn something close to what she herself knows, unlike the formulas and geography and English that fill his days at school, so far away up the road into town. She can't walk a mile to school in his shoes, but she can shadow him through the fields. He, too, is learning that he likes these formulas better than those of math, physics and chemistry, where the laws are those of the physical world and cannot be bought or bent.

Starting from the fourth week of Muchami's convalescence, though, Vairum grows increasingly circumspect. One day, as Sivakami serves him his morning meal and he silently eats, she asks lightly, with no trace of resentment, "Why do you not tell me any longer, of the little wars between tenants, of daily variations in monthly projected income? You have not said a word about your work, not for days."

He looks up, a little surprised. "Are you interested?"

"Of course. I studied all this, too."

"Yes, but only because you had to."

"Yes, the same reason as you." She smiles.

"But it's different for me." He frowns.

"How is it different?" she asks, happy to be having a conversation about their mutual interest, but curious about his silence.

"It's different because you kept count, money in, money out, revenues, expenses, salaries and taxes." He is impatient. "Counting is no challenge for me. Don't worry, everything and everyone will be looked after. But land is for growing, after all, and even if Brahmins are not farmers, I am going to make ours grow."

"Brahmins should not be acquisitive, either." She feels it's important to remind him, in his father's absence, that he has a responsibility to the traditions of their caste.

"I don't care about money!" he bleats, and she is cowed and impressed by his outrage. "I'm doing it for the challenge only." He sounds far away. "To prove I can."

Dreams of dominion? That's not what he said. As Sivakami serves him his breakfast, she looks at him closely. His eyes are as dark as ever, the future too far back in them to be seen.

18.
The Arrival of Children
1915

IF SIVAKAMI WERE TO BE ASKED—though who would ask her?—
she might say she knows there's a war on in the world, but when is
there not? She doesn't read the newspaper—she used to browse the
headlines and advertisements, but she stopped the subscriptions after
her husband died. She thought she would restart them if or when
Vairum asked, but shortly after Vairum started making rounds of the
fields, he also began stopping in on Minister daily, in late afternoon,
where he reads the English and Tamil papers.

Gayatri tells Sivakami that Minister has told her that Vairum is
indifferent to politics.

"Then what do they talk about?" Sivakami asks.

"Politics!"

When Gayatri carries gossip from her husband she almost always
repeats it verbatim—she says she doesn't understand it well enough to
paraphrase, but appears to get enough to take an interest.

"My husband is called to politics by his nature, that's what he says,
but he says Vairum is calculating, neutral, that he never expresses a
preference for one party over another, never seems to have an opinion
about a political gain or loss, but still wants to know all the details. You
know, on days when he doesn't have classes, he comes in the mornings, when all the other men come. If he weren't in school, I'm sure
he'd be a regular."

Minister hosts a daily salon where local men air and contest matters of power and political control. Only privileged men attend—the language of exchange, Minister insists, is English, even though all of the attendees are Tamil. Despite their wealth and power, Sivakami disapproves of the gathering because the majority are not Brahmin.

"But why would he go if he's not interested in politics?" Sivakami frowns, though more with curiosity than worry. She is still pleased Vairum is spending time in Chinnarathnam's house. "Isn't that what they . . . do, there? Or, talk about?"

"I suppose he is interested in the information, or the contacts, or . . . well, who knows, really?" Gayatri founders, and so goes on to tell in engaging if excessive detail about some mutual corruption charges between a developer and the Taluk Board on which Minister is a seatholder; and thence to ribbon-cuttings recent and forthcoming, while Sivakami mulls vaguely on her son's increasingly opaque facets, and what to make for tiffin and how the cowshed thatch needs replacing.

Vairum is ever laconic, about his school day, or the news, business or the war, which, for Sivakami, remains almost imaginary, much like those battles Vairum twirled through on twiggy horseback in the Samanthibakkam of a dimming childhood. Maybe mothers like Sivakami would take the far-off wars more seriously if they knew that the battles were so similar to battles they witness daily in their own villages, and that the issues fought over were so close to their own hearts: territory, status, gold.

Thangam returns home to wage a related battle in the back room where she passed the days of her maturation and whose walls will now witness the appearance of her baby.

Thangam is no howler, and there is no sound from the room but grunting and the grinding of teeth, accompanied by the incessant tinkle of glass bangles, given to every expectant mother in her seventh month. Thangam didn't tell Sivakami she was in labour and was quite far along by the time Sivakami noticed. As soon as she did, she hustled Thangam into the back room and sent Muchami to find the old ladies who will help, as well as the astrologer. Before they arrive, though, the head has shown and Sivakami has no choice but to hold out her hands and pray. A little girl slips from the womb into Sivakami's shaking hands, as three old ladies appear at the door, their lips moving with mantras, their eyes large.

Sivakami, holding the baby up like a magician with a rabbit, shouts to Mari to alert the astrologer, who is squatting in the garden. She turns the little one upside down, then rights her, as though the child is an hourglass with a few final grains to dislodge before she can be restarted. The baby coughs up a little goo and begins to cry primly, not too loud, nor very long. Sivakami jiggles the child gingerly and makes clucking noises, then permits the ladies to take over while she staggers forth from the gloom into the courtyard sunshine. She collapses against a wall and listens to the cows moan from the shed beside her and recalls herself as a mother at fourteen.

When the placenta emerges, Thangam is covered, her brow daubed, water dribbled between her cracked lips. The baby is wiped and bundled. Thangam's colostrum is expressed and discarded, according to custom; the baby is fed a little castor oil to get her meconium moving, a little sugar water to hold her until she is allowed the breast.

Thangam rests for thirty-one days, confined to the back room, where she sits or lies on the cot. Sivakami leaves her food in the doorway, and while she eats, girlfriends and matrons and Gayatri, who is both and neither, sit in the doorway and chat. They bring Thangam betel-stuffed leaves smeared with calcium: wisdom has it that, in the weeks after a birth, the new mother should consume a quantity of calcium equal to the size of her child's head. "For every child born, you lose a tooth!" Thangam is advised by half a dozen neighbours and her mother as she tucks the spicy bundle into her cheek. The visitors chew too, mouths dyed red as they jaw.

Thangam's complexion is shockingly bright. She looks childlike and charming. She is exactly where she is supposed to be.

And all the village seems lighter of foot, knowing the golden girl is back in its midst. When she emerges from her seclusion, a horde seethes round the veranda from morning to night.

Sivakami smiles hidden smiles: she not only gained a granddaughter, she may be regaining her daughter. The birth of the child added years to Thangam's life. The astrologer said so, in response to the secret requests Sivakami sent along with birth time. He responded yes, the birth of this girl-child had altered the relationship of her parents' stars, that she had worked a lengthening of her mother's years on earth. That the child had done for her mother what poor Vairum failed to do for Hanumarathnam—the note says nothing of that.

Good fortune can become a burden in its own way, though, so Sivakami hugs this knowledge to herself.

SEVERAL MONTHS AFTER THANGAM'S SECLUSION ENDS, Sivakami asks her, "You know how happy we are to have you here, kanna, but did the son-in-law say he would be coming to fetch you? I just want to make sure we're ready."

Thangam looks back at her with wide, soft eyes.

Sivakami continues, "You know that if your father were alive, he and I would have taken you back, but of course Murthy and Rukmini can take you."

Thangam looks uncomfortable and non-committal.

"He didn't say, one way or another?"

Thangam shakes her head.

"Do you want me to ask your in-laws and arrange an escort?"

Thangam nods but looks miserable.

Thangam's in-laws write that Goli will come to get Thangam, and Sivakami writes back that they will wait for him. Another month passes, then nearly two, and she writes again, very diplomatically asking if she has misunderstood and offering to send Thangam under escort if Goli's work prevents him from coming.

"Let her stay here, Amma," says Vairum, though Sivakami has assiduously not raised the topic with him. They are all sparkling faintly with Thangam's dust: the shedding began again, as soon as Sivakami broached the subject of her return to her husband, and hasn't abated.

"Don't worry, Thangam," she says. "That won't happen. You'll be back where you belong in no time." She won't even acknowledge the suggestion: the shame! What is Vairum thinking?

"I don't care," he says. "She could stay and we would take care of her."

"She has a husband, Vairum," Sivakami says. "The topic is closed."

Thangam's in-laws write accepting the offer. Murthy and Rukmini will escort Thangam to her home in the district where Goli is currently the revenue inspector in charge, some three hours away by train.

Sivakami talks to Muchami about the arrangements.

"You'll need to buy the train tickets."

"Of course, Amma."

"One would have thought he'd be curious to see his child," she says, and regrets having spoken it. It sounds like a curse on the baby.

"He's not an ordinary sort of man, Amma," Muchami says and purses his lips as if he, too, wants to prevent himself from speaking further.

"No, he's not," she agrees, but it is an acknowledgment that Muchami knows more than he is telling. She doesn't want to know.

Two weeks later, Muchami drives Thangam, the baby, Murthy and Rukmini to the station.

"Goodbye! Goodbye!" shout the teary villagers, an expression whose literal translation is "Go and come back! Come! Come!" Children run after the bullock cart, trying to touch its sides.

The next morning, returning at four from Sivakami's bath in the Kaveri, Sivakami and Mari are startled by someone asleep on the veranda. It is Goli. Sivakami invites him in, gives him coffee and explains that his wife has already departed for their home.

"What's that?" he says, sounding irritable. "My parents said to come and get her, so here I am."

"I'm very sorry." Sivakami is full of questions she cannot ask: who will greet Thangam on her arrival at their home? Has he made any provisions at all?

Vairum descends the stairs with a towel, scratching his head sleepily, and pulls up short at the sight of his brother-in-law. "Oh, priceless. You know she waited for you for months?"

"Vairum!" Sivakami indicates the back of the house with her chin. "Go take your bath."

Vairum gives an exaggerated sigh of disgust and turns to go as Goli replies in an ugly tone, "I'll look after my family, imp, and you take care of yours."

"You see that you do that," Vairum tosses back.

"I will."

It's a thoroughly adolescent exchange. At least Vairum is an adolescent; Sivakami wonders if Goli is much more.

PART FOUR

19.
Keeping Faith in Kulithalai
1917

IN THE YEARS THAT FOLLOW, Sivakami continues giving arm's-length advice on agricultural business, though she more often shares her opinions with Muchami than with her son. The servant faithfully reports all matters in which he feels he needs her approval, as well as discussing with her issues in which different approaches might be entertained. Vairum tells her nothing of what he sees or learns on his rounds, but he does discuss these in detail with Muchami, either at the end of the day or when they make rounds together, and so Sivakami knows her feelings are being communicated, though in the guise of Muchami's own opinions. In this way, then, Muchami functions as her proxy, even with her son, when it comes to matters from which the world—and Vairum in particular—thinks her better excluded. She's not sure why Vairum doesn't discuss these matters with her: he seems to consider it a waste of time since she has no direct involvement. Nor has he ever indulged her basic curiosity about his life and interests, or about the world that has been, for so long, beyond her witness. It never seems to occur to him that she might have a perspective of value, and in this arena, where he has the right and confidence to do well on his own, she doesn't want to press.

Thangam returns for the birth of her second child, bringing her first. When the time comes, Sivakami births this child, as she did

Thangam's first. Why? Because she attended the first, and both children have lived. One of the principles of a superstitious society is: don't fool with working formulas. If once a practice has a good result, it becomes a tradition; to change it would be arrogance against fate.

One day, at her usual time, Gayatri comes brimming with news and sits in the courtyard, within earshot of Thangam in the birth room, Muchami and Mari weaving thatch and sorting rice at their posts and Sivakami in the kitchen.

"I don't know if you heard," she says. "It's too terrible. That woman, Madam Besant, who has been agitating for independence, was interned a couple of weeks ago. Anyway, it has made her more popular than ever!" She holds a rolled-up newspaper in her lap.

"Jail?" Muchami asks doubtfully.

"Oh, yes! Do you remember who she is, Sivakamikka? She's the English lady, head of that theosophical society, the crackpot."

"She's a great friend to Brahmins," Mari contributes without raising her eyes from the rice grains she is sorting, tossing them in a shallow three-sided basket. "One of my relatives said she thinks we should return to Manu's laws."

"True, but she doesn't even know what she's saying." Gayatri might sound as though she's questioning non-Brahmins who admire Brahmin principles too intensely, but in fact it's simply that it spoils her pleasure to tell a story to anyone who disagrees with her, even by a shade. "She doesn't know any Sanskrit, or any other Indian language, and she advocates breaking down caste and giving full voting representation to everyone." Gayatri knows Mari can't approve of this. She continues. "It's of real importance that she be brought down. The talk is that she is heading for Congress leadership. She says everything those independence types want her to." Gayatri reflexively lowers her voice as though she doesn't want to be overheard. "There has been a rash of articles lately, mostly written by one very interesting doctor, a Nair. He started the Justice Party—you know, they are firmly against this independence nonsense. So this week, he wrote a column about the behaviour of Madam Besant's theosophical colleague, that Mr. Charles Leadbeater. You don't want to know the details, but he behaved very improperly, with young boys, and it's not good for voters—well, for anyone, to forget that kind of association. And so my husband added his voice to the chorus. Look!"

She opens the paper that she has been clutching, the *Madras Mail*, an English-language daily aimed at the Madras Presidency's British business class. She folds it back to the letters page and points at one item, a few paragraphs long, circled in ink. "My husband wrote it." She holds it longer than necessary under each eager nose: Sivakami is only functionally literate in Tamil, and Mari and Muchami not even that; none of them could pick English out of a lineup. Even Gayatri knows only from the position of the masthead whether she's holding the paper upside down.

"He signed it 'Keeping the Faith.' It's mostly about the need to preserve the empire, you know, continuity, India's rightful place in the world."

Vairum arrives at the salon as Minister is arranging the papers on a settee: the *Madras Mail* is on the top of the pile, folded to display the letters page. One letter is circled in red ink, and Vairum picks the paper up to have a closer look at it. Minister winks at him.

One reason Vairum attends the salon whenever he can is to work on his English, which is still rudimentary, though quickly improving. While some of the conversation eludes him, he finds phrases echoing in his head later and tries them on his English tutor, or on Minister himself, who has agreed, at Vairum's request, to speak to him only in that language.

Vairum runs his eyes along the lines of print with controlled desperation.

> *Sir—*
> (At least he knows that word, commonly used in Tamil for "teacher.")

> *I am pleased to add my voice to the welcome cacophony which has greeted Mrs. Besant's internment. Nothing is resolved without discussion, and I am certain this tempest*

*will be confined in an appropriate teapot before long. I
want to register my displeasure with Madam Besant's
reported increased popularity of which we, even so far
away as Kulithalai Taluk, Thiruchinapalli District,
have heard. Be assured that there are many in the
provinces dedicated to the progressive aims of the
Empire, Brahmins and non-Brahmins alike, and who
understand that membership in the British family offers
our motherland, India, her best chance for continuing her
advance into the ranks of the world's great nations. If
there are those who now know nothing more than Madam
Besant's name and fame, and think, on that basis, to be
led by her, this is but mere fad—which always shortly
changes to "fade."*

*Respectful regards,
Keeping Faith in Kulithalai.*

"Kulithalai!" Vairum exclaims. "Was it written by one of your, um, friends?" He's not sure what to call them, since they seem held together by something other than friendliness, a feeling he doesn't quite understand but intends to: another reason he comes whenever he can.

"Better than that, son," Minister says, going into his library, an adjoining room through a set of double doors. "It was written by yours truly."

Who is mine truly? Vairum wonders, vaguely embarrassed. It sounds romantic.

Minister looks back when he doesn't respond, and laughs. "Me! I wrote it. It's about time they knew what we're thinking out here about all that nonsense."

"Oh! Quite," Vairum says, one of his favourite English expressions of assent. "Quite." He perches on the settee to read the papers and wait for the regulars to arrive, while Minister unwraps some new books, a package from Higginbotham's in Madras, and another from Penguin of London, and sorts them into his already substantial collection.

Vairum regularly borrows from him, things he finds and things Minister recommends, from Sir Wm. Wedderburn's book *A. O. Hume: Father of the Indian National Congress* to classical Tamil dramas, analyses of the *Periya Puranam* as well as Sarma's *Toward Swaraj*. Minister reads all the tracts published by the Indo-British Association, such as *Indian Problems: Caste in Relation to Democracy,* or *Indian Opposition to Home Rule: What the British Public Ought to Know,* and Vairum struggles through these also, still unsure of what will be important to him as he makes his own way. Minister also takes newspapers of every political stripe, and Vairum browses the political and social pages but finds he pays most attention to business and finance. Sometimes, the same stories are covered in Tamil and English, a great help to his comprehension.

Minister doesn't even keep track of which books Vairum borrows, trusting him to come and go as he likes, so Vairum has also groped his way through such reference works as *Kissing in Theory and Practice, Pandora's Letter Box: Being a Discourse on Fashionable Life by the Author of the Technique of the Love Affair* and Marie Stopes's *Married Love: A New Contribution to the Solution of Sex Difficulties,* which he found at least as informative as *The Indian Constitution: An Introductory Study,* though, again, to what end he is not sure.

He hears the first of Minister's cronies coming up the stairwell off the veranda. Minister exits his library onto the balustraded corridor that connects all the upstairs rooms. He leans over the rail to shout through a skylight into the main hall below, "Gayatri! Snacks!" and then turns right to open another set of double doors into the salon, sliding bolts into the floor to hold them open. He checks the soil in two pots of ragged posies and adjusts the position of an occasional table as his cronies enter.

The two men arrive already arguing. They are close acquaintances and colleagues. One, whom Vairum has never heard speak below shouting volume, is N. Ranga, a Chettiar by caste, moneylender and compounder by trade, who now has several storefronts. His successes interest Vairum keenly. Ranga opened a Thiruchi branch, Ranga and Sons, some eight years back, where he stocks patent medicines and toilet products that he has test-marketed at his original location. The other is a Brahmin, Dr. C. P. Kittu Iyer, an undistinguished and lead-fingered practitioner (Vairum gathers) of the medical arts, who never ceases to criticize the compounder for pimping quack medicines. Kittu Iyer still sends his patients to Ranga to have prescriptions filled, though, because, as a medicine-maker, Ranga is skilled and honest, the best in the district. His dealings in skin-lightening lotions and tuberculosis tonics haven't hurt his professional reputation, either because people don't distinguish these from his legitimate trade, or because they understand the nostrums are purely a business concern.

"The man is a traitor!" Ranga hoots as though through a venom-filled whistle. "To us, and to his own people!"

"It is a victory for the right and might, but we must remain vigilant. There is no guarantee this is not a trick," Kittu rejoins as though addressing a much larger audience.

"Do you get what they're on about?" Minister asks Vairum, as he takes a seat beside his protégé.

Vairum shakes his head.

"Look again at the headlines. Edwin Montagu, the secretary of state for India, made an announcement to the House of Commons, of Britain's intent to increase Indian representation in administration—see?" He points to one article, and then to another: "'... with a view to the progressive realization of responsible government in India as an integral part of the British Empire.' There was no warning. Stunning." He rearranges the papers so that the *Madras Mail* with his letter is once more on the top.

Vairum has heard enough about these matters in the salon, and from Minister, to have a sense of how its members will divide. Non-Brahmins such as Ranga, a Chettiar, will restate fears that granting India independence at this juncture would mean handing the country over to an elite coterie of northern Brahmins. Brahmins such as Kittu, an Iyer, believe this seems like a good idea. Minister will be the only Brahmin to oppose the move toward independence, and the one who will take the move most personally. His salon is decorated with drawings of Whitehall and the Houses of Parliament he made as a child, hung on the western wall above a row of fragile potted flowers; in one corner of the library is a stack of empty Peek Freans biscuit tins; on a shelf, his bottle of No. 1 McDowell's brandy, proudly displayed. He drinks a carefully measured inch each night after supper. "I live with my mother and father," he once told Vairum. "Loyalty. Habit. My country is a participant in—not victim of—a grand and noble scheme. The British do things better. Nothing wrong with the Indian way, but nothing to lose, wot?"

Vairum watches Minister now, one leg crossed over the other, bouncing nervously as the sportif Muthu, of the Reddiar caste, rounds the stairs. "The wires are buzzing—what a to-do!" Muthu says, puffing.

He mops his expansive brow and grins at the two first arrivals, who have taken seats as far as possible from one another, and at Minister, who smiles back paternalistically and responds, "But who are 'they,' dear chap?"

Vairum thinks, *dear chap, dear chap,* savouring the unfamiliar syllables as Minister goes on. "My impression is that much of the Commons was taken as off guard by this announcement as we. For whom does Montagu speak?"

Slim, chic K. T. Rama Sastri, another Brahmin—lawyer by training, lounger by inclination—recites from the doorway, "'Now is God's purpose in us perfected / Complete the work of Clive and Nicholson / When in this Empire that their swordblades won / Authority is mocked and buffeted / And England's voice, no more the lion's they knew / Becomes the whisper of this Wandering Jew.' Nothing like a bit of doggerel to start the day off right."

"Har-har!" Muthu Reddiar slaps his knee. "That was this morning's *Madras Mail,* isn't it?"

"Yes, by the editor," says Rama, pointing a pinky out as he accepts a china teacup from a tray the cook's daughter is bearing self-consciously around the room. "He could hold his tongue no longer."

Vairum tries pointing a pinky out, too, but can't keep it there as he takes the teacup. He forces himself to put his mouth to the edge and slurp. The thought that his mother would be scandalized to see him drink this way is some motivation: in his house, they hold a silver tumbler above their mouths and pour, to avoid pollution from any saliva that has ever touched the cup. Mostly, though, Vairum does it because it seems an important, cosmopolitan skill, though he overcomes a little revulsion to do so.

"It is a serious question, however," R. V. Mani Iyer is saying. He is the salon's most recent Brahmin addition and is politically committed— to Congress and independence, as is usual for Brahmins. Several years behind Minister at school, he did a B.A. at St. Joseph's College in Thiruchi, where Vairum has also decided he wants to go. "Montagu seems a man of real disinterest and integrity . . ." He ignores a "Pshaw!" from Ranga Chettiar, punctuated by a soaring morsel of onion *budji*. "But he is a Jew, and we know how deep communal loyalties run. How can we with all our hearts accept this promise from someone the English cannot truly claim as their own?"

The last of the salon regulars slinks in—S. Gopi, another Chettiar, a grain and dry goods dealer. He has a couple of rice mills and has also recently started vending "Modern Pots" in new shapes and alloys, yet his tone around Ranga, his Chettiar castemate, bespeaks a defensive sense of inferiority. Gopi has no sons, and no shop in Thiruchi. Though he employs several of his sons-in-law in his concerns, his failure to expand beyond Kulithalai district is seen by some as a reluctance to build a fortune that will simply pass out of the family line. He has been heard proclaiming that small business is good business, but his customarily sarcastic tone makes it tough for Vairum to tell when he is sincere.

"High time to organize, man!" Ranga Chettiar exhorts Gopi by way of a greeting, as though they are in the middle of a conversation. Ranga's youngest son has initiated a Chettiar Uplift and Cultural Preservation Society in Kulithalai and Ranga appears to have made it a project to needle Gopi—either pressing him for more support, financial and otherwise, than he is inclined to give, or suggesting backhandedly that he is a potential beneficiary. Vairum thinks often about this pair: same caste background, but such different fortunes. What has caused one to succeed and the other to fail, apart from dumb luck?

"Has your son made contact with the Justice Party?" Minister asks Ranga, not changing the subject but deflecting it from his guest.

"Oh, quite," Ranga replies, in a gay, vague tone: he clearly has no idea.

"It's a natural fit—I'm sure other Chettiar organizations are getting behind them," Minister presses charmingly.

The South Indian Liberal Federation, increasingly called the "Justice" Party after its English-language daily, was founded by well-educated and generally well-off non-Brahmins. It is dedicated to opposing the independence movement, whose ranks are dominated by Brahmins: while Justice Party-ites murmur that of course all Indians want independence, they are devoted to preventing its realization at present because of the fear that, under current conditions, an independently governed India means a Brahmin-governed India. They will gain an ear among Brits who, regarding the Jew Montagu with no little disapproval, understand antipathy to moneyed minorities with aspirations to govern.

Minister, ever the cross-caste campaigner, is promoting the party among his non-Brahmin associates. He's certain Justice will make a successful run. Even though, as a Brahmin, he can't join the party, he wants to ensure he has many fingers in their pie.

"It's a self-destructive concept, a non-Brahmin organization!" expostulates Dr. Kittu. "Moneyed non-Brahmins have no more in common with one another than they do with Brahmins. Except in this one enterprise, you fellows are always competing, always trying to set yourselves apart from one another." He turns on Minister, his fellow Brahmin, with gentler reproach. "You shouldn't be encouraging them."

Minister performs a likable shrug and offers the doctor a plate of assorted sweets. Later this year, he will stand for his first election: he hopes to make the leap from Taluk to District Board. In part, Vairum knows, these men gather here daily because they believe he will succeed—he is the best-connected man in the district and increasingly relied upon for those connections. These men connect to one another through him. Maybe someday, Vairum thinks, he, too, will be such a hub. Not for politics, though. He knows that already.

Rama Sastri, whose attention is rarely held by the conversation but seems, to Vairum, not to have anything else to do, has spotted the letters page and is frowning at the circled item.

"Special interest here, wot?" He flourishes it inquiringly, and Dr. Kittu irritably snatches it.

Mani Iyer, reading over the doctor's shoulder, starts, hurt in his voice. "Daily there are these criticisms of Mrs. Besant—"

"Drivel!" says the doctor. "Muckrakers!"

"Oh, now, gentlemen," Minister sighs sympathetically. "Why would we trust self-hating Britons to give us guidance? But that's not why I circled that item. What do you think of the prose?"

Rama Sastri re-examines and reads the letter aloud with special emphases to show he has solved the puzzle. "Do we have a stylist in our midst?" He pops his monocle and moues at Minister, who giggles in response.

"What's so special about it?" Muthu Reddiar asks thickly as the others attempt to look knowledgeably disengaged, and Vairum is reassured to see that there are others here who are trying to hide their confusion, as well as at least one person who doesn't mind showing it.

20.
Far from Home
1919

HER BROTHERS HAD BEEN RIGHT: Vairum is leaving her. Sivakami had known this, and still, boldly, baldly, made her choice.

The seventeen-year-old Vairum, though, looks indisputably happy and proud. His valise is packed, his shoes shined; Rukmini, Gayatri, Minister and their children, and Vairum's math teacher are gathered for the send-off. Murthy will escort Vairum and get him settled in the dormitory. Sivakami has nearly finished assembling a tiffin for them to eat on the train.

Muchami comes to the kitchen entrance to say the bullock cart is ready. With little to take, Vairum could easily have walked to the station, but what sort of fare-thee-well would that have been for a young man off to attend St. Joseph's College in Thiruchi?

Always, Sivakami glances at Muchami's face to gauge her own emotions, but today his expression is not her own. No one feels about her son as she does. Muchami has concern for the child, and pity, and the restrained affection that develops with proximity, but does not have Sivakami's passionate protectiveness. His pity is reflexive: Vairum is a child without friends. He is thought so sharp and so bright as to be unassailable. Even Gayatri, despite an interest in Vairum's welfare, feels no fear on his behalf. Thangam is not here to show affection toward her little brother, and so Sivakami alone worries for the diamond-hard boy. She knows he will succeed, at college and afterward. He will become all he was meant to be. So what is she worried about? She has the feeling that if she could see far enough into his dark eyes, she would know, but Vairum doesn't let her look.

Sivakami speaks in tones alternately too brusque and too indulgent: Has Vairum packed twenty neem sticks for his teeth in case he couldn't find a good tree right away? And what about the shoe polish Minister brought him from Thiruchi?

"I can buy shoe polish there!" Vairum says.

"Obviously: that's where he bought it," she says, peevish now. "But we have no use for it here!"

Vairum has no patience for his mother's sentimentality. He wants to rush out, rush forward. He hears the bullock snort and stamp outside.

Sivakami is not finished. "Every mother who permits her son to leave her asks him for a promise. I am the same as every mother."

Vairum looks away from her, toward the door.

"Look at me," Sivakami says. He looks at her feet. "Your father's first wife was lost in the river which connects our small village to Thiruchi. I worship our Kaveri Mata daily, the river that gives us life. I ask her to spare the precious lives of our children. Promise me." Sivakami strains toward him. "Promise you will not swim in that river. You drink her water, your clothes are washed in her flow. That's enough. Boys will try to tempt you . . ."

Fat chance, thinks Vairum. Muchami reads it on his face.

"It will look like fun, but I cannot afford this. It is sacrifice enough to send you so far."

Vairum looks troubled. "The cost, Amma?" He thought he knew all their financial ins and outs. They can afford this.

"The cost of losing you, to the city, to the river, to . . ." She can't go on.

Minister clears his throat, steps in. "Promise your mother, and then look lively. Only twenty-five minutes till the train." He nods at Muchami, who picks up the valise.

Vairum mumbles something.

"Huh?" The volume of Sivakami's voice startles both her son and herself.

"I promise, good?" he repeats. "Can I go?"

Sivakami is seeing two scenes at once. She watches her son mount the cart—shiny dark shoes and shiny dark head and large, slim hands dangling from thin adolescent arms, his father's hands, but for a large white patch emerging from one sleeve and encompassing two knuckles—as she also sees a moment from their past: their family, wading into the Kaveri. She recalls the feeling of her hair ravelling its binds and floating up in the breeze cooling itself along the water. Baby Vairum, arms clasped around her knees as Muchami calls to him from farther out in the current. Hanumarathnam, helping little Thangam out of her paavaadai on the bank.

Watching Muchami help Murthy into the cart, she feels as though she is looking at and through the river's surface, seeing her own world reflected and also seeing the otherworld of fishes and insects. The otherworld of her memory feels at least as real: Muchami is several steps out in the river, the water only as deep as his shins. Vairum lets go of Sivakami one hand at a time with Muchami's wiry grasp around his chubby baby elbows. Delighted, he floats in the water, little-boy face to the sun, with Muchami squatting, holding him up. Hanumarathnam squats to do the same for Thangam, but she doesn't float. He tries to lift her from the armpits, but she's too heavy. Hanumarathnam falls, a big splash, and gets up laughing. Thangam splashes, too, slaps the water in excitement, then covers her mouth with her hands. Sivakami claps in excitement, and Vairum claps, too, laughing in the sun. Oh, those eyes.

Before her now, in the Brahmin quarter, the bullock's back gleams, then dulls with dust up the fatty hump. The tail flicks once as the cart rocks around the corner and away. Vairum doesn't look back. No weeping crowd, no running children. There are no rituals for bidding farewell to a son.

───୭───

THIRUCHINAPALLI.

Vairum has read up a little on the history of the city, poring through the *Trichinopoly District Gazetteer* at Minister's house. He likes the British spelling—as though Thiruchi were a transplanted Greek city. In any case, this has been universally shortened to "Trichy" or "Thiruchi"—certain names are a mouthful for Tamils and non-Tamils uniformly. Families of the region, though, call the city Kottai—fort—for the city's most prominent feature, a small mountain fortified by the illustrious Nayaks in their reign, now the site of the city's favoured temple.

Kottai is the last stop before Thiruchi Junction, and Vairum remembers, when he was eleven and just learning to keep track of such things, panicking when he saw that Minister, who had brought him to Thiruchi on their annual shoe-buying trip, wasn't moving. He only knew Thiruchi by this name and naturally thought they were missing their stop. Minister laughed and patted his knee. "Kottai is Kottai, m'boy, and Trichy is Trichy. See?" he said, pointing at the sign as they pulled into the main station.

Vairum shakes his head at the memory as they pull into the big station now. He was so green! Murthy is still drowsing, his head lolling to all points of the compass, and Vairum shakes him. He waits for the two immense, slumbering barristers opposite them to wake and arrange themselves so he can extract his valise from behind their legs—brothers, they had explained in the early part of the journey, when everyone was alert and conversational. The young barristers, who were in Kulithalai doing an official and personal favour for an old friend, are also St. Joseph's alumni and heartily pleased to meet the young admittee. They are so obese that each occupies nearly half the wooden bench, their legs dangling forward over the below-bench storage area like mahogany pillars in some hall of justice.

As the train halts, Murthy wakes, smacking his lips, and rearranges his oily *kudumi*—the hairstyle, front of the head shaved, the rest in a ponytail, has not yet been thrust from fashion by British influence—so that it is equally but differently dishevelled. "We're here."

It seems to Vairum that the equivalent of the entire population of Kulithalai streams past on the platform. The thrill of arrival in the city never seems to diminish. And now he is to live here!

The barristers awaken with snorts, compose their linen jackets, put on their Parsi-style caps. Murthy follows them to the door with

Vairum's suitcase and they exchange addresses on the platform. The lawyers will change trains here to return home, and Murthy and Vairum are cordially invited to visit if ever they find themselves in Pandiyoor, a market town in the Madurai district.

Murthy leads Vairum along the platform, past the first- and second-class resting rooms, past the steamy tiffin stand, past the small station offices panelled in dark wood and full of uniformed men with moustaches, toward the exit, beyond which the city quivers, mirage-like and muscular.

Late that afternoon, back in Cholapatti, Sivakami has cooked a lot of food and is wondering who will eat it. She has little appetite.

She wanders into the garden. The birds are getting active in antic-ipation of the evening cool, and the yard seems very loud. Was it this loud when Vairum was still here? She checks on the progress of the papaya, notes the coconut palms look a bit dry. From the northeast, she can hear hoots of young male laughter—the Brahmin quarter's youth gathering to go to Kulithalai for an evening of loitering in the market square. Muchami tells her that the ones with money play cards at the club. She imagines her Samanthibakkam nephews doing exactly the same. Nice boys, but not brilliant. What if she had stayed, and seen those boys going to secular schools, and her own son in a mediocre local paadasaalai? He would have grown bitter, sharper than any of them, but with no potential to earn. His cousins were friendly when they were small, but during ten years of living on her brothers' good-will, their relations would have changed. It wouldn't have been char-ity; she would have paid all of her own costs and Vairum's, but no one would have been permitted to know or acknowledge this; that would be bad form. Vairum would not have been the king of that household, the way he is here, in his own home. She imagines her nephews calling Vairum's name and laughing.

But she is not imagining it. The boys on the other side of her gar-den wall, they are talking about her son. She moves closer, though there is no need, their voices are clear as well water.

"He came of age and was taken away!" one snorts, impressed at his own wit.

"Yeah, he came of age and rode away on a bullock cart!" says another, as though it was he who thought of it.

"Like a bride!" says another, as though no one had understood the joke before.

Sivakami knows, through her sources, that none of these boys made any mark, academically. There was only one other Cholapatti boy, apart from Vairum, who had done well. He had gone to Thanjavur, where one of his four sisters was married into a family of revenue officials. His parents had eight other sons, two of whom might even be in the crowd massed at her garden wall. Their brother was not being insulted.

Sivakami crouches by her wall, her face hot.

Then a neighbouring door opens: not Murthy's, to her left, but the other, to her right, Dharnakarna, the witch.

From beyond her eastern wall, Sivakami hears the young witch's slightly muffled voice: "Move away from my door with your dirty talk!"

The boys escape toward town, yelping with shared fear and collective bravado like skinny yellow pi-dogs.

Safe.

Dear Amma,
Murthy Periappa will have told you all about our trip, so I don't need to.

 The names of the three other boys in my hostel room are K. Govindasamy, an Iyer boy, C.S. Francis Lourdesamy, a Christian, obviously, and S.K. Natarajan, a Reddiar. They are all in the sciences stream, like me, though Lourdesamy really wants to be a priest.

 As Minister Mama coached me, I explained about my skin condition before my roommates could ask, and they have helped to defend me against those who don't understand. We in our cell are enlightened people, not given to old folkways.

 I know you want to know about every single meal I eat, but I'm not going to write about that. I won't lose any weight, that's enough.

*The masters really want to give us a challenge. This
is a big change from Kulithalai school where the teachers
were always afraid I would already know more than they
did. I didn't. (Not always.) But here, I can have as
much extra homework as I want. Most of the other boys
don't want extra, obviously. I am taking extra maths,
physics and chemistry—won't bore you with the details.*

Your son,
Vairum

Sivakami folds the letter exactly as Vairum must have, far away in
Kottai, in a room she will never see. She knows he knows she is upset by
the idea of his rooming with a Reddiar and can barely stomach the
thought of his sleeping in the same room with a Christian, probably
from a family of converted untouchables, she thinks, masses of whom
were convinced by missionaries that Christians don't have any truck
with caste. He's almost certainly descended from a lower caste, at the
least. She's amazed the other Brahmin boy's parents permit it, but
maybe they have as little control as she feels she does. When Vairum
was admitted to a Christian college, she worried this would be the
result, but Murthy persuaded her. St. Joseph's is an excellent college,
even if it's not a Hindu one.

She slips the letter back into its envelope, imagining his hands
doing that, writing his sums, eating his food. She tries to imagine the
food, picturing great steaming vats of rice attended by Brahmin
cooks. Chinnarathnam had made discreet inquiries on her behalf
and reported that there were both vegetarian and non-vegetarian
dining halls and that the cooks in the vegetarian hall were Brahmin,
one of a few concessions by the British administration to the Brahmin
parents, whose sons make up a significant segment of the student
population.

She places the letter before the Ramar. Later, she will haltingly
read it aloud for Muchami and Mari since they, too, relish news of
Vairum's great adventure.

VAIRUM FOLDS THE FINE PAPER in half and in half again and slips it into a pinkish-brown envelope. He scoops a crusty gob of official-smelling mashed-rice paste from the small pot on the corner of the worktable he shares with Francis Lourdesamy and smears it across the underside of the envelope flap. He addresses the sealed envelope to Minister and Gayatri: another brief but chatty note, another promise kept. He makes a point of thanking Minister for his advice and asking after their children. He does like the idea that he has people to write to, even if there is little he really wants to tell them.

He's alone in his room and, as he folds his jingling pouch of silver into the waist of his dhoti, he wonders where the others are. His money pouch doesn't include the silver piece he was permitted to keep from the gathering of coins that marked his return to Cholapatti. That coin is folded into his waistband, as always, separate from his spending money. It is, after all these years, as much a part of his daily toilet as hair oil and a fresh shirt. No one knows it's there, and he doesn't feel dressed without it.

He leaves the hostel and passes the temple tank, nervously putting his palms together to greet two of the maths masters, who overtake him, absorbed in serious conversation. They nod back, busy, friendly. Their recognition inflates him.

Exiting the campus gate, he takes the long way around the traffic roundabout, idly browsing the knick-knacks for sale. A woman squats against the wall of the main St. Joseph's campus, behind an array of Ganesha statuettes. The largest is about eight inches tall, the smallest about two. They are beautiful: crude, geometric, of a wood so light as to seem made of foam. Vairum picks the little fellows up admiringly, one by one. Vermilion dots the pointed crown, the noble forehead, the trunk, hands, belly, feet—thirteen auspicious red smudges. Three grooves mark the bridge between the beady black eyes, three grooves cross the belly to imply a modest garment.

Vairum bends over the elephant-headed gods, unmindful of traffic and dust in the road, ignoring the woman grinning in fear at his white patches while unceasingly extolling her wares' spiritual and artistic value.

He must have one—a companion to witness the commencement of this new enterprise, to help put the shoulder to unseen obstacles that may yet block his twisted road. He extracts from his pouch the price of a smart-looking fellow about three and a half inches tall.

His new purchase in one hand, his letter in the other, he waits now to cross to the post office when Govindasamy, one of his room-mates, pulls up in front of him on a bicycle, and the others on another bike just behind him.

"Where were you, man?" calls Nattu, louder than necessary, as he falls off the handlebars. "We were looking for you."

"Um, meeting with my physics tutor." He grins back at them shyly.

Govindasamy points to his own handlebars. "Get on. We're going swimming."

"Ah, I—" Vairum looks at the letter in his hand, savouring their insistence.

"Get on," Nattu yells again, already remounted. Francis wheels unsteadily through the traffic to turn left, narrowly missing a gourd vendor and his cart. They're going to the river, the Kaveri, whose vicious seductions his mother had explicitly instructed him to resist, the only condition of his departure. This very afternoon, arriving at the physics building, his eye had caught, not for the first time, on a high-water mark memorializing one time the river had flooded the campus, running across fields to embrace the city in a morbid hug. Then there are times when one or another of the river's dams are, without warning, released . . .

Govindasamy jabs his hand aggressively in the direction of his handlebars once more. "Get on!"

Oh, the sweetness of one's company desired!

Vairum hops up on the handlebars, smiling widely as Govindasamy pushes off through the traffic.

The sun jigs on the docile water like Krishna on the defeated serpent's hoods. Children splash and shriek, their mothers wash clothes. The city bakes. It's the driest time of year. Vairum licks his lips; they taste of dust, of a cracked, parched road. Does the river look so wet and cool in Cholapatti? So meek? His feet rub sweatily in his shoes as he approaches the ghat with his friends.

This part of the river is three miles from the college. Vairum, looking up, sees the top edge of the Rock Fort, Malai Kottai. Here, the river looks more hospitable than agricultural, tame as an embassy party. Govindasamy, Francis and Nattu shed their clothes and descend the stairs at a point where the river is deep and narrow, dive in and swim to the opposite bank. Vairum hangs back a moment, his mouth open a little, gaping or panting, then shucks his shoes and clothes.

Ganesha sits on the bank, atop the letter addressed to Gayatri and Minister, facing the river as Vairum takes his first tentative steps down the stairs of the little ghat. The water is cool and Vairum first squats and splashes water on his dusty skin, then topples joyfully into the wet.

A cooling wind skims the water. The wooden Ganesha, light as river spume, topples onto its back and gazes at the sky. The letter lifts into the air, drops into the water and floats downstream. Cholapatti is the other way.

21.
Two Blooms
1920

JUST PRIOR TO THE DEEPAVALI HOLIDAYS, in his second year of college, Vairum is required to attend a wedding. He is the family delegate to such occasions, since his mother is a widow and not invited and his sister, though invited, would be dependent on her husband to bring her. If the wedding is too far away, he can generally make an excuse, but at least three or four times a year it happens that the connection or location is too close for him to avoid it.

In this case, one of those Samanthibakkam cousins closest to him in age is marrying a girl from Thiruchi, so Vairum has no means whatever of wriggling free. He spends such occasions in a contemptuous funk, a quartz isle in what he perceives as a sea of mental poverty and ambitionlessness, and must employ elaborate means to keep himself from slumping into a puttylike pile of boredom. When he was small, he used to say multiplication tables under his breath for the entire time, three or five or, once, seven days running. The longer his attendance at the wedding the larger the final figure. These days, he occupies himself with the formulas of borders and business that will make him a big man.

His entire gang of Samanthibakkam cousins is in attendance, and Vairum vaguely recollects a great enthusiasm and warmth he had for them when he was very young, but age and time have intruded, and a shyness grown. They speak, but they don't really know what to speak about. He avoids his aunts and uncles, who, on greeting him, all made cracks about the fact that the cousin marrying is his coeval, and isn't it time Vairum got hitched as well? Sivakami has been asking him about this for the last six months, and he has firmly curtailed her: he is focusing on his studies; he isn't ready.

He has not talked to her about the extreme anxiety of the prospect of a girl-seeing, given the reaction of most people to his skin condition. He would prefer to put off even thinking about it.

He stands at the back of the hall, fingering the coin at his waist under his new woollen vest. The weather has just recently grown temperate enough for him to show it off. All at once, a hushed reverence falls upon the gathering, from front to back. From the front, a veena's lambent notes flow forward to occupy the quiet. A young girl plays, looking as if she had been born between the two gourd-resonators, her left hand maintaining the drone with rhythmic strokes while her right hand plucks the melody from the strings.

This is a new trend and the assembly is stunned. Only two kinds of music have ever been heard at weddings. The first is the *nadaswaram*, a six-foot horn with an obscene, nasal sound, with the *thavil*, a double-sided drum whose hard surfaces are staccatoed by fingertips encased in strips of cloth hardened with rice paste. Musicians are low caste—Brahmins expect them to be heard but not seen. Detached, uninterested, they play a particular song for each phase of the ceremony, and in crucial moments make a huge tootling din so as to drown out any sneeze. Sneezes are very bad omens at weddings.

The other music appropriate to weddings is religious songs, wheezed at prescribed moments by revered matrons. They know all the words, though their thin voices often disagree on tune and timing.

But now here is Vani, a young Brahmin girl, playing "Vallabha Nayakasya," the veena's tones breathed deep with devotion and training. Worthy of Madras concert halls (some think but do not say "brothels"), this Vani sits before them in the midst of a provincial wedding. Vairum hears the scandalized whispers start with the *mridangam*'s downbeat, as Vani finishes a brief but confident *aalapanai* like a first few raindrops against glass.

"What is this spectacle—a girl playing a concert at a wedding?"

"I have heard about such things. My son's wife's people are from Madras city. They have been doing such . . . concerts, at weddings, since two years now."

"Who is this girl?"

"Bride's mother's uncle's daughter's daughter."

"Oh, yes, yes, the bride's family does try to be far too fashionable. I knew it would not be the groom's side arranging such things . . ."

"Pandiyoor girl?"

"Yes, pretty, isn't she? Different, somehow."

"Very fair, isn't she?"

"That skin—almost, I don't know, something different . . ."

Luminous. Vani's light draws Vairum as a moth to a cool, white flame.

He goes home to Cholapatti for the Deepavali holidays. Sivakami brings him more snacks, in greater variety, than he would ever want to eat, and begins asking him a thousand questions about the wedding. It's bad enough, he thinks, that he has to go and represent the family because his mother is a widow and disallowed. Should he also waste his brain-space remembering sari styles and hush-hushed gossip?

He cuts his mother off, rude but not unkind; she should know by now he doesn't pay attention to those things. Sivakami quickly reins in her only greed, the greed for details. She can understand and almost sympathize with his lack of interest: she herself was far less interested in weddings when she was free to attend them.

But Vairum is speaking.

" . . . I have completed eighteen years, now, Amma. It's time for me to marry."

Sivakami smiles cautiously at what she thinks is a concession. She had said just these words to him on his previous visit, and he had vehemently denied every part of it then, even his age.

He nods and purses his lips, businesslike. "I will marry Vani, daughter of Parthasarathy of Pandiyoor."

"You will . . . who?"

"She is the only reason for speaking of this idiotic wedding I attended," Vairum answers, already heading for the stairs to his upper refuge, picking his college satchel up on the way.

She watches it banging against his bony hip as he disappears into the upper reaches.

"Who is she?" Sivakami calls after him, a note of exasperation in her question such as she rarely employs with him.

"The one I will marry," he calls from above.

The next time Sivakami sees him—the next meal—she protests in gentle, persistent tones. "Vairum, kanna, a boy's family never makes the first move. You should be thinking about your studies, now. The time will come soon, and I will initiate some proceedings . . ."

"Enough, Amma," he responds, though she has numerous wheedlings still to deploy. "This is my decision."

"You cannot make such a decision, you are just a boy!"

"Throughout history men have made such decisions," he informs her. "Nowadays boys wait for their parents to present a girl or two and they say yes I will have her or I like this one better. I have already chosen and I will not have anyone else."

"I will speak to your uncles," she responds weakly, because she doesn't really believe they will make any effort to change his mind. Perhaps, perhaps the girl will be suitable.

"Do what you need to do." Vairum speaks as though to a minion. "Just make sure I am married to her. Soon."

When did that awkward little boy gain such confidence, such command? Maybe in his classes, where his performance has been exceptional. Perhaps it is life on his own in the city which has toughened him. Or maybe it was that moment when he, standing before the stage, caught the eye of the beautiful musician and saw her miss a note and smile a little and look away shyly, and glance back.

That night, Sivakami lies awake. This girl, Vani. She might be fine.

Venketu, Sivakami's second brother, could object. His daughter is seven or eight, and Vairum should be hers, by rights. But Venketu has been cool to Sivakami ever since she left their house. The youngest,

Subbu, has been warmer, as if to compensate, but she thinks none of them realize what a bright future Vairum is going to have.

Barring serious objections, she expects she will give in to her son. Then all she will have to worry about is the family rejecting the blotches on his skin. Perhaps Minister will find some way to finesse that. On subjects of diplomacy, he seems inexhaustible.

She rises and exits the pantry, where she sleeps, to do her beading by the moonlight in the main hall, conscious of Vairum's breathing on the mat beside the northernmost pillar. He chose to sleep downstairs this first evening—a gesture of tenderness toward his mother? She wants to think so. The slight sound of his breath fills the room.

By discreet means, Sivakami issues a request for information.

Her mole returns from Pandiyoor: Kantha, a hustle-bustle busybody whose nine yards of sari, given mid-region spread, suggest a spindle bundled with bright thread. Her tongue pricks like a spindle, too. She enters already wailing, "Oohh, Sivakami, Sivakami, it is all too unfortunate."

Sivakami bids her sit and offers a tumbler of water on a tray, the minimal mark of hospitality. She asks, "What have you learned?"

Kantha pours the water down her throat, head craned back to receive the stream, completely still but for a pulse in her neck like the gills of a shark. She fixes Sivakami with a beady, knowing eye, then her face softens into a well-practised expression between pity and conspiracy.

"Such a beautiful girl," Kantha begins in an ominous tone. "So accomplished."

Sivakami cuts to the chase. "She is married already?"

"Oh, don't they wish," Kantha says as though the words are delicious. She wants to draw this out.

"They have unfounded provincial superstitions about skin conditions."

The phrase "provincial superstitions" sounds stiff and unfamiliar, especially pronounced by one so provincial and superstitious as Sivakami, but Kantha looks interested at the possible bonus of learning more about Vairum's troubles. She shakes her head slowly.

"I doubt it—they are hopelessly sophisticated. Practically foreign! But surely your son . . ."

"So what's the trouble?" Sivakami cuts her off.

"Her horoscope is very bad." Kantha pauses to measure Sivakami's reaction while Sivakami works to keep her face neutral. "Very bad. It says . . . she will not have children, and only a very small minority of configurations could counter this. How is your son's horoscope?"

"Don't know," Sivakami replies, after a significant pause, in a mechanistic murmur noted and filed by the spindle, who knows fully well the rumours about the causes of Sivakami's widowhood.

"There's not much chance of a match, sadly," Kantha continues. "Sadly for them, too: her parents are getting desperate. Two years now they have been searching."

Sivakami tries to stay all business. "Is there anything else? They are a modern family—does the girl travel well escorted?"

"Oh, yes," Kantha yawns. "They are all too interested in their arts-shmarts, but this girl is their precious gem. No chances taken, I'm glad to say." She's not glad.

"And how do they feel about horoscopes?" Sivakami asks with deliberate coolness. "Are they looking for a boy whose horoscope will counter hers?"

"But it is so rare, Sivakami Akka!" Kantha is authoritative, encouraging. "They have been searching for years! And these modern people, aristocrats—they probably don't even follow the horoscopes. They just did it because how else to find a groom?"

When Sivakami closes the door behind Kantha, she paces the length of the main hall, feeling her cracked heels grind against the brick tiles. She is sure she can smell the sandalwood box, tucked within the safe. She can smell it from the farthest end of the hall. She doesn't want to touch it.

It comes to her: she doesn't have to. Vairum has made up his mind, and nothing about the horoscope will change it.

A responsible parent, though, would try to dissuade him.

"Little one," she starts when he returns from the fields. "There is bad news on the marriage front."

"What?" Vairum is clearly not interested in hearing objections.

"She cannot have children."

"She is only ten years old, of course she cannot have children."

"Don't be obscene." She purses her lips primly. "Her horoscope? They have been searching for a groom for two years and have found none to accept her."

"Pah! No one believes in that stuff any more. You know what I think of horoscopes? This!" Vairum mimes setting a fire and watching it blaze. "Superstition! Folk tales and false science!"

Sivakami imagines firelight on his face and suddenly the image shifts so she is remembering him as a baby, standing by his father's funeral pyre. Vairum had, as instructed, tossed a burning faggot onto the dried cow dung patties and was pulled back by his relatives as the fire licked through the layers of wood and warmed his father's corpse. *Had he known what he was doing?* Sivakami wonders. She recalls that he was crying. *Does he remember?*

His horoscope consigned his father to flames, and now he'd like to set his horoscope similarly ablaze.

She says weakly, "You must have children."

"We will have children! We will have ten children! You will see. Horoscopes are nothing. Less than nothing. Ashes of something long dead." He blows imaginary ashes from his palm and dusts his hands one against the other. "It's a new century, Amma, science and religion have triumphed over astrology and superstition. Come. Let's ask God."

The next day, Sivakami and Vairum mount the hill to the Rathnagirishwarar temple. The rains have come, as they generally do around this time of year, and they use banana leaves to cover their plate of offerings—coconuts, bananas, betel, yellow and pink flowers, camphor, turmeric, cash—and two paper packets. One packet contains a small red rose and the other a large white jasmine. They are roughly the same size, indistinguishable one from another, as impartial and innocuous as most instruments of fate—lemons, for instance.

Red is auspicious, the colour of vermilion powder and wedding saris. If Vairum chooses this flower, the wedding will proceed. White is the colour of death and if he selects this flower, plans for a wedding with Vani will quietly die.

The middle-aged priest takes the plate and, without ever looking at them directly, asks brusquely their reason for coming. He gives the coconut to a junior priest who uses an iron blade set in the floor by the sanctum to cut off its fibrous hair and break it open. The older priest lights the camphor and fussily rearranges the things on the plate. He waves the plate around, muttering, professionally bad-tempered, stuffs the yellow and pink blossoms into a few niches around the bottom of the lingam, takes half the coconut, some bananas and the money, and hands back the plate. The younger priest smiles at them.

Sivakami receives the plate and nods to Vairum. His hand hovers. He chooses one packet. He untucks the first fold and unfolds the next.

Red.

The rose petals rise, freed from the paper wrapping, like a ruffled sigh.

They return home in the rain, a triumphant smile across Vairum's face, and a resigned one on Sivakami's.

Sivakami makes a few well-placed remarks, speaking within the hearing of others as well as encouraging Gayatri to pass along information. There is nothing wrong with Vairum's horoscope—she makes that clear—they are simply not interested in horoscopes. Others have said such things, progressives, people like that. Vairum is in college, it is believable that he might feel this way. He cut off his kudumi last year in favour of a Western style; he looks like a modern thinker. Sivakami had been dismayed, but it is not unknown, these days. She emphasizes her son's impeccable lineage, his stellar future. Not the future determined by the stars, but his likeliness to be a star in the future. He will be a leader of Brahmins. He will earn cash, not paddy. A good boy, from a good family.

Gossip takes its course. Soon, they receive an invitation, almost identical to the one Sivakami's father sent Hanumarathnam a lifetime ago. Originality is praised in very few areas of life. In the matter of a wedding, it is nearly unthinkable.

Vairum attends the appointment with Sivakami's eldest and youngest brothers. At the girl-seeing, Vani's family plays her to advantage. She is exceptionally beautiful and Vairum is even more captivated. Vani smiles at him—without shyness or apparent distaste at his progressive bleaching—and seals the pact.

And look at this coincidence: when Vairum enters Vani's house for the girl-seeing ceremony, he is greeted by the two young barristers he met on the train to Thiruchi when first he left home for college. They are Vani's own uncles! It must be fate's working, all jollily agree.

The girl's parents are plainly thrilled. Sivakami's brothers enjoy the food Vani serves and the song she plays. They give broad hints that everything is satisfactory, but they really don't much care. Returning to Cholapatti, they put on concerned and condescending airs as they advise Sivakami to go ahead. She perceives that they are being cavalier, but this was expected. Vairum floats in, dreamy, blissful. This is more significant. He has been pleased. His sharp edges are momentarily cloaked in cloud, but just as fog vanishes under heat, so any objections from his mother would unsheathe his will.

Eight months later, Vairum and Vani are married.

———⸙

SO LOOK AT VAIRUM, a college student, married to the girl who will become the woman of his dreams. At first glance, it would seem he is becoming exactly what his mother intended when she tore him from Samanthibakkam and reinstalled him in Cholapatti, sacrificing his happiness on his behalf. If he had known what he would receive in return for his suffering, would he himself have placed his contentment on the altar? None of us will ever know.

He lives in the carapace of a happy young man. He has routines that build on his interests and skills, that give his life the appearance of balance. At college, he works hard and is rewarded with knowledge, honours and respect. He has friends.

One of those boys is distantly related to two wealthy merchant families in Cholapatti and goes there for weekends from time to time, since his own family lives in Thanjavur, a bit far to travel for such a short break. When his friend visits, Vairum is invited to be a fourth for tennis at the Kulithalai club and finds it a pleasant diversion at the end of a long day spent in studies and land management. He begins to frequent the club whenever he is home for the weekend, becoming a regular in singles and doubles within a rotating set of sons and fathers of the landed classes. Often he stops on the way home for a lemon soda with a few of them, though never with the Brahmins.

Why not with the Brahmins? Sivakami wonders. Is he shunning his own caste or are they shunning him or is it something buried, less specific, which neither he nor the group would admit? Vairum doesn't feel he needs to admit anything, he simply has never had friends among the Cholapatti Brahmins, and age and distance are not changing this.

Distance is begetting distance, in fact—Vairum is tethered to the village, as they all are, by his land and history. The difference is that he is shod for a great step out into the world. The barbs are beginning to fly, and from this distance, they look a lot like the stones that hailed upon him as a child in his glass house. But now his carapace of contentment is formed, and hail what may, he can retreat within it.

22.
Yellow Money
1920–1921

THANGAM HAS RETURNED HOME heavily pregnant with her third child: It's a boy, a boy! Sivakami is more assured in this birth than she has been in the last two, and her confidence grows as she hands the baby, red and screaming with good health, to his mother. Surely, thinks Sivakami, surely his chubby hands will wipe away the worry lines that have settled on his mother's face in the years of her marriage. A boy will be active, mischievous. He will clutch and tear Thangam's dulling mask of anxiety.

Thangam and the baby emerge for the single day of his naming ceremony and then withdraw once more. Two more weeks pass, but Sivakami cannot tell: has the mask rent? On the nineteenth day, Thangam and the baby come out into the sunlight of the courtyard. They bathe, and Thangam's gold dust silts up the narrow courtyard gutters. She looks calmer than she did on arrival, but the sides of her tongue and the lower rim of her eyelids are tinged a bluish grey. Is she or is she not relieved to have delivered a boy?

The little girls must be relieved to have their mother back, though they might have mixed feelings about the new baby. Saradha, the older one, especially—she had immense difficulty in adjusting to Cholapatti. On arrival, her eyes the size of palm fruits, she had clung to Thangam so vehemently that twice the expectant mother had tripped and fallen, prompting Sivakami to wonder if the child wasn't jealous and trying to endanger the coming baby. Thangam told her, though, that it was the change of place: they had moved a year earlier, and Saradha had behaved in just the same manner. Saradha is not so much attached to her mother as attached to her routine, to things familiar. It's true: Saradha violently protested much of what was required of her the first few days, and then insisted, with equal, desperate, vehemence, on doing all the same things every day after that: prayers with her grandmother, whom she conscientiously never touches until after supper, breakfast with Mari, late-morning visit with Rukmini next door, off to Muchami's village with him, where she takes a nap in his hut, back for tiffin and games with the children who still gather around the veranda whenever Thangam is in town, nursery rhymes on Sivakami's lap at night, by which time this is permitted. When Thangam emerges from her childbed seclusion, Saradha schedules intervals when she will sit by her mother's side and coo at her new baby brother. She is not difficult to tend, provided any change, anything new, is introduced only as a modification of her routine.

"Will Saradha be as upset by your return home as she was by her arrival here?" Sivakami asks.

Thangam smiles mildly and shrugs.

Sivakami persists, "When are you going to move house again?"

In eight months.

If Saradha were like her younger sister, Sivakami muses, there would be no need to worry, but the two couldn't be more different. Where Saradha approaches everything with a seriousness beyond her years or understanding, Visalam seems to see everything as a joke. Every creature, every event makes her laugh, really laugh, good-naturedly; she is not mocking or spiteful, and she is obedient. Sivakami thinks perhaps she should be worried about her unconventional behaviour, but she has so many other more urgent matters to worry about.

Thangam's health, for example. She looks weak, too weak even, apparently, to have any interest in her newest baby. With the first baby, Saradha, Thangam showed at least some curiosity, at the child's tiny fingers and toes. Sivakami saw her once tickling the child's pretty chin, though with an absent air. She didn't see what she expected, the adoration that Thangam had shown her little brother all those years ago, that which holds most new parents in helpless thrall.

The little boy, since he was first given the breast, seems to have fed through every waking hour and Thangam has barely looked at him. Thangam's milk flows from her breast, the roses from her cheeks, the gold from . . . where? Her skin, her hair? How will she have the energy to relocate three children? And the last is a boy—when they next move, he will, at eight months, need constant attention. The girls also need at least minimal supervision. Goli's salary and status should permit a couple of servants, but Sivakami has deduced that there are none. Does he fire them, do they quit, does he forget to tell them when they move? How will Thangam cope?

Sivakami chews her lip and selects a bead, tilting her head against the moonbeam illuminating her work. She hears the baby suckling, the breathing of the little girls on their mats in the main hall. Saradha should stay here in Cholapatti, that's what. And when the next baby comes, Visalam should stay. And with the next, this little boy, whose burgeoning belly has already earned him the nickname Laddu, "sweet ball." Thangam need only keep her youngest two with her, need only move and tend two children. Sivakami is thirty-four but, having had only two children, feels she has the strength and energy of women half her age.

She proposes the idea to Thangam, who looks reflective and says nothing. Boarding one's children with a relative is common enough, after all. Gayatri's first son, whose father was determined to educate him in an English-medium school, had gone at the age of five to live with Gayatri's second cousin in Madras city. Nor is parental authority sacrosanct: it's Goli's parents who have the last word on the children. She will have to wait for their response.

Six weeks after Thangam finishes her seclusion, Goli comes to Cholapatti.

He comes at tiffin time, greets Thangam briefly and pats the new baby on the head. Sivakami had no warning of his arrival and is concerned that she has been caught with nothing fancy enough to serve a son-in-law. Goli looks a little more inclined than usual to wait, though, and in fifteen minutes she has made a semolina pudding with cashews, one of the quickest sweets in the repertoire, and Thangam serves it to her husband along with idlis, steamed rice cakes, and a coconut chutney while the baby naps in his hammock in the corner of the main hall. When she comes back to fetch the *mulaghapodi*, a powdered chili and lentil condiment, Sivakami tells her, "You should speak to the son-in-law about my suggestion." Goli will not stay with them—it's not appropriate for a man to take advantage of his wife's family to that degree—so Thangam's only opportunities would be ones like this, and perhaps only this one, since Goli is exceptionally immobile today. He looks tired.

Thangam goes to squat by him while he eats. She says something Sivakami can't hear. He takes a moment to look up, as though he hadn't noticed her. "What?" he asks. Thangam speaks again as he frowns at her. "This is your mother's idea?"

Thangam doesn't look at him.

Goli eats for a moment without speaking. "I suppose it makes sense, doesn't it? Chutney?"

Thangam comes to fetch the chutney. *The matter is not technically concluded*, Sivakami thinks, and wonders if the parents will overrule the son. She looks toward the courtyard. Muchami has finished his tiffin and observed this exchange. He looks at her but says nothing, and she knows they will speak later.

Saradha has eaten her tiffin in the back with Muchami as usual. Sivakami had asked if she didn't want to go eat with her appa, but the little girl shook her head, looking frightened, whether of her father or of the change in routine. Visalam is still too little to feed herself, but as Goli drinks his coffee, she takes him the top she has been playing with. He obligingly spins it a couple of times as she laughs mightily, and then he appears to lose interest, though she continues playing with it, without appearing to notice he is no longer involved.

"I'm off, then," he says, and leaves.

Sivakami, though gratified by the length and relative normalcy of his visit, is alarmed by the abrupt departure. As Thangam gets her younger daughter's tiffin, Sivakami asks her, "Did the son-in-law say how many days he would be in town? I have to get your things ready."

Thangam shrugs.

Later, while Thangam rests, Sivakami raises the topic with Muchami. "I've come up with a plan."

"Are the babies staying here?" he asks.

"One can't surprise you with anything, huh?" she asks, smiling a little.

"That's my job." He shrugs, also smiling.

"Only the eldest. When Thangam has another, we'll keep Visalam. And so on."

"It's a good idea. The son-in-law has been in Cholapatti a couple of days already, trying to find investors for a business idea. I take it that one of the friends he has made here has agreed to front for it."

Seeing Sivakami's look of confusion, he clarifies.

"That is, the friend put up some of the initial money and his name will be on it, but he has had trouble getting others to invest, so the son-in-law has come to convince others."

"Ah. What kind of business?"

"Hm." He wishes she hadn't asked. "Ah, a cigar and cigarette manufactory."

"What?" Sivakami is scandalized. At the very least, she thought Goli was a decent sort. She's sure he doesn't dabble in such vices himself, but even pandering to others is hardly upstanding.

"Honestly, Amma, I don't think it's going to move," he hastens to say. "There's so much involved: you have to convince a landowner to switch over to tobacco, teach the tenant how to grow it. It's a very particular soil type, I think, that is good for it. It's not an easy proposition. Of course, if anyone can sell it, it's the son-in-law," he continues, as though to himself. Looking at Sivakami again, though, he backtracks. "But I'm sure he won't."

What he keeps to himself is that Goli has been spending early evenings in the club and later evenings in places of even lesser repute, spending beyond what Muchami would guess to be the means of a low-level official with three children to support, as well as losing money at cards. Friends who deal in such things have told him this is how big men do business: "You have to spend money to make money, Muchami!" But Goli's prospects of making money on this seem to Muchami so dicey that he fears the son-in-law is just spending money to spend it. No wonder he didn't object to the transfer of one of the children to Sivakami's home: all the more available income for him to invest in his "outside interests."

Sivakami instructs Mari to wash the babies' things and Thangam's saris, then gives them a final rinse herself, so that they are free of lower-caste pollution, throwing them over rods in the courtyard with a pole that she also uses to spread them out to dry. The next day, since Goli didn't say when Thangam should be ready, Sivakami exhausts herself making snacks for Thangam to take with her: crunchy swirls of savory *thangoril,* fried patties of ghee-soaked *appam,* great for nursing mothers, and in honour of the new baby, a load of *laddus.* She packs them in aluminum tins while Rukmini folds and packs their clothes.

It's well she does, because the next morning, Goli steps into the house long enough only to call, "Hup, hup! Come! The next train leaves in forty-five minutes! I'm having a word with an associate, then we go." He vanishes along the Brahmin quarter.

It is only eight o'clock, more than two hours before the mid-morning meal. Mari has not arrived; Muchami is out in the fields. Sivakami is forced to go and ask Murthy to send someone to find Muchami, who must ready the bullock cart. Rukmini has Saradha over next door to play, as is their routine each day at this time.

Thirty minutes later, the cart is packed and Thangam settled in the back with Visalam and Laddu, but Goli has not returned. Fifteen minutes pass; the train will have departed. Thangam is unloaded, faint from the heat of the street. She trails her gold dust back into the house. It is the hottest season—no one with a choice ventures out from eight to four, when the day bubbles around 100 degrees. It should be forbidden to small children and women recovering from childbirth, Sivakami thinks.

She had not tried to explain to Saradha what was going to happen, though she had a feeling Thangam wouldn't either, unless Sivakami told her to. Sivakami knew the child would be deeply alarmed but also didn't want to prepare her too far in advance, not knowing when Goli had in mind for them to go. The little girl, seeing her mother loaded into the cart, had panicked and started screaming without moving, not wanting to get into the cart but not wanting to let her mother go. Sivakami had hesitated to pick up the child: she would merely need another bath, but she had been madi for so long that it was no longer her first response. Before she could, though, Muchami ran and scooped up the little girl, pressing her face to his shoulder, shushing and rocking her until she calmed down. He has carried her to his home village every day since her arrival—she is still too small to be contaminated by contact with the lower castes, though she is made to change her clothes in the courtyard before re-entering the house—and she is as close to him as to Sivakami now.

Once she stopped yelling, he explained to her in soft tones what was happening. She continued to cry softly on his shoulder; he carried her back through the garden to the courtyard, where she changed clothes and came back through the house to take Rukmini's hand on the veranda. She follows her routine for the rest of the day, though from time to time hiccups rack her little chest and tears track the peach-fuzz cheeks as she doggedly helps Mari to sort the rice or Muchami to feed the cows.

The next train is now not for two hours, and they wait nervously for Goli to come, ready to spring into action again. Two hours pass, then four. Muchami has moved the bullock every hour, to try to keep it in the shade. Finally seven hours after he first hollered, Goli leaps up behind the bullock and hollers again. As Murthy makes Thangam and the two youngest children comfortable in the cart, Sivakami attempts a few civil words with her daughter's husband.

"I understand you will next be shifting house at about the time we will celebrate my son's first Pongal with his new bride, but perhaps it will be too much to come with the babies and return in time to take up your next posting . . ."

"How's that? Preposterous!" Goli sounds as though he is addressing a crowd. "Would my wife miss her dear little brother's first real pot of pongal?"

"Also because Thangam's perhaps not strong enough . . ."

"Preposterous!" Goli snaps his shoulder towel at the bullock's rump to punctuate his exclamation. The bullock jolts forward and lumbers the cart around the corner with Muchami looking like there must be some better way.

Sivakami expects, for a time, an indignant reaction from Goli's parents. Indeed, she hopes for one. In her mind, she challenges them to fight for the babies. If they do, she will allow them to take the children. It is only right for children to live with paternal grandparents. Goli and Thangam are moving everywhere, helter-skelter, but strictly because Goli's job requires it. They *stay* in various places. They *live* with Goli's parents.

The paternal grandparents never challenge Sivakami. She assumes they don't have the energy or interest, let alone the will, to raise a brood. Their efforts on Goli's behalf appear to have been desultory, or ineffective: the results were not, she admits, very cheering.

They also perhaps haven't the means to take a child or children in. Not only do they not object, they don't offer assistance, nor do they even ask how she will keep them. But this is the question Sivakami must now confront.

She is the caretaker of her son's property. None of this, not the house, nor trees, nor lands, nor cows, belongs to her. It is her son's duty to support her, but his property does not belong to her, and it certainly would not be proper to use it to support a daughter of the family, or that daughter's children. She had written to Vairum to tell him that Thangam's daughter will now live with them, but had offered no explanations or ramifications, and he didn't ask for any. Perhaps he didn't want to repeat in writing the arguments they have had about Goli. She recalls his suggesting Thangam continue to live with them; he clearly would not object to her children doing so.

There is the income from the lands her brothers have been purchasing and managing on Thangam's behalf. But who knows how many children Thangam will have? How many girls' weddings to pay for, how many boys' schoolings? Sivakami's brothers are condescending, but they don't condescend to share many details of their acquisitions, especially since Sivakami made it clear that she is fully capable of understanding anything they choose to tell her. They are not particularly shrewd or active managers. Chances are that the income from those lands would not support the day-to-day costs of Thangam's family, which gives indications of growing large, in addition to the special costs of festivals and ceremonies. Goli's parents' lands would not feed their grandchildren, neither in their possession or in the hands of others. And Goli, well, it's probably safe to say accounting is not one of his primary interests.

Since Thangam's children will not be supported by any of the overt and respectable channels, Sivakami must gain access to a wealth whose existence depends on a measure of disrespect.

She doesn't know if her brothers suffered pangs of loss when she bundled up her offspring and rejected their plans, but then she didn't show them her pain at this parting, either. What was evident and accepted was that this action hurt their pride. If their relationship to her was not outwardly defined by affection, it was defined by duty, and if their duty was to carry out the responsibilities of the children's dead father, to get the girl married and the boy educated, it was her duty to comply with their image of themselves. Sivakami broke this implied covenant, apparently without a backward glance. Now, despite her having broken one agreement, she needs them to comply with another.

Manjakkani is an inheritance customarily passed from mother to daughter to daughter. Literally, this translates as "yellow money," as though this land, or money, or jewels, were rubbed with turmeric, as is the thread of the thirumangalyam that knots a woman into married life, as is a woman's skin, freshened by the cut edge of that root on finishing her bath.

Many a woman does not receive her manjakkani. Many a woman, married by the time her mother dies, is convinced by her brothers that they need not give her the mother's wealth. She is well enough provided for, they say, and her husband would get it if they gave it to her, and so better it should stay in the family. Many a woman buys this line.

Sivakami's mother, though, on her deathbed, called to her side her only surviving daughter. There, in confidence, she told Sivakami about the battle she had fought with her own brothers, her mother's battle against the mother's brothers, and so on and up and down through the generations to defend the wealth of the family's women.

"God's grace, you will never need this money, as, God's grace, I didn't," she had croaked. "But you may. And even if, by God's grace, you don't, your daughter may. You must therefore fight for it, as I did, and my mother, and my mother's mother . . ." Sivakami's mother trailed off, exhausted, a jewel of spittle nestled in the skin around her mouth.

And Sivakami, though she was very young, newly widowed, not sure how she could afford to confront her brothers, not certain that the unpleasantness would be worthwhile, promised, because what else could she give her mother then? Sivakami was to blame for her husband's death. So, too, for her mother's, whose death proceeded from his.

She had followed her mother's directions and obtained, from a trustee, the document stating the value of lands and gold that should be passed into Sivakami's hands. Now she takes from her safe that yellowed parchment, written by a scribe, inscribed by a judge, stamped with a seal, listing the deeds to three plots of land, adjacent to one another, and a *kaasu maalai,* a necklace of coins weighing eighteen sovereigns. Accompanying the testament is a letter from her mother saying that the ownership of the land transfers to her daughter upon her death. The necklace had come to Sivakami upon her marriage and had been passed to Thangam at hers. The plots of land—large, fertile grounds with old tenants, midway between Sivakami's native village and Cholapatti—are being managed by her brothers. All these years, the income from the plots of land has been going into the family coffers—her brothers'. Sivakami does not begrudge them the income so far. If she had continued to live with them, it would have in some way paid for her and her children.

Sivakami replaces the keys to the safe beneath the loose brick and sits on the floor by the door to the garden, in view of the back room where all her grandchildren have slipped and burst into the world. The light from the garden billows and waves like long gauzy curtains on her left. Before her is a floor desk, a foot high at the near end and sloping up to a height of sixteen inches. She pulls it toward her and smoothes the uneven yellowy paper against the jackwood surface.

Her mother and grandmother fought their battles against their brothers in British courts. Sivakami doesn't know how their foremothers fought before the British; she knows only how she must wage her struggle.

She takes a slate from within the low desk and makes a few calculations based on her knowledge of crops and yields and the recent strengths and weaknesses of the regional agricultural economy. She regards these for a few moments, then lifts the lid of the desk once more and tucks the slate into a ledger within. She sends Muchami to fetch a scribe, the son of the man Hanumarathnam retained all those years ago.

Sivakami is not illiterate, but, with no formal schooling, writing is a labour for her, and her nibs are not really of a quality appropriate to matters of importance. Vairum can write fluently, and has good pens, with proper ink, not the powdered stuff, but it is some time before his next visit. In any case, this letter would take some explaining and this is her initiative alone for now.

Muchami escorts the scribe into the courtyard and enters the house to bring out the small desk. The scribe, seated on the cobblestones, pulls the desk to and arranges upon it his pen, ink and parchment. He confirms that Sivakami, who sits, almost out of view, in the kitchen, has her own wax and seal.

She begins dictating and he writes with terrific grace and fluency, in perfectly straight rows with many flourishes. Muchami watches from the side, his mouth slightly open. He is fascinated by letters and words, the ability to drop them from pen onto paper and pick them up again in recitation.

Twice the scribe makes suggestions as to wording, and Sivakami accepts his suggestions. Though young, he has a lot of experience with official correspondence. He meticulously blots the first copy and places it on the warm stones to dry while he bends to the task of preparing a duplicate.

Sivakami reads the first copy and places it in the safe along with the testament and her mother's letter. She takes out a coin for Muchami to pay the scribe and tells him to pass on her regards to his father, who has inked letters for the town of Kulithalai for more than thirty years. She places the second copy, still slightly damp, at the feet of her gods, prostrates herself before them and sits back on her heels. After a few moments she rises and, by the light of the ghee lamps, readies the letter to go out in the morning mail. She folds it carefully into a homemade envelope and heats a stub of wax marbled with smoke. The wax lique-fies and is about to drip when she notices some dusky gold motes on the paper. They must have been carried, clinging to the document, from the courtyard cobblestones. She tries to blow the motes off of the envelope, but it is too late. The wax drips and churns up the gold flecks. Taking up the brass seal engraved with her husband's initials, she aims and presses.

The wax cools and hardens quickly. Sivakami runs her finger over the cold seal, and then presses her left thumb to it, so long and hard that her husband's initials are depressed in the pad of her digit. She watches the impression fade by the buttery lamplight until her thumb is once again grooved only with that signature which is hers alone, flecked with the odd dot of gold, like the sign of her husband on the fateful letter.

Sivakami's letter reads:

Safe.

My beloved elder brothers:

Greetings to You and my Sisters and Father. I trust this finds You all in the best of health. We are all well here. Vairum is performing well at college and I see him every month or so on those weekends when he has no Saturday classes. On this Deepavali, he will go to his in-laws in Pandiyoor. We are eagerly anticipating that you, also, might come to witness the half-wedding. Thangam, with God's blessings, has followed her two daughters with a son.

Now I must come to the reason for which I am writing. As You know, I have been managing my own financial affairs since the death of my husband and am quite con-versant in the same. This income is more than sufficient for me to run our household and educate my son.

[Sivakami is careful not to overstate this, lest it seem jeering or immodest. But she does state it, because she was right.] *I feel I am meeting my responsibility of maintaining the property here in Cholapatti, in safekeeping for him until he comes of age and can assume management. He also is taking an increasing interest. So, I have no concerns in that regard.*

I am writing to You with a concern of another nature. As you know, my son-in-law holds a very responsible and demanding position. It requires of him that he leave his parents and settle for two-two years in all manner of places and circumstances. It is my observation that although He copes up well with this situation, it is a strain which is telling on Thangam, no less because she is weakened from childbearing, and must care for the children. In light of this, I have kept her eldest child here in Cholapatti, and am planning on keeping each eldest child as another is born.

Which decision brings me to the matter at hand: How to feed and clothe these children under my son's roof? Clearly, I cannot, in good conscience, use Vairum's money to support his sister's children. Although I appreciate the nobility and breeding of the family which You chose so well for Thangam, I know, no less from things You have told me, of their financial instability. It worries me not only that they seem to have little capital but that they seem to be sliding into a worse and worse financial situation, selling off properties below value because they need more money to live than they earn from their lands, but making less and less because they have less and less income property. Please forgive my frankness. I know You will treat this as a matter of confidence. I am not confident they will be able to provide for the children. My son-in-law's salary, also, is still that of a young man, and he has many expenses of a professional nature. [That last had been Muchami's suggestion. Sivakami didn't know how her servant had the vocabulary, but expressed appreciation for it.] *I expect You might suggest the income from the lands You have so astutely purchased and are managing on Thangam's behalf, but those lands were always intended to provide for her children's weddings and schoolings, and I still think they are best suited to that use.*

In light of all this, I have decided it is time for me to make my claim to the manjakkani property which our mother intended to pass to me. I did promise our mother that I would do so at some point, even had I no need, in case Thangam or her daughters should someday require a cushion to fall back upon. I know You will understand and, in memory of our mother, make this easy for me.

Quarter-annually, I will send my man, Muchami, to collect the rent from the lands. Nothing should change for the tenants. I will honour your agreements with them, trusting that you have made arrangements both fair and profitable. I will send word of the first day when he will come.

My namaskarams to all of You. You are in my thoughts and prayers.

I remain, your affectionate sister
H. Sivakami

She had signed her name herself, volunteering as the owlish young scribe penned the last words, to spare him the awkwardness of either presuming she could write her name or asking her for a thumbprint.

She feels proud and nervous about her letter: this was a hard bit of business. And when, after a month, she has received no reply, she sends another letter. It summarizes the first in brief, in case they hadn't received it. It also says that Muchami will be coming on the seventh day of the next lunar month. She receives no reply to the second letter either.

MUCHAMI DISMOUNTS THE TRAIN and tidies himself on the platform, meticulously smoothing dhoti, towel and kudumi. Finding his way
to the first of the plots, he introduces himself to the men he finds in two
huts side by side, at the corners of two sub-plots, farmed by brothers.

Muchami is not surprised to be gravely informed by these men that
the tenants have been told not to pay him a single paisa. Muchami
doesn't know Sivakami's brothers, but their behaviour is predictable to
him. People are very generous about such matters as hospitality, but
that is because they must be. Hospitality is required, by society and religion. It often costs very little, and it gains a person cosmic points.
Generosity with property inheritance is quite a different matter—
especially when the inheritor is a woman. There are so many ways to
justify bilking someone. Muchami frankly admits—to himself and to
Sivakami—that he would challenge his own sisters in just the same
way, should they ever lay a claim to his mother's wealth. Not that she
has any, but if she did, he would try to keep it. As the male issue, he was
charged with the responsibility for his mother. He might someday have
his own inheritors to consider. His sisters left the family when they
married. They are not suffering for money. Let their husbands take care
of them. He can easily imagine Sivakami's brothers' thoughts.

Muchami makes his rounds of the tenants, just to check the information he's been given. They are a little suspicious of his youth and
cowed by the brilliance of his dhoti and the confidence with which he
wields his walking stick. He speaks their language, though his accent is
a little strange, being from that country to the southeast. They do not
make eye contact with him, but they answer his questions in the affirmative: yes, they have been told not to give him any money.

Muchami knows better than to try to muscle them. They are not
refusing to pay rent, they are simply refusing to pay it to Muchami.
Sivakami's brothers will not cease to demand their share, and these are
poor people. They cannot pay twice. Muchami does not put pressure
on them that would catch them between landlords. This feudal feud is
between Sivakami and her brothers. He goes home.

When he gives his report in Cholapatti, Sivakami is no more surprised than he was. This is a strategic game. She advances to the next level of play. She informs her brothers that she is legally entitled to the income from that land and that if they do not observe this entitlement, she will find some means of enforcing her right.

At least this merits a response. Sambu, her eldest and most pompous brother, reminds her on behalf of their side that she is a woman. She has no legal entitlement. Her legal identity resided in her husband and they are very regretful to have to remind her that he is no more. Poof went her legal existence, up in smoke and ash.

Sivakami, as might well be imagined, has not forgotten her legal and social status any more than she has forgotten that her mother intended for her to have that money. Her son has, as everyone knows, the right to act on her behalf in legal matters. Funny her brothers didn't remind her of this, too, in the course of all their other reminders. Perhaps they themselves forgot.

Some months have now passed since Sivakami's initial efforts, and Vairum's first Pongal as a married man is impending. To her brothers' recent disdainful volley, Sivakami replies with only a gilt-edged invitation—modern, as Vairum had insisted. Further pleading, in her solitary, feminine voice, will be of no use. Vairum must now become involved in the claim. She will consult with him over the holiday and they will draft a response together.

───❧───

SIVAKAMI BUZZES AROUND HAPPILY, arranging the house. Straight from college, Vairum will go to collect Vani, her parents and seven or eight other relatives and escort them to Cholapatti. It is out of his way and protocol certainly does not require him to go, but he will miss no opportunity to pass time in the company of his young bride. His affection and regard for her are so great as to be almost improper. Sivakami doesn't know it, but Vairum had journeyed to Vani's village about six weeks earlier, at the halfway mark between their first Deepavali and their first Pongal. He had gone alone and on some highly flimsy pretense. His in-laws might have been suspicious, had he not won them over with his good manners and respect. He made no attempt to speak to Vani, though everyone saw him looking and smiled behind their hands. Clearly, he had been properly brought up, poor boy, he was just enraptured by the household's well-favoured daughter.

The party arrive at an auspicious hour on Friday, late afternoon. Vairum leaves them at the Kulithalai chattram to freshen up, dashes home and can barely greet his mother through his throat-clenching excitement, then dashes back again to fetch his bride and her family.

Sivakami watches for them from her door. As they round the corner, Vairum appears so relaxed and expansive that, for a shocking moment, his own mother doesn't recognize him. He makes some small joke. Sivakami watches his face through the dusk, laughing, lit from the pale glow that hangs round Vani's visage, the moon shining through mist.

Vani is growing from a pretty child into an unusual-looking young woman, with a wide face, bluish-black hair and ivory skin, the legacy of some west-coast ancestor. But there is something about her that strikes the viewer as odd—her movements are not jerky but give the impression of being unconnected one to another, just as she seems unconnected to the world around her. And yet here: she is laughing at something Vairum said. She accepts him, she likes him, she puts him at his ease! For this, Sivakami murmurs a prayer of thanks, and another as they enter.

The evening passes pleasantly in chat and feasting. Vairum's new relatives are prosperous, educated, confident in the art of gay conversation. They are modern—witness their willingness to permit their daughter to exhibit her talents publicly in such forums as weddings—and accomplished—the family not only includes several rising lawyers, but a poet, a dramatist and a member of parliament—but characterized more by their passionate eccentricities. Vani's mother, for instance, is a collector of vintage and antique armaments. Her father had been good friends with a British Army chief of staff, who got her interested when she was a little girl. Vani's father is developing a set of calisthenics based on theories of yoga and medieval humours. The practitioner ingests and expels liquids at different points in the exercise routine, drinking five different juices and herbal extracts, as well as spitting, sweating, crying, leeching and urinating. They and the other family members chat about their pastimes, about politics and culture, while Vani sits quietly in their midst, not appearing, really, to be listening.

She is a little like Thangam in this sense, Sivakami must admit. Unlike Thangam, however, Vani's contented silence is regularly broken: during mealtimes, the girl unannouncedly begins to rattle on with abandon. Sivakami finds Vani's chatter far more unnerving than her silence, not only the suddenness of it, but the volume. Streams of stories rocket forth from the child while her food goes ignored. Her family accommodates seamlessly, reducing their own output and confining their topics to those that complement hers. Evidently, Vani's exhibition is a longstanding habit. Vairum leans forward and gapes without cease as though the words are nectar he would drink from Vani's rosebud lips, oysters he would suck from between her pearly teeth. Sivakami can see she will need to learn to tolerate Vani's odd habits, but this does not seem a high price for the happiness she can feel radiating from her son. She has not seen him so joyful and comfortable since . . . since, she thinks resignedly, before he left the house of his uncles.

And now, sometime over the holiday, she must ask him to take those uncles to court.

She doesn't introduce the topic immediately. Several of her brothers have come to witness the celebration, and it seems neither wise nor polite to raise the topic when they are so near. They are warm and effusive toward her and avoid, with what appears to her an effort at grace, any mention of their exchange. She surmises that they think their hasty and factually incorrect letter has won them this battle. She meekly serves all, showing gracious hospitality, and lets them think what they want.

She introduces the topic with Vairum as soon as her brothers leave, immediately after the morning meal on the Sunday, the day of the dawn celebration, when first light saw Vani stir the first milk into the first pongal pot of her married life. Vairum is rather at loose ends, since Vani, her mother and the two unmarried paternal uncles, who will linger a couple of days in Cholapatti, have all gone to pay some obligatory calls. He sits before the floor desk with a slate for rough work, a copy book for fine work and an advanced physical chemistry text on the floor beside him.

He has turned the desk to face the door of the garden, ostensibly to receive a little of the breeze. Sivakami, at work cutting vegetables in the doorway of the pantry, watches him for a few moments and sees that he is staring out the garden door and not at his slate and paper. Every quarter-hour or so, he starts, as though a bubble around his head has burst, and bends with violent discipline toward the desk. But little by little, as though his chin is being lifted by an unseen finger, his head rises until his gaze again dreamily mixes with the morning sunshine, the sounds and smells of the drowsy garden. Sivakami watches him go through this cycle three times before she decides his assignments cannot be terribly urgent. She snaps the blade down into its block and goes to crouch beside him.

His instinct with his mother is always to look self-important and preoccupied, but brusqueness is, in this moment, too great a reach. He succeeds only in looking as though he just woke up.

"Do you recall your grandmother?" Sivakami asks. Her carefully chosen opening line only disorients Vairum further.

"I thought my grandmother died when my father was small," he says cautiously.

"Oh, yes, no—that is to say, my mother."

"No." He is trying. "I don't think I do."

"You were very small when she used to come and visit us here."

"I was very small when my father died, and I remember him."

Sivakami was unprepared for this but tries not to show it. "You remember him?"

"Yes, of course, everything. Everything about him."

Vairum is getting impatient. She launches more firmly toward her point.

"Well, my mother didn't come when you and your sister fell sick with the fever, because she had visited recently, and I said we were fine here, we were managing. Then she would have come when your father took ill, she was preparing to come, but then he died and she fell sick herself. From the shock . . ."

She looks to see how Vairum is taking this. He doesn't understand why she is talking about all this now.

"Even if she had come, you might not have remembered her. There were so many people around at that time, it was hard for both you children." Sivakami shifts her position. Her knees crack. "When my mother fell ill, of course, I went to see her. Do you remember that? Murthy and Rukmini took care of you and Thangam. I meant to go for one week, but I stayed for three."

Vairum shrugs—maybe he remembers, maybe not. Murthy and Rukmini's house is like a second home. They always took their meals there when Sivakami was isolated with her period, for instance—who could remember whether they stayed for a few days or weeks?

"I stayed on then because she died, and, you know, there were things to be done. But before she passed on, there was something else. When I arrived, she already knew she was dying. She called me to her side, when no one else was around, especially your uncles or their wives, and she gave me an instruction. It was something I had to promise her, at her deathbed, as her only daughter."

A person would have to be made of stone not to be interested by a promise extracted at the deathbed. Vairum's rock-diamond eyes glitter. He is intrigued.

"Now, the time has come for me to fulfill my pledge. Do you want to know what it was?"

He nods, just a little.

"I will take them to court," he responds, rising, even before Sivakami has proposed it. His eyes shine with ardour to be a tool for justice. "It is the only way, Amma, and you must not prevent me from fulfilling your pledge to your mother and getting my sister the money that is rightfully hers. Now you have told me, you must stand out of my way."

Sivakami has not even told him about her worries on Thangam's behalf, only that this was what her mother had wanted, a pledge she must fulfill and a point of justice. It appeals to Vairum's sense of the noble, the romantic; he's perhaps more than usually susceptible to things of this nature at the moment.

Sivakami is glad that she didn't have to use Thangam's neediness as a motivation. Vairum doesn't, in her opinion, need any more reasons to despise Goli.

For his part, although Vairum says that Vani's uncles will certainly represent the case, he doesn't mention how he will relish being on their side, one of a team with them, his comparatively puny shoulder between their massive ones, breaking down his uncles' door (in a legal sense) and demanding his sister's due. Vairum knows he shouldn't be so grateful to be part of his bride's family, he knows he should have accepted her coolly into *his* household; she should be the grateful one. But that's not how he feels.

He notices his niece, Saradha, observing him unsurely. She has come through the kitchen from the courtyard and is flushed with heat. Fair skin, shining black hair: a perfectly attractive child. Vairum beckons her.

"Come. You want to draw a picture? Come and draw a flower on my slate."

She comes and sits and draws and smiles, as she will once a day until he leaves.

Vani's immense uncles come the following morning, as they have made it a habit to do on this visit, to take their coffee upon the veranda. They peruse newspapers Minister has sent through Vairum as a welcome gesture. They take snuff. Occasionally, one grunts and points out an article or announcement to the other. They don't appear to notice the children swarming the veranda's periphery, watching them, perhaps because it is not unusual to find swarms of curious children around any visitor to a village, perhaps because the uncles know they are a curious sight, with their linen jackets and wobbling, shiny cheeks. They are the largest specimens of humanity these children have ever seen.

After three-quarters of an hour or so, they go inside, abandoning the untidily folded newspapers and leaving the tumblers and bowls with sugary traces that soon attract ants. Vairum is looking over the document his mother has given him, the yellowed parchment that confirms the legitimacy of her claim.

He scrambles to arrange bamboo mats for the uncles while they cluck absently, "Relax, son." They beckon for the parchment and for him to open the second of the double garden doors to admit more light.

Each carefully reads the text on the scroll. To Sivakami, out of sight in the kitchen, each sound—the sniff of an uncle, the low crackling of the scroll—is a word fate is writing on the taut parchment of her eardrum.

Then they begin to discuss:

Uncles: "Why is your mother pursuing the claim now?"

Vairum: "She promised her mother that she would."

Uncles: "But why now?"

Vairum: "Because . . . she can, now. Because you can help her."

Uncles: "No, we think it's because she needs it, now."

Vairum: "Why does she need it? I look after her."

The uncles purse their brows.

Uncles: "Hasn't your mother begun to care for your sister's children?"

Vairum: "Yes . . ."

Uncles: "How is she paying for them?"

Vairum: "My . . . well, the children's parents, their grandparents . . ."

Uncles: "No, there must be some need, you understand, to convince the court. The grandparents have very little money, the father must maintain a household of his own. Your mother must need the money for the children."

Vairum: "No. My sister's children are not orphans. My mother is pursuing this because she promised her mother, a deathbed promise, that she would. Her dying mother. That's enough, isn't it?"

Uncles: "It is useful. It will give a good sentiment. But our argument is stronger. Your mother promised she would pursue this in case her daughter ever needed it. Now there is a need."

Vairum: "But, but . . . I can't, be seen not to—not support my sister . . ."

Uncles: "Would your mother permit you to spend your fortune, your father's fortune, on your sister's children? That money belongs to your children. To Vani's children. Think about it. We will meet again, in a few weeks, in Pandiyoor."

Vairum is quiet. Sivakami sends the Brahmin woman she has hired for the festival shuttling forth with banana leaves to serve the mid-morning meal.

After the uncles have left to go visiting, Vairum is pensive. He steps moodily around the garden, pulling at leaves and flowers, holding them to his nose and then dropping them, staring up at the sky, until Sivakami is afraid he will get sunstroke, if he isn't already sun-stricken.

He is not; he is guilt-stricken. He re-enters the main hall and squats with his back against the wall, his forehead against the heels of his palms, until Sivakami cries, "What, child? Tell me."

She bends and peeps through his arms. He is muttering, "I am married. My sister is married." He flings his bony arms out from the elbows. Sivakami jumps back, stumbling, narrowly avoiding his touch.

He looks like a marionette, waiting for a puppeteer to work his strings. "It won't look good, will it, if Akka's children are paid for with my money?"

He drags himself up the wall by the shoulders, arms rising, head finding its equilibrium. He holds his arms out to her in supplication, a rare open moment.

"I will cause resentment in my in-laws, won't I? If I spend the money that should go to my children, Vani's children, on Thangam's."

"I could never permit you to spend your own money on your sister's children," Sivakami agrees.

The defensiveness reappears. "You cannot forbid me to use my money for any purpose."

"Correct, you are correct." She is careful now. "I should have said it would trouble me."

His generous nature is perturbed, but adulthood is compromise. "There is a high probability that my brother-in-law will not provide for the children," he explains to his mother. A sense of outrage begins to flood him, curiously like relief. "There is every possibility of this. I will make sure my sister gets that property from my uncles. They, who arranged my sister's marriage to that . . . that . . . stingy deadbeat, they had better make sure she is provided for."

"They have been purchasing land from her in-laws and managing it," Sivakami reminds him.

"Yes, yes, I have seen how they 'manage.' It is good that they know enough not to put it in my brother-in-law's feeble hands, but it will never improve in their own. They won't lose it, that's the best one can say about that." He is a fury of indignation now. "I will win the manjakkani, and I will manage it, and it will grow, so my sister's children will never want."

Emotional now, he runs up the stairs into the refuge of the attic. It is the result Sivakami wished for, though she wishes it weren't balanced on Vairum's hard feelings.

———⟲———

ALTHOUGH THE SUIT TAKES NEARLY TWO YEARS to work its way up a backlogged roster, it takes barely an hour to fight. If this were covered by *The Hindu* or another newspaper—which it won't be, but if it were—it would be headlined "Battle of the Uncles," Vairum thinks, as he emerges from the courtroom, flushed with victory, amid the barristers and other concerned parties. His maternal uncles trail behind, looking grey, stricken, disapproving and shrunken, especially in contrast with Vani's hale and corpulent ones.

Vairum has never thought of becoming a lawyer and still would never consider it, unsuited as he is to semantic niggling and logical stratagems. But he wouldn't mind being embroiled in a few more legal battles. Ayoh, it was fun! For him, the extended lead-up only added to the excitement. Then the bureaucratic elegance of the courthouse, the stuffiness of suppressed desire filling the courtroom, the judge's wig, like a kudumi out of control—each beat drama's drum in his young heart, athrum with blood and power.

It wasn't only the victory, though he wouldn't have enjoyed losing. It was the sense that he was on the side of fairness, of modernity. He had read much of the controversies of women's rights in the papers, and feels he has entered the fray on the progressive side. He knows his mother would have a horror of any such characterization of her case. Manjakkani is a long tradition and she was fulfilling a promise to her mother—there is nothing whatsoever modern or progressive in what she is doing, she would protest when he bragged to her of his pleasure in her win. But he will insist, to her and others, on his version. He is finding his philosophical alignments, and they are far, far different from hers.

23.
No Harm Done
1923–1926

IN 1923, ANOTHER GIRL IS BORN TO THANGAM. She is named Sita, at Sivakami's request, for Rama's wife—that most virtuous of women, who, in Sivakami's opinion, is as much the guardian of their home as her husband. Sivakami admits Sita would be nothing without her husband, but Sivakami's greatest challenge now is to protect the virtue and reputation of her granddaughters. In this, the goddess alone can guide her.

At her daughter Sita's birth, Thangam's second daughter, Visalam, comes to stay with Sivakami. The first one, Saradha, incorporates her younger sister into her schedule. She appears equally pleased with the company and with having someone to boss, demonstrating an officious side that she has not previously had the chance to express.

In this time, Vairum finishes college with high honours. He takes a job in Thiruchi as an accounting supervisor in a paper plant but decides, when Vani comes of age, to quit and live with her in Cholapatti. Sivakami is distressed: she had sent him to school and college precisely so that he would be more than a village Brahmin. Vairum brusquely assures her that his plans encompass much more than she could understand.

"It has been an informative year, Amma, but I'm destined to be more than a wage slave."

Sivakami has no idea what this means. She asks Muchami, "Where is the slavery in a dependable salary?"

Muchami has no idea either, but Vairum will listen to nothing more from her, so she waits and observes.

The biggest change in the household, though, owes to Vani's arrival. Her music practice transforms their home. She plays for several hours each morning and afternoon, and sometimes deep into the night. When the moon is full, she rises before the sun, fresh and energetic. If the moon is dark, she drags herself sleepily downstairs after the sun has fully risen. In either case, she bathes immediately, does a brief puja to her veena, and does namaskaram for Sivakami. Sivakami was very pleased to see that a girl raised in so modern a household would perform a daily prostration for her mother-in-law. Perhaps Vani understands that almost no other mother-in-law would be so indulgent: Sivakami expects nothing from her in the way of household assistance. For her part, Vani seems to thrive in the piety and order of the house her mother-in-law runs, and shows her respect and affection, albeit in her own, oddly detached way.

Pervasive as Thangam's dust, Vani's music is everywhere there is air, in the house and spilling out onto the street: between two people in a conversation, in all the cooking pots, travelling in through nostrils and out in snores. Sivakami has become accustomed to it, and now, when Vani is not playing, there is silence in all those places where before there was nothing.

One morning, Muchami finishes his milking just as Vani starts her playing, and stands in the courtyard shifting from foot to foot as Sivakami mixes yogourt rice for the little girls' breakfast. They attend the village school together and need a substantial meal before they go, though the rest of the household adheres to traditional timings: rice meals at 10:30 and 8:00, tiffin at 3:00.

Sivakami takes the milk, the third pot he has given her, and starts skimming it. "Do you need a cup of *kanji* or milk before you go?"

"Oh, no. Well, all right, yes, but . . . I need to talk to you." He squats against a post.

"What is it? Kanji or milk?"

"A mix?"

She puts sugar in a cup, pours him some of the water strained from cooked rice, adds milk from the pot already boiling on the stove and puts the third pot on to boil. The second is cooling and almost ready for her to add the yogourt culture.

"Well?"

"It's good news," he says, pouring his drink from tumbler to bowl, either to mix in the sugar and cool the milk, or to avoid Sivakami's eye. "The son-in-law's next posting will be in Kulithalai. He arrived yesterday to inspect the quarters and meet with his supervisor. I saw him last night in the bazaar."

"They're coming here?"

"It seems so."

Sivakami is not sure what to feel. "That's wonderful," she says. Why had Thangam not written to let her know? "Isn't it?"

"Yes. Certainly. Wonderful," Muchami echoes.

Despite her gladness at the news, Sivakami feels annoyance with Thangam for the first time she can remember. Wasn't she raised to have better manners than this?

"I wonder how much he tells Thangam about where they are moving to, each time," Muchami says.

"You knew what I was thinking."

"I suspect she doesn't get much warning or information."

"You're probably right."

"And we can't count on him to let us know."

"No," she agrees.

"You have her most recent address, right? I was thinking. Could you spare me for a week or two? Vairum is more than capable of handling the tenants now, and I could get a couple of my nephews to cover the milking, driving, whatever, heavy chores. I'd like you to write to Thangam-kutti and ask if she needs help with moving here. The baby is only one, and the boy is rowdy, I'm sure, a boy."

Sivakami feels moved at his use of the diminutive in reference to Thangam—Muchami doesn't have children of his own. He should, she thinks with sudden fervour.

"Yes, yes. You must go. I won't ask, I will tell her you are coming. Good?"

IT MIGHT HAVE BEEN INEVITABLE that Goli would eventually get a posting in Kulithalai; Sivakami has no way of telling what the likelihood was. Thangam and Goli, put up so nearby, with the youngest grandchildren! For two years. And with Vairum and Vani home— what a luxury, in these modern times, to have her family gathered about her. These years will be happy ones. Who knows: they might even see another grandchild born to this household, a son of her son.

Goli eventually manages to visit his mother-in-law and drink a cup of coffee, at which time Sivakami lets him know that they will have Muchami's assistance with the move. Goli receives the news as though it is a confirmation of something they had already arranged.

Now Muchami brings Thangam and the babies from the train station to Sivakami's house. Thangam greets her mother, as well as Vairum and Vani and her elder daughters, who act shy for a moment then grab their little brother by his hands and drag him into the courtyard, promising to show him a couple of crickets they have trapped with Muchami's help. Thangam looks wan and worn, and Vairum asks his mother for a glass of water as he tells Thangam to sit.

"I hope the journey was not too taxing, Akka," he says, and takes the water from Sivakami to give to Thangam himself.

"No, no," his sister assures him, drinking the water and smiling as though to show she's drinking only because he told her to.

He has been squatting and looking at her. Rising, he says, "I'll go with Muchami to unload your things. Where's your husband? Leaving his work to others as always?" He exits the front door.

The littlest girl, Sita, lying in her lap, yanks violently on her mother's thirumangalyam. It has to hurt, but Thangam, mortified, sits as though frozen, the water a lump in her throat.

Vairum and Muchami ride in silence on the front seat of the cart, while Mari and one of Muchami's nephews ride in back with the trunks. During Vairum's years at college, his relationship with Muchami has changed in ways now cemented by his return. As a child, he took Muchami almost as much for granted as he would a parent, and

Muchami filled a number of parental functions, including those of playmate, protector and—when Vairum acquired some responsibilities for the family lands—educator. With the latter shift, Vairum began to act wary around the servant: he needed Muchami, but he, after all, was the owner of the lands they were discussing. Still, it was evident to Muchami (who never made this explicit) what Vairum knew and what he didn't.

Since his return from Thiruchi, Vairum has set the tone clearly: he is the employer, Muchami answers to him, not his mother, and acts on his behalf, not hers. Vairum asks questions; Muchami answers them. He is to bring information to Vairum first.

Now he gives Muchami his orders. "Keep a close watch on my brother-in-law."

Muchami wags his head sagely, his eyes on the bullock's back.

"No one else is going to tell me what all he's up to. I know he's going to get into trouble and I want to know exactly how, when and what kind, preferably before he's in too deep."

Muchami raises his eyebrows, impressed. He has eavesdropped on conversations between college-educated men: they often seem incapable of learning anything except from books. Vairum, by contrast, may turn out to be a man he can respect. Muchami is comfortable with their dynamic, as it has settled out: though he never would have predicted it exactly, it feels natural and right. Even Sivakami appears to agree: she has taken care of these lands for her son, but they never belonged to her. She has to be glad that Vairum is willing to accept responsibility for what is his.

Muchami doesn't even feel his relationship with Sivakami has much changed as a result: he still reports to her in matters of concern to family life, provided they aren't of the sort he simply looks after on his own. In such matters—none have arisen in the months since Vairum's return, but surely they will—he still might trust his own judgment above Vairum's. Vairum is, after all, a young man, hotheaded and condemnatory, without, perhaps, the necessary subtlety and feeling for tradition that Muchami and Sivakami share.

As Thangam and Goli get settled in the government housing complex at Kulithalai, Muchami makes a point of dropping in daily. He almost always finds Thangam on the veranda, alone with the children, and offers to bring her back to her mother's for a visit and a meal. She always accepts, and he returns her at dusk to a dark and empty house. Sivakami sends food back with her, which she always accepts, looking as vacant as her house does even months after they have moved in.

She has been shedding gold since her arrival, and people from Kulithalai and even from Cholapatti have taken to passing by their veranda with little squares of paper into which they scoop or brush these holiest of ashes, as Thangam sits there, alone or with the children. Sivakami had wondered if Thangam might ask to have the older girls come and live with her, or if they might ask, now that their parents are so close. But the girls take for granted that their home is with their grandmother, and Thangam and Goli don't press for any changes to their arrangement.

She certainly didn't feel as though Thangam could have handled having any more children at home with her. She has had few such chances to observe Thangam at length since she left to live with her husband, apart from times immediately before or after childbirth, when it's not too surprising that a woman might be listless. Sivakami herself never was, but she knows such behaviour is not entirely abnormal. She does feel there is something not quite natural in the way Thangam relates to her children, though. Where is the adoration she herself felt? She remembers surprise at her abject fascination: is this how it was for her mother? Her mother said it was for the first two kids; with the third and fourth, she had less time to think about it. Maybe Thangam is overwhelmed by numbers: when her children crowd around her, competing for her attention, she gives it politely, but with a slight hesitation. Sivakami would even think *distaste* if that weren't such a horrible notion. Thangam seems slightly afraid of her children, and far from enthralled.

They are all very good-looking children: fair, some with their father's high, square forehead, some with Thangam's shapely nose. Sivakami herself would have been proud to have borne them. *I thought my fate was to have a small family, but I have a large one after all.* Now all that remains is for Vairum to complete it, with children of his own.

GOLI'S PRIMARY ACTIVITY ON ARRIVAL appears to be that of using his position as a revenue inspector, which gives him access to the exact income levels and amenability to corruption of all of Kulithalai's prominent citizens, as a springboard for his business schemes. For the first few months, he attempts to revive his proposal for a cigar and cigarette plant, and nearly succeeds, but one important backer with political ambitions withdraws late, and the idea falls through. Goli's spirits are briefly dampened, but he rebounds with an imagined line of bottled cream sodas in innovative flavours. He convinces the would-be politician to invest—"No political liability in soda!"—and pays a dissolute young Britisher for market research and suggestions. The consultant advises Goli that for bestselling "Top Flavours!" drinks (a name Goli paid him a handsome bonus to invent), he can't fail with vanilla, chocolate and strawberry. Goli pays another huge sum to have essences imported from Italy and tries them, at an exclusive event, on half a dozen interested parties, all of whom concur that these exotic tastes are, if not repulsive, not exactly sure bets. No wonder newly arrived Britishers never like our food, if this is the kind of thing their tongues are trained on! They always come around, though, with time. A few of the men say they might consider going in on a line of coconut, mango and lime-flavoured drinks, but isn't the market saturated?

"No one wants to turn him down flat," Muchami reports to Vairum as they walk the fields together one morning, "because he's the revenue inspector. It doesn't do to get him mad: he might tax them at full percentages. Apart from which, there's something about him people like. Even when they don't give him money—and it's amazing how often they do—they want to stay friends with him."

Vairum listens in silence. Nearly every meeting he has had with Goli (always accidental, never planned) has ended in a row. These have been quick but unmistakable, and usually concerned Goli's not living up to his responsibilities. There is something about the very sight of his brother-in-law that is, to Vairum, like a torch held to his tail.

"I'm surprised he hasn't asked you to go in with him on something," Muchami remarks to him, a surprisingly personal incursion.

"He has no access to my finances," Vairum responds curtly, poking a fallen bunch of banana leaves out of a canal. "I told his supervisor right away that he cannot be impartial with me, and that I will show my books only to the higher-up. My brother-in-law has no idea what I might have to give, not that he would get a paisa out of me."

Muchami nods and they walk on.

One day, when Muchami pays his call to Thangam, he finds Goli at home. This has happened only once before: it was a Sunday, Goli had just finished his mid-morning meal and went to take a nap, so Thangam clambered onto the cart with the children, as usual.

Today, however, is a Wednesday, and Muchami dares not ask why Goli is neither at the office nor out on calls.

"What do you want?" Goli asks him, from the door. Baby Sita, learning to walk, clings to her father's legs, the only one of the children Muchami has seen take such a liberty with their father.

Muchami has removed his shoulder towel to bare his chest, as is proper for men of lower castes with Brahmins, and holds it at his waist as he speaks. "I was out on business and wondered if Thangam Amma would like to come to visit her mother." He has never used the honorific for Thangam, who is more like a daughter than a mistress to him, but it would feel equally strange not to use it with Goli, and risk offending him.

"She's there all the time," Goli says. "She's going to be staying home a little more from now on."

Muchami is not sure how Goli knows Thangam's whereabouts, since he is never at home when she leaves and returns. It's hard to imagine him asking about her day or her volunteering the information. But he respectfully takes his leave, and drives away. He returns at four-thirty that afternoon, in case Thangam is alone by then and wants to come home briefly, but she is not on the veranda. He comes every morning for the next week. The door is always shut, the veranda vacant.

Sivakami is worried; Vairum demands that Muchami tell him what is happening, but Muchami can give them nothing, other than saying that Goli bragged to his wealthier friends that he was about to embark on an unprecedented scheme: guaranteed success, no overhead. He was sorry they could have no part in it, but it might have spinoff ventures, he had mused; they would just have to wait and see.

The following Friday evening, nine days after Goli secluded his wife, Muchami hears a rumour in the bazaar that makes him go to Thangam and Goli's house. It's true: Goli is selling packets of Thangam's dust in little printed paper packets. Muchami accosts one customer who has just left the line, having purchased three packets, and asks him to read what they say.

"'Ash of Gold! Most powerful and holy cure from daughter of famous healer! Siddhic power alchemized with Brahmin wisdom! Use sparingly—only small amount needed.'"

Thangam is nowhere to be seen as Goli hawks the virtues of her dust from his veranda. "Once a week only, folks! Step up, step up! It's exclusive, it's rare, it's like nothing you've ever experienced."

"We had heard of it," says the man who so obligingly went over the packet's text with Muchami. "Twice we came to Cholapatti to see if we could get some. But when we would come here sometimes, there were only traces on the veranda. We had to content ourselves with that. Now we will be first in line weekly, and buy also for our relatives!"

Muchami feels sick to his stomach during the whole journey to Sivakami's but knows he has to tell Vairum, and immediately, not because Vairum would expect it, though he would, but for Thangam's sake. *Poor child,* he repeats to himself with pity and dread as he nears Sivakami's house. *Poor child.*

He would prefer to leave Sivakami entirely out of it but has to ask her to call Vairum, who is upstairs with Vani.

Out in the courtyard, Muchami tells Vairum in low tones what is happening. Sivakami stays in the kitchen, looking more frightened than curious.

Vairum explodes. "That no-good, exploitative lazy bum of a half-man . . ." and so on, exactly as Muchami predicted. The servant makes eye contact with Sivakami: she doesn't need details; she knows who this is about. Within minutes, Muchami has hitched the cart again and he and Vairum depart.

They arrive along with a couple of hopeful customers, who clap at the still-open doorway and call out to Goli just as Muchami and Vairum dismount the cart. Goli comes to the entrance, looking tired and sounding cranky.

"Wish I could help you, folks, but supplies are limited. I ran out in ten minutes. Come back next . . ."

He trails off as Vairum bounds up the steps, making as if to close the door.

"Get in the house, you . . ." Vairum pushes his brother-in-law in the chest and into the gloom of the main hall.

Goli pushes Vairum back and the door shuts as he falls against it. Muchami decides against trying to listen and instead flicks his switch at the bullock's rump, going to fetch a couple of Vairum's friends, sons of a Kulithalai moneylender, who live just outside the government housing complex.

"You can get out of this house if you don't know how to show respect," Goli screams. "I have had more than enough of your—"

"Oh, it's respect, is it?" As Vairum's eyes adjust, he sees Thangam, the children huddled against her, sitting in a corner of the main hall as though trapped there by unseen forces. She doesn't look up. "What kind of respect are you showing for my sister and our family by *selling*, you are *selling* her dust?"

Goli looks uncertain. "Thangam is part of my family now, and this is family business, Vairum. Butt out."

"Let me tell you what happens now. One, you stop this venture. Two, you never try it again." Vairum is a little surprised at the menace in his tone. He has never had to threaten someone and although he hopes he doesn't have to again, it's good to know he can.

"Oh, come, Vairum," Goli wheedles. "Rumour has it you're interested in business. Can you really see passing this up? You can have a part in it, as long as we can be clear on . . ."

"Don't you ever *dare* suggest I would make money by *using* my sister . . ."

"All right—I'm through negotiating with you. Get out of my house." Goli opens the door and sees Muchami standing at the bottom of the front steps with Vairum's friends and several of their neighbours: strapping, athletic youth, their arms crossed as they wait. Vairum sees them, too.

"This is the final word: stop, " he says, standing a little too close to Goli, who looks away. "I'll see you at home tomorrow, Akka," he says to Thangam. "Good night."

Vairum joins his friends, who pat him on the shoulder as he hears the door slam behind him.

Muchami assures him, in the weeks following, that Goli has made no more mention of that scheme. Thangam resumes her daily visits with the children. When Muchami drops her at their house the Friday after the confrontation, a puzzled crowd of would-be customers is milling outside. They raise a happy buzz at Thangam's appearance, but she smiles at them vaguely and goes inside. Muchami lingers for nearly two hours in the neighbourhood, but when dark begins to fall and Goli has not returned, he leaves, along with the remnants of the crowd, who have wiped up on their index fingers any traces of Thangam's dust from the veranda.

Several more months pass before they hear again of Goli advertising one of his ideas. This time, he has persuaded a local importer to loan him one of two vitrines, where he has arranged a display of three stuffed deer's heads, a blackbuck antelope in the centre, its ringed and undulating horns crossing the ramified tines of two *barasinghas'* antlers. Before long, Vairum sees these heads appear above the doorways to the homes of a local lawyer and a prosperous compounder, as well as over the entryway to the import shop itself. Goli replaces them, adding an axis deer with magnificent horns. These, too, sell as soon as they arrive.

"He's hit on a trend," Vairum remarks, when Muchami tells him Goli has bragged he can't keep up with demand. "Or created one."

"Yes, if anyone can do that, he can. He says he mounted one of the heads above his own doorway, but was convinced to sell it, too!"

The next shipment comes in three weeks later, nine heads; the next, three weeks after, is twelve. Goli no longer bothers to display them in the import-shop window but just sells them out of his main hall. They never remain longer than a day, so his higher-ups do not appear to catch wind of it.

Thangam shows up for her visit to Sivakami's one day in a rich-looking cotton-silk sari in coral, orange and pink. Her daughters finger it admiringly, and Sivakami asks, "New?"

Thangam nods, looking down and smiling. A couple of days later, wearing yet another new sari, she gives each of the little girls a small carved ivory box and presents Sivakami with a large, sandalwood representation of Rama for her puja corner.

"What is all this?" Sivakami asks.

"Gifts," Thangam replies shyly. "From my husband."

Sivakami is surprised, but when Gayatri comes for her daily coffee, she hears about the source of the riches.

"We finally came up on the waiting list for one of your son-in-law's heads, Sivakamikka!" Gayatri sighs as she seats herself against a pillar in the main hall, smiling at Thangam, who smiles back before looking away and swallowing.

Sivakami is staring at Thangam's sari, as opulent as the last one, if less gaudy, checked in three tones of violet. She can't tell why it looks strange, apart from the fact that she has so rarely seen Thangam in new clothes since she left home, and suddenly realizes: the only gold she sees on the sari is in the jeri-work threads outlining the checks. Thangam's shedding has significantly abated in the last month. That can only be good, she thinks, and then realizes what Gayatri has said.

"One of his heads?"

"We just had it mounted! A blackbuck, I guess it's called."

"I'm sorry." She gives Gayatri her coffee, the tumbler inverted in the bowl. "I don't know what you mean."

"Has no one told you about your son-in-law's runaway success?" Gayatri asks.

Sivakami, feeling slightly humiliated, says nothing.

"Well, it's very fashionable," Gayatri tells her cautiously. "Deer heads, wall decorations."

A Brahmin selling the heads of dead animals? Sivakami returns to the kitchen. It sounds barbaric, but she can't very well say that to

Gayatri if she and her husband bought one.

"My parents have, you know, just the horns," Gayatri goes on, chattering a little to cover Sivakami's obvious silence, "but Goli says this is a new thing, with this advanced science, taxi-something."

Sivakami smiles at her and helps her to change the subject.

"All the best homes have to have them," Muchami tells Vairum. "He has taken advance orders from some thirty more people. I think his supply has maybe slowed a little, though: he has said for the last few weeks that he'll be getting more in, but they haven't shown up yet."

They are in the bullock cart, returning from looking at a rice mill that Vairum is considering buying, on the far side of Kulithalai.

"What do people love so much about them?" Vairum snorts, and Muchami shrugs, but then realizes Vairum was not asking him. "Fascinating thing, fashion. He sold so many so fast, and they have to be hunted, stuffed, sent. I'm not sure the trend will persist, but if it settles down and becomes a fixture, maybe someone should consider domesticating, starting a farm or something."

"Now there's an idea." Muchami guides the bullock around a pothole.

"So what's he doing with his winnings? Putting them into some other crazy scheme?"

"Um, no." Muchami is quiet.

"What?" Vairum asks eventually.

Muchami would really rather not have to tell him, though there is no saying how Vairum will react. "He seems to be interested in acquiring . . . trophies, of a sort." What Goli is doing is not technically wrong, but Muchami has a feeling that Vairum will not like it.

"What sort?"

If Muchami doesn't tell him, someone else will. "He seems to have his eye on Chellamma. You know who she is?"

Vairum shakes his head.

Muchami keeps his eyes on the road. "*Devadasi.*"

A temple dancer—"servant of the gods"—a courtesan. Women of this caste are trained in the finer arts, given to a god in a ceremonial marriage but dependent on liaisons with wealthy men, preferably in an exclu-

254 ~ PADMA VISWANATHAN

sive relationship. It's a man of rare refinements who keeps a devadasi: he may father a line of dancers, a great contribution to the native arts.

"A devadasi?" Vairum asks. "I didn't even know there were any around here."

"Just one, in fact. Long story. Her mother was brought here from Madurai-side, by her patron, Chellamma's father. She came of age some five years ago but has only had one patron, for a couple of years. No one is supporting her now, and there was no issue from the previous union."

"He is such a fool," Vairum says.

"Yes," Muchami agrees.

Vairum sighs. "He can barely support his own family, and now he wants to take on another one? Besides which, he leaves in less than a year. Thank God."

"Status," Muchami says simply. "He's been buying gifts for Thangam and the babies, and new furniture."

"He'll go into debt," Vairum says. "Big trouble ahead."

"Yes." Muchami looks over. "Don't get involved."

"I don't need your advice."

Muchami, stung even though he should have expected this, falls silent.

The next morning, Sivakami draws him aside. "What's this about the son-in-law's business venture?"

"Yes, Amma. I didn't think you'd like it, and haven't told you about most of his business dealings since he arrived in Kulithalai. He has had a new one every few months. Who knew this one would be so successful?"

"Animal heads?"

Muchami shrugs, grinning a little.

Sivakami is quiet a moment. "I suppose there's nothing wrong with him trying to supplement his income, though I wish he would live more quietly. All this flash!"

"Yes, Amma," Muchami says.

Sivakami looks at him suspiciously and waits, but he says nothing more and she doesn't ask.

It is two weeks before Navaratri, and Thangam comes in glowing. "Amma," she tells her mother. "Look."

Muchami is unloading boxes from the bullock cart, and Thangam opens them to show her mother: dolls, every size and style, perhaps two dozen of them.

"He brought them from Thiruchi!" Thangam picks each one up in turn, caressing it and setting it back in its wrapper.

Sivakami turns away from her, feeling discomfited. It is very strange. She knows Thangam loves dolls, but she's looking at them as Sivakami feels she should her own babies.

Vairum comes in and sees the boxes. "What's all this?"

"Dolls," Thangam whispers. "For Navaratri."

"You deserve to be spoiled, Akka, but surely he would be better off saving his money? Investing it in something safe?"

Thangam looks away.

"I can't talk to him," Vairum sighs. "Don't know if anyone can. Can you?"

Thangam keeps her silence.

"I didn't think so," he says. "All this is going to blow up in his face."

The end to Goli's fast fortune arrives in a near-literal fulfillment of Vairum's prediction. A rush shipment of four deer heads arrives within a month, but as he is taking the last out of its crate to hand it over to a customer, the animal's forehead ruptures, one glass eye pops out, and maggots spill forth all over Goli, the customer and Goli's veranda. The customer runs out screaming, and that's the end of trade.

The customers from whom Goli accepted advance payment cancel their orders and demand refunds, and a number of people even try to return heads they had already bought and taken home, even though Goli assures them the maggot incident was an unfortunate but isolated chemical slip-up.

"I've been pushing the supplier too hard. They got hasty. If you will only be patient . . ."

He permits the others to cancel their orders but tells them that it may be some time before he receives a refund from the supplier.

Muchami believes Goli only ever paid on receipt of shipments, spending all the advance cash on frivolities and counting on future orders to pay for those already in. Vairum believes the same, but Muchami has been more laconic with him since the conversation about the devadasi and, apart from brief reports, has confined conversation to their own immediate business concerns.

Six months later, no one has received a refund. Goli has spent this time trying to convince those few remaining men who have not yet invested with him to back him in setting up a sesame oil refinery, but without success. A little jealousy may have entered their relations, and now, in the wake of his failure, a little *schadenfreude*. Goli's odour of indebtedness also means his charm isn't quite as effective as once it was.

Muchami hears things are getting rocky between Goli and his devadasi but withholds this information from Vairum, who doesn't ask but assumes as much.

Thangam has started to shed again, copiously, and is starting to show: she is pregnant once more.

For some reason, Sivakami doesn't dare tell Vairum about the pregnancy, but, one day, he notices.

"Ah, great," he says, clasping his hands, glittering ill will from his diamond-black eyes as Thangam appears to shrink. "That's just what you and your profligate husband need. Well, it doesn't matter—you'll pack another off to live with us. The boy is first in line, now, isn't that right?"

"Vairum!" Sivakami says from the kitchen.

He leaves, with a dismissive gesture at his mother. Sivakami stands watching Thangam, who is curved around her stomach as though trying to make it disappear. Could that be the problem? *Thangam is ashamed of her husband, ashamed of her children.* Vairum should be ashamed of himself. She wonders if she should say something to him later. How can she, though, when he has been so generous toward his sister and her children, and wants children of his own so badly? Who can blame him for being a little resentful?

And now, Muchami tells Sivakami, "I understand the house is vacated." Goli sold the furniture; all that remains are the few trunks of pots and saris with which they arrived. These will be sent along after him. Thangam will stay in Cholapatti through her delivery.

"It's God's will that they move on. I can't question."

Muchami nods.

"Are you feeling all right?" Sivakami quizzes him.

He tries to look a little more lively. He feels like he has spent two years putting out fires. It was wonderful having Thangam nearby, but he's not sorry to see Goli go.

Sivakami's feelings are even more mixed. She's not sure it has even been beneficial to Saradha and Visalam to have their mother near: they seemed more confused than enriched, and always looked scared of their father. Muchami looks exhausted. She's not sure why— surely the extra trips back and forth were not so great a strain? Vairum will certainly be more relaxed, and she will, too: she was always dreading the prospect of a confrontation between them.

But now the two years are over, and no harm done, she thinks with resolute cheer. Another grandchild on the way.

24.
Two Ramayanas
1929

SIVAKAMI CONTINUES TO OBSERVE VAIRUM, without asking questions, which he does not welcome. Her tension about his professional prospects has ebbed with his increasing success. He not only managed their own lands very effectively, but purchased other parcels not thought to be productive and turned them around, quickly saving enough to buy a rice mill, whose output he has also increased, Muchami tells her, by 40 per cent. She has stopped worrying about him in this regard, but he still has no child, and it wears on him, especially as Thangam's children continue steadily to fill their house.

. Thangam has given birth to two more daughters. The manjakkani money has been put to ample use for Laddu's poonal, and Saradha's wedding, which was contracted four years prior, her first Deepavali and trips to her husband's home, and her coming-of-age ceremony and departure last year. She married into a stable family in Thiruchi, distant relatives, and it is deeply satisfying to Sivakami to know she is so well settled. The relentlessly jolly Visalam has married but not yet gone to her husband's house. Laddu is nine, a resolutely unambitious boy; Sivakami would be tearing her hair out if she had any. Vairum tutors him in math and science, and she has just hired a tutor in Sanskrit, but none of it seems to help. Sita, who came to stay late last year, is six years old and already has the black tongue of a harridan, a curse or insult always at the ready. Thangam's first two children didn't prepare Sivakami for the second two, and she prays daily for energy and cunning enough to raise them as she must.

It is to this that her thoughts always turn as she does her chores, as today, when she is slicing a turnip and muttering a mantra in worship of Rama. *Rama Ramaya Namaha. Rama Ramaya Namaha ...*

"*Mundai!*"

The ugly word jumps like a toad across her thoughts and she hollers, "Sita!" She considers rising and finding her foul-mouthed granddaughter but decides it's better the child learn to obey a summons. "Sita! Come here!" Sivakami is shocked by the tone of her own voice. Guiding Thangam's first two through the maze of manners and comportment never required any but the lightest touch. Where on earth would the child have heard a word like that? What could cause her to think she could use it?

The little girl sidles into the doorway, eyes cast down.

"That word has never been spoken in this house before. You are responsible for bringing this ugliness into our home."

Sita pouts. It's clear she feels bad, but only because she has upset her grandmother. That she has called her older sister a shaven-headed widow—for this, she is not repentant.

"Go study and not a peep."

Sita slinks away, her beautiful features obscured by this deep yellow rage she seems to have been born with, and which her first five years, living in God-only-knows what kind of neighbourhoods, did nothing to temper. Sivakami hasn't tried to fathom it. Sita is here now and a good upbringing takes a small creature with all its quirks and kinks and trains it to behave like any worthy person, fulfilling duty and accepting fate.

From what she could hear, Sita was frustrated because she wanted Visalam to play a game, which Visalam cannot because she is menstruating, isolated in the back room. For the first time: Visalam came of age yesterday. Sivakami thought it a shame the child's mother-in-law lived too far away to come for the celebration but then it might have been better that she didn't see her son's wife giggling throughout the most solemn parts of the ceremony and guffawing through the gay ones. Visalam finds everything funny. Sivakami tells her to watch that the crows don't snatch the little rice flour morsels of *vadam* as they dry on the roof—hilarious. When, once or twice annually, they choose new clothes, Visalam must invariably be excused, laughing so hard she's useless. School, needless to say, has been a trial, but that's all over now that she is no longer a girl.

Anyone around her who is inclined to humour is compelled to laugh with her. Anyone not so inclined feels mocked. By some stroke of God's grace, however, she married into a relaxed and mirthful family, perhaps the only one Sivakami has ever met which is truly so. While they generally seem capable of the modicum of sobriety Visalam is never able to summon, they are indulgent toward the girl, who is, after all, obedient and respectful.

As Sivakami stands to reach for the sambar *podi*, she feels a little trickle. She clenches her thighs and hobbles out along the platform behind the house and back in through the door of the back room. There, she sees a bead of red releasing a trail of smaller beads as it rounds her ankle bone and descends her instep to soak into the brick floor. She reaches under the cot for the box of rags and discreetly fixes one round her hips before shouting for Sita, muttering, as she always does, against the inconvenience of it. "Really, it's too silly—a grandmother, widowed for how many years? Sita!" she calls again, and Sita, who had been crouched over a school book in the garden and pretending not to hear, pokes her head around the door. "Go next door and tell Rukmini that I am in the room with Visalam. Go and come, you."

Visalam is wheezing through her knuckles. Sivakami squats in a corner and chuckles a little, too. She normally doesn't look at her granddaughters during the days of their pollution, but must admit it is nice to have this extra time with Visalam, knowing that soon the girl will leave for her marital home.

Menstruation always makes Sivakami feel strange, though she merely trades one kind of untouchability for another. Where she is normally too pure to be touched, not to mention a potent reminder of feminine destructive power, for these three days she is too impure to be touched, and a potent reminder of feminine procreative power.

And now there is a knocking and hallooing at the front door:

Laddu's Sanskrit teacher. Sivakami shouts, "Enter, enter!" but cannot make herself heard above Vani's playing. Thankfully, Rukmini arrives at the front door in the same moment.

"Sivakami!" Rukmini shouts from the front. She has, for thirty years now, managed Sivakami's household during menstrual leaves of absence. "Sivakami?"

"I am here," Sivakami replies, closing to a crack the narrow double door leading onto the main hall.

"Sivakami, young Kesavan is here to tutor Laddu in Sanskrit."

"Is Laddu there?"

Now Rukmini starts shouting Laddu's name.

Sivakami tries to make a suggestion. "Is . . . Rukmini Akka! Is Sita . . . Rukmini Akka!"

Rukmini stops.

Sivakami asks, "Is Sita there? Ask her to find Laddu."

"No," replies the other woman. "Sita stayed at my house to eat biscuits and play with the dog."

"Oh. Young Kesavan, I'm very sorry." Sivakami speaks through the crack between the doors. "Only the third session and Laddu is absent again. I'm so sorry. Rukmini, ask Sita to go find her brother. Or find Muchami and ask Muchami to find Laddu."

"Yes, um, I reminded him," the young man answers as Rukmini bustles away importantly, "right after his Sanskrit class in school."

This does nothing to relieve Sivakami's embarrassment.

"I'd like"—he moves nearer the door and clears his throat—"to, um . . . there are other boys in the class who could use the extra help. I will tell you in confidence, however"—he coughs but sounds as if he's gaining surety—"that their parents cannot afford a tutor. Or they cannot see the necessity of Sanskrit. Though it is a necessity, as I have told you—the right colleges look very positively on those students who are familiar with the classical language. Perhaps, if you would agree, I can suggest that those boys attend, here with Laddu, to help lend more of an . . . atmosphere. They are boys Laddu likes. He would make sure to come home if they were coming also. He wouldn't miss it."

Laddu has been falling dreadfully behind in his studies, lacking aptitude, conscience and enthusiasm. Sivakami wonders, when she looks at him, whether she is seeing what Goli was like as a young chap. Pressure to play host might be just the thing.

"Certainly, Kesavan. You invite the boys. That's good." Sivakami feels slightly vertiginous and lifts her sari *pallu* off her back to her shoulders so that the cool wall is against her skin. "Is Rukmini there? Rukmini!"

Rukmini has just returned.

"Rukmini, give young Kesavan a cup of milk."

Kesavan makes clucking noises in protest, but Sivakami speaks over him. "Find some *murrukku* and laddu as well."

"If you have Laddu, I'll teach the class!" Kesavan lamely attempts to make light of the situation. Rukmini laughs a little and Visalam as if she will never stop, but Sivakami is glad no one can see her face and lies flat on the cool floor, willing the season of cramps to pass.

Rukmini takes the vegetables that Sivakami has already sliced back to her own kitchen, where she and her mother-in-law integrate them into their sambar. Sita, Laddu, Vani and Vairum eat there that evening, as do Muchami and Mari the next day. Rukmini brings food for Visalam, and leaves the monkeys' offering in the customary spot in the forest beyond the courtyard. Rukmini and Murthy even scold Laddu on Sivakami's behalf, though Sivakami scolds him, too.

The next day, Vani gets her period: Sivakami had been expecting this. They have been roughly synchronized for years. The mood in the room shifts, though, with Vani's entrance: five years, and she and Vairum have yet to produce an heir. Vairum's evident and mounting emotion at this lack gives Sivakami one more reason to feel ashamed whenever she has her period. But of course it isn't her menstruation that renders Vairum unable to meet anyone's eye during his wife's isolation, it is Vani's. Vairum becomes visibly depressed each month, skipping meals, becoming curt with the rest of the family.

A week later, Saradha arrives in preparation for the delivery of her first child. A woman normally goes to her mother's house, to be looked after in the comfort of the home she has known, but Thangam is setting up house in yet another part of the presidency and is in no position to pamper Saradha as she deserves. In any case, Sivakami has come to be called Amma, "mother," by the children, who refer to their mother as Akka, "big sister." Sivakami is not sure when this started or whether she should do something about it, but it does reflect the children's reality at least in part. So Saradha comes to her amma's, at seven months, for her bangle ceremony, and now, to deliver.

The day arrives, and Sivakami sends Muchami to fetch the old women who deliver babies, but, when they arrive, she and Sivakami stop short at Saradha's look of panic. "No, Amma!" she says, gripping Sivakami's arm, which shocks Sivakami as much as anything. Even as a small child, Saradha never violated her grandmother's madi.

"What is it, kannama?"

"You have to deliver my baby, Amma. You have *kai raasi*. Just like you delivered me and my brothers and sisters. You have to do it, Amma. Please, Amma!"

Kai raasi: lucky hands. Sivakami feels like Saradha has tied them. She is scared of her own inexperience, but superstition scares her more: after Thangam had her first, Sivakami would not turn the job over to anyone else, and now it appears she may have to do the same for her granddaughter. Now that Saradha has said the words, *kai raasi*, it would be bad luck to say no.

The old women hang back—they will not put themselves forward now even though they all feel they have kai raasi. Sivakami has only delivered seven babies, while they have delivered hundreds, but it's true that Thangam's babies all lived—thrived, in fact, despite their sickly mother and the uncertainty and strangeness of their vagrant early lives. Sivakami must once more perform her magic.

Any magician will tell you, though, that magic is nine-tenths labour and one-tenth luck. After nine hours of labour, Sivakami is praying for an hour of luck. She instructs Visalam to dribble some boiled rice water between Saradha's dry lips. Saradha has permitted the old women to sop the sweat from her thick eyebrows, but only Sivakami is allowed to massage the spasming abdomen with sesame oil. Saradha's forearms, as she bears down, squatting, are locked in Sivakami's, and she will be persuaded to release them only because Sivakami needs her hands to catch the baby, whose head has finally, fuzzily, shown. The lucky hour has arrived.

A girl! She's small but screams at a pitch that would be admirable in a child twice her size. Saradha, relieved, whispers, "Kai raasi, Amma. You should never deviate from tradition. You have always birthed the babies in this house."

All the old women say as much and more to their families when escorted home that night. "Will she do the same for her son and daughter-in-law, do you think?" they whisper. "When?"

Sivakami is thinking the same thing. Vani has begun to do a daily puja for a dark-barked tree a furlong northwest of the house, on one of whose branches she has tied a pink ribbon, circling the tree nine times each morning. She has poured milk down every snake hole in the vicinity—Muchami would inform her whenever he spied one and she would journey out with one of Thangam's children carrying the milk jug. (Presumably, if the snake didn't drown in her generosity, it would be so grateful as to wish a child on her.) She has pledged a pair of little golden feet for the altar of the Krishna temple—Krishna is often worshipped in the form of a baby, chubby, sunny, mischievous—on condition of her pregnancy and safe delivery of a child.

Vairum never demonstrates blame toward his wife. Does he blame himself? He is a math genius and this is the simplest of equations: one plus one equals three.

And, daily, he is taunted by the evidence of his sister and brother-in-law's proficiency in this regard. His actions, in the main, have been gracious toward his nieces and nephew. He is not by any means affectionate with them, but it is clear he will do whatever he can to ensure their current and future material well-being. For instance, tutoring Laddu. He says he is doing this for Thangam: he said he would never take from her but only give, and if he doesn't offer this instruction, this boy will forever be a burden on his mother, causing Vairum indirectly to rob her. Having said that, the instruction does little to lessen this probability. Laddu attends his uncle's tutorials out of fear, opening his school books and staring at them in bewilderment as Vairum prods and ridicules him for an hour and a half.

Laddu's attitude toward his thrice-weekly Sanskrit tutorials is different. The first day his school chums attend, he does too, clearly intending that the time be spent in ribbing and chortling. This turns out to be more difficult than it is in school, where they have the cover of serious students, and because Laddu's companions refuse to misbehave in the home of the most respected widow on their street.

Laddu does not appear for the next session and Sivakami sends Muchami out to track him down. He finds the boy lying within a rough circle of smooth, large stones, the remains of a Jain monastery abandoned eight hundred years earlier but still outlined in stone dots and dashes like a telegraph from history. For generations, this has been one of those places where boys go to smoke and brag, boys with and boys without promising futures. Muchami knows the place well; he was never interested in smoking or bragging, but he was interested in boys and so was a regular.

"What is this?" Muchami begins haranguing Laddu from five yards away, and the boy jumps up guiltily. "How is it possible that there are four boys learning Sanskrit in your uncle's house and you are not one of them? Are those boys smarter than you, that they can find your house and you got lost in the forest? Maybe we should send you to school with a string tied around your waist and pull you home like a flapping fish when classes are over, shouldn't we? Can't you feel how your grandmother is suffering? She has brought all the knowledge of the village into your home and your portion is going to waste. She would give you everything, but she cannot afford to waste, not food, not clothes, not knowledge. It will rot there and smell bad and be thrown to the dogs in the street who will eat it and be fat and then maybe get sick, too! See how you are hurting your grandmother and all the creatures of the world by not following your dharma? Move! Back to the house! Look smart!"

Laddu doesn't look smart at all but does move fast. The tutorial has already begun, young Kesavan reciting noun inflections in a mesmerizing singsong, and his glazed-looking students singing each phrase back at him, "Ramaha Ramow Ramaaha, Ramam Ramow Ramaaha . . ." Laddu starts singing along while still in the courtyard and bursts over the threshold, expecting to garner a laugh on his entrance. No one even looks at him, and he creeps to a place on the floor, farthest from the tutor.

So now there are four boys learning Sanskrit. Or . . . ?

Sivakami, peeping in to check on the group's progress, notices Muchami, sitting in one of the doorways to the garden, agape at the proceedings. No sounds issue from him, but his lips are moving and he is hanging on each syllable as though it contains the mysteries of birth, death and cinema. Seeing him sit so wholly absorbed in the vicarious act of learning, Sivakami recalls one of her earliest impressions of him, that he aspires to be something more than most of his class. She recalls her own hope that she might assist him in realizing this aspiration. She already has—he is, at forty-two, among the most highly respected members of his caste. But here is a skill none of them has, something even she does not possess and never will, because she hasn't time nor would she consider it decorous. But now that Vairum has taken over much of the management of the property, and Sita has entered school, Muchami has more free time, and why shouldn't he consider some self-improvement?

The next day, Sivakami tells him to make a new slate and purchase some more chalk.

"Ayoh," he sighs. "Has Laddu lost or broken yet another slate? Honestly, I . . ."

"No, Muchami, it's for you," Sivakami says proudly, glancing at Mari, who is washing the vessels following the mid-morning meal, squatting in the courtyard and scrubbing the pots with soap-nut powder and a puff of coconut coir, splashing them with water from the well.

"What will I do with it?" he asks, understandably confused. Mari, having overheard Sivakami conferring with young Kesavan, starts to grin.

"As long as you are chasing Laddu and making him attend the Sanskrit tutorial, you may as well attend it yourself," Sivakami replies with mock gruffness. "I'm adding it to your responsibilities."

Muchami feels his mouth shape into a silent "o," much in the way he has tried, silently, to mouth the syllables of Sanskrit. He feels dismayed, as can happen when we receive something for which we did not dare hope. He is not a person who has spent time in self-definition. He is too busy, his personality too strong. It would have been a waste of his time. Now, though he would never describe it thus, his self-image is undergoing a jolt.

He is a member of what was once a warrior caste. His ancestors may have defended kings in a time before memory, which in their community is limited to a lifetime. Now their lot is with agriculture and service. They are a proud caste and, when serving, they serve fiercely. There are members of the generation after Muchami's who attend school—those young relatives of his who were Vairum's schoolyard defenders, for instance. One or two of his own generation may have done so, never for more than a few years. He didn't attend. It didn't matter.

He has altered as a result of his life in Sivakami's household, from the time he subtly adopted Hanumarathnam's Brahminical gait and manner. He has been further changed by his marriage to a woman who succeeds in observing Brahmin custom and prejudice more rigorously than most Brahmins—elevated, in Muchami and Mari's opinion; estranged, in that of their families.

And now he is to sit with the children of the scholarly caste and repeat with them the sacred phrases of the ancient language, the language of the distinguished, the learned. Was it even permissible?

"Young Kesavan thought it a terrific idea," Sivakami reassures him.

Is Muchami trembling?

Kesavan would think it a terrific idea: he is a progressive and positively delights in the idea of teaching Sanskrit to a servant in a Brahmin household. What hasn't occurred to him, or to Sivakami, is that were Muchami to learn to read and write Tamil, he would be well qualified for some other job. He would have choice and mobility. Sanskrit, on the other hand, qualifies him for nothing.

Filled with a cautious, unfamiliar joy, Muchami finds a scrap of board, paints it black, leans it on the back of his hut, checks to make sure it's drying smooth and gives it another coat the next day.

"Cha, chha, ja, jha, gna."

"Cha, cha, cha, cha, gna."

Laddu and his buddies suppress giggles as Kesavan turns to the garden door to address his newest student.

"Muchami. Try again. Cha, chha, ja, jha, gna."

"Cha, cha, cha . . ."

"No, Muchami, listen. *Chha*." Kesavan's voice betrays impatience. His other students are not nearly so interested, but they can, at least, pronounce the syllables of this language they are purporting to learn.

Muchami's brow is knit. "Cha," he chokes out hesitantly.

"Oh, never mind."

They move on to the next group of phonemes.

Muchami leaves his first class as dejected as he has ever been. He can hear that these syllables are distinct. But how to make them? He has no idea. How could it be as hard as this if children are doing it every day? Muchami speaks a different Tamil from the Brahmins'—one without Sanskrit inflections and terms. His tongue has not been accustomed to forming these sounds, which the sniggering boys have been instructed to use from birth, for words as common as "cooked rice" and "banana," items for which he has either another word entirely or another pronunciation.

His inability puzzles him—he is, as he well knows, among the most perceptive men in the village, no caste barred. He is a magnet for information and he knows how to use it. These sounds, though, and the words formed from them, they seem to have no place to roost in his head. They fly at him like frantic pigeons. They make him panic. He tries to retain them but feels them flutter off.

Each of those first few days, Sivakami eagerly inquires what it's like, to take a class. She expects his usual entertaining accounts, full of mimicry and insight. But all he says is, "It's good! Good! The teacher is very good, smart boy. Could I have more sambar?"

How to say he has never learned a thing in a classroom and can't figure out how to do so?

Mari does not ask him questions about his lessons. She flashes through her daily chores with defensive pride, and when Gayatri jokes that now it is not only Mari who is more Brahmin than the Brahmins, but her husband as well, Mari's pride shrills fiercer still, daring anyone to prevent this.

As the fifth year of Vani's residence in their home drizzles to a close, Sivakami feels pressure to perform some greater supplication on her son's behalf than the pujas she has done daily for the Ramar. She resolves on commissioning a dramatization of the Ramayana, the story of Rama's life and deeds. Vairum finds out for her which troupe in the region has the best reputation for flair and piety and writes a letter of request on her behalf. The troupe writes back; the dates and price are confirmed; she places their response at the feet of the four stone figures who govern her home and begs them again, be pleased with her and this re-enactment of their trials and victories. *Send me a grandchild, one who will belong to this house and to you.* The house drums around her with the noises of all those grandchildren who don't belong, welcome as they are.

Now, two days before Sivakami's dedicated Ramayana dramatization is to commence, Muchami brings unwelcome intelligence: another Ramayana will be performed in the village at the same time as hers, a different version.

Sivakami straightens from bending over a vat of oil, where eight vadais bounce and bubble. "Another Ramayana?" she repeats after him. "There are two Ramayanas: one written by Valmiki and one by Kamban, one Sanskrit and one Tamil, but they are one and the same. There is no . . . what did you call this?"

"It's called the Self-Respect Movement, Amma. They call this the 'Self-Respect Ramayana,'" Muchami reiterates shamefacedly. "I have heard it's a version where Ravana is, well . . . ahem, the hero."

Sivakami grimly squats and plunges the tongs amid the vadais to make them flip. Visalam squats beside her, patting vadai dough into sticky dumplings on a round, oil-blackened board, pressing her lips together and looking down, to keep herself from laughing.

"Will people go to see this, this . . . spectacle?" Sivakami demands. She lifts the crisped vadais from the vat and drops them into a vessel of yogourt, using her sari to wipe sweat from her upper lip and the corners of her eyes. Visalam slides a half-dozen more raw vadais into the pan, where they sink, begin to emit streams of bubbles and rise.

Visalam starts to giggle, and when Sivakami asks, "What?" points to the pan.

"Please, Sivakamikka," Gayatri says from the main hall, blowing on her coffee. "Don't be discouraged."

"Who is discouraged by these dirty, low types? Will Rama and Sita pay attention to these Brahmin-haters?" She stops herself from saying aloud the rest of her thoughts. *Would my husband have gone to the "other" Ramayana? He used to go with them, the ones who said there is no caste. Did they say "Long live Ravana"? What appeal is there in a topsy-turvy world?*

"I'm sure I don't know, Amma," Muchami solemnly replies, and Sivakami realizes she may have spoken her last question aloud, though sometimes, with Muchami, it doesn't seem she has to.

Visalam has patted out two more batches of vadais.

"Go," Sivakami tells her. "The kitchen is too hot."

The girl springs out to the courtyard and douses herself with well water, guffawing with delight.

The performance troupe Sivakami invited is setting up a stage in a mango grove about two hundred paces east along the cart track that leads from the southern exit of the Brahmin quarter. A number of children lucky or devious enough to have escaped work or school are goggling at the performers, who, even without makeup or costume, display a high theatricality of bearing. Several tease the children and make them shriek with gorgeous terror.

A mile directly east of Sivakami's back door, beyond the canal and the tracks, another stage and canopy are being erected, by performers physically indistinguishable from the first group in any significant way, though Sivakami's supporters will claim they are crude in looks and comportment. Even if they hadn't been so congenitally, the supporters splutter, they would have become so as a result of their crude tampering. How dare they touch the untouchable, alter the unalterable? The Ramayana is a foundation stone, a touchstone, a hero stone inscribed with the glorious events of some bygone day so they may never be erased nor forgotten, nor changed.

It's probably coincidence that the interloping troupe has come to play in the same week as Sivakami's scheduled performance, but both sides claim it's deliberate. The performers Sivakami hired are silent in the face of all political questions, while the other troupe and its citified supporters proclaim their mandate loud and proud:

"While Rama is seen by the ignorant Brahmin-followers to be a valiant hero, we will show him to be a cowardly schemer!

"While the ignorant Brahmins and the uneducated masses they have duped see Ravana as a licentious demon, we will show him to be an honourable man, taking no more—and no less—revenge than he must to vouchsafe his reputation!

"While the ignorant and the duped exhort their young virgins to uphold Sita as the model of virtuous womanhood, taking no initiative, living by the word of her husband, as instructed in that vile manual, *The Laws According to Manu,* this drama will expose her as the wanton and lusty strumpet she really was!"

The most skilled of the criers explain and extemporize; the least skilled recite, halting but loud, from block-printed, hand-sewn booklets. They thrust their manifesto into the hands of numberless unlettered villagers, cajoling, mocking, seducing them into attending. They roam and comb every caste neighbourhood, except the Brahmins', where they dump piles of the pamphlets at each exit.

In the hands of any other caste member, the pamphlets look like invitations. Littering the Brahmin quarter, they look like warnings. The wind blows them through the street, plastering them against the red and white stripes of the verandas. Some blow up beyond the reach of indignant reactionaries gathering them to thrust in their fires; some blow into eavestroughs and the little space between roof and walls. Perhaps they will be forgotten there for seasons on end and then discovered by an inquisitive grandchild in a time when all such conflicts are obsolete.

"Come one, come all!" the pamphleteer politicos scream.

Understand how the stinking Aryans flooded our Tamil country from the north with their weapons and their myths of our inferiority. Come and we will reveal what the Brahmins really mean when they say "all the monkeys of

the southern country welcomed Rama and pledged their
services to him." What do you think, noble citizens? These
Brahmins see us real Tamilians as monkeys! And devils!
Who is this Rama who is so celebrated for overcoming the
rightful ruler to the "monkey" throne by devious means
and waging war on the "devils"? Ravana might have been
a king from any of our luminous dynasties: any regal
Pallava, valiant Pandyan, noble Chola, or high born
Chera, who once ruled and battled and upheld our Tamil
pride. Are we so stupid that we will continue to accept
these distortions?

"Invaders out! Down with Brahmin raj! The day of the elite has
ended! They don't respect us—we have Self-Respect! Long live the
real Tamil people!"

Tonight, the seven-night-long performances commence. Which will
draw the larger crowd?

Vairum overhears men taking bets at the Kulithalai Club, when he
goes to play tennis. Manifold factors weight the odds. As with *bhajans*
or big temple events, only a small proportion of audience members
attend Ramayana recitals or dramatizations out of religious devotion.
Most come for entertainment, but devotion and diversion usually need
not be separated. Tonight, the townsfolk face a strange choice: should
they or should they not go to the new Ramayana, which, as a novelty,
is a much surer source of entertainment than the smooth and well-
worn passages and postures of the classical presentation? Will it be
blasphemous? Worse, disrespectful?

And there are other concerns: Will there be violence? Riots?
What does this performance signify?

The members of Minister's political salon have, as always, an
irreconcilable variety of opinions on the matter.

"It's an insult and an affront," foams Dr. Kittu Iyer, "and quite
wholly unnecessary and—"

"False." Mani Iyer interrupts, agreeing emphatically with the
older Brahmin man. "It's all lies."

Vairum, since returning to Cholapatti, has been a regular attendee at the salon, though he doesn't come daily, because he is too busy with his work and because he prefers to maintain a slight distance from these men who are nonetheless useful to him.

"It is the expression of our youth." Muthu Reddiar sweeps the space before him good-humouredly. "They are impatient. Don't take it so seriously."

Vairum had chatted with Minister on arriving, before the others had come. This "Self-Respect" Ramayana seems to Minister to be the harbinger of a fate that has already begun to strike. The years have not been great for him, politically, and he is serving as Taluk Board president—again. He had stood for election last year at the urging of his numerous friends. While it was not in him to turn down any opportunity to be a figurehead, he was acutely conscious of not having held so lowly a position (the first time, it was a pinnacle!) in over ten years. Back then it was a position given by appointment. In the years since, these decisions have increasingly been made by election. Minister progressed into ever-greater circles of influence, elected to the District Board and then to the Legislative Council, but as the franchise expanded beyond the elite, his decline was drawn: he can no longer drum up a majority vote beyond the *taluk*. Now, Brahmins will vote for him because he is one of them, and select non-Brahmins if he can still do something for them. But he never thought to court peasants—it never occurred to him that they could have any impact on his political future.

While the Self-Respecters' politics take something from each of Congress (they are for independence) and Justice (they advocate rule by non-Brahmins), they are resolved on overturning the elite class to which all the salon-goers belong, regardless of caste. These men enjoy debating Self-Respect politics, and even take the Dravidians' side in the safety of their small gathering, but they are scared of the Self-Respecters and have no intention of going near that performance tonight.

Dr. Kittu Iyer's eye softens as it lands on Vairum, who rarely speaks here, despite his frequent attendance. "You, at least, we can count on to take the right side in this debate: it's wonderful of your mother to be doing this for you, and the whole community will benefit, especially the illiterates, who get so few such uplifting opportunities."

Unsurprisingly, the conventional audience gets by far the greater share that first night. Vairum attends, as he is expected to, with Vani, and feels acutely self-conscious. He thinks at first that this is because those in the audience fawningly make a place for him at the front, expressing gratitude that his mother has done this for them. Perhaps he is uncomfortable because they all know the reason Sivakami has sponsored this: his and Vani's childlessness. He realizes, however, over the course of the performance, which he finds predictably conventional and uninspiring, that, although he is religious, he has nothing in common with the Brahmins who surround him.

He unconsciously fingers the old silver coin flipped into his waistband as he thinks how he has no friends among the Brahmins here. Since returning, he has made friends mostly among upper-caste non-Brahmins in Kulithalai while his Cholapatti neighbours remain as distasteful to him as ever, in their narrowness and lack of generosity, which he thinks he sees in his mother, also: she will help anyone of the clan, but her goodwill, he thinks, stops at the exit to the Brahmin quarter. He has also heard them complaining about his generosity, *of all things,* he thinks, getting worked up even as he sits before the decorated stage, his mind far from the action. He has bought a number of their plots of land, which they had let go through their laziness and bad decisions, and turned them around. They got a better price from him than they would from anyone else, but then they complain to one another! Jealousy. And they can't stand that he is friends with non-Brahmins, and that he hired a non-Brahmin manager for his rice mill: the best applicant, a born leader, even if he is from one of the peasant castes.

Why should I pretend solidarity with my caste? he is fuming, as they sit around him, smelling of holy ash and hair oil, gasping at all the familiar plot points. *What have they ever done for me?*

He waits out the performance, more for Vani's sake than anything, but it is a torment.

THE NEXT MORNING, when Muthu Reddiar arrives at the salon entrance, mopping his brow with an outsized kerchief and twirling the ends of his moustaches to guard against wilting, he wheezes, "Bets are being paid out at the club."

"The people have shown their might!" an unfamiliar voice crows in Tamil behind him. It's Murthy, his hair oiled and slicked back with care into a kudumi, minus one lock hanging before his ear. His kurta is stained with what might be squash. He occasionally drops in at the salon to tout Brahmin uplift: communal politics have led Brahmins, too, to realize they might claim some unified identity. "Tradition offers reassurance, consolation," Murthy puffs. "It will always win out over sensationalism. Clearly, the people's affection for the real Ramayana will triumph over childish stunts."

Minister always welcomes Murthy (despite the man's disregard for the English usage rule) as a link to a constituency best cultivated via its zealots. Still, he hates having to think in communal terms and yearns for the times when he had only to fulfill promises to important individuals.

"Bah! The people are scared." Ranga Chettiar jabs his finger aggressively at Murthy, who looks surprised and pained. "You and your ilk have cowed them for eight thousand years. But someday"— the Chettiar's voice dives deep into his most profundo basso—"someday, he will break the chains of Aryan domination and come into the full flowering of his Dravidian manhood . . ."

"So breaking the chains of British domination and coming into our Indian manhood takes no place in your scheme?" Dr. Kittu Iyer's narrow jowls quiver.

"Now, now." Minister's tone is more censorious than he would wish, but the doctor has hit a nerve. "If one is born and comes of age within a united empire, loyalty to it is as loyalty to parents and ancestors. If one renounces one's heritage, one is nothing."

Minister catches Vairum's eye and suddenly feels fiercely annoyed with the younger man for observing all, daily, in silence, never taking a stand. Vairum clearly has no political ambitions—why is he here?

"Isn't that right, Vairum?" Minister lobs. "Look at what your mother is doing for you—you owe her the world, isn't it?"

Vairum wags his head noncommittally. Such statements, his gesture might imply, are self-evident and need hardly be spoken.

Vairum goes again that night to the Ramayana Sivakami sponsored but finds himself unable to bear being surrounded by Brahmins. Several of his friends told him that day that they would be attending the other Ramayana because they were interested in supporting its message of non-Brahmin liberation. He is interested in that, too, and thinks, *They are my gods. Can I not worship them as well in an atmosphere I find more sympathetic?*

He takes Vani home, then goes and joins his friends. He is a little shocked by what he sees: Rama and Lakshmana as comic villains, Sita as a harlot, and Ravana made to seem a hero—as though this story were written on the other side of the world from the one he knows. He isn't sure how to reconcile this with his daily prayers to the Ramar in his home, except to think that his prayers are private. He has his convictions and can't escape his heritage. *They are the gods of my home and I am obliged to worship them,* he thinks, but he is not obliged to worship them in the company of people he cannot like or respect. How can he share their religious feeling if he doesn't share their caste sentiment?

He decides that the Self-Respect Ramayana is not an act of devotion, but it doesn't need to be. He prays at home. This is something different.

When Sivakami serves him breakfast the next morning, she asks Vairum to report on the performance, which she will not attend until the last night. His response is predictably disappointing.

"Amma, even weddings are more unique than these Ramayana performances," he dryly points out. "Why waste breath? Attendance was good."

Muchami reliably gives a much more satisfying account, taking nearly an hour to describe the costumes and mimic the highlights of the evening. Gayatri, who had attended, claims she is entertained all over again by Muchami's show, but also assures Sivakami, "It's a *first-class* performance, Sivakamikka, take it from me." She repeats, with emphasis, the English phrase that has passed confidently into bourgeois Tamil. "*First-class.*"

Muchami also, however, brings the unwelcome wisdom that nine-year-old Laddu, who had been given permission to attend, was spotted at the wrong tent. Sivakami mentions this to Vairum, who catches Laddu up by one arm from the corner where he is napping and delivers a brief but thorough thrashing.

"You were given permission to attend the performance your grandmother sponsored. You were not given time and freedom to do whatever you want. As long as you live under this roof, you will abide by what you are told. Clear?"

Laddu drops back onto the floor, sobbing.

The next day, Sivakami doesn't bother asking Vairum for his report but rather waits for Muchami's, which he delivers with all the enthusiasm and verve of the days prior, though he omits one detail. Gayatri notes this omission and says nothing: Vairum was seen once more under the canvas roof of the other troupe's performance tent.

"You all have enjoyed terrific success," Dr. Kittu Iyer says stiffly, in a rare acknowledgement, that same morning. The night before, that of the third performance, Self-Respect's audience equalled Sivakami's. "With the kinds of concessions the Justice Party has achieved for the non-Brahmin sector, one can't help but see a time when very few Brahmins would want to live in Tamil Nadu," he mumbles tangentially. "Opportunities are becoming scarce for us."

"Oh, pshaw!" Ranga Chettiar ejects. "The presidency's Brahmins have had their rampant nepotism but slightly curtailed. This hardly heralds your starvation, my good fellow!"

"Well may we all starve if our country is run by an administration chock full of fellows whose ICS examination scores are deplorably below par." Mani Iyer trembles indignantly.

"Yes, none of you fellows has been able to satisfactorily explain the continued inadequacy of performance by non-Brahmin castes on all academic and standardized measures," Dr. Kittu Iyer accuses. "And these reserved positions in colleges and the government can hardly offer much motivation to improve."

"Oh, come now." Rama Sastri, the lawyer, waves an orangewood stick at them and goes back to his cuticles. "All of your nephews and cousins and the brothers of your sons-in-law have profited from your acquaintance with our host. This is why you have so consistently returned him to office."

The remark is all too accurate, but none of them needs to be reminded. Minister, as their host and the subject of this most awkward moment, grasps for a remark which will smooth it.

"I'm sorry," the Sastri smirks. "That was tacky."

Young Kesavan, the Sanskrit master, attending for a second day, rises, stretches and yawns. "I agree that the administration is far too Brahminically weighted. It's not healthy for our future. But I, too, wish that non-Brahmin lobby groups could put the energy into self-improvement that they have invested in divisiveness and political manoeuvring."

"I ... I think," Minister begins, "I know you all have real evidence of my esteem for you and your families. You have been my constituency and will remain so. What benefit could I expect if I didn't return your trust?"

"You are a beacon, Minister," Muthu Reddiar rejoins with hearty ambiguity. "We are all looking to you in this difficult time."

"I have been waiting for that boy, that traitor—where is Vairum today?" Dr. Kittu Iyer springs to his feet, then looks a little dizzy. "You all have heard that he is now attending this Self-Respect whatever-it-is-called?" he spits.

Minister had not heard this and becomes grave. "I . . . he must have business in Trichy today. Are you quite sure? He didn't attend the performance his mother sponsored for him?"

His cronies shake their heads, not sure whether they are glad or regretful to be delivering him this news.

At 3:30, Minister descends to eat his tiffin. Exiting the stairwell, he padlocks the door behind him. It's only mid-afternoon, but with alien elements about the village, it's best not to take chances. Crossing the veranda, he steps into the narrow hallway that opens into the great hall and pauses to let his eyes adjust to the dimness.

He's sleepy. He's been attending only the first portion of the performance each night, just long enough to show his support for Sivakami. Even this brief appearance, however, has meant he gets to bed later than usual. And the daily salon inevitably leaves him too stimulated to manage an afternoon rest.

Gayatri smiles at him and shoos the children from the dining room as he sits. She lays a banana leaf on the floor in front of him and goes to the kitchen to fetch a serving vessel full of freshly steamed idlis. She puts five on the leaf and returns to the kitchen for okra sambar. The oily crescent moons beneath her eyes are darker than usual—it's been a busy week and she can't get to sleep at night until her husband comes home.

"How is Sivakami Mami?" he commences.

"Resigned. We didn't even speak of the other Ramayana today. Muchami gives such an entertaining—"

"Vairum has been seen at that other Ramayana."

This is not a revelation to Gayatri. "He punished his nephew for the same transgression," she says, though she is aware, on a level she can't articulate, that it is not the same transgression at all. "Are you going to say something to Vairum?"

"I don't understand his motives!" He shakes his head. "Does Sivakami Mami know he's been seen there?"

"I would hope no one would dare tell her." Gayatri stands to accept the baby from her mother-in-law.

"This is how big St. Joseph's College graduates behave?" Minister jabs the air with his eating hand, scattering beads of okra, then jabs again at his food. "What can he be thinking? He's not a child."

"No, yes." Gayatri jiggles the baby vigorously on her hip. "Maybe he needs a child of his own before he feels that."

"Hm," Minister grunts.

"He won't say it, but I think he thinks Cholapatti Brahmins don't accept him," Gayatri ventures.

"They don't," Minister responds pragmatically. "So what?"

"So maybe this is a kind of revenge."

"But no one cares but his mother!" Minister expostulates. "All he will do is give food for gossip and wound her."

Gayatri murmurs agreement, because if she didn't, she would have to suspect that Vairum may see this all too well, that his attendance is not a youthful caprice, nor a gesture of ignorance or naïveté, and Gayatri, while she is shrewd, can't think that way about a boy she likes.

The next day, when Vairum arrives in the salon, after the other members, Minister shouts at him. "What do you think you are doing? What about your mother?"

"My mother belongs to an old order," Vairum responds evenly. "I am interested in a new one."

The salon is astounded. Vairum has never expressed an opinion before and they, with the exception of Rama Sastri, realize now that they have been a little afraid to find out where he stands.

"You . . . you are worshipping Ravana?" asks Dr. Kittu Iyer, too shocked to reprimand him.

"No—neither of these Ramayanas is an act of worship. My mother's is supplication. The other is a political statement." Vairum accepts a cup of tea and a biscuit from a maid. "I worship the gods of my home in my home, every morning and night. I ask them, too, for the blessing of a child, but I will worship them no matter what they choose to give me in my life. I have been fortunate in most respects, so far. And I am interested in witnessing what all these Self-Respecters have to say."

Rama Sastri takes him up. "Come now, Vairum: you know very well *you* are making a political statement by attending one and not the other."

"Fair enough. By that reasoning, staying home would also be a political statement." Vairum watches the men watching him hold his own. "These are political times. The Self-Respecters offer an amusing spectacle. And they have a good point: the caste system *is* unfair."

Murthy, returning from a trip to the outhouse, hollers from the door. "I have been waiting for you! How could you betray your mother and your people in this fashion?" he berates Vairum in Tamil.

Although most of the other salon members would have said the same thing, they find Murthy somewhat distasteful and hearing him speak their thoughts makes them wish, a little, to take some other side.

"Your father was like a brother to me and I am as a father to you. I forbid you to return. You will attend the real Ramayana from tonight forward, yes? Good boy."

Vairum gives his father's cousin a hard look, shrewd and not unaffectionate. "I am not as confident as you of how my father would have advised me in this situation. But I have my reasons, and I will attend the performance of my choice. Excuse me."

Vairum rises and departs the salon before Murthy has a chance to react. Several seconds later, though, Murthy toddles stiffly down the stairs to give chase. He sees Vairum heading toward their houses at the other end of the Brahmin quarter and scurries after his swiftly striding form. At the end of the street, however, Vairum doesn't go into his house but continues on as the road turns left—toward town, toward the river, who knows. Murthy stops, panting, at his own veranda, the other salon members looking on, down the street, from Minister's door.

The next morning, Vairum comes back to the salon and, as always, peruses the newspapers, not speaking because he is not spoken to. Murthy is not in attendance, and the others hash things out among themselves. In a lull, Gopi Chettiar, who is also more observer than participant, asks Vairum's opinion on a newly formed cereals-processing unit going up in Thiruchi.

"It will do well. I have invested," Vairum responds, his fingertips joined, so his hands form a loose cage at his mouth.

The men are clearly surprised.

"Ah," Gopi Chettiar clears his throat nervously. "They asked me..."

"Get in now," nods Vairum. "It will soon get expensive."

"While we're on the subject of investment," Muthu Reddiar breaks in, smiling, "I wanted to let you know, Vairum—well, let all of you know," he expands graciously, "my man, the Sikh, has telegraphed me that our shipment of Australian horses has arrived in Madras harbour. I wanted to thank you for your support in this project, Vairum. They are evidently sturdier than our Indian breeds, and the stallions should stud nicely with my line of carriage horses."

"Glad to know it," Vairum says, poker-faced. "Clearly a winning proposal."

Minister is taken aback. Business matters are often referred to in the salon, since they are inseparable from the workings of politics and power, but this discussion verges uncomfortably on transaction. He thinks, though, that he may now understand how Vairum has been benefiting from these years in attendance. Now he quickly starts to feel pride in having drawn the boy in: Minister's not a minister at present, his political fortunes may be at a low ebb, but he is still an influence peddler. The boy knows which way the wind is blowing, Minister thinks. And he is my friend.

Vairum catches his eye and they exchange a slight smile.

The morning after the sixth performance, Rama Sastri treats them to a recitation of the concluding stanzas of each of the performances. Both showed the episode in which Ravana is slain in battle by Rama. The Sastri has sent his reluctant servant to the performance each night, and the man has turned out to be an excellent reporter.

"This is our performance, close to Kamban's words, if not quite," says the Sastri, clearing his throat and proclaiming:

"With Ravana's death, the field grows still
At such long last, the end.
Sita and Rama, reunited with dignity,
Paid respects by each foe, each friend.

And this is theirs—rather innovative," he smiles, shifting position, dropping his right hand and lifting his left:

"Ravana's noble head and body
Rejoined on the funeral pyre.
Dravidian pride and sorrow now
But battlefield's bloody mire.
The flames of truth and purity

Must in your eyes leap higher.
Ravana's children! Avenge this death!
Unite in the name of your sire!
Loose the blindfold of Aryan deception,
Every Shastri, Iyengar, Iyer
Is a manufacturer of illusions
Yet these are the ones you hire
For your weddings, your blessings, your babies and homes
Whether you be Panchama or Nair
Self Respect, man! Do it yourself!
Beneath Ravana's flag: the lyre!"

The Sastri concludes with a flourish.

"It's not a *lyre,* it's a veena," Dr. Kittu Iyer snorts.

"Poetic licence, dear chap," Rama Sastri responds.

"You can only take poetic licence with *poetry,*" the doctor explodes. "This is *drivel.*"

"Does anyone know why the so-called Self-Respecters ended one night early?" Mani Iyer deepens his ever-present brow wrinkles. "Surely not to actually enable the populace to celebrate Rama's return and recoronation in peace."

"Surely not." Muthu Reddiar strokes his upwardly waxed moustaches. "I passed their tent on my way here—they're readying for performance, not packing up."

"Curiouser and curiouser," remarks Minister, and the others frown in agreement or perplexity.

"My foot!" Murthy, who had held his tongue till then, screams in English. He has leapt up, fists and eyes clenched, face flushing from pomegranate to mangosteen. "Day after day this talktalktalk and no action. These fellows cannot fling about insults and expect best citizens would accept simply! Though they must think so because of you!" he spits at Vairum, who looks away, mild and skeptical.

"Have you . . . a . . . proposal?" Minister asks, though his tone makes it sound more like "Sit down . . . you're . . . embarrassing yourself."

"Yes!" Murthy cries, returning to his native tongue, ablaze with inspiration. There is a patch of dirty grey stubble on his dewlap, missed while shaving. It wobbles at the men as he reveals his idea. "I will lie down! I will lie across the path that these asses of the audience must take to attend the debacle, and prevent them from entering."

"Bravo!" Rama Sastri starts to clap. "Take a stand, man—lying down! The show must not go on!"

Murthy heaves for the door, muttering and crying, "Must not go on, the show!"

"The peasants will never step over him," Mani Iyer offers.

"No—they will go around him," says Ranga Chettiar with exasperation.

Minister tries to intervene. "Please, dear man. Don't be rash"—and he grabs for Murthy's hand, but it is slippery and Murthy, inflamed by his vision, descends the stairs.

"Well, thank God *that's* taken care of," snorts Muthurunga Chettiar, half-reclined on a divan.

After some moments, Minister speaks. "I shan't let him go to that place, alone—I shall try again, this evening, to dissuade him, and if he won't be dissuaded, I will follow him. He is my good friend, like all of you, one of my constituency, and I owe him a debt of good faith."

There follows a silence in which it seems several of the men mean to speak and change their minds. Rama Sastri finally breaks it.

"Ah—I had thoughts of slinking over there myself. Curiosity, don't you know, the last night. Theatre is hardly theatre when performed by my man."

"I am not curious—I am interested by this message of non-Brahmin uplift," declares Ranga Chettiar.

"Tsk, let us join!" Muthu Reddiar waves dismissively. "It's a spectacle!"

"Wouldn't miss it for the world," Gopi Chettiar offers in response to Ranga Chettiar's expectant look.

"We are not to be outnumbered," Dr. Kittu Iyer says with stiff and evident reluctance. "There may be those still amenable to the Congress message."

"Quite," whimpers Mani Iyer. "Oh, quite."

Vairum clears his throat. "I'll see you all there, then." He smiles, templing his fingers, lowers his head and can't help starting to chuckle, then laugh. Rama Sastri joins in, and then Minister, and the Reddiar. The others are not so compelled but smile perplexedly at their solidarity. It seems almost fated.

"Ho, ho, what is this?" the actor playing Rama exclaims jocularly. "Hoi! Jambu, Bala, come, quickly! See what I have found!"

Ordinarily, Murthy would bow before an actor dressed as Rama, but this is not a Rama he recognizes: painted-on leer, unimpressive profile, sloppy clothes. Rage and hurt start to pump him full again with bravado. Anyway, he can't bow: he's flat on his back.

Two more heads bend over him: Lakshmana and Sita, they can be none else, but, again, what perversions!

"Brahmin," says Lakshmana with glee, drawing a line from his own shoulder to hip to indicate the holy thread visible beneath Murthy's rumpled kurta.

"What do you want?" Sita demands. Stubble pokes through "her" rice flour face powder and kohl beauty marks.

"The show," Murthy squeaks, "must not go on!"

Rama turns to the others incredulously and Lakshmana starts a high-pitched giggle.

"Oh, come, let us get ready." Sita turns away. "Leave him until big boss comes and we have an audience."

"We have an audience!" Lakshmana jumps up and down a few times at Murthy's head, to make him wince, then follows the others.

Murthy can tell from their nasal voices and funny gaits that they are comic actors—what sort of Ramayana features comic actors in the lead roles? What was the English expression Minister Iyer was using, some months back . . . cave of inequity? Lair of inquiety? It means something very sinful. He was talking about opium smokers in Calcutta: white people, women. Shocking. Murthy sighs and looks at his hands, folded on his chest, chubby fingers and stubby nails, and up again at the sky. It's still blue, though each cloud blares orange off its western slope, heralding the dusk. He hears voices from around a bend in the path and tightens his bearing so he looks like a toy soldier at attention—knocked down.

"Ayoh! *Enn' idhu?*" It's a woman's voice, accompanied by running feet. A family group looks down on him.

"Who is it?"

"An Iyer!"

"Is the Iyer hurt? Does he need assistance?"

They do not make eye contact with him, and stand at a respectful and non-polluting distance, slightly bowed, rigid.

"No, you silly people, the Iyer doesn't need help," Murthy bellows. "As long as he knows you dolts are not participating in this scandalous and disrespectful so-called Ramayana, he will be fine." He returns his attention to the sky.

A crowd has dribbled in behind the first family. As they grasp Murthy's intentions, some begin to look guilty. Others begin to smile behind raised hands. Yet others appear worried. None, however, passes him by and the crowd grows as fast and thick as the darkness, bottlenecking some four feet from Murthy's prone form. A continual murmuring passes the message back and along.

A familiar voice rings out above the hum—Rama Sastri. "By Jove, it's working!"

Murthy straightens still further. The next voice, Dr. Kittu Iyer, sounds pleased and pompous. "Well done. Well done, I say. Move aside! Step aside, here. At once!"

In the instant before they achieve the front of the crowd, however, something transpires to Murthy's other side.

Rama! Sita! Lakshmana! Hanuman! Each springs from the bushes and takes his pose until they form a grotesque caricature of the classic formation, the very one that graces Sivakami's main hall. Murthy is lying at their feet. As one, they glance down and their faces light up with exaggerated pleasure. They present Murthy to the crowd with a sweeping gesture, as though his is one more body on the battlefield of Lanka, and a great cheer rises up. Minister and the members of his salon emerge and break this sound bubble; at their appearance, a nervous hush falls like soap film upon the masses.

Now another shout is heard from behind the crowd, and all turn and crane to see: it is Ravana—tall, handsome, noble-looking, as he would not be in the conventional Ramayana—who at the end of the previous performance was borne away, cold and ashen, on a funeral bier. Now he brandishes a sword atop a silk-jacketed steed, which capers and snorts as vigorously as his master.

"He lives!" shouts the shrimpy Rama, and cowers, the heel of his hand pressed to his mouth. Lakshmana hides behind his brother; Sita bats her eyelashes at her former captor; Hanuman, a large-cheeked fellow with a tail, yawns and scratches.

Vairum approaches through a group of not only lower-caste labourers, but Panchamas (as untouchables are coming to be called), Christians, even Muslims, though each sub-group has clustered and holds itself subtly apart from the others.

"He lives! He lives! He lives!" The chant begins in the crowd.

But which crowd? For Ravana not only faces a crowd but leads one. Which is composed of . . . strangers. Vairum will later learn that the 5:40 Thiruchi local pulled in and deposited them—mostly young, many urban, some from as far away as Madras, all chanting Self-Respect slogans—on the Kulithalai platform, where this Ravana had met them.

The local crowd pulls back to form a ring with more of their own numbers, who have continued to appear at the rear of Ravana's guard. Murthy has not moved, though he lifts his head and strains to see.

"How charming," sneers Ravana, and suddenly turns his horse's flank toward the salon members and sweeps his sword downward. The sun reflects red off the blade and they cringe into one another. "Nay, how convenient. The Brahmins and Brahmin-lovers have come to us." Ravana looks beyond them, toward the tent, and they turn, also, to see the rest of the cast—some twenty actors—assembled behind Rama.

"Gentlemen," Ravana booms. "The moment of justice's proof has arrived!" Three of the actors take hold of Rama, Sita and Lakshmana, three others snap them into leg irons. In the same moment, Minister's arms are pulled roughly back and his wrists tied. He looks back wildly to see a fiendish young face with huge white teeth and snapping black eyes.

"Release me at once!" Vairum hears from Ranga Chettiar, though he can't see exactly what is happening.

"Brute!" This is Rama Sastri. All the salon members have been apprehended, except Vairum, who is not with them.

"As a rightful and invincible monarch of the Dravidian people, I declare the trial of our oppressors, betrayers and false prophets open. Lead the prisoners to the dock!"

Ravana wheels his charge and then stops with a puzzled frown, as though he's heard something but can't place the source. His glance breasts the crowd and then descends to a form at his feet.

"Halt," Vairum hears Murthy squeak.

"Naptime?" asks Ravana.

"Sabotage, my liege," offers an actor with a gaudy band around his arm reading "bailiff." "He thought he could prevent the audience from coming in if he lay across the path."

Ravana dismounts with a jangle and clank—earrings, chains, bangles, belt, hilt, scabbard, anklets—and steps up to Murthy, whose features contract in fright as he draws his hands to his breast like a dog showing its belly.

"How you Aryans under-esteem us," Ravana tut-tuts. He takes a great stride, led by an immense foot clad in a gold-embroidered, curved-toe slipper with a stamped-leather sole, across and over Murthy's sunken chest—a gesture of magnificent disrespect. Ravana's horse follows suit and Ravana remounts.

"On with the show!" he cries, and gallops toward the tent.

Murthy is hauled to his feet by a couple of bailiffs and dragged along with the crowd toward the tent.

The painted backdrop, which, for the last week, has displayed scenes of palaces, forests and rocky beaches—Rama's castle was mysteriously identical to Ravana's, down to the personnel—now provides the atmosphere of a courtroom, with a ragged St. George flapping forlornly off the same flagpole as Ravana's flag, which stands out straight, starched with rice paste. On a podium stands a statuette, dangling scales from one hand; instead of classical Greek garb, however, the female figure is wrapped in the manner of a Tamil country tribal.

As Vairum surges forward with the crowd, he realizes that his salon-fellows are not the only detainees. There are others who must have been frog-marched in with the crowd from points distant. But— that one, with the wire-rimmed spectacles and bald head—is he supposed to be . . . ? If he were reduced by about three stone, perhaps he could pass. And why is that other prisoner clad in the jaunty cap and buttoned-up jacket of . . . ? But the hat is tied on with string, and that dark visage, with teeth poking out in all directions, hardly cuts the profile on which so many hearts are said to have been dashed. The men of the salon don't look up often, but when they do, they are even more frightened to find themselves surrounded by characters whom they recognize from newspapers and books, but whose likenesses here are to those photos as the Self-Respect Ramayana is to the original. Vairum is concerned for the salon members and glad to be out in the crowd, should anything untoward happen. But until it does, he has to admit this Ramayana is far more entertaining than the other.

"And now, who is our judge?" demands Ravana of the crowd. "Who will sit in judgment on all those who, in weakness and greed, have downtrodden the rightful people of Dravida Nadu?"

"You, Ravana!" several young men chorus back. "You judge!"

Ravana blushes and fawns. "No, no, I really couldn't."

Uproarious laughter rises from the crowds and Ravana turns serious.

"No, I refuse to judge because I myself must be judged. I want to submit to trial along with all the others who have purported to rule and lead you. Let us put a halt to blackmail and subterfuge, and let the people judge who is to rule them!"

Cheering.

"But someone must guide and order the proceedings, at least, and for this task I propose our Mariamman, never bent nor bowed." He kicks off his slippers and makes an elaborate prostration to the tribal goddess. All those present do the same, though the salon members must be rolled into and lifted out of the position, unable to help themselves with their hands.

Ravana settles himself on a bamboo mat. Two curvaceous young women fan him. "I declare the proceedings open," he announces lightly.

This is the night Sivakami is to attend the Ramayana she sponsored. Muchami has minimized the degree of attrition it has suffered, so she is shocked, when she approaches the *pandal*, to find no more than twenty people in attendance, made up of a few neighbours, with some Kulithalai Brahmins she doesn't know, even though the coronation of Rama has already begun. She has brought Vani, and had called for Murthy and Rukmini before leaving. Rukmini came but said it seemed her husband was already at the performance. Gayatri, sitting on her veranda with her children as they passed, said the same thing.

Now Sivakami turns to Muchami, who is following with Mari at a respectful distance. "Muchami! Where are Murthy Anna and Minister Anna?" she whispers loudly.

Muchami, miserable and mortified on her behalf, looks around. "I can't imagine, Amma."

Sivakami takes a place on a mat to one side of the stage and says to Vani, "I suppose Vairum was meeting some associate and will come when he's done?"

Vani doesn't answer. Sivakami looks at her hard and looks for Muchami again, but he has taken a place with the non-Brahmins, too far away to ask him the same question.

Back at the Self-Respect Ramayana, each of the characters is tried, one by one. Vairum, caught up in the mood of the crowd, finds the hearings eerily convincing. It never would have occurred to him to fault Rama and Sita for behaving as they do in the story, but it's really quite arguable. He doesn't think he'll ever be able to see his gods as he did before. Perhaps this is what it means to be a Hindu in the new age. Mother and father are to be worshipped as gods, and they have their limitations, as Vairum increasingly can see. Why shouldn't the gods, too, admit their faults?

Next, the politicians are tried: the chubby Gandhi, the buck-toothed Nehru, a host of others, found short-sighted—nay, blind; neglectful; unwilling to face their own prejudices. The crowd is in a frenzy.

Finally, the men of the salon: Brahmin and non-Brahmin but all clearly elite, marked unmistakably by their fine clothes, soft hands, softer bellies. They are given no chance to speak because they are clearly guilty, guilty, guilty.

Vairum recalls his euphoria at that long-ago courtroom victory when he won his sister her due. Here it is again, the triumph of right over might. The excitement of the crowd, unbelievably, is still mounting. Their clamour coalesces into a chant: "Parade! Parade!"

Like a snake with a belly full of squirming mice, the throng surges out along the path where, so recently, Murthy stretched his now defiled body, and heads toward the other tent.

"There's another Brahmin!" shouts one of the hired goons. "Take him!"

Vairum is alarmed as two of the bailiffs reach for him.

"Ugh!" The one to reach him first pulls back. "Stop! Leper!"

The thugs surround Vairum but none is willing to touch him. One throws him a rope. "Tie your own wrists, leper."

"No!" Two of Muchami's nephews push through the crowd and shove them aside, defending Vairum against attack as they had when they were all lads in school. "He doesn't count. He has attended every night of your Ramayana."

"It's lascivious curiosity, just as they like our women," sneers the roughest-looking bailiff.

"Yeah, take advantage, but don't take it home," says another.

"Really, he is different. Even the Brahmins know it," says the older nephew gently. By then, several of Vairum's friends, who were willing to defend him but, unlike the nephews, unused to having to, have advanced with similar protests.

The mass has continued to flow around them, and now Ravana comes past on his horse, with the prisoners of the salon, roped together, trudging abjectly behind.

"What's this, a stray?" Ravana trumpets from far above, then squints at him. "Leper?"

"They say he's an *exception,* sire," the tubby bailiff explains.

"Oh, they say so, do they?" Ravana glances from one nephew to another. "Well then, it must be so. We must trust the locals, fellows, or how will they ever trust us? Hop to, my nasties," he calls to the salon cortège. "There's more than one way to conquer," he nods to the foiled vigilantes. "In making war, as in making love, you must use your head as well as your hands."

He gallops on with a laugh and wink.

—☙

VAIRUM IS SWEPT ALONG in the crowd to "The Coronation of Rama," the grand finale of the conventional Ramayana.

Thus it is that Sivakami witnesses her gods arrested and tried, in a monkey court where the only monkey is found innocent, and the enemy of her gods, whose painted demon face revealed little intelligence and much vanity, is surprised but gratified to find himself revered as a hero. She sees her gods and her neighbours pelted with shoes (no one should have been wearing shoes on ground that had been consecrated for the performance, she thinks—did they bring them in bags?) and thus turned into untouchables. Rama is defiled, hit with the very sandals—his own—that his younger brother had placed on the throne when the god was sent into exile.

From her vantage point, backed safely by Muchami and Mari into a corner of the clearing, along with Vani and Rukmini, Sivakami feels curiously unsurprised to see Vairum arrive with the crowd from the other Ramayana, more surprised to see Murthy and Minister arrive as prisoners.

She had been wondering whether all this was her fault, whether she attracted the other Ramayana with her extravagant gesture. Gayatri and Muchami had assured her, no, no, this could never be the case. It's not the kind of thing she would say to Vairum. She and he make eye contact now, across the crowd, but she can't tell what he is thinking. From her protected corner, she tries but can't tell if he is wearing shoes, as has been his habit since Minister bought him his first pair.

Hours later, the hoopla shows no sign of abating, and in fact feels as though it might turn ugly. Muchami edges Sivakami, Rukmini, Vani and Mari along the clearing to the path and signals to Vairum to join them. Vairum says a word of farewell to a couple of friends and comes to them. He is barefooted, but as they make their way along the path, he dives for a moment into the brush and recovers his shoes.

They are all silent as they walk and Sivakami soon realizes she is the only one who can break the quiet. None of the others will speak before she or Vairum does, and Vairum never feels the need to account for his actions.

"If you didn't want the Ramayana, I never would have commissioned it," she says, not trying to keep the reproach out of her voice.

"I never said I didn't want it," he replies, aware that this doesn't begin to explain his behaviour.

"How could you humiliate me so?" she whispers.

"I had no intention to humiliate you. My convictions are different from yours, that is all."

It's true that he attended the other Ramayana because he couldn't stand to attend Sivakami's, and yet, even as he says he didn't mean to humiliate her, he feels the statement turning into a lie. Could he have borne his neighbours' company for her sake? Another son might have, but what other son is subjected to all he must endure, for the sake of caste?

"I can't stand to be a Brahmin sometimes. If you weren't a Brahmin, you wouldn't be in white, with your head shaved, hiding in the house, living constantly in a state of victimhood while thinking yourself better than everyone else."

"We are better," Sivakami says simply, bewildered. "Why are you not proud?"

"I just can't stand it!" he roars at her, turning backward along the path to face her, and the others, arrayed behind. "That there is no escape. Can't you . . . I want to see things differently sometimes!"

He stalks ahead, and they follow him home.

The next morning, he feels moody and stays in the house. As the older children leave for school, he puts a mat to one side of the main hall, where he can listen to Vani play. He lies, his elbow on a bolster, letting the music ebb around him as though he is lying in a few inches of warm ocean at the beach.

One little grandchild is creeping around the house still: Sita. She comes in from the garden but stops when she sees him, and backs away again. *Unpleasant-looking child,* he thinks, and then is overcome by throbbing, choking, desirous sadness. He turns back to watch his wife. *Why haven't we had a child, my love?*

I killed my father, he killed his father. He doesn't remember when he first heard the chorus in his brain, sounding as though it has murmured there since he was born. Vani, without ceasing her music, looks at him suddenly, and he, feeling her glance, looks back. Even to him she speaks little, but she can still, as she did from that first day, drown out the deathly chatter with her music and her eyes.

She completes me, he thinks, breathing shallowly with gratitude, grasping at this as though at a branch overhanging a now-swollen river, *but marriage is not marriage without children.*

To escape his origins; to embrace them.

I just want a baby to raise. It may be possible that I am worthy of this.

PART FIVE

25.
Janaki Starts School
1931

MUCHAMI HAS CARED FOR ALL of Thangam's children with as much tenderness as their personalities and his station permitted, but he has never grown so attached to one as he has to Janaki in the months since she arrived. He tried with all of the children to distract them from their grief at losing their mother, tried to compensate with games and amusement for the affection Sivakami was unable to give them during the day. Only with Janaki, though, has he formed such a bond. She shines with a brighter light than her siblings, he often thinks, as she trots along beside him, helping with his chores and chattering.

Janaki considers the calves to be her special responsibility and helps especially by coaching the calves in comportment, telling them to stop licking the wall, for instance, where their craving for lime has worn a smudgy brick border into the whitewash. Muchami does the tending and milking. It's a very particular procedure. A calf is unroped and led to his mother. He roughly butts and nudges her udders before he clamps on. After a few moments, he's pulled off her belly and tied so that she can reach him but he can no longer reach the udders, and then she is milked while she licks her calf's back and shoulders. The very young calves stay close by their mothers even after they are untied. They're allowed more milk. But a slightly older calf, once untied, will dash straight to the water trough. The mother cow will look on for a few moments, then turn her face toward her feed. This calf is not really hers to mother, anyhow. He was born on someone else's account.

When the milk is handed to Sivakami, that is Janaki's cue to rouse her sleepy-faced siblings. She gleefully taps heads and shakes shoulders, saying officiously, "Hoi! Hoi, lazybones, what do you think this is, a hospital?" She has heard hospitals are places with cots where everyone stays in bed all day. "Get up!"

Each child sips a cup of boiled milk flavoured with sugar and the scents of cow and woodsmoke. Chores and baths follow and last urgent sums of homework. Janaki usually gets a piece of chalk and makes marks on the floor as her siblings do on their slates, her markings as incomprehensible to them as theirs are to her.

More important than any of these activities, though, is listening to Vani play. After Laddu and Sita have departed for school, Janaki creeps close to listen to her aunt. She's not sure if Vani sees her; sometimes Vani smiles, but it's a mysterious smile and could as easily be a response to a moment in the music or some fleeting sensation as to Janaki. From all around, from street and kitchen come the sounds of people working, talking, solving problems and creating new ones, but Vani responds to none of it. She is not startled by loud noises, not disturbed by shouting.

As Janaki listens, she pretends to tap out the beat structure, the *taalam*, of the song on her lap. She has seen knowledgeable listeners do this, tapping the front and back of their hands, and each of their fingers, in arcane and particular orders.

When Vani has finished playing in the morning, she eats her meal. Janaki eats hers at the same time, not least because Vani talks while she eats. She never talks at any other time, and even at this time, no one—except, now, Janaki—really listens. Sivakami comes in and out with food, but not appearing to pay attention to the daily discourse.

Vani's method is to tell, on average, a different story each week, repeating it daily with small variations. She often draws from her childhood, telling tales of grandeur and aristocracy. Her uncles are lawyers and ministers; her father is rich. Their house in Pandiyoor is full of music, culture, the latest fashions in clothes, slang, comportment. Most of the time, since Vani doesn't speak, it's difficult to tell that she is the product of such a home, but when she does, the influences are obvious.

After a week or so, however, Vani will change the story—fundamentally, but not superficially: most of the details will remain the same, but the moral import or the conclusion will be entirely different, all the pleasant people might become rude and the mean ones heroic. Once, for instance, it was a story of how a wedding was almost stopped by a death; in the variant, the death was almost stopped by the wedding. After delivering this reversal, she stops telling that story, and goes on to another one.

Janaki is as often confused by Vani's stories as by her music, but she never asks questions. She knows that questioning will get her nowhere with her aunt. She must find other ways.

As Janaki is currently the pre-school-age child in Sivakami's house, she is looked after by Muchami for much of the day. After his morning chores and mid-morning meal, he goes to his own small house and neighbourhood. Janaki goes with him, as the youngest child in Sivakami's care always has, and runs through dust and groves while he naps, gossips and has a cup of *ragi* porridge with his mother.

Sivakami's grandchildren will each have a very different memory of his or her pre-school months in Muchami's care. Saradha will remember organizing Muchami's nieces and nephews into games whose rules they continually broke or forgot—deliberately, she felt. Visalam will remember the whole time as a series of unbelievably funny mishaps. Laddu will forget most things about this epoch, though he will retain the rudiments of gambling, acquired while practically losing his shirt to Muchami's young nephews day after day. (Muchami made them return to him whatever they won.) Laddu will also never forget the most effective ways of tormenting chickens, though he will not remember having learned them. Sita will recall Muchami's small relatives as snotty-nosed, insipid, ill-mannered, repulsive, his neighbourhood as offensive.

Janaki will forever regard this epoch as the happiest of her childhood. In the late morning, each day, Muchami finds her squatting in one of the garden doorways, listening to or thinking about Vani's story. If the story is not finished, he waits; if it is, he whistles from the courtyard and Janaki comes trotting out to meet him. As they walk, they ask each other questions about things they see or have been thinking about.

"Janaki-baby, why is it that the dust of our Cholapatti roads is so red?" he might ask as they exit the Brahmin quarter, the big houses falling away, replaced by mud huts with thatched roofs.

"I don't know," Janaki might reply, trotting to keep up. "Do you think it's because the sun stains it when it comes up in the morning?"

"Never thought of that." Muchami squints penetratingly at a field—one of Sivakami's tenants.

"Yeah, and the night stains it black, did you ever look?" Janaki is starting to pant.

"Ah, yes." Muchami crouches so that she can put her arms around his neck and he can piggyback her the rest of the way.

"And, Muchami, what happens to notes of music when they disappear?" she asks from his back.

"I can't say I ever thought about it," he admits. "Did you ever try following one?"

"I . . . don't think so." She wishes she could see his face—is he serious?

So they agreeably pass the journey, stopping if he has work he must do en route from her home to his, whereupon she is released to her recreation, and he to his rest. After an hour or so, she creeps into his hut and lies down beside him to take a nap herself. At the afternoon's end, they make a return journey.

By then, Janaki's siblings are returning from school, ravenous. They pluck tiny bananas from the stalk that always leans, drooling sap, in the pantry corner, the ripening bananas winding up it like stairs. Sivakami gives each child a cup of milk and a globe of *thaingai maavu*, coconut ground with palm sugar and lentil flour and formed into a ball with the adhesive of a little milk. Fortified, the children go about their business until nightfall.

Vani, who rests upstairs for some time after her morning meal, comes down to wash her face and comb her hair about the same time the children and Janaki return. She then has Muchami carry her veena up onto the roof, where Vairum has erected an awning for her, and there plays hot and vigorous afternoon ragas until the sun goes down.

While Vani conducts her afternoon session, Janaki sits in the chalky-smelling cool at the top of the stairwell. Sometimes she's permitted to remain there, sometimes lured or forced away by other happenings in the house. This is the hour when Laddu has his tutorials, for example. If Vairum is tutoring him, Janaki stays away. She tried, once, to take part, but it didn't go well.

Vairum and Laddu had been sitting down to work in the main hall, Vairum glaring dismissively at Laddu, who fidgeted nervously with his books and slate.

Vairum lobbed an opening, his mind clearly already on his tennis. "What's news, Laddu? Fail any tests today?"

Janaki had already figured out that whatever school is, Laddu is not very good at it. The boy made no attempt to return the volley. Vairum served a few more, underhanded. "What if your parents never have another boy? You'll have to support them all alone. You must feel very ashamed and frightened, being the first boy and not having a future. Well, there is always your grandmother's money, and my help, of course."

Janaki, listening to this from one of the doorways to the garden, felt a response was merited and looked to her older brother to see what he would say. Laddu scratched at a peeling patch on his slate. He didn't even look worried, just dull and patient.

Janaki piped up. "Actually, Laddu Anna's going to do a big job and be very rich."

Vairum had started to laugh and Janaki felt encouraged.

"Laddu Anna's pockets will be so full of gold," she improvised, "that his shorts will always be falling down and his bum will show, but no one will laugh because they'll all be sad because he's so much richer than they are. Yep. That's what's going to happen."

Vairum had laughed harder, then stopped on a single snort and fixed her with a look. "Oh, ho, is that how it will be? Good. Very glad to hear that."

Janaki looked to her brother for approval.

"What nonsense is this?" Laddu snarled. "Get out of here before I beat you!"

He shoved her toward the garden while Vairum said to him in much the same tone, "And I want to see some sums before I beat them out of you, get it?"

The episode left a bad taste in Janaki's mouth, and she treated herself to a mouthful of dirt from the garden. She passed Muchami, wrestling with a rogue plaintain tree. Pretending to examine the rosebush, she scooped a rich, moist handful from among the roots and swallowed quickly, barely bothering to chew. Licking morsels of earth from her baby molars, she went from there to visit with the calves.

Janaki never tried to get near one of Vairum's tutorial sessions again.

During Sanskrit lessons, however, Janaki sits with Muchami, in one of the garden doorways. The teacher sings out the slokas and she sings out her version of them—Laddu has told her she's yelling gibberish, but she thinks she sounds pleasing and accurate. Muchami is far less assertive in his responses, and one would suppose Janaki's high-volume participation wouldn't help him, but he never objects to her presence and always compliments her afterward on the subtlety of her pronunciation. Sometimes Sanskrit even enters their midday to and fro.

"That last sloka, Janaki: how does it affect the meaning that it's on an upward instead of a downward tilt, at the end?" he puzzles one day. "I keep wanting to do it downward."

"I was thinking about the very same thing." Janaki purses her lips. "It sounds more like birdsong the way it is."

"Quite right and well put, but is that the point?" Muchami challenges, smiling.

"Oh, I don't know." Janaki's brow is furrowed. "We'll have to ask Kesavan Master tomorrow."

A few times, she really did try to ask Kesavan. That was another mistake. Kesavan is willing to put up with Janaki's participation because her presence has injected Muchami with some greater degree of commitment, if no greater competence. But he'll not stoop to ridiculing the ancient tongue because the granddaughter of the house sees it as a lark. After a couple of barked responses, Janaki learns quickly to confine her questioning—on Sanskrit, on nature, on anything, really—to Muchami, the only person in the household who sees her questions as worthwhile.

She has also learned to confine her questions to times and places when her elder sister Sita will not overhear her. It had happened once, that, in a good mood, Janaki had called out to Muchami as he ate his tiffin, "Muchami, when a bunch of stick insects get together, do they make a tree?"

Before Muchami could answer, Sita, walking past, had supplied a response. "Sure, the same tree your wooden head fell off of."

Seeing Janaki absorbed in Vani's music, Sita chitters from the bottom of the stairs or the pantry until Janaki can't help but look.

"Janaki, this is you," Sita says, and makes an expression like a monkey sunk, drunk, in a pile of rotting fruit, batting her hand idiotically against her knee.

While Janaki earnestly sits by Muchami's side, singing out her phrases of "Sanskrit," Sita parades past in the garden and yodels perfect imitations.

So now, when Sivakami tells Janaki she must come back early from Muchami's because the tailor is coming to measure her for a school uniform, Sita clarifies, "Amma wants to make sure you have a uniform because then you'll blend in even though you don't know anything."

"Blend in to what?" Janaki frowns.

"The rest of the know-nothing babies, what do you think?" Sita smiles her perverse smile and leaves for school.

"What happens at school, Muchami?" she asks that afternoon.

"Well, you know I've never got past the door, Janaki-baby," he explains, "but I imagine it's all the things you like, writing and reading and learning, only more and you can do it all day and all the other children are doing the same."

That sounds all right. Janaki likes the idea of the uniform, also. And Muchami is making her a new slate.

She goes to tell the calves her news. From the cowshed, Janaki hears Sivakami talking to Vairum in the courtyard. Vairum is washing his hands at the well following his own morning meal.

"Have you given it any more thought, kanna?" asks Sivakami. "I think we must pledge another—"

"I never said we shouldn't," he cuts her off efficiently.

"I . . . okay, I'll look up which is a good day." Sivakami goes to take the almanac down from the ledge in the hall where it is kept, about six feet off the ground, so she must stand on a small stool to reach it. Janaki watches from the kitchen doorway.

"I want to do the puja at home, for our Ramar," Vairum says, slowly now.

"Good, kanna." Sivakami squints through the thick, wavy-paged book. "Next Friday is auspicious." She spots Janaki. "That would also be a good day for Janaki to start school. Janaki-baby, we'll do a puja for you to start school, next Friday."

The tailor comes to take Janaki's measurements. She starts to feel important.

Preparations begin for the puja. Supplies are bought for sweets, for example, and their manufacture begun.

The tailor returns to fit the uniform.

"Will I wear the uniform for my puja?" Janaki asks her grandmother.

"No, kanna, we do the puja for your uniform, your slate, your books, put it all in front of goddess Saraswati, right? Ask for her blessings so you will study well. You can wear your usual paavaadai, and then put on your uniform afterward."

"Can I wear a silk paavaadai?"

"If you like, yes. You feel like wearing something special?"

"Yeah."

Janaki was pretty sure she had heard her uncle and grandmother discussing a puja for the Ramar, not Saraswati. Things sometimes, often, change out of her hearing, hard as she tries to keep on top of all household developments. They must have decided it's more appropriate to do the puja for Saraswati, the goddess of learning, all things considered. Yes, that must be it.

Friday morning arrives. As her grandmother returns from the

Kaveri, Janaki awakens and informs Muchami she didn't sleep a wink all night for excitement. She bathes and puts on a paavaadai, teal silk bordered in yellow. She hears her grandmother instructing Sita to bathe and dress, and reminding Vani, also, that today is the day of the puja. Vairum has gone to bathe at the river, something he does only on big occasions. This school matter is even bigger than she had realized, thinks Janaki. The uniform had been delivered the day before and is ready to be blessed, together with her slate, ink powder, writing stick and nib, paper, books and a new tiffin box engraved with her name, G. Janaki.

Sivakami sees her come in from her bath and asks, "All ready, Janaki? Come, the *raahu kaalam,* the inauspicious hour, has just ended and the good hours begun. Let us do your puja now, before the priest arrives."

Janaki follows but doesn't understand. "How can we do the puja before the priest comes and everyone is ready, Amma?"

"No, kanna." Sivakami moves briskly into the hall. "*Your* puja, for school."

Vairum is already before the gods, doing his regular morning prostrations and prayers, clothes and hair still wet from his bath.

Sivakami takes the brass plate on which Janaki's small pile awaits, and dots a little vermilion powder on each item. Janaki shifts foot to foot, chewing on her lip, looking anxiously at the door where Sita has emerged from her bath. "Hurry up, Sita, my puja is starting."

Sita slows down to a insolent saunter. "So?"

A look from Sivakami speeds her along.

Sivakami is lighting camphor and offering Janaki's things along with flowers, sugar rock-candy, a coconut and a piece of turmeric. She prays to goddess Saraswati that Janaki will work hard, appreciate this great privilege and succeed. When they think the goddess has had enough time to grant them the blessing, the plate is set down and Janaki prostrates for the gods, her grandmother and uncle, and Sita, because she's older than Janaki and happens to be present. From the gods, Janaki believes she receives benevolent approval. From her grandmother, she receives solid encouragement. Her uncle looks uninterested and skeptical but tells her to make the best of this and sounds like he expects to be obeyed. Sita lets Janaki get close before she whispers, "You'll be a disaster." She beams at her little sister, saccharine and malign.

Then Vani arrives to do her morning prayers, after which she sits and begins playing.

Laddu comes and sits to one side, morning-befuddled, but clean and dressed for a special occasion, and everyone else is clearly waiting for something more. Janaki sees Muchami in the garden and goes to the door. "My puja is over," she tells him. "What is everyone waiting for?"

She spoke her question a little too loud. Everyone turns a puzzled look on her, except Sita, who hoots and cackles, "She thought every-one was dressing up because they were so excited that the little dimwit's off to learn some learning!"

"Sita, stop that." Sivakami turns toward the little girl. "We're doing a puja for the Ramar, today, Kanna. Vairum Mama and Vani Mami are asking to be blessed with children. You forgot?"

Had Janaki known, she surely would not have forgotten. She has participated in many rituals already to this end and was especially enthusiastic about the one where Vani poured milk down snake holes.

A priest arrives as Janaki sulks in the garden door. The priest begins to set up the fire. He needs to start the puja within this hour and a quarter: one of the auspicious times that checkerboard the day. Sivakami bustles back and forth from the kitchen with things the priest needs as Vani plays on, more intensely and virtuosically than usual, though all Janaki can tell for sure is that it seems louder.

The priest does the preliminary incantations. Vairum comes and sits where he is directed to by the priest. Sita is sitting beside Laddu, looking disgusted. She whispers something to him and he shrinks like he's been jabbed with a hot poker. Vani still plays. Janaki decides to go change into her uniform, but when she rises, Sivakami shakes her head. The priest looks at Sivakami and at Vairum; he's done all he can do without Vani's participation. They look back at him as though they don't understand what he wants.

The priest turns to Vani but senses something about her that makes him unwilling to address her directly. So he casts another, more obviously plaintive glance at Vairum, who sighs and raises his eyebrows back. The priest points at the hourglass. They don't have much time to get on with it. All the household watches with eyes narrowed as Vairum approaches the woman who should regard him as her lord.

As he crouches beside her, she gives no indication that she is aware of him. Finally, in a natural pause in the music, he says tentatively, *"Ma?"*

She launches passionately into the next movement of the improvisation, her left hand, above one gourd, strumming and plucking the melody, right hand, at the frets above the other gourd, stroking out the accompanying drone. Sita and Laddu break into vicious chuckles and don't stop despite Vairum's withering stare. Vairum flushes. He rises to standing, like a hawk poised in the air before a dive. Janaki, from her vantage point, sees his lips seal into a tiny knot.

Fwoosh—he stoops and catches Vani's left wrist, arresting the melody.

Without breaking the drone sound, Vani's right hand forms a fist and knocks him in the forehead. He falls, stunned, onto his bottom as he releases her wrist. She resumes her virtuosic swells. Now every eye in the room is open very wide, except Vairum's, which are screwed shut. He keeps them that way as he rises and stumbles through Janaki's doorway into the garden. She tucks her legs in so as not to trip him.

Only Janaki can see him as he leans his desecrated forehead against a young papaya tree. He stays that way for a very long time, while the notes climax and come to rest. Vani places her hands on her knees and takes one breath, staring at her instrument. Upon exhaling, she raises her head and her eyes come into focus. She gets up and seats herself in place for the puja. The priest awakens in a fluster from his own reverie, finds his place in the sloka book and begins to chant.

Vairum detaches himself from the lacy, leafy papaya tree and returns to the doorway. The sun is behind him and Janaki cannot see his face. He turns to take his place beside his wife. On his forehead is the deeply imprinted double X of the papaya trunk's bark—a wavy diamond with a half reflection on each side. The hourglass runs out as they complete the puja for a child. The papaya skin diamond melts from his forehead, as his diamond-dark eyes, too, melted briefly into something soft and hurt.

As the auspicious time dribbles to an end, Janaki jumps up and runs off to change into her uniform before her grandmother can object.

Her white shirt and blue skirt are starched as stiff, it seems, as her books. The buttons of the shirt are at the back, so she has to ask Sita for help doing them up. Sita deliberately buttons her wrong; Sivakami notices and makes her do it again, and then squats in the kitchen with a brass pot of yogourt rice. The children seat themselves in a semicircle around her and she feeds them their breakfast, dropping a mouthful of the mixture into each of their palms in turn as they eat.

When they finish, they run to the well to wash their hands, rinse their mouths and gather their things. Muchami secures Janaki's books in their strap as she picks up her slate, writing stick and ink, and they run for the door.

He lifts her onto the cart. "Janaki-baby, go to the centre, away from the edge."

He points and then stands, twisting his shoulder towel around a finger as Janaki crawls to the centre, moving her things in two trips. As the cart lurches around the corner, she seats herself in a puff of relief, and then looks up to see Muchami watching her from the veranda. She suddenly realizes he needs to do all his regular things today: go to his home, take a nap—how is he going to do all that without her? She had gotten so excited about going to school that she hadn't considered the fact that she wouldn't be at home.

She tries to stand but stumbles on a couple of other children. The last sight she has of her home is Muchami gesturing impatiently and yelling, "Sit! Sit!"

Muchami enters the garden (he had run through the house to help Janaki but, as a matter of course, doesn't walk through the main hall), walks through the cowshed and into the courtyard.

"I suppose I'll get the marketing done, Amma," he calls to Sivakami. "Anything particular I should look for?"

"No. Whatever's good." She doesn't look up from preparing the mid-morning meal. He doesn't go, however, but continues standing in the courtyard, half out of sight, beyond the kitchen door. Sivakami stands to dump out the water in which she has been rinsing okra, and sees him. "I said, whatever's good."

He looks at the ground. He doesn't understand how Sivakami could not feel as he does, bereft, though the course of her day is relatively unaltered by Janaki's departure.

"You know, Mari and I have talked, sometimes, about adopting a child," he tells her.

She slices the okra against the blade, tossing it into a pan. "I think that's a good idea. No one should be without a child."

"I think, maybe a little girl."

"A girl? Why would you do that?" She doesn't think she has ever heard of anyone adopting a girl. Childless Brahmins generally adopt some poor relative's son, so that they themselves will have a son to perform their death rites. Muchami's community's customs are unknown to her, though. She suspects they may not have annual death rites; they barely even observe time the same way as Brahmins.

"You're right," he says hastily, unwinding his shoulder towel yet again from his sweaty palm. "I don't know. I'll go to market now."

Sivakami shrugs. She has no idea what's on his mind, but expects either he will tell her, or she will guess, in good time.

At the entrance to the schoolyard, Sita jumps off the cart and walks toward the school without looking back. Janaki finally figures out a way to pile everything on her slate and balance it as she walks, but she has to stop every few steps to look up and check where Sita is going.

They enter the school, a long mud building with six classrooms, their doors opening directly onto the yard. At one end are three offices, occupied by the headmistress and some lesser functionaries. Their doors open onto a hallway that traverses the width of the school, and opens onto the schoolyard at either end. There are only sixty girls in the school, so the first-, second- and third-standard students are together. Sita and Janaki will be in the same class.

"Miss, this is Janaki, Miss, my sister," Sita mumbles to the teacher for form's sake as she crosses to deposit her tiffin box in the coolest corner of the room.

It's then that Janaki notices she is without her own lunch. Did she leave it in the cart? But no, it took her two trips to move her things, one for books and pen, a second for slate and ink. It must still be in the kitchen, where her grandmother leaves Laddu's and Sita's lunches after packing them. But she cannot take any more time to think about it. Sita has already taken her seat on the floor among the other third-standard girls. Janaki pivots from one side to another on her heels, trying not to upset her little stack of supplies, unsure as to where she should go. The teacher, Miss Mathanghi, points her toward the opposite side of the room, where eleven girls of roughly Janaki's size and level of uncertainty are sitting. They all started school this month; three are starting today.

Miss Mathanghi, an ancient and dour twenty-five, waits for the shuffling and gossip to peak. The last girls are just entering as she launches into the morning's prayer, some twelve couplets from the Bhagavad-Gita, which she bellows line by line, and which the girls yell back. She does this once through with the entire classroom in some semblance of chorus. She then sings out each line a second time, looking at the ceiling or out the window. At the end of the line, she points to a student, who must repeat it alone. Sita is among the first; she gets perhaps half of her line right. That is typical for her, but today she has an additional distraction: she is smiling a calculating smile at her sister, implying that Janaki will be chosen and that she should be scared.

Janaki is scared. One of her standard-mates is selected, a little girl like her, who has only begun school that day. She just gapes at the teacher, who stares back a second before rolling her eyes and pointing to a second-standard. Janaki feels herself petrifying and turning red; perhaps, she thinks, perhaps she can blend into the brick floor. Perhaps the teacher will see only an empty space, an empty uniform starched stiff enough to stand alone.

But there is the pointer, aimed at Janaki.

And Janaki responds, repeating the entire line perfectly. Or so it sounds to her, but then it always does. But yes, it's true: the teacher is nodding, surprised, approving. She sings out the next line and the next, the final line of the prayer. She indicates Janaki for both of them. Janaki repeats them. She looks cautiously at Sita, expecting her sister to be shaking in triumphant hilarity while Janaki makes a fool of herself, but Sita is gaping at her jealously and looks away when Janaki turns to her.

The first class of the day for the youngest girls is arithmetic; the first exercise is writing the numerals one through ten. The teacher props a slate near the front of the classroom and writes, "1, 2, 3." "Those of you who can, copy this. Those of you who can't, well, then we will know you can't!"

Janaki thinks she can do this. The first figure on the board looks like a walking stick, the next an ear, with a dangling earring blowing out in the wind, the last like a bird, tipped sideways to round a corner in flight. She thinks the teacher has been too hasty in making the drawings and does her best to make each figure more realistic and accurate.

If only she could stop the tears that keep blurring the image in front of her, the job would be much simpler. She can't seem to stop herself from thinking about the calves and cows, who must be feeling lost without her there to instruct and reassure them. And Vani—will she even bother to change her story when no one at all is listening? Worst of all, Muchami is walking home alone. He'll be leaving any time now, his head heavy with questions he can ask no one. Three tears plink onto her new slate and she wipes them off with her skirt quickly before anyone can see. But when she blinks, swallows and blinks again, the design she worked so hard to produce is also gone, and she has a smear of chalk on her navy blue skirt.

Meanwhile the teacher has given a reading assignment to the second-standards. The third-standard girls have been asked to write out multiplication tables.

"I'm so looking forward to reading Sita's times table—three days ago she wrote all the figures so small no one but she could make them out. I'm sure they were all absolutely correct," Miss Mathanghi says in a tone implying the opposite. Her face is grim as concrete.

Sita, already seeing red due to Janaki's recent triumph, bends to her work with a grimness bordering on the teacher's own. It's not the only way she resembles the teacher. Sita has a talent for hurting people, but she has learned a lot in Miss Mathanghi's classroom.

Miss Mathanghi is making her way back to the first-standard girls. She has a small waist and low hips behind which clings a flat bottom. Her skin is greyish and her shoulders so rounded that her trunklike arms give the impression of emerging more from the front than from the sides of her torso. She has taught these classes for eight years, more than long enough to know that, in this tender phase, she need do little more than look at the first-standards to set them aquiver with fear and self-consciousness. Janaki, though, is a harder nut. She is not, as most of her classmates are, fixed desperately on the teacher, searching her in vain for signs of approval or affection. She is weeping, which is common, but, despite the tears, seems fully absorbed in the scene she is elaborating on her slate.

Janaki's slate shows a small flock of 3's, headed by a fantastic bird of prey. She is sitting back from the slate so that her tears drop onto her skirt and don't interfere.

Miss Mathangi chooses her approach instinctively. "You don't turn the world, Janaki."

The little girl sits up, as though the currents running between her brain and spinal cord have suddenly increased in voltage.

"Either you do as you please," the teacher continues deliberately, "which is to say, the wrong thing, or you do what I have instructed you to do, that is, the same thing as every other girl in this classroom."

It hadn't occurred to Janaki to look at what the other girls were doing. Now she looks around. Most of the children have done a passable job. Janaki looks at the brief and unattractive marks on their slates, and the detailed, dramatic tableau on her own. She's confused. She automatically looks to her sister. She knows, though she doesn't realize it until she's already turned her head, that she will see the usual cruel gloat. Even that, however, is reassuringly familiar at the moment.

But then a far more reassuring figure appears. Could it be? Muchami is silhouetted in the doorway. He stands and doesn't say anything, just moves a little, side to side, to draw attention.

All the girls crane to see him, tipping forward onto the knees of their crossed legs, though not rising. Miss Mathanghi glances at him and asks, "What?"

He holds out his right hand, a string tied into a loop hooked across his palm. At the other end of the string dangles Janaki's shiny new tiffin box.

"It's Janaki's lunch," he explains gruffly and looks furtively into the classroom, searching for her face.

Janaki is frozen, fixed on him, but her eyes dart to her teacher and back.

"Mmh!" Miss Mathanghi grunts and jerks her head toward the door to indicate Janaki should go take her lunch.

Janaki slowly rises and goes to the door, uncertain of how she should take her lunch from him. Why is he carrying it like that? She holds her left hand out as if to take the string, but he holds the tiffin box up and frowns to indicate she'd better take hold of it. She carries the box to the lunch corner as Sita starts to laugh, and soon the whole classroom is in gales, hysterical from the tension of the classroom.

When Janaki sets the tiffin box down, Sita yells, "Touch the water, touch the water!"

There is a jug of water in the corner by the tiffin boxes, and Janaki tips it with her left hand so that she moistens the fingers of her right, a ceremonial washing of the hand polluted by contact with cooked rice. As she does so, she looks over to Muchami.

Who is not there.

She drops the neck of the jug but catches it by the lip before it falls too far. The girls who see this gasp and then start laughing again as Janaki runs out the door and after Muchami. She throws her arms around his legs and clasps her face to his hip, clinging with the strength of immature fruit to the stem. Muchami pries her off: fruit drops away when it's ready, but unripe fruit can also be plucked and ripen on its own.

"Oh, Janaki-baby." He stoops toward her. "Don't you love school? What did you learn today?"

Janaki doesn't answer. Her small body strains toward him so that the second his elbows relax, she sticks herself again to his leg.

"Have you had enough for today already?" He knows he probably shouldn't even be asking, but he, too, had been wondering how he would get through his day without her. "Okay, just today. You can come with me."

She lifts her arms to him and he picks her up and starts to walk, her arms around his neck, her face in his shoulder. He can feel her calming, or is that him?

Her face in his neck, she asks, "Muchami, why did you carry my food with the string—because of cooked-rice pollution?"

"Um, no, Janaki-baby," he replies, feeling an unaccustomed sting of humiliation. "Because you are Brahmin and I cannot touch your food."

Vairum had left already to look after business in Thiruchi when they noticed the forgotten tiffin box in the corner, and they were about to send for one of the layabout sons of one of the Brahmin quarter's poorer families, but then Mari had proposed that, just as she used a stick to move the family's clean laundry and detangle the girls' hair, Muchami should be able to carry the food if there was some instrument intervening. Sivakami produced the twine.

Janaki raises her head. "How come you can carry me like this but not my food?"

"Because you can take a bath or change your clothes, but your food can't? Or maybe because you would be uncomfortable if I tied you up with string?" he suggests.

"Yes," Janaki smiles. "I'm too big for you to carry me that way."

"That must be it," he smiles back.

They return to the house. It's still early; Muchami has not yet had his morning meal. Even before reaching the little temple halfway along the road into the Brahmin quarter, they can hear Vani's music. She had resumed right after the puja. Does this mean the day has continued in Janaki's absence? Or is it now picking up where she left off? She would have believed the latter, were it not for the seed of doubt Miss Mathanghi had so accurately sown.

Janaki and Muchami enter through the courtyard door. As he washes his hands and feet, Janaki changes her clothes as her grandmother instructed her to do whenever she returns from her outings with Muchami. If she were older, she would have to bathe.

When she emerges from the bathroom, Mari, serving Muchami his meal, yells, "Ayoh! Janaki?"

Janaki runs through the kitchen, past her grandmother, into the main hall and drops herself into her doorway niche. She is sore all over. The music surrounds her and she starts to relax.

Vani raises her left hand and beckons in the child's direction. Janaki looks behind her to her right, into the garden, to her left, into the back of the hall, but she is the only one around. Vani looks directly at Janaki, something she's never done, her pale face solemn, her eyes canny and expectant. She beckons once more.

Janaki leaves her niche and seats herself, facing Vani and slightly to her right. Vani strokes the drone strings, upward, with her right pinky, leaving the melody for a moment. As she does, she taps the front of her left hand on her lap. Then she taps the back, then the front again, and as she does, strokes the drone. Then again the front of the hand, with a drone stroke, and she counts off, pinky, ring, middle finger. She repeats: front of hand, back, front, back, front, pinky, ring, middle, with the drone struck each time she taps with the front of her hand, and Janaki understands: this is how you count off the rhythm.

As Vani resumes playing, continuing to stroke the drone with her pinky on the taalam's downbeat, playing the melody with her ring and middle fingers and working the frets with her left hand, Janaki taps out the taalam.

"Adhi Taalam," Vani names it for her with a smile, and Janaki is elated because she hears it and doesn't have to pretend any more.

As she listens to the song, though, which has grown sleepy and tense, like the lull before an episode in a long-running quarrel, Janaki's teacher's words return to her. She blushes and happens to look to her right, where she sees Vairum standing on the spiral stairs leading down from his and Vani's quarters. He is watching Janaki with a look she will never forget, though she won't understand it for years: the remnants of that morning's humiliation, scattered against years of disappointment.

Janaki circles with her hands the space her aunt and the veena inhabit and cracks her baby knuckles against her own temples—a customary gesture of affection. Vairum charges.

"All you children, all of you think you own this place, don't you? This is your inheritance from your father—the belief that you have the right to a good life without working for it! How long did you last, a half-hour? The school uniform is a joke to you? This is not your veena! This is not your place! You do not decide, do you hear?"

Vairum advances six steps toward her with his speech and Janaki has to flee. She scoots back an equal distance on her bottom, then stumbles to her feet and backs away, around the veena and her aunt, both of whom continue as before. As her uncle reaches the spot where Janaki herself had been sitting, Janaki reaches the garden door. As Sivakami yells, "Stop! Stop, my son!" Janaki runs out into the green and embraces from behind the young papaya whose succour Vairum had taken earlier.

The earth in the pockets between the tree's roots tempts her. With one hand still fast round the tree, Janaki flips into her mouth a lump of dirt the size of the thaingai maavu balls the children have for their after-school snack. The soil is crunchy and damply acrid, and contains a couple of jasmine petals. Its dark comfort spreads in her mouth. She sighs and leans her forehead on the tree, both arms clasped round it, its parasol of leaves nodding above. Despite having her forehead pressed to the tree, Janaki can see her grandmother approaching from the main hall and Muchami from the cowshed.

Sivakami says from the door, "Tch-tch, Janaki-baby. Vairum Mama didn't mean what he said. He knows you are a good girl, a smart girl. But why are you home from school now? You were so excited to go."

But Muchami reaches her, turns her small shoulders from the tree and puts his arms around her. Janaki knows Vairum meant every word of what he said and now she has learned something else on her first day of school: to be afraid of her uncle.

She starts to cry on Muchami's shoulder and a dribble of black drool escapes the downpulled corner of her mouth and falls onto his bicep. He wipes it with his shoulder towel and frowns at its colour. "Ah, Janaki-baby," he sighs. "How many times do you have to be told?"

Mari, who had joined them by now, choruses, "Ayoh! Dirty girl! So much good food you get in this house! Don't eat dirt! Don't, don't eat dirt!"

Janaki's sobs, which had been pulling at her small form with increasing intensity, cease with a great inward yank, as though a line around her has been pulled taut. She fixes on Mari a look of weariness. Mari, who means well, clamps shut her lips. Janaki whips around and vomits on the roots of the young papaya.

Muchami takes her by the hand and leads her to the courtyard, where he washes her face and tells her to rinse her mouth. Vani finishes playing in the meantime, and Muchami sends Janaki back inside to listen to the day's story while he has his meal. This week, Vani has been telling the story of a mysterious reliquary that seemed always to appear during times of crisis in the family, and disappear when the crisis had passed. A box in the shape of a parrot, encrusted with a filigree of unidentifiable metals, it contained a rosewood bowl as big as half a hen's egg, still bearing faint traces of some pearly unguent; two coins, the smaller with a stamp of fruits and the other of two figures entwined in erotic counterpoise; and a wooden statuette that offended everyone who saw it: a dog with vermilion stains that indicated it was an object of worship. No one could hold on to the box, and no one could agree on whether it was bringing or banishing the family's episodes of ill fortune.

Janaki checks the vestibule and sees that Vairum's shoes are gone: he's out on rounds or wherever he goes. She sits across from Vani and sinks into the story as into a down-filled comforter, wondering where it will go today. In the last four tellings, the story has turned on Vani's uncle noticing the reliquary, in a time when he had been asking many pointed questions and receiving no answers. His suspicions of some misfortune afoot had been confirmed by the parrot box's appearance. Janaki wonders if the story will change today and hopes not. She's in the mood for continuity.

Maybe Vani senses this, because the story stays the same, with only the smallest additions or subtractions of detail. When the story is done, Janaki looks over to see if Muchami is ready and waiting. He is, and the two of them set off for his home. En route, Janaki asks the questions she had prepared. Muchami has a couple of his own. They are quieter than usual. At Muchami's house, Janaki falls promptly asleep and remains so for the entire afternoon. When she awakens, it is to find herself in Muchami's arms, and half of the homeward journey completed.

Back at home, Laddu and Sita have already arrived. Janaki tenses for a barrage of Sita's barbs, but Sivakami must have spoken to her because Sita says nothing.

An hour later, she and Muchami sit in their usual spot for the Sanskrit tutorial. Janaki sings out her responses with confidence and without expression, as though already taking for granted what the teacher notes with a congratulatory smile: she has had a breakthrough.

In a pause, while young Kesavan drills the other pupils in a phrase Janaki had gotten right the first time, Muchami leans over. "You are the smartest and the best, Janaki-baby." She smiles, embarrassed, and butts her forehead into his shoulder.

The next morning, Janaki rises, as usual, well ahead of the other children, and commences her morning routine. When Sita and Laddu sit to do their homework, she sits with them, bent over the slate Sita brought home for her the day before.

Sita is too sleepy and grumpy to be properly cruel and so only asks, "Where's your uniform, twerp?"

Janaki looks up from her slate as though irritated at the interruption and asks defiantly, "What do I need it for?"

"To go to school?" Sita yawns loudly.

"I went yesterday." Janaki bends again to her slate.

Even Sita is given pause by this, though she recovers quickly. "What, you think you're finished?"

"Yep. I'm needed here," Janaki confides with a return of her old assurance. She understands now that she can't be both at school and at home. People need to make choices in life; this is hers.

"Amma!" Sita bellows, and Sivakami comes running. "Amma, Janaki thinks she's not going to school any more."

"Janaki-baby, shouldn't you put on your uniform?" Sivakami asks kindly, and all Janaki's confidence deserts her.

She sits like a crumpled paper cut-out of herself. Sivakami doesn't say more. She tells the children to come to breakfast. Janaki doesn't come. The bullock cart arrives. Janaki stays in her hall-door niche. Vani invites her to beat the taalam on the final number. Janaki does—

Vairum left on business early that morning, and she doesn't need to worry about him.

Today Vani's story changes: now the uncle is the one on the brink of misfortune and trying to keep it secret from the rest of the family, and the family guesses, from the reliquary's appearance, that someone is hiding something, though not what or who.

And now Muchami is ready to depart and Janaki to depart with him.

On the road, she starts in with the day's questions.

"Muchami, how come rice and lentils get soft when they're cooked, but idlis and dosai get hard?" she asks in a let's-forget-the-past tone.

Muchami smiles at her sadly. "I don't know, Janaki-baby. Maybe you should ask your teacher that one."

Janaki slides him a wary look. "What teacher, Muchami?"

"Your teacher at school." He looks at her and back at the road.

"I'm finished school, Muchami," she explains. "It was spreading me too thin."

"But you have so many questions, Janaki, that you and I can't answer alone. We need your teacher."

Janaki is silent, wondering how Muchami could be so wrong in his judgment.

"Janaki-baby." Muchami clears his throat. "Did you learn Sanskrit in school?"

"No," replies Janaki, and it's the truth. She didn't learn it, she discovered she already knew it. "You can't learn Sanskrit at school, Muchami, that's why Laddu Anna needs to learn it at home."

"Laddu is being taught at home because he's not learning in school, but he's not learning at home, either," Muchami points out, and a little of Janaki's faith in him is restored. "But you could learn so much, Janaki-baby. Trust me: so much that you can't learn at home, that I can't learn unless you go and do it for me. Then you can teach me. Please go back to school, Janaki-baby. Do it for me."

Janaki is starting to see his point of view in spite of herself. Her practical mind begins rearranging her days. She could look after the cows before and after school. She and Muchami, too, can convene at other times to do what they must do. And she only need attend school a half day on Saturday, and Sunday not at all.

But what about Vani? Vani cannot be rearranged. Well—if Janaki is to be Muchami's eyes and ears at school, he can be hers at home. Janaki will spend as much time as ever she is able listening to Vani's music; he cannot help her with that. But he can listen to and relate the day's stories. If he promises this, she will go back to school.

He can offer this. "Done."

Done.

Janaki returns to school the next day, opening some doors, closing others. Muchami and she save their questions for the end of the day and weekends, but there are more and more questions never asked and never answered, and eventually, more and more she doesn't think to seek answers for.

26.
The Son of a Son
1932

THERE IS A BOY ON SIVAKAMI'S STEP holding out a piece of paper. She doesn't understand.

He explains that it is a telegram.

The telegram. Sivakami receives it with trembling hands. Vairum always has to be modern. He and Vani had travelled to her parents' house for Vani's delivery. If the telegram is arriving in Cholapatti today, that means he sent it . . . when? How long do they take?

These thoughts chase one another like minnows through the reeds of her mind. She has never been so nervous. She takes a short breath through her nose and opens the seal.

BOY BORN STOP VANI TIRED BUT HEALTHY
STOP I COME HOME TOMORROW STOP

A son of her son, a son of her son. She falls on her knees in front of the Ramar. *Thank you, thank you.* Her elation is so great it feels not unlike despair: how can this be? She wished for this so long and so hard that she had nearly given it up. Her happiness now is too near wonder—how can this finally have come to pass?—to be recognizable as joy.

Gradually, however, rocking back and forth on her knees before her gods, the telegram stretched between her hands like a cradle, she comes to accept and a grin starts to pull at her upper lip.

VAIRUM IS ON THE TRAIN HOME, wearing the same grin—that
seen on a stranger walking the opposite way, that inward smile that
makes one think, oh, someone has found love, has found a job, has
been paid a high or casual compliment; someone has been made happy.

In the train car, people make conversation with him, and though
he's always the silent one in the compartment, this time he shyly confesses: he's a father. He has a son.

I have a son, I have a son. Cradled in the train in the drowsing of
the day, Vairum's thoughts drift to his own father, and those
moments when he would have first learned he was father to a son.
His musing is interrupted by a strong, sudden headache. The left
half of his brain seems to throb, and the temple around it, one of the
body's irrational moments, the kind of pain that happens every so
often for no reason. His left eyelid twitches. He shakes his head and
holds his eye shut with his fingers until it is still. The train pauses at
an uncovered village platform and he goes out to take a drink of
water at the pump. When he sits down again, he can't remember
what he was thinking of and can't be bothered remembering. He
blissfully goes on conjuring his son and this mantle of fatherhood,
drifting through such lulling, abstract thoughts as only Vani has
ever before invoked in him.

He enters the main hall, falls at the feet of his gods, and then
does the same for his mother, who holds her hands over him in blessing. He stands and looks into her eyes, the only person, with Vani,
whose joy equals his.

He does not go out in the fields that day, which should have been
his greatest priority after three days away. No, Vairum takes a few
magazines and sits on the veranda. It is the strangest sight. Why is it so
strange when it is precisely how most other men on the Brahmin quarter spend their days? Well, precisely for that reason. Several neighbours offer shy congratulations as they pass. Vairum modestly accepts.
Murthy joins Vairum on the veranda and acts the proud senior uncle.

Sivakami lies awake that night, a night twelve long years in
coming. Her optimism had ebbed a little with each succeeding—or

should that be failing?—year, though she wouldn't admit it, even to herself. It wears a person down, hope. So many pledges and pujas, from the most public and dramatic to the last one at home—the one that worked.

Had the miraculous not occurred, the events of that day might not have stayed in Sivakami's mind at all, but as it is, she recalls the disagreement between Vani and Vairum over the puja. She had never seen them disagree and hasn't since. Sivakami recalls that her own first child was conceived on a night when she and her husband were together again after a rupture, one of his unforgivable sojourns, and though it is awful to think that the best unions may be born of discord, she thinks more than one couple may share this experience. Certainly, Gayatri has gone so far as to confess she occasionally provokes fights with her husband because he works so ardently to regain her favour.

But Sivakami doesn't think Vani was simply upset at having her playing interrupted, or at Vairum's not trusting her to finish in time. South Indian classical music tends to be devotional. Vani was making a supplication that day, Sivakami believes, the same request they would then make in the puja, the same they had been making all those years. Vani had to stop Vairum from interrupting it.

For the last nine months, Vairum has been buoyant and benevolent as never before: kind to Thangam's children, solicitous of his wife and mother. Sivakami and he have been united in their desire to care for Vani. Previously, Vani's energies had mirrored the moon's: she would be sluggish and sleepy while the moon was in shadow and shake with overabundant energy when it waxed bright. Pregnant, she was consistently inward-directed and content. Her playing became softer and more conventional—most often, she played paeans to Lord Krishna, favourite to children, songs she occasionally sang. She obediently drank the garlic rasam Sivakami prepared, even when she occasionally brought it back up. She had attacks of nausea through her first trimester that left her skin waxy and eyes dull. But she was obviously happy. She put on weight; her plummy figure and moon-like face grew rounder. She had always glowed, but in pregnancy, she looked less exceptional than she had before. Sivakami thinks this must be some portion of her happiness, as of Vairum's: finally,.they were like any couple. No longer the darkly repulsive business genius; no longer the eerily glowing musical genius. Just a young married couple expecting their first child.

Sivakami turns over to her other side. A son of her son, a son of her son . . . she falls into a long sleep, deep and dark as a stone well.

Though perhaps her sleep should rather be compared to the bed of the Vaigai River, which runs behind Vani's hometown: peaceful and solid in appearance, but with a current ever springing just beneath the surface, so that one need only rake the sand with one's fingers to find one's handprint immediately drowned.

While Vairum is striding about the fields the next day, shielded within the touching invincibility of parenthood, another telegram arrives.

While Vairum is out seeing that the earth will provide for his son, while he is gracefully accepting congratulations on this most natural and, for the father, effortless of achievements, while he stands gazing at the fertile fields and thinking how he never felt the goodness of sunshine before, Vairum's gold medal, his rose-tinted spectacles, his soft beating heart, loses grip on this world and slips away.

CHILD DID NOT SURVIVE STOP

Sivakami collapses. There is no other response. She crumples in a little bald and white heap on the brick floor and her granddaughters run to her, shrieking, not sure whether to touch her. They run around her screaming until she opens her eyes and finds some neighbours entering the front door and kneeling beside her. They look at the telegram and bring her a tumbler of water.

Like a pattern of sound waves radiating from a signal source, silence spreads over the Brahmin quarter, the village, the river and fields, until Vairum, some three miles away, notices a hush, shivers and starts running for home. He runs without stopping, the panicked Muchami struggling to keep up with him, and when he enters his house from the back and sees his mother on the floor of the hall and his nieces around her with tear-streaked faces and the neighbours all fearful and resigned, because babies are fragile and do tend to die, Vairum raises his face to his fate and feels it press him down to his knees. As he falls, though, he curses. He cannot change his fate, but he can object, and this he does, in tortured tones. Those who hear him talk of it for years: his scream, like no sound they had ever heard from any living being.

27.
Thangam Visits
1934

THANGAM HAS BEEN EXPECTED in Cholapatti for nearly a week now, and Janaki, for one, is tired of waiting.

"Is she coming today?" she asks Sivakami, as she has every morning since they were told to prepare for the visit and the arrival of a new baby. Their elder sister, Saradha, arrived a week ago, for the same reason—she is due in a couple of months—but she is bossy and Janaki, who has never lived with her, finds her a little hard to take. She longs to see her mother again.

Sivakami tells her wearily, as every morning, that she can't say for sure.

"Why can't you say for sure, Amma?" Janaki whines, while her siblings scramble to organize their school work. She always has hers ready the night before. She's eight now and can barely remember living with her parents but still aches for her mother at times.

"Because your father is a ne'er-do-well and a cad," Vairum remarks casually as he passes her and breaks a couple of bananas off the stalk leaning in the pantry.

Janaki shrinks back against the main hall wall to let him pass back out. She watches him leave through the front door.

"What does that mean, Amma?" she asks Sivakami, her lower lip trembling.

"Nothing, kanna, nothing," Sivakami clucks. Janaki keeps her head down, her hands folded in front of her. "Your father's work keeps him very busy. He can't easily get away when he wants."

Muchami overhears this exchange from the courtyard but is not close enough to participate. He watches Janaki turn away, *oh, my girl,* too old now for him to take in his arms. As badly as she clearly needs to be held, there is no one now for that.

It's lunchtime at school, and Janaki and her friend and benchmate Bharati go to pick up their tiffin boxes. "So has your amma come yet?"

Janaki momentarily can't think of what her friend means. "Amma?" Then she realizes: Bharati is referring to Thangam. She's not Brahmin and so has never been inside their home. She can't know they call their grandmother Amma and refer to their mother as Akka. When Janaki was telling her friends that her mother was expected, she used the term "amma," but as identification, not appellation. "Um, no. Probably today."

"I thought she was coming a couple of days ago."

"My appa's work means he can't always bring her whenever he wants," Janaki parrots, glad that Bharati's gone on ahead of her out of the classroom and doesn't appear to have heard.

They look to see where their little gang of friends are sitting in the schoolyard and head for a slightly different place to force the other girls to come and join them.

"I couldn't live without my mother," says Bharati.

Is she being sly? Tough to say: her eyes are downcast, toward her lunch, which Janaki notices contains chicken. Although Janaki still only vaguely understands caste distinctions, she has been inculcated with Brahmin disapproval of non-vegetarianism. Even if one's caste permits such practices, she believes better individuals behave as much like Brahmins as possible. Muchami and Mari would never touch meat.

"I don't really notice it," Janaki lies.

Bharati lives with her mother, but, like Janaki, in her mother's mother's house. This is unusual, and they have talked a little about this strange fact of their lives they have in common against the world. She has heard it whispered, however, that Bharati might not know who her father is. Janaki doesn't know how this works but figures the subject must be sensitive. Janaki doesn't live with her father either, but at least she's confident of his identity.

"Ayoh!" yells Bharati all at once. Only the newest girl of their set jumps, the others being more accustomed to her melodrama.

"What?" asks one of them finally.

"We have our music lessons with that horrible Nandu Vadyar today," Bharati groans. Janaki can't help noticing that even Bharati's complaints sound musical and appealing. "Everything I learn about music I learn only from Vani Amma. Nandu Vadyar may as well be teaching us to wash dishes. Janaki, when Vani Amma was playing 'Nannu palimpa' last night, oh I thought I would cry." Bharati leaps up and falls to her knees. Arms arching skyward, eyes softened, she holds the pose as though she is being painted. She's so pretty, with fair skin and straight jet hair, that all the girls easily imagine her as an illustration in a storybook about the gods. "It was as though I could really see her, pleading with Lord Rama . . ." She clasps her hands at her breast and bows her head, while somehow still ensuring that her face is visible.

"Do you think when Nandu Vadyar hears music he's hearing the same thing we are?" Janaki asks metaphysically.

"I don't care what he hears." Bharati resumes her lunch. "Anyway, that's why I must have courage to listen to Vani Amma even after the sun goes down and the ghosts come out!"

Their four little friends jump and shiver as if on command. Janaki, because she is lieutenant and foil, and because she's smarting from having had her question dismissed, remains icily still.

"I saw a ghost, Janaki, two days ago," Bharati gasps, her eyes dancing, "when I came to hear Vani Amma play and Draupadi was late coming to get me. Can you guess where?"

"Tamarind tree, again?" Janaki assumes a diagnostic expression. "By the gate?"

"Have you seen the ghost that lives there?"

"Oh, there's more than one," Janaki world-wearily informs her. "Describe it."

"Huge, skin of fire, dripping fangs, broken horns," Bharati lists as though cataloguing the merits of a recent clothing purchase. All four of their friends are squirming, stricken.

"No, I haven't seen that one," Janaki admits with a tone of detached interest. "I think it almost got my brother once."

"I shielded my eyes and ran." Bharati mimes the tableau. "I could hear it chasing me until its power sucked it back into the tree."

"But how can you bear to go back, Bharati?" One of their companions asks, reason and curiosity overtaking her fright.

"Because that's the only place I can hear Vani Amma play," Bharati harrumphs, adding dreamily, "I would overcome any fear, I would scale mountains and swim up waterfalls to live in her music."

The whole rest of their class, munching lunches, looks frumpy and discontent in contrast with Bharati. Even Janaki, despite their close association, can never come close to matching her friend in style or mystery. Bharati seems to have been born sophisticated; there is something tragic that twinkles about her, something real or tinsel, one cannot tell, but it is intriguing either way.

On the bullock cart ride home, Janaki thinks on what may await her. She hopes her mother has arrived. She hopes her little sisters look like her, especially the one, Kamalam, who is coming to stay.

Vani normally commences playing shortly after the children get home. Today, though, as the bullock cart rounds off the town road onto the Brahmin-quarter approach, Janaki can already hear the music—vibrant, furious. Vani must be well into her session to have the raga at such a pitch.

The front hall, as always, is dim and cool, but the floor is shimmering with trails and patches of golden dust, as though a character from fairy stories has wandered through their home and enchanted it. The hair on Janaki's neck stands up: her mother, loveliness itself, is seated against a pillar, smiling faintly. The contours of Thangam's shoulders are accentuated by shadows of fairy dust, the pleats of her sari spread against her swollen belly. Kamalam, a little girl who does look like Janaki, leans against Thangam shyly. Another, littler girl, Radhai, is galloping to and fro in the garden with Muchami, banging trees with a stick.

Laddu, Sita and Janaki all grin and shuffle their feet in front of their mother.

"Hi."

"Hi."

"Hi," they say.

"Kiss your mother," Sivakami says loudly from the kitchen doorway, and the children go to Thangam, bending awkwardly to peck her on the cheek. She touches them lightly with her hand as they incline toward her. She smiles as if to put them off, and Sivakami, watching, feels pained. Has Thangam been made unable to show affection, too embarrassed by her father's favouritism, and now by her fecundity? *But why make the children suffer for that?* thinks Sivakami. *Vairum is not even home.*

The children look at Sivakami as if to ask what to do next, and she beckons them to the pantry to receive their after-school snacks. Laddu and Sita sit against the wall in the main hall, Janaki in one of the doorways to the garden. Janaki expects to be asked questions, but she's not. Sita and Laddu look proud and anxious to be noticed. Sita creeps gradually closer until she can take Thangam's hand. Thangam lets her, without clasping the hand in return.

Saradha comes into the hall from the kitchen, bustling and bouncing, straightening things that don't really need straightening. Janaki watches her and understands that, annoying as her methods are, this is her peculiar way of giving herself a feeling of stability. She listens, disturbed, to Vani's music. It sounds mad this afternoon, twirling and popping like Deepavali fireworks off the roof above them. She thinks she recognizes "Jaggadodharana," a song of praise for Lord Krishna, but each note is scissored frighteningly into sixteenths, blurring its sound. She hums along—yes, it is that song—and starts singing the lyrics, about the god born to a mortal, and his mother playing with him, as though he is merely her plump, silken baby, hers to hold, out of the world's eye. Janaki first heard the song at a wedding a year earlier, and made a relative there teach her the words. Lord Krishna is humanity's essence and its saviour, says the song, and his mother plays with him as though he is no more than her precious baby.

Then Vairum blurs through the pantry door and pulls up sharp at the sight of his sister and her mass of offspring, and Janaki suddenly remembers when Vani went away to have her baby and it died. Janaki has often thought about this cousin who vanished before she ever had the chance to meet him. It took her a while to understand that, unlike her and her sisters and brother, who have all been taken away and all eventually returned, this baby will never arrive here. She has always wondered what he looked like—crystal crossed with a moonbeam? A bubble on a cloud, attached to the world by dew-covered spider lines. They tore and he floated away. Had he come to live with them, he would have been Janaki's special companion, her complement, she thinks. He would have seen light where she saw dark, he would have been Vani's melody to Janaki's taalam. She used to crave dirt; he might have licked whitewash from clean corners and she alone would know.

Vani hits and pulls furious strings. The melody hammers on the drone as Janaki's imaginings plink glassily onto the brick floor and she drowses, half in sun, half in shade, her hand half-consciously tapping the song's rhythm on her knee. She's awakened by Sita knocking on her head.

"I'm going to go have a veena lesson like I always do at this time," she remarks pointedly. "I'll wake you up when it's time for supper."

"I'm coming, I'm coming." Janaki starts toward the back of the house. "Let me change, wait for me," she calls over her shoulder as she runs.

At four o'clock, as every Monday and Wednesday, she and Sita have a veena lesson at Gayatri's house, with a terrible teacher of good family engaged by Gayatri's mother-in-law. Gayatri had invited Sita and Janaki to participate since her daughter Akila was quite young and it would help to have older girls along, since she knew Janaki would like nothing better, and since she couldn't invite Janaki without inviting Sita. Janaki ekes all she can from their teacher's limited store of knowledge, while Sita, though she loves the idea of having lessons, is terrible and never practises. Still, Gayatri and Sivakami privately agreed that any constructive activity could help curb Sita's destructive impulses, and Gayatri was glad to help Sivakami, much as she disliked having Sita in the house. Even if Sivakami had intended to give her granddaughters veena lessons, which she hadn't, it would be impossible for the girls to receive a teacher at home, given that teachers generally teach in exactly the hours when Vani conducts her own afternoon session.

Sita will, of course, have left by the time Janaki gets out of her school uniform and into a regular paavaadai, and Janaki knows this, but changes quickly just in case. Sita has gone, so Janaki trots to the back door off the courtyard and leans out peering to her left, so she can see Bharati, who sits beneath a mango tree as she always does at this time.

"Hi."

"Hi."

Bharati points up in Vani's direction with a mystified expression; Janaki purses her brows and shrugs in agreement. Bharati closes her eyes. Janaki goes to her veena lesson.

After he finishes with them, their teacher goes west, out of the Brahmin quarter, to the very edge of Cholapatti, to Bharati's house, where he gives his last lesson of the day.

It's midday break, at school the next day. Janaki and Bharati choose their position, and their friends close in uncertainly.

"I knew your amma had finally arrived," Bharati opens, "because Nandu Vadyar showed up for my lesson with a gold stripe across his forehead."

While Janaki and Sita had been at their lesson, Thangam had taken up her old position on the veranda, and Brahmin-quarter residents paid calls into the early evening. They would greet Thangam and, despite receiving little if any acknowledgement, would pinch stripes of gold dust off the veranda to apply to their foreheads and those of their loved ones.

"Yes." Janaki smiles, wondering why she feels shy. "She was there when I got home, with my little sisters."

"And she wants a boy, doesn't she?" Bharati is poking at the contents of her lunch, which, Janaki notices with a little inward shudder, includes eggs. "Brahmins always want boys."

Janaki doesn't really know how to answer. Who doesn't want boys?

Another of their friends, not Brahmin but close, blithely advises them, "My father wanted a girl by the time I was born. They had seven sons already."

Bharati's sneer startles them, though Janaki had noticed her gritting her teeth.

"My grandmother says all of your castes talktalktalk about how the good of the family is on the woman's shoulders, how she is the strength and wealth and culture, but no one really believes that, they just want dowries, so they want son after stupid son. Pooh! My mother wanted girls and she has girls."

They are too young to ask how it is that Bharati's mother got girls just because she wanted them. Some people are lucky that way, after all: they get what they want. Bharati gives the impression that she too will be such a person.

"Oh, Janaki!" Bharati claps her hands.

"What?" Janaki asks with irritation. Why does Bharati so often make her feel as though she is losing? Aren't they on the same team?

"It's Sanskrit lesson, right after lunch," Bharati says as though repeating herself. "We get to hear what happens next in *Shakuntalam*."

Their friends try to look interested but not too interested: as regards Sanskrit, Bharati and Janaki are in a class by themselves. By themselves in a class of girls two years older, that is: they are sufficiently advanced that they take Sanskrit with the sixth-standard girls instead of with the fourth. In the advanced levels, the girls' Sanskrit master is the same as the boys', young Kesavan (not really so young any more, but he will be called "young Kesavan" until his death at the age of eighty-four). It is partly for this reason that Bharati and Janaki participate in the advanced class: each of them already receives home tutoring from Kesavan. Bharati has taken Sanskrit tutoring since she was four; her mother considers it part of a girl's mandatory education. Janaki vaguely guesses this is some kind of a tradition in their caste but somehow feels shy to ask questions about it.

The fourth-standard girls are still at work on nouns, chanting them in singular, dual, plural, until, finally, the words become sounds without meaning. With the sixth-standards, Kesavan has taken it upon himself to introduce them to some classics of Hindu theatre, starting with Kalidasa's *Shakuntalam*. The well-loved story of a hermit's daughter, married in a secret ceremony to a king who later fails to recognize her owing to a curse, it is a challenge to the children, the vocabulary being sophisticated for the ten ten-year-olds, and the romantic intrigues even more so for the two eight-year-olds. Bharati alone seems alarmingly equal to both.

Rattling home in the bullock cart bound for the Brahmin quarter, Janaki reviews the *Shakuntalam* story episodes of that day, knowing they will form the better part of that afternoon's tutorial. She had read the part of the jester, a Brahmin. She would have loved to play the star role, Shakuntala, but that had gone to Bharati, and Janaki had to admit she deserved it.

Janaki tries to remember her longest speech, in which the jester complains about his forest sojourn in the king's company: " . . . drinking water from tepid streams fouled with dead leaves, eating badly cooked meat at odd hours . . ." Their teacher had shocked the class by saying this line showed that Brahmins likely once ate meat. One girl, taunted with this after school, had burst into tears and said it was a lie. Janaki thought she might be right. She has heard Sivakami and Muchami describe Kesavan pejoratively as a "progressive," and so is skeptical of anything he says about caste.

In front of her—that is, behind the cart—a creature with strong legs and puny waving arms gallops out of the banana groves to the left. Janaki flushes as the creature giddily hurtles into the groves to the right. She sighs hard, once, through her nose.

A moment later, Muchami and Kamalam, in piggyback combo, bounce out of the groves again and gallop and weave up the road. Kamalam waves in a manner Janaki thinks is ridiculous, as she plans to inform her sister as soon as they arrive home. For now she is limited to a dignified, reproving glare. Muchami and Kamalam both seem too exhilarated to notice Janaki's expression, though the jolt and shudder of the cart would make focusing on Janaki difficult even for the soberest of persons. Janaki clenches her teeth, trying at minimum to keep her cheeks from infantile jiggling, but the cart hits an anthill and all its contents are flung about. By the time Janaki collects herself, Muchami and Kamalam have turned up the path behind the Brahmin-quarter houses.

She wonders if Muchami asked Kamalam any questions today, as he used to do with her, which thought slows her to a stop in the vestibule. Her chest feels tight, her face hot. She is close to tears, but

Sita and Laddu shove her from behind and the three of them stumble into the main hall, where loud laughter clusters and breaks around them: their second sister, Visalam, has arrived—she is also expecting—escorted by an entourage of her relentlessly gay in-laws, all now momentarily incapacitated by the schoolchildren's brief physical comedy.

Already, Kamalam is seated next to Visalam and is laughing. The rest of the party is looking at the door, but Kamalam stares at Visalam and her husband, and bursts into delighted gales whenever they do. Sivakami is beckoning the schoolchildren from the kitchen, but Janaki's eyes are trained upon the treacherous Kamalam, who was to have been Janaki's shadow, her admirer, her imitator, and instead is insinuating herself into all those places that are rightfully Janaki's own. Sivakami calls Janaki by name but the child smoulders to her doorway niche with the intention of wasting away.

Ten minutes later, no one seems to have noticed her wasting. She keeps her face turned resolutely to the garden until she sees Muchami approaching from the cowshed, grinning broadly and toting his slate. Then she turns toward the hall to snub him.

Muchami sits on the ground behind her and asks, "Janaki-baby, where is your slate?" Normally, Janaki starts writing out the initial stanzas of the class in advance of Kesavan's arrival, and Muchami copies from her. When Kesavan arrives, they are often already mid-chant. They rub out and start over with the class, but the advance exercises make them feel unified and athletic.

"By the door," Janaki replies as though she can't imagine why he's asking.

If Muchami notices her tone, he doesn't let on.

"Young Kesavan is arriving, listen." He points into the hall with his chin.

Bursts of laughter issue from the hall. Kesavan nervously reciprocates. From the corner of her eye, Janaki watches the in-laws shift and roll apart with the motion of a flotilla.

"Tell Kamalam to fetch it for you," Muchami suggests.

Janaki straightens.

"Kamalam!" she essays. "My slate." She points to it.

Kamalam scuttles to the door in a single motion, more eagerness than grace. Delivering the slate, she awaits further instructions. Muchami indicates to Kamalam that she can sit. She does, cross-legged, not leaning against anything, but, like Muchami, facing Janaki expectantly.

"Kamalam-baby, you listen carefully to Janaki," Muchami says. "This is Sanskrit and it's not easy."

Janaki reminds herself that, even if she's less inclined to express it, her scorn for their earlier foolishness has in no way relaxed. For now, it's a special flavouring—essence of contempt—in the sweet sense of superiority flowing from beneath her tongue.

She clears her throat and calls to mind the cadence of the day's first syllables, but before she can mouth them, the hall is blustered once more by gales of laughter. Laddu's tutoring fellows are sidling in. They get laughed at a lot, however, and so neither hang back nor show alarm. One is tall, one fat, one handsome, but people tend to think they look alike because they share the tentative and hopeful bewilderment of the bad student who will never improve.

Janaki looks to young Kesavan, expecting him to be irritated or self-conscious at being stuck in this tittering tableau, but he has spied an opportunity. As Laddu and his three fellows sink to the floor, Kesavan rises and addresses the mini-multitude.

"I am hoping the majority of you are comfortable with Sanskrit pronunciation," he smiles eagerly and only wavers a little at the shouts of laughter he receives in response. It's not clear whether these are self-mockery or affirmation, so he has no choice but to plunge on. "Since you all are here, I hope you will permit me to take advantage and have you recite, along with the children, some scenes from *Shakuntalam*." Here he pauses to receive the hoped-for hoots. "I can tell you agree it is a splendid chance to help the young people of this house better appreciate this beloved play."

He casts everyone in the room in a role. Janaki is awarded the role of Shakuntala. Sita and Visalam are her girl chums, Visalam's husband the king, Laddu the jester, Muchami plays a charioteer and several minor hermits. Kesavan then begins to conduct them as though they are an orchestra. He sings out lines, and indicates individuals and clusters to echo him like woodwind or string sections coming in at the baton's behest. This is the largest audience Janaki has ever had, and she brings all her skills of diction and dramatics to the part. She doesn't look at Kamalam for the duration of the lesson but feels her sister's gaze. Kamalam has found an ambition: to play second fiddle to Janaki's first.

But if Janaki is first, what is Sita? Visalam is married and therefore Sita should be highest ranked in the household now. Was she hoping for the part Janaki had been given? Janaki, casting her eyes across the room, sees Sita's eyes burning like a cat's in a darkened corner.

By end of the second act, voices are flagging. Kesavan winds up the day's session; the crowd wants to know where the story goes next, so he knows he'll have his cast back the next day. Many of the younger relatives will stay a couple of days in Cholapatti and are likely to be around at tiffin times. He gives them a brief disquisition on the portion they've read and asks if anyone has questions. Janaki asks whether there is a written assignment, but Sivakami interrupts to say that young Kesavan has stayed much longer than his contracted period and should hurry home lest complete darkness overtake him on the road.

The lesson over, Janaki goes up the winding staircase to the roof to listen to Vani play. Kamalam creeps along behind her. Vani is playing "Jaggadodharana" again, just commencing a *charanam,* the improvisational segments that make up the last parts of a song in performance. The girls squat by the balustrade, under the awning's shade. This is one of the strangest charanams Janaki has ever heard Vani play, though Janaki suspects that more than her still elementary musical education prevents her from understanding Vani's playing. She descends the stairs to go out back of the house. Bharati comes there daily to sit beneath the old mango tree and listen to Vani play. Kamalam follows her sister.

Janaki exits from the cowshed to the courtyard and out the back of the house, and looks left to the mango tree roots. Bharati is not there. Janaki takes two steps out and squats to scan the forest's lower reaches. Some bird whistles a two-note signal. Where is Bharati? She can't have left yet. The bird signals again, from the same place, close to the mango tree, or in its branches.

"Hsst," Janaki hears. "Janaki."

Janaki trips over a set of margosa roots tangled across the path. Bharati's hennaed feet are waving from a low branch of the mango tree. One of her silver anklets keeps catching on the red-orange border of her chartreuse paavaadai—her favourite colours, distinctive anywhere except in a mango tree, where they serve as camouflage.

"Was that you whistling?" Janaki peers up at her.

"Who did you think it was?" Bharati grins.

"Why are you up in the tree?" Janaki asks, sounding grouchier than she intends.

"I thought I would be able to make the song out better," Bharati explains.

"Can you?" Janaki moves to the tree and looks up.

"No. Come up anyway. Is that your sister?"

"Yes, Kamalam." Janaki points at the littler girl, who hangs back, nearer the house. "How do I get up there?"

"Jump and grab that branch there and swing your foot up. Come." Bharati holds out a hand as though to help.

Janaki jumps for the branch and swings. She kicks her legs, which makes her swing harder, pedals her feet against the trunk, falls.

"Try again," Bharati suggests.

"Come down if you can't hear the song any better anyway." Janaki sits, leaning against the trunk, and beckons her sister impatiently to join her.

A minute's rustling later, Bharati drops from the tree in a pretty heap, thumping against the ground with a sound akin to mangoes falling on windy days, the promise of sweetness, even sweeter if bruised.

"I have a sister around your age," Bharati says to Kamalam, who sits, knees to chest, on Janaki's other side. "Maybe she'll be in your class at school."

"Isn't Vani Mami's playing so strange today?" Janaki shifts a little so Bharati's view of Kamalam is obstructed.

Bharati shrugs. "No one plays like her, but other people have kids."

Janaki doesn't know what Bharati means but is not going to admit that in front of Kamalam.

That night Thangam goes into labour.

The next afternoon, Janaki is listening to Vani play, again "Jaggadhodarana," with the strange improvisation, which has grown even wilder and more alien. And when the rips and hics of a newborn's cry rise from the room below the stairs to join the notes bounding across the rooftop, Janaki hears: Vani's version sobs. The song somehow remains intact—perhaps because the improvisation cycles back to the original raga—but a keening invades it, as if the song were a baby blanket impaled on a sword.

Abruptly, Vani ceases playing, takes up her instrument and carries it down the stairs to the chamber she and Vairum inhabit on the second story. Janaki and Kamalam edge along the balustrade. Janaki happens to glance east over the rail, into the witch's yard next door, where the slapping of laundry against laundry stone had been providing percussive accompaniment to Vani's music. Dharnakarna, the witch next door, is washing the clothes herself. It often happens that her servants quit. In the silence which seems extra silent now, the witch's sister-in-law's incessant obscene monologue crescendoes and recedes again within the witch's kitchen. Dharnakarna doesn't pause.

Janaki, her hand on Kamalam's shoulder, arrives at the bottom of the stairs as Vairum blows in from his business, a cold front in a warm climate. The door to the birthing room is closed. He goes to the pantry entrance and sees that the kitchen is empty.

"Amma?" He calls out. "Amma!"

Sivakami answers from within the birthing room. "A boy! Finally, another boy."

Vairum nods, walks toward the stairway, and pauses outside the birthing room.

"Congratulations, Thangam Akka!" Vairum calls out. "A second son, at last. Now you truly need worry about nothing. I could even kill your first son and you would still have another. Nice work. Your mind must now be so at ease."

Laddu, who had just emerged from the pantry with two bananas in each hand and his mouth stretched to encompass a generously proportioned sphere of thaingai maavu, retreats again. Janaki and Kamalam look at him, terrified, but Vairum looks back a little too late to see his nephew, then turns to mount the stairs. Kamalam holds on to the back of Janaki's shirt as they shuffle through the doorway and along the garden wall. Kamalam is crying, and Janaki looks at her sternly.

"Kamalam, Vairum Mama's not going to do anything," Janaki tells her little sister as they arrive at the cowshed, where Muchami is milking. "Muchami, Vairum Mama isn't going to hurt Laddu Anna, is he?"

"No, no, no." Muchami puts a hand on Kamalam's head. "Vairum was just . . . he was just talking. Aren't you glad to have a little brother?"

Kamalam nods, though she is still crying. Janaki doesn't reply, ashamed of her anger at the uncle who shelters them. Muchami seats Kamalam where she can watch the milking, but Janaki goes out back through the courtyard door. Bharati drops out of the tree beside her.

"Did I hear a baby cry?" she inquires.

"Yeah. A boy." Janaki scrapes up a handful of dirt, dry and pebbly.

"A boy, huh?" Bharati crosses her wrists elegantly over one knee. "Your amma must be happy."

Janaki shrugs—she has never thought of her mother as happy.

"My mother is never happy when she has a boy baby," Bharati says, tearing a long blade of grass into shreds. "And they don't live, except for my one brother." She drifts into silence, then sighs a quick breath and looks up. "It's okay though because my mother really only wants girls."

"My Vairum Mama and Vani Mami's boy baby passed on, too."

"But they wanted him. Trust me." Bharati looks like she knows more than she should. "What did your cousin die of?"

They hear Sita in the courtyard. "Janaki? Janaki? Okay, I've looked for her. I'm leaving."

Janaki gets up. "Veena lesson. See you tomorrow."

What did her cousin die of? Maybe Muchami can tell her. She has the feeling talking about it might upset her grandmother.

The next day, Janaki finds Muchami as he milks the cows. Even if she is too big now to go with him to his village, she still likes to spend time with him when he does chores, helping a little when she can.

"Muchami?"

He looks at her briefly and back at his work. "What do you want, Janaki-baby?"

She strokes the cow's flank—it's the oldest and the most calm of the three.

"I was wondering, do you know . . . how my cousin died?"

Muchami looks at her again, pursing his brow. "Vairum's son, you mean?"

"Yes."

"I don't know," he says gently. "I don't think there was a specific reason. It happens, unfortunately."

Janaki nods.

"What makes you ask?" He finishes the milking and stands, holding his back.

"I was just thinking about it because someone I know, from school, told me all of her brothers died when they were babies, except one."

"That must be very hard."

"I suppose, except"—he question bursts forth, held against Janaki's curiosity for so long—"my friend said that in her caste they only want girls! Have you ever heard of that?"

Muchami wags his head slowly.

"Why?" Janaki asks.

Muchami rubs his forehead. "There could be a few reasons. I'm not entirely sure."

Janaki waits.

"Is that the girl I see out back sometimes?" he asks.

"Yes," Janaki says. "She loves music. She comes to hear Vani Mami play."

"I see."

"She's my best friend," she confides, not that he would know what a privilege this is.

He doesn't respond, and she feels a bit disgruntled: he might appreciate it just because she so clearly does. In silence, she helps him carry the milk in.

Ten days after Thangam's delivery, Janaki and Sita are kept home from school to clean house and prepare for the baby's eleventh-day naming ceremony. They spend the day bickering and being separated. Janaki manages to arrange her tasks so that she can listen to Vani's morning session: she spends the time spinning wicks from cotton bolls and knotting jasmine blossoms, marigolds and roses into garlands with cotton twine.

Kamalam fills her day by doing whatever Janaki does, but less so: she spins more slowly, her wicks are thick and uneven, her garland knots loose. Today, she can do almost nothing, owing to tension: their father is expected. Kamalam has confessed to Janaki that she is afraid of Goli and wishes he weren't coming. Janaki, who hasn't seen him for a couple of years, recalls some feeling of fear, though she is also curious.

Sivakami is preoccupied and apprehensive, as much in anticipation of Goli's arrival as of his potential failure to arrive. Vairum will be unpleasant in either circumstance. Sita, who idolizes their father loudly and frequently (though never in Vairum's presence), is menacingly sweet today.

When Vani's morning session ends, Janaki winds up her garland weaving and reports for her next task—making murrukku, fried lentil-flour snacks. It's a chore the children compete for, and she has won the first shift. She takes up the tumbler portion of the murrukku-squeezing mechanism, selects a metal disk punched with star-shaped holes and drops it into the tumbler's bottom to form a sieve. She scoops batter from the basin where Sivakami has prepared it, and fills the tumbler, then takes the compressor, double-handled like the tumbler, and fits its end into the tumbler's top. Kamalam, too young for anything involving hot oil, squats in the doorway to watch.

Janaki holds the contraption over the bubbling oil and starts to squeeze, twirling it slightly to make the descending parallel lines loop as they hit the oil. The syllable "ka," "க," appears, floating in the pot.

"Look, Kamalam, I'm writing your name!" Janaki makes a "ma," "ம," a "la," "ல," and an "im," "ம்," which bubble and bob in and out of sequence, becoming "mamkala" and "lakamma" as Kamalam, who cannot read, bends open-mouthed above the wok. Janaki fishes the now solid syllables from the oil, and lays them on a plate in sequence, then pulls the tumbler from the compressor and refills it.

"Make Sita," says Kamalam, drawing closer and then back on a warning from Sivakami. Janaki does: the syllables "see" and "thaa," "சீ தா," sink and rise, gold against the black iron.

Muchami peeks in from the courtyard where he is washing up, and Janaki writes him into the pot. "Mu," "chaa," "mi"—but of course he cannot read Tamil.

"This is the last one, what should it be?" Janaki asks, scraping up the last of the batter under Sivakami's frugal eyes.

"Amma," Kamalam suggests. Sivakami smiles and turns away, though she keeps looking as Janaki spells "ah," "im," "maa," "அ ம் மா."

Janaki and Kamalam wash up and, with Vani, are served their late-morning meal. Kamalam appears fascinated with Vani's stories, though Janaki is not convinced her sister is really following them. Today's was particularly worth missing school for: the story of Vani's father's second cousin who was kidnapped by a renegade band of dacoits and made to serve them for twelve years as a laundryman and spiritual adviser. His thumbs were cut off so that he could not use their stolen muskets against them, and when he was returned home, he was never again permitted in the family's sanctum sanctorum because clearly he had not prepared his own food in that time and indeed had taken up with a concubine, who not only cooked for him but fed him from her own hand.

After the morning meal, the household naps. After tiffin, while Sita makes murrukku with unusual willingness but no attention at all to shape or symmetry, Janaki is excused to listen to Vani play.

She slips out the back, swings herself up against the mango tree, bracing her toes into near invisible notches on the trunk and standing, then sitting, on a branch about eight feet off the ground. She mastered this about a week ago, practising one Sunday morning when Bharati was not around.

Bharati arrives soon after and climbs up as well. Janaki has taken the better branch—slightly wider and higher up. Bharati takes the second choice—lower and narrower. From above and to their right, Vani commences playing "Akshayalinga Sankarabaranam," a song for Shiva.

Janaki and Bharati begin to tap out the rhythm—they have just recently deciphered it. It seems to be three and a half beats: a short and a long tap on the back of the hand, two long taps on the front.

And they are humming along. Occasionally, Bharati and Janaki find themselves humming different things, each anticipating a different turn in the song, just as happens with Vani's stories. But, increasingly, they find that even when they hum different things, neither sounds wrong, because they are both improvising on the raga, though neither will learn its name and formal properties for some years. And they don't sound bad together. So there they are, tapping and humming, their two pairs of feet dangling from the foliage. They can't see the back door from the courtyard and so don't see it open and Sita step out, hot and cranky from completing the coveted chore, blinking oil-smoke tears. She hears the two to her left, though she can't see them. She says, "Oh, you two songbirds fill our neighbourhood with beauty. We're so lucky! You must promise me, Bharati, that you will sing at my wedding. And Janaki, you must sing at my funeral. Promise?"

"Sita!" Sivakami's voice comes from the courtyard. Sita wheels and whacks her elbow on the heavy wood door. "Not one more word like that!"

The songbirds stop their twittering. Sita slinks back inside like a mean pet cat in a family of dog lovers.

It is shortly after midnight by the time the preparations are complete. The moon has waxed full and burns candle-bright, so Vani does, too. Janaki listens to the last strains of Vani's practice as she washes her face and hands, and Kamalam's, in the moonlight by the well.

Vairum steps off the stairs into the main hall as Janaki and Kamalam lay down their sleeping mats. He speaks to Sivakami with a roughness that has increased with the years.

"Still hasn't appeared?" It's not a question. "What will we do if he hasn't come by morning?"

Sivakami sighs. "We go ahead, even without him. We can use a stand-in, if necessary."

"Makes sense. He uses a stand-in for every other function of fatherhood—except the original one, pardon me."

Everyone else likes to sleep in the darker areas of the hall, but Janaki places her reed mat over a cold, striped mat of moonlight. Cold, milky moonlight pours in the window and runs over her face, along the grooves between her nostrils and cheek, collects in her collarbone, between her lips, in her cupped palm and the clench of her fist, and chills her finally to sleep.

The next day, the inauspicious period of raahu kaalam doesn't end until 10:30, so everyone has plenty of time to rise and bathe and grow hungry—none will be permitted to eat cooked food until after the puja. Thangam and the baby take their first bath since the birth and Thangam applies turmeric paste to her skin. It makes an ordinary woman appear golden, but on Thangam's arms and countenance it has a dulling effect. The baby is gently massaged with sesame oil, with special attention to shaping the features of his face.

From today, he will be called Krishnan, since he is the eighth child and a boy, just like the hero-child of myth. The name certainly fits, coo his sisters: just see his lusty yells, his kicking and writhing, his handsome face. He has all the strength and charm and mischief of the god. Clearly, he is more than equal to multi-headed sea serpents and poison-nippled wet nurses. Without doubt, he could steal butter and charm any village lady into forgiving him.

But just in case—and especially if all the admiration to which he will be subjected makes him vulnerable to the evil eye—baby Krishnan will receive today a black cord to be tied below his belly. On the cord, among a few other tiny trinkets, will hang a cup containing a snippet of his umbilical cord, and a bit of Laddu's, the older brother who lived, sealed in with gold. Sivakami stubbornly overrode suggestions that the cup include a pinch of Thangam's gold dust. She can't believe that others persist in seeing Thangam's dust as auspicious: to her it seems quite clear that Thangam sheds when she is at her lowest, that in some way, the dust is her essence, her promise, her vitality draining from her. It's no wonder it has healing properties—she has no doubt about that—but it is not indicative of fulfillment or joy.

The puja is to commence in about ten minutes. Priest, mother and child are assembled, along with Rukmini and Murthy, Gayatri and Minister and their children, and assorted other neighbours. Even neighbours not present for the ceremony will attend the feast—it's mostly of the feast that even those assembled are thinking.

Fortunately, this ceremony is not a long one. The question, as always, is how to plug the conspicuous Goli-shaped hole. Thangam is releasing dust in volumes as though the stuff might fill the void, or, failing this, mask it. Rukmini, clumsy and helpful, gathers it into a dish. Vairum, looking disgusted, finally clears his throat with a snort and looks at Sivakami as though challenging her to make a decision. She takes a breath and turns to the priest, wondering what she will say.

She is spared. There is a commotion in the street, then the front door swings open and their hopes and fears are confirmed: Goli has finally arrived. Sita runs gleefully to greet him. "Appa, Appa, a new little brother!"

He speaks over the little girl's head. "Hello, folks, hello!" His high, handsome brow and ruddy features shine as though he could make the sun sweat. "What's all this?"

Sita trails behind him, a weak smile at the ready in case he should turn and see her.

"The eleventh day," Sivakami responds. "The eleventh day after the birth . . ."

"What? Oh, I thought it was the . . . Wait until you—look what I brought! Son, you!" He is waving in Laddu's general direction. "You come, help me."

Laddu runs out willingly and they struggle back in with a large crate leaking straw. With a creak and tear of wood, Goli removes the top of the crate and digs through the stuffing.

"Catch!" he cries.

Luscious, exotic malgoa mangoes—Goli tosses them one by one by one by one over the austere, pious little hall. Shooting stars. The children run after them. The adults, bewildered, reach and jump on the spot. And starbursts: one, then another, explodes ripely against the clean brick floor. Visalam, eight and a half months pregnant, slips and falls in a mango slick.

A gasp goes up like a lost balloon, three more stars plop from the firmament and Gayatri rushes to aid the fallen girl. Visalam's face is crumpled, as if she is about—to—sneeze—or—cry—then . . . "Ha, ha, ha, ha . . ." She rolls over laughing, and the others, tentatively, do too. Sivakami looks relieved, then severe. Vairum only looks severe.

Thangam looks away. The priest has one eye on the hourglass, but he's as up for a good laugh as anyone.

Now Goli is reaching inside his coat again, and pulling out . . . what now? Pens. Shiny, new pens, far beyond the reach of every day. These, too, he tosses in the air. "Catch, children, catch!" he cries. The pens turn and glint. Gold like Thangam and straight like arrows, they circle in the late-morning sun that seeps in through chinks.

Janaki is thrilled and aghast. Such opulence, such waste! There are mangoes ripening on the trees in the yard, not malgoas, which come from far away and are terribly expensive, but still, perfectly tasty, or maybe not perfectly, but good enough. And if they need pen and ink at school, they dip a nib tied to a twig into ink mixed from powder. What need could they have, mere children, for such luxuries? It has never occurred to her to want them. But as she looks at Sita, Janaki sees it has occurred to her sister. Sita has no real taste for either food or penmanship, but her look implies she could cultivate both, given food and pens that were worth her while.

Goli is lugging in yet another crate, pronouncing like a street huckster, "And for my bride Thangam, as beautiful as the day I married her, the gift of music!"

Thangam blushes fast and deep under her turmeric mask, and all the other women blush briefly for her, too—such inappropriate comments . . .

But what could this be? A wooden box with a brass crank like a shrugging arm. Goli affixes something like an enormous trumpet-blossom to its side. The guests gape, the puja forgotten, as Goli pulls two large black plates out of the packing with a flourish. "Stand back, friends, a little room please."

He fits the disk onto the top of the box, turns the crank a dozen rotations, then lifts a lever from the box with a point he sets upon the record. Crackles, hisses and pops begin emerging from the great flower, but before the Brahmin-quarter denizens can start to fear the snakes or insects or whatever will follow, the hall is filled with music.

The good people of Cholapatti listen in astounded silence, motionless, until a few come forward cautiously to peer into the bloom's private depths. Surely a thumb-sized musician must sit there amidst stamens and pistils, writhing snakes and whirring beetles. They pull back from the flower's empty darkness to look, mystified, at Goli, who winks, raises his eyebrows, gestures toward the machine, offering no explanation. Thangam hangs back shyly. She doesn't try, as the others do, to find the music's source. She owns it, it is hers. Goli said it was. Here is proof, if anyone wants it: he does think of her. Sita stands proudly beside the contraption, policing the crowd.

The music is not nearly so impressive as Vani's, but few of those assembled appreciate this. Janaki is among them, aware of how dull and uninspired the playing is, but she must admit that this does not diminish the thrill. The player's absence gives her an appeal beyond Vani's reach. Oh, listen! The song ended and the tiny musician said her name. Where is she? Maddening. Several advance again to try to see her, as Murthy begins pompously explaining how the technology works.

Janaki looks at her aunt, who had finished her playing amidst the final puja preparations. Is Vani hurt at all the attention being given to a mediocre musician who is not even here? Most villagers don't appreciate her playing anyway, and since her melancholic phase began some weeks back, a few have actually complained. Her recent improvisations remind a person so strongly of old grief, it's been hard to get things done. Fights have broken out. Perhaps the appeal of the absent Madras musician's mechanical recital is increased by the villagers' recent feeling of estrangement from Vani.

Though she appears to be paying attention to the new music, Vani doesn't look in the direction of the gramophone or the crowd. As the record ends, Vani sweeps the room with a glance, her eyes narrowed, nostrils flared. Janaki, too, is caught in her net of disdain—the only person to notice it, the least deserving. Vani goes upstairs.

Everyone else is clamouring for the invisible musician's return, and Goli lifts the needle to the start of the record once more. Amidst the bustle and buzz now comes Vairum's voice, coldly inquiring whether they shouldn't think of commencing the puja, given that the hour ticks down.

All jump to. Goli must be instructed twice in each task and always looks as though he is about to break in and say something. Sometimes he does, comments neither amusing nor relevant, but everyone laughs and pays attention. When he sees his new son, he picks him up and swings him, making the baby shriek with justifiable fear.

"He loves it!" cries Goli. "Listen to those lungs!"

Then, distracted by some new thought, he hands Krishnan back to Thangam and doesn't seek his son again. Janaki, who had leapt forward in alarm when her father swung the baby in the air, sinks down beside her mother. Kamalam is already huddled there. She was a little too excited to feel afraid until that moment, and impressed by all the show, but now she is shaking a little. Was their father this careless with all of them?

Janaki leans on her mother, who doesn't respond. She feels a familiar whir of disappointment but no surprise. She had tried a couple of times, before her brother was born, to be affectionate with Thangam and found that her overtures were not reciprocated. The pain has begun to lessen, though, and she takes some comfort from the simple warmth of her side.

The puja soon ends and Sivakami begins insisting the male guests and children have lunch. No one would refuse, but they let themselves be pressed as a courtesy. Janaki sets banana leaves down in a row along each side of the main hall, and Sita follows her, holding in iddikki tongs the lip of a hot pot of semolina pudding, from which she deposits a blob on each leaf as the diners sit down. Kamalam begs to be allowed to serve also and follows her sisters with a vessel full of vadais.

One lunch guest begins polite conversation, asking, "How long have you leave, Goli?"

"Oh, my schedule is my own." Goli slurps up the initial daub of sweet. "This is a business trip for me."

"Revenue department business?" inquires another luncher. Some of these people tried for some years to extract what they are owed for undelivered deer's heads.

"Ha!" Goli sprays three or four morsels of rice with sambar back toward his leaf. "I'd not make any money at all, if that's all I did."

"What kind of a salary does the department offer?" asks an anxious-browed man from several doors away. "My son plans to take the civil service exam next year. I told him to talk to you."

"You wouldn't believe. Thirty rupees monthly."

"Oh, that's . . . well, it's a good salary, of course, but to feed a family of what, eight children . . ."

"No, no, absolutely unjust. Very difficult to make ends meet." Goli signals for more rice, and rasam, the next course, and Janaki and Sita run out with serving dishes. He conveys a sense of constant motion above his meal, and despite talking more than anyone, also eats more and faster.

Janaki, serving Vairum, whose indignation is writ large on his face, wishes her appa would just keep his mouth shut. She knows her father has never tossed more than a few odd paisa toward his kids' upbringing and she turns, blushing, away from her uncle's rage.

Another neighbour inquires with hesitant interest, "Where are you stationed currently, Goli?"

"One has somewhat just transferred to Malapura. But I am maintaining strong interests in Salem. Salem!" Goli reinforces. The man, who heard the first time, nods. "That's where everything is happening. Everything modern."

"Oh, is that so?" another politely remarks while belching.

"Oh, yes," huffs Goli. "Industries! Banking! Everything is there!"

"Ah . . ." several men nod.

"Yep." Goli gobbles both desserts and calls for more, and yogourt rice. "That's where my son here had better set up. Might even get him to do his college there first."

"College?" someone chokes lightly—another of Goli's unpaid creditors. Eyebrows rise in a ripple among the eaters: Goli's son Krishnan is yet a possibility but Laddu's poor school performance is no secret.

"Sure," Goli finishes, and drinks water, a long stream poured down his throat from a tumbler, which Janaki waits to refill, twice, from a brass jug. He belches monstrously. "If he's going to be an engineer, lawyer, medical doctor, he has to go to college—may as well be there!"

"Oh-ho, Athimbere," Vairum growls, making the honorific, "elder sister's husband," sound sarcastic. Goli turns slowly to face his brother-in-law. "How's your money situation? Problems?"

Sivakami is in the kitchen and doesn't hear Vairum's remark, but hears the main hall grow silent.

"Not at all, Vairum," Goli smiles tightly. "I don't know when things have gone as well. So many opportunities opening up. A person just has to know how to take advantage."

"You certainly know how to take advantage, Athimbere," Vairum spits. "That is definitely one of your strong suits."

"I'm sure we all prefer not to know what you are talking about, Vairum, but what I am talking about"—Goli opens his face like a late-season sunflower to the rest of the company—"is investment. I'm sure there are many present who wouldn't mind knowing how to improve fortunes grown paltry with time."

"Investing with you, Athimbere, would be the equivalent of burying one's wealth and forgetting the location." Vairum flicks his hand twice toward his leaf, folds it toward himself and stands. "But anyone stupid enough to give you his money deserves to lose it."

"Vairum!" Sivakami says from the kitchen. "That's bad manners."

"No, Amma." Vairum sighs fast and wearily. "It's a warning. I would hate, I would really hate to see anyone in this room lose money he can ill afford."

"How disrespectful can a man be? Listen to your mother!" Goli shrills. "You keep your head in the clouds and act superior to try to keep the people of your village beneath you. They are not fooled!"

"So they'll do what they choose." Vairum disappears out the back.

"You are not fooled," Goli commands those around him, and they all wag their heads, "No, no, yes, yes."

The hall empties of the men, who go to the veranda to chew betel and chew over the latest gossip. Inside, the women sit to eat, including Vani, whose bright chatter is not dulled by the events of the morning. Janaki receives a welcome bonus: Vani's story changes today. Now the dacoits cut off their own thumbs as part of their initiation ritual. Their weapons are adapted. Vani's relative cooks and feeds them from his own hand, as he also does his thumbless lover, who had cut off her own digits as a gesture of unity with her first lover, killed young in a raid on a Hyderabad *haveli*. None of the other children had paid attention enough to realize they are lucky to be present at the change; none is paying attention now.

Saradha has her daughter the next week. The house throbs and surges with children, children having children, children expecting children, steaming milk and screaming mouths and Vani's music, which beats like the sound of peace dovetailed with conflict.

Around this time, Sivakami is approached with a strange request. The neighbour two houses down, all of whose grandchildren have died at birth, asks Sivakami if she might birth her daughter's next child. Sivakami is insulted and flattered—decorum means she can't comply, while sympathy makes it difficult to turn the woman down. Gayatri hits upon a solution: if Sivakami can't lend her hands, she can lend her handiwork. Sivakami doubtfully offers the family one of the scenes she has worked, an episode in the life of Krishna, the invincible child. She threads beads onto a string and sews the ends to the piece to make a necklace. Her neighbours gracefully accept. Some weeks after the daughter of their house, with the talisman hanging around her neck, gives birth to a healthy child, Sivakami receives another request. Sivakami fulfills it but worries that there is something untoward in this. She hides it from Vairum, who doesn't pay much attention to the comings and goings of women and children from their house. She is not sure why she is uncomfortable disclosing the new vogue: perhaps because it is superstitious behaviour and she knows how he feels about that. Perhaps because she is helping others to have children.

Sivakami readies Thangam to go to Malapura. It has been thirty days since Krishnan's birth and so it's time for Goli to fetch her, but Thangam and Sivakami know how this usually goes: the packing and waiting, the unpacking and being taken off guard. This time, though, things might be different, since Goli hasn't left Cholapatti in the weeks since his arrival.

He sleeps at the local chattram, not only dropping in on Sivakami more frequently than ever he did when he lived nearby, but occasionally convening his cronies around the veranda, where he tosses out schemes and schematics, logics and logistics, and figures vague or specific but always theoretical. The small group of men around the veranda is composed, Muchami tells Sivakami, of men who have faith in him despite that earlier mishap, including a couple who are hoping that, if they support him a little more, they might make their money back.

Sivakami hears, via eavesdropping and Muchami, Goli promoting a train-wheel foundry; a touring, and then a stationary, rice mill; a stationary, and then a touring, cinema; a stable of stud bulls; and a soap and petticoat depot.

Now: Sivakami is no businesswoman, though she keeps well abreast of Vairum's instructions to Muchami with regard to the management of the lands. She rarely understands in advance how a purchase or sale or other strategic change will benefit them, but she more or less apprehends such matters in retrospect. She is also an excellent manager of household expenses, keeping Thangam's manjakkani entirely separate from her dowry, separate expenses and separate income. Weddings are paid for from the dowry lands and the children's daily expenses from the manjakkani, while Sivakami's own paltry expenses are paid by Vairum. She accounts for every paisa, recording these in a ledger kept in the floor desk in the main hall.

So Sivakami knows they are about to run a surplus on the dowry monies. The next wedding to be arranged is Sita's. She is ten, and were it not for a law recently passed against child marriage, it would be time to marry her off. As it is, they now must wait four years. *Why should that money sit gathering dust?* Sivakami thinks, influenced, it seems, by this new spirit of investment and improvement inflating her son and son-in-law. She doesn't pretend to know any method of increasing money other than saving, nor does she think Goli has much money sense, but what if they were to support one of Goli's schemes, with Vairum as a collaborator of sorts? Vairum has such an instinct for finance that it would surely then succeed. Sivakami starts to imagine the money being transformed into comfort for Thangam and her children, and a rapprochement between Goli and Vairum. Maybe Goli could become independent of his employment income! Maybe they could settle down in one place. Maybe close to here. Deep in a sleepless night, she conjures a good life for the new baby, Krishnan, her beading forgotten in her lap.

The next day, she opens the subject as she serves Vairum his morning meal.

"Vairum, kanna, let me talk to you about something."

Vairum looks skeptical, as always with his mother, as though he has more important things on his mind. Sivakami serves the sambar—pearl onion, his favourite—and bitter-gourd curry.

"You know that child-marriage outlawing nonsense means we must wait at least four years to marry Sita off," she says. "So we have a surplus of cash that you will surely double by the time we need it."

Vairum now looks wary.

Sivakami plunges on. "So I was wondering: why not give a show of family support? I know you will say your brother-in-law is not a good money manager . . ."

Vairum snorts at Sivakami's delicate understatement.

" . . . but if you were to give some advice, some consulting, he might do well. The schemes don't sound so far-fetched, and think how much it would mean to your sister." Sivakami is gaining confidence—Vairum is listening. "And really: that dowry money is under your management, but technically, it belongs to them."

At this last point of argument, Vairum's expression turns sour. "He does not need to be reminded of that, Amma, though it seems he doesn't dare remind us. Okay. I'll consider investing in the cinema. I've been thinking of something like that anyway. My own money, not theirs. For Thangam Akka. I have no confidence in my brother-in-law, but if this will shut him up, it might be worth it. It's obviously what he came here for. Maybe this will make him go away."

Sivakami overlooks the rudeness of the last in consideration of her victory. It's true that Goli has been obviously hoping to bring Vairum on board. Sivakami lets herself dream vaguely of a real success for Goli—a father capable of looking after his children, a man they can respect. Were she to force herself to think clearly and coldly about this, the fantasy would be unsustainable. She has seen no behaviour from Goli to make her believe in such a dream. But Vairum is dark, clear and cold, while Sivakami is none of these, and sees no need to be.

⁓

NOW VISALAM GIVES BIRTH TO TWIN BOYS, having had a girl here a couple of years ago. As is customary, though, until the babies are out of danger from the evil eye, close neighbours and more distant relatives will be lied to and one baby will be kept hidden at all times. Sivakami makes the children solemnly swear to keep the babies under wraps, but if she knew how to listen to Vani's music, she would hear that Vani is giving the secret away. Her music now features a strange new doubling, each note of the keening played in chorus.

And since there are only two people in Cholapatti who make a real effort to listen to Vani's music, the other one gets suspicious.

Bharati corners Janaki in the schoolyard and demands, "Okay, what happened with Visalam's baby? When little Krishnan was born, and Saradha's baby, Vani's music was strange, but now it's different."

"I can't say." Janaki stands in front of her friend, trying to think of how to get away. No information Bharati desires has ever successfully been withheld from her.

Sita passes them and hisses, "Get away from her, Janaki. Their kind kills boys."

Janaki feels Bharati shudder, and hisses back, "It's you, Sita, who'll bring the evil eye on the house with all your death talking. Amma said."

She leads Bharati away by the elbow as though from a secret wound as Sita taunts them, "Amma said. Amma said."

Bharati pulls her arm away from Janaki and walks quickly to a clump of coconut palms in the farthest corner of the schoolyard. Janaki trots after her, saying, "Wait. Wait." Bharati leans against one of the trees, looking hard at the ground.

"Bharati. I'll . . ." Janaki touches her friend's arm. "You know Sita is always talking nonsense, just for sport. Listen," she says, knowing she is about to betray her family for the first time. "Visalam had twins. Now you know. Swear you won't tell," she adds aggressively, as though her real motive had been to cement their friendship through the offering up of this sacrifice.

"Sita's right, for once." Bharati looks threatening and Janaki takes a step back. "Why do you think only one of my brothers lived? My mother can't afford boys. She thinks I don't know, but I watched her once, grinding pebbles into the baby's porridge, and a week later, he died. I get chicken and eggs, look how strong I am! And the baby boy gets stones."

Janaki takes another step back, and Bharati steps forward and yells at her, "Run, then! Run away!"

But Janaki is too bewildered to run, too scared to ask why boys would be expensive in Bharati's caste, and once she thinks about it, a little suspicious of whether Bharati might be making up stories.

"I'm not running," she defies her friend.

They are quiet for a time.

"Are you still going to come and listen to the music?" Janaki eventually asks.

Bharati looks at her. "Sure."

"Don't tell anyone about the twins," Janaki adds, now that they're speaking again. "Okay?"

Visalam's husband and a gaggle of in-laws arrive for the newest babies' eleventh-day ceremony. Kamalam adores the in-laws and follows them about like a small dog, smiling whenever they look at her. Janaki can't summon much jealousy over this temporary crush and is moved to joke during the feast, "Maybe you should marry into this family, too."

Kamalam, who takes everything Janaki says seriously, turns gravely to Visalam. "Please, Visalam Akka, can I marry your in-laws too?"

Visalam hugs Kamalam close, her maternal flesh wobbling as she giggles. "Yes, there are many eligible young men in the family. We just have to choose the right one for you. What should he be like?"

"I don't know." Kamalam's response is muffled by the hug.

"Oh, come now." Visalam pokes Kamalam in the ribs. "You don't want to end up with someone like my husband, do you?"

Kamalam pulls away and buries her face in her hands. "I said, I don't know."

Saradha, who is also looking a little broad and matronly following the birth of her fourth child, attempts to enter into the spirit of the moment. "It's Sita's marriage that we need to arrange next, isn't it? How old are you, Sita?" The younger girl doesn't answer so Saradha answers herself. "Ten years completed already! It's time, I say, time for a big party in Pudhukkottai or Pondicherry—somewhere French, where they haven't passed laws against girls marrying in time!"

The varied volume and quality of laughter around the room demonstrates the variety of opinion around Madras Presidency on the child marriage law, and its attendant problems and solutions. Saradha persists.

"What would be really nice, right now, Sita," she suggests, "is if you would play a little song on the veena for Visalam's in-laws. She's been taking lessons."

The crowd murmurs approval.

Janaki tries to catch her grandmother's eye: if they do have further designs on Visalam's family, Sita's playing won't help in this aim. But Sivakami doesn't notice her. And what is Sita thinking? She is taking her place behind Vani's veena, sporting a little grin. Even she cannot possibly think she will suddenly become a virtuoso player just because she wants to impress? Janaki slowly brings her hands up to her ears, whether in a gesture of dismay or to block out sound is impossible to tell, but Kamalam unconsciously imitates her, two little monkeys guarding against the same evil. Sivakami catches Janaki's eye then, and, annoyed, makes a gesture as though to bat their hands down, and the girls lower their hands to their laps.

Sita begins to play. Her song, "Sami Varnam," sounds like the breath of a wounded animal. At first, the in-laws look as if each has been hit on the forehead with a clay pot. Then, as each notices the look on the others' faces, they begin, once more, to laugh. They don't mean to laugh at the music: they are not rude people. They are laughing at each other. Sivakami looks uncertain, almost as if she wants to enjoy their enjoyment. Sita is oblivious, grunting a little as she tries to control the bucking beast of sound beneath her fingers.

A shadow falls on the veena and the girl looks up to find Vani standing over her. Vani makes a flicking motion with one hand, and Sita abandons her song mid-strain. She rises and stumbles back. The bubbles of laughter have nearly all burst, bright, wet, prismatic.

Vani retunes the instrument. Sita looks around, blinking as though she has just awoken, and the laughter starts up again. Vani begins playing "Sami Varnam," the same song, so naturally it sounds like a rebuke, though Janaki is willing to believe that's not how she intends it. An elementary item in the south Indian classical repertoire, it's a song occasionally used as a warm-up, and it is Vani's regular time to play.

There's a motion in the southwest corner of the hall, nearest the kitchen. Thangam is cranking the phonograph and laying the needle into its groove. Is this Thangam's own rebuke, or her way of joining in? Janaki had forgotten the record started with "Sami Varnam," and now Vani and the absent Madras musician are twinned, like the baby in the main hall, brought out for the naming ceremony, and the one hidden upstairs.

Sita, a tear starting down her cheek, runs straight out the back of the house, bumping into two walls in her haste.

Sivakami quietly tells Janaki to follow her sister.

Janaki doesn't find Sita under the trees, or anywhere on the way to the canal, so, at the canal, she turns right, toward town. Head down, watching one foot place itself before the other in the mud, she bumps into Bharati, walking in just the same manner toward Sivakami's house. Bharati's maidservant Draupadi follows behind.

"Have you seen Sita?" Janaki inquires.

"Yeah, where was she going?"

"Where did it look like she was going?"

"I don't know. Town?"

"I guess. I'm supposed to find her. Are you coming?"

"Isn't Vani Amma playing? Hey," Bharati stands and listens. "Have you got someone visiting you?"

"No, no. It's the gramophone." Janaki doesn't know whether to be proud or ashamed of the toy. "Come on, come with me."

They emerge at the main road and look in both directions. It is a market day, and the crowds are thick.

Bharati points east toward the next crossroads. "Is that her?

Janaki squints. She is hearing drums, bells and shouting, a non-Brahmin funeral procession, and now catches sight of Sita, a flash of terracotta paavaadai against the similar red-brown of the road.

"Yes, yes, come, let's hurry." She and Bharati weave up the road, dodging bullock carts and baskets, and then are engulfed by a huge herd of goats, going the opposite way. They cannot move until the animals are past, but the goats' motion makes them feel they are flowing forward, as in water. Janaki loves goats almost as much as calves. She thinks it's charming that the babies have just the same proportions as the grown-ups, tiny, like dolls. She taps each one on the forehead as it bawls past her.

There: Sita is halted at the fore of the crowd preceding the funeral procession, either stymied by the crush or watching the proceedings.

The dead man must be a Chettiar, Janaki thinks: he reclines on a huge bier of bright flowers. No Brahmin would go in for this kind of show. Ten impassive young fellows beat drums with curved sticks. Two or three men and one woman jump around, very worked up, nearly off their rockers with grief-for-hire. The drums and wailing are mesmerizing and though both Janaki and Bharati have received many warnings against getting too close to funeral processions, they draw closer.

Six little men carry the bier. It dips and rocks as they struggle against their sweaty palms and the surging of the crowd. One of them suddenly catches the fever of the paid mourners' dance and starts shaking the bier as the others struggle to keep it steady. He is thrashing his body around and moaning, but not letting go, gripping tight even as someone tries to prise the pole from him.

Edging and shoving through the crowd, Janaki has nearly reached her immobile sister. The head of the great big corpse flops to one side and Janaki catches a glimpse of the face. She is startled to recognize him: N. Ranga Chettiar. She hadn't heard that he died. She had seen Vairum chatting with him outside Minister and Gayatri's house several weeks ago.

As the bier passes Sita, the bearer who caught the dance leaps, frenzied, away from the bier. The man walking beside him catches it in time, but he is very tall, and as he rises to his full height, the head flops, forcefully, toward the girls. The Chettiar's eyes are open.

Janaki puts her hand on Sita's arm.

Sita shudders. Janaki glances toward the corpse and back at her sister.

"Sita?" Janaki shakes her sister's arm and repeats loudly, "Sita."

Sita ignores her. There's nothing Janaki hates more. She shakes her sister's arm again, roughly, then takes her shoulder and spins Sita around to face her. "Sita!"

Sita speaks. "Palani veeboothi!"

The voice that comes out is not her own and Janaki jumps. Sita says it again: Holy ash from Palani mountain! There is something odd about her face. She is looking not directly at Janaki, but slightly off to the right.

"Palani veeboothi!" Sita shouts again.

"I heard you!" Janaki, on tiptoe, examines her, and makes the tone of her voice gentler when she asks, "Is something wrong?"

"Palani veeboothi!" Sita booms again.

"Would you stop shouting this!"

Even under such strained circumstances, they bicker.

"I am dead!" Sita proclaims. Bharati has caught up with them, and takes Sita's other arm with a look of concern.

"Stop that, Sita," Janaki says sternly. "Amma said . . ."

"I am dead! I am Ranga Chettiar!" Sita exclaims. "She looked, I came! She looked, I came!"

"Shush." Janaki shudders. "What about Palani veeboothi?"

"Palani veeboothi!" Sita says loudly into the space to Janaki's right. "I must have holy ash from Palani mountain, to cleanse my soul of guilt and memory."

One or two people are looking their way. Janaki, feeling very strange, indicates that Bharati should help her lead Sita out of the crowd. Sita seems to walk all right, if a bit stiffly. Bharati speaks across Sita's glassy gaze.

"The Chettiar's life force must have jumped into her. I've heard of that."

"You have?"

"My mother's sister," Bharati says. "It happened to her when she was very young. That's why unmarried girls aren't supposed to see funeral processions. We're vulnerable."

"Oh, God." Janaki feels sick with anxiety. "Sita shouldn't have gone so close. God, Amma is going to be so mad."

"Palani veeboothi!"

"Shut up!" Janaki yells at whoever has taken up residence in her sister. "Is that all you need, to leave my sister? If we get you Palani veeboothi, will you go away?"

"Only Palani veeboothi can cleanse my soul of guilt and memory," the Chettiar affirms.

They lead Sita home, taking her in by the back entrance, partly because Bharati, as a non-Brahmin, cannot walk on the Brahmin quarter, partly because Janaki would rather the neighbours not know before her grandmother does. Vani is still playing, though the gramophone has stopped. For a moment, the girls stand at the back door. Even the dead give respect to Vani's playing, it appears: Sita is silent. Janaki leads her sister in and sits her in the courtyard while Bharati goes to sit under their usual tree, a few steps from the back door. Janaki takes a long look at Sita's face, its expression addled yet intent: the look of someone with a single desire. Janaki leaves Sita in the courtyard, telling her firmly not to move.

By now, the jolly in-laws have departed. Vairum lies on the floor of the hall, listening to his wife's music. Thangam is huddled in the corner by the gramophone. Everything looks highly normal. Janaki seeks Sivakami and finds her in the garden, looking critically at one of the mango trees, while Muchami squats beside it.

"Amma?"

"Mm?" Sivakami looks up. "Did you bring Sita home?"

"Sort of."

The song from the living room ends, and Janaki hears a voice boom in the silence, "Palani veeboothi!"

She and her grandmother look at each other and hurry from the garden to the back of the cowshed, and from there through a door into the courtyard. Sita is a terracotta streak of silk and skin exiting the back door where Bharati catches her and holds her fast. Muchami is with them in a flash and takes hold of Sita just as Bharati is losing her strength. As Muchami pulls the struggling, writhing Sita over the threshold into the courtyard, Sivakami asks, "What happened?"

Janaki begins to explain, and Sivakami goes to close the courtyard door, glancing quizzically at the girl standing just beyond the threshold, a girl she doesn't know. *What luck she was passing!* she thinks, though she doesn't say anything to her, just nods a little. *Perhaps a child of one of the Brahmin-quarter servants, though awfully well-dressed for that.* Bharati doesn't move, but stands looking at Sivakami, her chin raised, while Sivakami closes and bolts the courtyard door.

As soon as Sivakami hears the Chettiar's demand, she dispatches Janaki to get some holy ash from the people three houses down who just got back from the Palani hills day before yesterday. And to get the priest from the temple. Vani resumes her playing, which calms Sita once more. They induce her to sit on a mat in the courtyard, since she has been multiply polluted: by Bharati's touch, by Muchami's, and of course by inhabitation by the spirit of a dead Chettiar. Janaki pictures Bharati sitting out back and realizes they shut the door in a panic without saying bye or thanks. But for Bharati, Sita could have been God knows where right now. *I'll apologize tomorrow,* Janaki thinks.

The neighbour insists on bringing the holy ash herself, after changing her sari and refreshing her hair. She can sniff out a gossip opportunity anywhere within a ten-mile radius. By the time Janaki returns home with the priest, there are no fewer than ten people sitting and clicking their tongues in the front hall and occasionally going through the kitchen to peep at the now prone girl. The priest administers the ash externally, on the forehead and throat, and internally, a pinch on the tongue, then everyone sits around and waits.

After about two hours of muttering and twitching, Sita's skinny frame leaps to its feet. She goose-steps to the well and draws a bucket of water. Face skyward, she dumps the bucket of water unceremoniously over her head. Three seconds later, her body gives a great heave and a shudder and collapses to the ground.

A cry goes up among the watchers, and they pick her up and carry her into the hall. She is feverish and barely conscious, but restored to herself.

They are settling her in the hall and congratulating one another on the success of the treatment—Janaki thinks they are acting a bit too much as if they thought of it, forgetting it was in fact the dead man's own suggestion—when Goli bursts through the door like unwelcome relief. He has a wild look in his eye, and today is extra dandy, with bowler hat and cane.

"My brother-in-law has called me!" Goli announces. "Such an honour!"

What he says is true; Vairum awaits him on the roof. Goli sweeps through the hordes of gigglers and gossipers and general hangers-on in a single noisy motion. Sivakami and Gayatri join Muchami in the garden, where they can hear the conversation beginning above. Gayatri and Muchami, in whom Sivakami has confided, look at each other with conspiratorial hope and then turn their attention inward and upward.

"I'm interested in the cinema, Goli Athimbere." Vairum must not even have given Goli time to sit. Sivakami winces, wishing Vairum were better about observing niceties. He is standing, and they can see his hands and head for a second at the balustrade; then he walks away.

"The cinema is an enormously interesting proposition," Goli agrees. "Do you know——"

"I know, I know," Vairum interrupts. "Look——"

"Oh, I'm looking, Vairum," Goli says, clearly annoyed at the interruption. "I'm looking."

Sivakami shakes her head.

"Okay," Vairum goes on. "I don't know what you know, but you do know that these are tricky times for investment, which is the whole reason all these possibilities are . . ." Vairum is uncharacteristically searching for words.

"Possible? That's only a part of it. Naturally, a part of it, but a person needs a nose for these things. It's not everyone who can get on board." Goli's voice sounds as if he is marching pompously back and forth across the roof.

"It's a good bet, the cinema, Athimbere." Vairum is no longer hesitating. "The only aspect of the proposal that makes me nervous is the fact that you are in charge."

Sivakami, Muchami and Gayatri simultaneously lower their foreheads onto their palms.

"But the amount of investment you need takes the project largely out of your hands," Vairum proceeds, reasonable and direct. "I will front the rest of the money—because it gives me the controlling interest. You must admit, it's safer, for you and for everyone else involved."

Incredibly, Goli has said nothing through this speech, but now he sounds as though he is orbiting madly, an electron around Vairum's nucleus.

"I spit on your money, you cheap-nosed freak of a not-quite-man! How dare you insult me with your generosity! Don't you think for a second you are getting any part of this so let that be a lesson to you with your swell-headed individualistic ambitions and attitudes! I ought to—"

Vairum bellows, "You cannot for a second speak of what it is to be a man, you who leave your children to be raised by others."

Sivakami prays the children did not hear that. (They did.) She knows Vairum doesn't mind the children's presence, not at all. It is Goli he resents. Oh, why did she suggest this?

Goli's voice circles as he charges down the spiral staircase. He pitches into the hall from the stairwell, chopping the side of his right hand against his left palm.

"Pack your bags. We are leaving." He flies around the room, shoving each child in the direction of Thangam's baggage, which stands ready in the corner of the hall. "No objections, children! You will not insist any longer on living in this house. Time and again I have tried to make you all come and live with me. You always refuse: my Vairum Mama says this, my Sivakami Patti says that!"

What he is saying is untrue, but this is immaterial.

Sita is hauled to her feet, unprotesting but also largely unconscious. Laddu, Janaki and Kamalam mill into one another, bumping, confused. Radhai, the toddler, howls and shoves her mother's sari into her mouth as Thangam moves toward the door. Visalam has stealthily backed out into the garden with her baby. Chances are Goli won't notice her, but Sivakami closes the garden door just in case.

"No more!" Goli hollers. "This time, I will not take no for an answer. Go, pack!"

The children have no idea what this means as far as they are concerned.

"PACK!"

Sivakami indicates that Muchami should fetch a trunk from upstairs.

They all get on the 9:35 train that night. By morning, they will reach the Karnatak country, where Goli is stationed at present, the farthest they have ever been from home.

28.
In the Karnatak Country
1934

THEY ARRIVE AT TEN IN THE MORNING, by which time Cholapatti would have been sweltering and still. In Cholapatti, the packed air is so hot and moist that every villager feels a privileged proximity to Goddess Earth—each person feels her sweat.

In the Karnatak country, the air swirls and rustles round, cool as the children have known only water to be, water dippered from the big clay pot in the darkest corner of the pantry. The house is like theirs in Cholapatti; the same brick floors and clay-shingled roof, but smaller. It is a government-issue house and comes with a government-issue houseboy who bobs ingratiatingly as they arrive and then disappears.

The children watch their father take soap and a towel and stride toward the back of the house. He returns ten minutes later, shaved and washed. They are still in the front hall, mostly still standing and very quiet. The one or two who sat scramble to their feet. Goli looks at them with indignant expectation. He shouts, "Not clean yet? Move!"

Laddu and Sita rush to the back, grabbing towels where they saw Goli do so. There must be more than one bathroom, they think, if they were supposed to be bathing while Goli was. But no, there is only one bathroom. One by one, then, they bathe in cold water and then sit in the hall, uncomfortable.

Goli paces and mutters, to and fro, up and down, sometimes right out the front door. Each time one of the children stands to take her turn at the bath, he shouts, "Move!" at the receding back, which then jumps and runs for the bathroom.

Thangam is exhausted from the trip and lies under a thin dhurri with the baby in the other room. As the last child is bathing, Thangam calls out feebly, "There is no food in the house. You have to get them some food."

Goli boomingly echoes his wife, "No food in the house? No food in the house. Okay, we will eat out." He starts out the door, but no one follows him. He returns to the door and shouts, "Come!"

Kamalam is still in the washroom. The other children point that way.

"Hm? What?"

"Kamalam is still taking her bath," Sita says helpfully.

Kamalam comes hurrying along at that moment.

"Hm!" Goli sweeps his hand upward and starts out the door again. The children run to follow him. Their hair is still uncombed, and Kamalam's blouse is buttoned wrong, but they are reasonably clean. They turn two corners and stop in front of a low building: two parallel walls connected by a thatch roof, steam coming out the open ends. Goli enters, saying over his shoulder, "Don't you tell your grandmother. I don't want to be hearing about this forever."

It is a non-Brahmin establishment. Their grandmother would never let them near such a place. Janaki very much disapproves, but what is morality on an empty stomach?

A harried-looking boy looks up at them from the floor, where he is clearing disposable plates made from stitched-together leaves. He throws the plates, coated with the remains of meals, to two grateful dogs in a roadside ditch. His eyes swing to a man squatting shinily among vats and cauldrons. The place seats only five, and two places are taken. Goli has now taken a third. The man looks at the children, then addresses his pots. "They'll have to eat in shifts, that's all."

The children give one another looks. They didn't understand the man. It is as though his words come from funny places in his mouth. It hadn't struck home before: this is the Karnatak country they have learned of in school, where people speak the Kannada language. But why would they speak a language no one can understand? Tamil is normal, Kannada is strange, like a one-legged bird or two-headed cow—recognizable but not the way things are meant to be.

Their father is yelling, "Sit! Sit!"

The boy has laid out two more places. They all step forward together. Panic surges in the boy's face and he says something to Goli. Goli raises one hand to point at the dish the boy is carrying and says to the children, "Only two of you now. Not enough room."

Sita flounces forward to take her place, dragging Radhai. Kamalam, Laddu and Janaki politely watch the dogs instead of the diners. The dogs, dirt collected in the hollows between their jagged ribs, lap the sauces and grains from the ridges of the leaves, always licking twice where once would do. Finally, they do a quick sniffover. Finding no more pickings, one mounts the other and starts a dance. Janaki knows enough to look away and Laddu knows enough to know why, but Kamalam keeps staring, her mouth slightly ajar, until Janaki spins her by the shoulder to face the street.

The food is as strange as everything else. Goli vanishes upon finishing his meal, citing important business. By the time the children find their way back to the house, which is still cold and dark, homesickness is burling up in them. It will soon harden and form a ring, marking the end of one age, the beginning of another.

Only Sita is perfectly cheerful, bright-eyed and willing as they have never seen her. She arranges their bundles neatly in the hall. Thangam rises while she is doing this.

"Amma," Sita inquires, apparently having decided that now they are together as a family, her mother should be addressed as such, "shall I take the baby for a while? Don't you want to bathe?"

Thangam gives them the mixed blessing of her smile, like the sun shining through clouds. Sita takes baby Krishnan, and Thangam goes to her bath. When she returns, they sit together on the veranda, relieved that these are also a fixture in this strange new country. In the combined strength of Thangam's faint glow and the dilute sunshine, they begin to feel almost warm.

Neighbourhood children grow curious about them, but since they cannot speak to one another, they choose the shared language of sandlot cricket. Even the girls join in, but not Sita, who takes stock of the staples and purchases vegetables and milk, lamp oil and kolam powder out of the ten rupees Sivakami slipped to her as they left. She even cleans a little. When Goli returns from work, Sita bustles to the door and hands him a hot tumbler of coffee.

Goli appears sullen and takes his coffee wordlessly out onto the veranda. Janaki and Kamalam are out there, playing at catching the other's hand, like bear cubs slapping at river fish. They become quiet at the sight of Goli's face, but their giggles quickly escalate once more, until Goli howls, "Hush!"

They freeze.

"Am I sweating to earn your keep so that you can torture . . . ?" He jabs his hand at them, and then lapses back into his ruminations.

Supper is a silent matter. Laddu makes one attempt to tell the story of something funny he saw on their journey, but Goli breathes harder, the huff and puff of a coming storm. Janaki signals her less barometrically sensitive brother to abandon the story.

Sita is still suspiciously happy. She serves all of them first and eats afterward with Thangam.

The days pass, without school, almost without talk. Janaki has never lived with so few words. They continue to play with the neighbour children, games the children know from home; you don't need to talk to play kabbadi.

Sita, though, seems to be completely occupied in housework. Janaki is suspicious because she has always tricked others into doing her chores, faking a cut by making blood out of vermilion powder mixed in water, or trading tasks so relentlessly that Janaki would lose track of who owed whom and end up doing all the work. Here, Sita is industrious to the point of making them all a bit nervous.(Is Sita happy because all is finally as it should be? For the first time she feels part of the natural order? But few admit, even though they know, that the order's nature is that its elements line up only to drift apart again. Sita appears happy, but she smells of desperation.)

Thangam works alongside Sita, offering no instructions or suggestions even when Sita turns out rubbery dosais and powdered condiments one would sooner use to dust a baby's bottom than to fire up a meal. It is strange that the house and position don't come with a government-issue cook, Janaki thinks, but perhaps no stranger than anything else.

One evening, Janaki and Kamalam see their dad at the end of the road, talking with two dark and paunchy men. They are all laughing, slapping their thighs. Goli spots his daughters and calls them over. As they arrive he grabs them by the shoulders and tells the men, "Two of mine." He slaps his daughters on their backs. "Finally got them out of the grip of my brother-in-law. None of his own, you know?" He turns his head sideways and gives a wink. "None of his own. Right?"

The men laugh again.

"I've got more than I can count," Goli brags. "That brother-in-law, rich as a Chettiar, but will he share it? Ah, what to do? The poor fellow can't have kids . . ."

The two men giggle.

"I'll forgive him." Goli shakes his head and squishes the two girls together. They can't remember him ever touching them before. "You know, if it's true that a man's real fortune is his family, and you and I know it is, well then I'm a millionaire." Goli shoves the girls toward home and says, "Run. Tell your sister I'm on my way home, coffee better be ready. Scoot."

Generally, home supplies are purchased on credit, the bill paid quarterly. Cash is used only for the daily purchase of vegetables from the market or passing vendors. Here, in the Karnatak country, the merchants have told Sita they will not give credit. She doesn't understand and they will not explain. Is it because their father is not a local, because he'll move on? But he's been here a year and is posted here one year more, long enough, certainly, to have established a reputation.

Sita had pooh-poohed the merchants, rudely and with dignity. She bought supplies with the ten rupees Sivakami had slipped her; she had splurged, believing her father would want nothing but the best. She was right; he does want nothing but the best. But he clearly had forgotten to give her more money—poor man, she thinks, so much on his mind and now his household has doubled in size. She decided to remind him, show how willing and able she is to take over running the household.

While serving him his afternoon coffee, she asks, "Can I give the houseboy a shopping list, Appa? Will you give me money to give him?"

He looks at her as though he doesn't know who she is and how she came to be in his house. "Money?"

"For groceries, Appa, we need some—"

"Management, management!" He raps his knuckles hard and humorously on her noggin. She winces. He winks. "What have I been keeping you at your grandmother's for, if you still do not know how to manage money?"

"I . . ." She thinks she does know how to manage money, but she is probably wrong. That was Vairum's house, an upside-down world, everything wrong. She needs to learn things again.

"Payday is Thursday." She beams, but he is looking elsewhere. "Thursday I will bring home such food as you have never seen, squashes and cucumbers and sweets, yes?"

She happily claps her hands and retires to the kitchen.

The following evening, Janaki and Kamalam are sitting on the veranda. They forget the palanguzhi board between them when they see their father appear on the seat of a bullock cart. Radhai, who has been watching covetously, seizes a handful of cowries. Kamalam grabs her wrist but then releases it as Goli shouts, "Come! Come!"

Janaki and Kamalam's instinct is to run into the house, which they do, with Radhai following, scared, on their heels, but Goli soon follows, still shouting, "Come! Come! Come!"

When the girls run into the house, looking like a startled school of fish, Sita guesses the reason and decants the coffee. Flushed with pleasure, she trots it out with two sweets, but Goli takes no notice.

"Come, I say!" he hollers, waving. "Into the cart! Where is your precious mother? Thangam! Thangam!"

Sita looks anxious and eager to obey but unsure of what action to take to do so. Goli blusters past her into the next room, then reappears and clarifies, "Into the cart!"

Moments later, they are all nested in damp straw, trundling up the road clinging to boards that threaten to pull away. Janaki whispers to Kamalam, "There is a cow pulling this cart."

Goli hears and makes a grunting noise—"Huh?"—but has his nose pointed at the horizon.

Janaki whispers, "Cows are mothers, they give us everything. They must be worshipped, not made to work."

Sita's eyes narrow at them in a skilled imitation of her former self. "Hoi," she instructs. "Stop telling secrets against Appa."

Kamalam looks as though she's been struck. Goli whips round in his seat, glaring. Janaki hisses at Sita, "We weren't."

The cart rolls on and Goli's eyes roll reverentially back to his fantasies. Sita twists her mouth at her sisters. Goli leaps from his seat to the ground. He stumbles slightly and readjusts his dhoti. As the bullock cart jolts to a halt, Goli is already some distance away, gesturing to a building by the side of the road and asking, "Unh? Unh?" in a tone suggesting they should say what they think, and what they should think is that it's great.

They all climb out cautiously, Sita holding the baby while Thangam dismounts. Goli has already run up to the building, evidently a recently defunct cinema. He turns as they trudge toward him, and whispers as if all the world is a stage, "Criminal, really. The price. Got it for a song—a filmi song! Can you sing one, kids?"

The kids can't or don't, but he's not stopping.

"Lots of people going under these days. The stupid ones. Used to be you could get away with not being on the smarts. But not these days. These days it's be smart or die. Kids, the sinking has started— and you are hitched to a swimmer."

Thangam's voice is both unbelieving and utterly without surprise. "You bought it?"

Goli beams at her and calls back as he starts running around the building, peering and banging and measuring things with the span of his hand. "Lock, stock and barrel. Me and several of my associates. Opportunity is knocking down our door. The ground floor suddenly lowered and why, we just got on."

Thangam is whispering now, "I thought . . . it was a gamble . . . ?"

Goli is in front of her in a flash, the pockets under his eyes pulsing. The humidity is giving Janaki a slight headache.

"You are repeating your brother's words to me? He wanted me to work for him. For him!" Goli has begun chopping his right hand against his left palm.

Thangam speaks again, her eyes shut. "He wanted to be responsible—"

"No!"

The children step back in unison as the hot roar of refusal whips past them. Sita alone stands her ground and looks at her siblings triumphantly.

"He wanted to be my boss. No respect for me, me! His elder brother-in-law! Go and work for him . . . big shot . . ."

In the field before the cinema, they all privately recollect the scene between their father and uncle. One would guess from Sita's smug face that in her version, Goli is the winner. In Janaki and Laddu's memories, the victor's identity is less certain. Kamalam recalls words but not meanings. She thinks she wants to go home, but she is not certain where that is, just now.

As uncomfortable as all of this is, they all appreciate Sita's continuing good humour. The occasional lapse, such as that in the cart, reminds them of how good they have it now. That night, for example, Sita doesn't give Janaki any lentils from the rasam. Since Janaki hates that bottom-of-the-pot sludge, Sita usually stirs it up and dumps it on double thick. But not tonight. Janaki ascribes this to Sita's new-found mental peace. Then Sita eats—last, as she has taken it upon herself to do. Janaki sees her take the last of the rasam. It is nearly clear. There are almost no lentils in the broth.

Janaki presumes Sita forgot the lentils, a logical supposition given the quality of food Sita has been serving since their arrival.

The next morning, they eat pazhiah sadam, fermented rice with yogourt. ("Best thing for young tummies," their grandmother always says.) But the buttermilk is watery and they are all hungry by mid-morning. When they come to Sita mock-whining that they want a snack, they expect her indulgence with milk sweets, since she's been handing them out freely all week. Instead, Sita barks that if they've got nothing better to do than annoy her, why don't they spend their time finding some fruit in the garden. The children drift out of the house, avoiding the two stunted, barren banana trees that stand at the end of the yard like more children their father forgot. Lunch is rice, lots of rice but with rasam even thinner than it was last night. For supper, the same. Kamalam asks for more and is given a big chunk of plain rice with a pickled baby mango from the jar Sivakami packed with their luggage. Thangam doesn't eat, saying she's not hungry. She drinks half a cup of nearly transparent buttermilk and goes to bed. Their father still has not arrived and Sita will not eat until after he does. Nine o'clock, ten o'clock, eleven o'clock pass, and Sita sits in the dark. She says she wants it dark so everyone else can sleep, but she wiped out the bottom of the lamp oil can with cotton wicks the night before. At eleven-thirty there is a loud knocking on the doors and Goli's voice calls, "Thangam! Eh, Thangam!"

Sita lights a lamp and unbolts the doors. Goli drops his dapper hat and swinging cane in a corner. He drops himself onto a waiting bamboo mat. Sita holds the oversized lamp with the itty-bitty flame, so he can see. She asks, "Supper?"

He is prone and his eyes closed. He turns onto his side and gets comfortable as he says, "No. Ate at the club."

Sita blinks, then glances at the lamp. She hurries to the kitchen and eats in a race against the dwindling flame.

For breakfast and lunch the day following, they have rice with buttermilk so thin that it looks like kanji, water that old people strain from boiled rice and drink for strength. Each of the children pretends the runny white meal is something else: onion sambar, spinach curry, bitter gourd. Kamalam starts to sniffle a little as she bites into the tangy flesh of another baby mango. Janaki signals her, "What?"

Kamalam answers aloud, "I miss Amma."

Janaki's sinuses start to sting, too, at the thought of their grandmother, her generous kitchen and care. Sita ends this nonsense. "Hush. Stop that. You have your 'amma' right here. You want to go back to living with Vairum Mama, where we are not wanted?"

That night, Goli's work forces him to stay over in a neighbouring town. His family eat their poor meal early, all together, and gather in the hall. The moon has narrowed nightly and is almost ready to turn and begin its pregnant climb again. In the bluish darkness of the hall, the children lie or sit on their bedrolls and play word games, making up rhymes and riddles, laughing loud and free in the night that gladly does not contain their father. Sita shines brightest of all in the open darkness of this night. Why? Tomorrow is Thursday, payday.

It is afternoon. Sita is sitting on the veranda when Goli arrives home from work the next evening—empty-handed, but with a spring in his step.

"Coffee?" he asks, walking past Sita, into the house, with his head opposing the direction of his travel by about thirty degrees. Sita had put off making the coffee, hoping—not, though she would never admit it, assuming—he would bring some of the precious dark dust, since she has enough to brew only a thimbleful. She sits a moment longer on the veranda, where all sit to sun their cares or forget them by watching their neighbours, where private pains meet the life of the street, where decisions are made and deals contracted, along streets just like this one all over Madras Presidency. Different people, different language, but the same worries. And despite all this, Sita sits all alone in the rosy dusk, her toes over- and underlapping one another, her chin on her knees. In the rapid sunset, it is only moments before she can no longer see her toenails and is isolated even from herself.

Taking a breath, she picks herself up and walks into the house just like her father did, her head cocked at an unreasonable angle, trying to see what he sees. There is no more milk in the house. She brews the weak coffee and dumps three tablespoons of sugar through the pale steam. Thank God sugar and rice come in huge sacks. Plenty of those commodities remain. Looks like sugar and rice for supper tonight.

She places the tumbler and bowl on a saucer and carries it out to her father. No more English biscuits or store-bought sweets. Goli is pacing to and fro. He grasps the bowl and pours the coffee from the tumbler to blend and cool it. He is anticipating, as every drinker of great South Indian coffee does, the pleasure of foam and steam rising as the creamy liquid, falling from the lip of the stainless steel tumbler, hits the cylindrical bowl. He gets steam, but no foam. He frowns and peers into the bowl, fighting more the fog in his mind than that around the dish, trying to see what is wrong. Sita stands by, her mind a blank with hundreds of squirming questions nibbling its edges. Finally, Goli looks up, his spectacles opaque from the mist, and asks her, "What is this?"

She answers, reflexively obedient. "Appa, coffee, Appa."

"It doesn't look like coffee," he grunts.

"Appa, that's what coffee looks like without milk, Appa." She bobs in a sort of curtsy.

"Who drinks coffee with no milk?" Goli addresses the ceiling. "Am I an Englishman?"

Sita swallows the air in her mouth with great difficulty and asks, "Did . . . did you get paid, today, Appa?"

"Oh, yes, oh, yes." Goli smiles. "Stopped after work and put the whole thing down on that new cinema of ours. Ready to fire her up any day now." He makes another long waterfall of the coffee and remembers his displeasure. "Milk!"

"We have no milk, Appa," Sita explains gently, her face tense.

"Get some, then, are there no cows left in the world?" he jokes. "Listen, girl, you can hear them now . . ."

The questions in Sita's mind are taking big bites now, feasting on her eleven-year-old brain. She replies, "I need money, Appa."

"Money? You need money?" Goli rises. "It is not enough that I am slaving from dawn until dusk, working for the English, buying properties, doing business, you want money now too?"

"No, Appa, for supplies," Sita minces. "To buy milk, vegetables, lentils, butter . . ."

Goli throws the coffee onto the street. "Just like your mother, no management sense. Just like that stupid cook! I told her, get out!" He begins pacing, reliving the scene. "I said, My wife will cook, my daughter will cook! What else are you doing? I don't have infinite resources, you know. You have to learn to plan."

"But—" Sita attempts.

"Do not talk back to me!" Goli chops his left hand against his right palm terrifyingly. "I told you, you must learn. The budget is all used up—too bad. I'm going to the club."

That night, they eat plain boiled rice with a choice of side dish: sugar or baby mango. Breakfast: the same. Lunch: ditto.

At five o'clock, Laddu shows up with three onions and a sweet potato. Sita is elated, her salivary glands springing to action. The springs quickly run dry, though, when she thinks to ask, "Laddu. Where did you get these?"

Laddu's head cocks at thirty degrees, apparently the angle at which an individual can dissociate from any present situation. He replies, "My friend gifted them to me. They had too many."

Sita heaves half a sigh of relief. It is interrupted by the remembrance that Laddu cannot speak the same language as any of his friends. Now she asks, "Does your friend know he gifted them to you?"

Laddu is fascinated by a spiderweb in the northwest corner of the kitchen. Sita asks no more questions and prepares a decent meal. Her siblings relish it like no meal they've ever eaten, their delight pathetic. Sita gags on every mouthful and lies awake that night on an empty stomach.

In the morning, Goli sits groggy on his mat. This he does for long minutes each morning, sometimes rubbing his head or cleaning his fingernails. It is as though his internal mechanisms are winding. Soon something will snap and he will career for the bathroom as though released from a colossal slingshot, the mist evaporating from his eyes like clouds from a lake. Once this happens, he cannot be stopped. Sita has chosen this, his calmest hour (quarter-hour, really, but who's counting?), for her second approach.

"Appa?"

No sign of response. She creeps closer, and kneels. "Appa? Appa, I know I should have planned better, Appa, I know I splurged, but I . . . I really need to buy some more supplies, Appa. I can't . . . I have nothing left to cook . . ."

She trails off weakly, distracted by the oddness of his demeanour. He is only a yard away but peering at her as though from a long way off. Suddenly, he zooms in, his pupils dilating with the rush of landing. He springs to his feet.

"That's it. That's it, I've had it with your requests. If you will not stop bothering me, if you cannot take responsibility for yourself and live by my rules, you can all go back to live with your grandmother. Pack up, you're all leaving on the 9:30 train."

Sita works her mouth in horror and confusion. Janaki, Kamalam and Laddu are rising around her; they open their eyes to Goli's words. Thangam, who had already risen, lies back down. Sita replies, "That's not ... But ..."

"Nine-thirty," Goli thunders. "Be ready. If you won't be happy any other way, that's what you will have."

Sita doesn't turn to look at her siblings but feels their alkaline shock neutralized by her stinging helplessness.

Nine o'clock sees them trooping out the door. Thangam sits in the large room, by the exit, clutching Krishnan and Radhai. She is holding Radhai so tightly, in fact, that the child keeps trying to squirm out of her pale-knuckled grasp. As each of the older children files past, he or she drops a kiss on Thangam's powdery skin. She says nothing, nor even moves, but looks long and almost sullenly on each. Only as the last one leaves, a gold-flecked tear trails down her cheek.

Sita wonders why Goli couldn't give her grocery money yet can pay for their tickets back to Cholapatti, but decides it's not her problem. He strolls whistling from the bus stop toward the station, the snuff pocket of his kurta jangling. Each child carries some baggage or bedding, since Goli has arranged no bullock cart for them, nor have they seen the houseboy more than twice in the week since they arrived.

A shrivelled, cackling man waves bunches of faded paper pinwheels at everyone hurrying into the station. Goli tosses a rupee coin at him. The old fellow catches it with startling ease as Goli relieves him of the entire bunch, distributing one each to his faithless children and the remainder magnanimously among all the children in sight. The old man wanders off elated—a rupee is many times more than that bunch was worth. Kamalam had already been struggling under her baggage allotment and is a sad sight, trying to carry the pinwheel as well.

A freak of architecture has created a gale force wind in the doorway to the station. As the children pass through the vacuum, the curved petals of each of their pinwheels rip free of their moorings, so that the pointy ends dangle like seaweed out of water.

The four children approach the platform while Goli buys their tickets. One by one, they toss their pinwheels onto the track. May as well have saved the effort and just put the coin on the rails for the train to flatten, Sita thinks morosely. Three of the pinwheels lie limp and motionless, and the fourth rotates in futile quarter-turns, one direction, then the other, back, back again, until a beggar child wanders up the track and urinates on it.

The tickets are two and a half rupees each, ten rupees for the four children, just the amount Sita used to feed the whole family for the ten days that the experiment lasted. Goli gets a ticket for himself, too.

Their baggage is stowed and they are on their way. Goli is in a gleeful mood, buying snacks, cracking jokes, making a party with everyone in the compartment. Isn't this fun, his attitude seems to say. Charming man with his four beautiful children, off for a holiday. Listening to him speak to other passengers, the children learn he had had a good night at the club—another source of supplemental income, though this pursuit is often as expensive as it is profitable.

In the spirit of a game he asks his children, "What if . . . I were murdered? What if someone got on at the next stop and stabbed me dead, right here and now?"

They look like a naive painting of dismayed witnesses to a crime, their faces yet without depth or perspective. Smiles wiggle nervously on all their faces except Kamalam's, who starts to cry. Maybe on account of the fleeting thought that, scary as it sounds, she might be happier if he were dead. Her tears attract Goli's attention.

He asks sympathetically, "Missing Vairum Mama?" and slides down the wooden seat, shoving Janaki and Sita along and knocking Laddu off the end. Now he is across from Kamalam, her face filling his vision as he leans in closer and closer, head cocked like a father crow's. "I only let you all live with him because he can't have children of his own."

Closer.

"He can't have kids."

Kamalam is looking down. She is making an enormous effort at continence but it's not quite enough: one last slippery tear bubbles out to run over her cheek.

Goli bounds to his feet and roars at the people ramrod still all around the compartment. Chop chop chop chop goes hand against palm.

"He talks against me! He is a stingy coward who can't have relations with his wife! He tries to steal my children! *He* talks against *me*!"

Kamalam bellows through her weeping, her eyes still shut, "Don't talk about my uncle that way!"

Goli leaps over and hits her.

He stands and fumes at the door as the train pulls into a station. He gets out and paces around the platform, then buys fifty packages of snacks from another vendor who looks as if he hasn't had a sale all year. Goli throws them through the windows at everyone in the compartment, telling them to eat. Janaki hands one to her little sister, who will not take it. Janaki puts it in her lap. There the package sits untouched until Laddu points at it. She nods faintly. He eats it with alacrity.

Goli is strutting up and down, stuffing a couple of packages of the stale, greasy bits into his mouth. Like an aristocratic host at a royal banquet, he is aggressively hospitable, ordering everyone to eat. The new people in the car smile at his neighbourliness, his good spirit, and their mood affects even those who were present before, as they and the children nibble the age-old snacks. Janaki offers some of her own to Kamalam, who doesn't respond. There are finger marks on Kamalam's pale cheek.

In the city, their father puts them on the train bound for Kulithalai. He bids farewell to all of his good friends from the compartment and now to his children. He has business to which he must attend.

They reach Cholapatti slightly after sunset. Not knowing how to tell their grandmother or Muchami of their arrival, they walk home from the station, dragging bags, bedding, bottoms. Sivakami looks them over anxiously but asks no questions. Vairum, when he sees them, takes a breath as though to say something, but Sivakami raises a hand, and he keeps silent.

Late that night, Sita, Laddu and Janaki all rise with terrible diarrhea. Only Kamalam sleeps soundly.

PART SIX

29.
Time to Go
1938

GOLI AND THANGAM MOVE EVEN FARTHER AWAY in 1935, and then, in 1937, close enough that Thangam can consider coming to Cholapatti for Pongal, the January harvest festival. She is four months pregnant and, at Sivakami's suggestion, agrees to stay until her delivery. Her health is waning; she lost a baby two years earlier while stationed too distant from Cholapatti to come and receive the benefit of Sivakami's lucky hands. Krishnan, now a rambunctious three-year-old, needs companions to exhaust him, Sivakami believes. Sita, recently married, is preoccupied with her imminent departure for her husband's home, and Laddu has been given a job at a oil-processing plant Vairum is about to open. The younger sisters, however—Janaki, twelve, full of unspent creative energies; Kamalam, a sweet and pliant nine-year-old; and Radhai, an indefatigable six—welcome their little brother with the aggressive delight of children who don't have enough to divert them.

Goli brings Thangam, along with a business proposition, he tells his mother-in-law. They have arrived mid-afternoon, after six hours' travel. Thankfully, the weather is temperate at this time of year, and though it's the hottest part of the day, it is only about twenty-eight degrees outside. Still, Thangam, exhausted, is settled on a quilt to rest.

"Vairum is in Madras at present," Sivakami informs her son-in-law, "though we expect him back tonight. You know he does so much of his business there, now, he has even bought a house. He is there two or three days every week. Will you have coffee?"

"Yes, of course." Goli leaps to his feet. "You tell him to wait for me—when is it?"

"He gets back, I don't know, tonight some time," Sivakami repeats, unsure if he has said he wants coffee.

" . . . if he wants to make a deal." Goli has exited.

Sivakami sighs, unable to decide whether she should pass on the message. There's no guarantee that Goli has anything to offer that Vairum would want, and the chances of his returning the next day are so uncertain. After the previous fiasco, why try again? Goli ran his cinema into the ground within a year, Vairum told her.

She decides to ask Muchami what the chances are that Vairum would simply catch wind of whatever it is Goli wants of him.

"Oh, don't worry, Amma," Muchami tells her as he supervises the replacement of some bricks in the floor of the main hall. "No doubt the son-in-law will show up at the clubhouse tonight to play cards. The son-in-law will talk about his business as he plays and I will find out. When Vairum returns tonight, he will have to meet with his manager about the plant opening tomorrow, so word may reach him of the son-in-law's business, but if Vairum doesn't find out what is happening before me, I will tell him first thing tomorrow. Okay? Taken care of."

If Sivakami were still looking, she would have seen Muchami's reassuring smile fade as he turns back to his work. Muchami doesn't know what Goli plans on proposing to Vairum, but a few weeks ago an old Cholapatti acquaintance of Goli's had asked Muchami to give Goli a message: Goli, she said, owed her money. This was not someone who had bought a deer's head, though the debt dated to that period. It was the devadasi. Muchami had had to ask Vairum's assistance, being unable to write himself and wanting to keep the contents of the message within the family. The letter had probably prompted this visit and spurred an even greater than usual desire in Goli for some fast cash.

Muchami finishes his work with all the appearance of calm. His next chore is to whitewash the upstairs rooms. It is the season; the relatively cool, damp weather helps the whitewash to cure and so every house on the Brahmin quarter undergoes this makeover in preparation for the harvest festival. When Muchami finishes, around five-thirty, Vairum still hasn't returned. Muchami goes home, and after a bath and his evening meal, goes out again. He had had thoughts, anyway, of going out that night on a personal errand, the sort he still runs occasionally. He stops by the Kulithalai clubhouse on his way and makes a pretense of buying a bottle of *goli choda*, a lime-flavoured carbonated drink. Muchami hates the stuff but pops the wax seal on the glass marble stopper, and pretends to drink, just outside the door, where he can listen to the men inside.

The next day, Janaki arrives at school before Bharati. When Bharati shows up and takes her seat at their shared school bench, Janaki makes the signal that is shorthand for their latest big joke, something to do with their maths sir's stooped posture. Today, Bharati doesn't laugh, not even a snort, but stares straight ahead. Janaki looks at her in concern. Bharati turns as though she is going to ask Janaki a painful question, and enjoy asking it. Then their maths sir enters, loping under the burden of his body. The girls face forward in silence, looking down at the slates in their laps.

Their silence lasts until eleven-thirty, when their lunch gang joins them, pulling other benches over to form a triangle where the five meet daily. Bharati, of whom they are all afraid, narrows her fish-shaped eyes—liquid brown irises, whites shot with blood in the manner of classical beauties—and tells them, "Go away."

They all stop. She says again, "Eat somewhere else today." They back away without question.

Janaki asks, "What is wrong?"

Bharati freezes a look on Janaki and asks in a voice glittering darkly, "Why don't you ask our father?"

Janaki doesn't understand this, nor does she know how to reply.

Bharati replies for her. "'*Our* father, what do you mean *our* father?' Oh, I was surprised, too, let me tell you. Turns out your dad and my mother were friendly way back, before my mother met the man I've called Appa all these years. He's a Brahmin, too, a freedom fighter, a Congressman, and now he's in jail, and can't give us money like he always has. He's very honourable," she says pointedly, so

Janaki understands this to be a contrast with Goli. "He got to know my mother just after I was born. Now I know why my younger sisters don't look much like me! Anyway, now my mother told your father it's time he chips in, and he thinks he can sweet-talk and bully my amma into letting him off the hook." Bharati leans in close. "It's the age of Kali, my grandmother says: the brave are in jail and cowards walk free."

Janaki is trembling. She still doesn't understand much except that her family's honour is at stake. She points at her friend. "You are the coward. You are so full of lies you wouldn't know the truth if it punched you in the nose."

And then she punches her friend in the nose. Bharati comes at Janaki, scratching her temple and cheek. Janaki hits at her, and Bharati grabs her by the hair saying, again in that voice like mica, "Where does your father go at night, if you know so much?"

The other children have collected in a wide circle around them. Janaki is slap-scratching anything within reach but replies reasonably, because she knows the answer. "He goes to the club."

Bharati tosses her to the packed-earth floor and hisses, "Where does he go after the club?"

Janaki is weeping. Bharati walks away. As the teachers hurry over, Janaki yells, "I don't even know where your house is."

Bharati spits back over her shoulder, "Follow him tonight. You'll find it soon enough."

She pushes her way past teachers and students, to wash her face and clothes at the school pump. Neither girl is permitted to walk home unescorted, so, abject, stony, dishevelled, they finish out the afternoon on their shared bench.

As Janaki is learning things about her father that she doesn't want to hear and claims not to believe, the man himself mounts the steps of Sivakami's veranda. Vairum, having spent the morning inspecting the oil processing plant he is to open that afternoon, is lying down for a few minutes before leaving to drop in at Minister's salon.

"Hullo!" Goli yells from the door. "Hullo! Vairum! Big chances afoot—come on out."

Vairum slowly descends the spiral staircase into the main hall, as Sivakami, having her own meal in the kitchen, stands hurriedly and goes to wash her hands.

"Well, well!" Goli rubs his own hands together. "You are looking prosperous these days—filling out!" Vairum puts his hands on his hips as Goli continues, "So—I have a proposal."

"Want to sell me another tract of your family land, eh?" Vairum stands on the last step, looking down at Goli. "Must be getting down to the last few parcels now. I sent for the registrar first thing this morning to make sure this wouldn't take any longer than necessary."

The young official, who had been sitting in the vestibule between the front door and the entrance to the main hall, unfolds his gaunt frame and pokes his head in hopefully.

Goli looks at him stupidly and then points at Vairum. "You hang on—don't you assume anything, little man. We've got some bargaining to do."

"I pay better than anyone else in the presidency, Athimbere, in part so I don't have to waste time bargaining. Your father knew that better than anyone, and I know you know it, too, which is why you're coming to me."

"How dare you mention my late father," Goli snarls, advancing on Vairum.

The lands in question passed into Goli's possession the year prior, with his father's death. Before that, Vairum had twice made similar transactions with the older man, who had fallen into the same troubles as so many Brahmins, his need for cash outpacing his ability to coax income from crops, forcing him to sell off.

"Either sit down and do what you came here to do, you fool, or get out," Vairum tosses back. "We're not doing each other any favours."

Sivakami tries to intervene from the kitchen entrance with a civility. "Please, Vairum, offer the son-in-law coffee. It's almost ready."

"Fool? Fool? As if I need your stinking cash." Goli reaches into a document case he carries and flings a set of papers at the registrar. "Who is the fool here?"

Vairum indicates to the young official that he may begin. "I would say it's the one who fathers children he can't support. Ah—" He holds up a finger as Goli winds up with a retort. "One word out of you and this deal is off—I defy you to find anyone else who will buy these lands for as much money as you need. And you and I both know you need it now."

Goli makes a noise of strangulation and goes out into the garden. What, Sivakami is wondering, does he need the money for? It must be some debt. She knows he gambles—but surely he can't have lost this much money on cards? Another business scheme gone awry, she supposes.

As Vairum begins counting the stamp papers and checking the description of the property against the deed, he instructs the official to put the property in Thangam's name, carrying on the tradition Sivakami's brothers started.

"You may be willing to rob your children of their inheritance, Athimbere," Vairum comments loudly, "but I am not."

"Vairum!" Sivakami says again from the kitchen, and he looks at her sharply. She wants to say what he already knows, that he is the better man and that he need not remind Goli of that, but she cannot say that with Goli and Thangam present, even though Thangam has lain with her eyes closed, on a reed mat cushioned with homemade quilts, in one corner of the main hall, throughout this exchange, which she gave no indication of hearing. Sivakami's thought makes her feel slightly as if she is betraying her daughter. Regardless, Vairum already knows it, so she need not say it. Instead, she remonstrates, "The neighbours might hear."

Vairum's lip curls. He turns back to the paperwork, finishing it off with a flourish. "Your turn to sign, Athimbere," he says, rising. "Take it to my bank in Kulithalai. The manager is expecting you." He puts on his shoes at the door and leaves before Goli re-enters.

That day after school, Janaki makes a point of telling Sivakami that she is going to study up on the roof. Her books in their strap, slung over her shoulder, she treads the stairs with leaden feet, matching each step with a hand slap against the wall in the narrow stairwell. The fresh whitewash makes the pads of her hands chalky, and when she arrives in the sunlight, she claps her hands to make little dust clouds. She walks slowly around the edge of the roof as Vani plays. The sun is already slanting low enough to make two feet of shade along the western side.

Looking down into the next yard to the east, she sees Dharnakarna, the witch, feeding idli to her sister-in-law. Their tiffin hour is often amusing, the witch patiently timing the mouthfuls so they don't get slapped across the courtyard. The sister-in-law won't bite the hand that feeds her, but she snaps at it sometimes. Janaki moves across the back and looks down into her own courtyard and the woods behind. A brief breeze parts the lingering stillness of the afternoon air. Parrots are beginning to fly among the trees. She can't see if Bharati is in her regular spot behind the house: she's pretty sure Bharati won't have come but will not go down to check, in case she has.

She circles, coming up the western side of the house, from which she can see into Rukmini and Murthy's courtyard. Rukmini has fetched Krishnan to play with her, and Janaki hears his laughter. She moves again toward the front of the house, unable for once to sit still and listen to her aunt play. The sounds of the street dissolve as day thins into dusk.

Kamalam arrives from downstairs as Vairum comes to carry Vani's veena to their quarters. Vani follows. Kamalam and Janaki stand in silence at the front of the roof until the moment when—you can almost miss it—outlines of shapes disappear and become one with the dusky blue air. Then Janaki says to Kamalam, "I'm going out and I'll be back before suppertime. If I'm not, though, just say I have fallen asleep up here and don't feel like eating. Say I'm being cranky if you are sent to wake me up."

Kamalam is frowning. "Why . . . ?"

But Janaki just shakes her head and waggles her finger as she walks back to the stairs. She descends cautiously into the main hall, which is empty apart from their mother, who sits thin and pregnant against the back wall. Where is Sita? Talking with one of her friends out on the veranda. Janaki cannot leave the house, by front or back, while Sita is out there—she will be visible from the veranda as she takes the cart path out of the Brahmin quarter. She hides behind the stairs and calls out, "Sitakka! Sitakka!"

Sita shouts back, "What?"

"Come back and help me with this, just for a second." Janaki pops her head out to yell, and then hides again.

"What?" Sita says bad-humouredly from the vestibule. "Where are you?"

"By the well, just for a second, really." Janaki watches her mother, who doesn't react.

Sita says an exasperated goodbye to her friend and heads for the back by way of the kitchen. As soon as she enters the pantry, Janaki scurries for the front and slips out the door as the sounds of Sita's fury start to mount.

She picks her way along the edge of the cart path leading to the main road into Kulithalai. As she steps onto the road her heart begins to pound. She has barely been out after dark and never alone. Figures approach and she steps aside so they pass her without seeing her or inquiring as to her business. She doesn't want to give anyone stories to carry back to the Brahmin quarter. She is risking being seen and talked about; she is risking not being seen and not being missed, should anything happen. But what choice does she have? She turns onto the main road and keeps to the shadows.

The club is within a walled compound but there is no one guarding the big iron gate. At night, the grizzled old peon patrols the compound occasionally but must also make change and sell goli choda for the card players to mix with spirits they bring themselves.

Janaki looks for a place where she can spend the next few hours unseen, waiting for her father. The clubhouse faces the tennis court. Men approach it from one side. The other side is sheltered but smells of urine; one can imagine it is used often over the course of the evening. Janaki opts for a large neem tree at the back with a branch obligingly bowed into a seat, thick enough for her skinny twelve-year-old bottom.

From there she catches only glimpses of men as they walk past the barred window. Once they are seated they are hidden from view but a large gap between the wall and the roof thatch lets her hear the men's voices, including her father's, rising above the slap and shuffle of a deck of cards. From the few Janaki saw, she didn't think they looked like an appropriate class of men to be associating with her father.

"So you transacted the necessary business with your brother-in-law today, Goli?" a man says in a Brahmin accent. Janaki is surprised that there are other Brahmins here, though she doesn't know why she should be.

"He's going to get his comeuppance one of these days," Goli says by way of reply.

"I hope I'm around to see it," the first man says. "He owns half of my family properties now."

"Yes, well, today, he opened a factory on my ancestral lands," sputters another Brahmin. "And if that's not enough, I swear, half my tenants are going to work in it! I could kill that guy. I swear, if he wasn't the son of the most orthodox lady in the Brahmin quarter, I might think he's a progressive. Did you hear what he's paying?"

Janaki, wincing at his inelegant Tamil, listens harder.

"Vairum is canny—and fair-minded," says a warm, gravelly voice in a non-Brahmin accent that Janaki can't place. "Happy workers are good workers."

"Sure, I'm all in favour of non-Brahmin uplift," says the other Brahmin reservedly. "But for non-Brahmins like you, Mr. Muthu Reddiar, self-starters, of good family. Putting power in the hands of the illiterate masses, though—it's a recipe for disaster."

"The man wants to start a revolution, that's what," Goli cries. "He wants to be king."

"Seems to me the Brahmins around here have profited as much as anyone from business with Vairum," Muthu Reddiar insists, an edge to his voice. "He's generous, you have to say that for him."

"I don't have to say anything good about that man!" It sounds as if Goli has thumped the table.

"All right, all right," says the first Brahmin. "Let's take it easy. You can rest assured that most if not all the Brahmin quarter shares your opinion, Goli."

"What a week," Goli complains.

"Have you been to see Chellamma?" someone asks, and Janaki starts.

"Last night. She won't budge," Goli growls. "Bitch."

Janaki gapes at the crude language, feeling sick.

"Hasn't given me the time of day since Balachandran came on the scene, and now she expects me to pay for that pup? *Ravana!*" Janaki can't tell if he's cursing at Bharati's mother or just lost a hand of cards.

"So don't pay," the first Brahmin man advises.

"She's got me over a barrel," Goli says darkly. "She'll go to my boss."

"What—" the man starts, but Goli breaks in: "Deal. I'm done talking about that."

The clubhouse goes briefly quiet except for the slap and slide of cards and occasional muttered words. Then the night erupts in hooting and shouts as someone wins. Janaki listens to the chime of the men's tumblers and wrinkles her nose at a puff of tobacco smoke that has drifted from the clubhouse window.

The cycle repeats, the men's voices blurring and sharpening with emotion and drink. At one point, Janaki drowses, shakes herself, drops off again—and drops off the branch. It's a rude shock, but she is not hurt by the fall. She runs behind the tree when the peon looks out the window, and then remounts the branch.

It must be well on for nine o'clock when Goli finally wins a round—the biggest pot of the night, according to the ribbing he receives. He loudly claims that it only earns him back what he has lost, but it sounds as if he's being modest. Janaki, hearing him announce his departure, perks up.

"Lads, I'm sorry to say I must take my leave of you now."

"Come on, Goli, let us at least win back our dignity."

"Sorry, you'll have to face your wives without it. Not the first time, I would say."

More hoots.

"Last time Nallathumbi here stripped himself of his dignity his wife ran from the room in fright!"

Nallathumbi makes his rebuttal. "Naked, I inspire men and frighten women. Just as it should be."

They all laugh, satisfied. Goli takes his leave.

Janaki allows him a few moments before slipping from the tree, praying to herself, "Please go home just go home please go home just go home go home go home." She tails him to the gate. "Go right go right right right."

He hesitates, looking both ways, and turns left. Janaki pauses a second, to look down at her toes, bare and vulnerable as they emerge from beneath the paavaadai. *My toes look purple in the moonlight,* she thinks. *How curious.* She too emerges from the gate.

In the dark this is not the town she knows. The night forgives a lot; she doesn't want to imagine what sins it lets slip by. Kerosene flares make sinister shadows that dance and dodge no matter how still the body that throws them. Janaki is frightened and focuses on her father's back as though it is a magic charm whose powers she doesn't know and yet has no choice but to trust.

At the end of the commercial thoroughfare, Goli strikes east along the curving road that rings the town. Janaki is not so scared now. The velvet dust between her toes is like the dust behind their house when she relieves herself at midnight, and the shadows cast by moonlight are steady and sedate. She permits herself to imagine Bharati's house and her mother.

In her mind, Chellamma is slatternly. Lumpy mounds of flesh, conniving eyes ringed in thick kohl, scheming lips reddened by betel, layers of powder over a dark and uneven complexion. Janaki really cannot understand what her father would see in such a woman, when he has the most beautiful wife anyone's ever seen. Janaki gasps aloud: witchcraft! Bharati's mother captivates men with spells. That must be it!

She is walking faster and faster, working herself into a fury of indignation, and nearly overtakes her father but catches herself in time and drops back. Finally he steps onto a small path leading to a mud house with thatched roof. It is lit within by kerosene lamps, proof of their prosperity. Janaki, though hardened by anger at Chellamma's nerve, doesn't fail to note the tidiness of the swept path, the walls as freshly whitewashed and decorated for Pongal as any Brahmin's.

She sees her father stoop and enter the dwelling. Janaki paces the periphery clockwise until she comes to a window. She approaches it and startles.

Bharati's knowing smile matches Janaki's frightened face as though the window were a magic mirror. Bharati makes no noise, but, giving Janaki a sly nod, seats herself to allow Janaki an unobstructed view.

Bharati's younger brother and three sisters are clustered in a corner around their grandmother. Her mother, Chellamma, matches her house: she is a small, tidy woman with wrinkles around her eyes that seem to Janaki oddly familiar. She is not fat and slovenly; she is just . . . plain. And tough-looking. Her mouth is set in a hard line as she tells Goli, "Hand it over."

Goli hands her a packet of rupee notes. Janaki thinks of the day before, when she saw her first of the new five-rupee notes that have just come out, with a portrait of George VI. She wonders how much her father has paid.

"You could have had all the income from that land," he jeers, "but you had to make me sell it, didn't you?"

Chellamma turns away from Goli, and Janaki sees the hardness drop away for a moment. In its place is an expression tired and sad, and Janaki recognizes the lines around her eyes: they're like her own mother's. As Chellamma crouches and pours a tumbler full of water flavoured with palm sugar and ginger, Bharati's grandmother speaks from a corner, where she is assembling betel nut and leaves from a rosewood box.

"Oh, and how was she supposed to manage that land from here? If it was any good, you would have been able to keep it and pay us from the income."

Goli suddenly explodes, his hand chopping against his palm. "You have no proof! Why should I pay at all?"

The grandmother coolly looks down at the spade-shaped leaves in her palm, a winning hand of cards.

"What proof do we need, beyond your bragging of the strength of your seed?" the old woman says as she streaks the leaves with calcium paste and rose-petal gel. "Everyone knows you were the man my daughter was receiving at that time."

"Pah!" Goli appears at a loss for words.

Chellamma, the hardness returned to her face, turns back and holds out a plate to him, on which sits the cup of flavoured water.

"Look at Bharati's forehead, her eyebrows, her hair," Chellamma says. "Do they not look familiar?"

Janaki watches the old woman sprinkle the leaves with areca nut, cardamom and rock sugar, roll them into three-sided packets and pin them shut with cloves.

Chellamma places the betel packets on another plate and, pulling her sari over her shoulder, offers it to Goli.

Janaki waits for her father to slap the plate away and send the odious packages flying. Instead, he puts one in his mouth, then puts another in Chellamma's. The gesture has the ceremony of a pact-sealing and the intimacy of lovers' service. Janaki starts to cry.

"So our business is concluded?" Goli asks Chellamma in a low voice.

Chellamma inclines her head, lowering her eyes and lifting them again. Goli touches her cheek. "I'll be around a few more days," he murmurs.

Bharati's head pops up in the window and Janaki, unable to face her, turns her back to the house and sits on the ground. When she sees her father leaving, she follows him home.

Kamalam looks as though she has been holding her breath since Janaki left. She doesn't ask questions. When Janaki starts to cry again, Kamalam kisses her hand and strokes her hair, but Janaki only cries for a minute or two.

At lunch hour the next day, when their friends begin cautiously to pull up their benches, Janaki and Bharati say, "Go away," almost in unison. During the morning's lessons, they have been civil but serious—co-operating in maths, participating in history. Now they incline toward one another.

"I'm sorry," Janaki says.

"Me, too," Bharati quickly responds.

They are quiet for a few moments.

"Is your mother saving for your marriage?" Janaki asks. She's not sure why she put her question this way, other than that she doesn't know how else to ask what she wants to know.

Bharati smiles a little, wearily. "You don't know much about us, do you?" she asks.

Janaki shakes her head quickly, holding her breath.

"I'm married already," Bharati begins.

"You are?" Janaki is amazed. She had no idea. "Did your mom take you to Pondicherry?"

"Uh-uh. Madurai."

But that's the city closest to Pandiyoor, Vani's hometown, Janaki thinks. It's within the Madras Presidency.

"I didn't marry a man," Bharati continues. "We . . . in my caste, we marry a god. There aren't too many of us around here—my grandmother came from Madurai—so she took us back there for my wedding ceremony."

"How did—you married a god?" Janaki frowns.

"It's just like a wedding, you know. Except the groom is a god statue, dressed up. You even have a pretend wedding night, where you sleep with a sword, in a bed. I don't really get that part," Bharati admits, blushing. "But, anyway."

"What's . . ." Janaki begins, realizing she can't tell Bharati's caste from her name. "What's your caste called?"

Now Bharati looks at her sharply. "We're devadasis, Janaki. You didn't know that?"

Janaki's eyes widen but she tries to stop herself from looking too shocked. She is pretty sure she has heard the word "devadasi" whispered as though it is something scandalous. After a moment, though, she admits, "I don't really know what that means."

Bharati looks as though she's trying to decide whether Janaki is telling the truth.

"Well," she starts, cautious and a bit didactic, "you know we really believe in education, especially for girls. That's why I learn music, and I'm in school, and I have a dancing master, too, who comes to my home. My mother and grandmother had live-in instructors." She warms to her story, starting to sound more assured, and older. "My grandmother was quite famous in Madurai, so much so she got a big patron, a Kulithalai Brahmin, who brought her here. So that was my grandfather."

"Oh . . ." Janaki's trying to absorb all this. "You learn dancing?" This is probably the most incredible aspect of the story so far.

"Yes—*sadir*. You should come and watch me dance sometime," Bharati offers warmly.

"Sure," Janaki says, thinking she might have gone to Bharati's house before, but now she doesn't think she can face Bharati's mother. "So your father and grandfather were Brahmins? But you're not."

"Uh-uh." Bharati is emphatic. "Devadasis don't marry the men," she clarifies. "You got that, right?"

"I guess."

"We're artistes." She pauses, then elaborates, sounding now as though she's making an argument, to Janaki or herself. "And we're good omens because we're *nityasumangalis*—'forever married'— because a god never dies."

Janaki wonders what it's like to be a good omen. Her grandmother hardly ever goes out, in part because widows are a bad omen and she doesn't want to do that to anyone. Does Bharati always want attention because she's a good omen? But she still can't walk on the Brahmin quarter.

"It was funny when the census came," Bharati goes on. "My mother had herself put down as married, and me as unmarried. The census taker did it, but you should have seen how they looked at us— so self-righteous." She smirks, before growing reflective. "My amma is worried—people are talking about abolishing the devadasi system. There's a lady minister, a doctor, who's been pushing for it. Then what are we supposed to do?"

"You could marry, like everyone else," Janaki suggests, not meaning to sound derisive.

"First of all, there aren't many boys of our caste," Bharati says, looking at Janaki like she is slow. "No devadasi keeps more than one son. Not like Brahmins, where all they want are boys." Now Janaki does feel stupid. "Devadasi boys aren't educated much; they don't earn. All they can do is maybe play drums or something. Who would want one of those?"

They are quiet.

"You'll be all right," Janaki says after a few moments. Bharati looks at her. "I just know, things will turn out good for you."

Bharati smiles at her and shyly looks away. "You've never had a half sister before, huh?"

"No," Janaki says and politely returns the smile. She feels strange, aware that she no longer feels the urgent need to gain Bharati's favour.

When Janaki returns from school that afternoon, her father is sitting on the veranda, chatting with several neighbours, Brahmin men she knows slightly, not well enough to have recognized their voices at the club the night prior. Hearing them now, as she passes on her way into the house, the night scent and nervousness of her vigil come back to her. Her father doesn't acknowledge her.

She has a snack and changes her clothes. She is about to start up the stairs to listen to Vani, who has already begun playing, when she hears shouting from the front. Her uncle has come home.

"I don't want anything from you, you peasant-lover!" Goli screams.

"That's a nice change, then," Vairum spits back as he mounts the stairs. "I'm sorry I asked."

"Sooner help a non-Brahmin than anyone from your own caste!"

Vairum doesn't turn. "Keep your epithets to yourself." He shucks his shoes in the vestibule and enters the main hall. "Hypocrite."

Goli runs in after Vairum and, picking up Vairum's shoes, throws them. One hits his back. Vairum turns and seems to watch the other hit his front, not even lifting a hand to bat away this insult, the erasure of caste.

"You love untouchables so much, now you can be one," Goli sneers. He backs out of the vestibule, through the crowd, and disappears.

Vairum walks slowly out to the veranda and faces the Brahmin-quarter denizens staring from his stoop, fair, flabby men, fingering their holy threads and shoulder towels.

"Here—I stand before you, uncasted," Vairum softly proclaims. "Has he acted on your behalf?" he asks, gesturing over them as though to clear a small cloud. "A low and unscrupulous scoundrel, who has left his children for me to raise. *He* has thrust *me* beneath caste?"

He looks at them and they look away; one man clears his throat. They are thinking, variously, that Vairum is the scoundrel; that Sivakami, and not he, is raising the children; that Vairum may be in the right but it is best not to get involved in a family fight. But none speaks, and Vairum closes the door on their faces.

"You see, Amma, why I care so little for what the neighbours hear." Vairum turns to face his mother, who comes out now from the pantry, where she stood and watched the exchange.

"Oh, my child." She holds her arms out toward him and he looks at her incredulously.

"You understand you are party to this, yes? The man hangs around my front stoop waiting to insult me, Amma. Why do you protect him?"

"I never wanted, I . . ." *I would have done anything to save you from this.* "For your sister." What can she say—is it not obvious that she would give her life for him?

She looks around at Thangam sitting in the corner where she has lain since her arrival, her body rigid, her neck stiffly bowed to hide her face. Kamalam and Janaki watch from the corner by the kitchen, and Sivakami sees Muchami watching Janaki from the garden door, all of her feelings mirrored in his face: how to keep children from harm? She has done all she can to protect all of them—hasn't she?

"You have never done what is best for my sister," Vairum thunders. "The Brahmins on this street have never accepted me, and now your son-in-law has uncasted me like those ruffians uncasted your Rama. There is no reason for me to live here. You can have your precious neighbours, and your reputation. Vani and I are moving to Madras."

"Don't do that, my son," Sivakami says, confused.

He calls Vani.

They need take nothing: they each have a full wardrobe in their house in the city, and Vani a better veena, though she has gone there only twice a year till now. They take leave of Sivakami, doing a prostration for her. Sivakami doesn't know if Vairum means to force his mother to give them her blessings, or if Vani insisted on their paying Sivakami their respects. When they rise, Sivakami hugs them, though only Vani returns her embrace. Vairum keeps his arms stiffly at his side. She is crying, though from her right eye only.

She calls Janaki to offer Vani a plate of turmeric, betel and vermilion.

Sivakami doesn't know what "hypocrite" means, and doesn't know why Goli was accusing her son of loving non-Brahmins, but she knows Vairum has not shown nearly the sort of allegiance with his own caste that the times seem to demand. She feels small and old, and frightened.

It has been years since Janaki has helped Muchami with the cows, and she feels awkward and guilty as she goes to the cowshed the next morning. She feels she is being babyish. She can't even wholly admit to herself her motivation: she wants desperately to talk about what she learned about Bharati. She presumes her mother and grandmother don't know, and she can't be the one to tell them. What if they do know? It would be horrible to talk about it, especially now that Goli is responsible for Vairum's leaving. Kamalam is too tender; her eldest sisters are too far away. Sita would call her a liar, and Janaki would never talk to her about anything important or painful anyway.

She thinks Goli has done something wrong, but has he, and what, exactly? The man Bharati thought was her father sounds honourable, and Bharati made it sound as though his second family might not even be a secret from his first. Sivakami must not know about it. But maybe the only thing Goli did wrong was not paying. Janaki feels as though she is banging weak fists against her own unyielding head. Who can help her to understand this?

Once she sees Muchami at work in the shed, however, she is unable to talk to him either. He is a servant, she tells herself, even as she feels an ancient urge to climb into his lap and put her arms around his neck. He is not part of the family. *If he doesn't know, I can't be the one to tell him, and if he does know, it would be improper for me to discuss it with him.* She backs out of the shed without saying anything, and goes slowly toward the house. She doesn't feel like crying; she feels as though a black wind whirls dryly at her centre, obscuring something essential from her view.

Muchami had heard her come in. He turns and sees the hem of her paavaadai disappearing into the house. He guesses she wanted to talk. Perhaps it's about Goli, perhaps . . .

Of course: her school friend. She must have said something to Janaki about Goli owing her mother money. Nothing can be proven; he hopes neither girl has heard the rumours that the devadasi's daughter is his. It's not a subject he can raise with Janaki, though. Hopefully, she'll just let it go.

_____ &

FIVE MONTHS LATER, Thangam gives birth to another baby boy. The child is lusty and red, and when his sisters see him, they gasp at his beauty: he alone among them has inherited Thangam's golden eyes.

Thangam, though, is exhausted, and lies with her eyes closed, until Sivakami says, "Thangam? Thangam, kanna, do you want anything?"

Thangam raises her head and Sivakami freezes: Thangam's eyes are now stone cold blue. She shakes her head, *no,* and lies back down to sleep.

30.
Rainy Season
1940

IT'S THE LAST DAY OF SCHOOL. Janaki and Bharati hold hands up
to the schoolyard gate, then uncouple while their servants, Mari and
Draupadi, wait to escort each of them, and their younger sisters,
home. They are both nearly five feet, and wear uniforms of a half-
sari—a long cotton paavaadai in navy blue, with white blouse and
white *davani*, a cloth piece wrapped once about the hips, across the
chest, and over the shoulder—indicating they are now more women
than girls. They both came of age this year—Janaki is nearly fifteen,
Bharati has commenced her sixteenth year—and will not continue in
school, since all higher levels are coeducational.

"Well, see you later," Janaki says, at a loss. They know it's not
likely they will cross paths again.

"Bye," Bharati rejoins, with a sweet smile. "Good luck, with marriage and all."

Janaki reciprocates, open and genuine. "And good luck to you—
whatever comes next."

Bharati raises her eyebrows, amused and practical, but then Janaki
is alarmed to see Bharati gulp as her eyes brim slightly and she blinks.
"Yes, whatever comes next. G'bye, little sister."

It has become one of their private jokes, to call each other little sister and big sister, thangachi and *akka*, though Bharati started the joke.
Hearing the reference now returns to Janaki her guilty relief at this

parting. Ever since she learned of their blood relationship, she has felt mildly cool toward Bharati, in spite of their greater closeness. She both dislikes this feeling and feels it is justified. She doesn't think it shows; Bharati, she thinks, might not even have picked up on it.

Back when Bharati was uncertain of who her father was, Janaki and she remarked innocently on the coincidence that they both lived with their maternal grandmothers. Now that they share a father, Janaki frequently tells herself that she and Bharati really have nothing in common, because otherwise she would have to admit she identifies more with Bharati now than before. They both feel ashamed of their father, though he disappoints them in different ways.

Their slight estrangement had been facilitated by Vani's absence, since Bharati no longer had a reason to come and sit behind their house. They continued to spend all their time together at school but no longer had an after-school relationship.

When they had outgrown their first veena teacher, Bharati's mother had engaged a music tutor who came, once a week, all the way from Thiruchi. Bharati invited Janaki to come and participate in the lessons. It was tempting: Janaki had had to work hard to keep up with her music since Vani and Vairum moved to Madras. She practises at least an hour or two every day on the veena Vani left, which has, de facto, become hers. Once a week, there is an educational music program broadcast on the radio, and Janaki goes to Gayatri's to take it in; occasionally, she goes to weddings, where she makes a point of learning some new songs from whoever is the best musician in attendance. The few times Vani has come back to visit them in Cholapatti, Janaki, in her desperation to learn, has been persistent to the point of rudeness, but Vani is ever patient and indulgent with her: playing, listening to Janaki play, wordlessly making corrections and modelling improvements.

When Bharati asked again if Janaki would be coming over for veena lessons, Janaki shook her head. "My grandmother says I'm too old to be going to others' houses for lessons, that I should just practise at home."

Bharati tossed her head a little, lifting her chin as though something were flying past it, and said coolly, "Very conservative, your grandmother."

Janaki felt herself get hot: she had always understood "conserva-tive" to be a compliment—why didn't it sound that way coming from Bharati? But then Bharati appeared to correct herself. "So's mine, in her own way," she told Janaki with a return of the intimate joviality that Janaki now shrank from. "Too bad. It would have been fun."

In fact, Janaki had never asked her grandmother. She wouldn't have wanted to admit to having a devadasi as a friend, though she knows that, were it not for their other connection, she would have found a way to attend the special lessons.

And now Bharati is turning toward the rest of her life and Janaki, toward hers. Janaki knows her own near future, but not the far. She will stay home, but will receive a tutor, young Kesavan, who will help her maintain her Sanskrit and other basic academic skills. Next year, her grandmother will start to solicit potential grooms. Beyond that, she cannot see.

Janaki, Radhai and Kamalam, all of whom have come home from school together, wash their hands, face and feet, and change into everyday clothes. Radhai goes to play with Krishnan next door at Rukmini's house, where he spends every day, the first of Thangam's pre-school children not to pass his afternoons with Muchami. Though Muchami missed having a child with him, he had no means or desire to override Rukmini's proffered affection for the little boy.

Kamalam and Janaki take their embroidery and go to sit on the veranda, where they will be met by Ecchemu, a Brahmin girl of about Janaki's age, with whom Janaki has become friendly. Ecchemu is a dull, silly girl, but, by virtue of caste and age, is an appropriate companion for Janaki. Where Bharati has always made Janaki feel frumpy, Ecchemu causes her to feel her own attributes keenly. She has always known she was smart, but now she may have become pretty. She is of average build, unlike Kamalam, who, at five feet and five inches, is by far the tallest of the sisters. Janaki has inherited something of her father's square jaw and forehead, but her demure, perceptive gaze is hers alone, as are her creative talents, which always exceed available outlets.

Since Sita left for her husband's house, Janaki has taken over the drawing of the kolam every morning, the rice flour design that ornaments every threshold. Where their house used to display no more than a perfunctory few lines and dots of the required symmetry, it is now daily decorated with a kolam no less than three feet across, often embellished with birds and flowers. Janaki admires her latest—a cobra wriggled across the threshold in perfect diagonals—as she takes her seat on the veranda and smiles condescendingly at Ecchemu, who is just arriving.

As they work together, Ecchemu chatters vapidly about her sister's recent marriage. Janaki doesn't listen, but instead reflects on the academic career she has just ended. She performed well—better than any of her sisters did, and likely better than Kamalam or Radhai will. None of them have her desire for knowledge, her determination and application. She knew full well she would have no more than an elementary education, though, and it doesn't occur to her to be discontent at not going further. Rather, she is grateful to Sivakami for continuing to give her tutoring, more than most girls receive. Now she is looking forward to marriage and to raising a family, as much as she can look forward to events both inevitable and essentially unknown.

—⟳

SEVERAL MONTHS LATER, Navaratri approaches—festival of dolls. It's Janaki's favourite, not surprisingly, since it offers chances for imaginative play, and because it includes several days of tribute to Saraswati, goddess of music and education, the deity Janaki feels most personally inclined to worship. Gayatri, when she comes for her morning coffee, tells Janaki stories, innocent and repetitive, of how the holiday used to be Thangam's favourite, too.

It feels like a strange coincidence, then, when the day's mail contains a letter from Thangam, the first Janaki has seen. It is written in pencil, in Thangam's own hand. In places, the writing is so light that it disappears. In others, Thangam has pressed so hard that the thick, nubbly paper has torn, as though she were leaning on the pencil for strength.

"*Amma*," it begins, after the usual "*Safe*" in the upper right corner, and the date, in the left.

He has been moved again. He has already gone and I
must ready the things. I think my baby is due in some
three months. Can one of my daughters come to help me?
Baby Raghavan is very strong, red and chubby. Please
send a girl if one of mine can come to help. I know all of
my girls are very strong. Do not worry.

It finishes with her name, laboriously inscribed at the bottom.

Janaki is in the middle of her veena practice. Sivakami shows her the letter. "You'll go, Janaki? Muchami will take you."

"Yes, Amma," she responds rapidly. Why is Thangam asking Sivakami not to worry? What does her grandmother have to worry about?

Sivakami smiles, looking wan. "Good girl. Maybe you can be ready to leave day after tomorrow?"

It's a pleasant nine-hour journey northwest. Janaki has brought a slate, to pass the time, and gives Muchami a few Sanskrit lessons. He is too shy to work aloud in so public a setting, but she writes out lines for him to copy. He has continued to sit in on Janaki's Sanskrit tutorials, though young Kesavan practically ignores him. Once in a while, though, Janaki, in a didactic mood, will take it upon herself to quiz Muchami on the basics. He has grasped these, though his pronunciation continues to be atrocious and Janaki doesn't try to hide her impatience as she corrects him.

When they are done with Sanskrit, they watch the landscape shift outside the barred windows of the train. The greens and browns of the Kaveri delta give way to pinkish rocks and sparser settlements as they climb into the hills. It's the monsoon season, and the air smells of rain. Twice, they ride through cloudbursts.

They chat, but not much. There is a distance between them now, which both feel it proper to observe. Janaki is glad for it, because it indicates the difference in their stations—she is growing up and happily anticipating the small powers that will fall to her as a matron. Muchami, for his part, still feels the weight of the child she was on his hip. If she tends to boss him, if she is short with him over his Sanskrit, he indulges her. She is still his favourite and he is proud of her.

Once in the town, Muchami, carrying her bag, hurries ahead and drops behind, inquiring repeatedly. They find the house. Two-year-old Raghavan gallops out of the house. When they stoop to caress him, he whinnies and ducks and continues past them, into the neighbour's house. The neighbour emerges carrying him. She is a tall, thin woman with severe looks. Tics in either side of her face pull her mouth down in clownish grimaces. Raghavan seems to think she is making faces to amuse him, and to Janaki's mortification, imitates her and laughs, clapping his hands.

Thangam leans in the doorway and smiles at them, a smile below which stretch two cords in her neck, like the pillars of a suspension bridge. She is as grey as ash, and as incorporeal.

Muchami says, "Thangam? Are you well?" But Thangam just stands back silently to let Janaki enter the small dwelling. Janaki moves toward her mother to kiss her, but Thangam makes no similar move and her initiative fades. She puts her bag in a corner while Thangam makes coffee for Muchami, who squats at the front stoop.

They are living in a house with the well in the middle of the main hall, under an open skylight. Raghavan runs around the well, flings himself gaily against the walls, pulls saris and braids. Once he stops and walks delicately to a shrouded pile. He pats it gently, saying, "Amma. Ga'phone. Amma! Ga'phone." She smiles, goes to the mound and unveils the gramophone.

Raghavan sits and watches the turntable with the intensity of the little dog on the label waiting for his master's voice, while Thangam takes four records, one by one, from a high shelf. She fits the needle into the gramophone's arm and the key into the body and winds. Janaki and the neighbour sit, while Muchami moves into the front doorway. First they hear a loud scratchiness, then a single veena as though heard over a river's rush. It's "Sami Varnam," the same recording they heard when Goli first gave Thangam the machine.

Thangam plucks the disc from its bed, sheathes it and takes out another. The new record also rushes and shushes, riverine—but it is a vocalist this time, not a veena player. The singer is very young. Janaki has never heard Bharati sing, but she finds herself imagining her friend at home, in that pretty hut with no neighbours, plaiting her hair after her oil bath, kohling her eyes dreamily in a fragment of mirror, singing through barely parted lips.

They all know the song: "Balagopala Palaya Mam," a devotional song for Lord Krishna, composed by Dikshitr, one of the immortals of south Indian classical music. Janaki sings along, and even the severe-looking neighbour joins in. Thangam leans against a pillar with her eyes closed. Little Raghavan claps his chubby hands and occasionally cuffs one of them in delight.

But Thangam forgot to rewind the machine, and when the song is nearly at its end, the disc begins to slow. Seventy-eight rpm becomes sixty-five, fifty, thirty-five. Raghavan stops mid-clap to listen to this dying groan. Janaki giggles at the funny sound, at the expression on the little boy's face. Seeing her laugh, he begins laughing also.

Thangam opens her eyes, pulls out a third disc and slips it on the turntable, not forgetting to crank this time. She looks at her children and visitor with a sly expression, one that might almost be mischief. Janaki stops laughing in amazement, but many people are still laughing, more than are present: from the phonograph issues a river of giggling, chortling, guffawing and twittering, the laughter of a large number of people of all ages and sexes that, in ensemble, creates the cadences of a familiar, elementary tune, "Vara Veena."

It is a novelty record, a fashion item: music of laughter. Minister probably has a copy; he rarely misses a fad.

Raghavan doubles over, laughing louder and harder. At this, at him, Janaki starts laughing again; the neighbour joins in, and even Muchami, at the door. Thangam smiles, her eyes closed again, looking almost peaceful.

Oh, thinks Janaki, as she lies that night with her baby brother sleeping in her arms and the first monsoon rains thrumming through the skylight, *why could not every day of our lives have been like this?*

Janaki sets to work the next day, getting them ready to move. Muchami, seeing that there are no servants here, is arranging to transport their belongings to the new home, while Janaki, Thangam and the baby will take the train.

Not much has been packed yet but there is not much to pack. Still, progress is very slow at first because each item Janaki puts in a bag or trunk, her little brother takes out again. So instead she sets the things down beside the luggage and tells him to leave them there. He mischievously packs them one by one. In this way, things get done.

Janaki is shocked at how few furnishings there are and asks if some items have not gone ahead with her father. Thangam shakes her head. Janaki shrugs and continues to make arrangements, knowing her mother must have had more copper pots than this—there are gaps in the usual size sequence. She's sure they had more in the Karnatak country. And only one silver plate—unheard of. She admits to herself what is clear: her father must have pawned the pots and plates over the years.

The transfer of goods and persons to the village of Munnur is completed without incident. Munnur is to the east, a few hours closer to Cholapatti, back on the Kaveri. Muchami, after delivering them, takes his leave. When Janaki sees him off on the veranda of their new home, even more modest than the last, he inclines toward her and speaks in a low voice. "Janaki, your grandmother gave you a little money, yes?" Janaki confirms it.

"Keep that safe," he instructs, sounding reassuring, no longer the servant, but Sivakami's representative. "It's for an emergency. You never know what might happen. And you know how to contact us, if you need to? To send a letter?"

"Yes, of course," Janaki says—she's fourteen, practically an adult!—but also scared at the degree of responsibility this conference implies.

"All right," Muchami says, his brow furrowed. He's reluctant to leave.

"It's okay, Muchami." Janaki looks brave. "We'll be fine."

He looks at the ground. "You're a good girl, Janaki, a strong girl, smart girl. I know you will take good care of little Thangam. Poor Thangam."

Janaki is slightly offended that Muchami sees her mother—and probably her father—just as she does. But she cannot sustain this feeling; she is still too much the little girl she was.

"Don't worry, Muchami," she insists. "I will look after her."
He smiles slightly, bows and is gone.

Goli had appeared surprised to see his family, but he seems to be in a mood of regularity, going to the office every day and, better yet, coming home. He hasn't made friends yet, Janaki thinks sourly. She looks at her mother and thinks of all she has suffered, feeling self-righteous and wishing she didn't.

Janaki unpacks by leaving the bags and trunks open and letting Raghavan keep himself busy. She hangs the cuckoo clock—another of Goli's caprices—and a calendar she brought from Cholapatti, showing an image of the goddess Saraswati, signified by her veena. A servant is arranged for cleaning; Thangam will cook. The rains are coming reliably now and the family, too, settles into a routine of sorts.

Navaratri is fast approaching and Janaki turns her thoughts happily, if uncertainly, to the festival: they are in a house entirely without dolls and with barely five or six deity portraits. Buying dolls the way Gayatri would is not an option: Janaki doesn't want to ask her parents to pay and doesn't think this qualifies as an emergency, so she can't use the money her grandmother gave her.

As she sits on the veranda one morning, watching the rain and thinking on the doll question, Raghavan runs out to give her a murrukku, then trips and drops his own in a puddle. He howls briefly, then continues dunking the chickpea flour snack into the puddle until it is reduced to a sodden mess.

Janaki recalls making her family's names in murrukku and smiles as an idea occurs to her. She fills a bowl with wheat flour, which they have in abundance and don't much need. She mixes in some rice flour and blends it with water to make a dough. As she works beside the well, the rain clears up, and a timid sunshine leaks through the clouds.

From the paste, Janaki begins fashioning figures the height of her hand: a yogi, a teacher, a judge, laundryman, betel vendor, widow, farmer, iron-press man, priest, barber, soldier, rail signal man, mother, father, goddesses Meenakshi, Saraswati and Lalitha Parameshwari, a Sita, with Rama, Lakshmana and Hanuman, a

Ganesha. As the homunculi dry, she paints details onto them with kohl, crushed leaves, tamarind, turmeric, lime and ink. She anoints them, where appropriate, with holy ash, sandal and vermilion, using a lightly frayed green neem stick as a brush.

Over a few days, a small village grows in their small hall, where Janaki has created a golu stand of seven shelves, made of bricks and boards left by some previous tenant. On the floor, she places pigs, crows, puppies, a policeman, a village idiot, a labourer, a vegetable vendor, a bulk goods vendor, a Muslim shopkeeper and four musicians. Two village women argue, two pound rice grains; two men nap in the street, and two fight over a goat. A baby gets a massage; a little girl plays hide-and-seek; a couple get married. Set in a little garden of her own, one naughty little girl eats some dirt. A calf and a young Lord Krishna watch over her in attitudes of adoration.

Raghavan plays with them all. Though he's told to play gently, he breaks or loses a number of the figures. Janaki refashions them, not ungrateful for the extra demands on her time. The few neighbours who come nightly during the festival never fail to remark on the ingenious little village. The goddesses must certainly be pleased with Janaki, they tell her. Even more important for Janaki, Thangam is delighted. Janaki basks in her mother's pleasure as the small figures' industry, prosperity and cheer light the empty house.

The only gloom on their society of simple pleasures is cast by Goli. He goes out to work in the morning and returns in the evenings, giving them daytimes of freedom and evenings of trying to keep the baby quiet and out of his way. Goli does not remark on the doughy village within his residence, and Janaki thinks this is just as well. Thangam spends evenings sitting mute and inert in a corner. When neighbours come to pay visits, customary during this festival, Thangam greets them silently, while Janaki, trying to keep up appearances, offers refreshments on arrival, and a plate of turmeric, betel and vermilion as the ladies depart.

On the fifth day of the festival, a letter arrives from Sivakami. Janaki's hands shake as she steams it open, her eyes welling. It has not been easy, staying with her parents. Janaki loves Thangam in intense and complicated ways, but she loves Sivakami with a love light and clear.

The letter says Vani is playing in a special Navaratri concert series on All India Radio, to be broadcast from Madras. Vani has, since they moved, played a few concerts in Madras. She will play on the radio on the sixth night of the festival—tomorrow. Janaki's heart pounds and her mouth waters at the prospect of hearing her aunt. Sivakami says in the letter they must listen to the concert. Of course they must. Janaki will die if they don't.

When her father returns from work, Janaki hands him the letter and watches his face. She finds herself comparing him with his wedding portrait, on the wall behind him. He has the same wavy jet hair and sharp button eyes, but looks less restless now, more intent, and lines have formed on his wide, square muzzle, like big apostrophes around everything that comes out of his mouth.

He snorts, bringing her to attention.

"Yes," he says, "we *must*, we *must* hear your talented aunty."

He has said what Janaki wanted to hear, even if the quote marks around it give it some irony she doesn't understand. She scurries to prepare.

The first complication is that Munnur, where they are now stationed, is not electrified. Goli volunteers that his good friends in Konam, the closest town, own a radio and would be pleased to have them come and visit. The second complication is that the concert will run later than the last bus back to Munnur. They will stay overnight and catch the first bus at 3:30 a.m. The third is that some rule of Goli's position forbids him to overnight anywhere outside of Munnur. Goli scoffs when Janaki timorously mentions this. Janaki, well trained in strategic deceit, emphasizes to those neighbours who visit that they will return by the last bus at night. No one from the village is ever out at night, anyhow. They hope that in the morning they will be able to sneak in without the more zealous housewives and busybodies seeing them.

Janaki is bustling happily and pauses to ask Thangam if they should bring a second extra set of clothes for Raghavan and whether Thangam needs a shawl for the early-morning trip back. Thangam doesn't reply but rather looks on listlessly until Janaki stops, pursing her lips, and asks, "Akka?"

Thangam's eyes slide away beneath papery blue eyelids. She draws in a quick breath and says, "You must go and enjoy. Vani plays beautiful music."

"Akka, why, Akka?" Janaki is plaintive. "Why won't you come?"

"You are a good girl." Thangam reaches out. Her hands, which long ago were warm and golden-hued, are cold and blue-veined, white at the tips. She reaches out to lay her hands on Janaki's head and then cracks her knuckles against her own temples.

"*Chamutthu,*" she says, to accompany this touching, absurd gesture, the older person abasing herself before the perfection of the younger. "Good girl."

The gesture is commonplace—but not from Thangam. Janaki doesn't recall having ever received a sign of affection from her mother. She has wanted such a touch so badly, for so long, that her head burns where her mother's fingers stroked her. She feels small and close to tears.

In silence, Janaki prepares to go. Her mother plaits her hair tight and shiny, tying in the ribbons with gentle hands like dreams of alchemy and magic. In contrast, Sivakami's hands, the few times she has done Janaki's hair, felt rough, practical, reassuring.

Freshly pressed and dressed, in a half-sari made up of a snuff-brown silk paavaadai with cream-coloured davani, Janaki climbs into the bus behind her father. He had asked nothing when Thangam failed to accompany them out the door. But had he even noticed Janaki was there? The instant he drops into his seat, he falls asleep. Janaki, sitting in the aisle seat, watches him, his handsome head leaning against the algae-green rexine of the seat back. *In sleep,* she thinks, *he looks smaller and less dangerous than he does alive.* Oops—*awake, I mean. Why is he like he is? Why can't he just be nice?*

Less than two bumpy hours later, they arrive in Konam. Goli springs to his feet so that Janaki flies out of his way. Left behind in the queue to disembark, she gets down off the bus and looks frantically for her father. He is making a purchase, a few feet from the door of the bus—ugly, overpriced dolls. "Navaratri dolls!" the vendor is shouting while wrapping and making change. "Beautiful for your golu! Buy them all!"

"Look but don't buy," Janaki has been trained by Sivakami; her father clearly has not. His policy seems to be "Buy but don't look," she smirks to herself, then rebukes herself smartly.

They ramble toward their host's house, Goli buying sweets, flowers, magazines, generous with tips, generous with beggars. He keeps asking Janaki if she wants anything. She refuses mutely; he shrugs and buys more. He got paid the day before—Janaki had heard her parents arguing about whom he owes. The argument was short; Thangam fell silent as soon as he yelled.

Before they left the house, Thangam gave Janaki bus fare, which she tucked into the waist of her paavaadai.

They arrive at Goli's friends' house, a small bungalow set in a garden, a twenty-minute walk from the bus depot and market square, practically in the centre of town. Goli has not said how he knows these people.

They step over the threshold into the salon, a claustrophobic room crammed with several rattan-strung recliners, side tables with doilies, a mahogany display case full of dolls and the radio. While Gayatri and Minister's radio stands about two feet, on a table in Minister's upstairs salon, this one stands on the floor, almost four feet.

Janaki considers the radio the best invention ever. The gramophone she thinks a novelty item at best, though it brings music to those who are non-electrified and non-musical—because of course no machine can take the place of a veena and someone who knows how to play it. Tonight the radio will bring Vani herself, in all her mature genius. Oh, how Janaki has missed this music. Her fingertips throb, her forehead tingles, her heart is doing something akin to salivation as she waits to hear what she has heard so little in the two and a half years since Vani and Vairum moved to Madras. Before radio, only Vairum had the power to bring Vani and take her away.

Goli presents their hosts with dolls, sweets, flowers. The husband emits clucks of delight and dismissal. "Oh, you shouldn't have!" His wife raises her eyebrows as if smiling. She isn't. Janaki feels chilled. It has begun again to rain outside.

Goli and the husband sit in the chairs, Janaki in the little floor space remaining, close by the radio. The wife stands behind her husband.

Goli does not let slip a single opportunity to remind his hosts of how closely he is related to tonight's featured performer. The husband is impressed and excited. Janaki thinks maybe that little sneer mark to the right of her hostess's nose is just the way the poor woman's face is made. But when their daughter, who is about Janaki's age, comes in to say good night, the mark dissolves in a face suffused with pride and love.

The daughter sees the guests and asks, "What are they here for?"

In Tamil it is polite to refer to people in the third person, but the girl's tone is rude in any language. Her mother replies, "Their female relative is playing veena. On the radio."

The girl raises her eyebrows and scrunches her lips. She returns to the other room.

Goli says, "I'm sure your daughter would love to stay and listen! She can sit with my daughter. Vani, my own sister-in-law, would be honoured."

The sneer returns as their hostess explains, "We don't approve of Brahmin women playing in public. We would never permit our daughter to listen to such a display."

Her husband giggles as though in apology and leaps to switch on the radio, saying, "Not five minutes now! Best give it a chance to warm up!"

The radio's initial whine and crackle always make Janaki shiver with excitement. Even her hostess, whom she now hates, cannot dampen the electric thrill. The whine thins, the crackle settles like a good fire, and a sombre voice announces: V. Vani.

At the sound of tuning, Janaki closes her eyes to all those around her. The musician is unmistakably her aunt. The program mixes adventurous and conservative choices, though even the best-known songs are made unfamiliar by her aunt's rhythmic and stylistic innovations. Janaki keeps her eyes shut tight, listening for old favourites and for new songs she herself might learn.

Not bothering with an introductory varnam, Vani launches into an improvisational aalapanai in "Begada Raga," and then segues into the recital proper with "Vallabha Nayakasya," a meditative and richly emotional prayer to Lord Ganesha, god of new beginnings. Janaki recalls the little wooden Ganesha that Vairum used to keep in a lamp niche near the entrance of his and Vani's quarters. Janaki never entered their room but would see the statuette when she climbed the stairs to the roof. The roughly carved little figure was shiny with age, its back blackened with lamp smoke. Once, Janaki, curious, picked it up and was surprised at how light it was. The tiny statue went with her uncle and aunt to Madras when they moved, and Janaki felt that this signified more than anything the permanence of their leave-taking.

The second song in Vani's program is "Sakala Kala Vani," a melodious, feminine piece with tightly shaped verses, a tribute to the goddess Saraswati, one of the triumvirate of female deities whose festival they were celebrating. She wraps up the first part of the concert with a song Janaki has never heard. The announcer gives the title, "Chinnan Cheeru Killiyai Kannama," by Subramania Bharatiyar, whose name, at least, Janaki recognizes. He's not one of the ancients, but rather a Tamil nationalist poet who died not long before Janaki was born—it was an accident, she thinks, involving an elephant, maybe? Janaki has heard of musicians, recently, setting Bharatiyar's poetry to music. Listening to Vani now, she is intrigued and frustrated: each time she thinks she starts to get the raga, it seems to change. If Vani only lived with them still, Janaki would have heard her practicing. She might even have been able to play this piece by now.

She opens her eyes slowly. Her host is sitting rapt and respectful. His wife's sneer has deepened. Possibly, to be kind to her, she is unable to appreciate what she has just heard. Goli is sticking to the line that he is related to a genius.

"Marvellous, wasn't it? What virtuosity! What excellence of technique! To think, how many times have I heard her in the privacy of my mother-in-law's village home. And here she is playing for the whole of the presidency more or less. Isn't that something!" Then he stands, holding his palms together. "Well, we'd better make a move."

Janaki starts.

Their hostess looks at her and speaks to Goli, "Oh, must you?"

Janaki stammers, "We can't . . . the second half . . ." The announcer had told listeners to stay tuned through the interval—Vani would be playing "Jaggadodharana" on her return, one of her signature songs.

Goli turns on her. "Have some regard for your poor mother. She home alone. If we stay, we will surely miss the last bus. Thangam wi be worried to death." He turns to their hosts. "My wife is expecting, you know. And, of course, with the demands of my position, it really is not advisable."

The husband makes weak clucking noises to insist upon their staying, while his wife goes to fetch the vermilion to offer Janaki in farewell. Janaki tries something else.

"But . . . my grandmother will be very angry if we don't listen to the whole thing."

Goli's eyes, which always shine unfathomably, flash.

Janaki heedlessly continues, "Akka will be okay. She's not expecting us until morning . . ."

"Stop calling her Akka. She's your mother." Chop, chop, chop, hand against palm. "Don't you care for her at all? Why are you telling me what your grandmother wants? Am I not your father?" He flashes his eyes at their motionless hosts and his voice modulates into a soothing tone, somehow more frightening even than his explosion. "I know I told her we would be home in the morning." He smiles at Janaki as she shrinks from him. "We'll surprise her."

The lady of the house holds the silver plate of hospitality out to Janaki. Janaki, fuming, applies a vermilion smudge to her forehead and accepts the betel leaf.

It is better that they return that night, and Janaki knows it but doesn't know why he had earlier insisted they would not. This move to return the same night is not out of character: the only rule to Goli's behaviour appears to be that he does not keep his word.

Janaki dozes on the way home, the betel leaf crunched in her fist. Vani's music steams in her dreams and when she lifts her lids and looks through the metal shutters half-closed against the rain, she glimpses the silver moon, full and bright beyond thick clouds. The rains beat on the bus roof and become the mridangam in her dreams.

Soon enough, they arrive in Munnur and duck and dodge from tree to eave toward the tiny house. Lamps flicker in the windows. Goli says, "See? I told you she'd be waiting up for us. Good thing we . . ."

But Janaki knows Thangam wasn't expecting them until morning, and quickens her pace against the flutter of anxiety in her chest.

They bang on the door and look through the window. Thangam lies on a cot and one of the neighbours, who is with her, comes to open the locks. She tells us she was called by another neighbour when Thangam started vomiting early in the evening.

The lamps' golden glow cools and condenses as it reaches Thangam. Her brow is dewy. Father and daughter step across the threshold. Thangam opens her blue marble eyes, and Janaki's fast-beating heart is in her mouth when her mother's blue lips part: "If you had come in the morning, you would have beheld my dead body."

If you had come in the morning, you would have beheld my dead body.

"I can't hold on any longer. I'm too tired." She convulses, lips slack, eyelids small knots, nostrils flaring and closing.

Janaki runs to her side, calling out to her. "Akka, come back, Akka, my mother." Janaki tries to smooth her brow, but life pulsates under Thangam's skin, weighed down by lumps and bricks and dreams of gold, life held under the cold blue surface.

Goli pulls Janaki away and lays a finger on Thangam's shoulder. Immediately Thangam is still, as though the impulses have withdrawn, the way the touch-me-not plant closes its leaves on contact. She is still, except for a decorous, defiant throb at wrist and neck, and another life, in her belly, which kicks to be free of her.

Goli demands, diagnostically, "Too tired? Too tired how?"

No response. Raghavan sleeps on a blanket, snug and dry between three spots where rain drips through the roof. Goli swivels toward the two neighbours and begins shouting at them.

"What's going on? How long has she been sick like this?"

One tries to say what she knows, what she has seen, but Goli is pacing and muttering, every now and again returning to Thangam's prone form to say her name, "Thangam! Thangam. Thangam?" until he begins to wind down, like a gramophone record. Finally, he, too, is still. Above and around them is the chaos of the crashing rain. Janaki watches her father. For the first time that she can recall, he is still and present.

He looks at Thangam, a long time, and then he begins to speak. "Thangam? You look so different, Thangam. When did you change?

You were once so beautiful. This small house, it's a mistake. My sma.
salary, it is all the government bastards would give me. That's why I
was always trying to do more, Thangam, to get more money, so you
could have a big house. A comfortable life. This is . . . this is a mistake."

He backs away from her, toward a far corner where he unrolls a
mat, lies down and soon falls asleep.

One tear draws down from each of Thangam's closed eyes. The
rain begins to leak through the roof in a fourth place.

Janaki turns to one of the neighbours. "Mami, you must tell my
grandmother. Please, my grandmother. She must come."

If you had come in the morning, you would have beheld my dead body.
Oh no.

"I need my grandmother, please." Janaki gets the cash her grandmother gave her and holds it out. "Can someone go?"

The kind neighbours assure her, yes; one says she will send her
grown son.

Janaki sits beside her mother through the night. She presses
Thangam's legs and arms, rubs warmth into them, until the chill breaks
and fever burns through her brightly. Janaki soaks a cloth with rain-
water and lays it across Thangam's forehead, but the chill soon returns
and Janaki resumes the rubbing. All the while, she speaks encouraging
words. "Akka, you must hang on. Amma is coming. Amma is coming
and everything will be fine, but you must hang on and see her."

A leak springs above the dough village but Janaki makes no
attempt to move her creatures, and from top to bottom they melt,
sometimes in a slow bending, sometimes in a sudden collapse, until, as
morning nears, the seven shelves are coated in a cold lava strung with
puddlings of colour that were once red lips and emerald earrings, dark
hair and cheery skirts.

An hour before dawn, the young man returns. He had gone to the
next village and had a telegram sent—as quick as going himself, and
less costly. Janaki knows her grandmother forbids telegrams for any
but the worst news. She had forgotten to tell the young man. Anyway,
this may not be the worst news, but it is close. He gives her the change.

In the morning, when her father rises, Janaki prepares coffee. She
is a terrible cook, and her father makes a face as he swallows. Oh, well.

She takes the second steaming tumbler, holds it beside her mother and blows the vapours toward her, hoping that miraculous scent of richness, vigour and future unexceptional mornings will rouse her. It doesn't. Maybe the coffee is too weak; maybe Thangam is. Janaki keeps whispering in her mother's ear, as she has all night, "Amma is coming, Akka. Amma is coming, just hold on." She takes heart from the fact that Thangam has hung on, so far. Goli, saying nothing, goes to work.

On Tuesdays and Fridays, girls have oil baths. Today Janaki must administer her own, for the first time ever. She sniffs a little with self-pity as she works the oil through her hair as best she can, and goes to rub it out with soap-nut powder in the bath, leaving Raghavan and her mother under a neighbour's watch.

She comes back into the main hall, holding both ends of the thin cotton towel and snapping it against her hair, from neck to waist, then binding the hair into the towel so that it makes a knot the size of three hearts at the nape of her neck. She and her sisters certainly have been blessed with hair, she most of all.

Thangam is lying waxen and small on her cot, burning again with the fever.

Raghavan awakens and wants his mother. Janaki consoles him, giving him sweet milk, bathing him and singing "Jaggadodharana," with its lyrics about Lord Krishna: *His mother plays with him, as though he is no more than her precious child.* It is raining too hard to go outside. They play with pots and pans and two of the dolls their father bought. Janaki makes as much noise as he does. She wants their mother to hear them playing.

The servant comes to sweep and mop, quiet and fearful. When she leaves, Janaki breathes, relief: morning is past and Thangam is still alive. If she can just hold on until evening—they're only five hours from Cholapatti, so Sivakami should be here by what, five or six?

She removes the towel and mechanically binds just the ends of her hair, which is now so little damp it feels not so much wet as heavy. The small knot hits the back of her thighs, the hair loose enough to finish drying, but not unbound, since a woman's hair should never be unbound except when she performs her parents' funeral rites. "The

sight of a woman with unbound hair strikes sadness into all hear
Sivakami, very strict in this regard, would say.

Janaki scrapes the doughy mass that was the golu into some newspapers and tosses it out behind the house. The neighbour comes,
brings food and plays with Raghavan. Janaki again makes sure they do
it close to Thangam. They unshroud the gramophone and play each
record three times. The laughing one sounds stranger each time: at
first it sounds eerie, the second time as if it's mocking them. By the
third playing, it doesn't even sound like laughter any more.

The neighbour leaves to prepare her family's tiffin. Janaki isn't
hungry but feeds Raghavan. She sits by her mother and sings the first
two songs from last night's concert, which feels so long ago. She tries to
hum "Chinnan Cheeru Killiyai Kannama" but can't remember how it
goes. The baby inside Thangam seems to wake, kicking and swimming.

Five o'clock, six o'clock, seven o'clock . . . the cuckoo, which
Janaki is coming to hate, pops out each hour to announce to her that
her grandmother still has not come.

Thangam is breathing but not moving. She looks bluer and bluer,
or is that the fallen night? Janaki lights a lamp for warmth.

There is a knock. She leaps and unbolts the door, but it's her
father. He thrusts a paper packet into her hand. "Here."

Veeboothi—he must have passed a temple on his rounds. Janaki
carries it to Thangam, smears it on her forehead, throat and belly, and
puts a pinch between her lips. Previously, it would have shown grey
against gold; now it merely dulls the waxy blue surface of Thangam's
skin. Janaki rubs it in but the ash resolves into nubbins and disperses
into flakes, refusing to absorb.

Janaki serves her father the food the neighbour has brought. For a
second unending, undying night, Janaki sits beside her mother. She
prays without ceasing, saying Shakti Mata, Durga Mata, Saraswati
whose names are Uma, Vani, Saradha and nine hundred and ninety-
eight more. *Bring me my grandmother, oh don't let my mother die*. She
looks at the Saraswati calendar she hung on the wall, the face of the
goddess sweet and impartial.

She presses her mother's legs, holds her hand and strokes her forehead while her father sleeps. Her little brother sleeps, his golden eyes

nut tight. She doesn't know why Amma has not come. She fears she has been abandoned. She fears the rain rain rain has washed the world away, washed the universe clean, shining, empty. All the people she loves, all those she doesn't love, all washed away. Are they all alone, too, waiting for one another? Are they all together, waiting for her? Is she late and are they wondering what is keeping her? Has the rain washed her away, too, clean and empty, no guilt no ambition no short history of minor transgressions no unwanted wisdom left to pollute her and tear her gently limb from limb?

They are nine who issued from this womb that is even now still pulsing, poking and bumping, though not as much as before—the stubbornness, the wilfulness, perhaps diminishing. They are nine, and those kicks are of the tenth, but Janaki is sitting alone with only the soft whistle of her brother's nose to remind her that there are others too who will be orphaned to the world in the swirling raining dark.

But dark always turns to light and it does this time, too. The rain stops; morning breaks grey and awful. Janaki does not move. Her mother is still; her father is still sleeping.

―☙―

SIVAKAMI DIDN'T GO TO HEAR VANI'S RADIO CONCERT, but the children did, at Gayatri and Minister's house. That night, though, the sixth of the Navaratri festival, Sivakami didn't sleep at all. She rarely sleeps much, but the first couple of nights of the festival had been good and tired her out. From the third night, though, she had been waking with feelings of dread and finally, this night, couldn't muster the will to sleep. For the first time ever, she made mistakes in her beading, giving a poor cow five eyes before she realized what she had done.

Muchami arrived at 3:45, as every morning, and they walked to the Kaveri, where, as always, she bathed in the dark while he stood guard. This morning, as happens sometimes, she was accompanied at the river by a slim figure in diaphanous white, not unlike her own. It floated above the opposite bank, bobbing a bit like a current or breeze. The first time it happened, thirty years ago, she had asked

Muchami who it was. "Probably Mariamman," he had shrugged. Sivakami normally takes comfort in the village goddess's presence, though she thinks she shouldn't, since these Dravidian deities are generally malicious. The goddess had, however, meant no harm before this—or not succeeded in causing any. Why was Sivakami unsettled by her on this day?

At the house, she hung up her wet garment and readied her brass pot and travelling bundle in dread certainty.

This is the thirty-fourth year since the marriage of the girl of gold, the year the astrologers foretold for her death, and when the telegram came, Sivakami didn't wail or gnash.

THANGAM MAMI SERIOUS STOP COME AT ONCE STOP

The first births added years to Thangam's life, the astrologers had told Sivakami. The last births took them off again.

Sivakami took the telegram and walked the half-furlong to Gayatri's house. It must have been more than thirty years since she had walked on the street of the Brahmin quarter in daylight. Her feet felt detached, her body bobbing lightly above them, floating diaphanous white.

Minister read the telegram, set about replying, organized the journey. Muchami assisted. Sivakami returned home to awaken Laddu, Kamalam, Radhai, Krishnan and Sita, who was seven months pregnant and home for her bangle ceremony, to what might be the worst day of their young lives. On the way home, she encountered Rukmini, doing her kolam, and told her to prepare to travel.

By mid-morning, the party boarded the train. Muchami was made to stay behind for the sake of matters quotidian. On the platform, as the train gathered speed, he raised his face and, with the force of his eyes, gazed them safely out of the station.

They rocked silently in the carriage, all faintly nauseated. The atmosphere was so moist they felt they could chew it to slake their throats. Ten minutes out of Salem, the turgid air exploded into drops, stinging their warm faces like forgiveness as they shut the windows against the storm.

The closer they got to Munnur, the stronger the rain. Dismounting in the little station, they found the earth around the unsheltered platform eroded into sharp cliffs descending to choppy brown seas. They waited while Minister inquired of the station master, a droopy little man in a cubicle, where they might find the revenue inspector's home. He seemed at first reluctant to divulge directions, and Minister suspected him of being involved in one of Goli's schemes, holding a grudge or wanting to protect him. Then he realized that the station master was simply worried about their ability to negotiate the passage, which would involve walking about four furlongs, crossing the river and walking another furlong on the other side. With some relief, Minister dismissed the man's worries and set out, lifting the smaller children down from the platform and hurrying everyone up the flooded road-way, all the children's hands grasped tight. It was soon clear that the man's fears were justified, but, by a hundred yards, the rain descending like screens, the water filling their eyes, they could barely make out the station behind them and so pressed forward to the river, where they paused on her banks in respect and dismay.

The Kaveri was swollen and rough and in a lethal mood. It was mid-afternoon but even with the light at its highest, the streaming rain obscured the opposite bank. Minister, feeling valiant, made as though he would swim across, but Sivakami forbade it. Even in calm moods, this river made sport of men in the prime of their lives. Sivakami herded them into some bankside groves to shelter.

Curious villagers ventured forth and expressed sorrow when they learned of the circumstances. They were not so irreverent as to offer the travellers their homes—this was the non-Brahmin side of the village—but they brought sheets of thatch to shelter them and fruits Brahmins may eat without fear of pollution. The villagers told the party that the rain would clear by morning, when they would be able to cross by *parasal*, a round boat towed by swimmers.

Within an hour, Visalam arrived from Karoor with her baby and husband. The sympathetic villagers clucked and cooed and set up a baby hammock between some bamboo stalks, with a waterproof cross-hatch of thatch to protect the child from the elements.

Just before dark, Saradha came from Thiruchinapalli. After midnight, the rain ceased and the sky began to thin. The moon, thought Sivakami, was weak from crying. She shook the thought off disdainfully. She alone was awake in the party to recognize stooped and purposeful gait of her son approaching on the riverli road, Vani glowing beside him. Now Sivakami's tears began to fall, hard as the rain, from both eyes. Vairum and Vani approached, and Vani fell to embrace Sivakami's feet. Sivakami put her hands on Vani's shoulders and raised her into an embrace. Vairum said nothing but waited to speak until his mother's eyes were dry, the tears wiped away by Vani.

"I have spoken to several villagers," he said then, soft and brusque. "I believe we must wait until morning to cross."

Vani pressed Sivakami's hands and Sivakami leaned her forehead against that of her son's wife. They waited for the dawn.

Before dawn, all did their ablutions, the men saying the daily prayer for illumination, and then light broke saffron in the east. Six village men appeared, carrying a round, shallow boat of woven reeds, which they held at the river's edge. Sivakami, Minister and Laddu got in. Laddu tried to insist he would swim, but Vairum forbade it. When the village men tied gourds around their waists as life preservers, though, Vairum and Sita's husband did the same, and took places at the boat's side as they began towing the boat across. By the time the sun laid its palms on the water's surface, the first party was halfway across.

Through her fear, Sivakami wondered where Vairum learned to swim so well. She had made him pledge, when he left for college, that he would never swim in the Kaveri. She didn't need to ask him to study, to be frugal, to eschew bad habits. Vairum rose on the other bank, braced his hands on his knees and coughed. He turned toward Thangam's house. *At least there are no predictions against his life,* Sivakami thought. *None that I know of.*

Yesterday, Janaki had not felt the day on her face except in the hour before dawn when she did the kolam that the rain washed away even as the powder descended from her fist. Today she does not do kolam but opens the door only after the light is full. And opens her eyes wide because Laddu is running toward her up the road. He pants the news out hoarsely: "We are here, we are all here, we couldn't cross the river yesterday evening, too flooded, we had to wait for light . . ." His hands are on his knees as he stoops to catch his breath. "Parasals—they are bringing the others across."

Next comes Vairum. He strides first to the doorway where she is standing, her hair loose around her. Vairum goes past her into the house and looks at his sister lying blue on the cot, her womb an expectant silence.

Goli sits up in the spot where he has been sleeping, his forehead in his hands, cradling his big dreams. He looks up to see his wife's brother. He puts his head back in his hands.

Vairum runs back up the road without a word to them. He passes his mother and tells her, "She is there—go up the road, you will see the house. I'm going to fetch help."

He swims back across with the parasal, faster than riding in it. The villagers take a collective step back as he ascends the bank before them like a minor god and sets off in the direction of the rail station.

Sivakami places her feet carefully in the streaming road. She looks up to see where she must go and staggers, firebursts of fear in her tired eyes: here is Kali, goddess of destruction, her hair loose and rising about her, mouth open—Kali, running on water, bounding death.

No, it's Janaki. Just a little girl, helpless and scared, her hair streaming. What is she, after all, just fourteen? Fourteen years old. She is crying with sadness because her mother is dying, and with relief, even joy, because now she can say so. The world still exists; they didn't abandon her.

Her loose hair is stuck to her face and as Sivakami clears it from her mouth, Janaki suddenly becomes conscious of it and binds the ends together. Sivakami squeezes Janaki's arms, pats her back. They walk back together, Janaki holding her grandmother's arm. Once, Sivakami slips on the sliding invisible earth and Janaki steadies her.

Sivakami knows none of the people in the house, but she does not resent them. Sickness always draws a crowd. A pathway through the mass appears for her and at its end, the waxy blue figure of her daughter. Sivakami strokes Thangam's cheeks as though drawing out sadness, kisses her fingers where they touched her daughter and asks, "Enn'idhu, kanna?"

What is it, dear one? What brought you to this pass?

Janaki moves to a corner and slumps down, cradled by two walls and the floor. She thinks her grandmother and mother, alone in the nattering crowd, look like an island in the Kaveri, a still, holy place in the mad rushing river. Her neck softens and she drops into sleep.

Some three hours later, a beefy white face appears in the door. Everyone stops talking. Many are trying to remember whether they owe taxes.

But he is not a revenue officer, he is the district medical officer whom Vairum has fetched, along with two junior doctors to assist. Three white doctors, everyone whispers. This is the kind of influence Vairum exerts now. Such doctors come with strings attached: Vairum has evidently pulled some.

The DMO asks that everyone clear out. They laugh at his excellent Tamil and go, except Sivakami, who refuses to leave her daughter alone with these strange men. She resists efforts at persuasion, saying, "I know: they are doctors. They are good men, and they have come a great distance, but anything they have to do, they can do in my presence."

Vairum takes her aside and explains to her that she is an ignorant woman and the doctors need freedom to work. Sivakami says nothing, her lips set as tight as if sealed with wax, and finally, for the first time, his logic and will are bettered by her determination.

The DMO nods, impatient. "It's fine, sir, please. I can do the work with the lady present, as long as she doesn't interfere. I quite understand." He waves Vairum out the door.

Several neighbours try to rouse Janaki to come out with them. She resists unconsciously. Her eyelids twitch and she mumbles but does not awaken. They shake her, speak gently, then fiercely, until Sivakami says, "Leave her. She's not in the way." She looks to the DMO, her ally. He nods resignedly. So Janaki remains, a crumpled pile of hair and clothes, in the corner.

The nurse from up the road arrives, looking very hastily washed and combed, though it is approaching eleven o'clock. Her lethargy is legendary. Vairum had rapped on her door and called for her as he and the doctors waded up the road from the crossing point: the DMO had asked for a nurse and she is the only one, locally.

The DMO asks Sivakami to put some water on to boil. She does, compliant but suspicious, as the nurse, shaking her head, closes the bottoms of the shutters against the many who watch unashamedly from without. The DMO checks Thangam's pulse again and turns apologetically to Sivakami to explain, in his blocky, grammatical Tamil, "I must now check on the baby. I, have, concerns."

Sivakami squints in incomprehension then closes her eyes when she understands. No one in their family has ever been seen by a doctor. She knows there are woman doctors for women patients, but it's too late to get one. She knows she cannot interfere and knows it doesn't matter, that Thangam will not have to account for this loss of modesty.

The DMO checks: there is no sign of dilation. The instruments are boiled. He performs a Caesarean.

A girl. Big. Blue. Dead. Gently and with regret, they hand her to her grandmother. The child's blue lips are sealed stubborn and resistant in a frozen face. Sivakami looks deep into the lost eyes of her daughter's last child. She thinks she sees a gold band around the pupil narrow, fade to blue, and then to black. Sivakami carries the baby out the back of the tiny house.

After sewing Thangam up, the DMO palpates her throat, feels her forehead, opens her eyelids one at a time and looks into her eyes. He feels she is far away, already. He looks up at Sivakami and asks, "How many children does she have?"

"She has nine children, and five grandchildren."

"How can it be?" he murmurs, as if kind and gallant. "She looks so young."

But when he looks back at her, she looks very old. He blinks to clear a film and again she looks terribly young. Tragic, these people. He lifts her lids again and again checks the pulse at her wrist. He is buying time. The other two doctors are waiting for orders.

He says to Sivakami, "I will try," and reaches for a phial and a needle.

But he is lying. Her illness is serious and, as far as he knows, unnamed. He looks at his eager assistants, who are waiting for some instruction. He believes there is nothing he can do and believes the wee widow watching him knows this, too.

In his professional opinion, he needs to inoculate this dying woman with faith. He is a skeptical Christian but understands these people have their ways. He shakes the phial of saline and tries to think of it as liquid faith. It could work, in this country where so much happens that he cannot explain. He shakes the bottle faster, willing a catalysis within the worthless liquid, imbuing it with that chthonic quantity this woman needs to live. He shakes and shakes—the junior doctors are looking puzzled—shakes—he doesn't look at Sivakami's careworn face— shakes—he maintains a look of diagnostic concentration—shakes.

Chime! The clock rings out. The cuckoo pops. One o'clock. The phial takes flight, out of the DMO's hand, between the inclined heads of the neatly groomed junior doctors, to shatter against the picture of the goddess Saraswati on the wall calendar beside the window.

Janaki sits bolt upright from sleep. She hears her mother make a rattling growl.

Then Thangam is dead.

The tall white doctor opens the door and walks outside, and leans his forehead against a palm. Those who saw him claimed he cried a little, but that makes no sense.

The others cry, then, except Sivakami. She hears the wails of her grandchildren rise and fall in waves. She sees Janaki lower her head in the corner and recognizes, with a stab, that while joy can be shared, grief must be borne alone. She hears little Raghavan begin screaming and thinks, *He must be frightened.* She hears Murthy, gasping, "Gold. She was our pure gold, and we have lost her."

Sivakami goes to the back to bathe, dousing herself with water head to toe, as one must when a relative dies. As the others follow, she helps the nurse to tidy the room. She wipes the liquid from the face of the goddess of wisdom and music. It looks like tears, or like rosewater sprinkled in worship. Could that elixir have saved Thangam? Doubtful. Sivakami has little faith in medicine. No faith in that stuff she wipes from Saraswati's cheeks and the crumbling wall and the rain-damp floor.

31.
Gold to Ash
1940

WHEN MUCHAMI SAW SIVAKAMI and the family off at the train, he did so with some certain knowledge that he would not be seeing Thangam again. Sivakami told him, *The year has arrived,* in the way she sometimes talked to him: as though it were not too different from talking to herself.

The day after they left, Muchami was supervising the gathering of coconuts in Rukmini's garden. Rukmini and Murthy had recently engaged a new servant and they didn't trust him not to take a share. A small gang of his youngest relatives kept him company—the youngest sons and eldest grandsons of those boys who guarded Vairum in the days of his earliest persecutions. The children, inspired by a bunch of young coconuts hanging low to the ground, started clamouring for coconut water.

The coconut gatherers were taking a break, squatting in the garden. Muchami asked if he could borrow a scythe. Though a cut above his caste—agricultural labourers, generally handy with the implements of harvest—Muchami is not good with knives. He started lopping off coconut tops, concentrating visibly, his palms sweating. The labourers giggled as he handed the first off to the children, a rough hole hacked off the top, and some of the water spilt. He had just started on the second, determined to give his young cousins this treat himself, when from within the house the grandfather clock struck one o'clock.

Muchami startled. The scythe went awry and split the coconut lengthwise from tip to tip along one side. Falling to the ground, it yawed slightly, water slopping out, tears from a nearly closed eye. Muchami had nicked himself, and tried to staunch his thumb. He didn't know why the clock should return him to thoughts of Sivakami's mission, but he had a sudden feeling it was complete.

⁓ ☙

IN MUNNUR, THE FAMILY PERFORMS Thangam's last rites. Her body is cremated at a ghat downriver. The cremation grounds attendant, a bored and ill-tempered dwarf, pokes the pyre to ensure thorough incineration. His son, a tall boy, handsome enough to be in movies, assists.

Six priests chant around another fire in the small salon of the last house where Thangam lived. The house is filled with the mournful, waxy smell of things sacrificed to the flames: ghee, holy water, flowers, puffed rice. Thangam's ashes are gathered, and Laddu, looking solemn and unfamiliar, carries the urn to the river. An entourage surrounds and trails him—his siblings with their spouses and children, Vairum, Vani, Goli, Murthy and Rukmini, Minister and Gayatri, some neighbours.

As Laddu wades out into the current, he stumbles and begins to cry. Behind him, Murthy wails, "We have lost our purest gold, our darling!"

Saradha and Rukmini whimper agreement; Gayatri, her head bowed, stands behind her husband, weeping and not watching. The urn exhales several puffs of ash against the cool light of the season before Laddu tips its contents into the river's flow.

Sivakami, watching from the bank, recalls the first time she saw Thangam's strange golden dust silting the narrow gutter that leads from the bath. The dust would shift with the water but was so heavy buckets were needed to move it along into the drain. Now, Thangam's particulate remains, light as anyone's, float out and away in seconds. A thin ashen sheet billows in the air before dropping to follow the rest.

Sivakami's eldest brother died some three years back, but the next two brothers come and observe mourning with the family, repeating, as does Murthy, platitudes on the nobility of Thangam's death. Sivakami grits her teeth and says nothing. If it were anyone else's daughter, she would be saying the same sorts of things.

Rukmini tends Krishnan, who, at five, may not be entirely certain what has happened. He has lived with Sivakami since his younger brother's birth; Sivakami made the argument that Thangam could not handle two boys, and Thangam did not protest. Also, Sivakami believes that boys should be coddled, to give them confidence and a strong feeling of home. Girls don't need either, she reasons, since they don't need to meet and do business with the outside world. Because Laddu needed discipline, Sivakami had not been able to indulge him to the degree she would have liked, and fears that, as a result, he may have turned out nervous and remote. Krishnan, a brighter and more sensitive boy, gives her some hope of restitution.

It has been two years since Krishnan last saw Thangam, and as far as Sivakami can tell, he has forgotten her. He spends every day with Rukmini, who is childless and has lived alone with Murthy since her mother-in-law died. The little boy has become the light of her days and their companionship is as intimate as any between mother and child. It pains Sivakami and also makes her glad to see Krishnan so little affected by his mother's passing.

Raghavan, however, had not been fully weaned when Thangam died. Though he accepts cups of warm, sweetened cow's milk from his sisters, he sucks on their sleeves and bites their shoulders, crying for comfort they can't give him.

Janaki feels sad at her mother's passing, but also guilty. She wonders whether her sisters feel similarly. While they are motherless in a sense, she thinks, their state is not too different from before: they are still reliant on their grandmother, vulnerable to their uncle, suspicious of their father. Janaki and Kamalam still crave physical affection, a craving finally satisfied in the elder sisters now that they have children of their own. Radhai is just now getting too big to sit on Muchami's knee.

Sivakami watches Vairum and Goli circle, keeping their animosity within the limits of decorum. Goli is sullen but remains present for all the ceremonies where he is required.

During the day, Sivakami remains composed, busy cooking for fifteen people and watching the ceremonies. At night, her sense of devastation returns as if to feed on her. *I thought if I lightened her burden,* she thinks, *she might hang on.* And, *The horoscopes have defied me once again.*

On one of these nights, Vairum, rising to relieve himself, finds her huddled in a corner, her face hidden in shade, her body illuminated by moonlight. She sleeps directly on the cement floor, its grey turned shades of blue by the night, but now, at three, she is sitting up and weeping.

He pauses before her, hands on hips. "You think she died of a bad horoscope," he says, his voice ringing quietly. All the other family members sigh and snore, asleep in the hall behind him. He shakes his head. "May the day come when you admit it was his loutishness that killed her, not the stars."

Sivakami wipes her tears, then puts her hand to her forehead, not looking at him.

"I will arrange the marriages of my sister's remaining daughters," Vairum swears, standing over her. "I will . . ." he chokes, this little boy who swore never to take from his sister, only to give, and who, as she lay dying, could not give her what she needed any more than his mother could. "I will arrange their marriages on terms rational and religious," he sputters. "No more horoscopes. Let people take responsibility for their actions."

Thirteen days after Thangam's death, the priests are paid and a feast prepared to bid the soul pass on.

The next day, the Cholapatti folk make ready to return. Thangam's elder daughters will also go back there for a time with their children. Goli goes out at some point—no one sees him leave. Presumably, he has gone to back to work, his bereavement leave concluded. They are milling around, feeling it rude not to have bid him farewell, but Vairum hustles them to the train mid-afternoon, reminding them that Goli did not pay them the same courtesy.

At the Cholapatti station, they ask the children of the station master to run and alert Muchami to their arrival so that he can bring the bullock cart. When Sivakami sees Muchami's familiar silhouette emerge from the now-solid dark, she feels herself relax and come close to tears again.

Muchami jumps down and, putting his palms together and bowing quickly to them several times, sets about loading the baggage. Sivakami gets into the cart first, without saying anything to him. The family had not communicated with him from Munnur, knowing that he would intuit the reason for so long an absence. He fusses over them, asking, "Are you comfortable?"

Vairum has mounted the front. When Muchami hops up beside him and takes the reins, he asks, "So, Vairum, everything taken care of?" Vairum nods perfunctorily. Muchami glances one last time over his shoulder before starting. He catches Sivakami's eye, and his face crumples.

"Our gold," he whispers, turning to the front. He twitches the rein against the bullocks backs with a "tch-tch" to get them started. "Pure gold. Such a good girl."

"Yes, yes," Vairum sighs. "She deserved much better."

Muchami weeps audibly for the duration of the trip home while the occupants of the cart behind him are silent, having spent much of their grief during the formal mourning period and being tired from travel. Muchami is far less demonstrative than many servants in his position, who would weep for form's sake, as servants are supposed to weep for masters, more even than for their own families. Sivakami knows him to be sincere, knows he feels exactly as she does: that while Thangam's marriage may have killed her—by whatever means— Sivakami had no choice and did the best she could have done.

32.
Not Another Mother
1940

THE NEXT DAY, hordes of Brahmins from up and down the quarter come to pay condolences. Sivakami wishes she were more like others, like her granddaughter Saradha, for instance, who clearly takes comfort in hearing the same encomiums repeated again and again by people who barely knew Thangam. Instead, as when Hanumarathnam died, Sivakami wishes they would all keep quiet, or, better yet, stay away.

When Muchami's and Mari's families come to the back to pay respects, gnashing and screeching as is appropriate in their community, Sivakami wonders if it is within her rights to tell them to leave. Out of consideration for Muchami and Mari, she doesn't. But Mari does—telling her parents and her mother-in-law that their histrionics are not needed. Mari herself, when she arrived that morning, expressed her condolences to Sivakami with quiet dignity and went about her chores.

In the days after they return from Munnur, little Krishnan takes to sleeping at Rukmini's house. By the time Sivakami is fully aware that it has become a habit, she is not sure how to break it. It seems cruel to deny a motherless child all he is receiving from Rukmini: he accompanies her in every activity; at home, he sits in her lap; they play games, have secret jokes and a code language. Rukmini makes sweets for him daily and bids him bring his sisters to eat them.

Sivakami is in a quandary: she wants Krishnan to enjoy these attentions, but she feels she must remain responsible, in certain ways, for his moral and physical upkeep. She also thinks Rukmini might be too soft, too grateful for Krishnan's presence, to hold to certain old-fashioned child-raising practices.

So Sivakami requires that Krishnan come to take his breakfast at her house: pazhiah sadam, day-old rice, mixed with yogourt—the best thing for a young tummy. One of his sisters feeds him—Sivakami herself cannot touch it because it is kept to ferment overnight. Every Wednesday and Saturday, she insists he comes to take his oil bath and, every few months, a dose of castor oil. In other words, she asks only that Krishnan complete the severer and less pleasant of his basic requirements at her house because the sense of discipline and plain living these impart—the gifts of a conservative upbringing—will remain the measure of his origins.

Sivakami is motivated by concern not only for Krishnan's well-being, but also for the family's. "A house that gives a son for adoption has no sons for seven generations." The proverb reverberates in her conscience. Krishnan is with her for safekeeping; he belongs to the house of his father. Rukmini may tend him further, but she cannot be allowed to feel he is her son.

Rukmini understands Sivakami's concerns, though she doesn't think about them too deeply. She is flattered by the violent resistance Krishnan displays whenever his sisters come to fetch him. While she doesn't interfere with their missions, neither does she assist.

Krishnan is always reluctant to leave Rukmini—she is his favourite person. He doesn't respond to cajoling nor to ordering. He is becoming the boy Sivakami meant him to be: precious and headstrong. Nor can his sisters bribe him—little they offer can compete with his treatment at Rukmini's. Increasingly, they resort to tricks to get him to come home. Fortunately, Janaki proves herself a master of minor deceptions, and enjoys devising them—for a good cause, of course.

Sita stays on to keep company with her family and give them comfort in the wake of Thangam's death. (Or so goes the protocol. Sita's specialty has always been discomfort, and relative marital happiness has not gentled her. Her husband is a stable, timid man, a compiler of agricultural statistics who admires and resents her. She is not interested in his feelings, but his behaviour suits her well and she has seen no need to change hers.) When she is the one sent to fetch Krishnan, she blackmails him, explaining to him in a low, sincere voice that unless he comes with her immediately, she will fix it so that he never sees Rukmini again. Krishnan listens, wide-eyed, without reason to disbelieve her, and obeys.

"Poor Akka," she remarks the Friday after their return to Cholapatti, as she and her sisters sit, after their oil bath, drying their hair.

"Mm-hm," says Janaki, peering critically at her embroidery, a bouquet of flowers, none of which she recognizes. She drew the pattern after a photo in one of Minister's books on English gardens.

"Forced to give up her children one by one like that," Sita continues.

Janaki and Kamalam are silent, Janaki looking at Sita, Kamalam lying on a cot with her hair fanned and falling over the edges, incense burning beneath to perfume it.

"I could never." Sita shakes her head. "I'd rather die."

"Well, she didn't give us up." Janaki finally rises to the bait. "Amma just looked after us for them because Appa's job . . ."

Sita points at Janaki. "Vairum Mama stole us because he's jealous."

"No—" Janaki starts.

"And because he hates Appa. He would do anything to sabotage Appa. Poor Appa, just trying to make an honest living, and he has this business shark for a brother-in-law."

Janaki tries again lamely. "What—"

"Is your hair on fire, Kamalam?" Sita inquires sprightly.

Kamalam, who had let her eyes drift shut, springs up, trembling.

"Oh," Sita laughs, "I guess it was just the incense smoke. You know I never think you wash the oil out properly. Can't blame me for worrying!"

Janaki stands. "You look like you could use a nap, Sitakka." She gestures to Kamalam with her head and starts for the veranda. "Don't you feel tired?"

"No," Sita replies. "Where are you two going?"

Around this time, Murthy invites some cousins to stay with him and Rukmini. Down on their luck, as so many Brahmins are these days, they had lost their lands and home, and approached Murthy at a wedding a month or two earlier and appealed to him for assistance.

"We must help our own." Rukmini parrots her husband's words to Sivakami the day before the cousins arrive. "So much assistance available to those low-caste types, but Brahmins are as poor as they ever were and no one thinks about what services they give! Who will assist them?"

Sivakami agrees and congratulates her on their generosity. They are not the wealthiest family in the Brahmin quarter—that status has always been reserved for Minister's family, though she suspects Vairum might have exceeded even them, not that it has changed her lifestyle or the children's. Murthy and Rukmini are comfortable, though, and childless, and live modestly in a spacious house, built for the large, extended family that has dwindled to these two over the course of three short generations.

These relatives are expected to arrive by bus, and the next day, Murthy, a splash of betel-stained spittle ornamenting his fresh-pressed kurta, borrows Sivakami's bullock cart to meet them. When he returns the cart, he brings them in to meet her. They huddle together as if persecuted and have to be bid to enter several times, Sivakami calling from the pantry.

They have been travelling and need to bathe, they protest in whimpers. The wife is barely four foot nine, and her husband perhaps two inches taller. Their faces are pinched and ingratiating, their clothing poor. Their son, a strapping, touchy-looking youth, carries their little baggage.

"Welcome," says Sivakami with energetic friendliness, inspired by Rukmini and Murthy's caste feeling to ensure they feel warmly received. She sends Janaki and Kamalam out toward them, one with a tray of tumblers of water, the other with plates of snacks. "Eat something small at least. And you must come take a meal here soon. Our home is yours, just as it is Rukmini and Murthy's."

The couple, who had been casting looks of rapid appraisal at the Ramar, the safe and the girls' jewellery, thank her, wagging their heads so vigorously their bodies move. The son smiles meanly and turns to go.

"Ugh," Sita shudders, when they have barely gone. "Unattractive lot!"

"No more out of you, young lady!" Sivakami's sharpness startles both her and her granddaughters. "They are in need and it is an act of good to give charity. Rukmini and Murthy will do well in their next lives."

Sita doesn't retort but later tells Janaki, "I'm all in favour of caste solidarity, but I have a bad feeling about them."

Just because Sita said it, Janaki feels compelled to disagree. Privately, though, she fears Sita intuits malignancy all too accurately.

———⌒〇⌒———

WHAT A STRANGE FEW MONTHS this has been for our dear ones on the Brahmin quarter, Sivakami thinks, a couple of months later. January is drawing in, with the Pongal holiday. They won't celebrate this festival, nor any other, for a year, while they are in mourning.

In September, Thangam's death. Then, last month, Gayatri's mother-in-law had decided someone had hidden a cobra in her bun, and tried to use the scythe to cut off her hair. She killed herself—not as quickly as would have been merciful, but still, it was a relief to the family and probably to the old woman herself, who had for years been living in an increasing state of paranoia.

And now Rukmini is ill. She has been suffering from a severe digestive affliction since about the time Murthy's cousins came to stay with them. At first, it had seemed no more than heartburn. Rukmini confided in Sivakami: she feared her cousin-in-law's cooking didn't agree with her. The cousin was helping in the kitchen. Her cooking tasted wonderful, and it was nice to eat someone else's food. The cousin cooked Thanjavur-style, and the flavours were quite exotic. But Rukmini had grown scared of eating. She was mystified. The vegetables were not undercooked. She was being served items in the correct order. She had worried that perhaps the cousin-in-law was violating rules of *ecchel*, the contamination of saliva, and *patthu*, the contamination of cooked food, which orthodox Brahmins observe strictly. What if she was insufficiently superstitious, one of these progressive sorts, and so was not washing her hands after touching cooked rice, for instance? But the cook, who watched her, said she was quite above board. And no one else in the household was in any discomfort. Rukmini's stomach alone bloated and kicked after every meal.

And it grew large: it was only when Sivakami began noticing Rukmini's tummy that she inquired. Rukmini had been a sturdy woman, with the flat stomach and well-proportioned hips that are the preserve of childless women. Now she has grown considerably thinner, though her tummy has inflated like a rubber tire.

When Sivakami told Rukmini she was not looking well, Rukmini didn't understand, because saying someone has grown thin is also used as a formality, a greeting, to show concern. So it took a few tries before Sivakami could make clear that she genuinely thought Rukmini was looking very thin and that her swelling stomach might be a cause for concern. She asked if, perhaps, Rukmini could, after all these years, be pregnant. Rukmini laughed and blushed, clapped her cheeks and made slapping motions in the air with her hands.

"No, no," she said, "I'm not pregnant. Really, the thought!" She lowered her voice to a whisper. "You remember, Janaki came to help me just two weeks ago—I still get my monthlies."

Sivakami shrugged. "Sometimes—rarely, but I've heard of it— women get their periods even when they're pregnant. Or at least bleed a little."

"Possibly," Rukmini said politely, "but I really don't think I'm pregnant. I don't feel any different. Just a bit weak, maybe."

Sivakami gave her some holy ash from Palani mountain, known for its potency in expelling unwanted foreign bodies while strengthening desirable ones. She also told Rukmini to drink a broth nightly of her brother Venketu's patented Cure-All Concentrate™, as a purgative and blood-thickener. She had many extra jars, since Venketu's wife sent a care package of their products every time a granddaughter came to Sivakami's house to give birth.

Sivakami also advised Rukmini to take doses of their gripe water, since she had developed a terrible gas problem. Sometimes Sivakami herself would hear, from within her own house, Rukmini's prodigiously windy emissions. Neighbourhood children shamelessly imitated the poor woman's range of belches and farts. The sound rose even above the wash of the canal.

Rukmini conscientiously followed every prescription, but her misery did not abate. Her tummy was hard to the touch. She looked like a dying willow with a parasitic fungus clinging to its trunk.

As if all this weren't hard enough on a woman's vanity, Rukmini's hair began coming out in handfuls. Rukmini's hair had always been a bit thin, and she owned a couple of hairpieces, for special occasions. Now her own measly strands were barely sufficient to hold them on. Finally, she was reduced to sheltering her pate under her sari end, like a widow or Muslim. She was misery incarnate. Her only joy was Krishnan.

So Sivakami's heart burned at the thought of tearing Krishnan from Rukmini's bony bosom. How could she? How could she not?

Three nights running, Sivakami has awoken from the same dream, her heart thrumming and brow running with it, clear and cryptic as a telegram.

In the dream, Rukmini's long-dead mother-in-law, Annam, looked at an illustrated catalogue of hairpieces. The pieces kept trying to scurry away off the pages and into the scrub. The mother-in-law seemed to be charged with minding them, though she would occasionally pick one up and tug at it until it loosened a bit and then study it, flattening it or holding it up to the sun, making the hairpiece whimper or shriek.

Sivakami was puzzled: Annam was a widow when she died, and so she appeared in the dream, with a head stubbly as a coconut. A widow has no need or use for hairpieces. Annam replied that soon her daughter-in-law would come and take the hair from her stomach. Oh, said Sivakami. So Rukmini's stomach is full of hair? Yes, said Annam, she will come and take the hair from her stomach and fashion it into hairpieces.

Sivakami tried reason, the worst tactic one can attempt in a dream. "But why would Rukmini make hairpieces?"

"If my daughter-in-law is dead, she will not get my son's money," Murthy's mother explains. "She will need some income, so she will have to make hairpieces to sell."

"Who will get your son's money, then?" asked Sivakami. This was not reason, but curiosity: if she had been awake, she might have asked what use a dead woman has for money.

"Our grandson," the woman replied.

Halfway between wake and sleeping, she felt dread. In that dream voice that takes all the effort of shouting, Sivakami argued, "You have no grandson."

"Oh," said Rukmini's mother-in-law, "we have a grandson, you and I."

Here Sivakami really woke, gasping as though breathing through cobwebs. She didn't discuss this with Muchami on the way to or from her bath, but finally, three days later, they talked. Muchami had heard of a poison that causes a big ball to grow in the stomach and long hairs to grow from it, until the victim's life is crowded from her belly. They admit between them that they fear Rukmini's cousins are poisoning her to get her husband's house and possibly his money. They admit, shaking, that if the cousins consider him a threat, Krishnan may be poisoned next. They must remove him from that house.

That morning, Sivakami dispatches Janaki and Kamalam to fetch their little brother to eat pazhiah sadam at home. As he eats, she examines his stomach for signs of swelling, but Krishnan's shorts look as baggy as ever. She asks, "Have you had stomach aches lately, Krishnan-baby?"

Krishnan furrows his brow—is this is a trick to get him to take an extra dose of castor oil? Sivakami grunts in such a way as not to make him more suspicious, and says nothing more.

While Krishnan is eating, however, Muchami slips next door to have a conference with Murthy, and when Krishnan goes back next door, Rukmini wails, "Go home, kanna! You don't live here, you don't belong here, we don't want you."

Krishnan stands still, confused, not only because Rukmini is shouting all this, each phrase louder than the last, but because she has fallen to her knees and embraced him, so he couldn't move even if he wanted to.

Janaki and Kamalam appear, having been instructed by their grandmother to come and bring their little brother home again. He looks over his shoulder, sees them and flings his arms around Rukmini's neck, howling, "I won't go!"

Janaki starts to cry—she cannot do this, not so soon after Thangam's death. She leans against a wall, tears coursing from unblinking eyes. Kamalam, silent and alarmed, takes her elder sister by the hand and the shoulder and leads her home.

Three rooms away, in the courtyard, Murthy's cousins half-pretend they don't know what is happening. Murthy tears his hair quietly on the veranda, waiting to accuse his cousin once Krishnan is safely out of the picture. What a sorry state the world is in, he tells Sivakami later, thanking her for having sent Muchami with that alert, when one trusts a servant over one's flesh and blood.

Finally Rukmini tries to thrust Krishnan from her. His little hands pinch and scrabble and he starts again to yell, but Rukmini eventually pins his arms to his sides, kisses every feature of his face and runs from the room, her stomach visible on either side of her.

Krishnan tries to follow, but she closes a door against him. Sita arrives within minutes, with Muchami, who carries Krishnan home.

The cousins object when confronted, denying that they have done anything, saying the accusations are outrageous. Then they steal away in the night, more outlaws than in-laws.

It would have been safe then for Krishnan to return. Certainly, he tries it, meekly. He and Rukmini have visits, but Muchami and Murthy don't face protests when they carry him home each dusk. Over the next six weeks, Rukmini grows gaunt. Her stomach, though it grows no bigger, becomes painful. For the final ten days of her illness, she is confined to bed, able to take nothing but a little water. Then she, too, expires.

Circumstances being suspect, Rukmini is made to submit in death to the doctor's examination she refused in life. Cause of death is listed as cancer of the stomach, but in fact, the doctor has never seen a growth like this one—a wrinkled tumour, like a mammoth brain, but from it grow long, matted hairs, five feet long in places. He considers removing it for research—maybe he could write a paper?—but concludes the tropics have robbed him of his professional ambition—he has no desire to take the trouble of preserving and analyzing it. It is a curiosity, but it is not going to make him famous. It is too bizarre for that— just a bit of a novelty. He sews the woman's stomach up, the flaps baggy over the deflated cavern, and sends word that the family may have her back for her funeral.

Surely little Krishnan must have done something very bad in a previous life, Sivakami thinks, the night after Rukmini's funeral, watching the child sleep between his elder sisters. How else could it be that a child never really knows a mother at all and yet loses not one mother but two? It's a riddle fit for gods, who are fond of perversity.

She thinks back on the scandals she has been witness to in these months and wonders, trying to keep herself from feeling prurient, how many there have been on the Brahmin quarter that she doesn't know about. She wonders why she works so hard to keep up appearances— surely everyone's family has misfortunes. Surely they are nothing to be ashamed of. She doesn't condemn either Minister or Murthy for having madness and criminality in their families, but if she didn't know them better, she might. She might wonder if these traits would rear their ugly heads in others among their families. Say if she was considering a bride or groom from a family within which lurked such shadows.

This, of course, is why she has invested such energy and effort in keeping the facade of her family stainless. Thank God no scandal has enmeshed them yet, though she often senses a circling threat. Goli's behaviour is so unpredictable; Vairum's beliefs are so unconventional. *It's just my imagination,* she tells herself. *They would never do anything to hurt the children. Well, Vairum wouldn't. And Goli would never hurt them deliberately* . . .

She looks at the children, as blameless and earnest in sleep as in waking, and says a quick prayer to her gods against the evil eye: *please let it remain so.* Thangam's children's futures are precarious as it is. Sivakami is their only guarantor and all she can give them is their reputations.

33.
A Suitable Girl
1941–1942

WITH THE LONG, DARK YEAR OF MOURNING finally ended, Janaki becomes eligible for marriage. Horoscopes begin arriving, but Vairum insists that Sivakami disregard them. Every marriage begets another, as the saying goes, and it takes only one such function for Vairum to target a family he considers suitable: relatives of Vani's who live in her hometown, Pandiyoor, a market town close to the city of Madurai, some seventy miles south and inland from Cholapatti.

Closely related to Vani, and distantly to Gayatri, they are a grand and wealthy family. The eligible son is the youngest of three boys; there are also three daughters, all married and well-off. Vairum has a long-standing casual acquaintance with the father.

Sivakami does not see how this is going to work. It's well and good for Vairum to say he has no truck with astrology—he has always had strange notions and she has never been able to influence him—but, she asks him timidly, what sort of a family would marry their child off without the advice of the ancient science?

"It's not a science." Vairum is as brusque with Sivakami as she is gentle with him, as dismissive as she is credulous. "It's inexact and manipulative. I won't consider any family who can't recognize that."

Sivakami withdraws, suitably cowed. Astrology has brought her misery her whole life—she's not going to argue further for it. She has no doubt it will be operative, no matter what Vairum does, but maybe, for once, she would rather not know the future.

Vairum doesn't bother explaining that he doesn't yet know if this family is as willing as he to undertake a modern marriage. One of his reasons for targeting prospects above the middle class is that the upper echelons tend to be more sophisticated in such matters. The family's elder sons work as lawyers—they employ reason and logic, even in highly emotional circumstances. This detail, he thinks, bodes well.

But how to handle protocol when the usual formalities are so pointedly not to be observed? Vairum is a man of forethought and has considered this. The matching of horoscopes is the primary method his community uses to arrange marriage, but the *Laws of Manu* describe others: kidnapping, for instance, trickery, sorcery. Vairum opts for enticement, targeting the boy's mother, a formidable aesthete and lover of the intellectual arts, a woman who Vairum guessed might appreciate those virtues Janaki has so consistently cultivated. He need only find or create the means to display her in all her eminent suitability.

He suspects an opportunity will arise before long. The daughters of the Pandiyoor household are gadabouts and use any excuse to travel for functions. In November, he hears from Vani that they will come to Cholapatti to celebrate Gayatri's granddaughter's first birthday, and he hastens from Madras to brief his mother and Gayatri.

"Concocting such a womanish scheme," Gayatri marvels to Sivakami in a rare pause for breath amidst her preparations for the function. "Who would have suspected him capable?"

Sivakami doesn't respond, and Gayatri reassures her.

"I think it's wonderful, Sivakami Akka. I have met this boy, Baskaran. He is a nice boy, very devoted to his parents."

"Hm." Sivakami feels she needs more information. "Is he a college graduate?"

Gayatri raises her eyebrows. "I suppose not." She purses her lips and continues. "What I have heard is that Baskaran completed his second year at American College in Madurai. He is an intelligent boy. But then his grandfather died, and his father became sad, it's understandable. He was having difficulty managing at home, and so on. The father, Dhoraisamy, had inherited the responsibility for a charitable foundation his uncle . . . ?" Gayatri pauses, frowning. "Maybe his father? Someone established this charity—I don't remember. But there is a paadasaalai and a chattram, and Dhoraisamy now is the in-charge of managing them. The elder sons work as lawyers, perhaps they are too busy or not so interested in family affairs. So Baskaran stayed home and helped. He is very devoted to his parents."

Sivakami is not in a mood to discuss her reservations, and Gayatri leaves soon afterward, clearly hoping she has not said anything to con-travene the match.

Sivakami broods. So many Brahmin families have lost their prop-erties in the last thirty years, including many on their own Brahmin quarter, including Goli's family, because they failed to keep up with the times, thinking their wealth would continue to perpetuate itself. Perhaps this Baskaran is canny, a man, such as Vairum, able to recog-nize that Brahmins' old wealth must be transformed into new money, given new life through new methods of management. Her observa-tions suggest, though, that Vairum is exceptional. She would feel so much better if Baskaran earned a wage.

It's both too early and perhaps too late for her to object. Perhaps Baskaran's family will not be taken in; perhaps they will demand a horoscope and it will be unsuitable; perhaps some other obstacle will arise.

But if Vairum has decided on this match, she says later to Muchami, as they go over grocery lists, it's probably too late for her to do anything about it. Muchami tells her she's right.

"If Vairum decides on it, though," she says, "he will do everything to make sure it does turn out for the best. His pride will never let a match he makes go wrong." She shrugs and sighs. "At least I have that insurance."

On the morning of the birthday party, Janaki, Kamalam, Radhai, Krishnan and Raghavan walk down the Brahmin quarter to Minister's house. Radhai is under specific instructions, which Janaki and Kamalam are charged with enforcing, to behave in a ladylike manner. Radhai, ten, is never deliberately disobedient, but the force of her per-sonality is such that she is easily distracted. At the height of Kamalam's coming-of-age ceremony three weeks earlier, for instance, Radhai burst into the courtyard covered in mud, a frog in each hand, clamouring for a pot to put them in. Raghavan, at three, worships her.

The girls are welcomed by Gayatri's youngest daughter, Akila. While Raghavan and Krishnan run to the back to play with the other little boys, Akila invites Radhai to help her greet guests, offering them rock sugar, sprinkling them with rosewater. Akila is a placid girl, and Kamalam and Janaki encourage Radhai to spend time with her, while they seat themselves against a wall and examine, with disguised curiosity, the family Vairum has targeted. They whisper to one another: the family looks familiar, they must have seen them sometime; they may even have seen the groom—oh! They used the word! Now it can't be taken back! Janaki hits her sister unconvincingly and frowns, holding her braid in front of her mouth and trying to keep out of the sightlines of her potential in-laws.

Only the matron and her daughters have come. The daughters' saris are of a rich silk, with heavily embroidered pallus that slimmer bodies would not support. Fortunately the sisters are unvaryingly large, one plump and squishy, another bustling and broad, another solidly stout as though a slap to her thighs would ring like a brass pot. They all carry additional weight in the form of large gold ornaments and hairpieces. Their mother trumps them, though. She might be the largest person Janaki has ever seen, sitting in soft mounds that roll and break with each of her movements, though she moves rarely and slowly. Her eyes are small and sharp between rising cheeks and drooping forehead.

Watching them, Janaki feels skinny and unadorned. She is barely ninety pounds, wrapped in a conservative sari of serviceable silk, wearing a complete but understated set of earrings, nose rings, chains and bangles. Her thick braid, which she fingers as she watches them, is probably the weightiest of her ornaments, its end hitting just above her knees.

That afternoon, Janaki goes back to Gayatri's house, this time with only Kamalam as an escort. It is the hour when she normally practises veena. Vairum, on his trips through Cholapatti for overseeing purposes, will often sit in the hall and listen. Her playing has none of

Vani's unsettling genius, Janaki is far too sane and conventional for that, but it is very good. She has a light, fresh touch, the quality of mornings in the cool seasons after the rains, pleasing and restorative.

Gayatri presents Janaki to Baskaran's mother, whom everyone calls Senior Mami. She lies on her side on a bamboo mat. Akila's veena, the one on which Janaki and Sita learned to play all those years before, has been set up. Baskaran's sisters, also gathered around, compliment Janaki's slenderness and her hair, while the great woman's eyes glint blades of taste and discernment.

Janaki sits at the veena and tunes it. She has thought for days about what she will play, and decided to start with "Sami Varnam," a reliable favourite. She is aware, as she plays the varnam, that she is using it to demonstrate her level of command: she is not a concert artist, but she has some deserved confidence. As she concludes it and prepares to play "Sakala Kala Vani," she senses that she has won her audience's interest.

She has been practising "Sakala Kala Vani" hard for some months and begins with an aalapanai, not so ambitious or lengthy a one as a concert performer, but one that she knows demonstrates a degree of erudition. She plays, even to her own ear, very well. She has never really played for an audience and is surprised at how it heightens the emotional charge of the music—perhaps because she feels she has a message she must communicate—and makes her less conscious of those technical points she knows she has mastered yet still obsesses on. As she concludes the finale, an improvisational charanam, she begins sweating and blushing, the moisture on her fingers threatening her playing. She manages to finish, wipes her hands and doesn't look up.

The sisters burst into chatter, full of compliments and questions. Janaki plays divinely! Did Vani teach her? Who is teaching her now? She is too inspired—a real talent! Janaki ducks her head and bites her lip while Kamalam proudly answers the inquiries on her behalf.

Senior Mami says nothing, but looks approving. Gayatri urges Janaki to play one more piece. Janaki is uncertain, but the sisters press her until she gives in and plays "Jaggadhodharana," explaining it is a tribute to Vani, the first person she heard play it. When Janaki departs, she thinks she sees Senior Mami, faintly, smile.

"The sisters all seem nice. Unpretentious," Kamalam comments cautiously, as they return home.

"They do, don't they?" Janaki feels as though she is waiting for exam results, except that she's not really sure whether she wants to pass or fail. She has sensed that Sivakami might not feel as enthusiastic as Vairum about this potential alliance, though she can't guess why.

She passed: a letter arrives, written and signed by Baskaran's father, saying he has a son of marriageable age and understands Sivakami has a granddaughter, a beautiful girl of good reputation, and could they arrange a girl-seeing?

Vairum makes the arrangements and is in Cholapatti to greet Baskaran, who comes with his father, Dhoraisamy, one of the elder sons, a sister, whom Janaki has met before, and two nephews. Vairum ushers the party into the main hall with a tinge of the false heartiness Janaki so strongly associates with her father. Seeing him like this perplexes her. Baskaran, who is fair and chubby, balding a little and wearing round black-framed spectacles, seems quiet and well-behaved. He smiles deferentially at Vairum and, palms together, does a deep obeisance to Sivakami, who lurks at the entrance to the pantry.

In the kitchen, Janaki adjusts her sari, which is lush and appropriate, a maroon silk bordered in teal. She takes the refreshment tray from Sivakami. Her hands and feet have been hennaed for the occasion—the leaves, which Kamalam gathered and crushed, had been so fresh and potent that Janaki's palms and fingertips are nearly black. As she serves, she tries not to look at Baskaran.

Dhoraisamy, in contrast with his son, is animated and talkative, wiry and long-fingered. His daughters clearly inherited their bubbliness from him, if not their physiques.

"Such a good house—certainly it would be our great fortune to have an alliance," he assures Vairum, abasing himself. "Gayatri has assured us of how well brought up the children are, as though we didn't already know. We know! We know!"

Fathers-in-law are supposed to be aloof and difficult to interest, Janaki thinks, trying not to giggle. *Doesn't he know he's reducing his bargaining power?*

She returns to the kitchen and sees Radhai, arms out, walking the perimeter of the courtyard well. Janaki bids her angrily, *sotto voce,* get down, then returns to the hall entrance and, with Kamalam, peeks around the corner at the visitors. Just then Baskaran looks in their direction and Kamalam yanks Janaki out of sight. Janaki is not able to tell how he's feeling—curious? amused? He has a pleasant look about him, but that doesn't necessarily mean he's having a good time.

And now, as is customary at these things, and since they have reverted to custom as though the early part of this process had not been quite unconventional, Janaki comes to play and sing for them. She goes to the veena, head down, knees rubbing as she walks. Her potential father-in-law is leaning toward her, nodding and smiling. Janaki keeps her eyes fixed on the floor, biting her lip as though she were shy, instead of trying to hold in her giggles at her prospective father-in-law's manner.

Dhoraisamy is simpering to Vairum, "Tch—we hardly need to hear her play for ourselves. I mean, of course it is an enormous pleasure, but her reputation precedes her. My wife couldn't stop talking about her."

Vairum raises his eyebrows above a long, slow smile. He says to the man, while looking at Janaki, "Is that so? Well, let's hope the real thing is not a disappointment."

"Ah! No, no!" Dhoraisamy tosses his head back with a hearty laugh. "How could that be? Oh, to have a musician in the family! You are too, too fortunate!"

Janaki seats herself gingerly at her instrument, barely able to move her head for trying not to laugh, and commences "Sami Varnam." She is a little distracted at first, trying to imagine this man's wife, who did not say one word in her presence, going on and on to her husband. Probably she said something like, "She plays veena," and sent the entire house into an uproar over her unusual loquaciousness.

She sinks into her playing and feels the party float slightly away from her. Dhoraisamy exaggeratedly beats time, flipping his palm up and down and touching each finger to his thumb with extravagant waves of his wrist, crying, "Vah, vah!" and "Sabash!" as though this is a Mughal court. Janaki tries not to let it distract her. She can just imagine what her grandmother thinks of him, though it is nice to be so spectacularly appreciated.

Sivakami watches from her spot, remembering herself at ten, singing for Hanumarathnam, her eyes screwed shut as though to demonstrate how little she cared what he thought. She actually thought she didn't care. Janaki is evidently concerned with playing well, but to what end? Is she destined to find contentment with this family? Could this Dhoraisamy be sincere, with all his exclaiming and arm-waving? *He will be lucky to get one of my granddaughters,* she thinks, in a rare moment of arrogance. *They are exceptionally well brought up girls.* She happens at that moment to glance back out at the courtyard, but doesn't see Radhai, just out of sight, now balancing on a brass pot, one foot on either side of the lip.

When Janaki finishes playing, there is a strong feeling in the room that those present are merely performing the final scenes of a drama whose conclusion has been thoroughly foreshadowed. There will be no final twists in this plot. The guests part with friendly, matter-of-fact assurances that they will contact one another shortly. As they go out the door, Baskaran looks back at Janaki. She covers her grin with her braid. And he smiles at her, sweetly.

Vairum folds his arms and leans victoriously against the closed door. He points at Janaki and says, "I always knew you were the smart one. You did it. You deserve to marry this family, Janaki. You got them, just like I knew you would, given a chance. Ha-haaa!" He claps his hands just once and holds them together as though shaking his own hand. "Oh, my girl, you are going to have a good life. Just the life your mother would have wanted for you."

Janaki smiles warily at him. Kamalam turns and goes upstairs. Janaki leaves her uncle and grandmother to talk to each other. This is none of her business. She goes and changes out of her sari, smoothes its folds a last time and uses a stick in the corner to hang it tidily on the sari rod above her head. She goes to find Kamalam on the roof.

Kamalam is looking off the roof at the street and doesn't look when Janaki joins her. Her voice sounds funny when she asks, "So when do you think it's going to happen?"

"What, the wedding?" Janaki frowns.

"What else?"

"I don't know," Janaki shrugs.

"You're so lucky," Kamalam murmurs. "You're so lucky."

"Why? Because they're rich?"

"Everything, Janaki Akka."

Janaki doesn't say anything. She feels apprehensive, despite liking Baskaran. Being rich doesn't seem like a guarantee of anything. Minister's mother went mad; the people three doors down had to sell their grand house and move into a flat in Thiruchi where they share a bathroom with three other families; she even thinks her paternal grandparents once were rich. Where is her father in all this? Shouldn't he be making these arrangements?

Downstairs, Sivakami has screwed up her courage to the point of recklessness.

"This boy." She clears her throat. "He is not even a graduate. Rich boys have less motivation to work than boys from the middle class."

"His elder brothers are working." Vairum looks up from where he lies on a bamboo mat. This is exceptional—he never rests—so the morning's triumph must have worn him out, or maybe he is scheming further.

"We don't know under what circumstances." Sivakami gathers momentum. "So many families are losing their lands these days. Not everyone has done as well as we have. We have done well because of your efforts and your uncles'. What if they lose their wealth, like so many have?"

"Like the family of my dear brother-in-law?" Vairum is not about to permit his mood to be spoiled. "This is not such a family. Much of their wealth, I believe, is tied up in this charitable trust they have the responsibility for running. They are good Brahmins, Amma." He smiles at her, and she looks away from a wicked glint in his gaze. "Surely you appreciate that I have ensured that for your sake."

Sivakami has said all she is capable of saying. Vairum will do what he wants. Marriages, she thinks, are made in heaven.

Vairum, in a rare conciliatory mood, unintentionally echoes Sivakami's thoughts. "It's in God's hands, Amma. Let's settle it like we did my marriage. First reason, then religion. This is how to make marriages in the new world. Pay attention."

On an auspicious day shortly after, Janaki undertakes a visit to the Rathnagirishwarar hill temple with Vairum and Sivakami. Just as in Vairum's case those many years ago, they have taken a plate full of offerings and two small paper packages of roughly equal size. One contains a white flower, which would signify a bad choice; the other has a red flower, a positive sign. Vairum insisted on organizing the offerings just as he has everything else. Sivakami makes a surreptitious survey of the plate. He doesn't seem to have forgotten anything.

The priest, completing the puja, holds the plate out to them, admirably unconcerned with his words and actions, apart from an appraising look flicked at the girl whose fate clearly hangs in the offerings' balance. Vairum reaches out to choose a flower, but Sivakami clucks, and he pulls back his hand with an evanescent pout as she nods at Janaki. Janaki's hand hovers over the plate a moment as she glances at her uncle and then chooses one of the two packets. The priest hands the plate back to Sivakami. Janaki awaits further instructions.

"Open the packet, Janaki!" Vairum says, awfully jolly. "It's in God's hands now!"

Janaki unwraps the packet she has chosen and a red mass of petals unfurls in her palm, covering exactly the dot of henna, now faded to a deep orange, which Kamalam had patted onto her hand for the girl-seeing.

God must be on Vairum's side. He snatches up the other packet and sets it alight on the nearest oil lamp. Left hand on right wrist, he respectfully offers the flaming packet to the altar, giving it back to God. None but God will ever know its contents.

Janaki, her fate decided, begins picturing herself with Baskaran. His height matches hers well. She can't remember his eyes but she thinks they were kind. He spoke five or six words. Each one is burned in her mind—even though she was of two minds that day. He wore scent.

Kamalam awaits her on the roof and they go over every detail without restraint, Kamalam swallowing her sadness in deference to

Janaki's hoped-for happiness, even giggling guiltily at Dhoraisamy's manner and the mother-in-law's girth. By the time they get to the topic of the groom, they are a little giddy with anxiety and confidences.

"His skin is very fair," Kamalam judges.

Janaki says slowly, "Yes, he's very fair."

This is suddenly, illogically, very funny. "He's fair!" they say. "He's so fair! Oh, he's so fair," laughing until they are heaving and gasping on the floor, holding their cramping guts, resting their forehead on the shadowed strip along the roof's western edge.

Janaki sits up and leans against the parapet.

"Well, he is," she sniffs.

It's too soon. They're off again, choking tears, aching guts, and the big hot sun gone down.

~

SOME SIX WEEKS LATER, Sivakami receives her invitation, just like everyone else on the Brahmin quarter—and elsewhere in the presidency, and possibly beyond. Vairum has associates everywhere now. He's putting Cholapatti on the map, as empire builders have always done for their hometowns, even if he seems to be doing it more to spite his origins than to commemorate them.

Printed in Madras on pumpkin-coloured paper so thick and soft one could sew clothes from it, in royal purple ink with a stylized Ganesha stamped in gilt, the invitation includes both a Tamil and an English version, confirming that there must be foreigners on the guest list. Anyone would be pleased to receive it, and indeed, almost every family that does receive one saves it. What it says is this:

C. H. Vairum
has the pleasure of inviting you to the wedding of
Sowbhagyavati N. Janaki,
daughter of
Sri I. M. Nagarajan, called Goli
(Indian Revenue Service, Indrapuram) and
(late) Srimathi N. Thangam

with
Chiranjeevi P.D. Baskaran
son of
Sri P.P. Dhoraisamy (Landholder, Pandiyoor) and
Srimathi N. Kalpagam

Sivakami is disappointed though unsurprised that Vairum has issued the invitations in his name instead of Goli's. They have heard from Goli only once since Thangam's death, when he came to Sivakami's house for an hour and made noise about how it was time for Laddu to come and work for him. Goli did not look well. He had lost weight, so that his eyes and jaw seemed overly prominent and his clothes, old and expensive, were a bit big to flatter him the way they did when he was younger. It was midday and Laddu was out at the oil processing plant. He grew impatient and left. Sivakami never told Laddu and Goli never returned. Laddu has done well at the plant, against all expectations. Vairum has promoted him to overseer and Laddu would have been very ill-advised to leave.

"Perhaps," Sivakami speculates aloud, to Muchami, showing him the invitation, "perhaps Vairum didn't even know how to contact Goli?"

"Not likely, Amma." Muchami shakes his head. "Vairum could probably find anyone in the presidency. Didn't you say the invitation says your son-in-law is now in Indrapuram?" Muchami pauses, either to decide how plainly he should speak or to let his words sink in. "In fact, I'm sure Vairum might even have sent Goli an invitation, if only to provoke him. He didn't make the invitation in Goli's name because this is his show."

"People in our Brahmin quarter are going to think Vairum is trying to slap Goli in the face," Sivakami says, rueful.

"He is, but I think that's only a side benefit."

Sivakami looks at him.

"I don't mean to make a bad joke." He holds his hands up, conciliatory. "Amma, Vairum is doing something good for Thangam's daughter. Accept this. He is doing as much for Janaki as if she were his own daughter."

Sivakami wishes she could not see the wisdom in what he says, but he is right: Vairum is doing more for Thangam's children than her own brothers ever did for him and Thangam. *He is a better man,* she thinks.

"Amma," Muchami goes on slowly, "I have a concern." He has never talked to her in much detail about Goli's deal-making and is nervous to do so now, but feels he must. "I suspect that, as soon as Goli receives the invitation, he will be in Pandiyoor, trying to raise support for some investments. I'm sure Janaki's future in-laws are cautious people. But they may feel shy to say no, and then . . ." He has speeded up and pauses. "There's nothing like money matters to cause familial discord. I would hate for them to take a financial loss out on the girl. They think very highly of her, as highly as she deserves."

Sivakami is flummoxed. She never would have thought of this. She feels slow and he waits, giving her time to think through what he has said. "I absolutely do not want them to think that investing with him is a condition of the marriage," she says after some minutes.

"Yes, that's exactly one of my fears," Muchami responds.

"Vairum is so explosive when it comes to his brother-in-law," she continues. "I would rather we not go to him about this."

"Okay. Perhaps it won't be necessary." Muchami scratches his chin and his scalp. "What about this? Can we somehow inform the son-in-law that while Janaki's future family appears well-off, we have just learned that they are in fact in a very bad position financially? That they may well say they want to invest with him, but that he should beware, because they are wily—lawyers, after all—and will take him for all he is worth? That they are going down and he should be careful not to be dragged down with them?"

"We cannot say that ourselves," Sivakami objects. "He will ask why we are marrying his daughter to these people."

"Good, quite right—so who would he believe?" Muchami asks, like a schoolteacher, as if he knows the answer. He gives a hint. "Who would be only too happy to believe and pass on such a story, but be unlikely to pass it on to anyone else?" He pauses to give Sivakami a chance to respond, but she is silent. "Your brothers, Amma."

Sivakami frowns, impressed, as he goes on.

"Send them a letter in confidence, saying Vairum heard this from a reliable source after the arrangements had been made, but decided to go through with the wedding, because it's a good family otherwise, and that he pledged that he will not permit anything bad to happen to his niece. You don't need to say what they will recognize, that this is exactly what they did for Thangam. But say you are worried about Goli, and want them to talk to him, because it would not be appropriate for you or Vairum to do so. They will be only too glad to have this authority, and even if they spread rumours, those won't amount to anything more than all the usual rumours that are always in the air about rich families."

Sivakami has to admit it is an excellent scheme, and as it turns out, Sivakami's brothers are happy to do their sister this favour. She and Muchami are satisfied that they have done something to ensure harmony for Janaki in her marital home.

Sivakami has insisted that all the basic costs of the wedding be paid for from her money, the manjakkani, which has grown substantially owing to Vairum's efforts. He agreed but has insisted on paying for extras himself—this is to be a sumptuous celebration, far showier than Sivakami thinks advisable.

The wedding will be not only ostentatious by Sivakami's lights, but also, paradoxically, short. Efficiency is the hallmark of the new age, even in matters nuptial. A celebration that would have lasted a week in Janaki's mother's time will now be completed in three days. People have jobs.

Cholapatti is done up in style. An enormous canopy is erected, covering the entire length of the Brahmin quarter, which will be closed to traffic, from the witch's house to the temple. All Cholapatti's Brahmins are invited, as well as a number of wealthy non-Brahmins. They will be sufficiently deferential not to take cooked food in Sivakami's presence, but the Brahmins are abuzz at Vairum's urban bad manners nonetheless. Relatives of both sides will descend from all over the Madras Presidency, as well as a number of Vairum's associates from Madras, including foreigners with whom he does business. Vani will play a recital on the second evening, reprising the program, a little old-fashioned but still charming, of the concert where Vairum first saw her.

Baskaran's family, as has become the custom in certain circles, has not asked for a dowry, and Vairum has not offered one. Still, Baskaran's siblings and his parents will receive gifts of clothes and jewellery and Janaki will go to her in-laws with a substantial trousseau of high-quality pots, gold and silver jewellery, silk and blended saris, and other items modern and traditional, representing considerable expense. Sivakami is not sure how she feels about this advance on the old system. On the one hand, she recognizes their lack of demands as a sign of their graciousness. On the other, traditions offer protection. A girl is an asset to her in-laws—a cosmetic, material and moral asset—and a dowry is one way of assuring she is seen as such. If the bride's side keeps up its end of the bargain, so must the groom's. Sivakami fears that the loosening of certain controls may lead to the loosening of others, that families who don't receive dowries may not protect girls as they have been obliged to do in the past.

When she raised this question with Vairum, though, he told her that her knowledge of history and human nature is flawed and incomplete, and that people who take dowries these days are opportunists and not to be trusted. And, as Sivakami observes Baskaran and his family, she finds herself, a little grudgingly, coming to believe that the family is honourable and the match a good one.

Which makes her feel all the odder when Vairum confronts her, late in the afternoon of the third day. The main hall is full of relatives and guests, napping and gossiping, passing the time between meals and major ceremonies. She herself is lying down, in the pantry, her head on her wooden pillow. She hasn't the energy she once had, and the effort of making the sweets, which she insisted on, has tired her, as has the stream of people coming to pay their respects, and the instructions she has sent out with Janaki, Kamalam and Gayatri, each time the bride has come in to change her clothes and eat.

She feels she has just closed her eyes, when she senses a presence, breathing above her. Her mind flashes briefly—is it a dream?—to the semi-opaque figure she used to see by the river. The last time she saw it was the day she got the news of Thangam's illness. Then she opens her eyes: Vairum stands over her, black-diamond eyes snapping, nostrils flared. His hair fans like a dark halo around his mottled face, as much white now as brown.

He thunders softly at her, "You asked your brothers to warn Goli off from Dhoraisamy's family? *You* are spreading rumours about *this* family?"

Sivakami sits up, feeling frail and uncertain. She had felt so competent when she wrote the letter.

"You will go to any lengths to protect that man, won't you?" Vairum is in a fury.

Sivakami opens her mouth to respond—she wasn't protecting Goli, she was protecting Janaki. "What if Dhoraisamy broke it off, when they learned . . ."

"You think I didn't know Goli would try to milk them? I briefed them as soon as they agreed. They contracted with you and me, who are beyond reproach as far as they are concerned. They would never hold Janaki's father against her. And you spread rumours. About them. Which reflects badly on me. You can't just tell the truth about him, can you? That would be a blow to your pride." He looks ugly. "If only your pride extended to me." He thumps his chest with what sounds like a sob, and runs, so like a little boy, upstairs.

Sivakami can't follow him—the main hall is full of relatives—and she doesn't even know how to answer. She must talk to him, as soon as the wedding is done. She couldn't be prouder of him. Isn't that obvious? He is what she always wanted him to be. And she is ashamed of Goli—that's why she took this step. Has she made the mistake she feared others would make, all those many years ago, thinking Vairum too hard to be hurt?

Janaki thought the costume changes were fun, as were the ceremonies, which felt a little like play-acting. She is a bit embarrassed by the grandeur and finery, but also excited: these are harbingers of her new life. And she is mature enough to appreciate her in-laws' classiness. *They didn't even ask for a dowry,* she thinks with pleasure—they were happy to get her and didn't need a bribe.

As the ceremonies wind to a close on the third night, Janaki sits with Baskaran on the dais at the end of the Brahmin quarter nearest the temple and wonders, not for the first time this weekend, where her father is. She thinks back to the last time she saw him, the only time since her mother's death. He looked like a wraith, she thought—his hair nearly white, his eyes red, his clothes baggy and ghostlike.

As the sun begins to set, a chaotic figure runs hopping and gliding through the attendees of the wedding, from the other end of the Brahmin quarter—Padmavati, the witch's sister-in-law. She streaks past the dais, and toward the temple, her clothes creased and bunched, food on her chin, trailing a yeasty smell of confinement in her wake. A moment later, the witch's husband dashes frantically along the same path. When he reaches the dais, he asks Vairum, "Did you see her? My sister. Which way did she go?"

He points toward the temple, where Padmavati has achieved the top and begun shouting. First children, then other curious parties, crane and creep out to see what is happening. She has begun to tell a familiar story: the *Tale of an Anklet*, a Tamil classic. At least a third of the wedding's guests move out to listen to her. Her brother figures out how to get onto the temple roof and tries to apprehend her. She runs to the opposite side, lifts her rumpled sari and starts masturbating for the crowd, shouting at her brother to keep away. He chases her and pushes her hands and sari down, but she slips out of his grasp and shoves him over the edge of the roof. The temple is only about nine feet high, but the wind is knocked out of him and he gives up.

Padmavati returns to her tale:

"I," she declaims, "am Kannagi, the innocent daughter of a Thiruchi merchant, married to Kovalan, the handsome son of another merchant. At a festival some time back, Kovalan met Madhavi, a fish-eyed courtesan, and forgetting his faithful wife, went to live with her. Then they fought and he returned, but he had spent our entire fortune and I offered up to him my ankle bracelets, the thickest and best of my ornaments. 'Come,' I said, 'let us go to Madurai and make our fortune anew.' So now we go," Padmavati grins evilly and marches around the perimeter of the temple. "But when we arrive in Madurai, new misfortunes are afoot. One of the queen's ankle bracelets has been stolen and my husband, trying to sell one of mine, is accused. He is brought before the inattentive king and killed for a thief. I am waiting," Padmavati sinks sideways to her knees, batting her lashes caricaturedly. "Where is my husband? I go and follow and hear of my husband's destiny. I have fought and scratched my way into the king's court: 'What did your wife's anklet contain?' I challenged him. 'Pearls,' the queen tells me. 'A city ruled by an unjust king is doomed to misery,' I tell the king, and break mine open, from which gems roll and scatter. The queen faints; the king faints, too. 'May Madurai burn!' I scream. 'My happiness is ended!'"

From within her sari, the witch's sister-in-law withdraws a scythe and a bottle of kerosene. She douses herself while the crowd watches, still confused as to what she intends.

At that point in the story, the legendary Kannagi, that paragon of faith and chastity, cuts off her left breast and the city of Madurai bursts spontaneously into a cleansing flame, but Padmavati strikes a match on her scythe and sets herself on fire instead.

The crowd bursts into shouts and runs, but by the time they have fetched water and medics to the rooftop, the witch's miserable sister-in-law is dead.

This doesn't seem like a very good omen for a wedding, but Janaki is determined not to think that way. What has shaken her more than anything was the mention of the seductress who lured away a husband and made him spend on her the money he should have lavished, if judiciously, on his faithful wife. *I hate stories like that.* She is unable, however, to keep herself from wondering what becomes of the courtesan.

34.
Madras, the City by the Sea
1942

SEVERAL MONTHS LATER, Vairum comes to fetch Janaki and
Kamalam to Madras for a holiday. It is his final wedding gift to Janaki.
Though she is well brought up, he wants to encourage Janaki to be more
worldly, not only in her habits and tastes, but in her comportment.

Vairum's driver loads their luggage and the two sisters climb into
the car, a Ford woodie wagon with a royal blue nose and tan uphol-
stery, cool to the touch. Janaki faces forward; Kamalam faces her on
the jump seat. Vairum says little on the twelve-hour drive, and the girls
are absorbed in watching the countryside. It's their first time in a car,
and the scenery is so much closer than in a train. Twice, Vairum stops
for business. Before each meeting, he extracts a dossier from a pocket
in the door on his side, flips down a desk from the seatback in front of
him and double-checks the documents. The driver courteously inquires
if the girls would like "cooldrinks" and they refuse. At the first stop,
they eat, on their uncle's direction, the rice meals that Sivakami has
packed for them, washing their hands with water the driver brings
them. At the second stop, they accept a tiffin of dosai and idlis Vairum
buys them at a small hotel.

They arrive at Vairum's house in the city a little after dark. Janaki
and Kamalam are breathless at the activity between periphery and centre, the cars, buses, carts and cows competing with people for space on
the roads, the blocky houses, apartment buildings, churches, mosques,

temples and shops. Vairum lives in the thick of it, just off Cathedral Road, but in a neighbourhood of three-storey detached houses where tall, leafy trees muffle the urban noise. A peon pulls open the gate and they roll into a carport.

The driver opens their doors then extracts their things from the back of the car, a storage area Vairum calls the dickie. He runs up a curving outside staircase while they wait for Vairum, who has stopped to have a word with someone inside a large door on the ground floor, his home office, he explains briskly to the girls: reception room, guest quarters, small study and skeletal staff. A couple of staff members bow to the girls, palms together, as they stand in the carport, bleary-eyed from the drive. They follow Vairum up the stairs, polished granite, by appearance, but glittering with something like mother-of-pearl, and onto a narrow balcony edged with a plaster balustrade. The walkway widens into an outdoor reception area, furnished with bamboo sofas, in front of a pair of monumental carved wood doors. Vani rises, smiling, from a divan in the salon within, and waves them in to show them the room where they will sleep, off the dining area, opposite the puja room. Their things have been deposited there.

"Well, then, girls," Vairum says, clapping his hands softly. "Wash up and we'll have a bite to eat. I hope you're ready to have some fun here!"

Janaki and Kamalam murmur happy agreement.

The next morning, Janaki parks herself in front of Vani to listen to her morning recital. She feels shy, but not shy enough to keep away. Vairum, leaving for his office, bids her sit on the divan—"That's what it's for! Go, sit, relax!"—and stands at the door until she obeys, tipping awkwardly on its edge. Kamalam, who had sat behind her on the floor, follows. "If you don't learn anything else while you're here, please at least figure out how to look at ease without plopping yourself on the floor."

He leaves, and the girls remain rigid on the divan. Janaki doesn't really mind sitting on it, especially after Vairum is gone and there is no one left to see them, but wishes she were closer to Vani, the better to observe her fret work. At one point, Kamalam rests a hand on one of the bolsters, which are covered in woven Hyderabadi cloth, black and white to match the floor tiles, with cross-hatched embroidery in primary colours.

Vairum returns to take his mid-morning meal at home. Beforehand, he beckons the girls to sit with him in the salon a moment and shows them a small picture book.

"I had a meeting a few doors down from Higginbotham's this morning." He looks at their faces. "The big bookstore. You know of it." They are not sure they do. "I got this for you both. I imagine your English is as bad as mine was when I was at school, before I started going to Minister Mama's salons, yes? Let's give this a try."

Janaki sounds out the title and author: *Madras, the City by the Sea.* C. A. Parkhurst.

"Not bad," Vairum says. Turning the page, he holds the book in front of Kamalam, who stares at it, her hands at her sides. Janaki recalls having seen Kamalam through the window of her primary-grades class, when the teacher, Miss Mathanghi, was giving them Sanskrit lessons. When she pointed at Kamalam, the little girl simply didn't respond. The teacher berated her, but Kamalam kept her silence, looking straight ahead, her lower lip trembling.

Vairum sighs and moves the book back to Janaki. She takes it and haltingly reads a few lines of the text below the pictures of white children and catamarans. "Well, children, let us go on a visit to Madras. It is a city by the sea. I wonder how many of you have seen the sea."

"Right," Vairum says, standing. "That was painful, but I know you like a project, Janaki. Work on it, and work on your sister. I'll expect both of you to read it to me in turns, in a way that doesn't grate like a file on cement, next week sometime. Done?"

Janaki would love to learn English. She's sure she can help Kamalam, who still has not moved or spoken.

Vairum had told them that they should be freshened up and dressed for 3 p.m.: they are invited out for tiffin today. They are seated on the divan, their hair identically oiled and coiled, their faces powdered with Pond's Rose Talc, Janaki in the nine-yard sari of a married woman, Kamalam in the maiden's half-sari, when they hear the car roll up

462 ~ PADMA VISWANATHAN

downstairs. They stand and wait, some ten minutes, before they hear the soft clatter of Vairum's feet on the stairs. "Vani!" he calls, and she comes out, putting on a ring.

He stops in the doorway to watch her, and she smiles knowingly. She wears a silvery blue silk with a wide black border, very simple, utterly elegant. Janaki, who had felt so sophisticated powdering her own face and her sister's, shrinks again, frowsy, hopeless. She watches the look on Vairum's face. *He adores her.*

Vani walks past him. He notices the girls and beckons them impatiently to the door.

They go to the Theosophical Society headquarters in Adyar, where a woman Vairum introduces as Rukmini Arundale tours them aggressively around the grounds. Janaki read an article about her in a women's magazine: a Brahmin, married to a British man, she has learned and is marketing the devadasis' dance-drama in a new, respectable form. It was called *sadir*, but she has renamed it. Now it is "Bharata Natyam," the dance of India, and it carries, she says, a message of national liberation and uplift.

She is trying to get Vairum to sponsor a performance, in which she will star. "I know your politics are progressive, Anna," she presses flirtatiously, though Vani is standing close by his side, no expression but an air of hauteur. "And, being as you're married to such an illustrious artist, you know better than anyone the importance of preserving and promoting our classical arts."

Vairum looks amused. They have paused beneath the Society's famous banyan tree, beside the main trunk, surrounded and shaded by a grove of aerial roots. The sun through the large leaves dapples Vairum's already blotchy face as he smooths his moustache.

"I'm just not entirely convinced that what you're doing is progressive, my good lady," he says, sounding mildly jocular. "Stealing those poor devadasis' livelihood!"

"No one says they can't dance any more," Arundale responds tetchily. "Though certainly our performances demonstrate much greater scholarship and grace. But don't you agree they should find"— her voice drops—"that is, be encouraged into, more respectable means of supporting themselves? Think of their virtue," she insists, leaning into him and speaking as though not to offend the ears of the ladies.

Janaki, who had had doubts about this enterprise—a Brahmin woman, a married woman, dancing in front of an audience? How could it possibly be modest?—finds herself won over, despite being put off by Arundale's coquettishness. She's not sure whether the devadasis' self-respect is besmirched by all the arts and wiles they use to attract men to support them, but think of all the corollary damage they cause! Mrs. Arundale is right: it's a question of public morality.

Vairum remains non-committal and Arundale somewhat grudgingly escorts them to the guest suite, where an elegant tiffin awaits them in the company of her husband, George. While Janaki eats with appetite, drinking in the room's European-looking appointments, she notices Kamalam just picks at her food.

After tiffin, Vairum tells the driver to take them to Adyar Beach. Janaki and Kamalam have never seen the ocean and they wriggle in excitement, exclaiming when it comes into view. Vani shows some hesitation about disembarking, but Vairum persuades her to join them for a stroll. Janaki and Kamalam have to hold themselves back a little to stay within a decorous distance of their aunt and uncle. Janaki sniffs the salt air, feeling the breeze stick and sting on her cheeks.

A few family groups are out for a promenade. A father and son kick a striped ball back and forth. The boy must be about four, fair-skinned with curly hair in a high quiff that tosses as he runs and laughs. Vani slows to a stop, watching the pair, as Janaki and Kamalam go on a little ahead, looking for shells. At a certain point, the little boy misses the ball and it rolls up into a patch of beach grass. Vani scurries after it, with Vairum looking a little alarmed and starting as if to get it himself. She plunges through the high grass and emerges with the ball, squatting and holding it so that the little boy comes to her. She speaks to him momentarily and Vairum moves toward them as she suddenly hugs the child, who looks uncomfortable, and then starts squirming and pushing against her. Vani doesn't let go, however, until Vairum arrives and releases her arms.

The little boy runs to his father, looking panicked and close to tears. The father had looked as though he weren't sure what to do: Vairum and Vani are obviously prosperous and respectable. He might have thought, until Vairum freed his child, that Vani was just enthusiastic and affectionate, but now, as he pats the boy and they walk away together down the beach, he looks back and shakes his head.

Janaki and Kamalam raise their eyebrows at each other furtively as they collect shells, flat and white with regular red zigzags on the back. Vairum and Vani stay crouched together, where the boy left them. Vairum is talking to her, a hand lightly on her arm; she is rocking back and forth slightly. As the girls return to them, Vairum stands, telling Vani gently and repeatedly to do the same, until she does.

They return to the car, walking past catamarans beached for the evening, long logs lashed together so they look exactly like giant cupped hands, upturned to receive some offering.

As they get ready for bed, alone in their room, Janaki asks Kamalam, "Didn't you like the tiffin today?"

"Not much. It tasted funny," Kamalam says.

"Are you feeling all right?" Janaki asks.

Kamalam had eaten well at supper, but the cooks are people they know vaguely, from Cholapatti, where they had lived down the street. The husband had been a cook-for-hire there, and Vairum brought them to Madras, saying that they would prepare food with the flavours of home, besides which they were two other Brahmins, like him, whom the people of the *agraharam* didn't respect.

"I guess," says Kamalam, lying down with a sigh, her arm over her eyes. Janaki turns down the lamp and joins her.

"Tired?" Janaki asks. She herself feels lit up from everything they've seen and done.

"Yes," says Kamalam.

After a pause, Janaki asks, unsure if she should, "Why do you think Vairum Mama reacted that way to Vani Mami when she hugged that little boy? She wasn't hurting him."

Kamalam answers without hesitation. "She wants babies too badly, Akka. It's tearing her up."

Janaki is startled but knows Kamalam is right. She, too, had sensed something like this behind the scene they saw, but never would have been able to put it in words so clearly.

"Yes," she says. "They should have babies."

"Everyone should," Kamalam says through a yawn, "but it's in God's hands."

Within minutes, Janaki can hear that her sister is asleep, while she lies awake an hour or more, choosing and examining moments from the day as though they were snapshots in a holiday album.

The next day, Vairum takes them to his office in town, and then says the driver will take them shopping while he is in meetings. "Buy yourselves some new saris. Ask the salesmen what is fashionable—they will tell you. You can take the blouse pieces to Vani's tailor. And Janaki, get some nice fabrics to take to your husband's home, for quilts and cushions, that kind of thing."

Janaki has a gay time playing the young mistress. She feels a little frustrated at Kamalam's shyness, even while she enjoys being in charge. The younger girl stands always very close to and a little behind her sister, and tells Janaki to choose her saris and blouses for her. When they are finished, the driver skirts the city, taking them to Chromepet, where Vairum awaits them at a leather goods factory, one of a number in this district named for the chrome tanning process that took hold here late in the last century. The smell of leather, chemicals and dyes is faint outside but overpowering inside, even in the closed showroom at the upper reaches of the building. Janaki tries not to make a face and breathes shallowly as they browse the sandals. Vairum is on the company's board and has told them each to choose a pair while he finishes work.

Kamalam starts tapping her arm frantically. Janaki peers at her. "What?" But her sister runs out of the showroom and vomits in the hallway. Janaki, mortified, takes her outside to get some air while peons rush up to clean the mess. The driver opens the car doors the moment they appear. Janaki asks him to fetch some water.

Vairum comes out a few minutes later, looking concerned. "Kamalam? Are you all right?" He crouches beside the open car door and reaches in to feel her forehead. She starts and pulls away a little. Neither girl can remember ever having been touched by their uncle. He clicks his tongue and puts his hand again to her head. "You don't feel hot."

"I'm feeling better, Vairum Mama." Kamalam licks her lips. "I'm very sorry."

"Hm. Okay. Give me a couple of minutes to finish and we'll get you home to rest, all right? Good girl." He goes back into the factory, his dhoti snapping between his Jodhpuri jacket and huge black shoes.

"Are you really feeling better?" Janaki asks.

"It was the smell, I think," Kamalam whispers, not wanting the driver to hear, and shudders.

"Yes, horrible," Janaki says. "I don't know how he can stand it. Like a slaughterhouse or something, I imagine."

Each day of the visit, it seems, Vairum has some entertainment planned for them, and people of the city for them to meet. Often, guests come to his home: business associates, people who wish him to support their causes, others with whom he has had some similar association in the past. They attend a concert at the Music Academy in the company of a burly, red-cheeked Dane, an investor in a fertilizer company Vairum is starting up, and a sallow Russian who will become its chief engineer. At the intermission, Vairum introduces them to luminaries, including C. Rajagopalachari, former premier of Madras, and still one of the top men in the Congress Party, and Kalki Krishnamurthy, who has published articles and stories in the weekly magazine *Ananta Viketan* for as long as Janaki can remember. Gayatri and Minister now subscribe to the new periodical, *Kalki,* that he started after his release from jail last year. Janaki, taking her cue from Sivakami and Minister, disagrees with Kalki's politics: he is in favour of independence. Still, she can't help feeling impressed and has often enjoyed his lighter pieces. Rukmini Arundale is also in attendance and flutters up to monopolize Vairum, crowding his nieces to one side.

On the car ride home, Vairum asks them, "So, I assume you girls recall why Mr. Rajagopalachari resigned his premiership, yes?"

Janaki and Kamalam are silent.

"Janaki?" Vairum peers at her, over Kamalam. "You need to learn to keep up. He objected to the British here declaring we were in the war on their side."

Janaki is not sure what to say and not sure he expects her to say anything.

"You've read Kalki's work, though?"

They both tell him yes.

"There are pros and cons to independence, but it is coming and we will manage. Interesting challenges ahead. I want to see what Congress does about caste. Completely outmoded. We'll never progress as a nation, self-governed or otherwise, unless we can stop thinking people's birth determines their worth."

The girls are rigid in their seats, and he looks over at them and laughs.

"You don't like this kind of talk? Get used to it. You've been brainwashed by your grandmother, closed up with her in that house, in that village. Why should people put up with Brahmins acting like they're better than everyone else? I wouldn't, in their place."

They arrive at the house and Janaki lets out a breath she didn't know she was holding. The car doors open. She looks at the driver as she gets out and he smiles at her with what now feels like threat. Are the lower orders planning a revolt? What's wrong with everyone being in their places, doing the work that suits them? She has never questioned her place. Muchami has never questioned his place, and he and Mari admire Brahmin ways, as they should.

She doesn't feel offended so much as confused. If people don't aspire to emulate the Brahmins, what would they aspire to?

The next day brings more visitors, some of whom come to hear Vani play in the evening: a young Punjabi Sikh couple, she in a pale grey *salwar kameez*, he in a high red turban, and two Tamil Muslim men. Janaki doesn't mind the Sikhs so much; they are practically foreign and have to speak to her in English, which she responds to in monosyllables. It feels very odd to sit in the salon with Muslims, though—are they even interested in Carnatic music? They appear highly educated and flow between English and Tamil in a way Janaki finds dizzying.

It's like trying to listen to someone who, every few phrases, turns away and mumbles.

Afterward, they all go to the Dasaprakash Hotel, where the Punjabis are staying. There, the girls have their first taste of ice cream. For the first time since leaving Cholapatti, Janaki sees a look of real pleasure on her sister's face. They are wearing their new saris and blouses—eyelet with puff sleeves—and look sweet, if not chic. The Punjabi woman, only a couple of years older than Janaki, seems to feel more comfortable with them than with the rest of the group, and they speak to one another and laugh at their halting English. Janaki is fascinated with the henna work on her hands: leaves and flowers, an intricate design such as she has never seen before, and asks how it is done. Vairum nods approvingly at their having made friends.

The next morning, Vairum tells them he'd like to take them to a couple of attractions. "You can't leave Madras without visiting the San Thome Cathedral and the Kapaleeswarar Temple. I've told Vani we're having our morning meal out, at the home of one of the associates you met last night. Then we'll go see the sights."

Janaki can't think who he means: surely not one of the Muslims? But yes: the taller of the two men who came to hear Vani play last night. Mr. Sirajudeen greets them at the door of his home, slim and elegant in a pressed white jibbah, a skullcap on his silver hair. Unfamiliar smells wash over the girls as they enter the house and seat themselves on divans in the salon. The house is large and light, but doesn't otherwise look too strange: Janaki wasn't sure what to expect, but thought it would be more shocking and unhygienic.

Sirajudeen speaks more Tamil than he did last night, now that the company is less mixed, but still peppers his speech with English phrases.

"Mr. Sirajudeen is a close associate of Rajagopalachari," Vairum tells his nieces, and then tells his friend, "They met him at the Music Academy the other night."

"Ah, yes. He's a rare Congressmen, one who takes Muslim concerns seriously." Sirajudeen smiles evanescently and rubs the corners of his eyes. "We talk often."

A bell sounds elsewhere in the house.

"Come," he says, standing. "We'll take brunch? We can eat at the table, or, if your nieces find it more *homely,*" he says the last in English, "we can sit on the floor as we usually do."

Vairum turns to them. "What do you prefer?"

They look back at him: what should they say?

"I think they can manage a table," Vairum says.

"Good, then."

There are four silver plates laid on the table, and a servant starts bringing rice and vegetables as they seat themselves.

"Pure vegetarian, of course," Sirajudeen assures them, but Janaki and Kamalam are still struck nearly motionless in their chairs. They recall having eaten out, years earlier, at a non-Brahmin place while staying with their parents. But they were children, and there was no food in the house, and their father told them to. But why eat in the home, at the table, of a Muslim, by choice? They're not even eating from banana leaves, but from plates other Muslims have probably used. One layer of contamination on another.

Kamalam is looking at Janaki to see what she should do. Sirajudeen bids them, "Eat, children," and he and Vairum resume chatting intensely about construction materials or some such thing. Janaki looks at her plate and sees there are two curries, one wet, one dry, two pacchadis, of cucumber and green mango, and the rice with a *kootu*-like sauce on it. The worst thing to do would be to take the rice. Perhaps she can simply avoid it. But there's not much harm in eating raw vegetables and fruits. She nibbles on the pacchadis. Kamalam does the same.

Mr. Sirajudeen finally looks over at a pause in their conversation, and asks, "What's wrong? You're not hungry? Not feeling well."

"No, no," Janaki says politely. "We're eating, we're eating. Thank you."

He looks at them, narrows his eyes a little and inclines his head to his own plate, nodding slightly. He has guessed what is wrong, and he is offended.

Vairum glares at them, his nostrils flaring above his wide moustache. "Go on, eat!"

Janaki smiles at him and eats a pinch of green mango with salt and lemon. Vairum points at her rice; she shakes her head.

There is a silence between the men for a time, then Vairum breaks it. "Delicious. Please tell your wife."

"Certainly," Mr. Sirajudeen says without looking at any of them, and then changes the subject.

"That was a mistake," Vairum expostulates as he slams his car door. "I thought you might not humiliate me in front of my good friend, but, no—you're worse than your grandmother! You're part of a new generation. Freedoms, to know people, to travel—does this mean nothing to you?"

Again, Janaki can't think of any response and doesn't think Vairum wants one. Would he really have her turn her back on all the values of her childhood?

"Answer me," he bellows, and she jumps.

"I . . . I owe Amma my life," she says. She has never said it aloud, but she knows it to be true.

"Many people have given you many things," he says pointedly, and she blushes, thinking of her wedding, "but your life is your own now."

Janaki thinks this is a very strange notion: she belonged to her family, who kept her in trust to give to her husband. Since when does anyone invent their own values? She is getting a very strange feeling from her uncle.

"We don't have to live as Brahmins have for eight thousand years." He sighs hard and looks out the window. "Don't you like the excitement of the city, the sense of possibility?"

"Yes, Vairum Mama," she quickly replies, but he doesn't look at her and she is left to her thoughts. Eight thousand years. She can't fathom it. She thinks of the day each year when a family honours its dead and tries to imagine eight thousand years of grandparents, but the only foremother she has really known is her amma, and she is not sorry she honoured her by refusing food in the Muslim's house, though she will never tell Sivakami about the incident. She was sorry to hurt Mr. Sirajudeen's feelings—he seemed like a nice man. But what did he expect, really? She feels a pang of homesickness and then starts to worry: Vairum invited her for this holiday so that she'll fit into her husband's family better. Will this kind of thing be expected of her in her new home?

Vairum no longer feels like touring sites with them. He has the driver drop him at his office and take the girls to the church and temple by themselves. The church is wondrous and unfamiliar, and the temple magnificent and comforting. They return home in good spirits. Vairum is out, and won't return until late, so they have tiffin alone with Vani.

Janaki had not been sure whether Vani would keep up her story-telling habit throughout her time in Madras—what does she do when Vairum is not at home for a meal, tell the tales to the cook? During their visit, though, Vani spins her old magic, telling a story of a young woman, a relative of hers, whose husband passed away while she was pregnant. The child, however, grew, as did his elder brothers, to look uncannily like the dead husband: his features, his voice, his manner. Soon they took over the running of the household just as her husband had done, while she, grown dim in age, forgot her tragedy and thought her husband returned to her, multiply. Although the men married, she never recognized their wives.

Today, the story changes, and the child dies at birth. The husband, traumatized, regresses, becoming more and more childlike with the years, and the wife plays along, becoming, in increasing degrees, like a mother to him. Their elder sons, though, come with time to look and sound just like the man their father once was, and she finds them wives who agree to dress the same as her, as well as adjusting their hair and manner to imitate her own. The story ends with both wives pregnant.

Janaki is disturbed. There is a strange light in her aunt's eye, an intensity to her telling, in the reversal, that makes the story sound less like the entertaining and impersonal mysteries Janaki remembers and more like an allegory of the psyche.

She has been preoccupied, since that night at Adyar Beach, with Vani's childlessness and with her isolation with Vairum here in Madras. She is increasingly convinced that this is an unnatural way to live: no

472 ~ PADMA VISWANATHAN

parents, no children, no relatives nor even neighbours of their own caste and community, meeting strangers every day, strangers who want something. Vairum seems so enamoured of this loneliness and anonymity, but now Janaki is fearful of what it is doing to their aunt, and maybe even to their uncle.

She knows Vani grew up in a sophisticated household, but also that she had thrived, as much as the grandchildren had, in the order of their Cholapatti home. Her affection and regard for Sivakami was visible. With children and neighbours, she was never alone, even when Vairum was away overnight. Maybe Vairum thinks Thangam's children reminded Vani of the baby they lost, but what if it was better for her, not having a child of her own, to be surrounded by children? She had always been eccentric but had seemed content. Now she crackles with some weirdness. Kamalam, too, has noticed it.

"Vani Mami is not happy," she tells Janaki tonight, as they take out the postcards they bought that day.

Janaki nods. "I know. I'm not even sure she's well."

There is little more they can say: what can they do, two young girls? Whom would they tell? They trade off the postcards, writing notes to Sivakami, Muchami and Gayatri, about the sights and wonders of the city by the sea.

They have four days left, which pass without major incident. A trip to Madras Beach, where they eat roasted corn and take in such curiosities as a two-headed girl in a boxlike theatre; another ice cream at the Presidency Club, where Vairum plays tennis. One evening, Janaki, inspired by the Punjabi woman, crushes henna leaves from the garden into the finest paste she can, and extrudes it from a paper roll onto Kamalam's hands. On one hand, she does a pattern of lotuses and mango leaves; on the other, a zigzag, replicating the pattern on the souvenir shells they took from Adyar Beach. Vairum laughs when he sees her art, so different from the large, crude dots that are customary in the south. "So you are capable of departing from tradition!"

Janaki laughs, too.

"Do Vani's hands also, why don't you?" he asks.

Tickled, she agrees.

On their last evening, Janaki reminds Vairum that he had wanted to hear them read from the English book. Kamalam had begged her not to bring it up, but Janaki felt it was an obligation, and welcomed the challenge, so like school. She missed school terribly. Kamalam didn't. Janaki has also started inserting, from time to time, an English word in her speech, though she blushed a little when Kamalam looked at her quizzically.

"Ah, it's all right," Vairum says, waving them off. "I'm sure you've learned many things no book will ever tell you."

The three look at one another sombrely, knowing each takes away very different impressions of this holiday, though these impressions are, nonetheless, shared.

Vairum had planned to drive them back to Cholapatti but must attend to a water dispute that is turning ugly and affects several of his concerns. He asks if they might be able to take the train. The couple who cook for him are due for a trip home; he'll give them leave to escort them. The girls tell him it will be fine.

The platform at Egmore Station is crowded with people fleeing the city for the villages, against rumours of attacks. Though the girls are fearful, Vairum looks at the hordes with something like disdain.

"No one will ever target Madras. It seems big to us, but it's a backwater in the world," he says, rolling his eyes and looking as if he wishes this weren't so.

Still, for every reason, Janaki and Kamalam are glad to be going home. That morning, a cook had arrived to replace the couple while they were away: a non-Brahmin. Janaki and Kamalam were aghast, though Janaki felt nothing should surprise them any more: now Vani had to eat this kind of food in her own home?

She's had quite enough of the city. Soon she will be home, and thence to married life. She hopes she is sufficiently prepared.

PART SEVEN

35.
The Tumbling Stars
1942

"So THE PRETTY YOUNG THINGS HAVE RETURNED, have they?" Gayatri ribs Janaki and Kamalam, who smile back. "How did you enjoy your trip? That was a nice gift, I must say."

"Yes," Janaki can agree on that. "It was a nice gift."

"Did you enjoy?" Gayatri prods. "What is their house like?"

"The house is very nice," Janaki says. "Modern, you know: modern stove, divans. Indoor toilet! So different. City life."

"Mm-hm," Gayatri frowns. "Almost too much, sometimes, no?"

"I enjoyed the holiday," Janaki insists. "Certainly, for two weeks, it was excellent. I'm not sure I would want to live in Madras."

"Oh, yes, I understand." Gayatri smiles, patronizing and warm. Janaki remembers hearing that her family was one of the first in the town of Kulithalai to install an indoor toilet. "Well, that's not too likely. I suppose, after a time, one just wants one's home, isn't it true?"

"I suppose." Janaki blushes.

"Not too long now, is it?" Gayatri leans forward a little. "Just a couple of months, and then you're off to your husband's! Your real home."

Her real home. After all these years of feeling she was living on credit—not just because she is a girl, but because she was being raised in her mother's natal home—Janaki is departing for the place where she truly belongs. She has been in safekeeping all these years, for this family she will now join.

Vairum and Vani were to have taken her to Pandiyoor by car but, at the last minute, a business crisis prevents Vairum from coming. There are not many male relatives appropriate to take his place: Murthy has grown increasingly dishevelled since Rukmini died, Janaki's brothers are unmarried; Sivakami's brothers are dead, and Vairum never liked to ask them for favours in any case. Instead, in a radical departure from tradition, he arranges for Baskaran to come and fetch his bride himself. Sivakami finds the plan disturbingly casual, and insists they will have at least a ceremonial handing-over, even if it takes place three steps from the veranda. She recalls that Thangam's in-laws came for her, but circumstances were such then that she didn't want to draw attention to the matter.

Janaki doesn't feel undervalued by the change in plans; on the contrary, it flatters her that Baskaran is willing to come himself. But the unconventionality worries her in the way that every departure from tradition does. On her last night within these borrowed walls, Janaki frets: will she measure up? Their trip to Madras made her feel more sheltered than ever. She lies awake, holding Kamalam's hand. Kamalam squeezes back, her face against Janaki's shoulder, crying silently.

The next morning, upon seeing Baskaran, with a brother and one of Vani's lawyer uncles, ready to escort her, she relaxes. His smile for her is reassuring.

She takes leave of her grandmother, prostrating for her as Baskaran bows, palms together, at her side. She does the same for the Ramar. She hugs Kamalam, wiping tears from both their cheeks, saying she'll be back soon for a visit, not to worry. "Or you can come to visit me there! Please don't cry." Radhai, Krishnan and Raghavan come along to the station.

At the Kulithalai station, she is packed into a train compartment by Muchami and Baskaran, as carefully as she packed her trunks. Radhai and her brothers kiss her, and Muchami smiles at her long and affectionately, a smile she returns rather more quickly, with a little puzzlement at his apparent sentimentality. He holds the children back from the platform and they wave until the train is out of sight.

⁓Ꮕ

ON THE TRAIN, Baskaran's brother and cousin bury themselves in newspapers and lift their heads only to engage in heated debate with their compartment-mates on the subject of India's entry into the war on the British side: was independence worth such a sacrifice of lives and integrity?

Janaki is next to the window with Baskaran beside her so that no other man will sit next to her. Baskaran grubs in the left-hand pocket of his kurta and holds its contents out to her until she accepts. He boldly brushes her hand as she pulls it away.

It is a package, no bigger than her palm: slightly heavy, wrapped in brown paper and tied with string. She tugs at the coarse bow. It comes loose, and the soft thick paper opens to reveal a box of worked silver in the shape of a parrot.

Seeing it stirs some dim memory in her that she can't quite bring into focus. It's so touching that he planned a gift; what a shame it's so ugly. The bird looks vulgar and ill-intentioned. Perhaps parrots are not suited to being rendered in silver, she thinks.

"Do you like it?" he asks.

"It's beautiful," she responds.

He gestures. "Open it."

She lifts off the lid, which fits onto the bottom half by means of a latticework border. Inside is a small sack and, inside the sack, glossy peppermints in pink and white stripes.

"Take one," he urges, but she thinks they look too lovely to eat, and she feels so shy. She imagines playing palanguzhi, Kamalam's favourite game, with him, using pink and white peppermints for tokens.

She hands back the bird-shaped box, indicating Baskaran should offer the mints around the compartment. He tries and is ignored by the others, who are shouting now, evenly divided on a number of related political topics. Finally, he takes a mint, presses it into her mouth and chucks her lightly under the chin. Taking another candy for himself, he sits back to enjoy her discomfort.

⟋ᢒ⟍

Muchami finishes putting away the bullock and cart and comes through the courtyard toward the kitchen door, carrying Raghavan, who is nearly asleep. Sivakami is in the pantry, reading her Ramayana, only her forehead and hands visible above the book. The older children have scattered. Muchami calls out softly, "Amma?" then goes back around to pass through the back room, then the room under the stairs, into the main hall.

Sivakami lays a mat down in the main hall. Muchami deposits the little boy on it, and Raghavan rolls luxuriantly onto his side, already asleep.

Sivakami and Muchami take their separate paths, she through the kitchen, he through the other passage, out to the courtyard, where Muchami draws some water. He washes his feet, face, neck and hands, and takes a long drink.

"Everything went all right?" Sivakami asks from the small veranda at the back of the house.

"Oh, yes," he says. "Janaki's a good girl, very smart girl."

"Yes," Sivakami says. "They're all good."

"I will miss her more than the elder ones," he says, a little apologetically, "and probably more than the younger ones, too."

"Sure, who will practise Sanskrit with you?"

Muchami laughs. "She surpassed me so long ago, she has no use for this old man's stuttering!" He looks serious again. "Amma . . . seeing her in-laws, I couldn't help thinking again about how Vairum, what he said about how we warned off Goli. Ah, I felt so bad, all over again."

Sivakami is silent: she had tried to talk to Vairum about that after the wedding was over, but he wouldn't allow it. "What's done is done, Muchami. Don't torture yourself. I wouldn't even have told you what Vairum said if you hadn't asked."

"I should have known." Muchami hits his head with his fist. "Vairum is also so intelligent. I should have known he would anticipate whatever we could. I was just so concerned for Janaki."

"Yes, yes." Sivakami doesn't see the point of talking about it. They can't take it back and they'll never do it again. "The point is, she'll be fine there."

"I think she will." His face shines as he thinks of her, all dressed up, with her rich husband. "I think she'll really do well."

At the Pandiyoor station, the family's bullock cart, magnificently decorated and drawn by a majestic and fatty black bull, awaits them. Gopalan, the family's head servant, is driving. Before he mounts the cart, Baskaran pulls a small tin from the pocket of his kurta, inhales a few pinches of snuff from it, and sneezes. Janaki looks away, wishing she hadn't seen. He mounts the cart and Gopalan twitches the reins against the bullock's back.

Leaving the station, they cross a small commercial street and travel past the bus depot and a post office before turning into one of two streets that, intersecting at a T, make up the Brahmin quarter. Single Street, the top of the T, is composed of a row of houses facing the sides of two long houses on Double Street, including Baskaran's family home. Double Street, the T's stem, looks more like the Cholapatti Brahmin quarter, with two rows of houses facing each other. On both streets, the houses share walls with their neighbours, the red and white stripes of the verandas, as in Cholapatti, practically continuous. Double Street culminates in a Krishna temple, behind which stretches the Vaigai River.

Almost everyone on the street between the station and the Brahmin quarter recognizes the cart and puts palms together respectfully. Baskaran's brother gives the expected reaction: sometimes he nods in acknowledgement; mostly he doesn't react at all. Baskaran, though, puts his own palms together, offering namaskarams to labourers, merchants, a tailor, hardly conventional Brahmin behaviour. Suspicion inkles in Janaki's breast: she hasn't married a radical, has she?

Only one of Baskaran's sisters is at home, the one who married locally. She squeals delightedly, a habit Janaki noticed when they met earlier. The two sisters-in-law are more—what? Reticent or decorous? Surly or proper? Janaki can't read them. Vermilion water is swirled; songs sung. The bride and groom are instructed to step up onto the threshold with their right feet. Janaki, looking down, watches her own foot, hennaed in dots and lines, entering her real and forever home in unison with the wide, pale foot of the husband who brought her here.

Her mother-in-law has stood for the occasion and waits inside, Dhoraisamy tittering and bobbing beside her. Baskaran and Mrs. Baskaran prostrate themselves before the household elders.

Her sisters-in-law indicate that they will show Janaki around while her luggage is brought in, and Baskaran goes off to bathe. Janaki turns and, without thinking, blurts words of caution about her veena. She receives a look of pained hauteur from Gopalan in return—a servant of his calibre needs no such instruction. She cringes, but is also reassured.

The house is two or three times the size of the one she grew up in. The ground floor has not only a veranda and anteroom leading into the main hall from the street, but a front study that corresponds to the anteroom, with a desk on which are neatly arranged a blotter, pen and paperweights. Tidily labelled ledgers bound in red or brown leather line a rotating rosewood bookshelf beside it. After a peep into the study, Janaki is led back through the main hall and into a small extra room, lit by two windows that give onto yet another room. The windows have no panes, bars, or shutters, but they are a bit too high to see through, the bottom edge at the level of Janaki's brow. Vasantha, the elder sister-in-law, explains in a low tone that this is the women's room. It contains untidy piles of tatting and embroidery, magazines and novels, a harmonium and now her veena still within its jute wrappings. Swarna nods nervously and whispers, "We spend time here, you see—when we're not doing everything else we have to do." Janaki wonders why they are acting as if this is a secret.

There is a communicating door between the windows, and she is led to it but stopped before she goes through. There, she is surprised to see Senior Mami, her mother-in-law, in a bright room barely wider than the good lady herself, about three times as long as it is wide. It contains a radio, a gramophone, a floor desk, two more bookshelves fully stocked with books and a cot, currently containing Senior Mami, who is reading what appears to be a religious commentary. Janaki sees that, among the pride of children following them on the tour, only one aggressive two-year-old still needs to be told not to enter their grandmother's lair.

The set-up seems regal or Muslim, somehow, with its hierarchies and its rigorous division of the masculine and feminine. This impression is assisted by the fine latticework that covers the windows of Senior Mami's room. Such fashions are rare in areas such as this, where Muslim emperors never really gained a toehold. Here, the ruling classes are likelier to ape the British, a less threatening practice, as far as Janaki is concerned.

Janaki tries to look coolly appreciative as, inwardly, she frets—could such details possibly be in accordance with the Shastras' dictates on construction? She takes a deep breath and doesn't think about it. Doorways are lined up from front to back in two rows—that's one Shastric prescription she does know about. She can see clear from the door of her mother-in-law's zenana entrance, through the women's room, into the extra room, into the puja room, the pantry, the kitchen, straight out into the garden, whence wafts the smell of curry leaf, jasmine, tulsi. Janaki exhales. She's imagining—she couldn't smell all that from here. But she can see a patch of green. Everything will work out.

They pass back through the great hall and mount the stairs to the next storey, where each brother has a chamber that he shares with his wife. Janaki and Baskaran are in the last. Her luggage is already there, between the double bedstead and *almirah*. The windows are hung with strung flowers in what strikes her as a Rajasthani fashion. Her sisters-in-law, who probably hung the flowers, giggle nastily and Janaki's flushing shyness turns to annoyance. She thinks to shoot them a look but stops herself. Janaki had very much hoped to find things in common with these girls. Observing them now, she feels homesick.

Vasantha and Swarna attack her luggage, searching out a fresh sari, blouse and undergarments so Janaki will not contaminate her things by touching them before she has had her bath. They swarm like ants over a torn-open package of candy, appraising her bodices with the lace straps and trim she crocheted herself, putting her saris in order of their preference, yanking out sheets, hairpins, cooking vessels. The entertainment is too soon concluded and Janaki senses, astonished, that she has come up short. Her trousseau is the grandest and most modern that any of Sivakami's granddaughters has had—Janaki had felt both embarrassed and proud at its opulence. But Vasantha and Swarna are rich girls, raised for boredom and discontent.

Janaki's things have been left in heaps and tangles, but she doesn't mind—organizing will be something to do. She follows her sisters-in-law as they descend the stairs with the outfit they have selected for her. Gopalan is in the hallway when they reach the bottom, gathering some sacks and a basket to do the evening marketing. At the sight of the new daughter-in-law, the head servant's chiselled features turn stony. Janaki feels scraped by his expression: she can't be working to ingratiate herself with the servants, but it would be nice to be liked, if not respected. Or perhaps respected, if not liked. She didn't mean to offend him with her instruction. Isn't he employed to take orders?

Fuming, she is led to the back of the courtyard and shown the bathroom. Her sisters-in-law hang her clothes and towel on a rod that extends from wall to wall, and leave her to marvel. The bathroom is three times the size of theirs in Cholapatti, with a slanting tiled roof and sunlight streaming in the gap between roof and walls. She removes the small clay plate covering the mouth of the enormous curved brass pot on a woodstove. Using a small brass jug as a dipper, she fills a cylindrical pot sitting on the floor. Her bad temper is rinsed into the gutter with the first sluice of hot water. *The servants probably build the fire even before the family rises,* she thinks. *And my sisters-in-law take it for granted.*

She opens her soap and turmeric dish and rubs her skin until it smarts red beneath its veneer of gold. She is already quite fair and hairless, and she wants to stay that way. She washes her travelling clothes, wrings them and sets them on a high shelf.

After having drawn the bath out as long as she can, she combs, braids and ties up her hair and dresses with care in a dusty-rose sari with burgundy stripes and border. She has been wearing a nine-yard sari since she got married, several months now, but is still not yet entirely comfortable wrapping herself. She puts on her new wristwatch—her first, another item in her trousseau, with a slim, octagonal face and slithery metal band—and checks the time: 1:35. Her edges and rims still glowing bright yellow from the turmeric, she emerges fresh and dressed, and newly cautious. She hangs her clean clothes to dry. Seeing the household's tulsi plant, the holy basil to which housewives pray daily, growing from a vermilion-anointed stand in the courtyard, she does an obeisance for it. As she does so, she hears the sound of chanting from next door—Yajur Veda. A master sings out and young boy voices chime back.

This must be the paadasaalai, she realizes, the Vedic school Baskaran's family has charge of. It is one branch of the charity established by Dhoraisamy's uncle, who had accumulated a fortune as a moneylender but had no child to whom he could leave it. He had bought the house next door as a venue for the school. The little boys must take their lessons in the courtyard, under a tree, perhaps, in the traditional style, Janaki thinks, lingering to listen to the pleasing, timeless sound. She can see the top of a tree, over the wall that separates the two courtyards.

Apart from the paadasaalai, Vairum had told her in a briefing, the rich and childless uncle had instituted two other major works under the auspices of the Kozhandhaisamy Charitable Trust. One was the *odugal*, a concept new to Janaki. The Vaigai River, which she has yet to see, appeared dry most of the year, though its waters continued to flow just beneath its glittering sandbed. The odugal is a large T-shaped cut, eight feet or so along the top, about twice as long, and a few feet deep, into which the river's waters spring. Brahmins use the top of the T for their ablutions; the other castes descend the stem downriver of them. The cut needs daily maintenance lest the river's sands collapse back and fill it in; the charity pays for a servant to come and re-cut it daily. Were it not for this, each man or family would have to dig a separate hole for bathing and water gathering.

The third branch of the charity is the Kozhandhaisamy Chattram, a rest home for Brahmin travellers, in one of the concentric streets around the famous Meenakshi temple in the nearby city of Madurai.

Janaki finds it deeply reassuring that this family, however wealthy, is bound to a trust whose goals are clearly in the service of Brahmin knowledge and prestige.

On her way to the puja room, she glances into the kitchen, expecting that she will see enormous, hurried activity. Feeding a household of over fifteen people, not including servants, must take military-level organization, and she is curious to see how they do it. She is surprised to see just two cooks, an old woman and a young one, making snacks, even though tiffin is to be served in an hour. They nod and put their palms together ingratiatingly and she smiles shyly back. She supposes the mystery will be solved shortly and goes to her prayers.

Arriving in the puja room, she is seized with comfort and reassurance—finally, familiar faces! Some of the gods are in different settings or configurations from those she is used to, their skins or outfits tinted differently from the pictures in Cholapatti—artists will take licence. But they are still her idols: Ganesha, with his fat tummy and encouraging expression; Krishna, with his knowing smile and valiant chest; Lalitha Parameswari, who always promised to guide her when this time came; Lakshmi and Saraswati, money and erudition, the matters that brought her here. Rama, Sita, Lakshmana and Hanuman . . . Gazing at them with compassion and gratitude, she thinks of all they have endured, the private doubts, mental tests, failures, betrayals. And here they are welcoming her, shining and beautiful and so well put together. She performs a sincere series of obeisances and settles to the task of settling herself in.

Or she starts to and then stops. She thinks she should ask whether she is needed. But whom should she ask? Senior Mami, seemingly completely removed from the operation of the household? Her sisters-in-law—where are they? Baskaran is coming into the great hall now from the veranda—perhaps she should ask him. But what's the protocol in this house for talking to her husband?

He beckons her impatiently from the puja room doorway, where she stands like a golden deer, torn between stillness and flight. Relieved to have a signal, she goes to him and asks in a stage whisper, "What should I do now?"

"I don't know," he whispers back. He's wearing a fresh kurta and dhoti, and a different scent from the one he wore this morning. "Did my sisters-in-law tell you?"

Janaki shrugs uncertainly. She doesn't think they did.

"Are you hungry?" Baskaran asks with concern. "Tiffin is at three o'clock."

Janaki shakes her head. "What about—should I be helping to cook?"

"I really have no idea." He smiles helplessly.

"Where," she asks, "where is the tiffin being prepared?"

"The paadasaalai kitchen."

They stand there another moment, perplexed but not willing to part, until Janaki takes matters in hand. "I'll ask your mother what I should do. I can't go wrong that way."

"Yes . . ." He purses his lips. "Unless she's asleep or not in a mood to tell you. Or doesn't know herself!"

Janaki frowns at him reprovingly as he smiles at her. Are they flirting? How fun! She goes off to find her mother-in-law.

She finds her sisters-in-law first, strewn in the women's room with their children like more jumbles of fabric and feminine fancy. Janaki doesn't want to undermine their authority, but neither does she want to address questions to them, especially in hearing or sight of Senior Mami, that really should be put to the matriarch.

But Janaki has not only been raised to please. She has also absorbed—so thoroughly she doesn't even realize it—the finest points of strategy and diplomacy. She enters the women's room, greeting her sisters-in-law. She pauses as though to ask them something and then starts gently and advances to the door of Senior Mami's chamber. Her mother-in-law is semi-recumbent, listening to a radio discourse on Tamil poetry. Janaki addresses her question to the floor. "What work should I be doing now?" she asks with formal respect.

After more than several tense seconds, Vasantha emits a pip of breath and asks, in such a low voice Janaki can hardly make it out, "What were you thinking of doing?"

It's a risk, but Janaki decides to be honest. "I was thinking of helping in the kitchen or arranging my things."

After another pause, Swarna suggests, "They might need help in the kitchen."

"Go and arrange your things," Senior Mami orders decisively.

"Yes," replies Janaki with eager obedience.

Crying intermittently, she spends an hour putting the mattress on the bed—a mattress made from the fabric she got in Madras, stuffed with bolls she herself gathered and cleaned—and the sheets on the mattress. She had embroidered the edges of the sheets, even designed the pattern of English flowers. She puts her formal saris in the cupboard with the moth-repellant sachets she sewed from old blouses—she got the recipe for the herbal fillings from a women's magazine she found at Gayatri's.

At ten minutes before three o'clock, she descends. Never a trip wasted: she carries her four other everyday saris, two bright and new, two nearly so. She takes them through to the back and uses a pole to hang them in a free space on the sari rod beyond the bathroom.

The men and children are gathering for the meal, seating themselves in the main hall, along with Vasantha, who assists with the children. Senior Mami eats in her room. Swarna indicates that Janaki should follow her, and they go through a door in the courtyard wall, so that they are back of the paadasaalai, where three cooks are arranging serving dishes just behind the kitchen. The daughters-in-law, along with one of the cooks, carry these back to serve: silky idlis and *thayir vadai*, lentil nuggets swimming in creamy yogourt, with mint and coconut chutneys smooth as if made from flower petals. Every day *is* a festival in this house, Janaki thinks, trying to attune her pace and rhythm to that of her sister-in-law. She even succeeds in fulfilling one strange requirement against her training. Convention has it that anyone serving food must insist on further helpings, until the eater covers his banana leaf with his hands, pleading satiation. Senior Mami has a difficulty the daughters-in-law are charged with correcting, for the sake of her health: she is unable to refuse food or to leave it uneaten. Her daughters-in-law therefore have been instructed by their husbands to find artful ways of limiting her quantities: after she is served a judicious second portion and perhaps a minuscule third, the items are not offered again.

Janaki's contentment is only slightly dented by Swarna, who suggests Janaki is messily attired, that she doesn't properly know serving etiquette, that she is moving too slowly or too quickly, until Janaki is in a transport of irritation, and grateful for her grandmother's training, which enables her to mask her reaction and to feel confident that Swarna is wrong. At 3:45, she eats her own tiffin together with Swarna, while Vasantha serves them.

As she goes, after tiffin, to take up a place in the women's room, she feels a flash of pride at being so genteel, so protected. Silent and invisible in her passage, just like her grandmother in a way. Sivakami so respects herself that she has almost never been seen on the street after sunrise. Janaki can't think even of one time (except that time in Munnur, in the rain, but Janaki passes over that quickly). She thinks of the Brahmin women employed in the kitchen. Were they born poor, or did something happen? *God's grace, that's all that separates us from life's humiliations.* If she had chosen the other flower packet, she might not be here. And what if her father had been in charge of getting her married—would she ever have gotten married at all? She wonders what everyone, Kamalam especially, is doing back in Cholapatti.

Her veena is still in its wrappings—her sisters-in-law either are not bold enough for that or not interested.

"Shall I take out the veena?" she asks, again unsure of whom she is asking.

"If you want," says Vasantha ambiguously.

Janaki glances in at her mother-in-law's room, but the great woman doesn't look up from her reading.

Vairum had insisted on having the instrument packed professionally. Still, Janaki couldn't help fearing for it and so sighs with relief when it is finally unclothed, curving and gleaming in the late-afternoon sun like a cobra ready to be worshipped. "Shall I play?" she asks, not fully confident of the answer. Her sisters-in-law say nothing, but she hears an affirmative grunt from the front room. She tunes, and plays "Sakala Kala Vani" and "Jaggadhodharana," grateful for the leisure to practise. Her sisters-in-law continue reading and playing with the children, though once, when one of the boys gets noisy, Senior Mami shouts, "Hush, child!" from her hideout.

Janaki has another reason to be glad for moving to Pandiyoor: Vani visits her parents every few months, and Janaki is sure her sporadic lessons will resume. She is particularly hopeful that she will finally learn the Bharatiyar number she first heard on All-India Radio when Vani played her Navaratri concert. Vani's version of "Chinnan Cheeru Killiyai Kannama," is becoming famous. She set it to a *raga-malikai*, a garland of ragas, the scale changing with each stanza. There's talk, Janaki heard at her wedding, of having Vani make a gramophone recording of it.

Janaki concludes her second piece and her eye lights on the harmonium, which looks dusty. It should be covered with a cloth, she thinks, if it's not going to be cared for. Maybe she can sew a cover for it.

"Whose is that?" she asks politely.

"Mine," Swarna says.

"Oh, how lovely," Janaki soldiers on. "Perhaps you could sing something for us?"

"Oh, I don't think so." Swarna smiles sourly. "Perhaps you could."

Janaki is confused and looks down at her instrument, pretending to examine a string.

"Miss Perfect," Swarna whispers.

Janaki freezes, not entirely sure she has heard correctly, then hears Baskaran calling her from the main hall. She rises, grateful, with apologetic glances to her sisters-in-law, who ignore her, and takes her leave of Senior Mami.

It's time for them to pay the first few of the numerous required visits they must make, as a newly married couple, up and down the Brahmin quarter. Out of respect, they will visit Vani's parents first, their seniormost relatives on the quarter. They walk, slightly apart and not speaking, along Double Street in the direction of the Krishna temple, greeting neighbours on verandas. Vani's parents' house is, gratifyingly, not as grand as Janaki's in-laws', though it would have cowed her before she was married. The talk is strange and lively. Vani's father describes recent progress in his attempts to start a school based on his system of calisthenics and Janaki pecks at a silver plate loaded with murrukku and *halwa* as she eyes a china cabinet stocked with Vani's mother's collection of vintage weapons. At one point, the woman runs to it to extract a nineteenth-century French switchblade, whose mechanism she demonstrates with a cackle.

Janaki, dismayed, checks her watch surreptitiously. She inquires politely about Vani and receives an earful, including the welcome news that Vani will visit next month.

At eight-thirty, the evening repast is served in Dhoraisamy's household, a simple meal. Janaki, after having visited three homes in which she was rigorously required to snack, wants nothing but a little yogourt rice. She and Baskaran are seated together and served by the sisters-in-law, one of the few nods to tradition in this otherwise uncon-ventional first day. After today, Baskaran will eat with the men and Janaki with the women.

When the meal is done, the cooks of the house proper pour sweet hot milk with boiled almonds into silver tumblers, inverting a bowl on top, then turning them both so the bowl can be carried by its lip. Vasantha carries one to their father-in-law while Swarna carries another to Senior Mami. The brothers are chatting in the main hall. The children are asleep in various places. There is an ayah and a ser-vant to keep track of them whenever a mother is not available. Each of the wives then takes a tumbler of milk and ascends to her bedchamber. The husbands shortly follow.

Janaki sits on the bed, scared once again. Unlike city girls, she knows how babies are made. And she is sharp, so when she overhears things, she puts the two and two together. But knowing the facts of life doesn't prepare a person for living.

Baskaran looks down as he enters, glances up, then down, and smiles a little. He closes the door, fumbles the bolt closed and closes the shutters on that side, which give onto the corridor. He clears his throat and hesitates, then crosses the room and reaches through browning garlands to close the shutters on the street-facing windows as well. The house across the street—Baskaran's uncle's—also has a second storey.

Janaki had stood as he entered, and now holds the milk out to him. He takes it gravely and urges, "Sit." He again hesitates—there is a chair in one corner of the room—and opts to sit on the other end of the bed. "Sit," he repeats in a low voice. "Sit, ma." She collapses a tiny bit at this endearment, and slowly perches again on the high mattress-topped bedstead. He pours the milk into the bowl, stopping before the almonds at the bottom slip out. He pours it back and forth, twice, to mix and cool it, then pours himself several sips, and drinks, watching her, before he pours a little more that he holds out to her. She accepts wordlessly and drinks. He pours her another and then shares the sweet, milk-cooked almonds out between them.

He takes the tumbler from her and puts it and the bowl by the door, then turns down the flame on the kerosene lamp so the room is dim and seems to brighten again as their eyes adjust.

"I was listening to you play this afternoon," he says. He sits on the bed again, a little closer. "So beautiful, it was . . ." He speaks with real passion, or so it seems to her. "Everyone was touched, I could feel it. I imagine you don't even notice others, though, when you play, do you?"

"I . . . I haven't played very much for anyone outside the family. Visitors occasionally. But I like it." She feels a shy smile tugging her lip upward, covers her mouth with her hand, lowers it with a breath.

He moves closer to her, awkwardly, and as though forcing his arm through a thin barrier, touches her face. Gaining confidence, he begins stroking her brows, temples and cheek. What a strange way of looking at her, she thinks, and how good it feels to be touched. She likes how he looks, his chubby cheeks and receding hairline. He looks like someone who means what he says. And he looks gentle.

Her face and neck feel ticklish and warmed, as if the skin is puffing slightly as he touches it. Now he strokes her shoulder, her arm and the hand on the bed, now her back, the skin above and below the lines of her blouse. She stiffens a bit as he leans toward her and brushes the base of her neck with his lips. He leans back to look at her, and she relaxes as he takes her face in one hand and kisses her neck again, stroking her forehead with his thumb as though to draw from it the tension of this strange day.

He is succeeding—this is the strangest part of it. He stands and removes his kurta. A twirled gold chain and his sacred thread lie on his mostly smooth chest. He has a single patch of hair, just above where his belly starts to curve out. He sits on the bed again and draws the pallu of her sari from around her waist and shoulder as he lies her down. He reaches to lift her legs onto the bed and kisses her belly, all hollows below her blouse.

Looking up at her, he puts both his hands under her thin shoulder blades and lifts her toward him to kiss her eyes and cheeks and each of her lips, and puts his cheek to hers and to her lips and she kisses him back just a little, as if to see what will happen. He emits a sigh as though he had no right to expect it.

She kisses his shoulders and neck. She has no idea if this is what she is supposed to do, but he is not objecting. It's funny to be kissing a grown man she hardly knows, but he did it first. He sighs several times and then brings a palm to her breast and strokes it through the cloth of her blouse. Janaki gasps—such a sensation! He watches her face anxiously, then smiles tentatively and tries it again.

"Does it feel nice?" he asks.

"Yes!" she gasps. "Er—I think so."

"Shall I continue?" He smiles, bringing his other hand from her back.

The only direct instruction Janaki received on these matters was from Gayatri, who said, "Whatever your husband asks for, whenever he asks for it, say yes."

"Yes," says Janaki.

He unbuttons her blouse with difficulty and his face shows complicated emotions at the sight of the cotton bodice underneath, with buttons concealed under the arm. There is mutual awkwardness as the blouse and bodice are removed. Much later, they will giggle retrospectively at their own seriousness. Now he strokes his mouth between her breasts and over them, holds her large, young nipples in his lips, then, gently, between his teeth, and then takes her whole breast in his mouth, or as much of it as he can. Janaki, repulsed at the sight and the damp, mystified at her enjoyment, closes her eyes.

When she opens them, it's because he is now unwinding her carefully wrapped sari from her narrow hips. Terror shudders subtly from her feet to her shoulders as he slips off the last crumpled yards, and she crosses her legs and arms. He has unwrapped his dhoti and now lies on top of her in loincloth and creamy skin. He rolls her awkwardly from side to side.

"Will you—" his voice cracks. "Will you take it off, this?"

He is giving her the knot to his loincloth. She looks at him in disbelief and he at her in fear and they both start to laugh. She undoes the knot, it falls away, and she closes her eyes again.

He is petting her hair, his cheek against hers, murmuring, "You are so beautiful." Warmth waves through her legs and loins, before she is hit by unjust bumps of hot, insistent pain. He stops when she cries out and holds her face as she whimpers.

"Is it very bad?"

"Yes," she replies, as instructed.

"It hurts the bride, at first," he says, starting slowly to move again. He clearly received a different set of instructions. "Shall I stop?"

"Yes," she says again, tense and glistening now with a sudden sheen of sweat.

He stops, cradling her head as though to console her, stroking one leg as though to relax it. She does start to relax a little, and he kisses her temple and begins moving again. It still hurts, but differently, and she tries not to stiffen again. He lifts himself up on his elbows above her, looking at her hair and face with an investigative air, as though she can't see him. As he's inhabited by the act's presiding spirit, he groans the names of several gods, gasps, and then the spirit passes.

He slides off to one side and immediately begins snoring. She gathers herself and sees spots: red stains on the sheet. Oh no, she thinks, but only because the sight of blood is always distressing. Gayatri had told her there would be blood the first time, but now she remembers what to do about the stains, and that she can do it tomorrow.

She had wondered for a second whether he was going to sneeze and had hoped he wouldn't because sneezing is a bad omen. The temple fire and the madwoman's death at her wedding could also have been seen as a bad omen, but no one knew how to interpret that. Janaki might have thought it strange that Baskaran fell asleep as he did, but it was far less strange than what had come before. She doesn't feel offended or relieved. She rises, puts her bodice and blouse back on, and a cotton sari to sleep in, and twists down the kerosene lamp key to douse the flame completely. Feeling shy even though Baskaran is asleep, she creeps back into the bed.

The next day, Baskaran runs an errand in Madurai. On returning, he presents her with a glass unicorn that rotates on one hoof while the box beneath it, covered in dusty green velvet, tinkles a tinny Brahms lullaby. The day after, she receives a bar of Raja Snow's Musk Soap with matching hair oil. The day after that, he presses on her a nail buffer and promises he will ask his cousin how it works. On the fourth day, a block-printed Bengali blouse piece. On the fifth, a flat beribboned box of caramels. The sixth, a book of embroidery patterns. On the seventh day after her arrival, he gives her a leather-trimmed kaleidoscope and they take turns being dazzled, lying on the bed and aiming it at the lamp flame, gawping like children at the tumbling stars.

36.
At Home in Madras
1942

IT IS THE EVE OF VAIRUM and Vani's trip to Pandiyoor, where Vani will stay a month with her parents. Vairum slips in from work as Vani practises music in their salon. He reclines on a divan and closes his eyes, opening them again as she finishes playing just a few minutes later.

"Oh, my dear, is that all?"

She smiles and nods, flexing her fingers and rolling her shoulders. It was a long piece.

"I must have been later than I thought." He pats the divan next to him as she rises from the Kashmiri silk rug where the veena rests on two small ringed bolsters. "Come and sit." She settles herself and he absently strokes a tendril of hair from her forehead. "So tomorrow we go." He pats his legs. "I'm interested to see how my niece is faring. Your protégée!"

Vani is silent, but she talks only under rare circumstances. When they go in to dinner, she will tell one of her stories, and Vairum will listen as happily as a little boy.

"Poor, motherless, fatherless girl," he goes on, playing with his wife's hand. Vani looks at him sharply and his face darkens. "She is fatherless! None of those children has seen my brother-in-law in years. And he never showed them a father's love," he says, his mottled face now forming into an expression he recognizes by feel from a time before memory, the look of a child whose father doesn't see him. Now Vani takes his face in her hands, looking worried, murmuring consolations. "I need a child to raise, my love," he tells her, in tears.

She wags her head, her forehead to his. She knows this.

"We have so much to give," he says.

She continues rubbing her forehead against his, an obsessive, desperate gesture, as though trying to graft his dappled skin to hers, cell by burning cell.

"Please, Vani." He tries to pull away, but she won't let him. "I shouldn't have said anything."

He succeeds in moving away a little, but she grips his hands and rocks back and forth, moaning quietly. He has seen her get like this, very occasionally, when she feels her own terrific need meet his. Her grief at their son's death frightened him: for a week, she made this same low keening, a sound he felt he recognized from her music. Although he felt close to madness himself, he knew that losing her would have done him in and found the strength to coax her back, as he has several times since, as he does now.

"It will happen, my love. I know it will still happen." He puts his shoulders against hers to absorb her motion. "Look at us. God will not deny us."

37.
Married Life
1943

JANAKI GRADUALLY LEARNS about Baskaran's family from her husband, as they snuggle together nights in the upper room, as well as from observation.

Dhoraisamy looks after the institutions funded by the trust and enjoys and endures the social approbation, privileges and headaches that accompany this responsibility. He has to hire the cooks and other servants for the paadasaalai, for example, but has use of them for his own family. He is fortunate, as he is wont to say more often than necessary, in having an excellent overseer for all the charity's operational needs.

"Mr. V. Kandasamy." He presented the accountant to Janaki with a flourish. "A gem of a man, a bit excitable and perhaps over-efficient, perhaps takes things a bit too personally, but it's all in the interests of the trust!"

Mr. Kandasamy, a small square man with a nervous squint, stood, clutching one of the largest ledgers, which he nearly dropped as he tried to put his palms together in greeting.

Janaki meets a few of Baskaran's friends, Brahmins for the most part, much like him: well-dressed boys with acute senses of humour. Like most fashionable Brahmin youth these days, Baskaran is in favour of Indian independence, and though he has moments of genuinely lathered passion about this, he can't take any of it too seriously for too long. Confronted by anyone with very deep convictions, he treads between Gandhian glamour and Nehruvian practicality. He and his friends tend to laugh off fuming, sweaty types who care more about ideas than people. Janaki gathers that Baskaran is a friend whom friends count on, and a son in whom his father confides.

Janaki fully approves of Baskaran in everything but his snuff-taking and his apparent lack of caste feeling. He appears to believe everyone is created equal and is equally deserving of respect, but that is so clearly not the case—she doesn't know where to start, though, and so doesn't try. At least, it seems, he has no intention of making her eat in non-Brahmins' houses or do other improper things that would dishonour her and her upbringing.

Some nights, Baskaran asks her questions about her childhood, so different from his. He asks how it was that they ended up living at her grandmother's house, and Janaki dutifully gives him the standard answer, that her grandmother thought the children needed some place they could stay, that her mother's health was always fragile and it was better she not spread her energies so thin. When others have asked her this, her answer has sounded plausible. She's not sure why, now, it sounds inadequate, almost deceitful. Perhaps Baskaran picks up on this because he continues to ask.

"That's unusual, though—that you would live with your mother's mother, instead of with your father's parents, isn't it?" he asks gently but with real interest.

"Yes," Janaki replies hesitantly. "I'm not sure why that was. Maybe my mother's mother thought she could do a better job. My father's parents aren't too well off."

"Have I heard that they sold a lot of land to your uncle?" Baskaran shifts a little, on his side, his head leaning into his hand, the other hand on Janaki's stomach.

"Mm-hm," Janaki says. "But it wasn't my uncle's money that paid for us, mostly. For our upbringing, I mean. It was my grandmother's own inheritance, her manjakkani."

"Interesting." Baskaran furrows his brow. "But wasn't your dad's salary enough? It sounds like your grandmother wasn't exactly extravagant."

Janaki feels herself blushing. "My dad . . . isn't very good with money." She takes a breath, aware of the depth and luxury of this intimacy with Baskaran, of how protected she feels in this room, revealing to him things she has never said to anyone else. "I doubt he ever offered to pay for us. I don't think—"

She starts to cry and Baskaran sits up, alarmed, and puts his arm around her.

"I don't think he ever really wanted to keep us. I don't think he even really noticed we were gone. And my mother never fought to keep us." She is sobbing against his chest, Baskaran holding her, patting her head, his lips to her forehead.

He wipes her cheeks with his thumb. "But your grandmother loved you, didn't she?"

Janaki nods.

"She took good care of you. And your uncle," he continues, "he paid for your wedding. He's obviously very proud of you. Look at how puffed up he was when they came to visit at Navaratri."

Janaki sniffs and hiccups, calming. She knows he is trying to reassure and cheer her. But he has no idea of the trauma she has suffered (she's not sure she had any idea until she surprised herself with these tears), and she doesn't know whether to be glad of this or angry.

"And I think you are wonderful," he finishes, looking into her eyes. "You are a gem, and I will always look after you."

Now she knows: she is glad, glad, glad he has never suffered the humiliations of neglect.

Later, he falls asleep before she does, though she is drowsy, emptied of tears and of lust. In that state, she wonders why she didn't mention Bharati when talking about her father. Because the conversation took another turn? Because it's not directly relevant? She wonders when and if she will have the chance, and in wondering, realizes that, even if the chance arises, she may not tell.

Janaki spends several hours each morning and evening in the women's room at Senior Mami's request. Janaki dislikes the room because it is untidy and airless and filled with Vasantha and Swarna's tension. They dislike it because it's the only room in the house where they absolutely cannot speak their minds (such as they are) because Senior Mami is sure to hear.

Janaki had sensed between Swarna and Vasantha a relationship that seemed more complex than that of sisters-in-law, and Baskaran had confirmed for her that they had been neighbours and friends since childhood. Vasantha's elder brother had gone to law school with Baskaran's brother Madhavan, who met his classmate's sister and fell in love. When it came time for the second brother, Easwaran, to marry, Vasantha suggested her chum.

"I don't think my mother much cares for either girl"—Baskaran smiles apologetically—"but she didn't stand in the way of my brothers' choosing. Perhaps there was no one else better!"

Janaki, diplomatically, listens without responding. Senior Mami torments the sisters-in-law to a degree that makes Janaki wonder if she admitted them to the family primarily for harassment. The women are, in Janaki's opinion, vapid and spiteful. In Senior Mami's position, she would ignore them, but they are difficult to ignore.

When Vasantha and Swarna first enter the women's room after a meal has concluded, there is typically a long silence. The sisters-in-law settle themselves, picking up magazines or patting a child. Janaki sits neither with nor apart from them. Finally, one of the two introduces a topic.

"I hear," Vasantha might say, clearing her throat and speaking as quietly as possible, "I hear Mangala Mami's son has declared he will only marry a widow—so they have placed an advertisement!"

"Oh," says Swarna, certain of what she thinks but not of what she should say. "Terrible, terrible."

"Why is it terrible?" Senior Mami calls from her room.

Vasantha and Swarna, who know she must agree with them, have no idea why.

"Ahem," Vasantha might cough. Or she might attempt a rejoinder. "Well, it's wrong. A widow!"

"Hush." The disembodied voice of their mother-in-law silences them.

If neither sister-in-law speaks, Senior Mami says, "Say something, bring me some news."

So one of them starts, "My sister sent me a letter. Her husband took their children to see a movie with Rita Hayworth!"

Janaki waits to find out if this is good or bad. The other one also waits. Senior Mami, though they can't see her, is waiting.

Finally, one says, "How awful!" or "How wonderful!" Senior Mami says, "Hush," and silence is reinstated. Often, now, she follows this command with another: "Play, Janaki." Which Janaki does, her sisters-in-law striking daggers at her with glances so she's forced to close her eyes.

Her sisters-in-law, lying on cushions in the women's room, often read aloud from newspapers and magazines, sensational stories of freedom fighters Janaki listens to with disapproval while she labours at her handiwork. They also pass on local gossip, including politically themed stories: a Brahmin man who rents half of a ramshackle house on Single Street is known to be on the independence workers' message circuit. He is a cook who has three daughters and no sons, and therefore can't risk imprisonment, but whenever a freedom fighter is on the lam nearby, this man, who can barely afford pride, carries dosais to them. Janaki imagines men crouched in tall grass, mud caked in their hair, shaming their loved ones for a country that has never existed and probably never will.

Even one of Vani's two gigantic lawyer uncles is gradually and bitterly parting ways with his family by giving free legal defence to, as he puts it, "people who haven't done anything wrong." His family disputes his definition of "wrong," suggesting that breaking the law is criminal and therefore "wrong," but he informs them rudely that the laws themselves might be "wrong."

These are confusing times, thinks Janaki, as an excuse for not trying harder to understand them. She purses her lips and admires a strip of trim she has just finished crocheting for a baby's undershirt—something real and pleasing. She's sure Sivakami would disapprove of her holding political opinions, and she has no intention of forming any. Why do Indians need to run the country, as long as they can live freely and get jobs? Most often, the talk reminds her of Bharati's first father, as she has come to think of him. She wonders if he got out of jail, if he managed to stay out. This leads her to think of her own father. Will she ever see Goli again? And what is Bharati doing now?

Owing to Baskaran's family's wealth, Janaki had expected that festivals here would be celebrated with the kind of flair Gayatri used to display before her family fortunes started to slide. Instead, Deepavali and Pongal in the Pandiyoor household are marked by celebrations proper but not extravagant, a spirit more in keeping with her grandmother's. All the household members are given money, new clothes or both, and guests are received. Janaki has taken over the responsibility for drawing the kolam daily on the threshold and in the puja room. She is given a box of coloured powders she may use to make special designs, as is customary during this festival

Vasantha mutters bitterly throughout these festivals about how much better her natal house does them. Swarna readily agrees, in private corners of the house far away from the women's room. Janaki can't say the same, but had hoped for better and analyzes the reasons their celebrations are so relatively paltry. It is not that Baskaran's family can't afford to do better: the gifts given to all the family members are generous. Nor do either of her parents-in-law believe in austerity, the way Sivakami does. Rather, Janaki senses that Senior Mami has no interest in opening their house to pomp and chatter.

This family displays its bourgeois pedigree in other ways. One is in the distribution of charity during the festival for the goddess Meenakshi of Madurai. Annually, the temple goddess is married in grand style. There are daily processions, in which a smallish idol is dressed and pulled through the streets by worshippers in a two-storey wooden temple car, and lengthy pujas at her temple. The city floods with pilgrims and petitioners as each caste community commemorates the occasion in its own way. The Kozhandaisamy Travellers' Rest Home, run by Baskaran's family's trust, feeds Brahmin pilgrims for free and ladles water and buttermilk out on the street to anyone who is thirsty, caste-no-bar. Every family member boasts of how the drinks are offered to all without regard to caste, suggesting they think it a virtue to reach out to other castes, even if they wouldn't think of practising this in any other way. Family members themselves stay in the chattram and serve, which Janaki considers evidence of Brahmins' committed magnanimity. She, too, takes her turn in the hot sun with the ladle. They wouldn't serve untouchables, of course, but untouchables don't pass and don't ask.

And in May, when the hot weather is at its blasting peak, Janaki witnesses Senior Mami preferring the force of her hospitality on the Brahmin quarter of Pandiyoor. She sponsors a moral discourse, to last ten evenings, by a Thanjavur philosopher-orator of some repute. Janaki is told, by Baskaran, who thinks it amusing, and by Vasantha and Swarna, who find it tiresome, that hearing and talking with these *bhagavadars* is one of Senior Mami's favourite activities. She sponsors these events once or twice annually, erecting a canopy along half the length of Double Street so that the entire Brahmin quarter may attend and be edified. They are even offered coffee, water and snacks as the man declaims from the veranda.

Each afternoon, the young philosopher is invited to take his post-tiffin coffee in Dhoraisamy's study, so that Senior Mami may converse with him, from her room, on the previous night's lecture. He and Dhoraisamy sit in the study, and Senior Mami, whom they can hear through a high air vent between the two rooms, puts questions and comments to the scholar by addressing them, for propriety's sake, to her husband. At night, Baskaran, laughing until he cries, imitates his father, who looks from the air vent to the young philosopher as though watching a tennis match. Dhoraisamy doesn't read much; neither does Baskaran. It would never occur to them to take on wandering scholars, but Baskaran finds it vastly amusing to watch his mother engaged in her favourite sport. Janaki is, nightly, convinced by the young orator. She has never seen anyone extemporize like this, drawing on other commentators, quoting scripture extensively—and yet her mother-in-law, each afternoon, converts Janaki again with arguments demonstrating equal breadth and acuity of reference! Each afternoon, whether because he doesn't want to argue with his hostess, or because he feels himself defeated in the debate, the young scholar capitulates, complimenting Dhoraisamy on his wife's erudition.

When first she heard Senior Mami arguing with the scholar on his own terms, Janaki felt a flooding envy that she was not better educated. She wondered how long it would take her to read through Senior Mami's library and become such a complex and wide-ranging thinker herself. The impulse quickly passed, and by the time she hears the scholar's concluding arguments, at the end of the lecture series, when he, as required, delivers moral prescriptions and rules for good living, she has developed quite a different way of thinking. The point of educating women, in her opinion, is to train them to better uphold the virtue and well-being of the family. Otherwise, she thinks, they may as well be courtesans. Janaki's own ambition is to be a good wife and mother, an aim at which she is not convinced her mother-in-law has succeeded.

Even though Senior Mami observes the basic rules of propriety, never showing her face to their guest and never addressing him directly, Janaki, in thoughts so private she can hardly articulate them to herself, much less to Baskaran, thinks her mother-in-law is unladylike. Her children don't seem to have suffered from her seeming coldness, but Janaki thinks this is because her emasculated father-in-law, whom she adores, is so encouraging and affectionate, and compensates. The more she thinks about it, in fact, the more she wonders whether Senior Mami's erudition, which cows Janaki, robbed Baskaran of the motivation to study. *What would be the point?* he might have thought. His elder brothers are lawyers, his mother an intellectual. What did they leave for him but the position of assistant to his father, the part of the good son?

Janaki's reflections on her mother-in-law's style of domestic management are, in part, being provoked by Vasantha and Swarna, who have begun to mutter about getting out. Janaki hadn't been sure she understood correctly, when first they began their dark hints. Janaki, hurrying to serve food with Vasantha, mentioned that their father-in-law had suggested she might teach the rudiments of Carnatic music to Vasantha's eldest daughter, who had begun showing interest. Vasantha drew up defensively and told Janaki, "You know, an extended family household isn't the only way. Just for your information." Janaki had no idea what this meant, but when Swarna said something similar in response to an equally innocuous comment, Janaki asked Baskaran what was happening.

Baskaran smiled unhappily. "Yes, my brothers have spoken to me. Their wives want an independent household. Each. Vasantha Mani's eldest sister's sister-in-law didn't get along with her mother-in-law and they just took their share of the family property and set up on their own. Now Vasantha Mani thinks it's a done thing. And it's the type of idea Swarna would have come up with on her own, if Vasantha Mani hadn't planted it."

"But . . . that's a ridiculous . . ." Janaki felt short of breath, her stomach roiling. "Your father surely won't . . . your mother cannot permit this. I know she will not," she concluded, feeling she had reassured herself slightly.

Perhaps Senior Mami should be told, Janaki thinks. But if Vasantha and Swarna learn that Janaki was in any way responsible for telling her, they would be furious, and Janaki is not sure she wants to risk that. Further, while Janaki knows her mother-in-law would bridle and resist the parting, she also blames Senior Mami for not doing more to cultivate the attachment and affection of her daughters-in-law. Janaki and Baskaran choose to stay out of the matter. In the months following, it becomes clear that Vasantha and Swarna are pressuring their husbands. Neither man, however, is a master of strategy or courage. They try to approach their father, but sideways, like crabs, waving their eyes at their goal but afraid to face it full on. Their father, no fonder of confrontations than they are, scuttles away from them as fast as they can approach.

When they achieve no results, Vasantha and Swarna implement their own plans of action, using the slim means available to them. Perhaps inspired by Mahatma Gandhi's campaigns of passive resistance, they begin campaigns of passive aggression. They begin interfering in the kitchen, ordering the cooks to use quantities of ghee and sugar that would have befitted a wedding pre-war and are now a terrific expense and challenge to procure. None of the staff dares question them; Mr. Kandasamy sweats over the accounts; the paadasaalai boys start pudging up. They further deplete the family coffers by insisting that their husbands replace all their jewellery and buy only imported cloth in a time when the whole country is turning to native goods. But the genius of Vasantha and Swarna's campaign is its exploitation of Senior Mami's possibly fatal flaw. When they serve her, they no longer limit what she is offered, but instead press on her enormous quantities of the rich food, so that she becomes grossly flatulent. They also become flagrantly insouciant with her.

Finding the atmosphere in the women's room intolerable, Janaki looks for chores to occupy her elsewhere in the house, and comes up with the idea of offering Sanskrit tutorials to the paadasaalai boys. She asks Baskaran to approach the instructor in basic Sanskrit on her behalf.

The pupils are a proud and pitiable crew. Among them are two pairs of brothers, but all eighteen boys look similar: their heads are shaved, leaving a brief kudumi, which hairstyle is now found only in the priestly ranks. They wear a standard-issue dhoti and breast cloth of coarse cotton weave. They are here because their parents cannot afford to give them the quality of nutrition and education the charity will give them, and so have left the children here to be raised in orthodoxy. Janaki might identify with these children more than she would ever admit. She relieves the Sanskrit master of the younger students, delivering the drills and exercises whose practice she perfected in her own questing childhood, and finds, in this work, a release from the pressure-sealed jar of the household.

Baskaran suggests to Janaki that his brothers don't really want households of their own, run by their wives. "Who would," he shrugs slyly, "with wives like that?"

Janaki thinks it improper for her to answer, and disloyal, even though she feels little loyalty to her sisters-in-law, especially in this low enterprise.

Baskaran frowns at her. "Is this what you want, also? To have your own home?"

"I absolutely do not. *Chi!*"

"Good, good," says Baskaran, smoothing the quilt. "I want you to be happy."

"I am happy," she says irritably as she turns the lamp key down and gets into bed. "Very happy. I couldn't be happier."

Families should not even be permitted to think of splitting up. Authority is responsibility, unity is security, Gandhi wants to split from the British, Jinnah wants Muslims to split from India, the non-Brahmins want to split from polite society . . . how will it end? Think of Vairum and Vani. Janaki tosses and rails in sleep while Baskaran holds the quilt fast.

She dreams of visiting Vasantha Nadu and Swarna Nadu, two countries in a house so large she never sees more than two walls at once. The floor is covered in what Janaki first thinks are enormous kolams coloured in with bright powders, but when she draws near to admire them, she realizes they are maps drawn in rice powder and the differently coloured areas are territories and states, each with its own governor and laws.

Vasantha and Swarna swarm like ants through an anthill, continually brushing away borders and redrawing them differently, quick as Janaki herself erases and redraws kolam lines in the morning when she sleepily connects the wrong dots. Janaki yearns to return to Janakipattu, her own city, but it has been erased, or amalgamated. She is stateless and homeless. Responsible to no one; no one responsible for her. She knows, in dreaming as in waking life, that there is no worse fate—standing still, condemned forever to pass through the strange lands that appear and vanish beneath her unmoving feet.

Clerk ex machina: the meek and ever-reliable accountant, Mr. Kandasamy, provides a means of resolution.

"In chess," he explains to Dhoraisamy and Baskaran, having clearly rehearsed every word, "this would be called a defensive move, except that, for Sir, and Sir's family, there is no risk. At this juncture, all the higher castes have reason to fear. If—no, let us say, *when* Congress assumes power, they will work hard to prove they have no bias toward the Brahmin. They will treat with us severely. We will be thoroughly oppressed. There will not only be the reserved posts for the lower castes in government and colleges, the administrative and educational biases. I have started to suspect there will also be vengeful taxation. It is not without precedent." Mr. Kandasamy took a breath, marking the end of his magnificent preamble.

Dhoraisamy had worked himself into a complicit lather. "What to do? Our dear Mr. Kandasamy, you alone can advise us."

"Well." Mr. Kandasamy mopped his brow, looking earnest and purposeful. "We know that the charity's finances are thoroughly separate from those of the family. And we have kept them strictly and, more importantly, provably so. However, I do think it my responsibility to warn Sir of possible vulnerability to others who are adept at and interested in manipulation. This is my suggestion: you must house your personal assets in what is known as a 'tax shelter.' Have you heard this term?" Mr. Kandasamy looked suddenly a few inches taller, Baskaran reported to Janaki with a giggle, and as though he had more hair.

"No, no, no, no." Dhoraisamy looked to his son, who also shrugged.

"Permit me to be direct." Mr. Kandasamy smiled with greater assurance than usual. "Your greatest assets are your own sons, are they not? One thinks it could be wise to house them . . . in houses. Of their own."

Baskaran and his father made faces demonstrating shock and reluctant receptiveness. Mr. Kandasamy plowed on. "Give them their share of their personal inheritances and pretend—if only on the books, more than this you need not do except to revenue inspectors and their relatives—you no longer care for them. It is the one way to ensure Sir operates at a loss."

Mr. Kandasamy, who, Baskaran later remarks, has a surprising flair for drama, allows a decorous silence, within which the mood alters and settles. "I know it must seem a heartless and scandalous notion," he goes on, "not to keep one's children and grandchildren under one's own roof, but many respectable families are considering this, and naturally I would . . . ahem, one would never suggest that Sir's sons go further than Single Street." Finally, Mr. Kandasamy draws a breath to conclude his speech. "The charitable institution was established to propagate the values and good name of our caste. It is my duty to guard against any threat to the institution and its values. I urge Sir to take this suggestion. Avoid any whiff of caste betrayal. Long live the Brahmins!"

Janaki is quite sure Mr. Kandasamy did this because the charity's finances are not nearly so separate from the household's as they should be, and he would be out of a job if the charity's foundation were eaten through. Whether this is a philosophical end gained by practical means, though, or a practical end gained by philosophical means, the results are the same.

The household returns to its former deceptive and uneasy peace. Still, Janaki continues her work, leading Sanskrit tutorials with the paadasaalai students. She has always kept busy, and work is reassuring, especially in times of change.

⸻

OTHER CHANGES ARE IMMINENT, too, but these are expected and non-threatening. Janaki, who has always perceived more than she could understand, now embodies changes she cannot control. She has intense cravings for foods that, once she has eaten them, she never wants to see or smell again. She takes long naps and has fits of crying. With joy, relief and fearful apprehension, she watches two months pass without menstruating. The estimate is that she and Baskaran will become parents in summer of 1945, and she imagines herself going to Cholapatti for a visit and returning to Pandiyoor with a child.

Now, when she's in the women's room, she is making items for her own child's layette. Senior Mami has a radio; Janaki turns it on and off for her and listens to programs on current affairs and spiritual matters while doing her handiwork. She practises veena at least three or four times weekly, which is what she is doing when the telegram comes.

A paadasaalai boy peeps around the corner of the doorway to the women's room; they ignore him. He gradually edges over so that more than half of him is visible along the doorway's edge. Still, he is ignored. He is evidently here with a message—giving the boys small chores, everyone says patronizingly, is a way of making the pupils feel included in the family.

The boy, a jug-headed child of six with attention problems, starts to fidget and rustle, but Janaki doesn't notice, over the music. Finally, Swarna sits up and takes the envelope out of the tyke's hand. Senior Mami, noting the end of the standoff, immediately says, "Here." But the sisters-in-law, lest anyone forget that they are burrs and must be plucked, and because it amuses them, have kept up their

habit of disobeying their mother-in-law. Thus Swarna, hearing
Senior Mami's command, tears open the telegram.

Her eyes bulge, her jaw drops, and she gasps, "Janaki! Your sister!"

That evening, Janaki, accompanied by her husband, is on a bus bound
for the town of Kumbakonam. She is wondering how much longer
laughter can last in the world, now that it has been returned to its
source. Like the heroine Sita, in the Ramayana, swallowed by the
earth, Visalam has been taken by the giggling, gurgling River Kaveri
in flood.

Janaki knows what the neighbours will be saying. There's always
someone who is taken, in every generation—the question is only who
it will be and when. They all will have lost family members and will
want to talk about them, and Janaki and her siblings will be forced to
be polite while Visalam's husband and children . . . how will they bear
this loss?

Oh, how she hates the rainy season! Janaki slams the bus window's
shutter against the wet. Baskaran, at her side, says nothing. She starts
weeping again and eventually falls asleep on his shoulder. In the dark,
he lifts his hand to stroke her cheek and when she shifts, he brings her
head to rest on his shoulder once more.

At Visalam's family's house, three matrons Janaki has never met
rush at her, awash in tears. She feels her bile rising and dashes to
bend over some bushes. Baskaran explains about the pregnancy and
the ladies cluck. Janaki's sisters and Visalam's in-laws jockey past
the strangers to take her arms, ushering her in toward a bath and
sleep.

The stunned house is quiet. That's not always the way when
tragedy strikes a gregarious people. Visalam's in-laws had loved
Visalam as though she'd been born to them.

Her widower performs the necessary rites. He is in his early thir-
ties but looks ten years older than he did the last time Janaki saw him,
six months ago, his laugh lines like cuts in his gaunt face.

Saradha has come from Thiruchi; Sita from Tiruvannamalai;
Laddu has brought Kamalam and Radhai from Cholapatti. He will
return to Cholapatti for a week and bring Krishnan and Raghavan

back for the thirteenth-day ceremony so they needn't miss school. Vairum and Vani also arrive from Madras, in time to see Visalam's ashes committed to the river that took her life.

The night they all gather, Sita wonders aloud if their father knows. "Does any of you have the least idea where he is?" She looks around at them, facing blank, weepy looks.

"I . . ." Laddu clears his throat inefficiently. "I had sent Vairum Mama a telegram asking him to inform our father. He is the only one of us who might know where he is!" he says defensively in response to several incredulous looks. "And Vairum Mama is honourable. He would have done it."

Saradha looks at Sita with concern and says, "But maybe he didn't." Kamalam bites her lip. "Or couldn't find him."

But the next night, when Laddu discreetly asks Vairum, Vairum assures him, "Oh, yes, I certainly did. Sent him a telegram." Vairum smiles, softly sardonic, not without pity. "I didn't offer to pay for his bus fare, though. He might have thought that an insult."

"Where is he now?" Laddu asks, a bit too eagerly.

"He is very near, as it happens." Vairum wears an even, appraising expression. "Thiruchi. Barely fifty miles."

Laddu looks small and stammering. "And do you know he got it?"

"The telegram was sent to his home." Vairum rises and stretches. "Presumably, he got it." He looks around at Goli's children, who look back at him, with Sivakami's features, and Goli's, and Thangam's, and Vairum's own, and the looks of ancestors none of them will ever know.

"Good night," he bids them, and leaves for the chattram where he is lodged.

They are silent a while in this room they have been given, off the main hall. Everyone else is asleep. Then Sita explodes.

"Our father is a good-for-nothing! A good-for-nothing! Look at how he left us, vulnerable to Vairum Mama's insults and jibes all these years!"

Her siblings shush her, telling her in whispers to sit, as she marches around the room, incensed.

"Vairum Mama was right! All of his slights against our father were absolutely right and I'm going to tell him so. Visalam was . . ."

Here she gulps a little against a sob. "Visalam was a harmless soul and Appa couldn't even come to bid her farewell. I know what you all think of me." Saradha clucks in protest, but Sita doesn't appear to hear, and none of her other siblings say anything. "But even I can see what an innocent soul she was. I wish he weren't my father."

Her siblings are surprised. None of them has felt compelled to make a declaration of the sort Sita makes the next day, to Vairum.

"Vairum Mama, I was critical of you all these years, trying to be loyal to my father. I regret that now," she says, her voice trembling but clear. "You have done more than he ever has or will for our welfare. Thank you," she declares, breaking down a little.

Vairum looks bemused and unabashedly triumphant. "It was, ahem . . ." he smiles. "It was my duty to my sister, as I saw it, and duty is an honour to uphold."

"Yes." Sita wags her head with martial vigour, even through tears. "It is."

Janaki herself cannot help but contrast Baskaran's ministrations with her father's absence and her uncle's passions. Baskaran stays at a guest house some ten minutes away for three days, coming to ceremonies, helping with logistics and children, offering graceful words of consolation. At the end of three days, he returns to Pandiyoor, where he is needed, but Janaki knows that he will return for the thirteenth-day ceremony.

She thinks, not for the first time, that if only he had a job and didn't take snuff, he might be the perfect husband. When she speaks of him to Kamalam, though, as they lie side by side on their mats, taking this precious opportunity to exchange sisterly confidences, she emphasizes his faults, suspicious of the evil eye. Having seen two more households on the Pandiyoor Brahmin quarter reduced to penury through bad management of their family fortunes, she has started to wish, as her grandmother has from the start, that Baskaran were earning a regular income.

"But if he had a job," Kamalam says, "like Saradha Akka's and Sita Akka's husbands, he wouldn't be so flexible. It's very good of him to come here and help. The old ways had their benefits."

Janaki concedes. Baskaran is traditional in all the ways she likes:

loyal to home and parents, upholding caste strictures out of deference to them, and in the interests of continuity. She really shouldn't complain.

Janaki journeys to Cholapatti shortly after the passing-on ceremony to spend some time with her grandmother. Sivakami protests that she will be fine, that Janaki shouldn't be travelling more than necessary in her condition, but Janaki insists. Baskaran escorts her and stays three days on Gayatri's hospitality, since protocol forbids a husband from staying in his wife's home.

While Janaki feels proud of the simple graces of her grand-mother's home, she is also uncomfortably conscious of some differences between it and the home to which she has become accustomed. It feels a bit small and shabby; the servants are too visible and audible, too familiar and influential.

The shifting of her perceptions has been a gradual process. The first time she came home, she felt intensely nostalgic and wanted to pretend she never left. By her second visit, though, she could feel she was changing. She was shocked at Muchami calling her by her name, and he saw this, so now he doesn't call her anything. They both realize, though they don't speak of it, that she might have felt equally strange had he begun calling her Amma.

It was also on that visit that Mari had told her in low tones, after she had dressed, that she had forgotten her dirty clothes in a bucket in the bathroom. She rolled her eyes at her new habit, recalling how Vasantha and Swarna had laughed at her when they realized she had been washing her own clothes every day in Pandiyoor.

It irked and unsettled Janaki that she should struggle to find her place here. Even the act of getting up in the morning had become strange: at her grandmother's house, when one rises, one clears one's own mat, and at night, one lays it down again. In Pandiyoor, a servant clears and lays down the bedrolls. Janaki mentioned this difference to Radhai, within earshot of Mari and Muchami, pitching it in a falsely neutral tone, as though this judgment were mere observation.

Mari was rankled. "That is interesting," she cut in, without breaking the rhythm of her work, patting fuel cakes from a pile of cow dung. She slapped the most recent onto the courtyard wall, where several rows were drying. "And do your in-laws' servants take a bath afterward?"

Janaki blushed violently. She really had not been sure how she felt about this difference—on the one hand, she believes in upholding Brahmin practices and disapproves of any modern development that breaks down caste barriers. But the Pandiyoor customs don't break down those practices—servants are non-Brahmins. Perhaps they aren't polluted by sleep articles; perhaps they take a bath. How is that her business? She didn't reply.

Through the old routines, though—setting a plate out back for the monkeys at dawn, snacking on a ball of thangai maavu in midafternoon, standing on the roof to watch the parrots at sunset—the small satisfactions of her childhood are returned to her, and she enjoys them, knowing she belongs somewhere else.

She is most concerned, on this visit, with making sure her grandmother is all right, following the shock of Visalam's death. Sivakami looks lined, small and weary, the stiffness of her shoulder blades more pronounced than Janaki remembers. Suddenly awkward at being in the role of adult, Janaki tries to ask her grandmother how she is, and receives dismissive reassurances. She doesn't know how to press through to the truth.

"Having you here is a great consolation to me," Sivakami says. It's after dusk and so Janaki lies with her head in her grandmother's lap, Sivakami stroking her hair. "You must look after your health. Think peaceful thoughts. I'll make garlic rasam for you—good for your strength, and the baby's."

Janaki wants to say something more, about Visalam and her untimely death, but doesn't want to upset her grandmother, either by reminding her of their loss, or by crying, and so just quietly rests her cheek on the soft cloth over Sivakami's bony thigh.

38.
The Barber Lover
1945

FOUR MONTHS LATER, Janaki is expected back in Cholapatti for her bangle ceremony. Muchami is excited about her arrival, especially since the occasion of her last visit was such an unhappy one. He misses the child she was, now no more than a ghost or vapour dancing around the woman she has become. Still, she reminds him of that long-ago child, and some of those lost, warm affections return to him in memory when he sees her.

Because Visalam's death is still so recent, Sivakami has been anxious about the bangle ceremony: they must provide their relatives and neighbours a way to celebrate the new life while still observing grief, make Janaki feel happy and beautiful while not making her feel guilty. Kamalam, who had stayed behind in Kumbakonam to help Visalam's in-laws with her children, arrives a few days before Janaki. Though Sivakami would never admit any such thing, Kamalam might be her favourite among the grandchildren: perfectly demure, unquestioning and capable. Sivakami feels reassured by the girl's presence and puts her immediately to work, cooking for the feast day. Soon enough, Janaki arrives, escorted by Baskaran.

The day before the ceremony, though, some unwelcome but not unexpected information reaches Muchami via his regular channels. He had, a week or ten days earlier, put a word out requesting this information, after having seen something that didn't quite look right.

He doesn't go out every night as he did when he was younger but does still make his way through the woods and fields twice or three times a week, in search of other men, like him, who need physical satisfactions they cannot give or receive in their marriages. It happens that he sees things on these journeys. Some things he understands immediately; some he must work to interpret.

As has been said, the only people abroad at night are those (like Muchami, it could be argued) who have no choice. One of those who must be out is the barber who clips the heads of Brahmin widows, a work of shame and sorrow done in the dark hour favoured by demons. Sivakami has her head shaved monthly, usually by the same barber who sheared her curls in the days of her widow-making and left her light-headed under the moonlight. Now, occasionally, it is his second son who comes. The first son used to come, until his family decided he, meaning all of them, would be better off if he used his skill with a blade to get latex out of trees in Malayan plantations.

So it happened, one night, that Muchami was returning home and saw the barber's second son entering the rear courtyard of a Brahmin-quarter widow who lives three houses over from Minister and Gayatri. He didn't think it strange until, some ten days later, he saw the same thing again. It was then that he mentioned it to some cohorts who have now confirmed for him that the barber's second son, Karuppan, has been coming and going from the house of the widow, Shantam, four or five nights each week. No one's hair grows that fast.

Muchami is outraged. He stalks home as though burning the fields in his wake, like Hanuman setting Lanka alight with his tail. He knows he must decide what best to do with this information and that it might be his obligation to go to Vairum, who, as his employer and the master of a house on the Brahmin quarter, is most entitled to know and take action. He is in Cholapatti this week. But Muchami is not convinced that Vairum will do what must be done: he has never shown caste loyalty; if anything, he acts as though it would please him to see the entire Brahmin quarter in ruin. And if he tells Vairum and Vairum does nothing, it will be much more difficult then to redress this ill.

He decides to call a conference. He invites Minister and Murthy to come to Sivakami's house after tiffin. He tells Vairum not to go to play tennis. He tells Sivakami only that the others will be coming, not why. He is trembling at the impropriety of it. This is the sort of thing about which he could gossip to Sivakami were it to have happened several villages away. But so close to home, to the home whose honour it is his dearest duty to uphold?

That morning, the bangle ceremony is held for Janaki. Every woman on the Brahmin quarter pushes a pair of glass bangles onto Janaki's wrists, until her arms are covered nearly to the elbows. Sivakami watches from behind the kitchen door, smiling at Janaki's face, at the auspicious tinkling of the bangles, worn until the birth. Some women pull the bangles off in labour, as a way to distract themselves from the pain or count down the time until it is over. She catches sight of her own bare wrist on the door, the skin loose and wrinkled, and tucks her arm under her pallu.

That afternoon, Murthy and Minister arrive for the conference within minutes of each other. Vairum lounges suspiciously in the hall. Muchami has been pacing from courtyard to garden, and now sees them. Sivakami takes a position behind the nearly closed double doors in the pantry between the hall and kitchen. Muchami has told the children they must stay in the courtyard or go out to play, that he will beat them if he catches them listening. It seems to have worked, though he doesn't see Janaki, out of sight in the room under the stairs: she doesn't consider herself a child, doesn't fear a beating from Muchami, and is curious.

Now Muchami, standing in the door to the garden, tells them what he knows.

Murthy begins immediately to splutter and shake. Minister looks circumspect and deeply troubled.

How it came about they wonder but have no idea. Maybe Karuppan forced her, the first time, and has been blackmailing her. Or Shantam, the widow, may have permitted it all along. She is a sullen and feisty type. She and her husband had loud, frequent fights in the years of their marriage, and she has had loud, frequent fights with her in-laws since he died. One of Gayatri's regular jokes is about the fact that this woman's name means "peace"—what would she have been like if her name had meant "hot-tempered"?

Vairum looks exasperated.

"What concern is this of mine?" he asks Muchami, and then looks at the others to see if they can answer. "Let her bring shame on her own head and her house."

"No, son." Minister cradles his forehead in his forefinger and thumb. It looks as if someone gave him a gun and he can't decide how to use it. "He is the criminal in this situation. A woman's virtue is that of her family, and he has destroyed it, whether or not she chooses each night to open her door."

"I-I-I can't even—how—understand, how you c-c-can both still be sitting and t-talking!" Murthy has leapt from his chair. "Open her door! I-I-I'll open his head, that's what!" He is running for the door now, his hands over his ears. "Ugh! Ogh! My ears are poisoned by what I have heard today!" He stumbles in an attempt to mount the two or three steps to his own veranda, and succumbs to an attack of asthma, whereupon a few passersby stop to ask what is wrong. He tells them.

Janaki wants desperately to go to her grandmother and console her. Sivakami is so restrained in her behaviour and outlook that Janaki imagines news of such an atrocity would shake her to the core. Really, though, she wants reassurance as much as she wants to give it.

That night, Shantam's nearest neighbours' servants are posted in the brush beyond her courtyard gate. The unlucky lover arrives. He pushes open the door, enters, closes it behind him. Each of the servants slips from his hiding place. Each goes to the door of the house he serves and tells his employer that the barber is inside. Each goes to the next house and tells the master of that house. Moments pass and from each house emerges its master. Each master carries a big stick.

What is the barber's second son thinking? He must be about seventeen, she about twice his age, plump and fair, while he is dark as rosewood. Sivakami thinks of them as she does her beading, working fast, very fast. She hears one of the servants knock on their door to inform Vairum that the moment has come for action. Muchami, who is spending the night in the courtyard, tells him Vairum will not come because Vairum said he will have nothing to do with this nonsense, that mobs always chase phantoms, that he has to work in the morning, unlike these professional moralists in search of a night's entertainment. Minister also will not participate, because of possible political repercussions. There are more than enough hands, anyway—more than fifteen pairs, all holding sticks, heading for the house, the third rough-hewn gate east of Gayatri's.

Did he force her? Sivakami wonders. But why didn't she just bar the door and not permit him to come again? Could he really have blackmailed her? She would have been defiled and disgraced, but better that than going through it night after night, no? Unless she really did choose this . . .

Sivakami can barely bring herself to think it. A barber, one of the worst classes of untouchables. A Brahmin woman choosing to *be with* a barber. Sivakami casts her mind back to the years of her marriage and remembers, vividly still because barely a night has passed in forty years when she hasn't thought about the acts of love she and her husband performed with each other. She can't help it: her mind begins to imagine Shantam and the barber's son in these poses, and she shudders, disgusted, but her mind keeps picturing it. She tries to keep the bile down and her mind clear by concentrating on the image she is working in beads, Lord Krishna at Bhutana's poisoned breast. It doesn't work. She runs outside and vomits.

Janaki, lying in the main hall with her siblings, hears her grandmother go out back and rises to meet her in the kitchen.

"Do you want a cup of water, Amma?" she asks.

"I'm fine, child." Sivakami dippers herself a cup and drinks. "Go back to sleep."

Dimly, they hear the sound of shouting, getting closer.

"I heard, Amma," Janaki confesses. "I know."

Sivakami sighs, and shakes her head, then draws Janaki down to sit beside her. "Pray with me. You mustn't think about such terrible matters, not in your condition. Good girl." She takes out her beads and begins the mantra she repeats one thousand and one times daily. Janaki joins in chorus.

Karuppan has closed the door but not drawn the heavy bolt. He never does, why should he? Shantam is waiting for him on the wooden bench on the back of the house where she is made to sleep. She hates sleeping there, but each of the bedrooms is now taken up with one of her late husband's brothers. Each of them is married now, and so they need private rooms. She could sleep in a corner of the main hall with the children, but it's her mother-in-law's prerogative and she wants Shantam to sleep outside. Shantam makes up for it in small cruelties toward her nephews and nieces, and even, sometimes, toward her own children.

She is sitting, waiting for him on her bench. He crosses to her on silent feet. Her sari has already slipped from her head and now he unwinds it from her shoulders and buries his face in the soft flesh between her collarbone and breast, stroking his lips and eyelids across the pillow of silky, fragrant skin. She is so unlike the women of his class—not that he has had one yet, but he can tell. They stand and walk past the cowshed into the garden, her sari beginning already to unwrap. They pull it after themselves and spread it on the garden floor. And when the enraged men burst into the courtyard and run from there into the garden, this is what they see: the widow trying to wrap herself back into the white sari that has been serving as her illicit conjugal bed, and the glistening form of the barber's second son, reaching the top of the garden wall and jumping down off it.

By now, Shantam's mother-in-law and other family members, who had not been informed about the raid, have flung open numerous internal doors. Some of the men run through the house to the front and start shouting for those doors to be unlocked, while others have already run back out and through the neighbours' houses onto the Brahmin-quarter street, to see which way the scoundrel is going. Every woman on the street, except Sivakami and Janaki, is witness to the flight of the naked and terrified boy, who streaks straight up the Brahmin quarter, whistled along by the wind of the matrons' gasps.

The men give chase. They chase him far, through bramble and brooks. He is much faster than they, but two send their servants on bicycles to cut him off. He is caught. These weak, pulpy Brahmins, worked up by the chase, beat Karuppan very badly. Muchami helps in the chase but participates only a little in the beating.

Shantam is also chastised and lightly beaten by her mother-in-law, in front of her children and all her brothers- and sisters-in-law.

These are the events of that night. After the shouting mob passes and the sound fades away, Sivakami tells Janaki to go back to sleep.

Sivakami resumes her beading. She hears the men return and go to their homes. Muchami comes back, too, and tells her what happened. Then he lies down in the courtyard to sleep. She closes the kitchen doors, goes into the pantry and closes those doors, too. She lies where she normally lies. She is calmer but can feel the horrible images trying to re-form in her mind's eye. She tries to banish them again, and images of her husband—his skin sliding against hers, the smoothness of his back where she gripped it, her fingertips notching his spine—slip in with distressing ease to replace those of the barber's son, who is just a few years younger than Hanumarathnam was when he died. Sivakami doesn't permit herself to move—she lies, as every night, on her side, on the cool floor of the pantry, her neck on a wooden rest—but shifts her legs minutely against that delicious discomfort that now can never be eased. She had almost managed to forget that gnaw and tickle, brushed it away with busyness and prayer. The advance of age was a relief: in the last ten years, the craving has begun to diminish. Now her chest feels thick with anger at Shantam for having reminded her.

Shantam has been a widow for less than ten years, less than ten years feeling no touch save that of her children, and even that only after sunset—and Shantam's not even permitted to sleep with them. Sivakami recalls her first years of widowhood, when she slept curled around Vairum, the warm pressure of his milk-smelling, dream-twitching, little-boy body anchoring her to her own body, which seemed, in daylight, not to exist at all.

Sivakami wraps her arms around herself, biting her lip. She knows what Shantam has endured. But *it is their lot* to endure. If not, why else does Sivakami live as she does? What appeal is there in a topsy-turvy world and what place does a widow have, if not this one?

Janaki, sleepless among the children, desperately misses Baskaran. She could talk with him about this, as she can with no one else, and he would hold her and help her think of other things. What if she never sees him again? What if he dies before she returns? She would never again be touched. It would be like her childhood all over again.

She had never before thought beyond her grandmother's sacrifice and righteousness. She believed in everything Sivakami believed but never thought of her grandmother as sharing her feelings. *I'm exactly the age Amma was when she was widowed,* she realizes. *How did she bear it?*

Janaki wants to share the village's anger at Shantam's breach, but, in the grip now of this strange pity for the girl her grandmother was, she is unable. She, in Sivakami's position, might well have gone mad.

At first light the next morning, a bullock solemnly pulls a cart down the Brahmin quarter from Shantam's house toward Kulithalai (most bullocks look solemn, this one especially so). On the cart are two men and a big load of hay from which they are creating a wake, systematically depositing large handfuls behind them on the path and roadway. When this is done, a priest from the Brahmin-quarter temple drops three lumps of burning camphor at the edge of the straw carpet, which begins where Karuppan landed after vaulting Shantam's wall. Three palms of flame grow fingers, join hands and run up the Brahmin quarter. Where the fire hits a pocket of damp, it pops and hisses much like the good Brahmin folk of the village waiting for the street to be purified so that they can meet and rehash the night's events. When the veil of smoke lifts, the carpet of straw has magically changed into one of ash, with little straw bits here and there, and the Brahmin quarter, too, has been magically restored to its former untouchability, which the untouchable robbed by his touch.

That morning, at Sivakami's, Gayatri expresses perfunctory regret about the beatings but is philosophical.

"It's terrible, it really is, but what could they have expected?"

Minister has contacted a French mission doctor of his acquaintance, who would go and see the boy today.

Gayatri notices Mari scrubbing pots with extraordinary vigour and asks what she thinks.

"Such liaisons must be stopped!" Mari retorts in a tone of voice that implies she is more offended at Gayatri having felt the need to ask than at the subject of the question.

"Clearly, yes, clearly," Gayatri mutters, taking offence at Mari's tone.

Young Kesavan enters shaking his head and clucking his tongue.

"Why, why, why, why, why . . ." He shakes his head.

People so often think something becomes more profound if repeated. Sometimes it does.

"Why don't Brahmins permit widow remarriage?" he asks.

This is not what Sivakami and Janaki expected to hear.

"I think it is terribly wrong, what they did," he continues, because this is how he feels and because he would hate to lose this job due to some misapprehension of his position on Sivakami's part. "But if widows were permitted to remarry and if we could rid ourselves of this terrible caste prejudice, maybe this would not have been necessary for them."

"This was not necessary for them," Sivakami starts, and Kesavan replies, "Oh, yes."

"And remarriage?" she continues. "What is this 'remarriage'? Marriage is something that can only happen once."

"But men are permitted another wife," Kesavan says, after a slight, ingratiating, pause.

"If the first wife does not complete him. If there is no child," Sivakami splutters. "But then it was not really a marriage, so the second is really the first. Or if there are children who need a mother."

Janaki watches her grandmother. She has never seen her angry like this. *Her convictions are what sustained her,* Janaki thinks. *How dare Vairum Mama try to challenge her on her beliefs? They are the reason she is alive.*

No one ever knows Shantam's opinion on the subject, because she disappears the next day, taking with her jewels—those that should have been her daughter's—and six silk saris belonging to her sisters-in-law. She is never seen in Cholapatti again. From time to time a rumour floats back: Shantam seen in Thanjavur, thinner and darker, living with a pearl fisherman and selling pearls on the harbour road. Shantam, cheeks and ears pierced with tridents, hair grown matted and coiled atop her half-mad head, running up to pilgrims in the Palani temple and telling their fortunes whether they want them or not. Shantam, fatter and fairer, living in Benares, masquerading as a wealthy Parsee widow running a charity home for destitute or abandoned Brahmin widows. None of the rumours is ever corroborated.

Karuppan, the barber's second son, needs surgery and is taken to the French mission hospital to have it done, but by then he has been bleeding internally for ten or twelve hours, so it's too late and he dies. At the beginning of the following year, the company employing Karuppan's older brother fails. It's a bad time for rubber, and for companies generally. He is sent home on a ship that gets caught in a typhoon and founders on some rocks. If there are survivors, he is not among them. His parents have now lost both of their sons. They never have grandchildren. Their older son's widow, as is not uncommon in their community, remarries.

The elder barber goes back to shaving the heads of all his customers. Perhaps he still says "I'm sorry," as he did to Sivakami, before shaving a Brahmin widow's head for the first time.

Perhaps not.

39.
A Jasmine at Dawn
1945

JANAKI HAD THOUGHT SHE MIGHT STAY at her grandmother's house until the birth, but Baskaran comes to escort her home the week before the annual festival for the goddess Meenakshi of Madurai. Senior Mami has had a dream, in which the goddess appeared as a bride and reproached her for not coming to her wedding. Senior Mami tried to protest: it's so far away, the family contributes much to the festival through the charitable trust, her daughters-in-law are attending, but she could not utter any of this. It was as though she had been gagged by a wooden ball. The goddess, already at the end of her patience, yelled at her to defend herself but still Senior Mami could not speak. Just as the goddess turned away—to receive, as it happens, the supplications of their immediate next-door neighbours on Double Street—Senior Mami regained her voice. It was too late—Meenakshi was bestowing all her favours on the neighbours.

The next morning, Senior Mami decreed that every member of their family must make an extra effort this year. Senior Mami herself will visit the temple to donate a ruby pendant for the goddess, along with the sari and cash the family gives every year. She will even participate in serving water and buttermilk on the street in front of the chattram. She hasn't come in person for years.

Sivakami disapproves of Janaki travelling all the way back to Pandiyoor in advanced pregnancy, then courting illness by serving buttermilk in the hot sun, not to mention courting the evil eye by displaying herself, pregnant, to so many. Baskaran appreciates her concerns but cannot find it within him to contradict his mother. He promises Sivakami that Janaki will do no real work and return within a month.

Every family member participates in the serving, however ceremonially. Even Dhoraisamy comes—once—to dip the ladle, fill a cup for some passing wayfarer and offer it with wishes for his refreshment and renewed devotional strength. Senior Mami does nearly a dozen before collapsing in a sweat into the shade of the chattram. Each of the sons serves for several hours, with his wife and children. Baskaran and Janaki serve on the sixth day. They, too, drink the water and the buttermilk—yogourt churned with water, lemon, salt and asafetida—the best antidotes to the year's hottest season. Janaki serves a few people and then keeps Baskaran company, sitting in the shade on the chattram veranda and fanning herself.

Mid-morning of that day, a covered palanquin passes, carried by two men. The palanquin continues a few yards beyond the chattram, then pauses. With effort, the men reverse their strides and set the litter down in front of the buttermilk-filled cauldron and the brass water drum. A hennaed hand parts the curtains veiling the palanquin, and a pale, hennaed foot slips out from between them.

Everyone's eyes are on that foot, which is followed by a thick silver anklet, then by the wide red-orange border of a Kanchipuram silk sari, then by the sari's chartreuse ground—the colours of ripe mangoes in a tree. Bharati emerges as Janaki shrinks. She smiles, requesting cups of the buttermilk for her entourage—the palanquin was followed by two manservants and two maids. As they're drinking, Bharati asks Janaki, "*Sowkyumaa*? Are you well?" It's not an intimate greeting, and Bharati does not sound familiar, nor challenging, though she must have stopped the palanquin because she saw her old school friend. She does sound interested, though, which is more than is expected from a stranger. She glances at Janaki's belly and her husband.

"I'm well," Janaki replies.

Baskaran looks at Janaki and then asks Bharati, as his wife should have done, "Are you well?"

"I'm well, yes." Bharati inclines her head to Baskaran, then turns back to Janaki to inform her, "I am a devotee of Goddess Meenakshi."

"Of course," Janaki says mechanically.

How is Bharati living now? She must have done well for herself—the palanquin, servants, jewellery.

"You might recall, Janaki," Bharati remarks conversationally, "that my grandmother is from Madurai. She brought me back." Bharati smiles, as though Janaki knows how grandmothers can be.

"How is your mother?" Janaki blurts.

"My mother is well." Bharati cocks her head slightly as if trying to understand what Janaki is saying.

Baskaran is looking at them as though they're speaking another language, very like Tamil.

The two women stand looking at each other for a moment, then Bharati refuses the cup of buttermilk held out to her by one of the elder children.

"And how is Vani Mami?" she asks.

"She is well," Janaki replies, starting to feel a bit scared. Didn't Bharati used to call Vani "Amma," the non-Brahmin honorific? "Mami" sounds funny, coming from her.

"You both are friends?" Baskaran smiles broadly. "From Cholapatti?"

The women smile narrowly. "We were at school together," Janaki tells him.

"We had the same music master," says Bharati, almost simultaneously.

Janaki doesn't know what Bharati is doing but thinks there cannot be a bridge between them now. Bharati refuses the cup of buttermilk again.

"I have a ten o'clock puja," she says crisply.

"Come home some time!" Baskaran tells her, heartily sincere and more than a little puzzled.

"I'll go and come," she says, and this time it sounds just as anyone might say it: goodbye.

As she folds herself back into the palanquin, Janaki tamps a surge of affection. She wishes she could have told Bharati she thinks of her every time she plays the veena, that she could have asked her how her own music is coming. But she doesn't really want to know any of the other details of her half-sister's life.

"Not Brahmin?" Baskaran confirms.

"No," Janaki shakes her head.

"She has excellent diction," he observes with a hint of condescension. "Striking."

Janaki busies herself with a ladle.

Ten days later, Baskaran escorts her back again to her grandmother's house. They are embroiled in their first real fight and are silent for much of the journey, except when they argue. Baskaran has insisted to her that he will book a labour and delivery nurse to attend her delivery. "I will feel much safer if you are in the hands of someone with some medical know-how, and not prey to these village superstitions. Your grandmother will still be nearby," he had told her.

A nurse? Janaki feels indignant at his presumption, but not so much as she would if she had any intention of actually letting a *nurse* deliver her baby.

Baskaran repeats all his instructions to her when he takes his leave. "Okay, so: you know how you'll know, right? When it's time, you'll feel contractions, a kind of cramping. Send for the nurse immediately. Day or night."

Could this be the fiftieth time Janaki has heard this speech? How does he keep his phrasing and inflections so consistent? She respectfully refrains from mouthing along with him.

"I've paid her handsomely to be on call," Baskaran remonstrates. "And she knows she'll get the rest when she has done a good job."

No good woman contradicts her husband, so Janaki is silent. She knows Baskaran has talked with Muchami and Gayatri about this. He doesn't want to seem disrespectful, and so has said nothing to Sivakami. But as soon as he leaves, Janaki tells Muchami, "Listen. No nurse. I want Amma's kai raasi to deliver my child."

Muchami doesn't respond. He is embarrassed at being involved in this disagreement: now that Janaki has said "kai raasi," it would be bad luck to call the nurse.

GAYATRI, WHO STILL COMES DAILY to take her coffee with Sivakami, asks Janaki to come and visit with her at home. Janaki is feeling a little lonely and isolated, despite the company of her siblings, and welcomes the chance to gossip.

She updates Gayatri on the running of the charity and describes the partition plans. The older woman concurs on their impropriety. The Madurai Meenakshi festival comes up in the course of their meandering palavers. Janaki doesn't even realize how much she has been thinking of her old friend until she starts talking about her.

She describes the encounter at the chattram and asks Gayatri if she knows about the family.

"But it's incredible, Janaki, that you would ask me about them!" says Gayatri. "I had forgotten that you and the elder daughter were in school together."

"Why," Janaki probes, impassive but for a trace of a pout, "is it so incredible?"

Gayatri clears her throat. "Until a few months ago, I only knew what everyone knows: they're a devadasi family. I think there are, or were, at least four children from C. R. Balachandran. And I know there were a couple of other children from a couple of other fathers."

Gayatri glances away at that last statement and Janaki, aware of her own dull anger, tells her quietly, "Rumours connect my father with that family."

Gayatri's head snaps up. "Who told you that?"

"Isn't it a mark of prestige to patronize a devadasi?" Janaki doesn't see the need to reveal her source and is more interested in getting to the heart of the matter.

"It depends what you mean by patronize." Gayatri smiles kindly. "But let me tell you what happened. I heard about it from my husband. He, if you can believe it, went to their house."

There is a debate in the legislature at present, Gayatri tells her, as to whether the devadasi system should be outlawed. Janaki recalls that vaguely—maybe Rukmini Arundale said something when they were in Madras?

Minister, whose contacts in the Kulithalai area are very much trusted, had been requested to escort an investigatory delegation to Bharati's family home. The committee member most strongly opposed to the courtesan system opened the conversation by asking whether they wouldn't rather find more respectable ways of living. Bharati's mother had refused to talk to this committee or any individual on it. But Bharati's grandmother replied, "I respect myself," with dignity that surprised them all: the non-Brahmins, who wanted the system abolished, and the Brahmins, who were against declaring it illegal. "How dare you imply that you are attacking immorality," the old lady had thundered at them, "when all you're doing is attacking the carriers of culture in your shrivelled world?"

"My husband said she might have been beautiful once," Gayatri said, "but so peevish! Though my husband did say she had excellent diction."

Janaki is silent.

"'Do you think that Brahmin girls will ever conquer the expressive arts?' the old lady asked my husband. 'We were not even permitted to cook. Do you think you can domesticate the spirit of culture? Brahmin women suffer, oh, I know they suffer. But they don't suffer the hardships that temper steel into artistry. They suffer the hardships that make women insipid. You want their husbands neither to take pleasure in them nor to take pleasure elsewhere. As though we are p . . . p . . prostitutes!'"

Gayatri, who had quite entered into the spirit of the old woman's speech, jumps as Janaki snaps, "Well, I am utterly in favour of outlawing them. Nobody's going to make art illegal—they want to make it respectable. What's wrong with that? The devadasis' options will increase. They won't have to prey on men, breaking up families and living without any kind of security, resorting to blackmail and who knows what?"

Gayatri makes a motion to her to lower her voice—her daughters-in-law and grandchildren are about.

Janaki whispers loudly, "How do they explain an artist like Vani Mami, anyway?"

"You have a good point, Janaki," Gayatri responds delicately.

"But I can't blame the women entirely. Especially lately. The system has been breaking down. They don't have the protections they once had. You asked whether it is not a mark of prestige to support a devadasi. It was—when it was done right. But more and more now, these women are being forced to behave like common prostitutes, which is degrading. Men don't live up to their responsibilities like they used to."

This statement clearly applies to Goli in any situation.

"May I tell you what has happened in their family?" Gayatri asks.

The old lady apparently considered her life, after she was plucked from Madurai like a jasmine at dawn, to have been a parade of disappointments. The essential tragedy, she said, was that none of her daughters was very beautiful or talented. She had chosen the middle girl, Bharati's mother, as the most promising. She convinced her own sponsor to fund an education for the girl like the one she herself had had. But, she grumbled, there was not a sufficient appreciation of devadasis in Kulithalai.

"So many men who, somewhere else, in another time, would have had the ambition to patronize a dasi. Here they don't even think of it. Okay, this," she said, pointing the heel of her hand at Bharati's mother, "would not have attracted the wealthiest and most powerful, but she should never have been left scrambling!" Then, as Bharati bloomed into beauty with adolescence, the old woman grew bitter. "This is the girl I should have had," she shouted at the committee, pointing at her granddaughter.

Janaki startles. "Bharati was there? But I thought she was living in Madurai."

"I'll get to that." Gayatri holds up a hand and continues quoting Bharati's grandmother. "'This girl should have been born a hundred years ago, in the shadow of a famous temple's towering *gopurams*!' she said. 'Poets would have immortalized her. Corpulent Brahmins with diamond ear studs and betel-stuffed cheeks should have been kept awake at night scheming on means to finance her maintenance. Kings would have declared themselves unworthy!'"

Bharati's dancing and music masters had not even lived in. The committee was made to understand this had been a sore point for her grandmother. This prompted them to ask: many a live-in master is brutish and demands distasteful favours, which the family must permit because how else can they give the child the training she needs? This surely was the type of suffering Bharati's grandmother had talked about: did any of her teachers ever commit improprieties upon her young person?

The old woman was appalled that the committee would ask such a question, and as good as kicked them out of her house for their rudeness.

"So that was that, but I wanted to know what was happening with the girl—what is her name again?"

"Bharati," Janaki mumbles.

"Yes—Bharati," Gayatri repeats, a little quiet as though she just remembered Janaki's stake in this story. "A beautiful girl."

Janaki doesn't reply.

"I asked Muchami." Gayatri lowers her voice confidentially. "Bharati came of age around the same time as you. When she finished school, her mother let her be taken to Madurai. Their relatives there arranged a performance to try to attract a patron for her. She attracted a man in his forties. He is a Brahmin but not a man of good reputation. He had dropped two previous devadasis after he tired of them, and he . . ." Gayatri makes the signal for drinking, her thumb pointing at her mouth. "His family still has money, but I imagine Bharati must be concerned that he may well drop her, too. She came back here for an abortion. I don't know if it was the first."

Gayatri stops and they both are silent.

Janaki wants to remain angry but finds she cannot. Her own life seems so simple by comparison.

"Sometimes"—Gayatri looks almost scared to say this—"men are known to patronize more than one woman. Women get diseases . . ."

"Are you saying this is what my father does?" Janaki asks.

"You opened the topic, Janaki."

Janaki is too emotional to apologize. "Does . . . does my grandmother know about the rumours?"

Gayatri looks as though she would like to end the conversation. "I'm sure she doesn't. As we said, it is no longer the mark of a great family, and never really was, I think, for people like us."

"People like us?"

"Modest people. Conservative people. We who live a quiet, middle-class village life, and keep to ourselves."

Janaki nods—that's it, that's who she is. That's the only life she has ever wanted.

IT IS THE LAST WEEK OF JUNE 1945, and Janaki's water breaks. As she goes into the birthing room, she signals to Muchami. When he nears, she hisses, "Amma's kai raasi. I won't let anyone else touch me."

Sivakami's kai raasi are the first hands on Janaki's baby, and Janaki's own hands are next. The nurse is never called.

It's a girl, a strong one. She thrashes and yells and eats heartily. Even at birth, she looks like her father, with a strong nose and round cheeks. Janaki writes to Baskaran to bring a photo of himself when he comes for the eleventh-day ceremony, so that when the ayah comes to massage the child and mould her features, she can make the baby's nose even more like his.

He doesn't think this is funny. He shows up two days early and, in a temper, tells Janaki from outside the birthing room that she will never again come to Cholapatti for a birth.

Janaki says nothing, but thinks, *He's a fool, criticizing, when the birth could not have gone better.*

He has brought gifts for the baby and coldly thanks Sivakami for doing such a good job—he is all manners—but Sivakami is mortified and Janaki is most hurt by the pain she has caused her grandmother, who feels terrible at having unwittingly created discord between the young couple. Although Janaki insists that it is her fault, not Sivakami's, Sivakami mounts her own argument.

"I raised you, Janaki. If you can disobey your husband, I did a bad job. It's my fault."

"Did you never disobey your husband, Sivakamikka?" Gayatri, witness to all this, asks.

Sivakami looks as if she's trying to remember.

Hanumarathnam bolts upright from sleep. With a slight movement of his head, he summons her.

"No, never." To answer otherwise would be to fault her own parents. "Don't ever do such a thing again."

Vairum and Vani are coming to Cholapatti for the baby's naming ceremony—they didn't come for all the babies', but Vairum has a special interest in Janaki's family. Generally, this interest pleases Janaki, but now she is dreading their arrival. While she had been confident of her right to decide who birthed her baby, she fears Vairum's reaction when he finds out she disobeyed her husband and failed to take advantage of modern methods. Vairum is so derisive about so many of their traditions, though not consistently: he and Vani still do a daily puja in their home and observe all the Hindu festivals. But this may be on Vani's initiative. Vairum is vocal, even at family gatherings, about his disdain for the way most of Sivakami's grandchildren live, in fulfillment of her legacy of orthodoxy.

She also feels a bit weak at the prospect of seeing Vani at the baby's naming ceremony. The last time she saw them was in Pandiyoor, two months after Visalam's passing, six months after Vani's mother's own death. Vani had looked drawn and greyish, a little worse each time Janaki saw her. She still played beautifully but otherwise appeared listless, not even chattering much at mealtimes, though she occasionally mumbled something Janaki couldn't catch, something that might have been the fragment of a story. Janaki could only think of one explanation, Vani's despair at her barrenness.

From within the birth room, she hears them arrive at the front, greeted by Murthy, Baskaran, Minister and Gayatri, Radhai, Krishnan and Raghavan. Kamalam is staying with her in the birth room to help her and peers out, squinting against the sunlight from the open front door. Vairum bounds into the main hall and does a full-length obeisance for the Ramar, leaps up and calls to Vani, "Come! Come!"

Vani enters more shyly and does the same, and then stands beside Vairum as he beckons the family and neighbours to enter and calls out to his mother. "Amma! Come here."

Janaki and Kamalam are supposed to stay in the birth room, but they are too curious and know no one will notice if they peer around the door at Sivakami, who has inched up to the pantry door but refuses to come any farther in front of Murthy and Minister.

"Oh, Amma. You are going to have adjust your village ways if . . ." Vairum pauses dramatically and looks at everyone, "you are to come and visit us in Madras."

He enjoys everyone's bemusement for a moment: how will Sivakami get away, with all her responsibilities? Why would Vairum even think up such a scheme? The children wonder if they are going, too.

Janaki looks at Vani, who seems happy and peaceful: still thin, but untroubled. What is happening?

"It will be an extended stay, Amma, because we are very happy to tell you—" Vairum pauses again and breathes deeply—"that Vani is expecting."

Sivakami is staggered. Forgetting herself, she takes a step forward and holds out her arms. Vairum and Vani step into her light and unfamiliar embrace.

40.
Late Surprise
1945–1946

IN THE MONTHS LEADING UP TO HER DEPARTURE for Madras, Sivakami replays for herself again and again the moment when Vairum told her he and Vani would be parents once more, as though it is a prayer bead on the string she tells daily.

After his oblation for the Ramar, he had turned to her with a speed and intensity she found alarming, his eyes burning. She recalls that alarm now with amusement, and also remembers the warmth and the good humour of his glance. It made her shiver.

"We are going to have need of your services," he had said, after making the announcement. "You know I have no truck with superstition, but Vani has insisted that she will have no doctors and that your kai raasi must deliver our child. I don't have the power to deny her anything she wants." He threw his arms up happily, then continued in a softer, tenderer tone. "Since her mother died, there is no reason for her to go to Pandiyoor for childbirth and, in any case, she has always felt that you are as a mother to her."

Janaki had listened to the exchange with wonder mixed with relief: if Vairum was acceding to Vani's wish for Sivakami's lucky hands, he couldn't object to hers! And now she need not feel self-conscious at the blessing of her child: Vairum and Vani's witness will be an especially happy one. What marvellous news!

She and Kamalam talk about it that night as Janaki nurses her daughter. Vairum and Vani so needed this. Janaki is sure that if Sivakami delivers the child, it will be strong and healthy, though she is still concerned for Vani, who looked so ill so recently, and is thrity-five, an advanced age for child-bearing.

They agree that Sivakami should come to Madras a few months before the birth, to cook and care for Vani the way a mother would.

Kamalam will return to Visalam's in-laws' house. They have been clamouring for her to come back, especially Visalam's children, who have grown very attached. Saradha, who is well settled in Thiruchi, will look after the rest of her younger siblings there. She has a daughter a year older than Radhai, and Vairum had intended that Krishnan and Raghavan would soon go live in Thiruchi in any case, to attend English-medium schools there. Sita is pregnant and Vairum has invited her to come to Madras instead of Cholapatti for her delivery. Laddu still lives with his grandmother in Cholapatti and cannot leave: he has now been given responsibility for a rice mill. He will board at the chattram in Kulithalai, where he will have meals and company, as long as Sivakami is away.

Although there is little in her affairs that she needs to wrap up— Muchami will look after the tenants as usual and Vairum comes once a month or so—there is one matter she wants safeguarded. She entrusts a biscuit tin of completed beadwork pieces to Gayatri, those that are still requested, every month or two, by Brahmins along the quarter whose daughters are about to give birth. Sivakami still has never spoken of it to Vairum and has no reason to believe he knows.

She will take with her the scene she is at work on now: Krishna dancing on the five hoods of the monster cobra. This scene should be finished before Vani gives birth. Apart from that, she packs a satchel of snacks she has made as a gift for Vairum and Vani, and another, much smaller one, containing her spare sari, her copy of the Kamba-Ramanayanam, between whose pages she has stowed five ten-rupee notes, her beadwork and the small brass water jug she always drinks from, so as not to have to share a vessel.

MUCHAMI IS EXCITED FOR HER, but also concerned: Vairum is so unconventional. What if he forces Sivakami to do things that make her uncomfortable? She is not young any more, he thinks, as he weaves thatch to repair the cowshed roof. The least Vairum can do is permit her her ways.

He tears a piece of thatch by pulling it too hard and realizes he has been getting angry with Vairum before anything has even happened. He certainly did look happy, and Vani looked better than she has in years. Maybe their contentment and gratitude for Sivakami's help will soften Vairum's radical edge.

He wonders how he will fill his days while she is gone.

"It will be quiet around here," he remarks to her late one morning.

His routine has altered considerably. He no longer has a child to look after, and Mari has been having health problems for the last year or two. She has been increasingly nervous and irritable, prone to dropping things and occasionally fainting. Sivakami has relieved her of many of her duties. Though he looks in during the day to make sure she's all right, Muchami prefers to leave their hut to her.

"Maybe I should go in for some other work: start a business. Can you see me in import-export?"

Sivakami laughs over the vegetables she is cutting. "You could do anything you want. Yes, I suppose the house hasn't been left empty since I went to live with my brothers—what's that, forty years ago?"

"A lifetime." Muchami walks to the garden door to spit a stream of betel juice into the growth.

"How did you stay busy back then?" she asks.

"I don't know," he says, trying to remember. "It was easier when one was young. There was always activity at the market, gossip, scandals, friends needing help." He doesn't mention midnight liaisons that occasionally left him fatigued during the day: an extra hour for siesta was a welcome thing. He still indulges, but only very occasionally. "The properties also needed more managing then, before Vairum organized them all. Life starts to run itself after a while."

"You should rest up while I'm gone. Vairum may not want to

come here so much when he has a child, and the first year, things may fall into some disarray. You will be useful then."

"Yes, it could happen." He smiles at her, feeling nervous. Is he only fearful of how Vairum might treat her there, so far away from her routines and the village she knows? No, there's something else: "Amma, when you go, do a ritual over Vani against the evil eye."

Sivakami stops slicing okra and looks at him.

"I am afraid," he tells her, and it's true. He is chilled to the bone at the prospect of what might happen if this pregnancy doesn't succeed.

"You are right," she says, allowing herself to feel the fear she had suppressed with her own happiness. "I will do it, yes."

It's 7 a.m. when Vairum comes to fetch her in his new car, a red Buick sedan. She has been ready and waiting for a couple of hours, sitting in the door to the pantry while Muchami keeps her company from the courtyard. Vairum stops at the house only long enough for a drink of water. He has to draw it at the well because the big clay water pot in the pantry is drained and turned upside down.

"Ready, Amma?"

The house already has an empty feel, the shutters closed, the children gone. Sivakami begins locking all the doors in the house, from back to front, and Muchami goes through the garden to stand on the street beside the car to await his final instructions. Alone, Sivakami does a final oblation for the Ramar, thinking of the two other times she has performed a farewell for these gods: before going to her brothers' house and before going to Munnoor when Thangam died. She prays, innocent and hearty, that all should go well in Madras, stifling a moth-wing flutter of worry. Muchami was quite right to remind her to do a ritual against dhrishti.

She locks the front door behind her, inserts the key carefully into her travel bundle, and turns, feeling self-conscious, to the car, which has attracted a crowd. Vairum takes the bag of snacks with a small, sardonic grin as the uniformed driver holds the door open. Sivakami mounts the running board and enters the cavern of the car's back seat. It is a rare sunny day in November, the height of the rainy season, and the air inside the car has congealed into a warm stillness. Vairum is lending his ear to a man in the crowd who seems to have a proposal. The neighbours and children press in a bit closer, their interest renewed by seeing Sivakami within the car. Gayatri and Minister are here, too, waving cheerily, but Sivakami, feeling uncomfortably like a bride in this red chariot, can't smile back. She's a little irritated at being made the subject of a spectacle. It is inappropriate, but she couldn't expect Vairum to sympathize with that. Finally, Vairum enters the car. He settles himself on the grey upholstered seat while the driver closes the door and runs around the front to start the car.

It takes them some twelve hours to reach Madras, during which time Sivakami takes no food or water—no food because she eats nothing she hasn't cooked herself, nor water because she will only drink that reserved for Brahmins. Vairum and his driver eat at a grand restaurant in Pondicherry, where Vairum has a meeting. She waits for them in the car, watching the gawkers cluster, again, into a crowd. The gleaming, showy vehicle would have drawn an audience anyhow, but the sight of an orthodox Brahmin widow tucked inside inspires comments. Sivakami unwinds her prayer beads from her wrist and says mantras until Vairum returns.

He is silent for most of the journey. For a brief time, following the meeting, he looks over some papers, and he takes a short nap. Otherwise, he stares out his window and she out hers. She imagines the quiet between them is companionable, that they are both lost in the same rosy visions of the months and years to come—but he doesn't say and she doesn't really know what he is thinking.

It is after eight o'clock when they reach Madras. The city welters up around them, almost before Sivakami realizes it has. The houses on Vairum's street look, to Sivakami, grand enough to be government offices. In the car port, the driver opens her door, and she follows Vairum's striding form up the stairs, yearning to be invisible as she feels his employees' discreetly curious eyes. Upstairs, she creeps along the narrow balcony, keeping her gaze on the floor. In the outdoor reception area, Vani falls at her feet and ushers her through the majestic carved wooden doors into the sitting room. The black and white tiles are cool, like taut silk. Sivakami's callused feet make slapping sounds that ring in the airy room's besieged hush—the quiet of a house sheltered from traffic noise by tall trees and a serious class differential. The sound of her feet against the brick of the Cholapatti floor was immediately dulled by the roughness of the floor, and the sounds of the village, always entering without leave.

She is so happy to see Vani, especially with the glow of expectancy lighting her rounded features. She appears cheerful and girlish as she shows Sivakami around, a terrific contrast with her appearance in recent years. She is about six months along and is significantly heavier, an effect enhanced by her nine-yard sari. But one would not guess Vani was pregnant from her figure, Sivakami thinks with some satisfaction: all the better to protect her from the evil eye.

Vani leads her to her room. She is not sure she likes this: a room of her own. It has one set of narrow double doors leading onto the rear courtyard, and another leading onto the sitting room. It seems inappropriate to her, excessive, for a lonely widow to take up an entire room, but she puts her Ramayana and extra sari in a wall-niche cupboard, along with her beading, and follows Vani out into the courtyard, in the centre of which is a well and a depression for washing dishes. This feels relatively familiar. The toilet and bath stalls are in the far corner. No more four-in-the-morning-blue-air dips in the Kaveri, she realizes. Will she really feel clean without sand encrusting her feet? From the courtyard, Vani shows her into the kitchen, where Vairum has deposited the satchel of snacks. It has a second set of doors onto a dining room, and a third, onto a rear puja room.

Sivakami takes water—the first she has drunk all day—pouring it from the brass jug down her throat without touching the jar to her lips, and then bathes and performs oblations for the gods in Vairum's puja room. Taking up a fistful of salt, she beckons Vani, making sure Vairum doesn't see, and circles her three times each way with the fist, saying the familiar curses under her breath. "May your eyes burst open if anything happens to this child." She looks around, unsure of where to throw evil-eye-soaked salt in a house without a canal out back. Vani points to the bathroom.

She turns next to familiarizing herself with the kitchen so she can cook herself a meal. So this is what it feels like to be so near the sea she has never seen, she thinks: the air itself clings like damp cloth. She finds herself waving her hand in front of her face as though she has walked through a cobweb; she finds the cupboard contents limp and sticky. She greets the servant couple from Cholapatti. The man has been given other chores, since Sivakami will do most of the cooking while she is here, but the woman remains to help with washing, peeling and chopping, and Sivakami shyly asks her how to use the stove.

Vairum has never told Sivakami anything about his work. Sometimes she has asked Muchami questions, and he has explained what he understood, based on gossip and on his observations as he accompanied Vairum in the field. She understands Vairum has a reputation for fairness and has earned a great deal of respect from both their tenants and his factory workers in the Kulithalai Taluk. She knows he had dealings with non-Brahmins but doesn't believe he will bring them into his house. Janaki and Kamalam had sworn to her, on returning from their Madras visit, that they ate no cooked food in non-Brahmin houses. It didn't occur to Sivakami to ask whether non-Brahmins ate food in Vairum's house. What is the purpose of soiling himself thus? He eats in restaurants—can't he just meet them there?

The first time it happens, she is convulsed with disgust: *she* has cooked this food and Vairum and Vani are sitting *together* with three of those people, *in plain view* of those people, polluted by their gaze. She never shows herself in front of guests, Brahmin or non-Brahmin; the cook serves. But she glimpsed them as they entered—dark-skinned, evidently wealthy—and could hear them, using inflections and terms foreign to Brahmins, and imagined them eating the food she had prepared. She crouches in the door between the kitchen and puja room, feeling ill. The crowning insult is when they cut through the kitchen to the courtyard to wash their hands—they enter the kitchen! On their way back to the sitting room, they stop to compliment her lavishly on the food, mortifying her with their lack of manners.

That night, she performs purification ceremonies, waving camphor and muttering prayers, to make the kitchen usable again. The next day, unable to help herself, she tries to talk to Vairum about the breach.

"Kanna, I have heard that non-Brahmins are very fond of our food," she opens, timidly. "But shouldn't you consider Vani's feelings?"

Vairum snorts, looking amused. "What are you saying, Amma?"

"Vani is a good wife—she can't tell you this herself, and would never disobey you," she presses gently. "But you shouldn't make her eat with those . . . with non-Brahmins, kanna."

"Vani no more believes in such artificial distinctions than I do, Amma," he says sharply. "We keep Brahmin cooks only because they prepare food in the style we are accustomed to and like—not because we subscribe to your outmoded provincial prejudices. Got that?"

Sivakami is defenceless. Hanumarathnam never spoke rudely like this to anyone. Vairum is more polite to his peons than to his mother. How has she lost her son to a world turned upside-down? Was it for this that she educated him? Perhaps she should have kept him in the paadasaalai, she resorts to thinking, briefly indignant. At least he would have valued his Brahminhood then, even if his caste status were the only thing he had to be proud of.

In December, Sita arrives for her delivery, bringing her elder daughter and twin sons. Kamalam and Janaki also come, Kamalam to help Sita, and Janaki for company. Everyone but the expectant mother is accommodated in the guest quarters below. Sivakami's room becomes a birthing chamber and Sivakami relocates to the kitchen floor, where she feels significantly more at ease than she did taking up a room all on her own. Vani's nieces hold a bangle ceremony for her, and now the merry tinkle of glass mingles with her music when she plays, along with the sisters' chatter and the clamour of their children.

"It's like being back in the village!" Sivakami overhears Vairum telling Sita's husband, at the eleventh-day ceremony. "In the best sense, of course. Nothing like the sound of children's voices to gladden the heart, no?"

Sivakami sees Janaki's expression: all of the Cholapatti clan present for the ceremony are painfully aware that he has not always felt like this about the sound of children.

Visalam's in-laws come for the ceremony also, with a proposal for Vairum: the year of mourning for Visalam has ended and Kamalam is now eligible for marriage. She is already part of the household, they say; there's no sense in breaking the family bond. The children need a mother and she has proven already that she can be that to them.

Kamalam acts surprised and embarrassed, but it is clear to all of them how comfortable she has felt at her future in-laws' house. Vairum happily accepts.

That afternoon, Vani plays a short concert for the guests. Sivakami disapproves and again makes the mistake, as Vani settles herself, of telling Vairum, "I am surprised you are not concerned about exposing her to the evil eye. She is almost eight months pregnant!"

"Oh, is she?" Vairum arches an eyebrow with consummate sarcasm. "I never would have known! Thank you for telling me, Amma! Oh, my, my wife is nearly eight months pregnant!"

Sivakami withdraws, humiliated, to the kitchen, where Janaki is stirring tapioca pudding on the stove for Sita's children.

"Is she well?" Janaki asks, a faint prying note in her voice. "One would hardly believe Vani Mami is pregnant."

It's true: Vani is nearing her due date and no larger than she was when Sivakami arrived in Madras.

"She is ready to be a mother!" Sivakami answers, sounding stiff. "Sometimes, when Sita's baby girl cries, Vani's breasts begin dripping so, so! The front of her sari gets soaked!"

"Oh, listen!" Janaki says. "She's playing 'Jaggadhodharana'! It brings me straight back to Cholapatti, Amma, that sound. Next summer, we'll all gather there, all the cousins, and Vani Mami will bring her child, and we can all look after it while she plays."

Sita's children swarm into the kitchen, whining for tapioca, and Janaki leads them out into the dining room.

DECEMBER BLEEDS INTO JANUARY, January creeps away and February swells into fullness, but Vani does not go into labour. She exhibits all the torpor and discomfort of advanced pregnancy, as though her burden is too great to bear and too precious to pass on, but she looks no bigger.

Sivakami is a patient woman, but she's not accustomed to waiting so long for this particular gratification. Gayatri, who had planned to come for the baby's naming ceremony, finally comes anyway, nearly two months after Vani's supposed due date.

"What on earth is going on?" she whispers loudly, as Sivakami serves her coffee in the kitchen. Vani is playing her veena in the sitting room, providing them with a cover of sound. "She's not pregnant, is she?"

"Of course she is." Sivakami combines the decoction with milk and sugar, pouring it from tumbler to bowl to mix it. "They must have miscalculated, miscounted."

"How long has it been since she last had her period?"

"I can't ask that," Sivakami responds reasonably, setting the coffee down in front of Gayatri and fetching biscuits.

"Have they seen a doctor?"

"I should hope not," Sivakami ejects, tartly indignant.

After a pause, Gayatri says, "I'm going to ask."

When Vani, after playing, comes into the kitchen for a drink of water, Gayatri beckons her.

"Come, dear." She pats the place beside her, and Vani plumps herself down awkwardly. "You look exhausted. I know all too well what it is like to be in this stage—every day seems like an eternity. Tell me, though: when did you last have your period?"

Vani frowns and looks away.

"Come now. You don't want this to go too long. It's not healthy for the baby, nor for you. You know there are remedies to help the baby along. Shall I find out about some for you?"

"No doctors," Vani says loudly, and Gayatri startles.

"Has Vairum taken you to any doctors?" Gayatri inquires.

"No," Vani says emphatically, and Sivakami thinks she can imagine the scenes between them.

"I have in mind traditional remedies," Gayatri says soothingly, and Vani looks more interested and less wary.

"But you don't want to take them too early—it's important to know that your baby is fully matured," Gayatri explains. "When did you have your last period?"

Vani purses her lips. Gayatri sighs.

After some long minutes, Vani replies. "April."

"April . . ." Gayatri counts off on her fingers. "So you might have been due as late as February. Let's give it another week and I'll see if my daughter-in-law knows anyone who can compound what you need."

Through March, the weather grows hot, and the atmosphere in the house feels oppressive. Gayatri secures and brings several herbal composites, which Sivakami prepares, boiling five roots in water for ten minutes, mixing the resulting decoction into milk and giving it to Vani to drink on an empty stomach. Vani follows the regime for three days, until Vairum learns of it and throws the herbalist's packets out the window of the kitchen.

"How dare you endanger our child with this witchcraft?" he asks. "I brought you here at Vani's insistence, but if I catch you again doing anything to jeopardize this pregnancy . . ." He leaves the threat unspoken.

Sivakami hasn't slept much since her arrival in Madras, and she lies awake for a week of nights after the confrontation, desiccated by sorrow. How could he think she would do anything to endanger the grandchild she wants, as she would readily admit, more than any of the others? A son of her son, a son of her son . . .

April bloats, May bursts—and still no child. Sivakami was to have returned to Cholapatti by now—she has been putting off her grandchildren, who all expected to convene in their natal home for the school holidays. It has become a tradition for those with school-age children to return, for the cousins to sleep together in the hall, play together near the canal, visit Gayatri's grandchildren in gangs and meet other children of their age on the Brahmin quarter. And now there are the three youngest ones in Thiruchi, whom she is missing.

She cautiously broaches the subject with Vairum, who has become increasingly preoccupied and busy of late.

"I don't see how you can go," he replies, without looking up from the paper he is reading on the divan, "but they are welcome to come here."

Janaki and Kamalam decide against coming, not wanting to crowd, and having visited so recently, but Saradha brings her family, as well as Radhai, Krishnan and Raghavan, who are thrilled to have the chance to see the city. Vairum makes a car available to them, though Saradha spends most of her time with Sivakami. Janaki had come to see her eldest sister the week prior and has sent a large packet of holy ash, along with a letter.

> *My husband had to go and consult a seer. Two of our tenants' plows were stolen, and they asked him to investigate. So he went to this man we heard of, who has a very high reputation. The man told my husband: you will find your missing items in two separate places, one high, one low, but equidistant from the river. Seek and you will find. And it was true! But I also had him ask what is wrong with Vani Mami. The man said exactly this: "Your relative has a baby within her whose soul's growth is being stunted by the evil eye. Take this holy ash, and tell her to rub it on her belly daily as an antidote. Within a year, the baby will grow."*

Sivakami thinks that surely Vairum cannot see holy ash as in any way harmful to the child—he is not superstitious but he is religious. But when, two months later, Janaki writes to her to say that the seer was arrested for leading a burglary ring—his henchmen would steal agricultural implements and he would collect money from the owners for describing how to find them—Sivakami discreetly tells Vani to discontinue this treatment also.

When August blooms like an foul-smelling flower, Vani is still acting elephantine with expectancy, though she has gained no more weight. If anything, she may have lost some, and has begun once more to look dull and drawn, as she did in the long, empty years before her pregnancy. Nearly all the glass bangles she received have broken, a bad omen, but who ever wears them this long? The lonely chime of those few remaining sounds like the dregs of misplaced hope. Vairum's overinflated good humour has fizzled; he is short with his staff and talks to Sivakami as though she is a nuisance.

Gayatri, whose Madras son has had a child, visits, and Sivakami broaches the topic with her, saying Vairum has twice brought doctors to the house, but that Vani refuses to be seen by them.

"Akka," Gayatri sighs, and looks away. "Vani's pregnancy is not advancing because she is not pregnant. Something else may be wrong with her—early menopause? I don't know. But she's not . . . pregnant."

Is Gayatri suggesting Vani has been lying? Why would she do that?

"I'm not saying she's lying," Gayatri continues in a gentle tone. "I . . . I've never heard of something like this from a woman. But it happens, with animals. I remember my brother's dog acted completely—"

"Really, Gayatri," Sivakami shouts at her friend. Comparison to a dog is one of the grand insults. "Sometimes you just go too far."

"Please, Akka, don't take me wrong," Gayatri protests, "I'm sorry."

But Sivakami is furious and they part awkwardly.

Sivakami putters around the kitchen in a rage, prepares meals and goes through the motions of her day, before finally, in the depth of night, acknowledging that, of all the possible explanations, this one makes the most sense. She is surprised that Vairum, with his reverence for reason and science, has not seen it before now. Maybe he has and is not admitting it. The ways of the heart are obscure, though: how can he give up this hope? He can't.

But if they can help Vani, perhaps they can still have a child? That is another question. Sivakami, exhausted by the effort logic demands from her, nods off over her beading.

"But she's in exactly the same condition now that she was a year ago."

Did she say that? She didn't mean to. She didn't mean it.

Yes, she did.

"Go," he says.

Sivakami straightens and dizzies. She doesn't understand.

"Go," Vairum says again.

His meaning is becoming clearer.

"As always with you, it's about appearances. I don't know why I gave in to Vani's begging for you to come," he growls. "A Brahmin widow in the city—you have done everything possible since you arrived to hold yourself apart. I can see the blame in your eyes, always that blame."

"No, it's not true." She doesn't sound sincere, though she is. She has never blamed him—what does he think she would blame him for?

"Go home. You'll never have to look at a non-Brahmin again, except for Muchami and Mari, who will cower for you in the courtyard."

"I will stay."

What about Vani? Can't he see something is wrong?

"No. You will go." He pulls her clean sari down from the drying rod, goes to the shelves of her room, takes out her few belongings and pulls a wad of cash from his pocket. His eyes are white and desperate.

"I . . . I want you to have children!" she cries, stumbling toward him in desperation of her own.

"We will." He pushes her effects and the money at her.

"Ten children!" She echoes the prophecy he made when he decided on this marriage.

"Go." He means it.

Vani, in the sitting room, has broken off in the middle of her playing. Sivakami gives her the last square of beadwork she completed— Krishna surrounded by milkmaids—and lays a hand on the crown of Vani's head. She need not remain madi if she is about to travel. Vani grasps her hand, so hard that Sivakami nearly falls, and lays her cheek in Sivakami's palm.

"You will be a mother," Sivakami whispers and then she walks toward the door, with Vairum's eyes on her. She expected him to precede her, to arrange the car, but she looks back, and he points to the exit.

She descends to the street and the peon, though confused, pulls open the gate for her. It is evening. She breaks a small twig from a neem tree growing at the edge of Vairum's compound, and pushes it into her bundle, walks a few steps, and stops. This is the first time in her sixty years that she has gone anywhere alone. She feels naked, invisible, petrified. She can feel Vairum's house behind her, as Rama must have sensed his home at his back when he was banished to the wilds, driven from his kingdom. That story has a happy ending.

She clutches for her Ramayana, inside her satchel, and forces herself to shuffle along to the busy street at the end of the cul-de-sac, where she hails a horse carriage. The driver stops but looks to either side of her and asks, "You must not be travelling alone, Amma. Where is your son, your servant, your nephew? Who is helping you?"

"No." Sivakami clears her throat. "I am going to my village. Please, take me to the station where I can catch a train south." She remembers that she must change trains in Thiruchi. "To Kottai," she adds, using the traditional name to make herself sound practised.

"Yes. Yes. Sit, please." He gestures to the carriage as his horse snorts in her frayed blue harness.

At the station, he escorts her in with a great show of respect, points out where she can get her ticket and overcharges without apology. Sivakami brought the cash Vairum gave her—she didn't want to insult him further—but doesn't want to use it for this journey. She extracts one of the five ten-rupee notes she pressed between the pages of her Ramayana all those months ago and pays her own way.

Though India has been bound together by the iron ribbon, most people on a train will try to keep a respectful distance from a Brahmin widow. As the cabin fills, though, this space thins to a sheet the thickness of a single molecule. Sivakami appreciates the delicacy of the dark and noisy persons to either side, who avoid eye contact with her despite their thighs pressed length to length, their shoulder blades fitted together like parts of a rice mill. These non-Brahmins clearly have not yet been infected by that intimacy shown by Vairum's associates, an intimacy which, she thinks, breeds and festers in cities, especially among the wealthy classes.

Madras rolls away. It is already dark. Chingleput, Madurantakam. She feels the sea recede. It is hours before she must change trains for Kulithalai. The sound of Vairum's voice returns to her on the rhythm of the train. "Go ... Go ... Go ..."

One day, when Vairum was small, he came to her urgently, wanting to tell her a story Gayatri had told him, of Lord Ganesha and his brother Murughan. The young gods' father, Shiva, had set up a competition, saying that the brother to most swiftly circle the entire world would inherit all its peoples and riches. Lean, noble Murughan leapt onto his peacock. It spread its wings with a shriek and sped off, to return in moments. Like that! Vairum said, and snapped his fingers.

When Murughan returned, Ganesha was still standing where his brother had left him. Murughan dismounted with a swagger and bowed to receive the winner's garland from his father.

"Very good!" said Shiva as he stepped forward and placed the garland over Ganesha's elephant head.

Vairum let his mouth fall open, dramatizing Murughan's shock. Shiva explained, "While you sped through the heavens, your brother, not even summoning his mouse"—that's Ganesha's vehicle, explained Vairum, as Sivakami pretended not to know—"walked clockwise around his mother. 'Mother is the entire world,' he said, 'I need go no farther.' And he fell at her feet and received her blessing and stood back up just as you arrived."

"I'm surprised fatso could move that fast," Vairum improvised on Murughan's behalf. But he accepted defeat and also fell at his mother's feet, at which point Vairum had leapt at Sivakami, throwing his arms around her, burying his face in her stomach. She could feel the warmth of him, even now, her precious boy, his face making a veronica of her belly.

Mother is the entire world. This is what we believe, she wants to shout out the window. He will hear her, back in his enchanted, sorrowful house, because this is the truth. Did she not raise him any better than this?

At Vellur, a young couple board. The floor between the benches has just been vacated. They spread their bedding. Sivakami cannot see them but can hear from their speech that they are Brahmins. The girl wakes with the first beams of light and smiles up at Sivakami.

"Where are you going, Granny?" she asks, rubbing her eyes.

"Kulithalai." Sivakami is sitting by the window now, her feet tucked under her.

"Who is . . . is he your grandson?" she asks, pointing to a young man next to Sivakami, whose head, bobbing in sleep, Sivakami has been trying for some hours to avoid.

"No, I am travelling alone."

The girl pauses, and Sivakami winces.

"You are so brave!" says the girl, her voice different now.

"One must be brave in this life," Sivakami says, hoping for some distraction to end this. "When life gives no choice."

"I am lucky," comes the response, full of youth's smugness. "Life has allowed me the choice of cowardice."

No distraction has arrived, so Sivakami asks, "Children?"

"In about six months," with a sign to ward off the evil eye.

"Very good."

"This is my first time south. My husband has taken a job in Thiruchi. Water inspector. My mother is in Kanchipurum, and . . ."

They pull into a station platform with a roof and open sides. Sivakami has anxiously checked the name of every station they have pulled through in the night and now she sees the name she has been looking for: Kottai. Kottai! She is caught off guard. This is where she must change trains!

The young woman looks doubtful, but Sivakami hurries from the train along with a few rumpled families, squeezing past the rest of the passengers, still awakening, sitting up, scratching and yawning. She descends the rungs of the metal steps and hops onto the platform from the lowest, which is still high for her. She is some thirty paces from a pump and as she walks toward it she feels some cheer. It will be good to brush her teeth and wash her face. Soon, she will arrive home. She need only think of how to disguise her unescorted arrival. She is glad to have a mission to distract her from her terrible thoughts, her shame.

She takes out her neem stick and sets her bundle down. The water gushes out brightly and she moves the bundle out of its reach. She fills her brass jug and squats to scrub her face over the drain. She hears a voice calling "Granny, Granny!"—no doubt some young person meeting her grandmother after a long time, and she thinks of the grandchildren she might see soon. She wets her neem stick and puts it in her mouth as the train starts to pull away. She looks up at the train, then down. Where is her bundle?

The young woman who shared her carriage has come to the window and is waving and pointing, "Granny! Granny!" But then she is carried past into another void.

Did she see who took it?

Sivakami runs a little in each direction like a caricature of a woman in distress, then realizes she may as well finish cleaning her teeth, and stands chewing the stick like an imbecile. Her bundle is gone—her money, her ticket, her Kamba-Ramayanam. The only person left on the platform is a peon sleeping against the ticket booth at the far end. She savours the neem's bitterness as she scrubs its frayed end over her teeth and tongue.

The platform sits on a plot of scrubby dirt and there are colonies of some kind in the near distance. This doesn't look like a big station with frequent ongoing trains. She trudges toward the ticket booth, but it's still closed and she doesn't know what she would do if it were open. The dozing peon, in a rumpled uniform of khaki shorts and shirt with fewer buttons than advisable, rolls onto his back. From the west, a woman in a khaki sari arrives and starts sweeping the station—likely her husband died in service, and she was given his job because the railways take care of their own. Sivakami doesn't try to talk to anyone. She tries to think.

Saradha lives here somewhere. Somewhere in Thiruchi, on a street by the name of Rama Rao Brahmin Quarter, in house number "6," as she recalls. She probably lives closer to the main station than to this place called Kottai, which is not what she thought it was. So if Sivakami follows the train she just disembarked, she will eventually arrive. She hopes she encounters a Brahmin quarter somewhere before long. She is parched.

Sivakami walks to the end of the platform, climbs off it to reach the track, where she puts her right foot upon a tie, and then her left foot on the next one. That's the first step.

Or was Vairum's last word the first step? Or was the first step when she took Vairum back to Cholapatti to raise him on her own? Or was it Hanumarathnam's, fleeing to read his fate's fulfillment in the sky? Now she tries not to think.

The sun rises, hot and hard. She passes through the centre of a labourers' encampment, the unwashed wives tying sun-bleached hair back with other strands of hair, leaning over the day's fire, the day's gruel. The children point at Sivakami and run toward her, bellies out.

Their mothers approach, shyly and swiftly, until Sivakami is forced to stop because a cordon has formed around her.

"Amma, Amma, where are you going, Amma?"

"I'm going to find my granddaughter."

How dare they speak to her?

"Amma, Amma, why hasn't she come to fetch you, Amma?"

"She doesn't know I'm here."

Why are they not making way?

"Amma, Amma, please sit, Amma. Please sit."

"Please, please let me go on."

So many people she was never meant to meet.

"Amma, Amma, be careful, Amma."

"I will. I will. Please, let me go on."

They part to permit her egress, grinning at her distress, or so she feels.

God willing, her Cholapatti neighbours will never know she has gone through this. How many of their lives contain miseries hidden from her? She remembers wondering this when Rukmini, poor dear, and Gayatri were going through their troubles. But her compassion for them doesn't reduce her own desire for privacy: we are ill equipped to bear even our own sadnesses, she knows, and many burdens are only made heavier by sharing.

She sees a big hill and wonders if it is Malaikottai, the Ganesha temple she has dreamed of visiting. Maybe Saradha will take her there. She wonders how far she is from Saradha's house.

She squints against the rails' glare, the sun a feverish palm on her crown. A burst of laughter causes her to turn her head. She almost missed it: a pilgrims' pavilion, a stone gazebo, in a triangle formed by the rail line and two roads.

Sivakami approaches. She must get out of the sun for a moment. She would rather the place have been empty, but . . .

The bunch sitting on the cool stone rip into peals of merriment again and their babble, as Sivakami approaches, resolves into speech. She stops. They are Brahmins. They will wonder if she is known to them. She may be, by marriage or some other connection. They call out to her. "Mami, please, Mami, sit. But . . . are you alone?"

"Yes, yes, alone," she says, wishing she had just gone on.

"Please, sit." They rise to make room for her.

"Sit, sit," she insists, now that they are all standing. "Sit, I say."

She clears her throat and looks away. Her mind is working more quickly even than she can think. She has the first word, she should use it to her advantage. "Where have you all come from?"

"Namakkal, Mami. Do you know it?"

She grew up in its shadow.

"I went there once, as a small child, with my grandparents. I don't remember it. Wonderful, is it?"

"Oh, yes, a very fine place. And you, Mami, where do you come from?"

"Cuddalore."

That just popped out.

"Oh, our niece married into Cuddalore."

"Ah, so you have been there?" she asks, terrified they will make reference to some landmark or family she doesn't know.

"No, not us. This is as far as we have ventured. We are making a pilgrim tour, going to Palani, Srirangam, all the important places."

"Very good, very good." Sivakami is so relieved that she can no longer listen.

"And you, Mami?" they ask, their curiosity bursting to the surface. "How do you come to be so far from home, and alone?"

"A . . . penance," she responds. Penance? "For . . . the sake of my son . . . who was ill."

"Oh, no, Mami." They are all sympathy. Their curiosity, though, is unrelieved.

"Yes, yes. He is well now, recovering, in Cuddalore, with his wife and family." Sivakami listens to the sound of her voice. Has she ever been lied to as easily as she is now lying? "I pledged a pilgrimage," she continues slickly.

"But if he was sick, shouldn't he do the pilgrimage?" One of the wives asks, unable to contain herself.

"I pledged, I pledged to do it. Alone. Myself, alone. Maybe he will also do it someday. He is a good and pious boy, very attached to me. He protested."

Sivakami, relieved both of the heat and the pressure of possible acquaintanceship, speaks with increasing conviction.

"But I told him, God accepted a small price for your health, for a useless old widow to undertake a journey alone. He shouldn't be so attached. I have no husband; my children are grown. I wish for God to take me. My work on this earth is over."

It's what old people say, but this is the first time she has said it, and now it occurs to her that she might mean it.

"Will you take some of our food, Mami?" asks another of the wives.

"No, no, please, thank you." They understand, and don't press.

"But . . . water?" asks the first man who spoke.

"Yes." She holds out her jug and they pour water into it from one of their vessels.

"Where will you stay in Thiruchi?"

"With . . ." Oh, no, what if Saradha's related to them? "My grand-daughter." She didn't think quickly enough—she should have said a chattram. But they might be staying in a chattram and might have insisted on taking her.

"Her husband's good name?" asks the first man again.

It's easier to tell the truth now than lie. "Sivasamba Iyer."

"Ah." No recognition.

"And your good names?" she asks politely.

"Ranganathan Iyengar."

Oh, they are Iyengar—a different sub-caste from hers. She ceases listening again, relief pounding in her ears. No relation. She nods with real happiness as Ranganathan Iyengar introduces his brother, their wives, their children. They are slightly, almost imperceptibly, chillier toward her, which is as she prefers.

They have just finished their meal and lie down to rest through the heat of the day. Sivakami lies down too, but when the food in their bellies goes to their heads, she slips down off the cool platform back into the sun. She can't risk their accompanying her, which they surely would do. She is sure to be caught in a lie if she is forced to talk any longer and would rather her face be burnt by the sun than by embarrassment. It's terrible that she prefers her lies to the truth, but, she has learned, that's what some lies are like.

Three furlongs down the tracks from where she left the cheery pilgrims, she finds a crumbling roadside shrine hung with crisply browned jasmine garlands. The god within is everyone's favourite, chubby Ganesha. Sivakami smiles sadly at his friendly elephant face, grasps her left ear in her right hand and her right ear with the other and squats a few times, the traditional abasement for him. As she rises from her last squat, she falls forward onto her knees and grasps the shrine, sobbing.

Her tears turn instantly to dry pits in the dusty ground. She squints up at her old friend, and quietly shrieks, "Take me. Take me!"

The god responds good-humouredly, "I cannot take you. But I cannot stop you either. Come along if you want."

"Take me, I say! Please, Lord."

"Come, foolish lady," he smiles, but not as though he has time to waste, "if you want to so badly."

Sivakami circles the shrine thrice, in a temper. Has she not been a firm and doubtless devotee? Has she not lived by every prescription she knows?

The gods do love their jokes: human prayer is always earnest and divine replies so often ironic. Sivakami throws up her hands and returns to walking along the track, stepping from one tie to the next. She doesn't look back nor about. She maintains a dim awareness of her feet, one in front of the other, in front of the other, on the wooden ties which fall one in front of the other in front of the other in front of the other in front of the other in front—just like the train—in front of the other in front of the other . . . in fact there's a train on the track. There's a train on the track train on the track train on the track . . . She can't see it yet, but the vibrations are growing. She hasn't looked around in some time. Now she finds she is deep within a ditch, the track laid in a furrow with embankments on both sides taller than she is.

Here is her reward, the answer to her prayers. She need only accept.

The head of the train appears. Accept.

Its face nears. It screams and the noise hits her, a foretaste of steel. The rails sing all about her, showing her the way: this is how to die. This is how to die. This is how to die—

Sivakami flings herself against the steep embankment, reaching for a pole sticking out of it. Her body flat against the slope, she pulls herself up, toes pushing like a gecko's into crumbling dust, fingers grasping, beyond the pole, for the thin grass and roots. Her hands have reached flat ground when suddenly her toes slide away on something slick: the railway is everyman's toilet and Sivakami loses her toehold in some malnourished tot's leavings even as, with a thud, the beast of her possible deliverance arrives to flatten the space she left behind, singing, Don't you want to die? Don't you want to die? Sivakami slides back down to meet her fate, flashing beneath her feet, but then she hits the pole. She wraps herself around it, clinging upside down like a baby monkey to its mother.

As the train passes, a thousand startled travellers crane out their windows to gawk back at the little Brahmin widow, her dust-stained sari blown from her stubbly head. Their bewilderment almost matches her own. She has always thought of her life as a series of submissions to God. What if she has been making her own decisions all along?

The train has passed. Elation and disappointment pound in her head like the waters of the ocean she never saw. She steps down to collect her brass jug from where it fell to one side of the track, then she climbs again, slowly, from the moat, by stepping on stones and wildflower patches. She has eluded death—why did she do that?

She collects her breath and, trembling, waits for the sound of waves to subside. It doesn't. She is hearing water.

It's her beloved and reviled Kaveri. She leaves the track and walks over a hillock toward the sound, passes through a parting in some brush, and there it is, familiar and unknowable as ever. She fills her brass jug, and rinses the film from her eyes, the dust from her skin, and the residue of recent adventures from the soles of her feet. Her exhilaration is ebbing. Did she defeat her god? Is she now truly alone?

Sivakami glances up from her thoughts to see one of her Cholapatti neighbours—Visalakshi, from three doors down—coming toward her, a friendly but puzzled expression on her face. Oh, she has been spotted, now everyone will know. What is Visalakshi doing here?

But it isn't Visalakshi: it's some other young woman with the same figure, same round cheeks and frizzy hair, stopping at a respectful distance to ask, "Mami is all right? Does she need some assistance?"

"No, no, child," Sivakami replies, and then realizes she does in fact. "I am . . . I need to find, Rama Rao Brahmin Quarter."

"Hmm."

The young woman makes a great show of thinking. She calls her family over and they all think. Clearly none of them knows. Finally, the eldest man in the group speaks on their behalf.

"Well, you must go to Thiruchi proper. All right? Cross that bridge, then you will see it."

Sivakami intended on going that way regardless, so she is spared the embarrassment of not taking their advice. She bids them a decorous farewell.

Rested and cooled, but still as deeply shaken by her failure as her success in not dying, she follows the little path back to the road and starts following it toward the next bridge. She recites Kamban's Ramayana to herself—she knows it so well that she hardly needs the book, but it, too, had become a talisman—the only book she has ever read. Each verse falls from her lips like a curtain against the entry of thought.

As she reaches the end, she spots a Brahmin walking in the same direction. She hurries to overtake him and accosts him by asking, "To go to Rama Rao Brahmin Quarter?"

He turns: it's the priest from the Vishnu temple at the end of the Cholapatti Brahmin quarter! A vicious gossip. She recalls his pious, lascivious voice, like a bletted papaya.

But no, it's just some other paunchy, middle-aged Brahmin. He informs her officiously that Rama Rao Brahmin Quarter is close to Malai Kottai, and points, with confidence approaching boredom, back the way she has just come. He clearly assumes she is a cook or some equivalent. She must be quite black, she thinks, after all these hours in the sun. For her part, she suspects he has just performed a funeral on Saradha's street, at extortionate prices.

He at least knows where she needs to go, however. She returns to the bridge and walks back.

Every hundred paces, it seems, she sees some familiar old acquaintance from Cholapatti. Is that babbling and limping old man not the same one Dharnakarna the witch cast her spell over three years ago? He is lewd and foul-mouthed and she has forbidden her granddaughters' kids to get within twenty paces of him, but now he seems like a fixture of home and she wishes she had food to give him.

It's not him. That hiccuping laugh that turns her head is not Gayatri's. She asks directions again. She follows a bend in the road. That hoot and holler is not Raghavan's. Raghavan, such a robust and cheerful boy. Just the occasional grey shadow in those golden eyes, only to be expected. She has stopped to seek him out in a cricket ground, though she knows by now that the sturdy boy running at her out of the dust is not him, and the lanky silhouette following is not Krishnan.

But then why are they embracing her?

It is they.

Sivakami doesn't respond to their questions. Each boy takes one of her arms, and they walk across the field to the street. The sun is showing its colours in the west, but Sivakami can make out her eldest granddaughter's compact shape, leaning on a front wall, chatting with her mother-in-law and a neighbour.

Saradha shrieks. "Amma! Amma! What are you doing? Where are you? What . . . what did you boys do?" She looks ready to hit them as they guide Sivakami inside.

"We found her," Krishnan says defensively. "We were playing, Raghavan looked over, and she was standing by the edge of the field."

"What are you talking about? That's ridiculous!" Saradha is in a panic. "Amma, say something, Amma, why don't you say anything? Raghavan, go get water for Amma."

Saradha's in-laws graciously retire to other parts of the house. Her husband is still at work. Sivakami opens her mouth. She holds it open a second, then shuts it again. Saradha pours water into Sivakami's jug, and Sivakami moistens her mouth and throat, and after some moments, asks, "Where is the washroom? I have not had my bath today."

"Sit for some more time, Amma." But Sivakami asks again for the bathroom. As she locks the door, Saradha asks, "Amma, when did you last eat?"

"Yesterday," she says into the dank and welcome solitude—out of the world's eye at last. "Don't worry, child. Let me have my bath and then I will make my rice."

"Yes, Amma. I will . . . I will prepare vegetables for you to cook."

"Good girl."

Saradha's sons, Raghavan and Krishnan's coevals, had been out playing cricket with their uncles but not recognized their great-grandmother so readily. They followed them home, quiet and incurious, though it is obvious that something bad has happened. Raghavan and Krishnan also ask no questions but show concern. When Radhai returns from visiting at a friend's house, she is panicked, but her elder sister silences her with a finger.

When Sivakami is nearly finished eating, Saradha finally makes her first sally.

"Amma, when is Vani Mami expecting?" Sivakami doesn't answer. Saradha tries one more remark. "She must be very big."

"She is no bigger than she was a year ago at this time," Sivakami informs her.

"Ah." Saradha bites her lip.

Her kitchen is orderly to the point of excess, Sivakami has noted, with approval and without surprise. Each time she used a spice, Saradha, hovering, returned it to exactly the spot from which it came.

"Amma, why on earth did you leave Madras, Amma?" she asks.

"Because my son told me to go," Sivakami explains evenly.

"He thought you shouldn't be waiting around any more." Saradha nervously adjusts her sari.

Once more, Sivakami doesn't feel like replying.

"He didn't send a servant with you?" Saradha whispers sympathetically.

There is a long pause in their conversation.

"But you should have informed us that you were coming!" Saradha throws up her hands and rolls her eyes, as if Sivakami were just too spontaneous.

"I intended to go straight through to Cholapatti without troubling anyone else." Sivakami finishes her meal. Dribbling water around the spot where her banana leaf lay, so as to ensure no one will step on the polluted spot before she can wipe it, she folds the leaf away from her and carries it back into the courtyard to wash her hands.

"Why did you get down in Thiruchi then instead of going on to Cholapatti?"

"I don't know what happened. I got confused. And my bundle disappeared, someone took my ticket and money while I was washing my face."

"Oh, no, Amma." Saradha lifts her hand to her mouth. "Oh, no."

Sivakami waits for Saradha to stop wailing. She would feel worse if the girl didn't react like this, but it's not making her feel much better.

Saradha finally dries her tears and asks, "How did you find your way?"

"How does it matter? I found my way. How is your husband?"

"Very well, thank you."

"How are your in-laws?"

"Very well, thank you."

"Good."

"Come," Saradha says, after a pause, standing with the busy air of the excellent housewife. "Lie down now."

"Yes."

Saradha unfurls a straw mat for Sivakami in a corner of the hall as the in-laws return and exchange niceties from a distance.

From the floor, Sivakami tells Saradha, "I want to go to Malai Kottai tomorrow."

"Tomorrow?"

"Yes, tomorrow morning, before I get on the train for Cholapatti. I want to go to the top of Malai Kottai."

"Aren't you terribly exhausted, Amma? You must stay longer."

"No. I want to look on that god's face in the morning."

"All right, Amma," she capitulates, sounding concerned. "Sleep now."

But Sivakami is already asleep.

At dawn the next morning, Sivakami and Saradha go by cycle rickshaw to the foot of the hill temple. Sivakami wanted to walk but finally capitulates only because Saradha said she herself couldn't walk three miles to the temple and then climb it. In the rickshaw, Saradha asks if they are retracing the route she took. Sivakami thinks they must be but it looks even less familiar now than it did then, when she thought she knew everyone she passed. Now, with Saradha at her side, she can see the streets' real strangeness. She might have wondered how she made her way, but it had never occurred to her that she wouldn't. That was the least of her concerns. What will happen when next she sees Vairum? What does he think happened to her after she left—and how can such a son live with himself?

They dismount from the rickshaw at the entrance to a thickly crowded corridor into the temple's first vestibule, and walk along a cordon of small shops into the oil-lamp-lit, stone-floored room. Voices rebound with the sound of coconuts shattering, thrown hard in a trough, as offerings or thanks, while devotees mill in circles around a wide tree growing out of the floor and into the ceiling. The smells of burning camphor and incense press hard against the smells of sweat, soap and hair oil.

Sivakami bustles straight to the stairs that ascend through the mountain's centre to its summit, and begins to climb rapidly, one hand on the rough wall to steady her, only one impatient glance back to check that Saradha is following.

Their legs grow painful, then heavy, then numb. Saradha struggles to keep pace. A bat dips into the stairwell from a high cavern in the walls. Sivakami listens to the rhythm of her steps against the stone, the brushing of her hand on the wall, her heart pumping, her breath rasping. She hears it all as though she were a bat, both within herself and high above, both inside the mountain and climbing it. They pass by chambers and niches for worship and rest. She doesn't stop, not once.

When they come out into the light, they are beside a small cave, with a smooth, level floor, a pillar-framed entrance and walls carved with row upon row of writing. Finally, Sivakami pauses and thinks, as she is meant to here, of kings. Chola kings—did they build this? To guard the city against the marauding Pandians from the south? Was it earlier? The Pallavas? The walls might tell her, but the Tamil is archaic, and though she stands mouthing the syllables, they don't assemble into meaning.

Still, she moves her eyes along each and every line of the inscription, an exercise not unlike her incessant reading of the Kamba-Ramayanam. She looks at that book because she thinks it important that Brahmins not forget how to read, and for that reason, now, she reads the inscription without understanding any of it and then begins again to climb. She calls out to Saradha, who is leaning against an opposite wall, her eyes still closed but her chest no longer heaving. After one more long flight of stairs, they emerge from the mountain onto smooth, bald rock. Sivakami walks to the edge of the small plateau and beholds the city with the Kaveri River, its reason for being, streaking unconcernedly down its centre.

She sees people below. It is too far down to make out any individual, besides which her eyesight is not what it once was. But Sivakami imagines she sees the kings and armies of olden times, the Pallavas, Pandians, Cholas, Nayaks, battling to gain territory, struggling to keep it. She sees Kannagi and Kovalan, of the *Tale of an Anklet,* passing through the city on their great and terrible journey south to find their fate in the kingdom of a careless monarch. She sees pilgrims, she sees merchants. Seafaring Chinese and African traders; Ibn Battuta and Marco Polo, laughing with them. And, arriving from the northeast, she sees herself, small and determined, fighting confusion, indignity and peril, and finding her way, in an unrecorded triumph.

Saradha is sitting beside her, now, enjoying the view. Sivakami thumps her encouragingly on the back and Saradha gives her a watery smile. There is yet one more flight of stairs—to the belvedere.

Saradha has always liked this temple. She always brings visitors and enjoys with them a leisurely ascent, with many stops for exploring the cavernous temple chambers hollowed from the mountain's centre, savouring a strong flavour of self-righteousness on completing the difficult climb and a pleasing glow of fatigue in the thighs. This insane dash has deprived her of all the en route pleasure, and now the tearing sensation in her lungs and the weakness in her legs are preventing her even from enjoying her spiritual point-scoring. Worse, Sivakami exhibits no consciousness of all this, no sense of how it all should be done. She is not even mouthing about how healthy the climb is, how holistic Hindu worship, how superior every Brahmin devotional act.

Rather, Sivakami is bounding, without a word, for the final staircase to the tiny Ganesha shrine at the top. It is enclosed in a cupola with open frames on all sides. Saradha lets her go.

Sivakami joins the other pilgrims circling the god, one of the primary modes of worship. In the course of her first circumnavigation, though, her courage deserts her. Sadly, she confronts Ganesha.

"Are you still there?" she asks, quaking.

"I am."

"But I didn't come." She looks down, her lip trembling. "I didn't take the chance when the train . . . I must have been frightened."

"Mortals refuse most divine offers." He sounds sad. And amused. "You've done nothing new. It reflects well on you that you were tempted. But so few of you accept our gifts, even ones you have prayed for."

Ganesha is the god of new beginnings, and she missed her chance to end this life and begin another one, fresh. What other divine offers has she denied?

But now Saradha has reached her, and together they make several more turns around the idol. Sivakami thinks Saradha is acting a bit strange, looking at her nervously. She can understand that her dash and insistence might have been alarming. Saradha has had a shock—seeing her grandmother appear, walking on the street with nothing but a brass jug, as if she were some itinerant person—a siddha, for instance—and not the respectable grandmother she has always known.

Sivakami tries to speak reassuringly, says how glad she is to have visited the shrine, and how invigorating the climb was, and asking which way is Rama Rao Brahmin Quarter and can they see it from up here? They make their way slowly down again, stopping to see whatever Sivakami senses Saradha wants to show her.

She gives in and stays two days in Thiruchi; then it's Saturday and a half-day at school. That evening, Krishnan escorts her to Cholapatti. Muchami fetches a locksmith to open the padlock, and Sivakami, at last, is home.

41.
Private Cares
1946–1952

THE FIRST FEW DAYS AFTER HER ARRIVAL are spent cleaning the house and updating the accounts. Muchami waits until the second morning before asking, "And Amma, why did you return?"

She has nearly convinced herself that her banishment was her own fault: if she had gone about things differently, introduced the topic more gently, more indirectly, perhaps if she had talked to Vani first, she might have helped. As it was, she just made Vairum defensive.

Still, she knows that if she tells Muchami what happened, Vairum will come off looking bad.

"What could I do there?" She smiles at him. "They didn't need me. They needed a doctor." She tries to make the unfamiliar word sound natural. It's the first time she has told Muchami a lie; they have always colluded in such matters. "They're so modern! I just couldn't keep up."

"I would have come to fetch you," he says. "He only needed to send word."

She realizes Muchami feels guilty.

"He should have asked me to come for you if he couldn't bring you hisself," he emphasizes.

"Himself. I told him not to." It's getting easier to lie: the first is always the hardest, she has learned. "I left quickly so he would not insist. It was not difficult."

She falters at the last. Muchami is not fooled, even if he doesn't know exactly what happened.

"You should have called for me, Amma." He can know nothing of the feelings of a mother for her son, but he has dedicated his life to maintaining the propriety of this household and, out of consideration for her feelings, faults her for its dereliction. "You should have let me do my duty."

Sivakami dutifully writes Vairum and Vani to inform them of her safe arrival. Months pass without a response and without an appearance from Vairum, who has come every month or two since moving to Madras, to check on his lands and his business interests locally. Muchami walks the fields, as he has always done, though it takes him nearly two weeks now to visit all of the properties, so much have their holdings grown. He ensures that rent is paid promptly and fully, and Sivakami records the amounts in the latest ledger. Once, there is a minor dispute, but he resolves it handily without having to ask Vairum for his intervention, though he invokes the landlord in the mild threats he uses to bring the tenant in line.

Sivakami and Saradha had conferred in Thiruchi and decided that Raghavan, Krishnan and Radhai will all remain there, despite Sivakami's return. The boys have settled into school and are performing relatively well, Krishnan better than his younger brother, who has little interest or patience for study despite his evident talent. It would not do to disrupt them again, much less to return them to the inferior school in Kulithalai. Though Radhai is no longer in school, what would she do alone in Cholapatti? Saradha can use her help—Radhai is an able cook and tutors the younger children, who love her. Though she has been more or less tamed, she retains enough tomboy mischief to keep them entertained. The other reason Sivakami recommends this arrangement, the reason she doesn't tell Saradha, is that she hopes Vairum and Vani may call her back.

Laddu moves back in with Sivakami, but he is away at work for as much as twelve hours a day. After years of efficiently co-managing the hubbub of children, grandchildren, neighbours and friends, Sivakami and Muchami find themselves, when they have finished their daily work, with a lot of time on their hands. Sivakami mentions to Gayatri that her copy of the Kamba-Ramayanam got eaten by worms in Madras. "The damp, Gayatri!" she told her friend. "Bugs I've never seen before!" The next day, Gayatri brought her the gift of a new copy. She never asks why Sivakami returned.

Sivakami daily spends an hour or two reading from the Ramayana, usually aloud to Muchami. Often, they pass some time in the afternoon playing palanguzhi or Chinese checkers. It's just as well they don't need help from Mari, because her health has continued to deteriorate.

In October, Deepavali, the festival of lights, comes and goes without word from Vairum. She had written to ask if he and Vani might visit, but received no more response to this letter than to any of the others she has written, four since her arrival home. She observes the festival with nothing but a small puja at home since Laddu has gone to celebrate with the crowd in Thiruchi.

She feels similarly dispirited when the days of Pongal arrive in January. Without enthusiasm, she makes big pots of sweet and savoury pongal, the sticky rice and lentil dish that is the emblem of the holiday, enough for all their tenant-labourers. Laddu stays home to receive gifts from the tenants, pumpkins and sheaves of rice or millet, which they leave in the front hall before going around to the shed for their meal. Muchami has cleaned it out for them, and Sivakami has drawn a large, festive kolam on the floor. He and Mari will serve.

It would be a modest but proper celebration, were it not for Mari's strange behaviour. She has been complaining of odd ills for years, and on this day, the first in months when she has been required to come to Sivakami's house, she is more of a liability than a help. She spills several plates of food, saying she can't see the labourers' banana leaves on the floor, or can't see the floor. Then, when Muchami tries to tell her to rest, she loses her temper, yelling at him in front of the gathering. It is highly awkward, but she will not retreat on Muchami's orders. She stands defiantly in the shed until she hears Sivakami's loudly whispered command from the courtyard. She gives Mari a cup of warm milk and, when the feast is done, Muchami escorts her home.

A few days after Pongal, Sivakami hears shoes being kicked off in the vestibule and hurries for the door, trying to outpace a moth of nervousness meandering around her. It is shortly after noon, and she and Muchami had been resting, she in the pantry, he out in the court-yard. She hurriedly puts some snacks on a plate with a tumbler of water, and runs to greet Vairum, saying, "There you are! I didn't know you were coming, and haven't prepared, but I must make a spe-cial tiffin. *Uppuma* and *samiya payasam*, yes?"

Without acknowledging her, he calls out, "Muchami! Muchami!" Passing his mother, he goes to the floor desk. Without sitting, he takes the ledger from it and begins looking over the accounts. Muchami arrives at the doorway to the main hall from the garden. "Yes, here," he says, panting slightly.

"This Chellasamy's rent. Why are there brackets around it?" Vairum asks, frowning at the ledger.

Muchami looks past Vairum at Sivakami, and back at Vairum. Vairum looks at him and points at the entry.

"Uh," Muchami begins, "if I'm not mistaken, that was because his brother paid on his behalf, to repay a debt to Chellasamy, but the paddy was not of the same grade. Is that right, Amma?"

Sivakami, who records income and expenditures according to his reports, confirms, "That's right."

"All right. The rest looks good. Shall we go out?" Vairum asks Muchami. He snaps the ledger shut, stows it in the floor desk, puts his shoes back on at the front door and strides away. Muchami looks at Sivakami and, wiping his forehead with his shoulder towel, dashes to catch up with Vairum.

Sivakami stands alone in the main hall for a long time before she takes the plate of snacks back into the kitchen. She makes the tiffin, but Vairum doesn't return that day. Muchami, when he returns, eats the tiffin and takes leftovers home for Mari. Sivakami eats nothing for sev-eral days. He asks her no questions and says almost nothing. Laddu, perhaps, never knows what has transpired.

She doesn't feel angry, nor even, really, confused, but just empty of effort and of fear. Now she grows accustomed to that emptiness jut-ting against the emptiness of the house, which vaults around her men-acingly at night, silently shouting reminders of all she does not have.

Vairum visits Cholapatti in March, again coming and leaving without a word for his mother. At the end of April, the school holidays arrive, and with them, her grandchildren and their children, for their summer visit. The house brightens with noise and activity.

So when next Vairum comes, she doesn't hear him enter, she just hears the main hall go quiet. When she goes to the pantry doorway to see why, all her granddaughters are looking at the front entrance. They turn to one another busily, as if to comment on what they have seen, but then catch sight of Sivakami and fall silent again.

Sivakami knows Vairum must have come and gone, perhaps acknowledging them, though her granddaughters saw that he failed to say a word to his mother. She turns from them and goes back to the kitchen. She doesn't want to know what they will say to one another and doesn't want them to think they can ask her questions or offer her comfort. This has nothing to do with them. She's not even sure what it has to do with her.

When Janaki sees how Vairum treats their grandmother, she wants even more badly to stay on. She had already been dreading the return to Pandiyoor: her brothers- and sisters-in-law are planning to move into their own homes in July, and the tension in their home, over the division of possessions and other niceties of the break, was already mounting before she left. But Baskaran's letters to her have been full of the pain this is causing his parents, as well as his longing for Janaki's return, and she can't prolong her stay.

She can see how their presence here must be cheering Sivakami. Saradha had told Laddu and her sisters of Sivakami's bizarre appearance at their home, leaving them all to speculate on the circumstances. Their convergence in Cholapatti revived the painful topic and the way Vairum ignored Sivakami sealed their consensus that there had been a violent break of some kind. They have heard nothing more of a baby from their aunt and uncle, and indeed, have heard little at all from them in the last year.

Inevitably, Baskaran comes to escort Janaki home. Thangajothi, their daughter, has had a marvellous time with her cousins but is thrilled to see her father. He and Janaki dote on her: a precocious two-year-old, fair, a little too skinny, with jet-black hair that has grown out in curls since it was shaved and sacrificed to Palani mountain a month before her first birthday.

On the train, Baskaran briefs Janaki while Thangajothi sleeps. The new houses are ready to be occupied, but Mr. Kandasamy's modest proposal also included a division of the inheritance. The brothers will walk with their shares. The brothers have become accustomed to the idea of being household heads and are behaving with due combativeness. Shortly after Janaki's return, Senior Mami decides all dowry items and furniture belong to the marital household; her sons overrule her by saying there are now two more marital households. She is so insulted she weeps, terrifying rubbery sounds, and gets a nosebleed that lasts, off and on, for days.

There is much wrangling over how the land is to be divided, which pieces of land are the more productive, and whether this is owing to the tenant farmer, the crop or the location.

In the final moments, Vasantha and Swarna let loose on each other. At meals, they accuse each other of acts and thoughts that had been secrets between them. They try to take back gifts, even from each other's children. Things not given, they steal.

Janaki pities her father-in-law, as now the brothers accuse him and Baskaran of plotting to disinherit them and throw them out. Senior Mami has a mild heart attack, and her husband a sympathetic attack a week later.

It is as though they are living through a scourge, and when it is over, what lingers? Bad feelings that may persist through generations, Janaki thinks miserably, huddling with her husband and child at night, being exceedingly solicitous toward her parents-in-law by day. How can people not see—Vasantha, Swarna, Vairum—that even a family that fights is better than a broken one? Families belong under a single roof. She resolves that, after they move, she will make an extra effort to be friendly with them, and with Vairum. She must work, in every way possible, against estrangements.

It is mid-August when finally the two couples move into their own homes, the week India gains independence and Pakistan splits off: a country born, a country split, parturition and partition.

Northern corridors run with blood—families abandon homes, families abandon families.

Janaki, who has no interest in politics and has lost track of the news, is felled by a fever that keeps her in bed, shivering, for three days. Baskaran goes in search of Palani veeboothi, which she takes in pinches and makes him and Thangajothi smear on their tongues and foreheads as a preventative until she is better.

——⌒——

THE FOLLOWING MARCH, she returns to Cholapatti, a month early because she is pregnant again, due in April. She has made one trip back in the meantime, in November, to visit Kamalam there, who just had her first baby. By the time Janaki gives birth to her twin boys—she and Baskaran compromised this time; the nurse was called but stayed in the courtyard, close at hand, until the babies were safely delivered—the house is full again with her siblings and their children. Laddu has so far refused to marry, but Sivakami has asked his sisters to convince him this summer. He is almost twenty-eight and, given how he has advanced through the ranks of Vairum's concerns and how well he is now earning, a highly eligible bachelor. The women look forward to a little sport at his expense.

Only one concern mars the summer's gaiety, and even that provides them with gossip: Mari has shown signs of increasing delusion and Vairum has been taking her for monthly treatments in Thiruchi. The young women of Sivakami's household press Gayatri for details and she agrees to tell all of them but Radhai, the only one yet unmarried.

"Hysteria," she says, looking at them meaningfully.

They look at her and one another, and then Sita makes a small sound of recollection. "I have heard of that." She looks at her sisters suggestively. "Isn't it . . . a complaint of a, you know, intimate nature?"

"Exactly. I don't know exactly how long it has gone on, but it sounds like perhaps from the start of their marriage, Muchami and Mari never . . ."

She pauses and the young women lean in.

"Never had sexual congress." Gayatri nods solemnly. "It's a terrible thing. And now it has started to tell on her health."

"Ayoh!" Saradha exclaims.

"It is terrible," says Janaki, as Kamalam blushes, looking deeply reluctant to learn all this. "Poor thing."

"So how is it treated?" Sita asks, with more curiosity than concern.

"A machine." Gayatri uses the English word. "In the doctor's office. My husband said he had seen advertisements for such things, in mail-order catalogues, way back. It does . . . it's supposed to simulate what a husband should do."

"Ayoh!" Saradha exclaims again, with greater feeling.

Janaki is silent now, full of pity for the both of them. Good old Muchami and his poor, striving wife. Whatever went wrong? Why did they never adopt? They should have had children. It might have saved Mari. She's sure it would have, in fact. Maybe Vairum and Vani will give in and do that before Vani goes entirely the same way. If they don't think of it themselves, though, she can't think of anyone who would be brave enough to suggest it to them.

The treatments appear to be effective, Muchami admits. For a week or two after each one, Mari appears calmer, doesn't drop things as much or fall down, and recognizes him as her husband. The effects ebb, though, and by the time she is due for another treatment, she once more cannot be trusted to cook or serve, and will call Muchami by odd names, sometimes male, sometimes female, and accuse him of histories and doings that are plainly not his.

He is so ashamed, and it is worse for not knowing how he is and is not to blame. He, who has always held duty above all, failed to perform this sacred duty for his wife. He tried, a couple of times, but she rejected him, saying they had agreed: theirs was a celibate marriage. He was grateful, because he had not been confident that he would succeed in satisfying her. He loves her, but much as he loves his younger sisters. He was frankly repulsed by the idea of intimate contact. Perhaps she rejected him because she sensed that.

Inasmuch as he is her husband, though, he is responsible for her health and care. He had taken her to see a number of healers before finally turning in desperation to Vairum. The doctor Vairum took them to see was the first who tried to probe the malady's causes, instead of treating symptoms. Muchami had always feared that their lack of conjugal relations would in some way return to haunt him, and the diagnosis was both a relief and a deep humiliation. He returned feeling unmanned, a feeling that intensified with Mari's first treatment. He waited in the small vestibule of the office—Vairum, mercifully, had dropped them off and said he would return in an hour—while Mari was inside on the doctor's table. Muchami listened to the whir of the machine and then Mari's cries, escalating. They reminded him of his childhood, when, a couple of times, he spied on neighbours at night. This was the first time since then that he had heard a woman orgasm.

He could feel Sivakami waiting, the next day, for his report on this latest effort. She had been among the first to witness Mari's difficulties, and had been his confidant as he searched for a means to cure her. He had been mum on the results of the consultation with the doctor, except for telling her, when she served his morning meal, that he thought the doctor might have some idea what was wrong. Sivakami had not probed for details.

"That's good," she said gently, not incurious but trusting him to say what he could, looking at him with such compassion that he was almost tempted to confess.

It had made him feel strange about their relationship in a way he never had before. He has never thought their closeness odd; rather, it was the natural result of their shared life's work. He is so grateful now, though, for the succour of her friendship, something none of his male friends can give him, nor, clearly, his wife. Unlike them, she knows nothing of his inclinations, and yet she feels what he feels, because their missions, their heartbreaks, their triumphs have so long been twinned.

He had nodded at her, and she smiled a little and went to fetch more rice for him as he sighed, exhausted from concern but now resting for a moment in their precious, private complicity.

42.
Touring Talkies
1952

JANAKI UNFOLDS THE NEWSPAPER and comes face to face with a face she last saw in front of the Madurai chattram, seven years earlier, before the palanquin curtains fell and ended the scene.

She feels the need to smooth her kitchen-puffed hair and re-pleat her sari pallu, which is crumpled and tucked like a crying infant over her shoulder and into her waist. She feels as skinny and provincial as she did as a child, when Bharati used to look past her much as she is now looking past Janaki from Janaki's lap.

The photo accompanies an article, and half of the page opposite is taken up with a movie advertisement. It has a border composed of a drawing of Bharati in a three-quarter view expressing pleasure and dismay as though in response to a declaration of illicit love, blending into the valiant leading man, and then into the conniving, mustachioed villain. These images twist like a vine from a tableau along the bottom: Bharati, flowing hair escaping her widow's whites as she wrenches her wrist from one of the men.

The article in *Dinamani* is a packet of the standard glowing rot: "Miss Bharati, the product of a modest, middle-class home in Kulithalai, always had a great love of music and was encouraged by her mother and father to pursue it seriously. Of course, her parents expected her to perform at home only, but Miss Bharati has taken a vow to marry her art only. She has been most inspired by the example of Sri Rukmini Devi, alias Mrs. Arundale, whose thrilling debut onto the Madras stage helped Miss Bharati to convince her doting parents that the Indian classical arts can and must be practised by respectable girls. 'It is a necessary step in the building of an independent, modern nation,' said Miss Bharati, an ardent nationalist, who is twenty years complete." Janaki wonders if the paper colluded or was duped into knocking eight years off Bharati's age.

She folds the paper and lies back on the low, narrow cot she has had built for the women's room. She has done the kolam, bathed, dressed and fed her children, sent Thangajothi off to school, consulted with the kitchen staff and overseen the start of the day's preparations. The servants should be leaving any minute with her twin sons, taking them back to their village just as she went back to Muchami's. This gives her a precious half-hour to look through the newspaper before taking a bath, doing her puja and giving the Sanskrit tutorial at the paadasaalai. She's excited these days because there is one new pupil who is quite talented. His gifts took her by surprise because his skin is so dark: she didn't think he looked so bright when he arrived. Now, she finds herself planning special challenges for him, just as young Kesavan did for her and Bharati.

Her sons, Sundar and Amarnath, active two-year-olds, gallop in, damp and toasty from playing in the garden. Every day, they come in at this time and act as though it were a delightful surprise to find her, nearly prone, vulnerable to their attack. Today, they cheer: "Hip hip hooray!" She wonders if they learned the English syllables from their cousin Shyama, a bright boy bound for a bad end. Hers are good boys, she can tell already, and they will remain so if she can keep them from bad influences: Amarnath, a reflective boy who she hopes will outgrow his propensity to cry easily, and Sundar, a resilient bouncy sort who will certainly try his teachers and be beaten but never broken. They are inseparable, which as far as she is concerned is only good.

They throw themselves on her, Sundar with a roar, Amarnath with a squeak, and she submits, pressing their heads to her to quiet them, because grandchildren are not among Senior Mami's interests. Thankfully, she hears the servants call that the prams are ready to go. She kisses the boys and pulls from under the cot a box of wooden blocks they can take with them. The blocks are painted with English letters; Baskaran bought them in Madurai last year.

She returns to wondering how long it will be before *Clouds in the Eyes,* Bharati's debut vehicle, comes through Pandiyoor with one of the touring talkies.

Janaki used to say she had never been to the cinema; now she says she has not been yet. She waited until the most conservative families on the Brahmin quarter started permitting their children before she would consider it for hers, though she still has not gone, nor has Thangajothi. Movie-going doesn't cause the gossip it might have once, but it's one of Janaki's points of pride to do everything possible to uphold conservative values in their household.

Folding the newspaper with a noisy yawn, she curls onto her side for a catnap. *Clouds in the Eyes,* she decides, will be her debut experience, too.

At half past three, Thangajothi arrives home from school, cranky because she is ravenous, and unwilling, as always, to eat. She's a bright girl, but complicated. With her is her cousin, Shyama, who is singing.

"Caw! Caw! Caw!" he bellows, the refrain of one of the season's most popular songs.

Sundar leaps and hinges himself to Shyama's side, Amarnath falls in behind. They've already joined in the chorus, a terrible, joyful caw-caw-phony. Janaki ignores them in the way of young mothers, wearing her authority with little grace. She fetches balls of thaingai maavu and instructs them to break bananas off the stalk in the pantry, pulls Thangajothi onto her lap and force-feeds her while Shyama entertains them.

He went to the touring talkies last night with his elder brothers, neither of whom made it to college, but who make it to the movies several times a month. Shyama is the youngest child of one of Baskaran's sisters. She married into Tamapakkam, Pandiyoor's other half, across the Vaigai. The groom turned out to be a Communist, which unfortunately resulted in an aversion to work, a love of sloganeering, and a pressing desire to give away his inheritance the moment it dropped into his hands. As a result, he has a lifetime honorary membership in the Communist Party and several unions for trades he has never practised while his family lives on what Baskaran can eke out for his sister by investing the dowry her husband naturally refused. She had capitulated to her husband in naming their first three children—Stalin and Lenin, and a daughter, Russia—but insisted the last have the name of her favourite composer, Shyama Sastri.

Shyama spends more waking time in Janaki's house than in his own, because the food and the audiences are so much better. As he snacks, he renders for them, line by line, note by scene, the film he saw last night, one of the year's *causes célèbres*. It tells the story of the youngest of three brothers, doing business in Burma during the war, who travels home to Madurai for his sister's wedding. En route, however, he is duped and robbed, left penniless in the city. His sister marries, but loses her husband and her father in accidents on the very day she gives birth to a child. Their house is sold and she, too, embarks on a life of difficulty: she is forced to borrow money; she tries to make a living selling idlis; she works in the house of a corrupt, high-caste man who tries to seduce her. What she doesn't know is that her brother, Gunasekharan, has been, in the guise of a madman, keeping an eye on her.

Shyama acts out all the scenes with verve and conviction but reserves a special energy for the songs, whose lyrics are full of attempts at political subversion. One, a siddha song, goes, "If a rich man tells a lie, it will be taken as a truth . . . Money makes leaders of fools . . . Even when crying over a dead body, watch your pockets!" The song Shyama had been singing when he entered the house asks why all men cannot simply share with their brethren, the way crows do.

"Caw! Caw! Caw! Beggars fight for food in the trash, while the mighty fight for money! Crows always call one another to share food, but people, never . . . Caw! Caw! Caw!"

"But children, look." Janaki sees an opening. "Crows call other crows to eat. They're not calling sparrows and ducks and monkeys. We all look after our own families, our own community," Janaki points out, confident in her logic. "You see? Brahmins look after Brahmins, non-Brahmins after their own sort."

"Communists are different," Shyama retorts.

THE TOSS OF A LEMON ~ 577

"Don't talk back," returns Janaki. A pause follows. "Drink your milk."

Shyama, unoffended, continues the story. The political content of the film becomes increasingly pointed, including specific references to up-and-coming champions of the DMK, newest party in Tamil nationalism, though it is lost on him.

In the film's culminating scene, the brother gulls a corrupt Brahmin priest, castigating him in the voice of the goddess Parasakthi. When the hero reveals himself, it is to make a speech in classical Tamil, a language practically foreign to those in the land of its origins. The DMK is revitalizing it, making a gift to the masses of their own tongue.

The film is so popular that most audience members can now recite this curlicued speech, and the syllables thrum from them in the tents of the touring talkies, as they do from Shyama now. Janaki is just about to stop him—the children, who can't understand, are restless, while she can't bear any more polemic—when Baskaran comes in holding a letter and looking grave. He holds up a finger and Shyama stops speaking.

"Janaki." He beckons her to come close and she disentangles herself from her daughter and rises. "We need to go to Madras. Your sister Sita is travelling there for surgery. It's"—he clears his throat—"cancer. I'm sorry. She will stay with your uncle Vairum and need help with the children, though of course we would want to go anyway, at least for a few days."

They decide that they can go to Madras for ten days, so Thangajothi doesn't miss more than a week at school. The girl is a top performer and Janaki is keenly interested in making sure she maintains her grades. She and Baskaran have not discussed it with anyone else, but Janaki wants to break with tradition in one critical way, and Baskaran supports her: their bright girl will go to college.

Janaki recalls having thought she noticed a black patch on Sita's tongue last summer, but, with advancing age, parches and discolorations are not unusual. But it was, it turns out, malignant. Sita had gone to Madras for a biopsy some six months earlier, but treatments had failed to halt the spread of the cancer and now her tongue must be cut out in hopes of saving her.

Kamalam arrives in Madras a few days before Sita's surgery; Janaki arrives the day of the procedure. Kamalam minds Sita's elder children, girls of twelve and four, and seven-year-old twin boys, along with her own child and stepchildren, while Vani tends Sita's babies, twin boys as well. When Janaki comes, she offers to help, over the clamouring jealousy of her own twins, with Sita's babies, but Vani refuses. Janaki and Kamalam look at each other, remembering the Adyar Beach scene they witnessed on their first visit to Madras, all those years ago, and hope that Vani will be able to give the babies up when Sita recovers.

They also wonder whether Sivakami has been told. They're almost certain Vairum would not have told her. As far as they know, he has not spoken a word to her since he sent her away. All of Thangam's children have chosen to remain on good terms with him, and he has done nothing to discourage this but has made it clear he wants to hear nothing of his mother. Any time she is mentioned in his presence, he spits some disparaging remark, which wounds them so that they have all learned to avoid saying anything about their grandmother around him.

Janaki must return home but makes Kamalam promise that she will ask Sita, once she is stronger, whether Sivakami knows of the illness.

Janaki had framed that article about Bharati in creases, torn it out and stored it between the pages of a book of embroidery patterns, *Stitches and Pictures*, that Baskaran had given her in the early days of their marriage. She reread it several times in the weeks that followed.

Now, *Clouds in the Eyes* is coming to Pandiyoor. In contrast to *Parasakthi*, it has not been much of a hit and may be here only a few days. Janaki must act. She asks Baskaran to make arrangements for the next day.

Their bullock cart and driver are sent around to collect Shyama, his brothers and Baskaran's nephews and nieces. Amarnath and Sundar are installed at a neighbour's house and the paadasaalai cook will feed Baskaran's parents. They set off for a tent in a field. The driver is a great film aficionado, and already unfortunately politicized—he has seen *Parasakthi* seven or eight times, Baskaran's family servant Gopalan has reported, and Baskaran is considering sacking him before something happens. Tonight, though, he will enjoy some harmless entertainment.

As they walk down the centre aisle, people on both sides rise, a caterpillar undulation, men shucking shoes and lowering the flaps of their tucked-up dhotis, the few women hiding behind men and uncreasing a bit of sari to cover their shoulders. Baskaran puts his palms together, bowing to the sides, waving his hand in gentle slashes to tell the people to sit. The family has seats in the chair class, behind the benches and those who would be seated on the ground were they not now standing. Even in the costliest class, a number of people stand, shuffle and consolidate to ensure the Brahmins are seated together.

The movie is unmemorable yet will earn an entry in chronologies of significant works, owing to Bharati's presence alone. She plays the role of an upper-class girl, kidnapped and forced into servitude by a villainous landowner angered at not having her hand for his son. The hero is her sweetheart, who mourns her disappearance with her parents in their home village. He imagines that she escapes her abductors but becomes lost in a forest. In his vision, she wanders, singing to keep up her spirits, melancholy at her plight but full of faith that God will save her. In a glade, she encounters a harp. As clouds part to light her, she leans her fair cheek against the curve of burnished wood and strokes out rounds of a tune Western audiences would have recognized as "Greensleeves." The lover, wending his own melancholy way in search of a medicinal herb his aged parents asked for, hears her song and follows the notes to find her, the song from his lips joining hers while he is still out of sight. Her voice catches when she hears him, but when she pauses her song and darts futile glances into the woods from her large, kohl-rimmed eyes, his song stops. She trills a signal phrase that he answers; she sings a line or two that he echoes; the rest is easily imagined. The tented audience erupts.

Janaki went rigid with Bharati's first scene and has stayed in a state of high nervousness throughout the film. She has never seen a film before, and this experience is sufficiently incomprehensible, but seeing Bharati makes her wish she had some privacy in which to sort out the muddle of her feelings.

Baskaran nudges his wife. "You know what? She looks like you," he says and winks.

Janaki surges with rage against her old friend. It serves Bharati right, this destiny of performing in front of people one can't even see.

Cine-acting may as well be what Bharati was raised to do, though neither she nor her mother could have foreseen it. Bharati surely holds herself well apart from the descendants of obsolete theatre families who also drifted into this variant on their hereditary profession. They have all been cast out together by modernity, she thinks with vicious satisfaction.

Worse, Baskaran is right, though the resemblance, as far as Janaki can tell, is only in their features. She had never dared try to emulate Bharati's gestures, such as the way she moves her eyebrows ironically and hands sincerely, making the viewer feel she is being falsely modest. After seeing how Bharati hunches protectively over the bowl of the veena as though it is a cradle, however, Janaki wants to try it, though she knows she would never do so with anyone else watching. She wonders if an opportunity will arise to tell Baskaran about her connection to Bharati and, if so, whether she'll take it. But when they get home, they talk of other, more urgent, matters: Dhoraisamy's health, which is, perhaps, failing, and the problem of a squatter on one of their plots of land.

The big news of this week, though, is that the creators of *Parasakthi*—who are touring the eastern part of this region still known as Madras to present to their fans, live and in person, the beloved speeches and songs from the movie—will arrive in Pandiyoor in a few days' time.

A dais is erected in the largest town square and decorated in ribbon-works with the DMK logo—a stylized rising sun—winking from the centre of every pouf. That day, the town is overrun; the square over-flows. Every cinema-goer within seventy miles of Pandiyoor has come for the show, except most Brahmins, who stay home.

From the women's room, Janaki and Thangajothi make out the faint boom and echo of miked and undiluted Tamil together with the growing echo and boom of the audience, which spreads along the streets radiating south, east and west from the square so the gathering takes the form of an immense, palpitating DMK logo.

Thangajothi sits on the floor, playing at sorting her collections: tamarind seeds, cowries, pebbles, beads. Her lips move in exact accord with the speeches from the squares. With the first song, her brothers burst through the doorway, fists and hips punching in time, "Caw! Caw! Caw!" and scattering her precious *objets*. She screams and Janaki suggests they all move out into the main hall and try to disturb Senior Mami a bit less.

The doors to the anteroom and veranda are open, and Baskaran sits outside with his father. He had insisted, like all the Brahmin-quarter parents, that the children stay home from school today. Despite this, the quarter is unusually quiet, and seems even more so than it is in contrast with the noise at the square. Two rays of the rally stretch past the northern entrance of Single Street.

The applause and cheering has built for nearly three hours when it hits a sustained note, the sound of an effort to prevent something from ending. The celebrities must now be descending the dais, bodyguards sheltering them from their admirers. The stars make jocund attempts to sabotage the cordon, reaching across it to tap hands and clasp fingers. The bodyguards push puny, persistent peasants to the sides, creating a corridor for the stars, and then another for the cars, which begin slowly to pull away. The crowd is thousands deep—over half those present dance an escort for their departing heroes, and then depart after them, elated; others sit or walk away; yet another faction of some hundreds, farthest from the cars and closest to the Brahmin quarter, take their feelings to the streets.

Seeing the crowd approach, the Brahmin quarter rises from its verandas, goes inside its houses, closes its doors. Janaki glimpses the distorted faces of the impassioned oppressed, trying to renounce God and caste for a better life, as Baskaran ushers his father into the vestibule and slides the great upper and lower bolts into place. "Janaki, make sure the back gate and the back doors are all locked."

Janaki hurries to follow his instructions and finds Gopalan already carrying them out, while Baskaran enters his father's and mother's redoubts to close and bolt the shutters inside the barred windows, and then does the same for all the high windows facing Single Street. Janaki finishes by shunting into place the upper and side bolts for the garden doors, where little Thangajothi is sliding their lower bolts down into the floor.

"I want you all to stay together down here, is that understood?" Baskaran looks at each of their faces in turn. "I am going up onto the roof to keep track of matters."

"No, *pa*, please," blurts Janaki.

"It's all right." He pats her hand and mounts the stairs. "They won't even be able to see me, much less reach me, but I want to watch what they're up to."

When Baskaran looks down from the edge of the roof, the horde has rounded from Single Street on to Double Street, filling the empty road as they pour toward the Krishna temple. Three or four other men are on their roofs and they acknowledge one another without sign or sound, lords now serving as their own sentinels. Some in the massing throng carry flags or pennants; three *badmashes* hold aloft a giant portrait of Ganesha, wearing an insult, a garland of sandals, and some others, when they reach the temple, pelt it with their shoes. Baskaran thinks it is this that causes one Brahmin man at the end of the quarter to point, then make gestures as though signalling someone to go. Another joins him. Baskaran shares their outrage at the insults, but thinks, *Surely they can't believe these deranged and unthinking semi-citizens will pay attention?* But now one of his neighbours is shouting west, and the others on their roofs are turning, and their message, relayed without distortion, reaches Baskaran.

"It's Shyama. He's in the crowd. Below."

Baskaran is at his stairs and dashing down even before he comprehends what has happened.

Shyama is a hard child to pen. He had arrived at the Krishna temple from the side near the river in time to meet and be engulfed by the swarm. A young man with a bright face had mounted the temple platform and begun declaiming the atheistic speech. The crowd recited along, as did Shyama, bringing to bear all his own powers of oratory. The men around him smiled down at him, so young, so cute, so full of conviction. Then one of them noticed his holy thread and signalled to his mates by running the point of his finger and thumb from shoulder to hip and back—*Brahmin*—a gesture that stilled a small ring of men around him.

Shyama stops singing when a shoe hits him on the forehead. He looks around and finds he is surrounded by a half-dozen leering, jeering men, calling him names whose literal meaning he doesn't understand.

The men lift their dhotis in thrusting gestures of insult, for forty or fifty seconds, a long time for a child, before their fellows set upon them and slap them resoundingly. Shyama is picked up, patted and placed on the shoulders of a man who either finds it amusing to have a Brahmin mascot for this exercise or thinks this the safest place to put the child for the moment.

Raised above the crowd, Shyama is spotted by the last man on Double Street, but, absorbed again in the action of the rally, he doesn't see the man shout and wave to him, then start to run.

When Gopalan sees his young master run shouting from the stairwell, he slips out the back, telling the cook he is summoning the police, who are circling but not interfering with the demonstration. At the front, Janaki bolts the door behind her husband as he has told her to, and presses her ear against it, sobbing silently so she can open it the instant he returns. Baskaran's father opens his window a crack and sees his son set upon with blows and kicks on his own doorstep, as have been his two equally reckless neighbours along the road.

Two police constables fight their way through the crowd with billy sticks now. With Gopalan's help, they carry Baskaran inside, his nose broken, scalp cut, blood crimsoning his kurta. Five minutes later, Gopalan bangs on the door again, this time with an unhurt Shyama in his arms.

Janaki spends a week nursing her husband back to relative health. Fortunately, most of his wounds are superficial. The first time she sees Shyama, she castigates him.

"Can you see now, what kind of sentiments those are? All men are equal! Bah! Why would they hurt someone, then, who never harmed them?"

Shyama doesn't respond, except to stop coming to their house after school.

Baskaran, once he recovers, speaks to his nephew and persuades him to return, though Janaki cannot help but have another talk with him, in a gentler but still firm tone, and with Thangajothi as well, who she feels is at an impressionable age.

584 ~ PADMA VISWANATHAN

"My own uncle, he is very progressive in his politics. And you know what? He doesn't even speak to his own mother. Can you imagine?"

She hadn't wanted to use Vairum as an example, but feels it is urgent to alarm Shyama.

"We must look after one another, care for our own. Like crows, yes. Otherwise, we will no longer know ourselves."

She has no idea, from Shyama's expression, what he has taken from her speech, but she can see that her daughter is listening.

⁓

TWO MORE LETTERS COME FROM MADRAS and this time Janaki is the one to receive them. The first, from Saradha, says that Sita has said, in notes on a slate, that she doesn't imagine their grandmother knows anything of her illness. She herself did not tell Amma, but wanted to wait until she recovered to go and tell her in person and seek her blessing. The sisters feel they must permit her this, but the next letter, which arrives two months later, from Kamalam, says that Sita will not recover. Evidently, the cancer has spread: Sita is now dying.

Gathered in Madras, the siblings confer.

"I told Amma I was coming here on business," Laddu confesses, "like I did last time. How can I tell her? She will want to come, and you know Vairum Mama doesn't want that. It would be a debacle."

Raghavan alone among them is in favour of bringing Sivakami to Madras. "Think: it could make them reconcile, when Vairum Mama sees her. Some good could come of this."

His reasoning is not without validity, though all of the others are deeply skeptical. If Vairum felt pity for his mother, wouldn't he have brought her there himself?

It is Krishnan who suggests, "Why don't we ask Sitakka what she wants?"

Sita is now lucid only for brief periods, when the morphine wears off or when it is first taking hold. Just after she receives a dose, but before she drifts off, they put the question to her. She takes up a piece of chalk and scratches dim letters on a slate: "No. It would hurt her too . . ."

Three days later, she dies. Among her effects, they find a sealed letter to Sivakami, and one to her brothers and sisters, whose contents are roughly the same. When the funeral is concluded, the granddaughters all go with Laddu to Cholapatti, to deliver the first to their grandmother.

Sivakami is instantly alarmed on seeing them. Saradha asks her to sit, and when she has, Laddu gives her the letter.

Dear Amma . . .

Sivakami starts to cry, in fear, it seems. Five months have passed since she last saw her grandchildren, all together for the holidays. She puts the letter down, dries her eyes and her palms on her sari and picks it up again.

> *You used to tell me I had a malignant tongue, and that it would be my ruin. Well, God is finally punishing me: I won't see my children grow up. I didn't know my sins were so great, but what do we know? My illness has taught me how small and insignificant I really am.*
>
> *I don't have much longer now, I can feel that. My sisters will tell you details if you want them: I had cancer of the tongue, but even after the doctors removed my tongue, the cancer was not gone.*
>
> *The one blessing that I have received is that, just as you and Vairum Mama cared for us when we were growing up, he and Vani Mami will raise my sons. They have wanted and deserved children for so long. It is some consolation to me that my sons will have a mother. My husband and I have given them leave to adopt.*
>
> *Please don't blame my brothers and sisters for not having brought you to Madras to see me. It is better you remember me as I was.*
>
> *Your ever-loving granddaughter,*
> *Sita*

Sivakami shudders. She considers chastising her grandchildren but feels a cool cloud of reason settling over her: Sita evidently told them not to bring her, and why? She didn't want to jeopardize the adoption by going against Vairum's wishes. Sivakami doesn't think it would have, but now Sita is gone, and Vairum is a father.

She realizes she has been silent a long time and looks at Saradha, Kamalam, Radhai and Janaki, who are holding hands and weeping. Their sorrow must be combined with guilt, for shocking their grandmother, especially after the fact, for not having liked Sita more, perhaps even for questioning Sita's motives in the adoption: her sons, born to a lower-middle-class household, will be raised in riches. Their house may not have sons for seven generations, Sivakami thinks ruefully, but who knows whether those old rules even hold sway any more.

She goes to take the ritual bath that must follow immediately on news of a relative's death. She is feeling, also with guilt, another emotion she can't stop. A son of her son, a son of her son. As if borne on a train, a rush of images fill her mind's eye: Vairum with two children, coming to show them to her, his snapping black-diamond eyes softened by affection, delight, pride, all the emotions denied to him all these years. Now that her wishes for him have all come true, he will bring the boys and they will all be hers again, the house lit with their laughter.

Some weeks later, Janaki's daughter Thangajothi, is coming home from school, her cousin Shyama absorbed in a book beside her. Their bullock cart passes a row of huts they pass every day and a woman emerges to scrape a pile of rice out of a pot into the shallow roadside ditch. As the children's bullock cart continues up the road, Thangajothi sees a crow circle and land, find the rice and start to eat.

He eats alone for a full five minutes before he calls his fellows. "Caw! Caw! Caw!"

43.
Bharati Moves In
1957

A HULLABALOO STARTS UP in the back of the concert hall, and
Vairum and Vani's five-year-old sons, Kartik and Kashyap, jump
onto their folding chairs to have a look. As Janaki reaches for them
with an angry warning, Sundar and Amarnath clamber up to copy
their cousins. When she turns to yell at them, Kartik's chair folds and
he falls through. Janaki pulls the crying child up and sits him on her
knee to dust him off, and glances apologetically at Vani, who is
onstage tuning her veena, and apparently as oblivious to the commotion in the front row as to that in the back. The other boys have been
distracted by the accident, but now Thangajothi is wandering toward
the aisle to have a look at who is arriving—some politician or musician they wouldn't even know, probably—and Janaki orders her
back unceremoniously. Celebrities are everywhere through the
Madras concert season.

On stage, a man in his twenties, tipped toward a polio-stunted leg,
his wavy hair slicked into a kudumi that now looks like a proclamation
of adherence to old fashions, squawks through acknowledgements
and sycophancies on behalf of the group that sponsors this venue, one
of the best attended in the Madras concert season. Eventually, two
assistants weighed down by fat floral garlands emerge from stage left.
The MC sways and swivels toward Vani and her accompanists to pay
them the honours, which they accept and refuse at once—removing

the decorations even as these hit their shoulders—in the spirit of this democratic age: "ThankyoupleasenothankyouIamnotworthy."

Janaki and the children, as special guests of the featured artist, are in the front row. She gets the children settled as the rest of the audience clap, but they get restless again within minutes of Vani beginning the *kirthanai*, and Janaki rearranges them, so that Kartik is on the other side of Thangajothi, and Kashyap between her and Janaki. Sundar is to Janaki's right and Amarnath on the other side of him—if Janaki can separate her children from their younger cousins, she can trust them to behave, but Vairum and Vani's boys are difficult under any circumstances and she is already grimly anticipating that she will miss most of the concert. She would have preferred to leave them at home with the help, but she wanted her own children to come and it was difficult to bring them without pointing up the younger boys' unmanageability.

She's made her peace with not paying full attention to Vani's playing; she has had the equivalent of a private concert each of the last few days as Vani has practised at home, and she will stay with Vani and Vairum ten days longer. It's Janaki's first time attending the Madras concert season. She intends to relish it. She taps Kartik's and Kashyap's knees sternly. Thangajothi stares dreamily at the stage. It's already breaking Janaki's heart that her daughter is not musical. Amarnath is the only one of her children with real promise in this department. Baskaran got him a first-class mridangam two years ago, and an excellent tutor. Sundar is made to participate in the lessons and makes no pretense of gaining anything from them, but is not jealous of his brother's talent. Thangajothi attends veena and vocal lessons with two of her school chums at a neighbour's. Janaki insists on the lessons but never makes Thangajothi practise at home because she can't bear to listen.

Intermission. Alone, Janaki might have made some attempt to move into the crowd, see if she recognizes anyone, have a glance at the new fashions, but today, she does no more than herd the children around the back of the concert hall to relieve themselves. Thangajothi refuses, feeling herself too old, at ten, for public urination.

When they are seated again, Vairum arrives, clearing a path through the noise to join Janaki in the front row, creating more noise in his wake as people realize who he is. She's relieved to be able to turn his sons over to him. He sits one on each knee and whispers to them through the second half. By the end, Kartik is asleep on his shoulder and Kashyap appears to be paying attention to the music. Who could have guessed Vairum, with his passionate tempers and dogmas, would make such a patient and attentive father?

Afterward, they go backstage, a large lean-to with a thatched roof like that over the concert hall. On one of the mats, Vani reclines against a bolster and accepts a tumbler of hot lemon water. Her children bound toward her and Kartik steps in the ill-tempered *ghatam* player's coffee. By the time Vairum has finished apologizing, the mat is aswarm with ants attracted to the sugar. Vairum offers the artists lifts home, but other patrons are in wait to pay similar favours and the children have great and inadvertent powers of dissuasion. At home, they alight into that urban dusk Janaki loves, its glow intensified by layers of dust and pollution.

All through the evening, Vani receives gifts with notes from admirers who were present and those who could not attend: boxes from The Grand Sweets, garlands that putrefy in the puja room, statuettes of goddess Saraswati. There are visitors—international businessmen, political petitioners, fawning philanthropists—all of whom are received with efficient grace.

The next morning, the gifts resume. Servants transport them to the appropriate corners of the house even as Janaki listens to Vani's daily practice and readies herself for a 1 p.m. concert. She will leave the children at home today, and frets over this, though the children are pleased. Thangajothi has books, the boys have each other, meals and snacks appear exactly when they should and none of them can get out—Janaki repeats all this to herself as she rattles in a cycle rickshaw toward the Music Academy, not far at all, she tells herself. A servant can run and fetch her in twenty minutes if anything . . . nothing will happen, she tells herself until, with relief, she returns home at four. The children have hardly noticed her absence, and she resolves on relaxing when she attends the festival in subsequent days.

She has finished her bath and is combing her hair when she hears yet another visitor arrive. Vairum is not home from work yet; Vani doesn't entertain. And it is her practice hour, so this person will be snubbed. Janaki has seen this here before—for a visitor in the know, it's a mark of inclusion not to take offence. She strains with curiosity to hear what will happen, as, her plait coiled at her nape, she hurriedly drags the comb from her part to her ears, once on each side. She dabs vermilion onto her forehead and freezes, her finger in her part, as the visitor's voice resolves out of the household hum.

It's not a voice Janaki would have recognized any longer had it not been restored to her through film, given as a gift to all Tamils. She is a provincial treasure, now that there is a Tamil province, that face, that grace, those now-beloved gestures.

Vani begins her evening session. The music's effect is as familiar as its form is unfamiliar, and Janaki hesitates, but can't wait long before entering the main hall to join the audience of one. Bharati, arrayed on the white divan, stands and nods a greeting, more composed than Janaki, as always. But how has she come to be so coolly sitting in Vairum's salon? Is Janaki's appearance, for her, a surprise? They sit in silence, giving Vani their full and companionate attention—a familiar and unforgotten state, though Janaki is soon distracted by her own thoughts.

She has changed out of the heavy-bordered maroon silk she wore to the concert, but makes a point, in Vairum's house, of always wearing a sari suitable for receiving guests of standing. She's glad she's not embarrassed by her own appearance, though she is awed and mildly dismayed by Bharati's. In contrast with Janaki's matronly nine-yard windowpane-check sari, Bharati is splendid in the latest thing, a five-yard "sugar silk," a fine silk spun roughly so that, woven, it gives a crystalline effect, in her signature colours, which are now all the rage: baby mango green with a marigold border. Janaki thinks the sari is a bit young for Bharati—not for her public age, true, but for her real one. But Bharati is, in the modern sense, unmarried, and—as far as Janaki knows, she thinks with a retrospective wince—childless, not to mention that she's part of the world of showbiz, all of which makes such display less inappropriate than it might be were her situation comparable to Janaki's own.

She steals looks at Bharati, whose beauty has been sharpened by age and experience, though the camera doesn't show the faint lines evident now to Janaki. On screen, Bharati looks like a sheltered innocent miraculously graced with the best effects of age—poise, wisdom, temperance. She appears to combine, Janaki admits, the best qualities of her half-sisters—Visalam's light humour, Janaki's creative spirit, Kamalam's inviting warmth—and none of the worst: not Sita's bile or Saradha's stodginess.

Janaki tries to keep face forward and listen to the music—she's only here for twelve days, she doesn't want to miss anything. Once, she looks at Bharati inadvertently and finds Bharati looking at her. Bharati raises her eyebrows slightly and smiles; Janaki smiles, too, briefly and with strain, and looks back at Vani.

When Vani's session ends, they sigh in concert, by then unconsciously and wholly absorbed in the music and regretting its close.

And now, they must talk.

"I suppose you're in town for the concert season," Bharati begins without awkwardness.

"Uh, yes, yes, that's right." Janaki wishes she could sound more natural. "I brought the children."

"Were you at Vani Mami's concert yesterday?" Bharati rolls her eyes and shakes her head. "I thought it was just marvellous."

"Yes, yes, you were there?" Had that been Bharati, creating such a stir in the concert hall? "We, uh, were in the front. With Vani Mami's children, and mine."

"Right. The children."

Is this a sore point? Just then, the children and Vairum arrive, Vairum's sons borne in his arms, Janaki's brood clustered behind.

"Hello, hello!" Vairum hails them.

"Hello, Vairum Mama, are you well?" Bharati bounces up, addressing Vairum with a familiarity that surprises Janaki. "Yesterday's concert was just too good, was it not?"

Vairum gestures to her to sit. Janaki's children come to stand beside her, but as soon as Vairum sets down his boys, they run to Bharati.

"Bharati Mami, we were playing kabbadi."

They lean competitively onto Bharati's knees.

"Bharati Mami, I won!"

"I won! I won!"

"Well, you can't have both won." Bharati picks up one of each of their small hands in her own. "But fortunately, that's not the important thing. If you played well, you will always win in the end."

"I played well!" cries Sundar.

"I played well!" accuses Amarnath.

They all seem very familiar, Janaki can't help but notice.

"And these are your children?" Bharati asks Janaki.

Thangajothi and her brothers are jostling genteelly on the side of their mother away from the movie star, nearest the wall.

"Yes, Thangajothi, Amarnath, Sundar, say hello to Aunty."

They do. Janaki prays that Thangajothi will say nothing about how her father teases her mother for seeing all of Bharati's films. It's unnecessary: Thangajothi is so shy around strangers that her parents worry for her. She's not the one who's going to spill embarrassing details.

Vairum has called for tea. "So you've met my niece, Janaki."

"Yes, it's funny . . ."

"Yes, we were . . ."

They begin once more in concert, Bharati warmly and Janaki wanly, so that it is clear Bharati would have told of a long acquaintance and Janaki might have said no more than that they had been chatting as he showed up. They stop, realizing this. Vairum is looking from one to the other closely.

"Did you ever meet in Cholapatti?"

Bharati wags her head while Janaki is too tense to respond. Vairum turns to her children.

"Bharati lives just across the street—that big white house, did you see it?" he asks.

Janaki's children nod, silent, awed.

"Oh, well, don't I always run into someone famous when I come to this house!" Janaki exclaims in a high and brittle pitch.

Bharati blinks.

There is a pause. Vani has put aside her veena and joined them. Vairum follows her with his gaze. "I came too late to hear you play today," he says wistfully. "I tried to get away."

"Did you know, children," Bharati says, "I grew up in your mother's hometown, and when I was a little girl, I used to sit in a

mango tree back of Vairum Mama's mother's house and listen to Vani
Mami play."

She doesn't look at Janaki, and Janaki wonders if she was supposed
to have said something about their childhood chumship, so long ago
now, improbable, irrelevant. In movie lore, it's common knowledge that
Bharati is from Janaki's hometown, but still no one has ever thought to
ask Janaki if they know each other—what could a girl from Janaki's
family and a girl like Bharati have in common? Many suspect the sort of
matters Gayatri confided, and even those who don't think about such
things, even Baskaran, who has long forgotten that brief encounter on
the Madurai bazaar, would never make such a connection and so why
would Janaki make it for her uncle and aunt? There is no need.

"Yes, and now she comes here, morning and evening, to listen"—
Vairum takes a tumbler of tea from a tray held out to him by a maid—
"whenever she's not filming in Kashmir or Kerala or some exotic place!"

Bharati, smiling, also accepts a cup. "I can never get enough of
Vani Mami's music!"

"Yes, I miss it terribly." Janaki, who doesn't take tea, refuses the
tray. "You're awfully lucky."

Bharati doesn't look at her, but smiles a little at Vairum, who is not
paying attention.

"I like your movies," says Janaki.

"Me too," Thangajothi squeaks, and Bharati reaches across Janaki
to pat her head.

"Well, Vani Mami doesn't see films," she responds, "and so has no
idea what I'm about to ask her, but I hope she might consider it."

They all look at Vani, now covered by her sons. It's impossible to
tell if she's listening.

"There is a film in the works where I am to play a musical genius,"
Bharati continues, now addressing Vairum. "You know I play, but veena
is not at all my genius, and it would be such an honour were Vani Mami
to consider playing the music for the film. It would be all classical—in
fact, she would have full rein to choose whatever she wants to play. The
composer and orchestra conductor will adjust. I would make sure she is
treated like a maharani, and it would be recorded here in Madras, at
Sagittarius Studios, so she would not have to travel at all."

"I think that sounds like a fine idea, don't you, kannama?" Vairum says and then notices one of the office workers from downstairs, hovering with obsequious insistence at the door.

Vani smiles vaguely, and Bharati, who clearly can't tell what Vani is thinking, looks back from her to Vairum.

"Excellent," Vairum says with finality, rising. He seems to think Vani has concurred, which probably means she has. "Just let us know the schedule. You'll come, bring the conductor, composer . . . ?"

"Oh, yes. I think it will be some months from now before we start, but yes, plenty of notice, plenty of freedom. Oh, I'm so honoured!" Bharati claps charmingly.

"I'm off—have to meet some Canadians." Vairum pauses in the doorway. "You're here for some time?"

"Sadly, no." Bharati has stood also, and Janaki wonders if she should. "We start filming tomorrow—in Sholavandan, near Madurai. Do you know it?"

"Of course—beautiful country. Get in touch with my office there, in case you need anything."

"Thank you, Mama, I will, certainly."

"Sit, stay!" Vairum is gone.

Janaki is by now also standing, and wonders if she looks inhospitable, as though she is trying to usher Bharati out. She is resentful—she feels it now, rising in her like heartburn—that Bharati would have invaded this salon and be entertained here like anyone else, like their equal. This is the sort of thing she hates most in the city, and most of all in Vairum and Vani's home. None of Baskaran's relatives would consider such a thing, even those who have lived in Madras for generations; it almost makes her uncomfortable to stay here, to permit the children to eat here. If it bothered Baskaran more, she might find somewhere else to stay, but Vairum's house is so well situated to attend the music festival, and she gets so few chances now to hear Vani play. She also prefers not to chance alienating her uncle by refusing his hospitality. He still mentions, from time to time, with pride, the role he played in her marriage.

"How is it that you have come to live—" Janaki pauses and gestures toward the street—"so close?"

Bharati's smile fades. "Yes, isn't it fortunate? I have known Vairum Mama and Vani Mami for some years now, through mutual friends. They knew I was looking for a house—Vairum Mama made a point of letting me know when that one became available. I love this neighbourhood. And how is your grandmother?"

"She is well. Your mother?"

"She is well. She and her mother, and my brother and sister, they are all living here with me now. I know if ever they need something while I'm away on tour, we can always count on Vairum Mama. You must come some time," she says, though her smile has not returned.

"Yes, you also." Janaki looks at Thangajothi, who she fears is a close observer, much like herself. "You must come if ever you are in Pandiyoor."

"Well, I must get ready to travel," Bharati says, gathering herself with a briskness that reminds Janaki that she is a working woman. Bharati turns and Janaki smells her perfume and rouge, and her silk, which smells light and crisp, like lemons and new rice, very different from the nutmeggy scent of Janaki's own, and the Pond's talc that dusts her face. "Goodbye, Vani Mami," Bharati calls. "I'll go and come. You can count on me to pay a call when I return."

Vani goes and fetches vermilion from the other room. Bharati dots it on her throat. Janaki walks her out to the balcony, Thangajothi's arm around her waist.

"Go and come." Janaki uses the formal conjugation.

"Go and come," Thangajothi echoes her mother, faint and intense.

"I'll come," the star rejoins.

A servant has been waiting on the ground floor, and now opens Vairum's compound door for Bharati, battling one of Vairum's servants to do so. He scoots across the street ahead of Bharati to open the arched wooden door in the whitewashed wall of her compound. Bharati pauses there and looks up. Thangajothi waves. A few seconds later, Janaki does too. Bharati raises her hand in response and disappears inside her home.

44.
Summer Hols
1958

SIVAKAMI CLUTCHES A LETTER—holds it out from her bosom to read it again, a terse four or five lines, and then again brings it close: Vairum is bringing his sons.

His letter says he will come during the school holidays and stay a week. She will see her grandsons, not as she first met them, at their birth, when they were Sita's children, but now as sons of her son, sons of her son . . . the little boys will play with the crowd of Thangam's grandchildren, and all will be as she imagined, as it was meant to be. All she had to do was endure.

She is not exactly sure why, but she doesn't tell Muchami about the letter for several days. Eventually, though, she must, because he needs to get the upstairs room ready to accommodate them. Her great-grandchildren play in that room but no one has slept there in years, and she's not sure what state it's in. Her granddaughters and their children sleep either in the main hall or on the roof; the second-storey room is hot, and since none of the husbands stay in the house, there has been no need for private quarters.

After she has gone over the details of routine summer preparation with him, she clears her throat. "There is something else, Muchami."

"Oh?"

He looks polite and weary. They are both getting old. Since Mari died last year, he has had fewer reasons to make the trek back to his own home at night, and often just sleeps in Sivakami's courtyard to avoid it. He spends most days there, too, in semi-retirement: Vairum has a full-time agricultural overseer for the lands, and the brightest of Muchami's nephews now does all his heavy work.

"Yes. Vairum. He is coming with Vani, and bringing the children." She beams; she can't help it.

His reaction is as disappointing as she knew it would be: this is why she waited to tell him.

He nods. "Ah. So—I'll ready the upstairs room."

"Yes," she says, and he goes.

She knows what he thinks of Vairum's behaviour: that his grudges have gone past the point of reason, that his priorities are wrong. This letter is proof of Vairum's basic good nature, she thinks, but how could she expect Muchami to see that? She doesn't need to prove it. *Let him see, when Vairum comes.*

Muchami cleans cobwebs and dust from the upstairs room. Presumably, the little boys, after the first day or two, will sleep below, in the hall, or above, on the roof, with their cousins. He'll have to check whether they have enough bedding for everyone. Janaki, Saradha and Kamalam usually bring their own. He'll dispatch a letter this afternoon to make sure they do. They probably won't leave their homes for a couple of days yet.

He squats, his head in his hand. Why can't he believe, as Sivakami obviously does, that Vairum has had a change of heart?

In the two years when Mari was taking her treatments, he had had the chance to observe Vairum more closely than he has in the years since, but he has seen nothing to make him believe Vairum has changed his thinking. He came to Cholapatti as recently as a couple of months ago, and was as cold to Sivakami as ever. In all these years, Muchami has never told her more than he felt she needed to know, and he never talks to her of her son: not of the things Vairum says, against caste, against her; not of his own unspoken responses. Muchami has endured his treatment of Sivakami for her sake, but his anger on her behalf is bright and ready.

JANAKI HAS THE SONG GOING THROUGH HER HEAD—the theme from *Saraswati*, the summer's big hit movie, starring Bharati, music by Vani. Gopalan's nephew was singing it as they waited on the train platform this morning; she heard someone humming it as he passed by her on the way to the lavatory at the end of the car.

Yesterday morning she had clipped two more articles to add to her stack of six about the movie. She has nearly a hundred articles about Bharati, collected over the years, clipped and pressed in books, like blooms from a path not taken. Both of yesterday's repeated the now well-known story of how Bharati grew up listening to "Sri Vani" play, sitting in the mango tree behind Sivakami's house. The media circulated and recirculated romanticized images of the future star as a child, sitting on a sturdy branch, ankles crossed, eyes closed and hands miming at playing her own veena in time to the notes emanating from the forbidden household, until dusk, or dark, or until a servant maid fetched her firmly home.

Her co-star, an actor rumoured to have political aspirations, was quoted in one of yesterday's articles.

"This unforgivable and humiliating segregation is the tragic fact even in today's village Brahmin quarter, all over Tamil Nadu. Sri Vani and her husband, Sri Vairum, are among the very few upper-caste persons willing to welcome their own non-Brahmin neighbours into their homes. How fortunate for all of us that they welcomed Bharati, that little girl hidden like some unspoken shame in the woods behind the house where Sri Vairum himself grew up! Would that the rest of Tamil Nadu's upper-caste bigots could cast aside their false race pride as Sri Vairum and Sri Vani have done! We must make it clear they have no choice."

No choice, no choice . . . The words sing in Janaki's ears with the rocking of the train, filling her with anger and disgust at politicians and actors—all the same, in her mind. *The articles have actually downgraded her caste background, compared with when they first started writing about her!* Fomenting discontent. *It's practically fashionable to be lowercaste these days,* she sniffed, mentally. No understanding of the village—of the mutual dependence and respect. *Look at Muchami! He has had everything he could want—more than most Brahmins! Would he have had the chance to learn Sanskrit in that actor's Tamil Nadu? Brahmins are the servants of society. Why is all of India out to get us?*

Greed, she thinks, *nothing more than that.* She lifts an arm around her daughter, reading a novel on the seat beside her, pinches her cheek. "Always reading," she whispers. "College girl, college girl."

Thangajothi doesn't look up but snuggles into her side. Amarnath and Sundar sit on a newspaper on the train floor, playing jacks. Janaki counts the baggage on the rack above them and below their bench. A dozen pieces, same as when they left Pandiyoor. All is in its place and soon they will arrive in Cholapatti, where the fragmented world becomes briefly, yearly, whole again. She sighs and feels her ire dissipating, grudgingly soothed by anticipation.

Kamalam comes to fetch Sivakami. "Amma! Janaki Akka's here!"

Sivakami, slicing bitter gourd as she squats by a blackened, bubbling rice pot, folds the blade down into its block and, pushing herself to standing, sets it on a high shelf, out of the reach of toddlers. She tries to catch her breath against the pain flexing through her lower back and right leg. While sitting, she can almost believe she is forty again, but this pain plagues her whenever she tries to stand, walk or lie down, so much so that she has been tempted, for a couple of years now, to give up those activities.

Kamalam makes anxious, sympathetic sounds as she waits for Sivakami to recover, but as soon as Sivakami is able, she impatiently shoos Kamalam along to greet her sister. She rejects Kamalam's hand, held out to help, out of pride, not because she's madi: she will have to take another bath today because she intends on hugging Janaki and the children.

Thangajothi feels the gossamer folds of Sivakami's sari flutter against her face, so different from the stiff, coloured silks and cotton blends that her mother wears. Sivakami's sari could be woven from spider webs, she thinks as her great-grandmother embraces her, seeing her hand through the pallu and inhaling Sivakami's soft-sour scent of rice and age.

She watches her mother's familiar transformation as Janaki inquires aggressively about everyone's health and whereabouts. Thangajothi has seen this every summer of her life but only recently begun to understand it: here, Janaki sheds the deferential diplomacy of the daughter-in-law and gets bossy. She's the second-eldest sister now, and a child of this house.

Thangajothi, feeling shy, makes similar but politer inquiries, as she has been trained to do. Kamalam arrived, some days earlier, with her three children. Visalam's first daughter is pregnant and has come here for her delivery, though she will be attended by a nurse, and no one will complain or even look askance. Saradha will come from Thiruchi any day, bringing Raghavan, who is living with her as he finishes college at St. Joseph's. Krishnan is teaching at a small college in Salem and lives there with Radhai and her family. They are also expected. And Laddu never left Cholapatti; he had finally married in 1953, and Vairum helped him to buy the house next door when Murthy died, leaving no heirs. His wife and children spend nearly as much time in Sivakami's house as in their own, and Muchami plays with those children as he did with Thangam's, though he is too old now to take them all the way back to his own village every afternoon.

Within days, Thangajothi knows, the house will hum and throb. She is more excited than usual: Shyama will come, at some point, for a week or so—her favourite cousin. He had left Pandiyoor at the start of the last school year, sponsored by Baskaran to study in Thiruchi. Infuriated that a boy so obviously bright was doing so poorly at his studies, Baskaran had sent him to stay with Janaki's sister Saradha, to attend the same high school as her sons for tenth standard—a crucial year, if one were to go further. Shyama, as though he had had something to prove, had excelled in his new school, and Baskaran had rewarded him with a summer holiday in Cholapatti. He will stay with Gayatri, his relative. Thangajothi had missed him terribly, despite his brief visits home. She had been hoping he might already be here.

But Sivakami is excited for another reason. "Vairum is bringing the children," she tells Janaki, whose expression changes, as Thangajothi watches, from happiness to circumspection. "The boys will receive their poonals here. Did you hear, Janaki? He is bringing Vani and the children, to spend time with you all!"

Even as Sivakami leans toward Janaki, her lined face lit with excitement, her voice quavering a little, Janaki catches sight of Muchami, listening from the garden door, his expression suggestive of pessimism and pain. When he notices Janaki watching him, he smiles at her and ducks away. Janaki might have been able to believe that Vairum had finally decided to stop punishing his children and his mother unfairly by keeping them apart, had she not seen Muchami. Though she has never articulated it, she is accustomed to seeing Muchami share her grandmother's feelings. Today, she sees her own feelings mirrored in her old friend's face: doubts about Vairum's motivations and anger over her grandmother's long years of suffering.

Now, in charge of preparations for the poonal ceremony until Saradha arrives, she finds she can't fully enjoy herself. Vairum was apparently too caught up in city life to have yet granted his sons the holy thread. She wonders how he will justify putting his sons through this most Brahmin of transformations, given his political stances. Will he say he is doing it because he can, back on the Brahmin quarter where he was humiliated and uncasted by his brother-in-law? Will he say he believes in education of any kind, and that his sons need to know their identity even if they must critique it?

Regardless, Janaki sees it as an opportunity for a real celebration of Brahmin values—just what the community needs about now—and tries to throw herself into the work with renewed enthusiasm.

On a morning two days after their arrival, Thangajothi pokes her head into the vestibule and calls out, "Gayatri Mami! It's Thangajothi." She holds a P. G. Wodehouse novel, which she had borrowed the previous afternoon from Minister's library. She enters the dim cool of the main hall, in the middle of which Minister lies on a four-poster bed. Gayatri lumbers from the rear of the house, and hands a stainless steel saucer with some snacks to Thangajothi.

"Yes, child, here. Sit." She looks a little nervously at her husband, who is so thin as to look like a long wrinkle in the woven bedsheets.

Minister says nothing as Thangajothi obediently squats against one of the pillars.

"Shyama came last night," Gayatri shares conversationally.

Thangajothi stands again. "He's here? Upstairs?"

"Of course. All you kids—can't stay away from the books, huh?" Gayatri sounds disgruntled.

Thangajothi thinks she must be lonely: none of their sons live here any more. One by one, they had all got jobs elsewhere. Yesterday, Thangajothi had overheard Gayatri telling Janaki how her sons in Madras had been asking their parents to join them there, and how Minister refused.

Thangajothi feels bad—she likes Gayatri, but the main reason she comes to their house is for the books. Now she's feeling worse, because all she wants to do is bound up the stairs to see Shyama.

"The time!" Minister cries from among the bedclothes, and Thangajothi, Gayatri and the nurse, who is squatting in a corner, all jump. "What is the time, ma?"

"Eleven o'clock," Gayatri responds, looking at the floor. "Go and come," she says to Thangajothi, waving her away. "Take your tiffin here, with Shyama, this afternoon."

That morning, a day after all of Thangam's children have assembled in Cholapatti, Vairum and Vani arrive. It has seemed, to Sivakami, an interminable wait. She is so proud as she comes to the door to meet them. She makes no effort to conceal her happiness, or herself. *This is the new way,* she thinks, a little giddy as she watches them get out of their shiny black automobile, and then backs into the house to admit them. *I, too, can be modern,* she thinks, though she's still too shy to meet the neighbours' eyes.

In the dim hall, which smells of cool brick, camphor and holy ash from the many who have performed morning prayers that day, Vani's sons clutch at her sari as she falls to do namaskaram for Sivakami. Vairum gestures toward Sivakami's feet and his head, and says to his sons, "This is my mother."

Sivakami advances a few steps, reaching toward the children as Vani plucks the boys off of her hips. Muchami, standing at the garden door, turns away from what he sees, what Sivakami can't and doesn't want to see: Vairum is not smiling and still has not said a word to her.

The boys receive kisses from Sivakami, stiff with terror as though she is a wraith. The aunts and cousins flood forward to engulf them in a warm tide, and Sivakami smiles, brittle and joyous.

Holding her paavaadai up with the hand clutching the book, bracing herself with her other hand against the wall of the stairwell, Thangajothi climbs to the second level. She crosses a room full of recliners and coffee tables whose random placement confirms their long disuse. She has often lingered in this room, searching out Minister's face in the many framed photos: large groups of sombre men, faces dark between white caps and kurtas, apart from the occasional white man in a suit, or Indian man in a uniform or princely regalia. The photos are annotated with occasions and purposes, sometimes with the names of all the men present, written in English.

This time, though, she goes purposefully to the original library. Shyama's not in there, so she goes through to the walkway. As she traverses it, she hears through the skylight, which gives onto the main hall, Minister's voice. "The time, ma! Tell me the time."

At the end of the corridor, she pushes open the door to another small room. It is, like the library, filled with books—lining the walls, in piles on the floor—mixed in with a jumble of other curiosities: an Eastman Kodak camera like a jack-in-the-box, a non-functioning radio, an empty binoculars case, all home to dust mites, scuttling spiders and an occasional scorpion; a stuffed mongoose with the tail peeling back to show wires and straw; posters of foreign movie stars; a hinge-lidded tin with printing on the side: "500 Scissors Cigarettes," and another dented tin bearing the puzzling "Peek Freans." Nothing has moved, from one summer to the next, in the years since Thangajothi first came upon them. Last year, she picked up a flyer for something called the "Self-Respect Ramayana," because it was exactly like another she had found in the attic room at Sivakami's house and used as a bookmark, until she lost it. This time, she stuck the flyer under some books on the bookcase, and it was still there when she returned.

Shyama turns from the shelves and indicates the book in her hand with his chin. "What have you got there?" He speaks as though they had just seen each other at breakfast, not as though they had seen each other only twice in the last year. He is taller, his voice suddenly deep, the skin of his temples and neck bubbled with acne. Thangajothi holds him her book out to him, feeling tongue-tied. "Oh," he says. "Good, no?"

She sneezes from the dust. "Yes, very. What have you got?"

He holds it out to her and turns back to the shelves. *Confessions of a Thug*, by Meadows Taylor. She had seen it and passed it over for no particular reason, and now is mad at herself: she would have liked to have read it first and recommended it to him. She goes back to the main library, Shyama following, and puts the Wodehouse back on the Wodehouse shelf. She picks up *Sivakami's Vow*, a novel by Kalki Krishnamurthy that she had read the year before. Her mother had read it when it was first serialized, bought the book for Thangajothi, and read it again when Thangajothi finished: a 1,000-plus page historical epic about a dancing girl named Sivakami who wants to marry a king. Thangajothi's uncle Raghavan had teased his grandmother: a courtesan named Sivakami! Raghavan wasn't much of a reader, though, and only Janaki, among the sisters, has finished it. She has told Thangajothi that Kalki is one of Vairum's acquaintances in Madras, that she herself met the great writer on her first visit to the city.

They wander back into the old salon to sit, facing slightly away from one another, reclined in the stillness of Minister's salon. Only the faraway sounds of Gayatri's kitchen, and the flip and ruffle of their own pages, break the hush.

The next morning, Shyama enrages Janaki by telling her, when she talks about the big poonal celebration, that he has removed his holy thread. "What do I need a caste marker for? I believe in education for everyone."

"So do we!" Janaki splutters inadequately, and Shyama shrugs.

Sivakami is sitting in the kitchen doorway now, watching them eat, and Thangajothi notices that Muchami, too, has come to squat in one of the doors to the garden. After returning from Cholapatti last summer, Thangajothi had bragged to Shyama of how progressive her great-grandmother's household is in its treatment of the servants and dared him to find another Brahmin household that so elevated the staff, where servants are permitted to be in view during meals, where they refuse to touch the bedding, where they have actually been given Sanskrit education!

"Elevated!" he had scoffed. "Brahminized, you mean! What's wrong with their own customs? What's wrong with Tamil? What's so polluting about bedsheets, for God's sake? You're brainwashed, all of you."

"All of *us*?" she had shouted, surprising herself out of a tight silence. "What about you? You're as Brahmin as we are and all you do is parrot your father, anyway."

As they end their meal now, she watches him observe all the Brahmin conventions—drinking water without touching his mouth to the tumbler, ringing his banana leaf with water against the pollutions of saliva and cooked food—whether out of mere habit or so as not to offend. She wonders if he remembers that conversation.

Having heard that the musical star of *Saraswati* is visiting, dozens of neighbours drop in daily to Sivakami's house, cluster in the hall, on and around the veranda, clamouring for the famous theme song. Sometimes Vani obliges, rousing a cheer with the opening bars and then a singalong, especially at the chorus. More often, she plays something else, and all those gathered look trapped. When she finishes, they try without success to talk to her about the movie.

When Thangajothi goes out the back, she often sees as many as eight or ten children sitting in the trees beyond the courtyard wall, and others, adults, squatted on the ground. She has heard her mother proclaiming her satisfaction with this turn of events. "Good for them. None but Brahmins ever take an interest in classical music. I think it's excellent that the lower classes have finally come to it, even if it had to be because of a film."

Thangajothi winces at her tone. Most of the time, she doesn't think much of Vani's playing and it's not hard to tell that most of those in the living room and out the back don't know what to make of it either. Her mother does, though, which fact Thangajothi respects.

Janaki sits in the main hall, working a kingfisher in bright threads. She peers too closely at it and wonders if it is obvious that she is sulking and trying to avoid talking to the visitors. She just can't decide if these people deserve to listen to Vani. This is the Brahmin-quarter majority and they are no fonder of her music than they were ten and twenty years ago. But they should humble themselves here, thinks Janaki, those same neighbours who disgraced Vairum, and who have, resentfully, sold him their properties at inflated prices. The tide has turned a little, though, with the rise of a new generation that knows only of Vairum's magnanimity. He never stays to visit the Cholapatti Brahmins in their homes, but it seems the chill of estrangement from the quarter may have abated a little. The simple charm of passing time.

Kamalam sits beside her, teaching palanguzhi to her four-year-old twin sons. One of the boys is prone to gestures of theatrical generosity; the other is conniving; both are disinclined to stick to the rules. (They are in the swell of their personalities, in their purest moment; they are impossible.)

Raghavan had been trying to help Kamalam but got bored and left to see if his older nephews were up for cricket. Janaki had charged her own sons with making sure they were all back for lunch. Krishnan reclines, his head on Radhai's knee, both sweetly attentive to the music. Laddu's wife is helping in the kitchen and Laddu will stop in for supper after work.

A horde of hollering boys—with Vairum's sons nearly, but not yet quite, at the front of the pack—swarm down the stairs, through the hall and out to the street.

Thangajothi comes to sit beside her mother, and without saying anything, slumps into her and opens a book. Janaki sets down her embroidery with a sigh. All the poonal preparations are done; the ceremony is the next morning. She pushes Thangajothi's book up to see what she is reading: Kalki, *Sivakami's Vow*. She smiles.

This is as close as we can come now, she thinks, *to what it should be like.* Her sentimentality smarts and she enjoys the sting. There are the missing—she feels the loss of Sita's darkness as much as Visalam's light—but this is close: Sivakami in the kitchen, Gayatri and Muchami lingering at her sides, Vani playing her veena, Vairum out on business, and the rest of them, Thangam's children, and her children's children, looked after, safe and happy.

During the poonal ceremony, Sivakami gets occasional glimpses of Vairum's sons at the ceremonial fire, as she stands at the kitchen door. Laddu and Vairum, shirtless, in silk dhotis and shoulder cloths, huddle under cloths to pass on to the little boys the prayer for illumination, but as Sivakami's eyes blur from the smoke, she is seeing another little boy, who had no father, receiving his holy thread, earnestly repeating the syllables an uncle is speaking into his ear—a little boy who was happy then, and proud, inducted into the traditions of his caste, surrounded by his cousins.

She turns away to wipe her eyes and sees Muchami, crouched at the far end of the courtyard, his head in his hands. A mild anger shudders briefly through her, riding a snake of puzzlement: why can't he feel happy for them? Clearly, Vairum's participation in this ceremony—of all ceremonies!—shows his desire, his *need*, to be accepted into the fold of his community, to be together with the family he supported. If not for Vairum's intelligence, his know-how, where would they be now? Yes, they suffered at times, but for this, to gather like this, prosperous and happy.

How sad for Muchami, she thinks, *that he cannot see what I see*. No one ever saw what she did: that tender child. (*A gem, a coin, all elbows and iron.*) A mother should know. *All is forgiven.*

Janaki lays down banana leaves for the third round of feasting, when the family can finally eat. Visitors from up and down the quarter are leaving for their homes with promises to return to hear Vani play that afternoon.

The family members are seating themselves when a car pulls up outside the front door. Vairum looks unsurprised, and Janaki thinks he is smiling slightly. Perhaps some business associate is coming to meet him here? That would be strange; he always has them meet him at his Kulithalai office.

No, it's a woman. Janaki can't make her features out against the light, until the visitor steps into the hall's cheery gloom. A shout fades in from the street. "Bharati! It's Bharati!"

So it is.

Vairum is striding up to greet Bharati. She holds her palms together. "Namaskaram, Mama. Namaskaram, Mami. Namaskaram." She offers graceful greetings to Gayatri, who, though gaping, reflexively puts her own palms together and then brings them apart an inch or two, unsure of what to do.

"How are you?" Bharati greets Sivakami's grandchildren, who stand and stare. She directs a particular greeting at Janaki: "Are you well?"

Janaki waggles her head with fearful rapidity, and Bharati gives her a hard and subtly victorious smile.

"So good you could come home, Bharati." Vairum is waving her toward the line of banana leaves. "You must take lunch with us."

"Oh, not necessary, I . . ."

"I insist," he says. "Sit. Sit."

Kamalam stands stock-still, while Saradha splutters and turns half away from the sight of a devadasi preparing to take food in her grandmother's home. But it's not her grandmother's home, Janaki is reminded as she catches Vairum eye—it's his. He doesn't even bother holding her glance. They have no right to challenge him—they are guests in his home. And before this, he gave them everything good. They owe him their lives.

Sivakami sees the visitor arrive—a sophisticated-looking young woman, not one she recalls having met before. She sees Vairum usher her to eat. There is plenty, of course. Saradha comes to fetch another banana leaf but doesn't appear to hear Sivakami asking who their guest is. Sivakami looks for Muchami, but he has gone. She beckons Gayatri back, signalling, a fist with thumb extended: "Who is she? What's going on?"

"Bharati, Akka." Gayatri can barely meet her eye at first, then looks at her with concern. "It's Bharati, the star of the movie, of *Saraswati*."

Sivakami looks into the main hall. Vairum is watching her.

⟍ৎ⟍

SARADHA, KAMALAM, JANAKI AND RADHAI ferry out the food, carrying vessels from the kitchen out to the main hall and back, stiff and regular as figures moving in and out of a cuckoo clock. They serve *payasam*, appam, pickles, curries, pacchadis, *applam*, rice, sambar. Somehow, though, they are all present to witness the first fistful of rice Bharati lifts from the leaf to her mouth.

There—there.

The house is defiled.

She lights them with her famous smile. "Delicious. My compliments."

The four sisters look back, variously, but all unsmiling. A flash-bulb pops—a reporter from *Anantha Viketan* who must somehow have caught wind of the visit. As though his intrusion has broken some film-thin membrane between public and private, the life of the home and the life of the street, neighbours pour back in.

"The devadasi's daughter," Gayatri finishes gently, and Sivakami sees a low-caste intruder take rice in her home, in front of her mother-in-law's Ramar, in front of all the neighbours.

Vairum is still watching Sivakami. Now he smiles.

Muchami has gone around to the garden door. Too late, he sees. He looks toward the kitchen. Sivakami doesn't look at him. She is seeing for herself now. Muchami hangs his head.

Thangajothi has never met her mother's father. She knows him only from the wedding photo hung on the pantry wall. She has spent hours looking at that photo; she used to ask to have it taken down for her. She thinks her grandparents the handsomest couple she has ever seen. Since last year, though, she has stopped looking at it so much. It's true that when these photos are taken, the subjects hardly know each other and often look shy and mildly surprised to find themselves in the same frame. In the photo of her grandparents, though, each looks wholly alone. It has begun to make her sad.

From the back of the salon, she watches the hubbub of neighbours part to make way for a man she now recognizes as her grandfather. His high and distracted beauty has not altered, though his face is lined and hair grey. He flutters and booms greetings to the crowd and the family.

Janaki feels faint. Bharati looks at her, alarmed, and makes the same signal as Sivakami did—a fist shaken, thumb out, emphasized with a thrust of the chin—*What's going on?*

Janaki signals her back with a hand flipped, fingers spread, bewildered and accusatory: *How would I know?*

"Ho, ho!" Goli is making his way through the crowd of Cholapatti Brahmins, offering namaskarams. "Yes, quite a while!" he says to one stiff greeting. "Very well!" he answers another coldly formal inquiry. "Very, extraordinarily, well."

Goli's clothes are worn, he carries no briefcase, no walking stick. Janaki cannot imagine where he has been all this time, and with whom, and shudders to think what he has been doing. She wonders if he held on to his job with the government.

Vairum has risen. He walks across the room to the garden door, and Muchami steps back as he holds his hand out over the ground and washes it with a tumbler of water, all without taking his eyes off Goli. He wants to see Goli see Bharati, Janaki realizes. He has set this up.

"And you, Vairum!" Goli crows. "Your man told me you had come around and I'm here to tell you bygones are bygones, but don't think you're getting off that easy." He spies lunch. "Don't mind if I do . . ." As Bharati rises, though, he halts cartoonishly, mid-stride, and then tries to fling himself back into the crowd. "Is that the time? Duty calls, my friends! Lovely to have seen you!"

But the crowd won't part. Janaki sees faces she doesn't know—has Vairum enlisted help? Goli can't get out.

"Amma!" Vairum calls. "Come! Some visitors!"

Sivakami thinks she hears Goli's voice. It can't be. He hasn't come since Thangam died; her sons do the yearly death anniversary rites for her. Sivakami has trained herself not to think of him.

She peeps out from the pantry. It is Goli. Well, she must feed him. She sees Muchami, at the garden door. Why doesn't he look glad? She is glad. Goli can do no more harm now, and what does no harm does good. Children need a father. Why is she shaking like this? And are these tears running down both her cheeks? She can't tell: one of her cheeks feels numb.

"Amma!" Vairum calls.

Vairum has called her "mother." How long has it been? *All is forgiven.*

"Come!" he calls.

Now: no Brahmin widow walks through her main hall in front of guests. How the neighbours would talk! But Sivakami is not the woman she used to be. Her house is not defiled—this is not her house. And she left her fear walking a train track near Thiruchi. She can't lose her son the way she lost her husband: without a word. She goes to Vairum.

"This is a great day!" Vairum proclaims to all assembled, arms outstretched, as Sivakami stands hunched beside him, twisting her fingers. "Finally, all my prolific brother-in-law's *known* kin are gathered."

Bharati, ashen, crosses the room to the garden door. Muchami fetches a brass jug of water and pours water for her to wash her hands. Janaki throbs in sympathy with her friend's embarrassment. Vairum should not have invited her, she thinks, but Bharati never should have accepted.

Sivakami looks very small as Vairum leans toward her. "You have, in marvellous conscience, sheltered and raised all of my sister's children by this man, but this man has at least one more child and she, too, deserves to be recognized, don't you think, Amma? You, who have such concern for the children of this village, who has ensured all of them survive their passage safely into this great world? Can we make up for what this cad has wrought? He killed my sister, robbed me of caste, never gave his children any more than a paltry legitimacy and didn't even give Bharati that. Let us make it right. Let us admit the truth. All together."

Sivakami can feel a numbness spreading through her left side but not quickly enough to prevent her from understanding what he has said. *He hates me,* and now she sees why. This poor girl had no father; none of Thangam's children had a father; her son had no father. *It was all my fault*; she deprived them all of the fathers they should have had. Vairum had no children—*also my fault.* She never should have permitted the marriage with Vani. *He was young; I should have decided for him what was best.*

Yes, let me shoulder the blame. Maybe now Vairum will stop blaming himself, throw away the knife he has used all his life to cut his own great heart into bits.

She sees Muchami step into the main hall, open his mouth and raise a hand, but then she sees him collapse.

He has brought us here, thinks Janaki, running forward with everyone else, *to shatter us.*

Epilogue

WE WERE NOT SHATTERED, but that's what my mother told me she thought, so I have recorded it here. I myself didn't know what to think at the time, but having now thought through these events, I suspect that Vairum Mama, in spite of all his disregard for Brahmins, might have thought he was doing something good for Bharati. Vairum was both a man of honour and one governed by his grudges, and certainly a gesture that would both force Goli to do the right thing and take revenge on my great-grandmother for whatever pain Vairum Mama thought she had caused him—it must have been irresistible.

I don't know what he thought of the aftermath: we were all watching Sivakami Patti, who appeared at first not to be responding. She swayed a little, and the room, which had been silent, started buzzing. Everyone swarmed her, and my uncle Raghavan took her arm firmly and led her to the kitchen to lie down. No one would look at Vairum Mama and I don't remember what he did, because suddenly there were shouts from the garden door: Muchami was lying on his side, his eyes rolling. I was near the door and saw Vairum pick the old servant up himself and put him in the car. Sivakami Patti would not have seen this. Vairum drove Muchami to a hospital: he had suffered a stroke and lost the use of his left side. It wasn't until a few minutes after Vairum had left that we all realized Sivakami Patti had also had a stroke, also lost the use of her left side. We had to borrow a car to get her to a hospital. I wonder if Vairum was troubled by not having been the one to look after her in that moment, as he had cared for his sister and all of us.

Others had already largely taken over Muchami's functions as regarded the lands, as well as occasional repairs and whitewashing of Sivakami Patti's house. Now they took over responsibility for her one cow and little bit of garden. At least half the year, though, Sivakami Patti would stay with us in Pandiyoor or with one of my aunts. When she was in Cholapatti, one of them would go and stay with her, as much for company as for care: Minister Mama died not three months after that summer, and Gayatri Mami relocated to Madras, where she lived in her eldest son's house. She never shaved her head or gave up contact with her grandchildren, though: times had changed, and widows didn't much do that any more. She visited Cholapatti a couple of times after that but would stay with her cousin in Kulithalai. Their sons sold off their house and their few remaining lands, so their family, in that generation, effectively severed all relations to the village. This was already the case for at least four other households on the Brahmin quarter by that time.

I moved to Canada, married to a man who had grown up on the same street in Thiruchi where my Saradha Athai lived. His family, too, had sold their house—to non-Brahmins, as those distinctions became increasingly eroded by economic pressures. Even Pandiyoor's Brahmin quarter would remain "intact," as my mother would have it—I would say unintegrated—only a few years more. My future husband's parents moved into a small apartment, and a few weeks after that, he left for Canada on a graduate scholarship, off to find a means to earn and support his family back in India.

My husband and I would eventually sponsor my twin brothers to emigrate, and they would bring my parents, who had run aground financially along with so many of their peers—the lands gone, the privilege gone with it. We were among the increasing numbers of displaced Tamil Brahmins whose stories were superficially different and fundamentally the same. Many of them brought with them their misguided race pride. They hope that here, we might rise again.

Bharati's story was different. The Cholapatti revelation never made it into the news—that photographer had not stayed to hear it and the Brahmin-quarter denizens must have held their tongues. Certainly, they had known the rumours all along. A couple of years later, she married a radical journalist and together they started a new magazine of popular opinion, satirical humour and cutting-edge fiction. She and her husband moved to a rambling house in Adyar, near the beach, far from my great-uncle's house, though I assume they still moved in similar social circles. I doubt they ever spoke about what had transpired that afternoon.

My mother wrote to me of Sivakami Patti's death in 1966. I received the aerogram weeks after her passing. At that point, Muchami was already several years gone. Sivakami Patti was staying in Pandiyoor when she heard the news of her old servant's passing and she went immediately to take a ritual bath, dousing herself with water as one does only for the death of a close relative. My mother wrote and told me this, too; I think she had been almost puzzled by her own feelings about Muchami's death until she saw her grandmother's gesture.

I remember once, when I was in college, my cousin Shyama came to visit me. He had not gone on to finish his education—despite his performance in tenth, he ran away right after that summer in Cholapatti. He returned five years later, taking us all by surprise, and came to visit Thiruchi, where I was in my final year of a physics degree. My marriage was already arranged; I would be leaving for Canada at the end of the year.

We had gone to my favourite temple, the Rock Fort, climbed to the top and were sitting looking out on the Kaveri plain as he told me about people he had met, movements he had been part of. I wasn't sure how much to believe—I wanted to delight in his adventures but had an inkling that the truth might be grimmer, or duller, and I preferred merely to hear the story he wanted to tell.

I think it was then that I realized I would need, at some point, to try to tell the events of my family's life. Because as he spoke, I imagined between us a huge, illustrated book. The illustration showed us, sitting high on a rock temple, the valley of the Kaveri spread below us. The ornate, block-printed text told the story of Shyama's adventures—as they really were, not as he was telling them. I felt that if I might turn back a few chapters, I would see Shyama and myself as children; a few more chapters and I would see my mother as a child; a few more and I might see Sivakami, coming to Cholapatti as a child bride. Maybe I could cross out some passages and scribble in the margins, make Vairum kind to his mother, or make Hanumarathnam live in spite of his horoscope.

Or maybe I would try, and find I could change nothing on the page, that all I could do was tell it differently, and maybe I would understand it better for that—the story of a world that, while it has not vanished, for those who know how to see, no longer exists for most of us.

And my story, too, may no longer exist for those who lived it, because it is in English and they knew only Tamil, maybe some Sanskrit. In any case, it's not the story they would have told. The tale has transmuted, passed from my great-grandmother into my mother into me, from old world into new, little piles of ash, little piles of gold, a couple of long-petrified lemons—an inheritance I carry around and read alone as I did those novels of long ago.

So it is that I sit here with you, the book of our lives between us, telling my story, and my people's, in lands and languages I know but that are not my own.

Acknowledgements

The Toss of a Lemon, while fictional, grew from stories told me by my grandmother, Dhanam Kochoi. I often asked my mother, Bhuvana Viswanathan, to translate, explain or elaborate; she and my dad, S. P. Viswanathan, answered countless questions on details and customs. The heart of this novel is, in many ways, as much theirs as my own. The rest of my Manathattai, Sholavandan and Senapratti families also contributed knowledge and histories, as did friends. I particularly thank Ravi Kumar, Vaidhehi Kumar, Lakshmi Athai, Janaki Athai, Ecchemu Athai, Sethurathnam (Ambi) Chithappa, Shyamala Chitthi, Dr. Ramaswamy, Sukumar Anna, Sujatha Akka, Raju Anna, Raju Mama, Pattu Mami, Kitcha Mama, Padma Mami, Vasantha Murthy, Nagy Nageswaran, Christine Agrawal, Dipak Saraswati, Raji Athai, Meenakshi Athai, Chellu Mama, Seetharaman Periappa, Visali Athai, Krishnan Chitthappa, Radhu Chitthi, Indhi Athai, Venketu Mama and my other grandmother, Vijayalakshmi Patti. Some of these dear ones have passed on since I began this endeavour; I hope I have honoured their memories.

Many books and articles assisted me in the writing of this work, but I must make special mention of S. Theodore Baskaran's *The Message Bearers: Nationalist Politics and the Entertainment Media in South India, 1880–1945,* Eugene Irschick's *Politics and Social Conflict in South India: The Non-Brahman Movement and Tamil Separatism, 1916–1929,* Saskia

Kersenboom's *Nityasumangali: Devadasi Tradition in South Asia,* Rajagopal Parthasarathy's translation of *The Cilappatikaram of Ilanko Atikal,* R. K. Narayan's *Ramayana,* K. S. Narayanan's *Friendships and Flashbacks* and M. S. S. Pandian's *The Image Trap.* The siddhas' song is an amalgamation of various songs translated in Kamil V. Zvelebil's *The Poets of the Powers.* Those kind enough to share their expertise in person include V. Amarnath, S. Theodore Baskaran, Eugene Irschick, K. S. Narayanan and family, Rajagopal Parthasarathy, M. S. S. Pandian, S. Ramaswamy, K. V. Ramanathan and A. R. Venkatachalapathy. Their scholarship and storytelling propelled me toward a more complex understanding of my subjects than I otherwise could have achieved.

Catherine Bush, Ven Begamudré, Elizabeth Evans, Suzanne Feldman, Tom Kealey, DD Kugler, Ian McGillis, T. Jayashree, Shelley Tepperman, Malena Watrous and Siân Williams—dear friends and valued mentors—read this manuscript in parts or in its entirety. Their suggestions and support were invaluable. Thanks, also, to my professors and colleagues in the programs at the Johns Hopkins University and the University of Arizona, who read and responded to segments of the book, as well as to Brenda O'Donnell and Ruth Smillie, who vetted my first Canada Council application, and to Stephen Elliott, who gave me a computer.

My thanks to the friends and relatives who hosted me for periods of writing and research, the course of which they paved in many ways. There were many, but those on whom I imposed the most were Sethurathnam (Ambi) Chithappa and Shyamala Chitthi, Raju Mama and Pattu Mami, T. Jayashree and Madan Rao, Merrily Weisbord, Joe and Maureen McGillis, Sujatha Akka and Raju Anna, Rathna Anna and Janaki Mani, Dhorai Anna and Padma Mani, Chris Yanda and Vicki Thoms, and, once again, my parents.

I am deeply grateful to Anne Collins of Random House Canada for her warmth and incisiveness; to Ann Patty of Houghton Mifflin Harcourt for making our vision hers; to Bruce Westwood and Carolyn Forde at Westwood Creative Artists for taking this book so many places it would not otherwise have gone; and to Shyam Selvadurai, who got the whole process started. Their buoyant enthusiasm has been a gift.

My mother, father and grandmother, whose humour and compassion inspire me, believed in *The Toss of a Lemon* long before it existed and read it for me when finally it did. So did Geoffrey Brock, my companion and anchor, who, with our children, ensures that my life is full with satisfactions books cannot provide.

The writing of this book has been generously supported by the Canada Council for the Arts, the Alberta Foundation for the Arts, Le Conseil des Arts et des Lettres du Québec, a PEO Scholar Award, a Milton O. Riepe Summer Fellowship, a Monique Wittig Writer's Scholarship, the MacDowell Colony, the Sacatar Colony and the American Academy in Rome. Excerpts have been published by *AGNI Online* and *Prism International*.